勇奪新[illegible]益

完整3回實戰演練＋試題完全解密攻略

試題本

MP3

寂天雲 APP

Yoo, su-youn——著

關亭薇／沈家淩
蔡裴驊／蘇裕承——譯

如何下載 **MP3** 音檔

❶ **寂天雲 APP 聆聽：**掃描書上 QR Code 下載「寂天雲－英日語學習隨身聽」APP。加入會員後，用 APP 內建掃描器再次掃描書上 QR Code，即可使用 APP 聆聽音檔。

❷ **官網下載音檔：**請上「寂天閱讀網」（www.icosmos.com.tw），註冊會員／登入後，搜尋本書，進入本書頁面，點選「MP3 下載」下載音檔，存於電腦等其他播放器聆聽使用。

勇奪新制多益 950

完整3回實戰演練＋試題完全解密攻略

作　　者　Yoo, su-youn
譯　　者　闕亭薇／沈家淩／蔡裴驊／蘇裕承
編　　輯　賴祖兒
主　　編　丁宥暄
校　　對　吳思薇／劉育如
內文排版　謝青秀／林書玉
封面設計　林書玉
製程管理　洪巧玲
發 行 人　黃朝萍
出 版 者　寂天文化事業股份有限公司
電　　話　+886-(0)2-2365-9739
傳　　真　+886-(0)2-2365-9835
網　　址　www.icosmos.com.tw
讀者服務　onlineservice@icosmos.com.tw
出版日期　2023 年 1 月 初版二刷 （寂天雲隨身聽 APP 版）

國家圖書館出版品預行編目 (CIP) 資料

勇奪新制多益 950 : 完整 3 回實戰演練＋試題完全解密攻略 (寂天雲隨身聽 APP 版) / Yoo, su-youn 著 . -- 初版 . -- [臺北市] : 寂天文化 , 2023.01
，面；　公分
ISBN 978-626-300-175-6 (16K 平裝)
1. 多益測驗
805.1895　　111021438

郵撥帳號 1998620-0 寂天文化事業股份有限公司
訂書金額未滿 1000 元，請外加運費 100 元。
〔若有破損，請寄回更換，謝謝。〕

高分答題策略

PART 1 照片描述

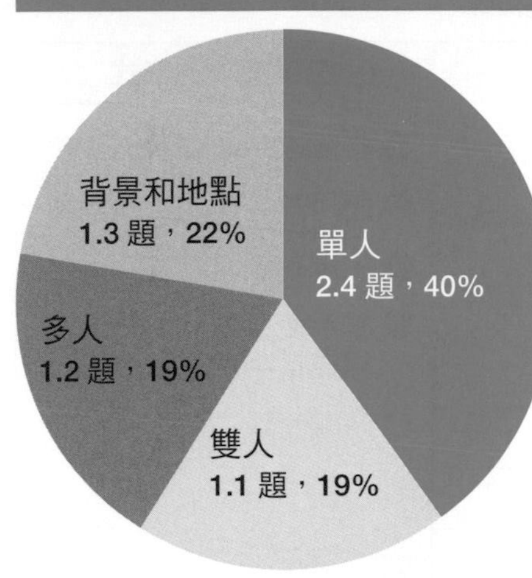

PART 1 照片題型

答案的描述方式

眼見為憑，千萬別任意推測答案。

❶ 針對全體描述 > 針對細節描述
❷ 事實描述 > 抽象描述
❸ 客觀描述 > 主觀描述

正確答案會針對事實或全體動作進行描述，不太會描寫抽象概念或著重在某個細節上。請以照片所看到的東西為依據，千萬不能自行推測。

基本解題策略

STEP 1 確認照片——在選項內容播出前，請務必緊盯著照片。
STEP 2 聽寫重點——聆聽選項內容時，請快速寫下一至兩個關鍵字。
STEP 3 刪去法——聽到照片中未呈現的單字（動詞或名詞）時，請馬上刪去該選項。
STEP 4 確認答案——請先刪去錯誤選項，再從剩下的選項中挑出正確答案。

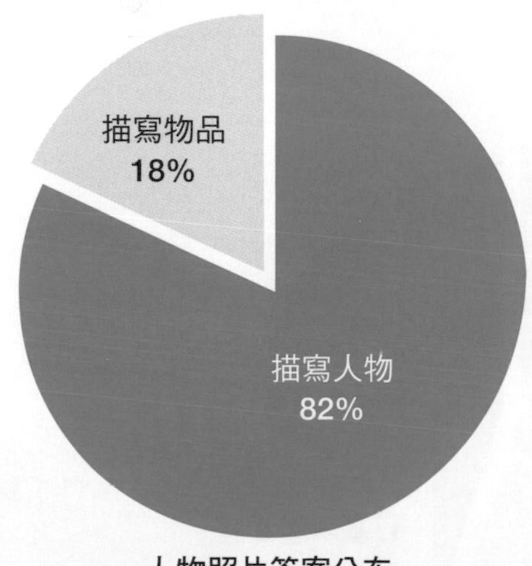

人物照片答案分布

破解新制考題

❶ 即使選項敘述與照片中的動作相符，也請務必確認敘述句末的名詞是否正確。

❷ 部分選項雖然以進行被動式 being p.p. 描述，仍適用於無人照片。

❸ 請務必多熟悉針對物品和自然現象的描述方式。

人物照片的答案中，有 18% 的機率為針對物品的描述。
而描寫人物的照片中，出題比例為單人照片 67%、雙人照片 23%、以及多人照片 10%。

PART 2 應答問題

基本上，PART 2 問句和答句的類型僅分為 15 大類。

PART 2 基本題型		錯誤選項的形式
Wh- 問句	❶ Who 問句	❶ 不能以 Yes 或 No 回答 ❷ 適用其他疑問詞的答案 ❸ 主詞有誤 ❹ 故意使用相似、相同或相關單字誘答 ❺ 時態有誤
	❷ Where 問句	
	❸ When 問句	
	❹ Why 問句	
	❺ How 問句	
	❻ What/Which 問句	
一般助動詞疑問句	❼ 間接問句	
	❽ 助動詞疑問句	
	❾ 選擇疑問句	
	❿ 表示勸說、建議、要求的問句	
	⓫ 附加問句、否定疑問句	
直述句	⓬ 直述句	
非正面回答	⓭ I don't know	
	⓮ 反問	
	⓯ 間接回答	

各題型出題率分析

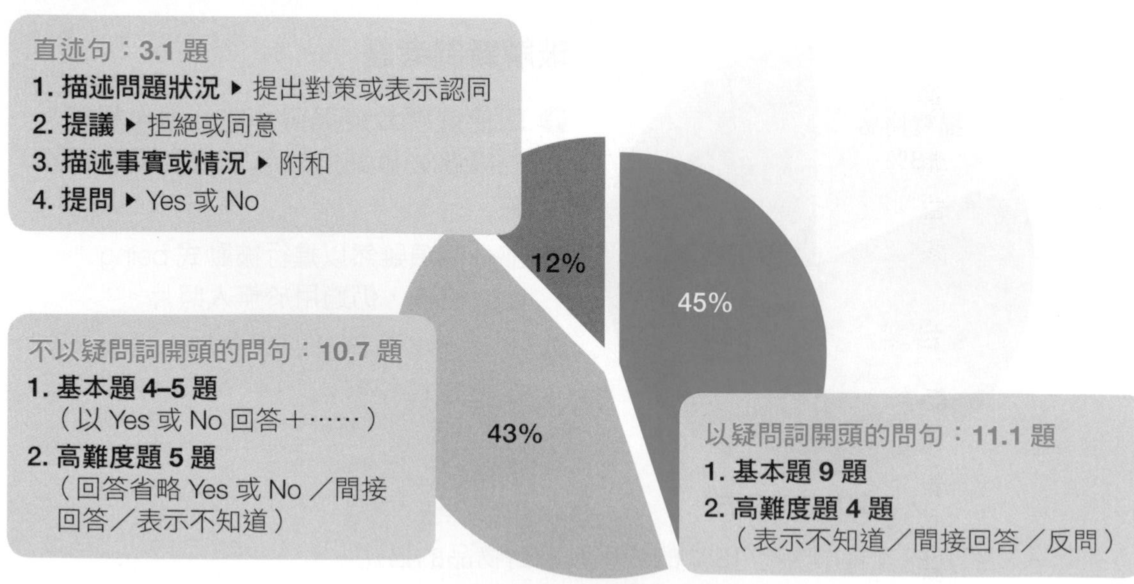

PART 3 簡短對話

PART 3 不變的原則
❶ 按對話先後次序提及答案內容。
❷ 題目皆有固定的提問方式。
❸ 對話中會詳細說明事實或情況，而答案則會採較為籠統的回答方式。
❹ 題目若針對 Man（男子）詢問時，答案會出現在男子所說的話當中。

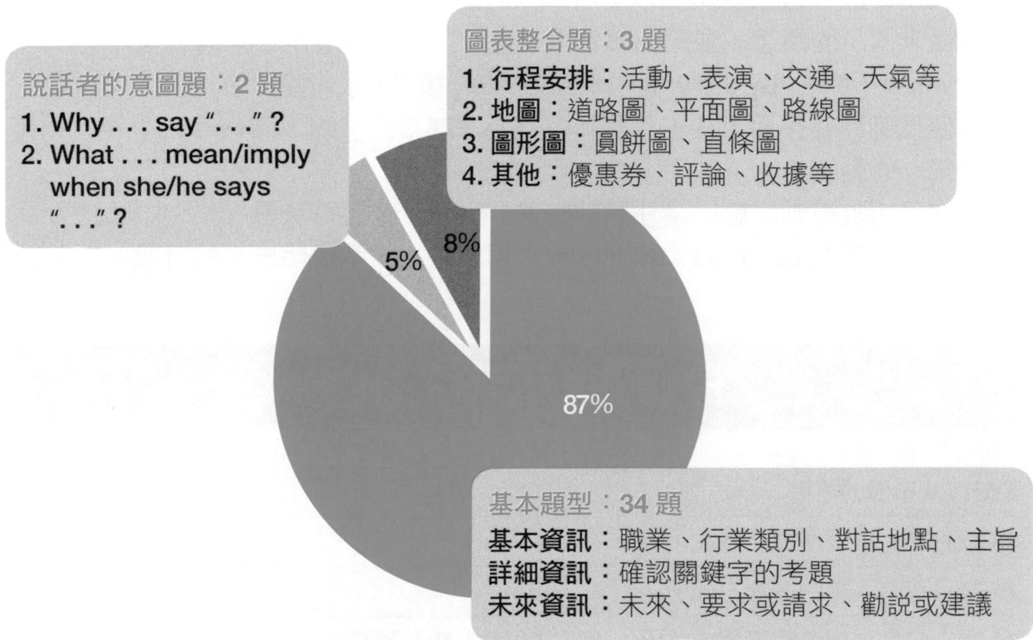

說話者意圖題的解題策略

❶ 刪去與該句話字面上意思相同的選項。
❷ 答案會採較為籠統的回答方式來說明情況。
❸ 確認該句話前後連接的轉折詞。

圖表整合題的解題策略

❶ 若對話中直接說出選項內容，該選項就不是答案。
❷ 確認行程表中是否有更動或取消的部分。
❸ 若圖表為地圖，答題關鍵為表示地點的介系詞。
❹ 若圖表為圖形圖，答案會出現在提到排名、最高級或數量之處。
❺ 若圖表為說明手冊、優惠券或收據，不符合圖表資訊的內容通常就是答案。

破解高難度題型

❶ 若前兩題詢問的是主旨、地點、職業或目的，答案可能會同時出現在開頭前兩句話當中。
❷ 若三道題皆屬於詢問主旨、職業或問題所在之處的考題，答案可能會同時出現在某一段落中。
❸ 「I'll . . .」開頭的句子指的是建議；「You'll . . .」開頭的句子指的是要求。
❹ 先提到答案後，才提到關鍵字。
❺ 若題目詢問有關未來的內容，答案會出現在對方所說的話當中。
❻ 若有兩個選項皆出現兩個以上所聽到的單字時，請確認選項當中是否有出現對話未提及的單字，並刪去該選項，選擇另一個選項作為答案。
❼ however、but、by the way、unfortunately 後方會出現答題的關鍵線索。
❽ 若題目詢問往後將發生的事情，答案為「I'll . . .」或「Let's . . .」後方連接的第一個動詞。
❾ 若題目出現被動語態，請注意聆聽表示勸說、建議的句子。
❿ 對話末出現 Let's / next / from now 等用法時，表示說明未來的行動。

PART 4 簡短獨白

PART 4 不變的原則
❶ 按獨白先後次序提及答案內容。
❷ 題目皆有固定的提問方式。
❸ 獨白中會詳細說明事實或情況，而答案則會採較為籠統的回答方式。
❹ 獨白的敘述方式有固定的模式。

新制測驗中，最常出現的獨白（talk）類型為會議、解說、演說和電話留言，因此請務必熟悉獨白的敘述方式。

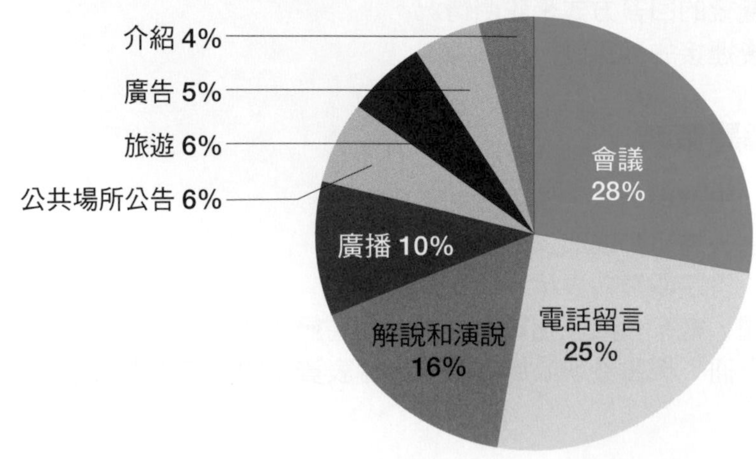

PART 5 & 6 句子 & 段落填空

PART 5

1

透過句型結構分析，根據詞類的排列和文法找出答案。

2

整理出有助於答題的文法重點。

3

找出句中的答題關鍵字，按照客觀性和邏輯性判斷出答案。

4

一併熟記單字會搭配的時間點和人物。

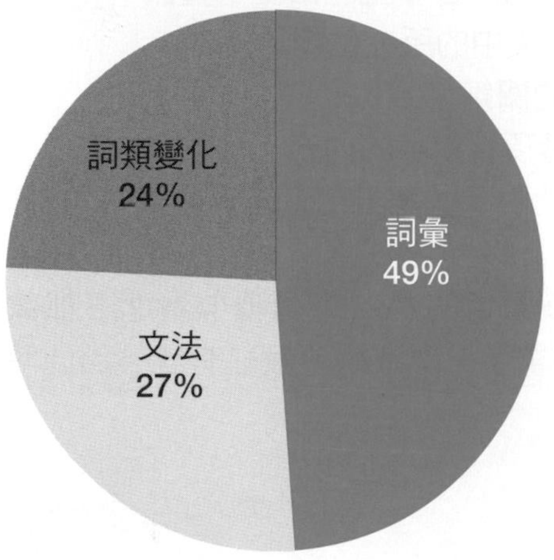

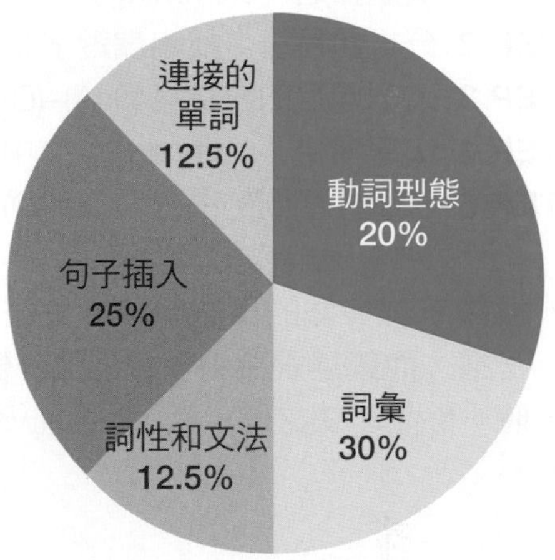

PART 6

❶ 詞類選擇 1–2 題

1. 詞類變化
2. 相關文法

❷ 動詞的型態 2–3 題

1. 動狀詞的個數
2. 主詞動詞單複數一致性
3. 主動被動語態對應受詞的有無
4. 配合其他動詞的時態

❸ 詞彙題 4–5 題

→ 符合邏輯的選項未必就是答案。

1. 句中決定答案的關鍵字
2. 同義詞
3. 廣義的單字

❹ 連接的單詞 1–2 題

1. 確認是連接詞還是介系詞
2. 確認是指示代名詞還是形容詞
3. 確認是連接副詞還是副詞

❺ 句子插入題 4 題

1. 整理出選項的關鍵字
2. 空格前後句中決定答案的關鍵字
3. 根據全文內容刪去不適當的句子

PART 7 單篇 & 多篇閱讀

閱讀測驗四大原則
❶ 按文章先後次序出現答案。
❷ 先分析題目後，再找出該題於文中的所在位置。
❸ 文章會詳細說明，而答案則會使用較為籠統的回答方式。
❹ 陷阱選項中可能僅隱藏一個錯誤單字，導致該選項敘述有誤。

策略答題五步驟

STEP 1 快速掃過（skimming）前半段文章的內容，整理出基本資訊。
STEP 2 分析題目後，找出關鍵字和答案於文中的所在位置。
STEP 3 確認題目的關鍵字和 (A)–(D) 選項的關鍵字。
STEP 4 快速掃過（skimming）文中出現選項關鍵字的內容。
STEP 5 將剛才找到的內容和 (A)–(D) 選項比對，並選出正確答案。

★ 根據新制多益的出題趨勢，會碰到很多題目的 (A)–(D) 選項乍看之下都像是答案，而錯誤選項中僅會隱藏一個錯誤單字，導致選項敘述有誤。因此解題時，除了求快之餘，請務必細心確認。

目錄

TEST 1

開始作答 ____ 點 ____ 分

完成作答 ____ 點 ____ 分

• 建議一次寫完整份試題，避免分次作答。
• 答題時，請比照實際考試，將答案畫在答案卡上。

目標答對題數 ____ /200

實際答對題數 ____ /200

• 將答對題數乘以 5 即可概算出分數。

LISTENING TEST

In the Listening test, you will be asked to demonstrate how well you understand spoken English. The entire Listening test will last approximately 45 minutes. There are four parts, and directions are given for each part. You must mark your answers on the separate answer sheet. Do not write your answers in your test book.

PART 1 01

Directions: For each question in this part, you will hear four statements about a picture in your test book. When you hear the statements, you must select the one statement that best describes what you see in the picture. Then find the number of the question on your answer sheet and mark your answer. The statements will not be printed in your test book and will be spoken only one time.

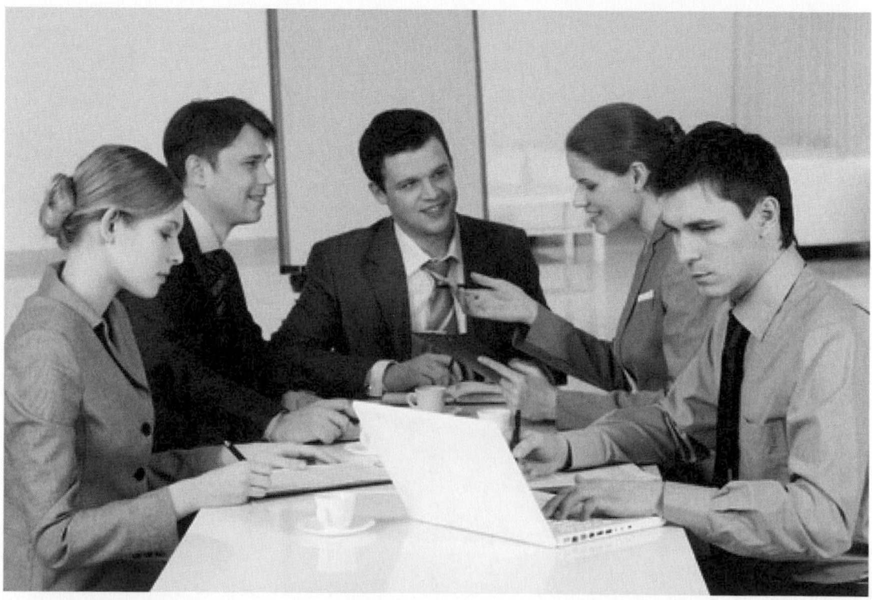

Statement (B), "They're having a meeting," is the best description of the picture, so you should select answer (B) and mark it on your answer sheet.

1.

2.

GO ON TO THE NEXT PAGE

3.

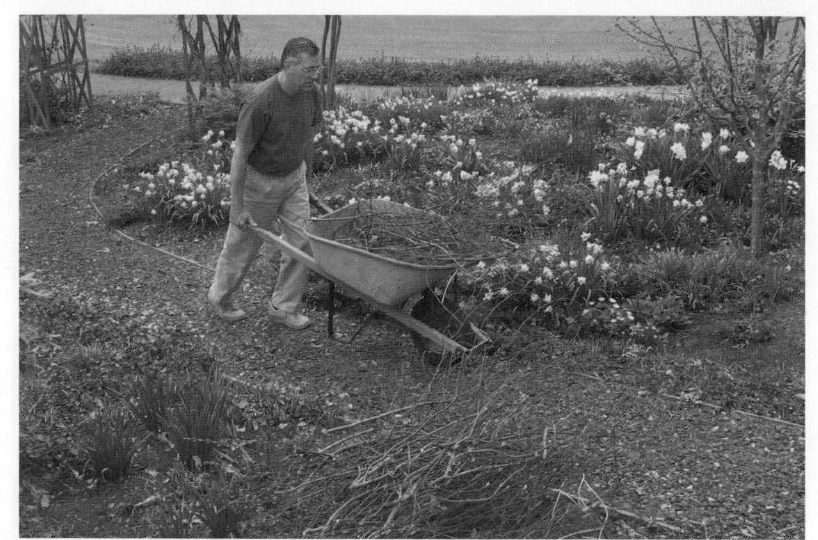

4.

5.

6.

GO ON TO THE NEXT PAGE

PART 2 (02)

Directions: You will hear a question or statement and three responses spoken in English. They will not be printed in your test book and will be spoken only one time. Select the best response to the question or statement and mark the letter (A), (B), or (C) on your answer sheet.

7. Mark your answer on your answer sheet.

8. Mark your answer on your answer sheet.

9. Mark your answer on your answer sheet.

10. Mark your answer on your answer sheet.

11. Mark your answer on your answer sheet.

12. Mark your answer on your answer sheet.

13. Mark your answer on your answer sheet.

14. Mark your answer on your answer sheet.

15. Mark your answer on your answer sheet.

16. Mark your answer on your answer sheet.

17. Mark your answer on your answer sheet.

18. Mark your answer on your answer sheet.

19. Mark your answer on your answer sheet.

20. Mark your answer on your answer sheet.

21. Mark your answer on your answer sheet.

22. Mark your answer on your answer sheet.

23. Mark your answer on your answer sheet.

24. Mark your answer on your answer sheet.

25. Mark your answer on your answer sheet.

26. Mark your answer on your answer sheet.

27. Mark your answer on your answer sheet.

28. Mark your answer on your answer sheet.

29. Mark your answer on your answer sheet.

30. Mark your answer on your answer sheet.

31. Mark your answer on your answer sheet.

PART 3 (03)

Directions: You will hear some conversations between two or more people. You will be asked to answer three questions about what the speakers say in each conversation. Select the best response to each question and mark the letter (A), (B), (C), or (D) on your answer sheet. The conversations will not be printed in your test book and will be spoken only one time.

32. What problem is the woman having?
(A) She doesn't know where the hotel is.
(B) She doesn't know the reservation number.
(C) She is late for the meeting.
(D) She wants to make a reservation for a meeting room.

33. What does the man imply when he says, "My shift just started"?
(A) He is a new employee.
(B) He cannot answer her question.
(C) He lacks experience.
(D) He could not find any reservation.

34. What is the woman asked to do?
(A) Call a supervisor
(B) Come back later
(C) Stay in the hotel
(D) Check the reservation record

35. How did the man hear about the hotel?
(A) From an online advertisement
(B) From a coworker
(C) From a newspaper article
(D) From a media commercial

36. According to the woman, how is the hotel different from its competitors?
(A) It offers a high-quality service.
(B) It has a great reputation.
(C) It has proximity to local attractions.
(D) It has many locations.

37. What will the man do in London?
(A) Go sightseeing
(B) Watch movies
(C) Visit an exhibition
(D) Work in city renovation

GO ON TO THE NEXT PAGE

38. What are the speakers discussing?
(A) Cooking recipes
(B) Home appliances
(C) Electronics stores
(D) Brand logos

39. What does the woman like about the product she bought?
(A) It is fully functional.
(B) It is inexpensive.
(C) It is energy efficient.
(D) It comes in various colors.

40. What does Patrick agree to do?
(A) Visit an office
(B) Call a store
(C) Forward a message
(D) Apply a discount

---

41. What did the woman ask the man to do?
(A) Organize a meeting
(B) Review her application
(C) Check some data
(D) Submit some documents

42. What does the woman plan to do today?
(A) Reserve a table
(B) Meet a client
(C) Give a presentation
(D) Book a train

43. Why does the woman say, "I don't have enough experience to handle such an important meeting"?
(A) To express concern about working alone
(B) To give an excuse for a delay
(C) To get feedback from the man
(D) To ask the man for some advice

---

44. What are the speakers mainly discussing?
(A) A road repair
(B) A construction project
(C) A train delay
(D) Public transportation options

45. What does the woman imply when she says, "Oh! I wasn't expecting that"?
(A) She has not prepared for a meeting.
(B) She has forgotten the deadline.
(C) She was not informed of the change.
(D) She is happy to hear some news.

46. What will the woman receive soon?
(A) A progress report
(B) A signed contract
(C) A construction invoice
(D) A traveler's check

---

47. What type of company do the speakers most likely work for?
(A) An advertising company
(B) An office furniture store
(C) A medical equipment manufacturer
(D) A digital camera store

48. Why is the man disappointed?
(A) An actor did not appear.
(B) A medical center was unavailable.
(C) Sales figures did not meet expectations.
(D) Some products were defective.

49. What does the man suggest doing?
(A) Replacing an agency
(B) Advertising through social media
(C) Offering additional discounts
(D) Improving the product quality

---

50. Which part of the company does the woman most likely manage?
(A) The factory
(B) The store
(C) The mail room
(D) The warehouse

51. What are the speakers mainly talking about?
(A) Placing an order
(B) Inspecting workstations
(C) Recruiting new employees
(D) Preparing a meeting

52. What does the man ask the woman to do?
(A) Update a document
(B) Complete a daily task
(C) Contact an agency
(D) Research some prices

---

53. What does the woman offer to do?
(A) Review a document
(B) Confirm a timetable
(C) Provide contact information
(D) Reserve a meeting room

54. What is Kate needed for?
(A) Translating an e-mail
(B) Contacting a keynote speaker
(C) Preparing a contract
(D) Writing an article

55. Why does the woman say, "You lived in China for about six years"?
(A) She corrects some information.
(B) She suggests her colleague for a position.
(C) She needs some travel tips.
(D) She wants to help her colleague.

---

56. What is the conversation mainly about?
(A) Advertising approaches
(B) Internet providers
(C) Employee communication
(D) Real estate properties

57. What does Jeannie suggest?
(A) Buying some supplies
(B) Comparing some results
(C) Using a Web site
(D) Reading an article

58. What will the man ask Lucy to do?
(A) Coordinate a project
(B) Organize a business trip
(C) Talk to the supervisor
(D) Interview job candidates

GO ON TO THE NEXT PAGE

Wellington Seminar room	
Name	**Capacity**
Bonnie	20
Lakeside	25
Phoenix	30
Jackson	40

59. What information did the man receive this morning?
(A) The number of participants
(B) The budgeted money
(C) The topics of a seminar
(D) The preferred menus

60. Look at the graphic. Which room will the speakers choose?
(A) Bonnie
(B) Lakeside
(C) Phoenix
(D) Jackson

61. What does the woman offer to do?
(A) Consult her supervisor
(B) Revise a budget report
(C) Arrange transportation for employees
(D) Reserve a seminar room in a hotel

Perrel Art Center Events	
4 September	International Toy Expo
9 October	Kids Jazz Concert
17 November	Aston City Orchestra
25 December	Christmas Traditions

62. Look at the graphic. When does the conversation take place?
(A) In September
(B) In October
(C) In November
(D) In December

63. Why is the woman unable to go to the orchestra's concert?
(A) She will be visiting some clients.
(B) She will be preparing a presentation.
(C) She will be on vacation.
(D) She will be participating in a trade show.

64. What does the man offer to do?
(A) Purchase a ticket
(B) Revise a schedule
(C) Attend a conference
(D) Research for a project

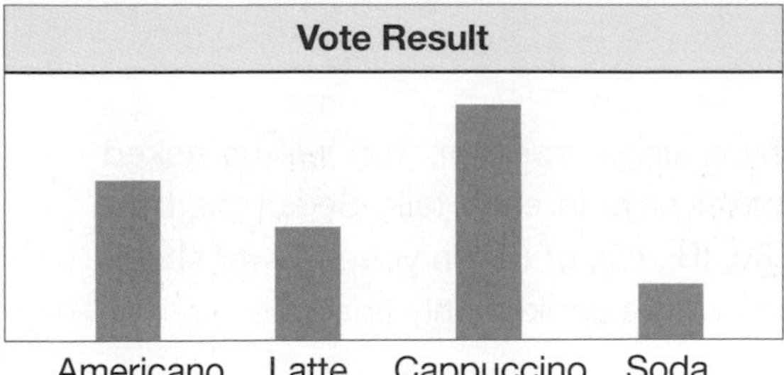

65. Look at the graphic. Which beverage will be discounted this week?
(A) Americano
(B) Latte
(C) Cappuccino
(D) Soda

66. What does the man thank Jason for?
(A) Developing a new beverage
(B) Organizing a chart
(C) Sharing helpful information
(D) Suggesting a sales promotion

67. What does the woman remind the man to do?
(A) Talk to other colleagues
(B) Join the project
(C) Ask for advice
(D) Make some suggestions

Name: Derek Moreno
Office ID: 124034

Department Code: 3111
Office number: 422
Phone number: 243-8876

68. Where is the conversation most likely taking place?
(A) At the security office
(B) At the maintenance department
(C) At the training center
(D) At the human resources department

69. Look at the graphic. What employee information does the man say is incorrect?
(A) 124034
(B) 3111
(C) 422
(D) 243-8876

70. What does the woman ask the man to do?
(A) Leave a message
(B) Change a badge
(C) Present an employee ID
(D) Return the call

GO ON TO THE NEXT PAGE

PART 4 (04)

Directions: You will hear some talks given by a single speaker. You will be asked to answer three questions about what the speaker says in each talk. Select the best response to each question and mark the letter (A), (B), (C), or (D) on your answer sheet. The talks will not be printed in your test book and will be spoken only one time.

71. What product is being advertised?
(A) An Internet provider
(B) Some audio equipment
(C) A musical performance
(D) A magazine subscription

72. What does the speaker say is unique to the product?
(A) It is the cheapest on the market.
(B) It has a variety of functions.
(C) It has the longest warranty.
(D) It has received the best reviews.

73. What can listeners do at a Web site?
(A) Read customer reviews
(B) Sign up for a free trial
(C) Download a coupon
(D) Listen to some samples

74. Where most likely do the listeners work?
(A) At a restaurant
(B) At a design company
(C) At an employment agency
(D) At a textile factory

75. What is suggested about XQ-1000?
(A) It can save more time.
(B) It improves product quality.
(C) It is easily operated.
(D) It is safer than the old model.

76. What are the listeners asked to do?
(A) Sign up for a seminar
(B) Attend a safety training session
(C) Clean the lounge room
(D) Take their belongings with them

77. According to the speaker, what is special about the restaurant?
(A) It serves many dishes.
(B) It has original appetizers.
(C) It owns a local farm.
(D) It offers low prices.

78. Who is Stewart?
(A) A business owner
(B) A famous chef
(C) A server
(D) A talented actor

79. Why does the speaker say, "I eat them all the time"?
(A) To complain about a menu
(B) To recommend a dish
(C) To explain a waiting time
(D) To clarify a menu item

80. What is indicated about Gail Nelson?
(A) She is running an online business.
(B) She is well known in her field.
(C) She has many years of work experience.
(D) She owns a small restaurant.

81. Why does the speaker say, "Running an online promotion can be expensive these days"?
(A) To reduce the marketing expenses
(B) To acknowledge a common opinion
(C) To suggest alternative promotional methods
(D) To contradict the marketing expert's claim

82. What will the guest most likely do next?
(A) Promote her restaurant
(B) Talk to the audience
(C) Give detailed suggestions
(D) Prepare a speech

83. Where does the speaker most likely work?
(A) At a doctor's office
(B) At a delivery company
(C) At a construction firm
(D) At a furniture store

84. What problem does the speaker mention?
(A) Damaged office furniture
(B) Road conditions
(C) A missing check
(D) A wrong address

85. What does the speaker imply when she says, "All I see are houses"?
(A) She is very impressed with the houses.
(B) She is confused with all the addresses.
(C) She claims a mistake has been made.
(D) She thinks there are too many buildings.

86. Why does the speaker thank the listeners?
(A) For attending the exhibition
(B) For designing a Web site
(C) For working overtime
(D) For being punctual

87. According to the speaker, what is scheduled for next week?
(A) A clothing release
(B) A trade show
(C) An apparel show
(D) A car exhibition

88. What does the speaker imply when she says, "It's a large space"?
(A) There is room to display new merchandise.
(B) The building is much bigger.
(C) The number of companies participating this time has increased.
(D) High attendance is anticipated.

GO ON TO THE NEXT PAGE

The International Management Workshop	
9:00 A.M.	Business Operating Systems, Mitchel Kim
11:00 A.M.	Human Resources, Vanessa Romero
1:00 P.M.	Small Business, Sung Park
2:00 P.M.	How to Start a Business, Kelly Scott
4:00 P.M.	Q&A

89. What is the purpose of the call?
(A) To make a job offer
(B) To attend the workshop
(C) To give a presentation
(D) To arrange for a meeting

90. Look at the graphic. Who is the speaker calling?
(A) Mitchel Kim
(B) Vanessa Romero
(C) Sung Park
(D) Kelly Scott

91. What does the speaker ask the listener to do?
(A) Consult the report
(B) Provide some information
(C) Work more efficiently
(D) Get a discount

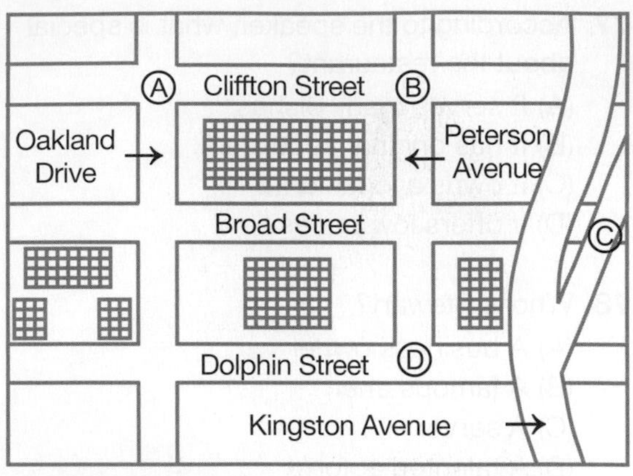

92. What caused a problem?
(A) A broken-down car
(B) An incorrect road sign
(C) Road construction
(D) Bad weather

93. Look at the graphic. Which location is the speaker describing?
(A) Location A
(B) Location B
(C) Location C
(D) Location D

94. What does the speaker say will take place tomorrow?
(A) A city tour
(B) An outdoor event
(C) Repair work
(D) A special election

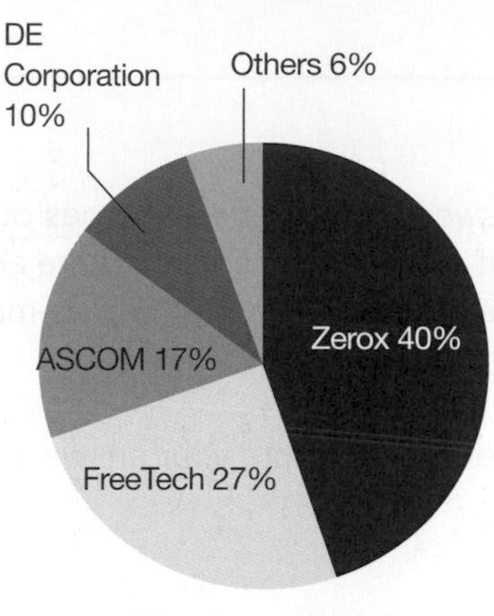

Market Share

95. What does the speaker point out on the report?
(A) A team has been nominated for a monthly award.
(B) Sales are higher than expected.
(C) A new executive has been hired.
(D) A business will be merged.

96. Why is the speaker concerned?
(A) The company seems to have lost its competitive edge.
(B) The operating costs have increased.
(C) The production capacity is limited.
(D) Numerous complaints have been received.

97. Look at the graphic. Which company may be acquired?
(A) Zerox
(B) FreeTech
(C) ASCOM
(D) DE Corporation

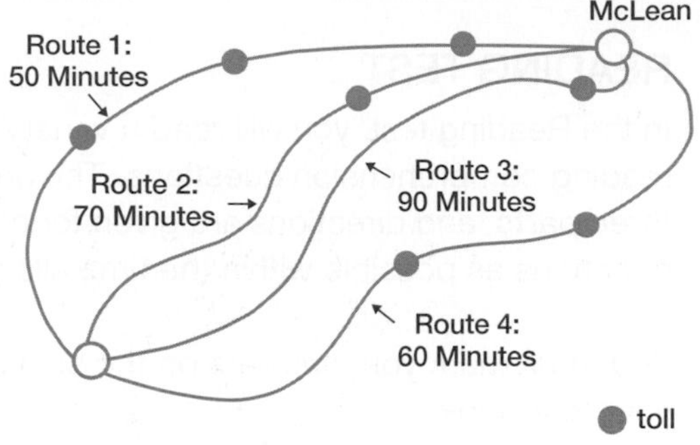

98. According to the speaker, what type of event is being held?
(A) An international fashion show
(B) An annual picnic
(C) An industrial conference
(D) A job fair

99. Look at the graphic. Which route does the speaker recommend taking?
(A) Route 1
(B) Route 2
(C) Route 3
(D) Route 4

100. What is the listener asked to do?
(A) Reschedule an appointment
(B) Confirm a reservation
(C) Check a timetable
(D) Sign up for an event

This is the end of the Listening test. Turn to Part 5 in your test book.

READING TEST

In the Reading test, you will read a variety of texts and answer several different types of reading comprehension questions. The entire Reading test will last 75 minutes. There are three parts, and directions are given for each part. You are encouraged to answer as many questions as possible within the time allowed.

You must mark your answers on the separate answer sheet. Do not write your answers in your test book.

PART 5

Directions: A word or phrase is missing in each of the sentences below. Four answer choices are given below each sentence. Select the best answer to complete the sentence. Then mark the letter (A), (B), (C), or (D) on your answer sheet.

101. Before taking on a managerial position, you must have enough experience and qualifications and understand how -------- aspect of your company runs.

(A) all
(B) each
(C) whole
(D) complete

102. Elizabeth Zane's teaspoons, in varying decorative shapes and sizes and approximately between $25 and $45, can be sold as a collection or ----------.

(A) separately
(B) separate
(C) separation
(D) separated

103. The elevator could carry -------- of five thousand kilos per day, which means it could deliver over a million kilos of material per year.

(A) loaded
(B) load
(C) loads
(D) loader

104. The Committee was not -------- convinced of the need to establish an additional facility and branches in Vietnam.

(A) fully
(B) enough
(C) almost
(D) surely

105. These days, for brands that want to provide -------- social customer service, it is more important than ever to establish close relationships with their customers.

(A) personalized
(B) personally
(C) personality
(D) personalization

106. In order to connect to the Internet, you will need to put in the user name and password that was given to you when you set up your account -------- the Internet Service Provider.

(A) of
(B) at
(C) on
(D) with

107. -------- our marketing team had expected the GLOBE Innovation Expo to be a success, the reviews from the attendees still overwhelmed all of us.

(A) Whenever
(B) Although
(C) Even so
(D) Because

108. FedEx makes three -------- to deliver a package, and following the third one, the undeliverable package will be held at our local office and available for pick-up for seven days.

(A) attempts
(B) purposes
(C) goals
(D) experiences

109. The tasks involved in maintaining this apartment -------- within the responsibilities of our on-site maintenance personnel who are always happy to assist you.

(A) have
(B) cover
(C) present
(D) fall

110. If -------- of these products are available at a store where you normally shop, then visit our Web site and place an order.

(A) no
(B) not
(C) nothing
(D) none

111. Only when stepping back -------- analyze a complicated situation from various aspects, so that we can handle any kind of problems related to our job.

(A) is able to
(B) our ability
(C) in order to
(D) are we able to

112. These proposals, some of -------- have already been accepted by the government, include the reform of fuel policies and the expansion of social safety net coverage.

(A) them
(B) that
(C) those
(D) which

GO ON TO THE NEXT PAGE

113. The latest reports suggest that Samsung's next mobile phone will be its most expensive --------, exceeding the $1,000 mark for the first time.

(A) just
(B) later
(C) yet
(D) very

114. This versatile table, model no. 2301, is designed to fit compactly for daily use and conveniently -------- to seat a big party of ten for special occasions.

(A) expand
(B) expands
(C) expanded
(D) be expanded

115. Lake Front Towers, located in the heart of Toronto, has one hundred rooms, -------- with a view of the city.

(A) much
(B) most
(C) almost
(D) such

116. Please note that employees are not able to take paid annual leave -------- they have completed at least one year's continuous service from the date of employment.

(A) until
(B) whether
(C) when
(D) by the time

117. In most cases, all outdoor activities for students -------- when school has been closed all day or closed early.

(A) were canceled
(B) have canceled
(C) would have been canceled
(D) will be canceled

118. Our new gift package with -------- health-care products will be released next month so as to meet the needs of current or potential customers.

(A) valuable
(B) comparable
(C) worthy
(D) raised

119. One of the reasons Mr. Hicks is widely respected -------- so many people is his great insight and a wealth of understanding of consumer behaviour.

(A) plus
(B) from
(C) in
(D) by

120. Our new customers -------- receive a ten percent discount on their first order at the site by entering their membership number and password.

(A) customarily
(B) exactly
(C) repeatedly
(D) almost

121. In order to ------- a refund request, a customer should contact the Internet service provider directly as set forth in the applicable policy.

(A) initiate
(B) appoint
(C) proceed
(D) ask

122. During the military parade, motorists were stuck in traffic for two hours on a five-kilometer --------- of road between Lancaster City and Hamilton.

(A) journey
(B) stretch
(C) duration
(D) period

123. Southwestern Energy Company is hosting its 10th Annual Convention next month where all of our employees will experience a ---------- range of expert presentations, seminars, and hands-on demonstrations.

(A) diverse
(B) various
(C) few
(D) assorted

124. Many options are being ---------- as the city discusses the future of the old church, the historic brick building which was constructed two hundred years ago.

(A) found
(B) famous
(C) known
(D) considered

125. Ford Family has sold more than 100 million albums worldwide, making them one of the most successful bands, ------- only The Philips in record sales.

(A) except
(B) over
(C) among
(D) behind

126. Please notify your customers that air or hotel ------- made through a third-party payment account or online travel agency will not be refunded.

(A) purchases
(B) purchase
(C) purchasing
(D) purchaser

127. The tenth International Movie Festival is held this weekend, but the celebration was held one week ----------.

(A) advanced
(B) following
(C) earlier
(D) previously

128. Should emergency assistance be required ------- our regular business hours, you can contact our emergency office number at 062-343-4111.

(A) at
(B) outside
(C) next to
(D) off

129. After much -------- by the judges, the finalists have been selected in all five categories of the World Music Awards.

(A) deliberately
(B) deliberated
(C) deliberate
(D) deliberation

130. Private investors for this project will receive financial benefits, such as dividends, right issues, or warrants, ------- they had invested in a company's ordinary shares.

(A) otherwise
(B) unless
(C) as if
(D) so that

TEST 1 PART 5

GO ON TO THE NEXT PAGE

PART 6

Directions: Read the texts that follow. A word, phrase, or sentence is missing in parts of each text. Four answer choices for each question are given below the text. Select the best answer to complete the text. Then mark the letter (A), (B), (C), or (D) on your answer sheet.

Questions 131-134 refer to the following information.

Call for Volunteers
Fall Bio Blitz

The Office of Sustainability is looking for 20 volunteers to help run our Fall Bio Blitz event on Sunday, February 10 next year. Volunteers will assist with registration, escort Bio Blitz participants out to join hikes, and will also be welcomed to participate in all event activities. We want you to encourage event participants and help to facilitate a positive experience for them. —**131**—.

What is Bio Blitz? Spend the day with us identifying plants and animal species on the Niagara-on-the-Lake Campus. Expert scientists lead citizen scientists like —**132**— on hikes around the property —**133**— identifying and cataloging the bugs, birds, amphibians, mammals, and plants. Niagara College is hosting the Fall Bio Blitz on Sunday, February 10 from 2:00 P.M. to 9:00 P.M. at the entrance to the Wetland Ridge Trail. Students, staff, and community members —**134**— to this free event and help collect information that can inform our species inventory of the campus!

If you are interested in volunteering for this event, please e-mail Amber Schmucker, Sustainability Engagement Officer, by Monday, December 27 at aschmucker@niagaracollege.ca.

131. (A) However, any issues and incidents should be reported to the volunteer coordinator directly.
(B) For more information on our campus schedule, please visit the event page on our Web site.
(C) Furthermore, attendance on all four days is preferred.
(D) In addition, volunteers are asked to attend this orientation one day before the event.

132. (A) them (B) ours
(C) himself (D) us

133. (A) that (B) during
(C) while (D) on

134. (A) have invited
(B) are invited
(C) will be invited
(D) would have been invited

Questions 135-138 refer to the following advertisement.

Mars Office
Renovation Experts

MORE creates a new atmosphere and interior to suit every single office, no matter the size. Most office designs are uninspired. Therefore, work environments create uninspired and stressful employees. Things like lack of privacy, poor lighting, poor ventilation, poor temperature control, or inadequate sanitary facilities can create a stressful work environment. So just let us do our job! Our designs have —**135**— small traditional offices as well as large-scale projects commissioned by architects and property developers. —**136**—. However, no single supplier can offer office furniture for all spaces and sizes. That is why MORE has developed close relationships with many professional furniture manufacturers —**137**— to provide us with the custom designs we need. Such resources give us the variety necessary to complete any —**138**—. In summary, we can bring you the most ideal office you've ever dreamed of.

135. (A) transformed
(B) related
(C) associated
(D) assembled

136. (A) A work environment is one of the most important issues you should consider.
(B) For most projects, we use furniture from our own factories.
(C) Some furniture needs special care.
(D) Under normal conditions, our furniture is guaranteed for one year.

137. (A) readily
(B) readier
(C) readiest
(D) ready

138. (A) research
(B) form
(C) order
(D) agreement

GO ON TO THE NEXT PAGE

Questions 139-142 refer to the following e-mail.

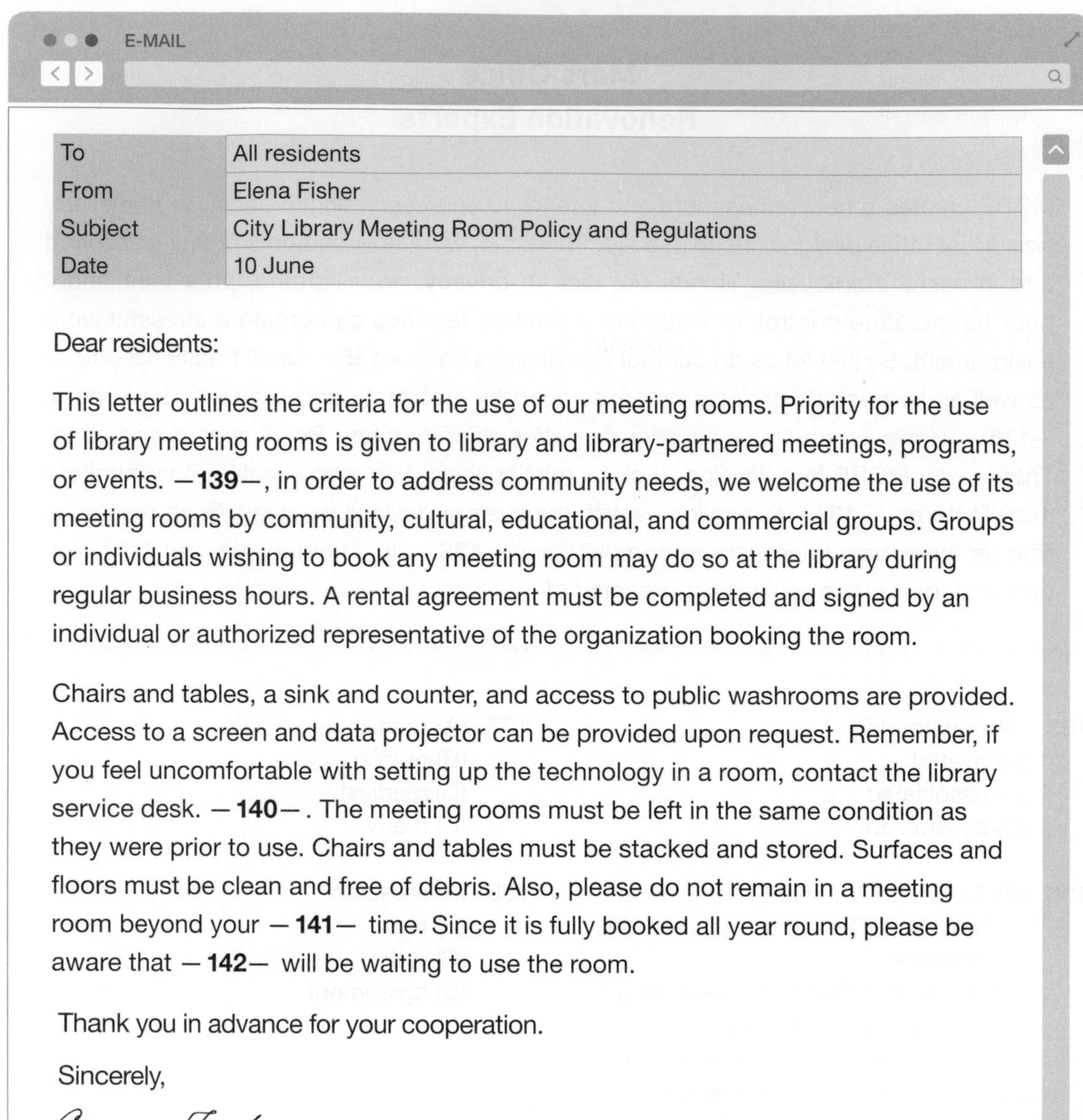

E-MAIL

To	All residents
From	Elena Fisher
Subject	City Library Meeting Room Policy and Regulations
Date	10 June

Dear residents:

This letter outlines the criteria for the use of our meeting rooms. Priority for the use of library meeting rooms is given to library and library-partnered meetings, programs, or events. —**139**—, in order to address community needs, we welcome the use of its meeting rooms by community, cultural, educational, and commercial groups. Groups or individuals wishing to book any meeting room may do so at the library during regular business hours. A rental agreement must be completed and signed by an individual or authorized representative of the organization booking the room.

Chairs and tables, a sink and counter, and access to public washrooms are provided. Access to a screen and data projector can be provided upon request. Remember, if you feel uncomfortable with setting up the technology in a room, contact the library service desk. —**140**—. The meeting rooms must be left in the same condition as they were prior to use. Chairs and tables must be stacked and stored. Surfaces and floors must be clean and free of debris. Also, please do not remain in a meeting room beyond your —**141**— time. Since it is fully booked all year round, please be aware that —**142**— will be waiting to use the room.

Thank you in advance for your cooperation.

Sincerely,

Elena Fisher

139. (A) However (B) Therefore (C) Whereas (D) So that

140. (A) Access to library data can be approved within five business days of your request.
(B) Only groups larger than twelve will be eligible for meeting rooms.
(C) One of our technicians will be on-site for you prior to your meeting.
(D) Ms. Fisher is able to make an exception in such cases.

141. (A) allotted
(B) allotting
(C) allotment
(D) allot

142. (A) it
(B) some
(C) there
(D) others

Questions 143-146 refer to the following article.

A spokesperson for NYC University —**143**— that Shepherd Nolan, a local entrepreneur, made a sizeable donation toward the expansion of the Fairland campus. "Without his generous support," said Stacy Mckinney, director of facility management, "our school would have been limited in our renovation plans going forward."

—**144**—. Now, a couple of new wings will be constructed on the south end of the —**145**— main campus building, as well as on the northeast corner of Lloyd Research Center. Additionally, a new fitness center will be located —**146**— the current student lounge. During the construction period, the closest entrance to the west side of the main campus building will be at the north end of the West Wing. These changes will be in effect for the duration of the construction period for the fitness center, which is scheduled to continue until the winter of next year.

143. (A) will confirm
(B) confirmation
(C) will be confirming
(D) has confirmed

144. (A) Ms. Mckinney's performance at Lloyd Research Center was outstanding.
(B) The renovation plan had been delayed because of budget cuts.
(C) The number of research projects has decreased over the past ten years.
(D) The original fitness center is being converted into the on-site laboratory for students.

145. (A) temporary
(B) existing
(C) located
(D) proposed

146. (A) adjacent to
(B) although
(C) instead of
(D) besides

GO ON TO THE NEXT PAGE

PART 7

Directions: In this part you will read a selection of texts, such as magazine and newspaper articles, e-mails, and instant messages. Each text or set of texts is followed by several questions. Select the best answer for each question and mark the letter (A), (B), (C), or (D) on your answer sheet.

Questions 147-148 refer to the following e-mail.

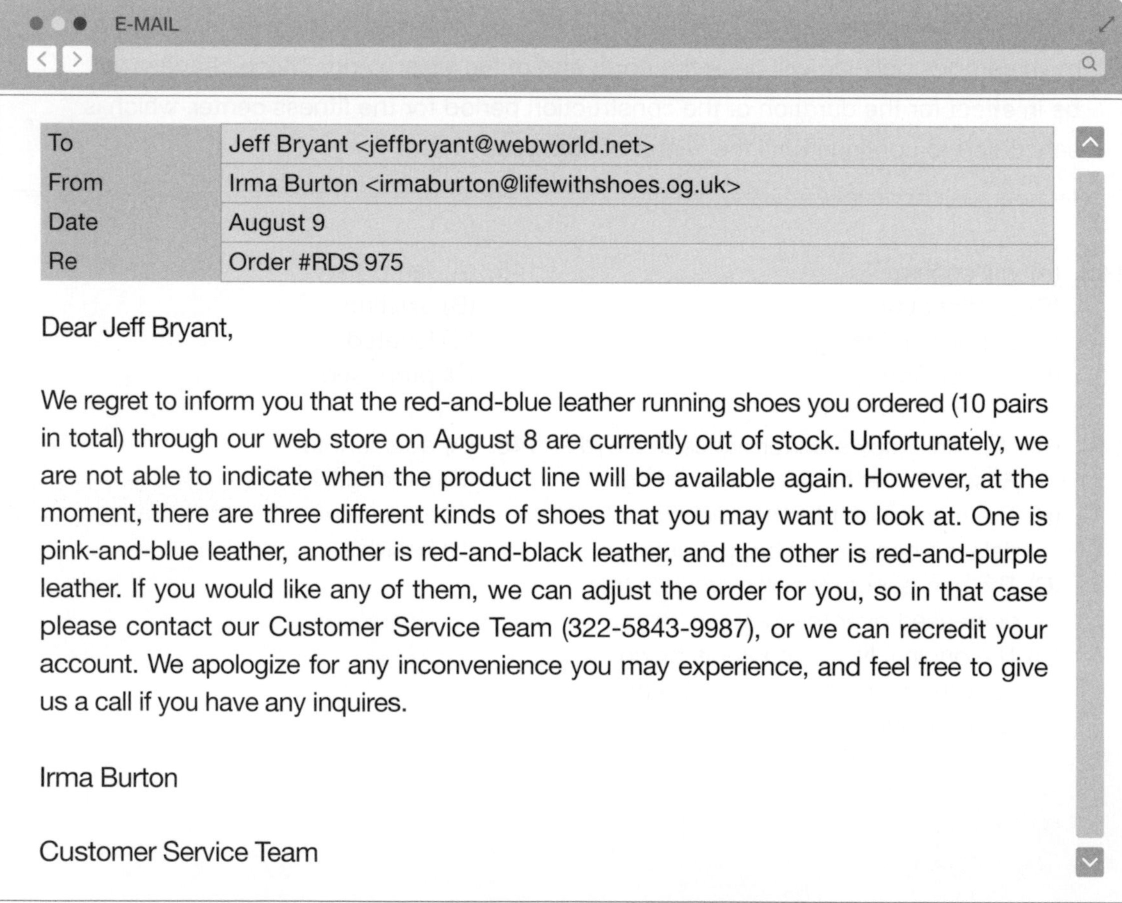
E-MAIL

To	Jeff Bryant <jeffbryant@webworld.net>
From	Irma Burton <irmaburton@lifewithshoes.og.uk>
Date	August 9
Re	Order #RDS 975

Dear Jeff Bryant,

We regret to inform you that the red-and-blue leather running shoes you ordered (10 pairs in total) through our web store on August 8 are currently out of stock. Unfortunately, we are not able to indicate when the product line will be available again. However, at the moment, there are three different kinds of shoes that you may want to look at. One is pink-and-blue leather, another is red-and-black leather, and the other is red-and-purple leather. If you would like any of them, we can adjust the order for you, so in that case please contact our Customer Service Team (322-5843-9987), or we can recredit your account. We apologize for any inconvenience you may experience, and feel free to give us a call if you have any inquires.

Irma Burton

Customer Service Team

147. What is the main reason the e-mail has been written?
(A) To schedule a return of a product
(B) To report a problem with an order
(C) To confirm a shipping date and time
(D) To reply to a customer

148. What is Mr. Bryant encouraged to do?
(A) Choose a shipping option
(B) Return the shoes and get a refund
(C) Get in touch with a certain department
(D) Cancel the order and make a new purchase

Questions 149-151 refer to the following leaflet.

Pop & Jazz
Concert

The Canonbury Community Center (CCC) is hosting its seasonal music event, Pop & Jazz concert, free of charge this coming weekend. This concert is held every summer for Canonbury citizens. As many public places CCC is running, this city park provides a place for citizens to gather for citywide festivals and public events. However, the CCC is largely dependent on donations to arrange and coordinate outdoor events such as this concert. We are gratefully accepting donations either at the event site, the Canonbury City Park or online at www.canonburycity.org/donate.

Become one of our CCC members by signing up online at www.canonburycity.org/membership or visiting our information desk. CCC members receive various benefits including a bimonthly newsletter covering current and upcoming exhibitions, a yearly city calendar highlighting our major events, and free invitations to every exhibition. Members are required to make a minimum financial contribution of £50 yearly.

149. Where would the leaflet most likely be given out?
- (A) In a community center
- (B) In an art school
- (C) In a public facility
- (D) In a concert hall

150. What is mentioned about the Pop & Jazz concert?
- (A) No admission fee is required.
- (B) Famous musicians participate every summer.
- (C) It will take place only at the city park.
- (D) A minimum financial contribution of £50 is required.

151. What is NOT stated as an advantage of members?
- (A) Members receive periodic publications.
- (B) Members' donations are listed on a Web site.
- (C) Members are invited to some activities.
- (D) A copy of a schedule covering some events is sent to members.

GO ON TO THE NEXT PAGE

Questions 152-155 refer to the following e-mail.

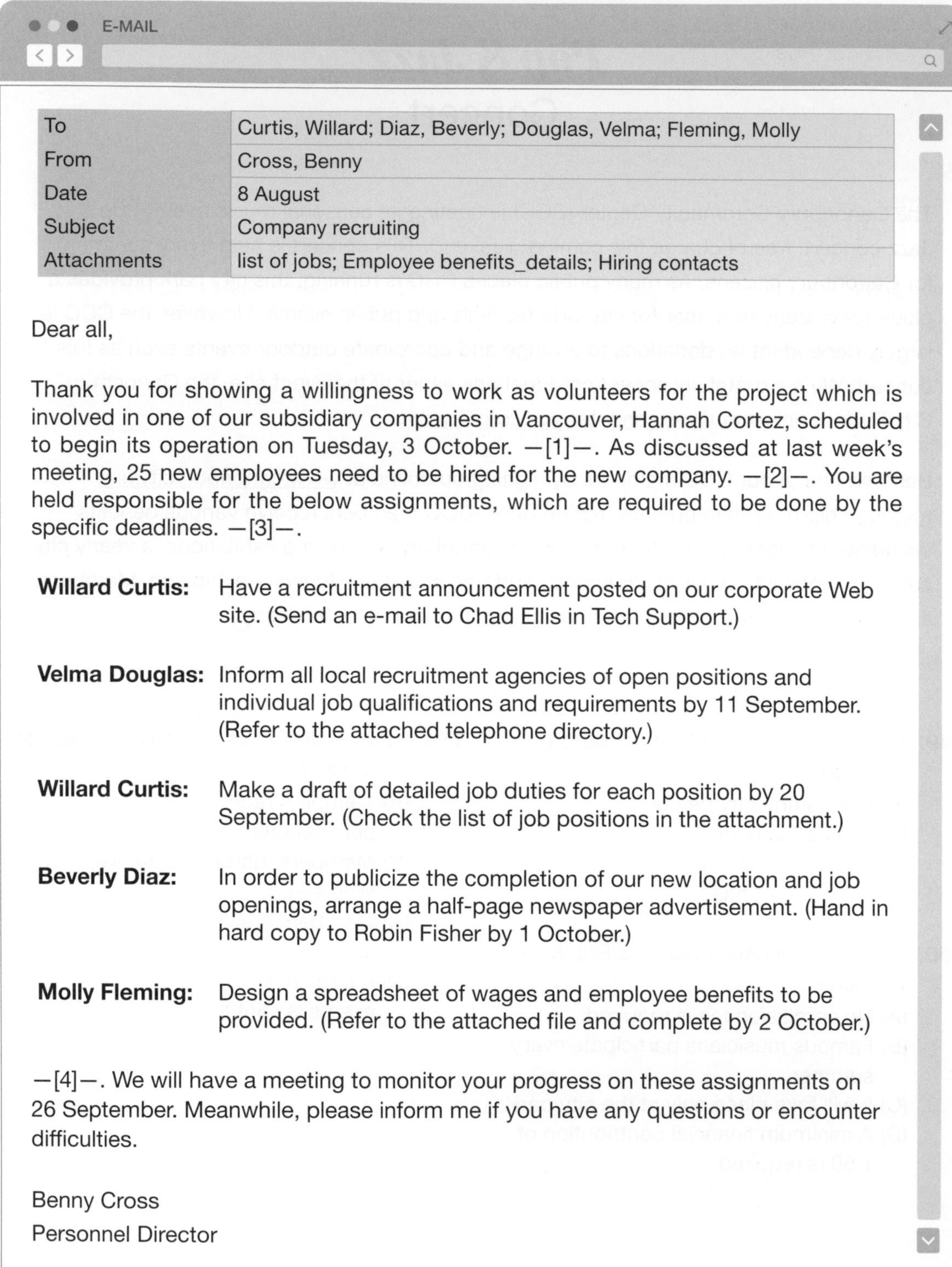

E-MAIL

To	Curtis, Willard; Diaz, Beverly; Douglas, Velma; Fleming, Molly
From	Cross, Benny
Date	8 August
Subject	Company recruiting
Attachments	list of jobs; Employee benefits_details; Hiring contacts

Dear all,

Thank you for showing a willingness to work as volunteers for the project which is involved in one of our subsidiary companies in Vancouver, Hannah Cortez, scheduled to begin its operation on Tuesday, 3 October. —[1]—. As discussed at last week's meeting, 25 new employees need to be hired for the new company. —[2]—. You are held responsible for the below assignments, which are required to be done by the specific deadlines. —[3]—.

Willard Curtis: Have a recruitment announcement posted on our corporate Web site. (Send an e-mail to Chad Ellis in Tech Support.)

Velma Douglas: Inform all local recruitment agencies of open positions and individual job qualifications and requirements by 11 September. (Refer to the attached telephone directory.)

Willard Curtis: Make a draft of detailed job duties for each position by 20 September. (Check the list of job positions in the attachment.)

Beverly Diaz: In order to publicize the completion of our new location and job openings, arrange a half-page newspaper advertisement. (Hand in hard copy to Robin Fisher by 1 October.)

Molly Fleming: Design a spreadsheet of wages and employee benefits to be provided. (Refer to the attached file and complete by 2 October.)

—[4]—. We will have a meeting to monitor your progress on these assignments on 26 September. Meanwhile, please inform me if you have any questions or encounter difficulties.

Benny Cross
Personnel Director

152. When is the draft of detailed job responsibilities due?
(A) September 11
(B) September 20
(C) October 1
(D) October 2

153. According to the e-mail, who will NOT use one of the e-mail attachments?
(A) Mr. Curtis
(B) Ms. Diaz
(C) Ms. Douglas
(D) Ms. Fleming

154. What does Mr. Cross ask the recipients to do before they meet?
(A) Send him their completed work
(B) Visit the subsidiary company
(C) Get in touch with him as needed
(D) Cooperate with each other on assignments

155. In which of the positions marked [1], [2], [3], and [4] does the following sentence best belong?
"Before then, there is a lot of work to do."
(A) [1]
(B) [2]
(C) [3]
(D) [4]

TEST 1 PART 7

GO ON TO THE NEXT PAGE

Questions 156-159 refer to the following text message chain.

Nellie Bishop 11:29 A.M.
Hello, everyone. Does anyone know Karla is working today?

Randy Bennett 11:30 A.M.
I am pretty sure she is on duty today. What's the matter?

Nellie Bishop 11:30 A.M.
I just checked the meeting rooms and found out that one of our speakers seems defective. It makes a crackling sound.

Randy Bennett 11:31 A.M.
Oh, no way. When is the marketing forum supposed to begin?

Nellie Bishop 11:32 A.M.
At noon. Some people have already arrived, and more than 100 are expected.

Naomi Brewer 11:33 A.M.
I am just calling the maintenance department. Give me a second. Well, there aren't any spare speakers in the storage room. Nellie, we have only about 30 minutes left, and we haven't finished setting up the microphones and the projector. Could you drive over to the nearest audio shop and borrow or buy some?

Randy Bennett 11:34 A.M.
That's a good idea. Nellie, while you are away, we will check this floor. I think I saw one around the corner on my way here this morning.

Nellie Bishop 11:35 A.M.
All right. I can do that for you.

156. Where most likely is Ms. Bishop?
(A) In her office
(B) At a storage room
(C) At a conference center
(D) In a maintenance department

157. At 11:31 A.M., why does Mr. Bennett most likely write, "Oh, no way"?
(A) A coworker has not come to work.
(B) Some equipment is not working properly.
(C) They don't know how to get a new speaker.
(D) Attendance is more than expected

158. What is suggested about Ms. Brewer?
(A) She is going to quit her current position.
(B) She was recently recruited.
(C) She agreed to go with Randy's idea.
(D) She takes the initiative.

159. What will Ms. Bishop most likely do next?
(A) Drive over to her office
(B) Try to find Karla
(C) Repair some equipment
(D) Go to a local store

GO ON TO THE NEXT PAGE

Questions 160-163 refer to the following letter.

RTCQ Australia
983 Gunnersbury Avenue
Melbourne, VIC X7R 3R1

21 October

Mr. Julius Shelton
214 Sloane Road
Sydney, NSW R3A 5T2

Dear Mr. Shelton,

We are happy that you have accepted our half-year paid internship position with the Products Development Team at RTCQ Australia. —[1]—. The first day of your internship will be on Wednesday, 5 December. You may have other scheduled commitments in the beginning of December, so if necessary, the starting date can be adjusted. This can be discussed further in November when your schedule becomes clearer. —[2]—.

Your supervisor will be Mr. Martin Soto, our head of Quality Control, who specializes in improving products' durability using eco-friendly materials. Mr. Soto said to me that he happened to find your report in the magazine Life with Nature last year, which impressed him. —[3]—.

Please find the enclosed contract and review it thoroughly. If there are no concerns or questions about the terms of the contract, you can sign and send it back to us at the address above by 29 October. As soon as the signed contract arrives, our personnel department will get in touch with you to prepare a staff ID badge, an e-mail account, and a parking space. —[4]—.

Janie Terry

Managing Director of Personnel

160. What is NOT mentioned about Mr. Shelton's internship?
(A) The division he will be working in
(B) The duration he will work
(C) The manager he will report to
(D) The wage he will receive

161. What is suggested about Mr. Soto?
(A) He read a report written by Mr. Shelton.
(B) Mr. Terry is working under his supervision.
(C) He is a well-known specialist in a field.
(D) Mr. Shelton was interviewed by him.

162. What will Mr. Shelton probably do next?
(A) Arrange a meeting with Mr. Soto
(B) Discuss a starting date
(C) Mail a signed document
(D) Open an e-mail account

163. In which of the positions marked [1], [2], [3], and [4] does the following sentence best belong?
"Not to mention, he was certain that you will be a great addition to his team."
(A) [1]
(B) [2]
(C) [3]
(D) [4]

GO ON TO THE NEXT PAGE

Questions 164-166 refer to the following contract.

Renewal Contract for Maintenance Service
Tooting Vehicle

We appreciate your loyalty to Tooting Vehicle!

Client Name: Jamie Crawford
Address: 432 Fulham Broadway, London, UK
Post Code: RC12 5Q3
Telephone: 345-3215-4432

Client Signature:

Jamie Crawford

Amount Due on Acceptance:
£99.00

Basic Plan: £99.00

This six-month service plan includes cleaning of your vehicle as well as conducting regular inspection.

Advantages provided:
- Verifying the engine for the best function
- Inspecting the overall tires
- Securing connecting components
- Sanitizing cooling and heating systems
- Filling cooling water

Super Plan: £149.00

Subscribers with this twelve-month service plan are offered relief-care service. On top of the basic cleaning and inspection of your vehicle, subscribers are provided with night and weekend services at no additional fee.

Inspection:

Subscribers are able to use the inspection service during usual opening hours, Monday through Friday, 9 A.M. to 6 P.M.

Service Request Calls:

Except for Super Plan holders, an extra £25.00 fee will be charged to the client account when a request is ordered during nights and weekends.

164. What is suggested about Ms. Crawford?
(A) She got a car insurance quote.
(B) She has contracted Tooting Vehicle before.
(C) She will have her tires changed immediately.
(D) She will be exempted from the extra service fee for weekends.

165. What is NOT part of the Basic Plan?
(A) Checking car tires
(B) Inspecting the engines
(C) Cleaning cooling and heating systems
(D) Changing engine oil

166. What additional advantage is included in the fee of the Super Plan?
(A) Cooling water supplement
(B) Replacement of components at no charge
(C) Servicing after operating hours
(D) Inspection service every month

GO ON TO THE NEXT PAGE

Questions 167-169 refer to the following letter.

Dear Editor,

It is always a great pleasure to read your thoughtful articles. I am writing to discuss your recent article "Inviting Arenas for Music – The Imperial Concert Hall" that was put in the June edition of *Life with Music Magazine*. The article made me pleased to read about such a splendid place that I am familiar with, and the photos in it were really great. It contained one thing I'd like to point out, though. —[1]—.

In the article, Cindy Walters was introduced as the founder of the Imperial Concert Hall; actually, although she was engaged in the initial stage of the business, she was just one of the investors. —[2]—. It was Alicia Warner who was the actual owner of the arena. I happened to learn about this since I had several opportunities to perform at the arena with my band, which naturally gave us chances to interact with Ms. Warner sometimes. —[3]—.

I think who the owner of the business is was not the focus of the article, but still it is, I believe, an essential part of the story of the Imperial Concert Hall. Ms. Warner tried to give many new gifted local musicians more chances to perform through her business. In spite of that, she is hardly recognized enough for her contributions. —[4]—. In order to avoid doing her a disservice, she should be given her due.

Sincerely,

Ricky Webb

Ricky Webb

167. Why has the letter been written?
(A) To review a concert hall
(B) To correct wrong information
(C) To publicize upcoming events
(D) To recognize a performer's accomplishment

168. Who most likely is Mr. Webb?
(A) An editor
(B) A reporter
(C) A musician
(D) An entrepreneur

169. In which of the positions marked [1], [2], [3], and [4] does the following sentence best belong?
"She didn't want to be co-owner when the business wasn't stable."
(A) [1]
(B) [2]
(C) [3]
(D) [4]

Questions 170-171 refer to the following e-mail.

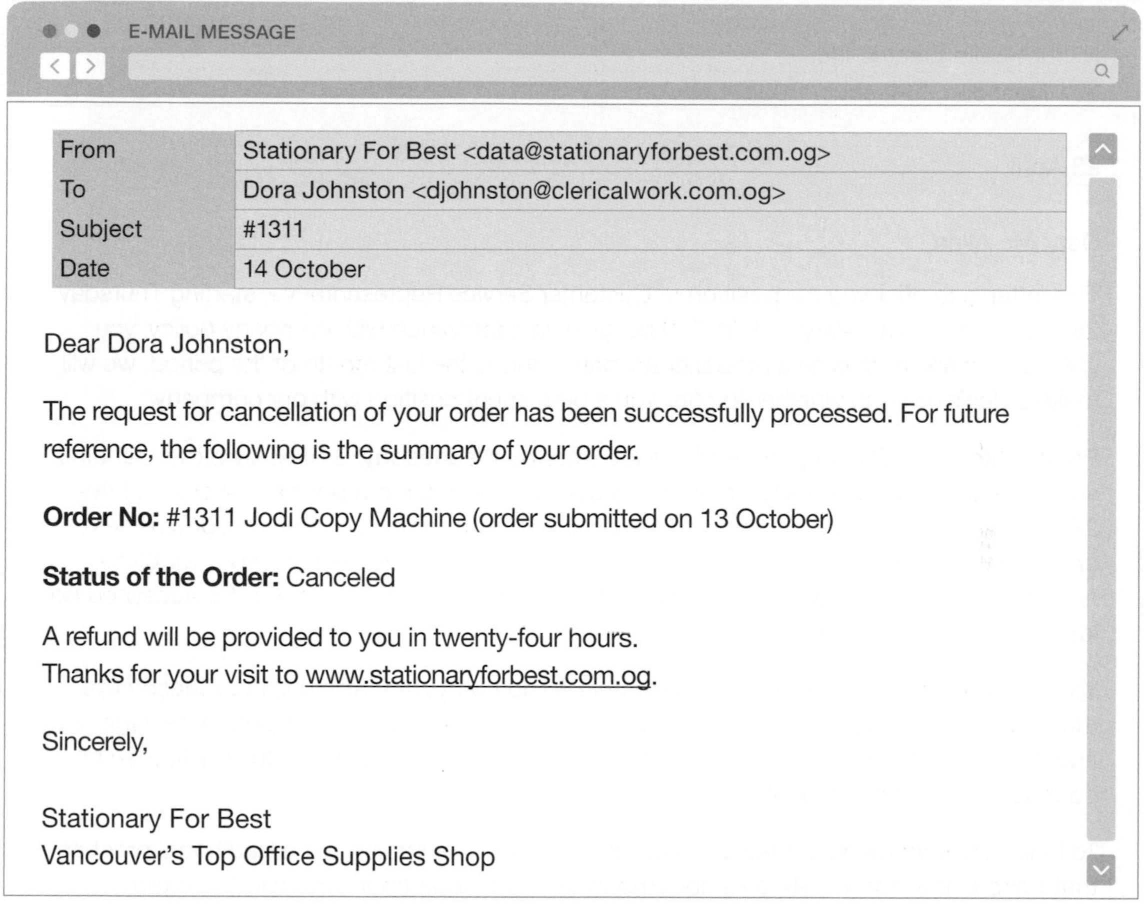
E-MAIL MESSAGE

From	Stationary For Best <data@stationaryforbest.com.og>
To	Dora Johnston <djohnston@clericalwork.com.og>
Subject	#1311
Date	14 October

Dear Dora Johnston,

The request for cancellation of your order has been successfully processed. For future reference, the following is the summary of your order.

Order No: #1311 Jodi Copy Machine (order submitted on 13 October)

Status of the Order: Canceled

A refund will be provided to you in twenty-four hours.
Thanks for your visit to www.stationaryforbest.com.og.

Sincerely,

Stationary For Best
Vancouver's Top Office Supplies Shop

TEST 1 PART 7

170. What is the reason the e-mail has been sent?
(A) To announce a new policy
(B) To inquire about an item's availability
(C) To confirm a modification to an order request
(D) To apologize for a delay in delivery

171. What information is given to Ms. Johnston about payment?
(A) She should already have got a refund.
(B) She does not need to pay for the product.
(C) She has paid for the order in full.
(D) She will pay a bill in twenty-four hours.

GO ON TO THE NEXT PAGE

Questions 172-175 refer to the following letter and agreement.

Kilburn Gold Electric Inc.
661 Neasden, Kingsbury Road, London

23 April

Dear Mr. Allen,

This letter is to offer you the position of Customer Service Representative, starting Thursday, 24 May, at the initial salary of £31,000 per year. In compliance with company policy, you will work for six months on a probationary basis, and at the last month of the period, we will make a decision as to whether to offer you a permanent position with our company.

Please inform us of acceptance of the job offer by Wednesday, 9 May, by either sending an e-mail to our Personnel Division, pd@kgei.com, or making a phone call at 21-3346-2211. If there are any circumstances keeping you from taking on your responsibilities on the date stated, please let us know at your earliest convenience in order for us to accommodate you. However, be advised that a new starting day cannot be accepted no later than Tuesday, 5 June.

You are required to report to the Personnel Division on your starting date. Please note that you need to bring a copy of this letter with you to let the head of personnel sign and date it. Moreover, you have to show official documents like your driving license or passport, and bank account number.

To help new staff members adjust to our organization, we implement a traditional practice that pairs a new comer with a senior employee in the department. Hence, Mr. Alton Baldwin has been assigned to answer any questions you probably have such as your responsibilities and department's ambience. You can reach him by calling at 31-3342-4495, or sending an e-mail at a_baldwin@kgei.com. Keep in mind that the new employee orientation you are required to attend has been scheduled for Friday, 25 May. At that time, we will let you know about employee benefits and company policies. Lastly, thank you for joining Kilburn Gold Electric Inc., and we hope you will be our invaluable asset.

Sincerely,

Ruby Morales

Head of Personnel Division

Agreement on Employment Conditions and Terms

I have hereby accepted employment with Kilburn Gold Electric Inc. under the conditions and terms specified.

Signature: *Scott Allen*
Name: Scott Allen
Starting Date: 1 June

172. What is a new staff member NOT required to do?

(A) Hand in a copy of their degree certificate
(B) Get in touch with the personnel division prior to their first day
(C) Present proof of identification on the first day
(D) Work with an experienced coworker

173. What is indicated about Mr. Baldwin?

(A) He is a personnel officer.
(B) He has worked for Kilburn Gold Electric Inc. since its founding.
(C) He is working in the customer service division.
(D) He will direct Mr. Allen to the personnel division.

174. When will Mr. Allen officially be notified of the organization's rules?

(A) On Tuesday
(B) On Wednesday
(C) On Thursday
(D) On Friday

175. What is indicated about Mr. Allen?

(A) He will get a raise after his probationary period.
(B) He will not be eligible for employee benefits for a half year.
(C) He postponed his starting date.
(D) He will be working with an experienced employee for the first six months.

GO ON TO THE NEXT PAGE

Questions 176-180 refer to the following information and form.

ENJOYING THE WATFORD CONTEMPORARY PHOTO ARCHIVE (WCPA)

The Watford Contemporary Photo Archive (WCPA) boasts not only various digital photos and prints but also a wide range of periodicals, books of paintings, and genuine materials acquired from many accomplished photographers and private collectors. Our invaluable collections are displayed throughout the whole ground floor of the building; the rare collections are exhibited on the first floor.

All visitors are required to follow the below guidelines to keep WCPA's possessions safely preserved.

- Upon each visitor's first visit, they need to fill out a membership application form at the reception office. In order to obtain membership cards, every member must provide credit card information and a photo ID.
- The entire materials we have collected are available to the members. When looking through them, please keep in mind that the order of the materials should remain as arranged. If you find any of them is missing or out of place, please inform one of our employees; do not make any effort to correct errors yourself.
- Our archive possessions should be handled in ways that avoid any damage, so do not leave any traces or marks during usage. Any damage may result in members paying a fine.
- Copy machines are accessible throughout the ground floor.
- Each material from any archive section has to be returned by 5:00 P.M.

Please comply with these special guidelines to look through the rare collections.

- Through a rare collection request form, rare items can be requested from one of our employees. Each visitor is allowed to view no more than four materials at once. The materials need to be returned to the reference office when a visitor requests more than four.
- Visitors are permitted to examine these items only in the rare collection area.
- All personal belongings such as jackets, laptops, and bags must be kept in a cabinet before getting into the rare collection area. For taking notes, writing materials can be provided upon request.
- Visitors are not able to request rare collection items after 4:30 P.M.

Watford Contemporary Photo Archive (WCPA)
Request Form for Rare Collections

Name: Jeff Bryant

Membership No.: 9321

Date: February 22

E-mail: jeffbryant@y-young.com

Telephone: 321-8872-8723

To help us locate the materials you would like to view, please complete the two sections below.

	Item Number	Brief Account
Material 1	TO 822210	Original flyer: Museum show of Henry Carter's artwork
Material 2	TR 474382	Henry Carter's work of art (India, 1941)
Material 3	JU 008331	Henry Carter's personal exhibition (Indonesia, 1943)
Material 4	CV 103469	Latimer Monthly News (published May, 1942)
Material 5	RO 339201	Henry Carter's family photo (New York, 1944)
Material 6		

176. What is suggested about the WCPA?
(A) Its opening hours differ from day to day.
(B) It is imperative for visitors to apply for its membership.
(C) It allows only local residents to access the first floor.
(D) Its items are kept in several buildings.

177. According to the information, what are visitors prohibited from doing?
(A) Touching delicate materials
(B) Leaving personal belongings at a desk
(C) Arranging misplaced materials
(D) Reserving items before their visit

178. How can visitors to the rare collection area take personal notes?
(A) By borrowing digital recording equipment
(B) By using writing tools distributed by the WCPA
(C) By asking for photocopies for notes
(D) By using one of the WCPA's tablet PCs

179. What most likely is Mr. Bryant's research about?
(A) A collection of rare photographs
(B) Belongings of a specific individual
(C) The works of a certain artist
(D) The preservation of historical photos

180. What does Mr. Bryant's request for materials indicate?
(A) He has to return materials before 5:00 P.M.
(B) He cannot view all his requested materials at once.
(C) He has never been to the WCPA.
(D) He needs to pay a fee to request some items.

GO ON TO THE NEXT PAGE

Questions 181-185 refer to the following agenda and letter.

Finsbury Business College

One-day event at Golders Hotel Headquarters (GHH)
Tuesday, March 21, 10:15 A.M. to 3:30 P.M.

Timetable

10:15 A.M. Finsbury students and their instructor come to the security office to get access cards
10:30 A.M. Lecture: What an Internship Is Required to Do for Operations
11:10 A.M. Lecture: Qualifications for an Internship in Public Relations
11:50 A.M. Lecture: Possible Difficulties in Administration
12:30 P.M. Lunch after a guided tour of the office building
2:00 P.M. Lecture: How Things Are Going as an Intern in Sales and Marketing
2:45 P.M. Open discussion including Q & A and Closing

If you are interested in this event, you must register in advance or on-site. If you register in advance, you'll only need to pick up your name tag and other materials on-site.

April 23

Mr. Corey Gardner
Finsbury Business College
754 Stanmore Avenue
Croxley, RW 43 1Q4

Dear Mr. Gardner,

About a month ago when I visited Golders Hotel Headquarters (GHH) with the schoolfellows from Finsbury Business College, I was lucky to have an opportunity to converse with you right after your seminar. You and your coworkers' presentations were very impressive, particularly Dana Frazier's speech about her operation management responsibilities and Clark George's wider perspective on his duties publicizing GHH's services and products.

Considering my goal to be a GHH's intern, however, your talk was the most relevant one among them. It was fascinating to hear about your managerial duties and your previous experience as an intern. It seems like the path you have come along is almost the same as the one I am planning to follow. Therefore, if you could give me some guidelines regarding what skills and knowledge you needed to fulfill your daily duties as an intern in sales and marketing at Golders Hotel, it would be greatly appreciated. Any advice I could have from you will definitely help me secure the skills and knowledge that I am going to need.

Thank you for your help in advance and I hope to meet you again. It would be great for me to have a chance to work with you in the near future.

Sincerely,

Delbert Acosta

181. What was most likely the purpose of the event?
(A) To inform the employees of the seminars
(B) To publicize a new training program to students
(C) To encourage students to participate in an internship
(D) To help business school students to complete their project

182. In what field is Mr. Acosta most likely majoring?
(A) Operations management
(B) Public relations
(C) Hotel management
(D) Sales and marketing

183. When did Mr. Gardner most likely deliver his speech?
(A) At 10:30 A.M.
(B) At 11:10 A.M.
(C) At 11:50 A.M.
(D) At 2:00 P.M.

184. In the letter, the word "secure" in paragraph 2, line 7, is closest in meaning to
(A) keep
(B) safe
(C) acquire
(D) purchase

185. What is indicated about Mr. Gardner?
(A) He signed up for the seminars.
(B) He worked as an intern.
(C) He met business school students after the event.
(D) He is working at the Golders Hotel Headquarters.

TEST 1 PART 7

GO ON TO THE NEXT PAGE

Questions 186-190 refer to the following e-mails and press release.

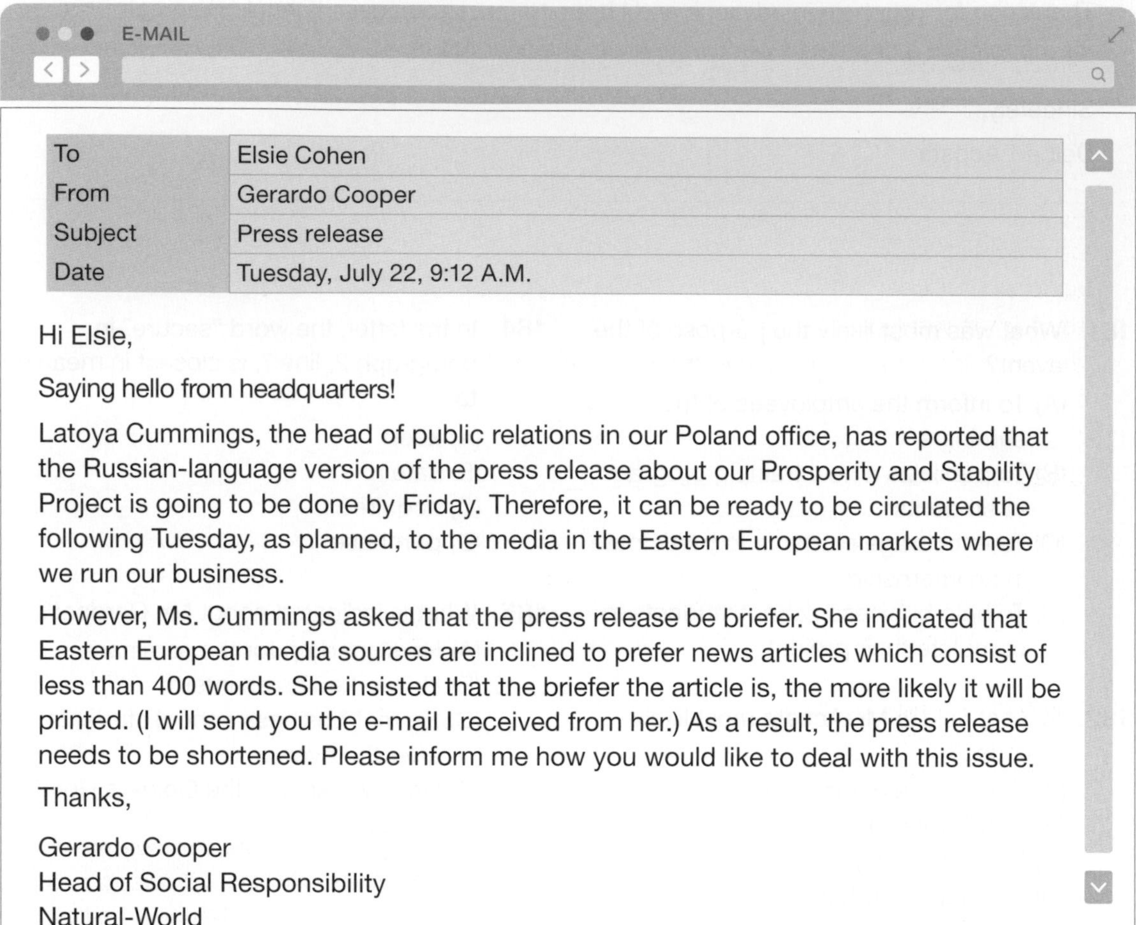
E-MAIL

To	Elsie Cohen
From	Gerardo Cooper
Subject	Press release
Date	Tuesday, July 22, 9:12 A.M.

Hi Elsie,

Saying hello from headquarters!

Latoya Cummings, the head of public relations in our Poland office, has reported that the Russian-language version of the press release about our Prosperity and Stability Project is going to be done by Friday. Therefore, it can be ready to be circulated the following Tuesday, as planned, to the media in the Eastern European markets where we run our business.

However, Ms. Cummings asked that the press release be briefer. She indicated that Eastern European media sources are inclined to prefer news articles which consist of less than 400 words. She insisted that the briefer the article is, the more likely it will be printed. (I will send you the e-mail I received from her.) As a result, the press release needs to be shortened. Please inform me how you would like to deal with this issue.

Thanks,

Gerardo Cooper
Head of Social Responsibility
Natural-World

E-MAIL

To	Gerardo Cooper
From	Elsie Cohen
Subject	RE: Press release
Date	Tuesday, July 22, 11:43 A.M.
Attachment	Important Project.doc

Hello Gerardo,

All of our team members have shared the e-mail you sent me earlier today. We have made some corrections to the press release according to Ms. Cummings' recommendation and attached it. Please look through it to make sure that the information does not have any mistake. Then, you can send it to her as soon as you can in order for her to translate it into Russian. In addition, could you remind her to contact all related social media to have it posted?

Thanks,

Elsie Cohen
Head of Communication
Natural-World

Official Announcement for Natural-World Announces Important Project

Natural-World is pleased to announce its Prosperity and Stability Project. Over the next four years, the firm will put a minimum investment of $600 million throughout all the nations where it runs its business to enhance availability of educational reading materials, which are very important for children in need. In cooperation with national and global child welfare associations, educational publications and programs will be provided to educators and professionals in the childcare industry. Furthermore, schools and local childcare institutions will offer a wide range of educational materials to children while nursery schools will offer educational toys and storybooks. Check out more information about the project by visiting www.naturalworld.net/project.

(Natural-World is a publishing company based in Canada, which also boasts its presence in Poland, Romania, Russia, and Ukraine.)

186. What is suggested about Ms. Cummings?
- (A) She has approved the Prosperity and Stability Project.
- (B) She has met Mr. Cooper in person.
- (C) She is knowledgeable about news formats in Eastern Europe.
- (D) She has recently transferred to the Poland office.

187. What did Ms. Cohen do recently?
- (A) She translated a press release herself.
- (B) She visited the Poland branch.
- (C) She revised a publicity material.
- (D) She has information posted on social media.

188. What is the main reason the project will be carried out?
- (A) To promote the education industry
- (B) To encourage teachers to make educational materials
- (C) To establish more childcare institutions
- (D) To offer children better educational items

189. What is stated in the press release?
- (A) The location in which the materials are produced
- (B) The number of Natural-World's international branches
- (C) The industry where Natural-World operates
- (D) The annual profit Natural-World earns

190. Where does Mr. Cooper most likely work?
- (A) In Poland
- (B) In Romania
- (C) In Canada
- (D) In Ukraine

GO ON TO THE NEXT PAGE

Questions 191-195 refer to the following e-mail, advertisement, and article.

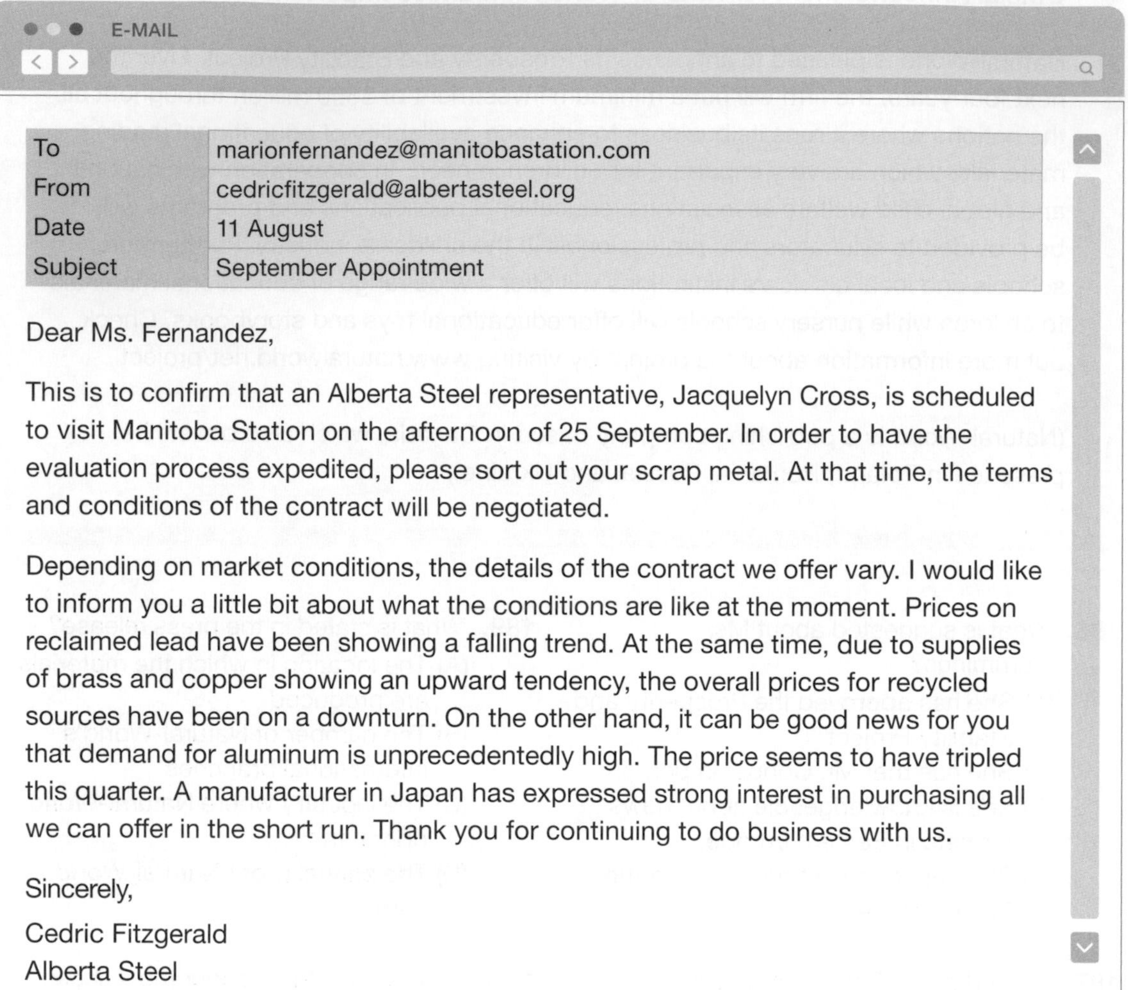

E-MAIL

To	marionfernandez@manitobastation.com
From	cedricfitzgerald@albertasteel.org
Date	11 August
Subject	September Appointment

Dear Ms. Fernandez,

This is to confirm that an Alberta Steel representative, Jacquelyn Cross, is scheduled to visit Manitoba Station on the afternoon of 25 September. In order to have the evaluation process expedited, please sort out your scrap metal. At that time, the terms and conditions of the contract will be negotiated.

Depending on market conditions, the details of the contract we offer vary. I would like to inform you a little bit about what the conditions are like at the moment. Prices on reclaimed lead have been showing a falling trend. At the same time, due to supplies of brass and copper showing an upward tendency, the overall prices for recycled sources have been on a downturn. On the other hand, it can be good news for you that demand for aluminum is unprecedentedly high. The price seems to have tripled this quarter. A manufacturer in Japan has expressed strong interest in purchasing all we can offer in the short run. Thank you for continuing to do business with us.

Sincerely,

Cedric Fitzgerald
Alberta Steel

Manitoba Station

Manitoba Station is the largest recycler of electronic parts in the area.
Do you intend to throw away any electronic devices?
Please drop off the materials in the proper place.

Shelves: Desktop and Laptop computers

Blue container: Miscellaneous and Accessories like mouses and other devices
Yellow container: Speakers, Monitors and any External storage devices

The demand for rare metals is strong in the current market. Thus, all small devices like game systems, tablets, and cell phones, for a while, will be accepted until the end of September.

Our priority is always to provide assistance for you. Should you have any further questions, please do not hesitate to contact us at 080-434-5353.

TOKYO (14 Oct.) - Dixon Appliances announced yesterday the earliest launch of its newest tablet PC, the R2Q-1000. The new tablet will be the most affordable as well as the lightest and fastest one in its class. The use of newly created capacitors made these high-quality devices possible. In addition, the R2Q is one of the first mass-manufactured tablet PCs using up to 60 percent recycled material, most of which is taken out of outdated electronic products. The Japanese firm's flagship shop in Tokyo will begin selling the R2Q models to a limited number of customers starting next week. Dixon is going to make the device available at outlets across Japan by 20 Oct., even though consumers abroad need to wait until 31 Oct.

191. What field does Ms. Fernandez most likely specialize in?
(A) Developing computers
(B) Recycling electronics
(C) Mining for rare materials
(D) Producing computer parts

192. According to the advertisement, where should a small item like a keyboard be put?
(A) On the shelves
(B) In the yellow container
(C) In the blue container
(D) At the service desk

193. Why did Manitoba Station ask that the rare items be dropped off through September?
(A) Because the prices for items will decrease.
(B) Because the market condition for the items is good.
(C) Because it will relocate to another region.
(D) Because its ownership will change soon.

194. What is Dixon Appliances most likely using in its new tablet PC?
(A) Lead
(B) Brass
(C) Aluminum
(D) Copper

195. When will the new tablet PC be available on the international market?
(A) On October 14
(B) On October 17
(C) On October 20
(D) On October 31

GO ON TO THE NEXT PAGE

Questions 196-200 refer to the following e-mails and meeting minutes.

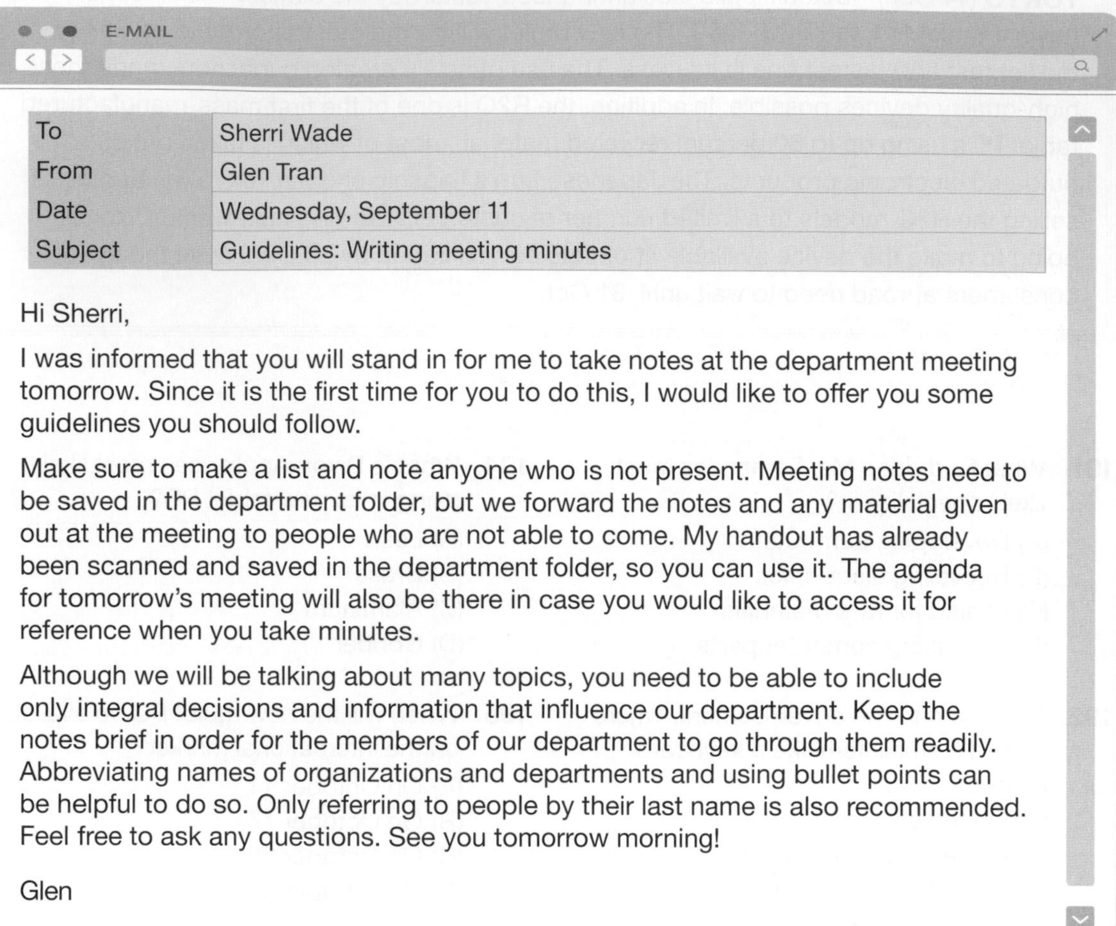

E-MAIL

To	Sherri Wade
From	Glen Tran
Date	Wednesday, September 11
Subject	Guidelines: Writing meeting minutes

Hi Sherri,

I was informed that you will stand in for me to take notes at the department meeting tomorrow. Since it is the first time for you to do this, I would like to offer you some guidelines you should follow.

Make sure to make a list and note anyone who is not present. Meeting notes need to be saved in the department folder, but we forward the notes and any material given out at the meeting to people who are not able to come. My handout has already been scanned and saved in the department folder, so you can use it. The agenda for tomorrow's meeting will also be there in case you would like to access it for reference when you take minutes.

Although we will be talking about many topics, you need to be able to include only integral decisions and information that influence our department. Keep the notes brief in order for the members of our department to go through them readily. Abbreviating names of organizations and departments and using bullet points can be helpful to do so. Only referring to people by their last name is also recommended. Feel free to ask any questions. See you tomorrow morning!

Glen

Accounting Services Department Meeting Minutes

On September 12

2:00-3:30 P.M.

Absent: Ana Stephens, Willie Walters

Attended: Kay Schneider, Ella Romero, Ella Rilay, Roy Reed, Eleanor Porter, Sherri Wade, Glen Tran, Celia Sharp

- Romero noted that RX has been experiencing data-loss issues with its accounting software program. Since Tran is handling the same problem with another client, he will take care of that inquiry.
- Reed and Porter attended the Accounting Symposium in Sydney from September 7 to 8 and were asked to deliver a talk at next year's symposium in Washington.
- The department's outing will take place at St. James Park on Friday, October 2. As Schneider will be temporarily helping the New York branch this fall, Rilay will be held accountable for this year's outing arrangements.
- Tran reported that his team is about to review the budget for monthly operating costs. He reminded staff members to avoid making excessive printouts and copies.

Minutes Taken by Sherri Wade

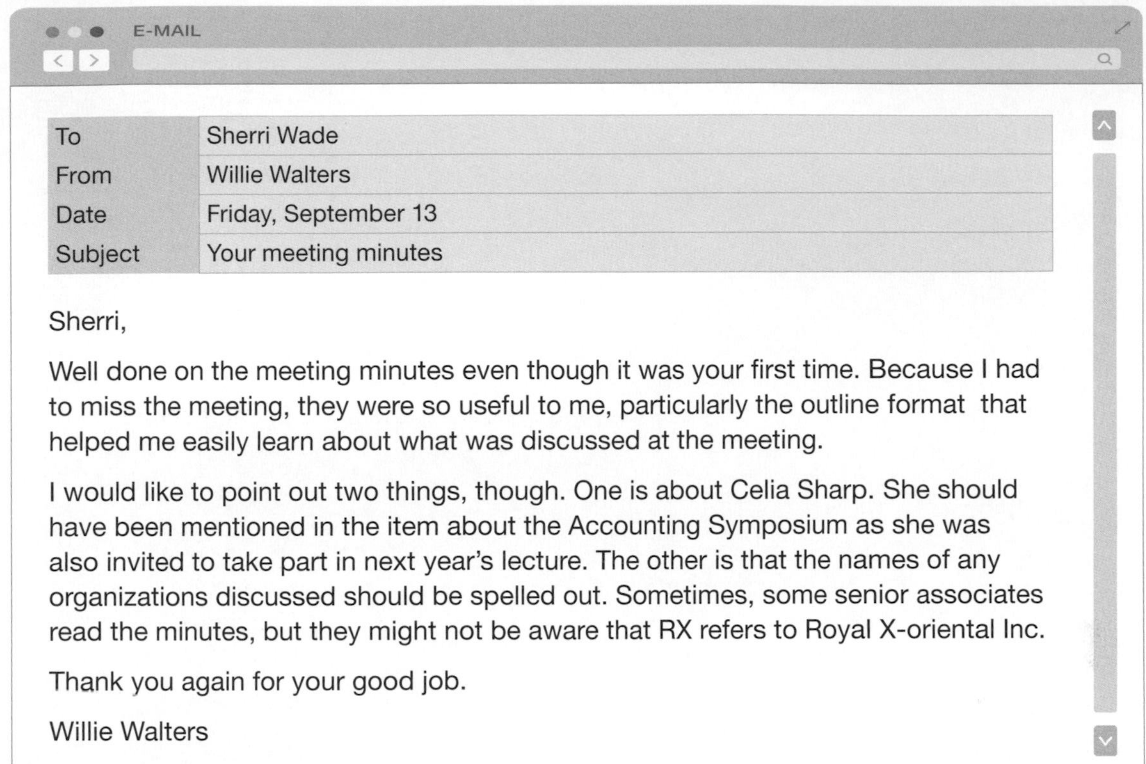
E-MAIL

To	Sherri Wade
From	Willie Walters
Date	Friday, September 13
Subject	Your meeting minutes

Sherri,

Well done on the meeting minutes even though it was your first time. Because I had to miss the meeting, they were so useful to me, particularly the outline format that helped me easily learn about what was discussed at the meeting.

I would like to point out two things, though. One is about Celia Sharp. She should have been mentioned in the item about the Accounting Symposium as she was also invited to take part in next year's lecture. The other is that the names of any organizations discussed should be spelled out. Sometimes, some senior associates read the minutes, but they might not be aware that RX refers to Royal X-oriental Inc.

Thank you again for your good job.

Willie Walters

196. What is indicated about Mr. Tran?
(A) He had to miss the department meeting.
(B) He distributed handout materials at the department meeting.
(C) He will keep the meeting agenda in the department folder.
(D) He will have to visit Sydney to participate in an event.

197. In the first e-mail, the word "include" in paragraph 3, line 1, is closest in meaning to
(A) back up
(B) memorize
(C) capture
(D) review

198. What task is Mr. Schneider usually in charge of?
(A) Dealing with client complaints
(B) Preparing a yearly social event
(C) Handling the monthly budget
(D) Taking notes at every meeting

199. What has Mr. Reed recently done?
(A) He has visited a branch office.
(B) He has contacted Royal X-oriental Inc.
(C) He has given a talk at an event.
(D) He has been to Sydney.

200. What suggestion for taking minutes do Mr. Tran and Mr. Walters disagree on?
(A) Only recording members' last names
(B) Using initial letters of organizations' names
(C) Checking who is present or absent
(D) Entering information into a computer

Stop! This is the end of the test. If you finish before time is called, you may go back to Parts 5, 6, and 7 and check your work.

TEST

開始作答 ____ 點 ____ 分

完成作答 ____ 點 ____ 分

- 建議一次寫完整份試題，避免分次作答。
- 答題時，請比照實際考試，將答案畫在答案卡上。

目標答對題數 ____ /200

實際答對題數 ____ /200

- 將答對題數乘以 5 即可概算出分數。

LISTENING TEST

In the Listening test, you will be asked to demonstrate how well you understand spoken English. The entire Listening test will last approximately 45 minutes. There are four parts, and directions are given for each part. You must mark your answers on the separate answer sheet. Do not write your answers in your test book.

PART 1 05

Directions: For each question in this part, you will hear four statements about a picture in your test book. When you hear the statements, you must select the one statement that best describes what you see in the picture. Then find the number of the question on your answer sheet and mark your answer. The statements will not be printed in your test book and will be spoken only one time.

Statement (B), "They're having a meeting," is the best description of the picture, so you should select answer (B) and mark it on your answer sheet.

1.

2.

GO ON TO THE NEXT PAGE

3.

4.

5.

6.

GO ON TO THE NEXT PAGE

PART 2 (06)

Directions: You will hear a question or statement and three responses spoken in English. They will not be printed in your test book and will be spoken only one time. Select the best response to the question or statement and mark the letter (A), (B), or (C) on your answer sheet.

7. Mark your answer on your answer sheet.

8. Mark your answer on your answer sheet.

9. Mark your answer on your answer sheet.

10. Mark your answer on your answer sheet.

11. Mark your answer on your answer sheet.

12. Mark your answer on your answer sheet.

13. Mark your answer on your answer sheet.

14. Mark your answer on your answer sheet.

15. Mark your answer on your answer sheet.

16. Mark your answer on your answer sheet.

17. Mark your answer on your answer sheet.

18. Mark your answer on your answer sheet.

19. Mark your answer on your answer sheet.

20. Mark your answer on your answer sheet.

21. Mark your answer on your answer sheet.

22. Mark your answer on your answer sheet.

23. Mark your answer on your answer sheet.

24. Mark your answer on your answer sheet.

25. Mark your answer on your answer sheet.

26. Mark your answer on your answer sheet.

27. Mark your answer on your answer sheet.

28. Mark your answer on your answer sheet.

29. Mark your answer on your answer sheet.

30. Mark your answer on your answer sheet.

31. Mark your answer on your answer sheet.

TEST 2 PART 2 PART 3

PART 3 (07)

Directions: You will hear some conversations between two or more people. You will be asked to answer three questions about what the speakers say in each conversation. Select the best response to each question and mark the letter (A), (B), (C), or (D) on your answer sheet. The conversations will not be printed in your test book and will be spoken only one time.

32. What was the man missing?
(A) A computer
(B) A notebook
(C) A pencil case
(D) A book

33. Why does the woman say, "I'll let the cleaning staff know"?
(A) To ask for some help
(B) To complain about a service
(C) To correct some mistaken information
(D) To inform them of a schedule change

34. What will the man do next?
(A) Give her his contact information
(B) Locate some items
(C) Contact the staff
(D) Check a floor plan

35. Why is the woman at a hotel?
(A) To organize a conference
(B) To make a presentation
(C) To stay for her business trip
(D) To visit a hotel guest

36. What was the man asked to do?
(A) Offer her free refreshments
(B) Guide her to the site
(C) Make copies for her
(D) Prepare for the presentation

37. What is available upstairs?
(A) A copy machine
(B) A restaurant
(C) A microphone
(D) A gift shop

GO ON TO THE NEXT PAGE

38. Who is Mr. Gallahan?
(A) A receptionist
(B) An owner
(C) A manager
(D) A sales representative

39. According to Patrick, what is suggested about the café?
(A) Its food quality is good.
(B) It is located on the rooftop.
(C) It offers a morning set.
(D) It is restricted to building visitors.

40. What will the woman do next?
(A) Install a new computer program
(B) Check her schedule
(C) Meet Mr. Gallahan
(D) Go to the café

---

41. Where do the speakers most likely work?
(A) At a warehouse
(B) At a museum
(C) At a gallery
(D) At a factory

42. What is the main topic of the conversation?
(A) Making an exhibition
(B) Hiring a new employee
(C) Increasing the budget
(D) Planning another schedule

43. According to the man, what has been changed?
(A) A display
(B) A class
(C) A Web site
(D) A policy

---

44. Why did someone from Humston Manufacturing call?
(A) To inquire about the prices
(B) To make a reservation
(C) To check the status of the event
(D) To visit the hotel

45. What is mentioned about Kelly Flowers?
(A) Its quality was not good.
(B) It was used by the company last month.
(C) Its style was imitated by other stores.
(D) It was owned by Humston Manufacturing.

46. What will the woman do next?
(A) Call a business
(B) Provide contact information
(C) Check customer reviews
(D) Reserve a hotel

---

47. What does the man explain to the woman?
(A) Some unexpected weather is coming.
(B) A computer system is not working properly.
(C) She should come back tomorrow.
(D) She needs to wait for some time.

48. What does the woman want to do?
(A) Attend the conference
(B) Meet Dr. Parker
(C) Reschedule an appointment
(D) See a doctor immediately

49. What does the man tell the woman to do?
(A) Sit in a waiting room
(B) Fill out a form
(C) Return later today
(D) Postpone a meeting

---

50. What are the speakers discussing?
(A) Replacing an old system
(B) Planning a training session
(C) Assigning a budget
(D) Operating a factory

51. Why does the woman say, "It costs a lot to travel to Denver at this time of year"?
(A) Another option for the transportation will be needed.
(B) A different location should be chosen.
(C) She doesn't want to transfer to Denver.
(D) She needs to take her vacation.

52. What will the man do next?
(A) Review the task
(B) Postpone the event
(C) Send another director
(D) Contact his colleague

---

53. What kind of business do the speakers most likely work for?
(A) A clothing store
(B) An advertising firm
(C) A resort
(D) A travel agency

54. What does the man imply when he says, "It's toward the end of the season"?
(A) He wants to encourage staff members to cheer up.
(B) His team will finish a project soon.
(C) A clearance sale should be held.
(D) The promotion will begin too late.

55. What does the woman offer to do?
(A) Compile a list
(B) Send some vouchers to guests
(C) Select some items for discounts
(D) Make a reservation

---

56. What is the main topic of the conversation?
(A) Revising a document
(B) Seeing a contractor
(C) Finishing a report
(D) Meeting a client

57. Why does the woman say, "I'm leaving for a meeting now"?
(A) She's asking the man to extend a deadline.
(B) She is not able to attend the meeting.
(C) She has already prepared for the project.
(D) She does not have time to look at a document.

58. What does the man say he will do this afternoon?
(A) Attend the board meeting
(B) Meet with a client
(C) Contact a colleague
(D) Prepare a budget

GO ON TO THE NEXT PAGE

Cafés Near Me	
Café	**Distance**
ARRIS Coffee	0.5 km
Towers Break	1 km
Hasbro's House	2 km
Adobe's Café	2.5 km

59. What will happen at 8:00?
(A) Some equipment will be delivered.
(B) A film will be premiered.
(C) A tour will be held.
(D) A presentation will start.

60. Look at the graphic. Which café do the speakers decide on?
(A) ARRIS Coffee
(B) Towers Break
(C) Hasbro's House
(D) Adobe's Café

61. What will the man do next?
(A) Get a recommendation
(B) Pay a parking fee
(C) Give some instructions
(D) Make a reservation

1 Sign up at the information desk	**2** Enter a dustproof room
3 Wear protective garments	**4** Leave all items

62. Look at the graphic. Which sign does the man refer to?
(A) Sign 1
(B) Sign 2
(C) Sign 3
(D) Sign 4

63. What did the woman bring today?
(A) A collection of documents
(B) A signed contract
(C) A journal
(D) A cell phone

64. What will the man do at the end of the tour?
(A) Submit some documents
(B) Meet her supervisor
(C) Fill out a form on the first floor
(D) Receive a souvenir

You're Invited to the 10th Anniversary of Marcus Marketing Firm!

Friday, November 21, 6:00 P.M.
Emerald Hall, Montreal Boutique Hotel

RSVP to Cindy Wong 532-4661

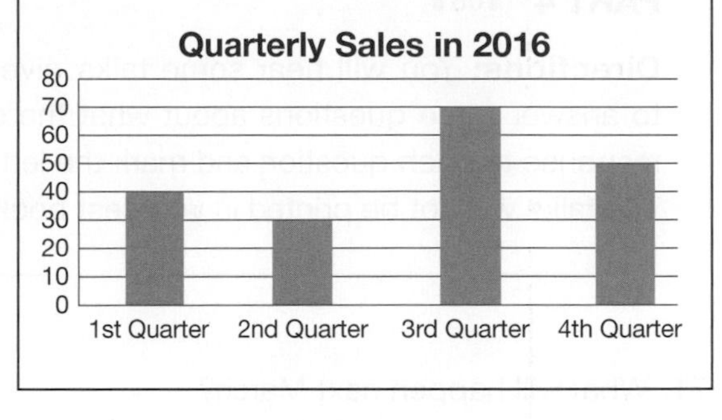

65. What did the woman ask the man to do?
(A) Review some work
(B) Send an e-mail
(C) Check a reservation
(D) Visit a printing shop

66. Look at the graphic. What should be changed?
(A) The title
(B) The date
(C) The place
(D) The phone number

67. When will the man probably receive the delivery?
(A) On Wednesday
(B) On Thursday
(C) On Friday
(D) On Saturday

68. What did the woman do in the morning?
(A) Called some clients
(B) Wrote a report
(C) Attended a meeting
(D) Sent a manual

69. Look at the graphic. Which quarter is being discussed?
(A) Quarter 1
(B) Quarter 2
(C) Quarter 3
(D) Quarter 4

70. What does the man suggest?
(A) Using some fruit
(B) Increasing prices
(C) Launching promotional events
(D) Opening new branches

GO ON TO THE NEXT PAGE

PART 4 (08)

Directions: You will hear some talks given by a single speaker. You will be asked to answer three questions about what the speaker says in each talk. Select the best response to each question and mark the letter (A), (B), (C), or (D) on your answer sheet. The talks will not be printed in your test book and will be spoken only one time.

71. What will happen next March?
(A) A proposal will be accepted.
(B) A construction site will open.
(C) A new building will open.
(D) A shopping mall will be closed.

72. According to the speaker, what has changed?
(A) The construction site
(B) The road expansion
(C) The public hearing date
(D) The transportation system

73. Why does the speaker ask the listeners to visit the Web site?
(A) To sign up to participate
(B) To raise some questions
(C) To take a survey
(D) To check residents' opinions

74. What type of business does the speaker work for?
(A) A fitness center
(B) A sporting goods store
(C) A newspaper company
(D) An automotive repair shop

75. What does the speaker say about Mr. Leed's order?
(A) Some of the items are no longer available.
(B) It was mistakenly canceled.
(C) It will be delayed.
(D) All of his order has been delivered already.

76. What will the speaker offer the listener?
(A) A free delivery
(B) A beverage voucher
(C) A shipping service upgrade
(D) A discount

77. What did the speaker do last Saturday?
(A) She stayed at the hotel.
(B) She gave a presentation.
(C) She participated in the reception.
(D) She went to a hospital.

78. What does the speaker mean when she says, "I have hired five receptionists through the agency"?
(A) Her business was successful.
(B) She couldn't complete the work.
(C) She had authority to hire workers.
(D) She wants to make a recommendation.

79. When will the speaker return to the office?
(A) On Tuesday
(B) On Wednesday
(C) On Thursday
(D) On Friday

---

80. What will the weather conditions be like until Thursday?
(A) Warm
(B) Rainy
(C) Humid
(D) Snowy

81. What will be held in the park?
(A) A road repair
(B) A sports event
(C) Musical performances
(D) Some exhibitions

82. What does the speaker imply when he says, "Lexington road crews will work around the clock"?
(A) There will be no traffic congestion next week.
(B) The temperature will be higher than expected.
(C) Some roads will be closed for clearing.
(D) Some of the residents will take a detour.

---

83. What happened last week?
(A) A summer event was discussed.
(B) A marketing presentation was made.
(C) A performance evaluation was conducted.
(D) Certain research was undertaken.

84. What information is the speaker showing?
(A) Feedback from a focus group
(B) Details of a new contract
(C) Reviews of the new packaging
(D) Updates on safety guidelines

85. Why does the speaker say, "This meeting room is reserved for the new employee training in an hour"?
(A) To encourage employees to attend the next meeting
(B) To ask for permission to extend the meeting
(C) To require people to leave the room
(D) To ask for understanding

---

86. What is the purpose of the introduction?
(A) To review a series of lectures
(B) To introduce new machinery
(C) To request donations
(D) To describe a support program

87. According to the speaker, what is suggested about Ms. Cooper?
(A) She was given an award for her success.
(B) She has participated in the program before.
(C) She is one of the well-known authors.
(D) She recently opened her own business.

88. Why does the speaker say, "She will receive questions after her presentation"?
(A) Not to interrupt during her talk
(B) Not to send her questions by e-mail
(C) To ask questions at any time
(D) To leave a question in advance

GO ON TO THE NEXT PAGE

Saturday	Sunday	Monday	Tuesday
Partly Sunny	Cloudy	Rain	Sunny

89. What event is being described?
(A) A technology fair
(B) A national festival
(C) A cooking show
(D) A food contest

90. According to the speaker, what can the listeners find on the Web site?
(A) A schedule for the contest
(B) A weather report
(C) A food sample
(D) An entry form

91. Look at the graphic. Which day is the event being held?
(A) Saturday
(B) Sunday
(C) Monday
(D) Tuesday

Item name	Manufacturer
Kids chair	Jerry
Home chair	Kahn
Office chair	Duke
Premium office chair	Raon

92. Look at the graphic. If you are a member, what chair can you purchase at an additional discounted price?
(A) Kids chair
(B) Home chair
(C) Office chair
(D) Premium office chair

93. According to the speaker, why do customers like Tidlis Furniture?
(A) It offers reasonable prices.
(B) Its products are easy to assemble.
(C) It provides a complete product.
(D) There is no delivery charge.

94. What can be found on the Web site?
(A) A special offer
(B) A list of products
(C) A coupon
(D) Contact information

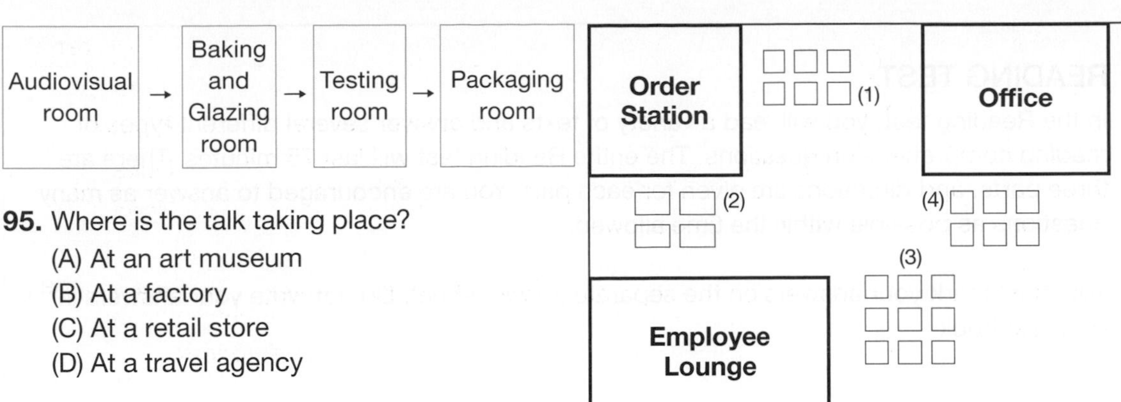

95. Where is the talk taking place?
(A) At an art museum
(B) At a factory
(C) At a retail store
(D) At a travel agency

96. Look at the graphic. Where will the listeners get souvenirs?
(A) Audiovisual room
(B) Baking and Glazing room
(C) Testing room
(D) Packaging room

97. Why should the listeners turn off their mobile phone?
(A) They will likely break.
(B) The system is likely to be affected.
(C) The area needs to stay silent.
(D) Some information needs to be kept confidential.

---

98. Why is the change being made?
(A) To address complaints from customers
(B) To get more feedback
(C) To improve the order fulfillment process
(D) To check for errors

99. Look at the graphic. Where is the place being described?
(A) Area 1
(B) Area 2
(C) Area 3
(D) Area 4

100. Where should the interested listeners go?
(A) To the employee lounge
(B) To the office
(C) To the meeting room
(D) To the Sales Department

This is the end of the Listening test. Turn to Part 5 in your test book.

READING TEST

In the Reading test, you will read a variety of texts and answer several different types of reading comprehension questions. The entire Reading test will last 75 minutes. There are three parts, and directions are given for each part. You are encouraged to answer as many questions as possible within the time allowed.

You must mark your answers on the separate answer sheet. Do not write your answers in your test book.

PART 5

Directions: A word or phrase is missing in each of the sentences below. Four answer choices are given below each sentence. Select the best answer to complete the sentence. Then mark the letter (A), (B), (C), or (D) on your answer sheet.

101. HSBC Bank is not responsible for any ------- arising out of the use of a local Internet service provider or caused by any browser software during an online transaction or electronic transfer.

(A) losses
(B) losing
(C) lose
(D) lost

102. ------- is retiring at the end of the year, so the chance that a position will open is minimal.

(A) Few
(B) No one
(C) Any other
(D) Anyone

103. Only qualified researchers will be granted ------- for the use of secondary data obtained from the National Health Service.

(A) permit
(B) is permitted
(C) to permit
(D) permission

104. A bunch of customers have complained that there is an ------- rattling noise coming from the front driver's side once the window is down.

(A) annoying
(B) annoyed
(C) annoyingly
(D) annoy

105. Women account for half of the world's population and represent the ------- purchasing decision makers, so even cosmetic brands for men need to appeal to both the targeted men and their wives.

(A) most
(B) plenty
(C) certain
(D) primary

106. -------- her consistent efforts, achievements, and higher-educational background, Jade will rapidly moved up from an entry-level position to the marketing manager within five years.

(A) Since
(B) Given
(C) Among
(D) Upon

107. ---------- found in his field, Chester Guzman's vast knowledge of international trade gives him a unique perspective and a great reputation.

(A) Less
(B) Enough
(C) Apart
(D) Seldom

108. -------- the following location not work best for you, notify one of our managers so alternative arrangements can be made.

(A) When
(B) If
(C) As well as
(D) Should

109. Southland will host the Global Trading Forum next year, although it has --------- alternated between Otago and Cantebury.

(A) traditionally
(B) positively
(C) nearly
(D) exceptionally

110. Holiday Inn has ------- from a single motel to a multi-national hotel franchise with well over 400 locations in operation worldwide.

(A) planned
(B) established
(C) furthered
(D) evolved

111. Now that our technical support team has taken all the necessary steps, we ------- that there will be no more technical issues preventing our customers from shopping online.

(A) suppose
(B) estimate
(C) expect
(D) guess

112. ------- two factories in London and one in Sydney have been closed, the Melbourne facility will remain open.

(A) Besides
(B) Rather than
(C) Although
(D) Before

GO ON TO THE NEXT PAGE

113. ------- among the reasons BAP World is the premier operating system available is the fact that it's open-source software, meaning that anyone can change or modify the source code.

(A) Many
(B) Proper
(C) Chief
(D) Straight

114. According to the recent marketing research, only half of U.S. households read ------- of their advertising mail.

(A) each
(B) few
(C) everything
(D) all

115. Jeffery Lambert ------- the weekly sales meeting this morning, but he had a scheduling conflict.

(A) should attend
(B) must have attended
(C) wants to attend
(D) would have attended

116. The board of directors will not move to the next stage of the project ------- those opposing it number more than 100 shareholders.

(A) if
(B) so that
(C) whether
(D) depending on

117. In a competitive insurance market, most customers are more -------- in which services they choose and which company they would like to purchase those products or solutions from.

(A) dominant
(B) punctual
(C) rigorous
(D) selective

118. The new capital city was ------- by chief architect Andrew Evans educated at Cornell University, and his assistant Rudy Ferguson.

(A) planned
(B) proceeded
(C) involved
(D) supposed

119. Lloyd's Distance Learning Course is by far the most --------- we have seen and offers innovative e-learning classes and degree programs through a digital learning platform.

(A) detailed
(B) detail
(C) details
(D) detailing

120. Our Richmond office is located slightly ------- the Golden Cinema on 23 Winspear Avenue.

(A) across
(B) over
(C) opposite
(D) past

121. The agenda of this meeting is to discuss what we need to know about ------- to promote the new product on social media.

(A) decision
(B) try
(C) how
(D) after

122. During the summer, we ship packages with frozen gel packs to prevent dairy and meat products and other ------- items from deteriorating.

(A) plentiful
(B) perishable
(C) spoiled
(D) adverse

123. If you can schedule a meeting ------- 9:00 tomorrow morning, our director will rearrange his flight to be in attendance.
(A) at
(B) to
(C) for
(D) in

124. CIBC Bank offers more sophisticated online banking systems to help our clients run their businesses more -------.
(A) broadly
(B) greatly
(C) efficiently
(D) potentially

125. The decision about whether the factory can reopen will be ------- until the Ministry has carried out a thorough investigation of this risk.
(A) deferred
(B) resolved
(C) informed
(D) agreed

126. At Molson Coors Brewing Company, we do ------- we can to help our employees achieve their full potential.
(A) so
(B) those
(C) everything
(D) whichever

127. Debra Mason, a widely recognized ------- on Northwestern Asian cultural history and art, was a curator of the Toronto Museum.
(A) authority
(B) authoritative
(C) authorizing
(D) authorization

128. ------- member is assigned a task depends on the speciality required for a project.
(A) Which
(B) Each
(C) Any
(D) Some

129. Recent studies from the University of California indicate that the ------- of visual aids to a presentation can provide the presenter with a lot of advantages.
(A) feature
(B) addition
(C) pictures
(D) tool

130. ------- poorly the customer may be treating them, customer service representatives are required to treat customers with professionalism.
(A) Although
(B) Seldom
(C) However
(D) Rather

TEST 2 PART 5

GO ON TO THE NEXT PAGE

PART 6

Directions: Read the texts that follow. A word, phrase, or sentence is missing in parts of each text. Four answer choices for each question are given below the text. Select the best answer to complete the text. Then mark the letter (A), (B), (C), or (D) on your answer sheet.

Questions 131-134 refer to the following instructions.

Why don't you install a Programmable Thermostat?

Save money and energy by installing Homeassistant, our new programmable thermostat, to control heating and air conditioning. This programmable thermostat can save more than 40% of your energy bill by turning on only during the daytime, and automatically shutting off when the desired temperature has been reached. And you can program it to **—131—** your home's temperature when you are away and raise it at a specific time.

The process of programming this thermostat is quite simple and does not consume a lot of time. Begin by pushing the home button of the device and **—132—** long press any blank section of the screen for a few seconds. Select the Choose Option to display the CHOOSE screen and the selection menu will pop up. **—133—**. When you're finished, press the OK button to save your selection. Your **—134—** will be applied immediately.

131. (A) show
(B) lower
(C) see
(D) review

132. (A) simple
(B) simply
(C) simpled
(D) simpler

133. (A) Using the drop down arrow, you can select your preferences.
(B) Before setting your device, check for any missing items.
(C) You can return it within 14 days of purchase.
(D) Press the red button on the left to see how much energy it has saved.

134. (A) settings
(B) savings
(C) screen
(D) device

Questions 135-138 refer to the following notice.

July is high season in Hawaii, so we recommend you make a reservation at your earliest convenience. Hotel accommodations here are very —**135**—. Reservations will be required with a deposit of $200. This amount will be charged to your credit card upon booking the reservation. Cancellations made more than seven days prior to your scheduled arrival date —**136**— in full.

However, if the reservation is canceled within one week of arrival, it will result in a full charge of the entire —**137**— of your stay booked. —**138**—.

135. (A) restricted
(B) difficult
(C) confirmed
(D) limited

136. (A) will be refunded
(B) will not be refunded
(C) are refunding
(D) had been refunded

137. (A) room
(B) degree
(C) length
(D) week

138. (A) Also, our new facilities will make your future stays with us even more enjoyable.
(B) This policy applies to early departure as well.
(C) In fact, we will soon open more hotels in July.
(D) Thank you for leaving a review of your stay at our hotel.

GO ON TO THE NEXT PAGE

Questions 139-142 refer to the following notice.

Notice: Shipping Fragile Items

Thank you for using Florida Logistics. Our mission —**139**— the best and most reliable service to all customers. We always handle all our shipments with care and caution, but we do not guarantee special handling for packages even marked "Fragile." Therefore, it is your responsibility to make sure that your contents are protected from any damage that may be caused during the delivery. When you ship your items, we do not recommend using old boxes but new ones. Old and used ones do not offer their —**140**— rigidity and adequate protection. In case you use a used box, any labels on it should be removed and any damage such as punctures and tears should be checked. —**141**— may result in damage to the contents. And please remember that it is important to use internal cushioning for items that are fragile. —**142**—. This way, all items are separated from each other, so your items will be safe from bumps, vibrations and shocks of any kind.

139. (A) provides
(B) is provided
(C) is providing
(D) is to provide

140. (A) creative
(B) original
(C) ready
(D) various

141. (A) Most
(B) Neither
(C) Others
(D) These

142. (A) Doing this is not advisable.
(B) We can purchase insurance for one single item.
(C) To do so, wrap them individually.
(D) Customers will learn that it is quite unsuitable.

Questions 143-146 refer to the following e-mail.

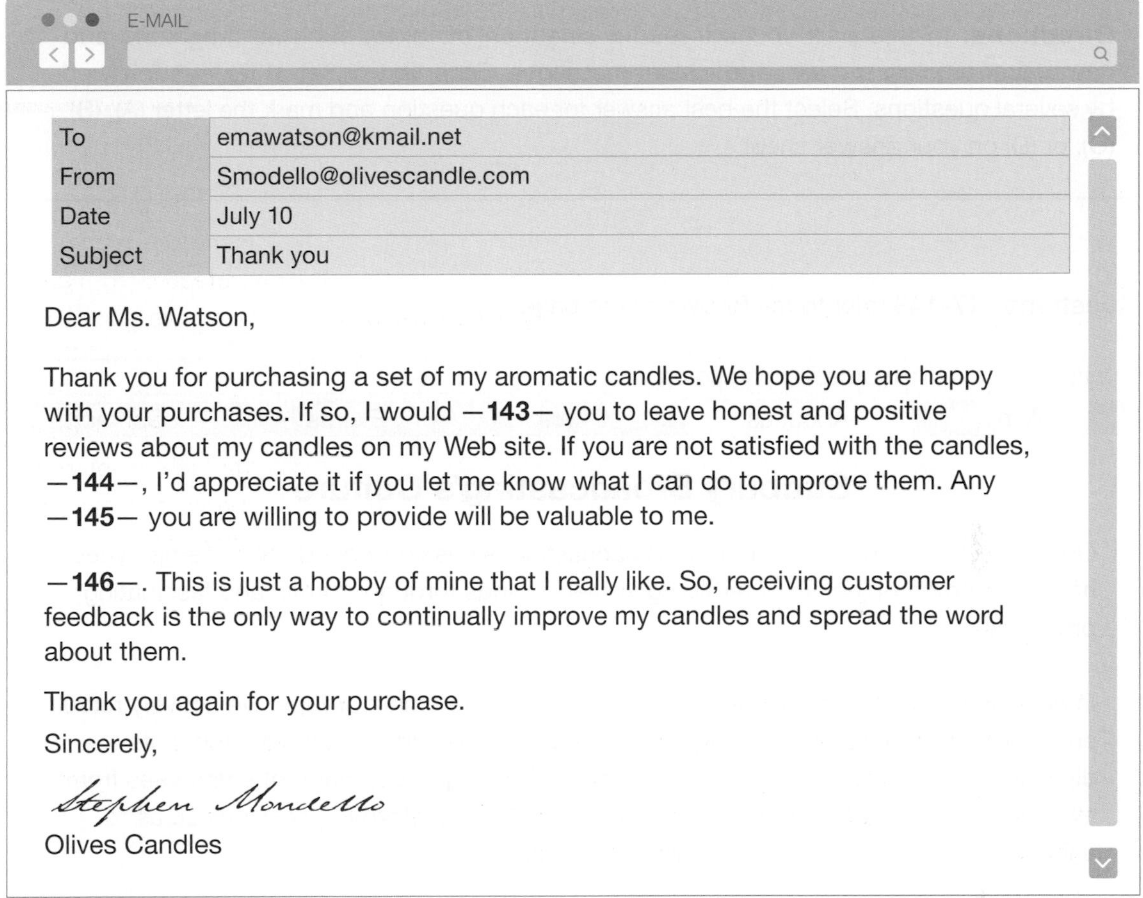

E-MAIL

To	emawatson@kmail.net
From	Smodello@olivescandle.com
Date	July 10
Subject	Thank you

Dear Ms. Watson,

Thank you for purchasing a set of my aromatic candles. We hope you are happy with your purchases. If so, I would **—143—** you to leave honest and positive reviews about my candles on my Web site. If you are not satisfied with the candles, **—144—**, I'd appreciate it if you let me know what I can do to improve them. Any **—145—** you are willing to provide will be valuable to me.

—146—. This is just a hobby of mine that I really like. So, receiving customer feedback is the only way to continually improve my candles and spread the word about them.

Thank you again for your purchase.

Sincerely,

Stephen Mondello

Olives Candles

143. (A) like asking
(B) like to ask
(C) have liked to ask
(D) have liked asking

144. (A) in the meantime
(B) however
(C) such as
(D) therefore

145. (A) proof
(B) ingredients
(C) request
(D) feedback

146. (A) All the candles can be purchased from retail stores in the area.
(B) I regret that there was a mistake in shipping your order.
(C) In order to fulfil customized orders, I have a variety of candles in stock.
(D) As you may know from my Web site, I am not a corporate seller.

GO ON TO THE NEXT PAGE

PART 7

Directions: In this part you will read a selection of texts, such as magazine and newspaper articles, e-mails, and instant messages. Each text or set of texts is followed by several questions. Select the best answer for each question and mark the letter (A), (B), (C), or (D) on your answer sheet.

Questions 147-148 refer to the following Web page.

http://www.sudburybroadcasting.co.og

Main	About us	Offers	Events	Contact

Sudbury Broadcasting's Culture

Our organization culture at Sudbury Broadcasting is mission-based. All our employees have a common objective of fertilizing viewers' minds through truthful and fascinating programs.

In order to reflect our audiences who belong to diverse ethnic groups, we actively recruit employees from a variety of backgrounds. Sudbury Broadcasting's devotion to its diversity can be also seen in our Mars Groups. These groups, made of employees from all different levels of the social groups, have regular brainstorming sessions so as to enhance not only productivity but also efficiency.

Sudbury Broadcasting provides a wide range of chances for career development and helps keep people motivated and inspired.

147. What is suggested about Sudbury Broadcasting's workers?

(A) They are all highly experienced in a field.
(B) They do not mind working overtime.
(C) They have multiple backgrounds.
(D) They need to regularly attend a training course.

148. What is a purpose of Sudbury Broadcasting's Mars Groups?

(A) To raise funds for the community
(B) To offer a wide range of career opportunities
(C) To provide creative solutions
(D) To encourage work-life balance

Questions 149-150 refer to the following text message chain.

Alton Baldwin 10:21 A.M.
Janice, when do you think you can get here? The job applicants have already arrived. We should start job interviews in ten minutes.

Janice Bailey 10:22 A.M.
I apologize! The tunnel is still closed. Our taxi had no choice but to take a detour. We should get there in 20 minutes. Could you go ahead and start without us?

Alton Baldwin 10:23 A.M.
All right. We will be meeting Gregg Mclaughlin first.

Janice Bailey 10:24 A.M.
Sure. He is the one I talked about who has some experience at another beverage firm.

Alton Baldwin 10:25 A.M.
Yeah. I am so surprised that our firm needs to employ more workers to keep up with orders. It's growing so fast.

Janice Bailey 10:25 A.M.
Same here! I'll get there as soon as possible.

149. What does Ms. Bailey want Mr. Baldwin to do?
(A) Publicize an open position
(B) Deal with some orders
(C) Speak to a job applicant
(D) Put off a job interview

150. At 10:25 A.M., what does Ms. Bailey mean when she writes, "Same here!"?
(A) She has reviewed the applications.
(B) She has already talked with Mr. Mclaughlin.
(C) She wants the man to arrive as soon as possible.
(D) She is also excited by the firm's rapid growth.

GO ON TO THE NEXT PAGE

Questions 151-152 refer to the following flyer.

Immediate Shipping

Do you need your package delivered as soon as possible? We expedite any delivery of items you need to send urgently anywhere in the nation. Just contact us at any time 24 hours a day, and your package will be picked up and processed on the same day. By visiting our Web site, the total cost of your delivery request can be calculated. However, keep in mind that the calculated cost is only valid for the day it is estimated. On request, a specific code will be provided, which can be used to check the status of your shipment such as its current location and arrival time.

151. What is mentioned in the flyer?

(A) Packages can be delivered within a week.
(B) Discounted prices are available for loyal customers.
(C) The quote can be provided online.
(D) A text message is automatically sent upon request.

152. Why is the specific code issued?

(A) To adjust a shipping schedule
(B) To keep track of a package's progress
(C) To verify shipping insurance
(D) To pay for a delivery service

Questions 153-155 refer to the following booklet.

Ruislip-R2Q!
Your lifelong electric device

Thank you for purchasing Ruislip-R2Q, the nation's best rechargeable electric toothbrush. To maintain your device in its best condition, clean your R2Q right after using it by running the part of its head under clear water. —[1]—. Every week, disassemble your R2Q and clean the under parts as instructed in the user handbook. Please be advised that the brush should be replaced with a new one every other week. —[2]—.

The lithium-ion battery installed in the device makes Ruislip-R2Q last much longer than any other electric products on the current market. —[3]—. You can charge your device any time you wish, but it is best for the battery to recharge your R2Q after it has fully discharged. Please keep in mind that only the charger that comes with your device should be used. Using other chargers from the third party may cause unexpected malfunctions not covered by the warranty. —[4]—. Check our Web site for more details : www.ruislipr2q.net/product.info

153. What is suggested about the Ruislip-R2Q?
(A) It does not need to be cleaned often.
(B) A new part is regularly required.
(C) Some parts should be changed every week.
(D) It can be purchased only online.

154. According to the booklet, what should users do with their devices to prevent malfunctions?
(A) Bring them to a designated store when it is broken.
(B) Go to a Web site to request a repair service.
(C) Avoid using other brands' battery chargers.
(D) Recharge them after it has fully discharged.

155. In which of the positions marked [1], [2], [3], and [4] does the following sentence best belong?
"This rechargeable battery will last longer than one year, if you perform complete draining every month."
(A) [1]
(B) [2]
(C) [3]
(D) [4]

GO ON TO THE NEXT PAGE

Questions 156-157 refer to the following advertisement.

Borough
Apparel

All items at our main store in the center of the city are on sale now!
Borough Apparel is replacing everything for next-season products.
Every summer item is on a clearance sale!
Unique designer accessories and clothes
can be purchased at reduced prices.
Every product is eligible for 30 – 60% discount.
Beginning on 15 August until 1 September
Opening hours: 11 A.M. to 8 P.M., Monday through Saturday;
Closed on Sundays.
Our store is on the ground floor of the high-rise building
located at 324 Borough Street.
Check our Web site at: **www.boroughapparel.com**

156. Who most likely released the advertisement?
(A) A clothing manufacturer
(B) A property developer
(C) A business owner
(D) A well-known accountant

157. What is indicated about Borough Apparel?
(A) It opens seven days a week.
(B) It is located in the downtown area.
(C) It offers a regular sales promotion.
(D) It operates only one store.

Questions 158-160 refer to the following letter.

Flora Mckinney
Valerie Supplies Inc.
Churchill Avenue
Watson Town, Regina EQ2 R12

Dear Ms. Mckinney,

Your final issue of *Luis Weekly* was sent to you last week. However, we have not received your signed renewal contract yet. —[1]—. Over the last four years, *Luis Weekly* has become well-known as a reliable authority in the areas of fishing equipment, camping news, and the best outdoor activities. —[2]—. Without doubt, the value of your business can increase by subscribing to our publication for £25. —[3]—. Enclosed is a special offer for 30 percent off the yearly subscription rate, which is only valid for the next 4 weeks. You would not want to miss a chance to acquire the latest information which should be essential to your business! Don't miss this great offer. —[4]—.

Sincerely,

Laurence C. Payne

Subscription Renewal Services

TEST 2 PART 7

158. What type of business does Ms. Mckinney most likely work for?
(A) A government agency
(B) A publishing company
(C) A leisure goods store
(D) A car rental company

159. According to the letter, what does Mr. Payne offer?
(A) A free guide for outdoor activities
(B) A discount for a limited period of time
(C) A complimentary copy of a magazine
(D) A gift voucher for future purchases

160. In which of positions marked [1], [2], [3], and [4] does the following sentence best belong?
"We believe that this is not intentional determination, but oversight."
(A) [1]
(B) [2]
(C) [3]
(D) [4]

GO ON TO THE NEXT PAGE

Questions 161-164 refer to the following e-mail.

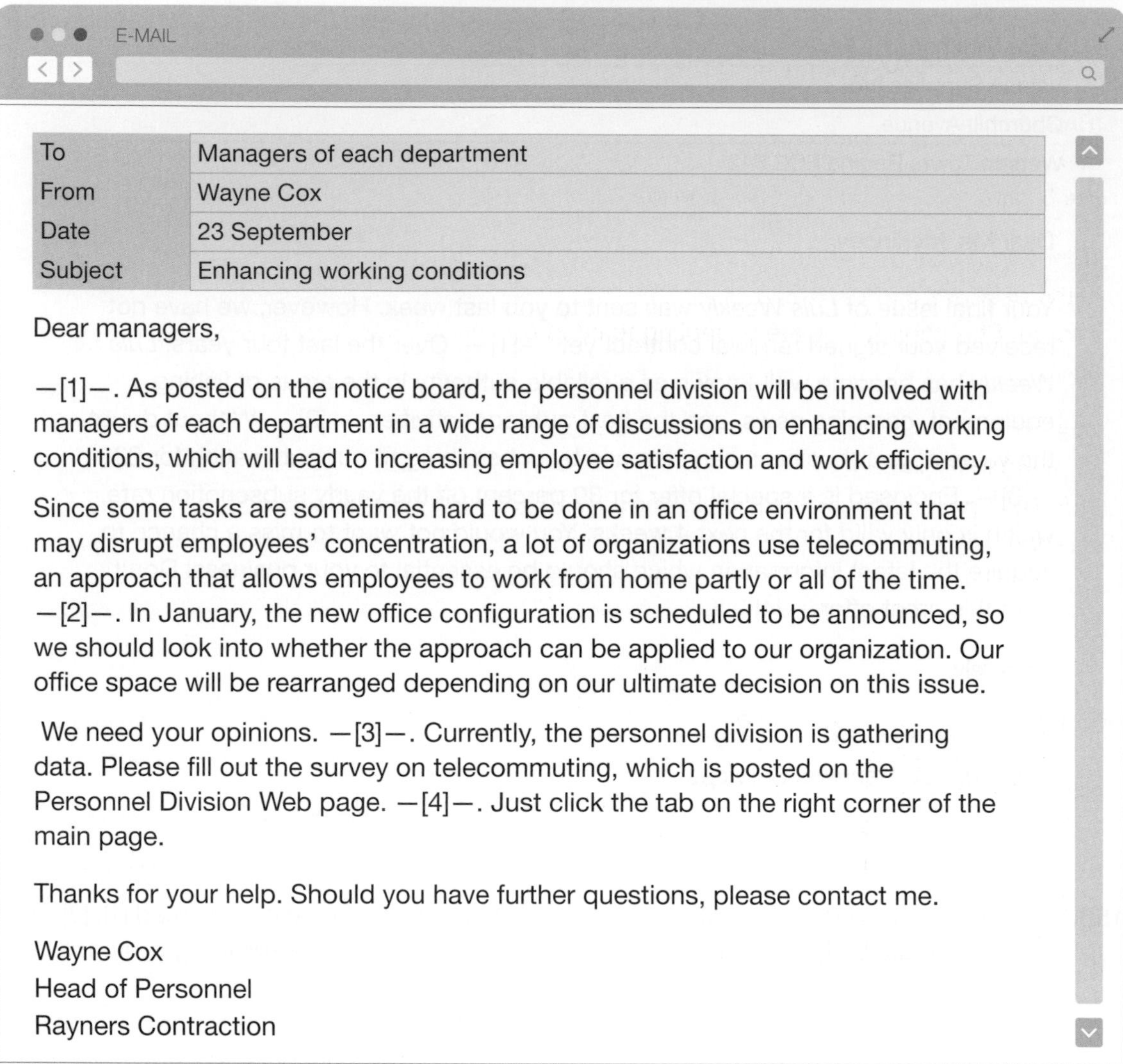

E-MAIL

To	Managers of each department
From	Wayne Cox
Date	23 September
Subject	Enhancing working conditions

Dear managers,

—[1]—. As posted on the notice board, the personnel division will be involved with managers of each department in a wide range of discussions on enhancing working conditions, which will lead to increasing employee satisfaction and work efficiency.

Since some tasks are sometimes hard to be done in an office environment that may disrupt employees' concentration, a lot of organizations use telecommuting, an approach that allows employees to work from home partly or all of the time. —[2]—. In January, the new office configuration is scheduled to be announced, so we should look into whether the approach can be applied to our organization. Our office space will be rearranged depending on our ultimate decision on this issue.

We need your opinions. —[3]—. Currently, the personnel division is gathering data. Please fill out the survey on telecommuting, which is posted on the Personnel Division Web page. —[4]—. Just click the tab on the right corner of the main page.

Thanks for your help. Should you have further questions, please contact me.

Wayne Cox
Head of Personnel
Rayners Contraction

161. What is the purpose of the e-mail?
(A) To announce new employee policies
(B) To remind staff of an upcoming meeting
(C) To ask for participation in a survey
(D) To increase employee satisfaction

162. What is stated as an advantage of telecommuting?
(A) It provides more room for employees.
(B) It can help staff work without distraction.
(C) It lowers overall operating expenses.
(D) It is an environmentally friendly approach.

163. What does the organization plan to do next year?
(A) Redesign a Web page
(B) Recruit a new personnel manager
(C) Carry out its restructuring
(D) Adjust the layout of the office

164. In which of the positions marked [1], [2], [3], and [4] does the following sentence best belong?
"Be advised that any decisions about the approach have not been made yet."
(A) [1] (B) [2]
(C) [3] (D) [4]

Questions 165-168 refer to the following article.

Halifax Factory to Open

(Brockley, June 21) — Canadian appliance manufacturer, Halifax announced its plan to start operating a fourth production plant in Brighten, UK, in October. It will open the facility on Peckham Rye Avenue in Brockley. —[1]—.

"Since there are a lot of experienced and skilled workers living in the region, the town is the best place to open a new manufacturing facility," said regional director Isabelle Theron. She added, "We are expecting to keep our infrastructure facilities in Brighten and are thrilled to expand into this area, getting friendly support from the town." —[2]—.

The Ontario-based appliance manufacturer also built a plant close to the town of Portland in Australia. —[3]—. Moreover, it has another plan to contract a factory in Indonesia next quarter. Its management is considering cities such as Medan and Cirebon. —[4]—.

165. What benefit of the new location does Ms. Theron mention?
(A) The population growth
(B) The plentiful labor force
(C) The cheap building rental fee
(D) The government support

166. Where is Halifax's headquarters?
(A) In Cirebon
(B) In Ontario
(C) In Brighten
(D) In Brockley

167. According to the article, what does the firm plan to do in the near future?
(A) Close a plant in Brighten
(B) Attract more infrastructure investment
(C) Expand into Indonesia
(D) Acquire another company

168. In which of the positions marked [1], [2], [3], and [4] does the following sentence best belong?
"The other plants are in the cities of Haxton, Camden, and Algate."
(A) [1]
(B) [2]
(C) [3]
(D) [4]

GO ON TO THE NEXT PAGE

Questions 169-171 refer to the following schedule of events.

The Headstone Global Publishing Expo

11-13 October,
Perivale Convention Center, Montreal

Schedule for Thursday, 13 October

The Winds of Change in the Digital Era
1:00 P.M. – 2:00 P.M. Lecture Hall 301
Debate on whether digital media promotes or degrades literacy hosted by Benny Cross.

Beginner Course in Visual Design
2:15 P.M. – 3:15 P.M. Graphic Images Auditorium
Terri Anderson and Killi Ball, experts in visual design, will address useful skills and trainees will gain hands-on experience of what they have learned.

Workshop on E-Publishing
3:30 P.M. – 4:30 P.M. Latimer Center
Publishing and advertising e-publications including audio books online. After and before the workshop, attendees will be able to purchase all accompanying materials on the Web site.

Presenters: Jancie Bailey, Chief Editor of Canons Books Ltd., and Willard Curtis, Head of Marketing at Canons Books Ltd.

Considering Readers' Views
4:45 P.M. – 6:15 P.M. Hall G1
In order to publicize her new book, "Considering Reader's Views", through a book-signing event, writer Nancy Cole participates in the Headstone Global Publishing Expo to talk about her new topic, answer questions and autograph her books.

- Keep in mind that since the number of seats is limited, arrive early before the programs you intend to attend start to secure a seat. Reservations are not accepted for any programs. Please be advised that video recordings are prohibited while photos are allowed.
- Purchasing a daily pass for $ 9.50 is required to attend the scheduled programs.
- Refreshments and meals can be purchased at snack bars across Perivale Convention Center. Visit our Web site at www.hgpe_events.com/inf.hotels. for information about accommodations.

169. Where will publishing expo visitors be able to attend interactive activities?

(A) In Lecture Hall 301
(B) In the Graphic Images Auditorium
(C) In the Latimer Center
(D) In Hall G1

170. What is stated about accompanying supplies for the workshop?

(A) They must be ordered in advance.
(B) They are offered in limited numbers for free.
(C) They are provided through a Web site.
(D) They can be bought at the venue.

171. What are publishing expo visitors asked to do?

(A) Avoid taking photos
(B) Come early for programs
(C) Bring their own lunch
(D) Prepare questions before programs

GO ON TO THE NEXT PAGE

Questions 172-175 refer to the following online chat session.

●●●○○

Xavier Parker 11:02 A.M.

Hello, all. It is time for us to begin thinking about the department meeting on Thursday. Our sales have been continuously decreasing. I would like us to consider looking at new ways.

Tamra Pansy 11:03 A.M.

Right. What do you think we should do?

Xavier Parker 11:04 A.M.

As the demand for cleaning products doesn't seem to be strong as it used to be, it could be a good move for us to expand Wilda Supplies with additional items.

Rhea Maura 11:05 A.M.

There has always been a high demand for small fancy electronics. Let's look into it.

Twila Vonda 11:06 A.M.

I believe that is a good idea. And, probably we should consider toasters.

Tamra Pansy 11:07 A.M.

I can't agree with that more. Electronics such as Blue-tooth speakers and coffee makers can be possible options.

Xavier Parker 11:08 A.M.

Great ideas, everyone. These ideas should be presented at the meeting. Please research more details about manufacturers and estimates and have those included in the presentation each of you will make. I'll need that information later in order to prepare a preliminary budget proposal for the board.

Twila Vonda 11:09 A.M.

No problem.

Xavier Parker 11:10 A.M.

If you have any concerns or questions, please inform me. I'll forward everyone some guidelines by fax.

172. What kind of goods does Wilda Supplies currently sell?
(A) Cleaning supplies
(B) Household appliances
(C) Business machines
(D) Office appliances

173. At 11:02 A.M., what does Mr. Parker mean when he writes, "I would like us to consider looking at new ways"?
(A) The firm should carry a wider range of products.
(B) The event should address various topics.
(C) The firm has to relocate its main office.
(D) The event should be postponed to another day.

174. What will Ms. Vonda most likely do next?
(A) Draft a proposal
(B) Fax a document to Ms. Pansy
(C) Collect some information
(D) Have a budget approved

175. What will Mr. Parker give to the board?
(A) Suggestions for new sales guidelines
(B) More information regarding manufacturers
(C) An invoice of recent orders
(D) A proposal for updating equipment

GO ON TO THE NEXT PAGE

Questions 176-180 refer to the following Web page and e-mail.

http://www.aoni.uk

Main	Items	Equipment	Details

Activities Outdoors with Nature Inc. (AONI)

The Pioneer in Innovative Hiking and Camping Gear

We process almost all standard orders made through phone or Internet and make them promptly prepared for delivery. Tailored and custom requests may take around four days to be processed. Please feel free to forward any concerns and questions to our Customer Service Team at cst@aoni.uk. Customers will receive a reply within a day. Regarding our delivery schedule, please consult the list below.

Order cost including tax	Under 20	£ 20 – 70	Over £ 70
Overnight (24 hours)	£ 5.00	£ 8.00	£ 11.00
Express (36 hours)	£ 3.00	£ 6.00	£ 9.00
Regular (up to 1 week)	£ 1.50	£ 3.00	Free

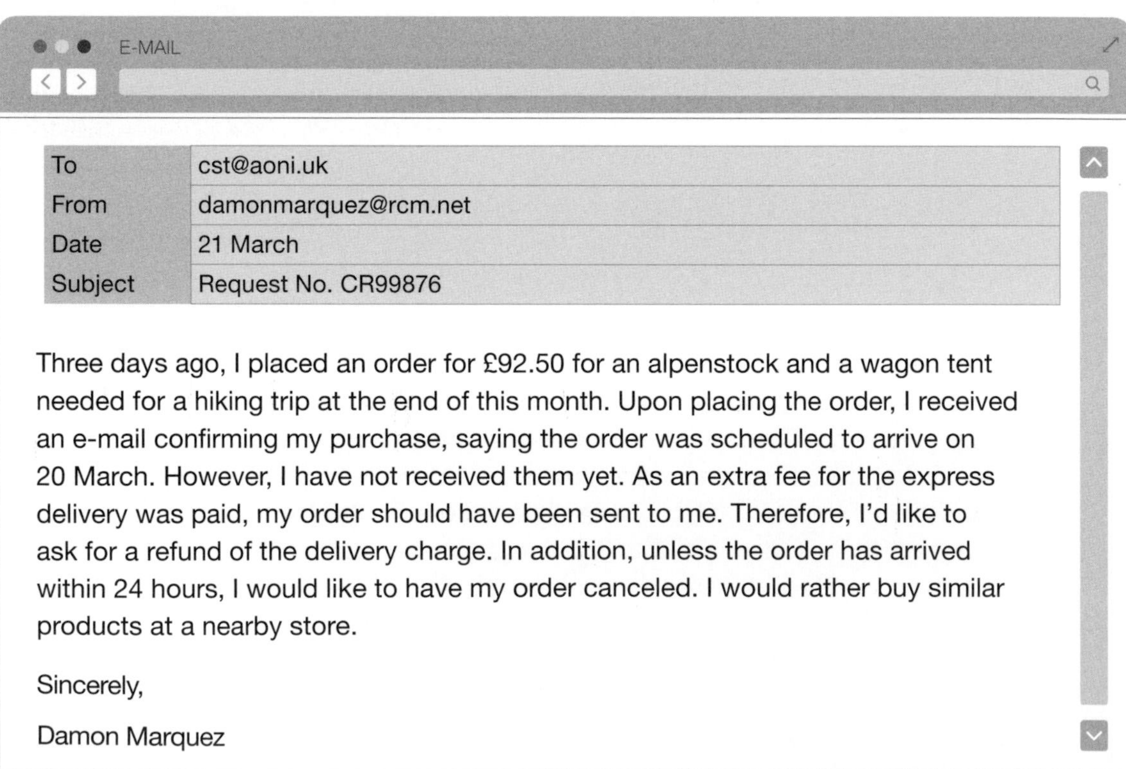
E-MAIL

To	cst@aoni.uk
From	damonmarquez@rcm.net
Date	21 March
Subject	Request No. CR99876

Three days ago, I placed an order for £92.50 for an alpenstock and a wagon tent needed for a hiking trip at the end of this month. Upon placing the order, I received an e-mail confirming my purchase, saying the order was scheduled to arrive on 20 March. However, I have not received them yet. As an extra fee for the express delivery was paid, my order should have been sent to me. Therefore, I'd like to ask for a refund of the delivery charge. In addition, unless the order has arrived within 24 hours, I would like to have my order canceled. I would rather buy similar products at a nearby store.

Sincerely,

Damon Marquez

176. In the Web page, what is suggested about the AONI's delivery?
(A) Regular delivery is free for orders under £20.
(B) Some delivered orders can take about seven days to arrive.
(C) The delivery charge depends on the total number of items.
(D) Tailored orders are not entitled to regular shipping.

177. In the Web page, the word "consult" in paragraph 1, line 5, is closest in meaning to
(A) advise
(B) refer to
(C) discuss
(D) ask

178. Why has the e-mail been written?
(A) To expedite a delivery date
(B) To report a shipping problem
(C) To cancel an order immediately
(D) To ask about an order status

179. How much did Mr. Marquez pay for shipping?
(A) £5.00
(B) £8.00
(C) £9.00
(D) £11.00

180. According to the e-mail, why might Mr. Marquez choose to visit a nearby store?
(A) He decided to cancel the previous order.
(B) He wants to use his order on a certain day.
(C) He intends to get a refund in full.
(D) He needs to buy a cheaper product.

GO ON TO THE NEXT PAGE

Questions 181-185 refer to the following e-mails.

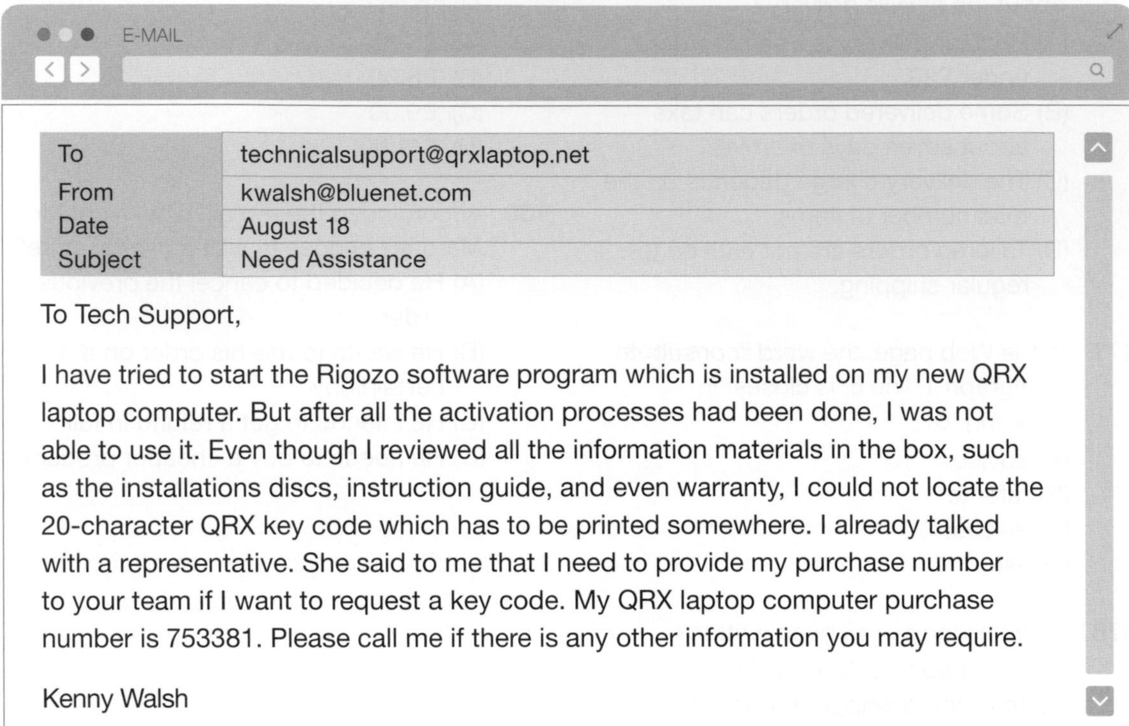

E-MAIL

To	technicalsupport@qrxlaptop.net
From	kwalsh@bluenet.com
Date	August 18
Subject	Need Assistance

To Tech Support,

I have tried to start the Rigozo software program which is installed on my new QRX laptop computer. But after all the activation processes had been done, I was not able to use it. Even though I reviewed all the information materials in the box, such as the installations discs, instruction guide, and even warranty, I could not locate the 20-character QRX key code which has to be printed somewhere. I already talked with a representative. She said to me that I need to provide my purchase number to your team if I want to request a key code. My QRX laptop computer purchase number is 753381. Please call me if there is any other information you may require.

Kenny Walsh

E-MAIL

To	Kenny Walsh <kwalsh@bluenet.com>
From	Tech Support <technicalsupport@qrxlaptop.net>
Date	August 19
Subject	Re: Need Assistance

Dear Mr. Walsh

Thanks for your call to QRX Laptop Computer Tech Support. After referencing your e-mail address and the information we have received, we are able to confirm that you have bought the QRX Model T14 with service label code 1-09832. Basically, we had the Rigozo software program set up at the plant, so entering the following key code will make the program activate; 212C93-22V99-45R87-1WCT.

In case you would like to get in touch with us in the future, please keep the service label code accessible for reference. The code is printed on the underside of your computer. By providing your service label code, your inquiry can be directly forwarded to a technician acquainted with your previous issues with your laptop and its configuration.

If you give a reply to this e-mail, it will be easier to contact our tech support. Please briefly describe your problem and indicate the most convenient time for us to call you along with your contact information, and your service label code. You can also find answers to frequently asked questions at www.qrxlaptop.net/fre-questions.

Sincerely,

Monica Weaver
Head of QRX Laptop Computer Tech Support

181. What did Mr. Walsh do before writing his August 18 e-mail?
(A) He provided a purchase number.
(B) He changed his computer configurations.
(C) He called to get technical support.
(D) He reviewed answers to previously asked questions.

182. How did Ms. Weaver verify Mr. Walsh's purchase?
(A) By checking a key code previously provided
(B) By using a purchase number and contact information
(C) By inputting a product key number
(D) By reaching the software program company

183. Where can Mr. Walsh find his service label code?
(A) On the bottom side of his computer
(B) Inside the laptop's warranty statement
(C) Attached to the computer's battery part
(D) On the front cover of the instruction guide

184. In the second e-mail, the word "forwarded" in paragraph 2, line 3, is closest in meaning to
(A) secured
(B) routed
(C) located
(D) advanced

185. How does Ms. Weaver suggest that Mr. Walsh contact a representative if he has an issue with his item?
(A) By leaving a question on the QRX Web site
(B) By registering for a membership program
(C) By making a phone call
(D) By sending an e-mail

GO ON TO THE NEXT PAGE

Questions 186-190 refer to the following leaflet, comment, and e-mail.

Learn Business From the Best in Dubai

The International Dubai Business College (IDBC) can be found in the center of Dubai's business district. This college provides a wide range of highly informative courses targeted at those who intend to pursue a master's degree. Students may explore the city and extend business networks. Various content-based sessions like economics, domestic and global sales and marketing, and finance are offered. There are also sessions only for those who intend to pursue a master's degree, involving improving résumés and other relevant materials. Hundreds of students receive help from the college in obtaining acceptance into master's degree courses around the world every year. The college features many highly distinguished lecturers who have expert knowledge in each of their areas, such as Marvin West, General Manager of Hongkong Financial Consulting, and Brian White, President of Horace Union Bank (HUB). Please check our Web site at www.idbc_programs.org for further details on our excellent course offerings and faculty, or to register.

www.idbc.programs.org/comments

Main	Courses	Comments	Contact Info.

Evangeline Gwen
November 11

At the moment, I am studying at a business college in Washington. I took one of the business courses at IDBC since I was not able to complete any prerequisite study after acquiring my bachelor's degree.

During my stay there, even though the public transportation was not convenient, I had no choice but to commute from the suburb area due to the incredibly high rent in the area around IDBC. I think there should have been students housing or other affordable accommodation options. The classes were excellent. My instructor was Marvin West. His classes were rather fast paced, but he covered many subjects in the seven-week course. Yet, I was able to keep up with the course by studying a lot of reading materials provided by IDBC. His commitment to his class was very impressive, and was helpful for me to get ready for joining a master's degree course.

Thank you.

E-MAIL

From	fwells@idbc.org
To	evangelinegwen@skynetmail.com
Date	16 December
Subject	Your comments

Dear Ms. Gwen

Thanks for your comments. Many students have voiced the specific issue you indicated. According to your suggestion, we plan to complement it. Those who intend to take courses with IDBC from the beginning of February will receive this new advantage. Please tell anyone willing to take a course with us about this.

Sincerely,

Frederick Wells

186. For whom is the leaflet intended?
(A) Students who want to improve their résumés for employment
(B) Lecturers willing to change their career path
(C) People planning to receive further education
(D) Business experts who intend to join an educational institution

187. What is suggested about students studying at IDBC?
(A) There are internship opportunities for them.
(B) Employment assistance service is available for them.
(C) They go through a busy area to attend their classes.
(D) They can receive financial support.

188. What does Ms. Gwen mention about her instructor?
(A) He graduated from a business school in Washington.
(B) He provided various reading materials.
(C) He presented a lot of examples.
(D) He rushed through his classes.

189. Where does Ms. Gwen's lecturer work when he is not giving lessons?
(A) At the International Dubai Business College
(B) At Hongkong Financial Consulting
(C) At Horace Union Bank
(D) At a company in Dubai's business district

190. How will IDBC be dealing with Ms. Gwen's complaint?
(A) By making a dormitory for students
(B) By providing shuttle bus service
(C) By extending the length of courses
(D) By recruiting additional faculty

GO ON TO THE NEXT PAGE

Questions 191-195 refer to the following advertisement, form, and letter.

Looking for Full-time Assistant Chef

The Highgate Bistro is a well established eatery operating in Golders Green since 1934. We are looking for an assistant cook to arrange salad and appetizer items under the direction of the main chef. More than one year of relevant cooking experience is required and a six-month apprenticeship has to have been filled in a high-profile establishment. A high level of ability to create not only new but also traditional style cuisine is required for the ideal candidate.

To apply, visit www.highgatebistro.net/recruitment.

---

www.highgatebistro.net/recruitment/assistant_chef/apply

Name: Amber Ward **E-mail:** a-ward33@skye-mail.net **Phone:** 421–265–3898

Attachment (1): Résumé (√) **Attachment (2):** Reference list (√)

Related Education: Bachelor's degree in Culinary Arts at Goldhawk National University

Current Employer: Chiswick Restaurant

Position: Assistant Chef (Length of Employment: Seven months)

Previous Employer: Vacation Inn

Position: Apprentice (Length of Employment: Three years)

Previous Employer: Clapham Café

Title: Cook (Length of Employment: Four months)

Cover letter: I would like to fill the position of assistant chef at the Highgate Bistro. I am currently working as an assistant chef for a restaurant cooking traditional style meals. Because the restaurant has neglected to fill the position of main chef, I am taking care of almost all items on the menu. I served an apprenticeship at the well-known Vacation Inn, working closely with distinguished chef Linda Williams. On top of these, I am capable of creating new innovative recipes as Hazle Washington (my instructor and mentor at Goldhawk National University) can confirm. Moreover, I won the Great in Creative Award for my East Asian-style seafood recipe, which is served at the moment at the cafeteria in Goldhawk National University.

Submit Application

GOLDHAWK NATIONAL UNIVERSITY

Department of Culinary Arts

Trevor Vega
Highgate Bistro
2678 Highgate Avenue
Putney, London 32Q1 2N1

Dear Mr. Vega,

This is in reference to Amber Ward's application for employment at Highgate Bistro. As Ms. Washington is away on holiday this semester, she wanted me to assume her role for a while. Ms. Ward, who completed our course in the top three of her class, proved her excellent culinary skills and showed strong initiative to be taught. She was recognized by well-known Chef Sherri Wade, who helped Ms. Ward finish her four-month internship successfully. I am sure that Ms. Ward will be an invaluable addition to your organization.

Sincerely,

Horace Warner

Horace Warner
Head Instructor of Culinary Arts Department

191. What is suggested about the assistant chef position?
(A) It includes working on some weekends.
(B) It requires cooking a limited range of food.
(C) It is a six-month contract job.
(D) It involves training apprentices.

192. What is indicated about Ms. Ward?
(A) Some of her recipes have been published in a publication.
(B) She led a class on cooking East Asian seafood at a university.
(C) She has already applied at a few establishments.
(D) Her qualifications seem to meet the requirements for the job.

193. Who most likely is Ms. Washington?
(A) A culinary instructor
(B) A cafeteria owner
(C) A celebrity chef
(D) A head teacher

194. What is true about Goldhawk National University?
(A) A renowned chef is invited every semester as a guest lecturer.
(B) Culinary awards are given to its students.
(C) Cooking seminars are provided for free.
(D) A new chef for its cafeteria will be hired.

195. Where did Ms. Wade most likely finish her internship?
(A) At Highgate Bistro
(B) At Clapham Café
(C) At Vacation Inn
(D) At Chiswick Restaurant

TEST 2 PART 7

GO ON TO THE NEXT PAGE

Questions 196-200 refer to the following leaflet and e-mails.

Roger Roofing Materials

Over the past few decades, builders and roofers have chosen Roger Roofing Materials for their roofing work including placing and replacing roof panels. Here are some of our best-selling items.

Bertie PRX 22: Without any screws, installed with durable clips. Please note that this model should be placed by a skilled professional because aligning the panels tends to be challenging.

Carey PRX 31: Best choice for properties whose roofs are steeply sloped. Smooth rainfall drainage is ensured by its slick surface.

Madge PRX01: Sturdy, less time-consuming installation, with a choice of 20 appealing shades.

Marcie PRX12: Quite similar to Madge PRX01, yet with only four shade options (blue, red, green, yellow). In addition, wave patterns are imprinted in it.

Please check out our latest brochure for more pricing information and specifications. Send us an e-mail at customerservice@rogerroofing.net or call us at 220-2235-6654 for any inquiry about our service and products.

Be advised that the degree of overlap can be different depending on roof panel products. Our online calculator is available at www.@rogerroofing.net/overlapdegree to find out the appropriate number of roof panels for your property. Just type the name of the model you would like to purchase with the size of your roof surface.

E-MAIL

To	customerservice@rogerroofing.net
From	malloyalisa@lourdesbuildingservice.org
Date	November 19
Subject	Purchase order

To whom it may concern,

I recently submitted an order, #339013, which includes some of your roof panels in dark gray. One of my clients called me to ask a question about whether the shade could lead to his gradually-sloped, east-facing rooftop heating up in the afternoon, especially during the summer. I informed him that theoretically, bright shades tend to reflect heat a bit better and are definitely not bad choices for warmer climate regions. Is it possible to give me some advice as I believe you may have experienced similar issues in the past? He has no intention to switch, and wants to stick to the shade if possible.

In addition, I heard that you run a Web site containing detailed installation instructions. I am worried as it is the first time for me to install this type of panel using the screws provided, so I would like to have the information downloaded. Could you give me the link to the instruction page?

Thank you,
Malloy Alisa

E-MAIL

To	malloyalisa@lourdesbuildingservice.org
From	bernardowood@rogerroofing.net
Date	November 19
Subject	Re: Purchase order

Dear Ms. Alisa,

Thank you for your inquiry about our product and service. In order to reflect sunlight and avoid heat gain, the roof panels are finished with a special coating material. There are several houses in the area that have the same panels in similar shades. But we have not received any complaints about the interior heating up thus far. Still, we are certainly happy to provide another model if the client wants to change his mind. Please just inform me no later than tomorrow.

As for the Web page you mentioned, as the manufacturers of the particular models have up-to-date and accurate information about their products and service, we encourage customers to talk with them directly. So only the lists of contact information for each manufacturer are now available on our Web site.

Best Regards,

Bernardo Wood

196. According to the leaflet, how can consumers decide how many panels to purchase?
(A) By taking advantage of an online tool
(B) By contacting a roofing specialist
(C) By e-mailing a request form
(D) By downloading a special software program

197. What aspect of the roof panels does Ms. Alisa want to learn more about?
(A) Their life compared to other models
(B) Their possibility of retaining heat
(C) Their capability to resist moisture
(D) Their popularity among consumers in a region

198. What kind of roof panel did Ms. Alisa most likely purchase for her client?
(A) Bertie PRX22
(B) Carey PRX31
(C) Madge PRX01
(D) Marcie PRX12

199. According to Mr. Wood, why would Ms. Alisa need to contact him again on November 20?
(A) To confirm the status of delivery
(B) To receive a refund
(C) To visit a manufacturer
(D) To prepare a different product

200. What is indicated about the installation instructions?
(A) They clearly show additional equipment to use.
(B) They used to be on Roger Roofing's Web site.
(C) Ms. Alisa has lost her copy of them.
(D) Roger Roofing will send them to Ms. Alisa by e-mail.

Stop! This is the end of the test. If you finish before time is called, you may go back to Parts 5, 6, and 7 and check your work.

TEST 3

開始作答 ____ 點 ____ 分

完成作答 ____ 點 ____ 分

- 建議一次寫完整份試題，避免分次作答。
- 答題時，請比照實際考試，將答案畫在答案卡上。

日標答對題數 ____ /200

實際答對題數 ____ /200

- 將答對題數乘以 5 即可概算出分數。

LISTENING TEST

In the Listening test, you will be asked to demonstrate how well you understand spoken English. The entire Listening test will last approximately 45 minutes. There are four parts, and directions are given for each part. You must mark your answers on the separate answer sheet. Do not write your answers in your test book.

PART 1 09

Directions: For each question in this part, you will hear four statements about a picture in your test book. When you hear the statements, you must select the one statement that best describes what you see in the picture. Then find the number of the question on your answer sheet and mark your answer. The statements will not be printed in your test book and will be spoken only one time.

Statement (B), "They're having a meeting," is the best description of the picture, so you should select answer (B) and mark it on your answer sheet.

1.

2.

GO ON TO THE NEXT PAGE

3.

4.

5.

6.

GO ON TO THE NEXT PAGE

PART 2 (10)

Directions: You will hear a question or statement and three responses spoken in English. They will not be printed in your test book and will be spoken only one time. Select the best response to the question or statement and mark the letter (A), (B), or (C) on your answer sheet.

7. Mark your answer on your answer sheet.

8. Mark your answer on your answer sheet.

9. Mark your answer on your answer sheet.

10. Mark your answer on your answer sheet.

11. Mark your answer on your answer sheet.

12. Mark your answer on your answer sheet.

13. Mark your answer on your answer sheet.

14. Mark your answer on your answer sheet.

15. Mark your answer on your answer sheet.

16. Mark your answer on your answer sheet.

17. Mark your answer on your answer sheet.

18. Mark your answer on your answer sheet.

19. Mark your answer on your answer sheet.

20. Mark your answer on your answer sheet.

21. Mark your answer on your answer sheet.

22. Mark your answer on your answer sheet.

23. Mark your answer on your answer sheet.

24. Mark your answer on your answer sheet.

25. Mark your answer on your answer sheet.

26. Mark your answer on your answer sheet.

27. Mark your answer on your answer sheet.

28. Mark your answer on your answer sheet.

29. Mark your answer on your answer sheet.

30. Mark your answer on your answer sheet.

31. Mark your answer on your answer sheet.

PART 3

Directions: You will hear some conversations between two or more people. You will be asked to answer three questions about what the speakers say in each conversation. Select the best response to each question and mark the letter (A), (B), (C), or (D) on your answer sheet. The conversations will not be printed in your test book and will be spoken only one time.

32. What is the main topic of the conversation?
(A) Reviewing market trends
(B) Taking a job training
(C) Going to a conference
(D) Renting office space

33. What is the man concerned about?
(A) The office size
(B) The deadline
(C) The market conditions
(D) The location

34. What will the woman do next?
(A) Consult a book
(B) Refer to the Web site
(C) Send a report
(D) E-mail some information

35. Where do the speakers work?
(A) At a law firm
(B) At a design firm
(C) At an advertising agency
(D) At a water manufacturer

36. Why does the man say, "I can ask Morin to update me later"?
(A) He wants to update the policy.
(B) He needs to process the work later.
(C) He plans not to attend an event.
(D) He disagrees with a request.

37. What will the man do next?
(A) Inform his coworkers
(B) Contact his client
(C) Send a sample
(D) Print a design

GO ON TO THE NEXT PAGE

38. Why did the women travel to Hong Kong?
(A) To negotiate a merger
(B) To get new business
(C) To take some time off
(D) To deliver some merchandise

39. What does Kate say about the trip?
(A) She had some problems during her presentation.
(B) She just helped her coworker do them.
(C) She has lots of overseas experience.
(D) She had a good time with her family.

40. What is the man working on?
(A) A sales report
(B) Presentation materials
(C) A product sample
(D) A project proposal

---

41. What is the conversation mainly about?
(A) A budget for advertising
(B) A proposal for new business
(C) An upcoming sale
(D) Accounting procedures

42. What does the man mean when he says, "They want to reduce it by 20% for other ads instead"?
(A) A total amount of budget has been changed.
(B) A new advertising method should be added.
(C) A plan should be revised.
(D) A report has some errors.

43. What does the man say he will do next?
(A) Review some documents
(B) Replace a file
(C) Contact another agency
(D) Reserve a meeting room

---

44. What will take place at the end of June?
(A) A department meeting
(B) A repair of a heating system
(C) Computer maintenance
(D) Implementation of a revised company policy

45. What should the employees be aware of?
(A) They have to bring warmer clothing.
(B) They should turn off their computers when they leave.
(C) They need to return the laptop computers to the company.
(D) They will not be able to work on a weekend.

46. What is the man asked to do?
(A) Return his computer
(B) Write an e-mail
(C) Ask for an estimate
(D) Submit a vacation request

---

47. Where do the speakers most likely work?
(A) At a restaurant
(B) At a hotel
(C) At a medical clinic
(D) At a fish market

48. According to the man, what do customers like about the business?
(A) The quality of the service
(B) The convenient location
(C) The reasonable prices
(D) The business hours

49. What does the woman mean when she says, "Seaweed is well known as being good for your health"?
(A) She hopes to change her business.
(B) She has some concerns about the man's health.
(C) She wants to use a certain ingredient.
(D) She is about to explain nutritious food.

---

50. According to the man, what is the problem?
(A) A machine is not working properly.
(B) A meeting is canceled.
(C) A book has an error.
(D) Sales are disappointing.

51. According to Sarah, what will most likely change at the business?
(A) A printing machine
(B) A version of book
(C) A launching date
(D) A safety procedure

52. What will the man do next?
(A) Arrange for a meeting
(B) Ask for investment
(C) Schedule a consultation
(D) Report to the management

---

53. According to the woman, what happened last week?
(A) She posted a job opening.
(B) She applied to be a volunteer.
(C) She provided some documents for a job.
(D) She developed a new Web site.

54. Who most likely is the man?
(A) A job applicant
(B) A business consultant
(C) A personnel manager
(D) A real estate agent

55. What does the man imply when he says, "That's interesting."?
(A) He wants to hear more about the woman's experience.
(B) He agrees to take an interview.
(C) He enjoyed the discussion about a job trend.
(D) He accepts the woman's suggestion.

---

56. What is the purpose of the man's visit?
(A) To review an estimate
(B) To inspect safety standards
(C) To conduct an interview
(D) To pick up an ID card

57. What does the man agree to do?
(A) Sign up for an event
(B) Provide contact information
(C) Perform a regular checkup
(D) Show his identification

58. What will Dr. Nunez most likely do next?
(A) She will cancel an appointment.
(B) She will get back to a meeting.
(C) She will take the man to her office.
(D) She will lead an inspection.

GO ON TO THE NEXT PAGE

	Monday	Tuesday	Wednesday	Thursday
9-10			Staff meeting	
10-11	Team building			
11-12		Directors' meeting		Survey Day
13-14				

Documents Folder		
Title	**Date**	**Size**
Palcon's strategy	2015-11-07	32KB
Employee schedule	2015-11-02	92KB
Payroll records	2015-11-04	120KB
Sales projections	2015-11-03	2.2GB

59. According to the woman, what did the business do?
(A) It replaced some equipment.
(B) It hired new employees.
(C) It changed safety policies.
(D) It had a meeting with a client.

60. Look at the graphic. On which day will the workshop be held?
(A) Monday
(B) Tuesday
(C) Wednesday
(D) Thursday

61. What is suggested about Mom's Sandwich?
(A) It offers reasonable prices.
(B) It is located nearby.
(C) It has only one menu item.
(D) It owns its own farm.

62. Look at the graphic. What file is the man suggesting?
(A) Palcon's strategy
(B) Employee schedule
(C) Payroll records
(D) Sales projections

63. How will the woman help the man?
(A) By forwarding an e-mail
(B) By printing a document
(C) By calling a colleague
(D) By fixing a computer

64. What will the man do next?
(A) Go to the office
(B) Have a meeting
(C) Have lunch
(D) Park his car

Title	Date checked out	Date due
The Unicorn, Book 7	October 1	October 5
The Temperature of Love	October 2	October 5
Her Name is Matilda	October 3	October 8

65. What did the business recently do?
(A) Hire more employees
(B) Purchase some software
(C) Check the inventory
(D) Inspect the system

66. According to the woman, how can users find the due date?
(A) By reading a text message
(B) By calling a business
(C) By visiting a business
(D) By checking their e-mails

67. Look at the graphic. When is the conversation taking place?
(A) October 1
(B) October 2
(C) October 5
(D) October 8

Day 1 only	Members $85 Non-members $100
Day 2 only	Members $110 Non-members $125
Both days	Members $160 Non-members $170

68. What problem does the woman mention?
(A) A contract has expired.
(B) A Web site is not working.
(C) A demand for registration is higher.
(D) Research has some errors.

69. Look at the graphic. How much will the woman most likely pay?
(A) $85
(B) $100
(C) $110
(D) $125

70. What does the man ask the woman to provide?
(A) The number of attendees
(B) Her membership number
(C) Identification information
(D) A deposit

GO ON TO THE NEXT PAGE

PART 4 (12)

Directions: You will hear some talks given by a single speaker. You will be asked to answer three questions about what the speaker says in each talk. Select the best response to each question and mark the letter (A), (B), (C), or (D) on your answer sheet. The talks will not be printed in your test book and will be spoken only one time.

71. What kind of event will take place next month?
(A) A conference
(B) A concert
(C) A festival
(D) A sports match

72. Why won't Main Street be available during a particular time?
(A) The road will be resurfaced.
(B) The sewage system will be fixed.
(C) The road will be blocked by snow.
(D) The site will be inspected.

73. When will the last bus of the day arrive at Carlisle Stadium?
(A) 11:00
(B) 11:20
(C) 11:40
(D) 12:00

74. What did Rachel's company do last month?
(A) It gathered customer reviews.
(B) It received an award.
(C) It expanded its office.
(D) It announced a merger.

75. What does Mr. Powell want to do?
(A) Have a meeting with a business
(B) Expand to an international market
(C) Visit a fair in France
(D) Give a woman some advice

76. Why does the speaker say, "He'll be at his desk for the rest of the week"?
(A) To recommend a suitable meeting time
(B) To suggest changing a meeting time
(C) To complain about some tasks
(D) To indicate that he will work

77. What kind of department do the listeners work for?
(A) Advertising
(B) Accounting
(C) Sales
(D) Research

78. What does the speaker say has recently changed?
(A) A payday
(B) A meeting location
(C) A survey
(D) A hiring process

79. What does the speaker imply when she says, "The 30th is always a busy day at our company"?
(A) To encourage employees
(B) To delay the date
(C) To ask for overtime
(D) To explain an excuse

---

80. What is the speaker mainly talking about?
(A) A job interview
(B) A flower shop
(C) A new chef
(D) A business opening

81. What does the speaker tell the listeners to do?
(A) Order some samples
(B) Decorate the business
(C) Put on their uniforms
(D) Review their uniforms

82. Why did Cathy Paluza make some samples?
(A) To get some opinions from staff
(B) To collect some money
(C) To offer them for free
(D) To try them on

---

83. By whom is the handbook used?
(A) Journalists
(B) Teachers
(C) Engineers
(D) Business owners

84. What did the speaker recently receive?
(A) Complaints
(B) Handbooks
(C) Sketches
(D) Samples

85. Why does the speaker say, "The handouts are in your folder"?
(A) To arrange something properly
(B) To correct some errors
(C) To make his coworker surprised
(D) To ask for some assistance

---

86. What industry do the listeners most likely work in?
(A) Accounting
(B) Electronics
(C) Engineering
(D) Logistics

87. What does the speaker imply when she says, "But look at these numbers"?
(A) Sales are higher than expected.
(B) A different promotion is necessary.
(C) Some figures must be corrected.
(D) A location for the event will not be spacious.

88. What does the speaker ask the listeners about?
(A) What to bring
(B) Who to invite for the event
(C) When the event should be held
(D) How to get to the convention

GO ON TO THE NEXT PAGE

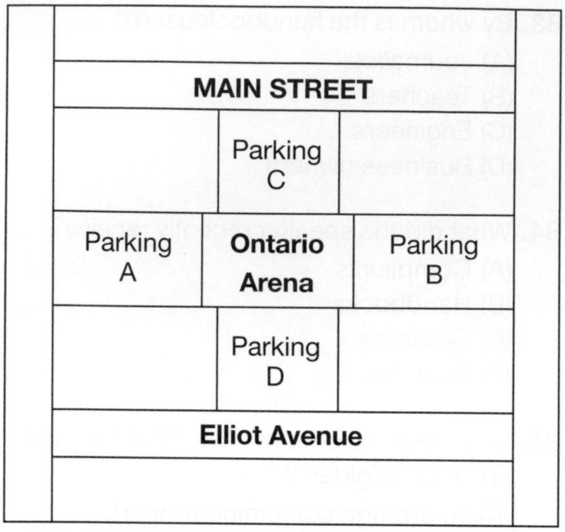

MAIN STREET

Parking C

Parking A

Ontario Arena

Parking B

Parking D

Elliot Avenue

89. According to the speaker, what happened yesterday?
(A) A concert
(B) A festival
(C) A competition
(D) Construction

90. What will the interested listeners most likely do next?
(A) Visit a Web site
(B) Get a signature
(C) Call a program
(D) Use public transportation

91. Look at the graphic. Which parking area will be closed?
(A) Parking area A
(B) Parking area B
(C) Parking area C
(D) Parking area D

Seminars	Place
Interpersonal and Analytical Skills	Diamond Hall
Planning and Writing a Blog	Emerald Hall
Information and IT Literacy	Sapphire Hall
Effective Negotiation	Prestigious Room

92. Where do the listeners work?
(A) At a conference center
(B) At a restaurant
(C) At a newspaper
(D) At a hotel

93. Look at the graphic. Which session has been changed?
(A) Interpersonal and Analytical Skills
(B) Planning and Writing a Blog
(C) Information and IT Literacy
(D) Effective Negotiation

94. What will the employees do this week?
(A) Give out some sweets
(B) Distribute some vouchers
(C) Apply a discount
(D) Conduct a survey

Fityou Shoes 25% Discount until This Weekend!	
Sale Item	**Store Location**
Sandals	Peterborough
Sneakers	Kingston
Ankle boots	Rochester
High tops	Kitchener

95. Why is Fityou Shoes having a sale?
(A) To celebrate a new season
(B) To make room for stock
(C) To attract more tourists
(D) To close the store

96. Look at the graphic. At which store location is the announcement being made?
(A) Peterborough
(B) Kingston
(C) Rochester
(D) Kitchener

97. Why should listeners visit a Web site?
(A) To shop for more items
(B) To check for job openings
(C) To participate in a survey
(D) To become a member

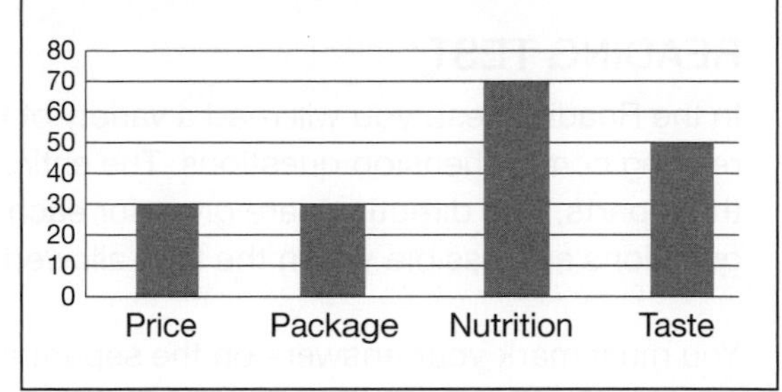

98. What product does the company sell?
(A) Glasses
(B) Shoes
(C) A drink
(D) A cereal

99. Look at the graphic. Which feature will the company begin to work on?
(A) Price
(B) Package
(C) Nutrition
(D) Taste

100. What will the listeners do next?
(A) Sign up for a workshop
(B) Submit their preferences
(C) Work on brainstorming
(D) Return to the office

TEST 3 PART 4

This is the end of the Listening test. Turn to Part 5 in your test book.

READING TEST

In the Reading test, you will read a variety of texts and answer several different types of reading comprehension questions. The entire Reading test will last 75 minutes. There are three parts, and directions are given for each part. You are encouraged to answer as many questions as possible within the time allowed.

You must mark your answers on the separate answer sheet. Do not write your answers in your test book.

PART 5

Directions: A word or phrase is missing in each of the sentences below. Four answer choices are given below each sentence. Select the best answer to complete the sentence. Then mark the letter (A), (B), (C), or (D) on your answer sheet.

101. At the company's tenth year celebration, Shane's Italian Cuisine will provide ------- which consists of various Italian menus offered at the restaurant.
(A) cater
(B) catering
(C) caters
(D) catered

102. After the president of the company had passed away, his son, the ------- living relative of the president, inherited his properties.
(A) sheer
(B) stark
(C) select
(D) sole

103. The number of customers who visited the store has increased tremendously ------- the unprecedented sale it has offered for a limited time.
(A) since
(B) though
(C) during
(D) while

104. The change in the firm's board committee ------- better working conditions for the employees as the members of the board have decided to shorten working hours and raise wages.
(A) promising
(B) promises
(C) will be promised
(D) would have promised

105. ------- the firm to avoid bankruptcy, the workers did their best in united efforts but they could not evade the crisis.
(A) Onto
(B) Until
(C) For
(D) Forward

106. As the marketing department has been augmented, Raymond Spencer has been transferred to the new section ------- his former division.
(A) in
(B) from
(C) across
(D) of

107. After years of hard work and successful results in important contracts, Kristi now has ------- over her colleagues and superiors.
(A) authority
(B) consequence
(C) significance
(D) reaction

108. The lounge may be ------- by anyone with a small entrance fee but the lack of information about the place holds people back from using the service.
(A) informed
(B) accessed
(C) prevented
(D) advanced

109. We are one of the leading companies in furniture manufacturing, ------- it took us ten years to get where we are now.
(A) since
(B) before
(C) even though
(D) instead

110. Before funding the project, the corporation sent experts to have the proposed product ------- to estimate its potential value and verify compliance with the national standards.
(A) invested
(B) assessed
(C) conducted
(D) developed

111. The regulars of Isaac Design who spend more than $20,000 a year will be ------- of any upcoming fashion shows with invitations.
(A) notified
(B) regulated
(C) announced
(D) determined

112. Most of the customers of our mattress store decide to buy the product that they ------- comfortable after lying on it for a short time.
(A) find
(B) stay
(C) relax
(D) spend

GO ON TO THE NEXT PAGE

113. Paul Academy, a non-profit online organization, is dedicated to making their program -------- to children who live in inadequate conditions by allowing them to receive quality online learning experiences.

(A) educates
(B) educate
(C) educational
(D) educationally

114. Jacob's sales records have been steadily ------- since he entered the company; this phenomenon answers the question of why companies think highly of experienced workers.

(A) improve
(B) improves
(C) improving
(D) improvement

115. In large companies like -------, it is nearly impossible to get to know every single employee, so it is normal to pass by strangers.

(A) us
(B) our
(C) ours
(D) we

116. The president of the charity organization, Eduseed, visits the school he has built in Burma ------- to restock the supplies that have run out.

(A) shortly
(B) deeply
(C) finely
(D) regularly

117. Quality, reputation, and service are usually given high priority by many business owners ------- these are easy for the customers to inspect.

(A) when
(B) so that
(C) as if
(D) since

118. Ms. Greenhill, ------- vehicle had been destroyed in a bad accident, had to take public transportation until she could afford a new car.

(A) who
(B) whom
(C) whoever
(D) whose

119. We ensure that our newly released automated sprinklers and mowers are much faster than those ------- by hand.

(A) accepted
(B) operated
(C) publicized
(D) intensified

120. Once you get to Highway No. 65 which leads ------- to the city center, it will take less than half an hour from the airport to our office.

(A) straightened
(B) straightening
(C) straighten
(D) straight

121. It will take months to negotiate the ------- to the urban development issues in downtown Chicago since most building owners voted against it.

(A) occasion
(B) resolution
(C) impression
(D) situation

122. The texts and images in the brochure have been provided ------- of the Tourism Administration Department.

(A) courtesy
(B) courteous
(C) courteously
(D) courteousness

123. Only after realizing the importance of satisfying the local customers, Jessie, the owner of Jess Cafe ------- on serving various Asian foods has developed a localized menu.

(A) focused
(B) to focus
(C) is focused
(D) focus

124. ------- given above, any claims for refund will be rejected, as the customer is accountable for all damages to the product after purchase.

(A) As
(B) While
(C) After
(D) For

125. Due to their modest stipend, anyone usually working under twenty hours a week is ------- from the income tax.

(A) subject
(B) operated
(C) built
(D) exempt

126. The Green Belt Action, in which construction of buildings and destruction of nature are strictly prohibited, is part of an effort to preserve more ------- for wildlife to dwell and reproduce in.

(A) benefit
(B) space
(C) project
(D) journey

127. Ms. Lewis is ------- that Timothy, under her supervision, will smoothly carry out orders assigned to him.

(A) designated
(B) remembered
(C) important
(D) confident

128. The shareholders hurriedly disposed of their shares ------- they would sink in price once the corruption in their firm received coverage.

(A) as for
(B) meanwhile
(C) for example
(D) because

129. The critics highly praised the seemingly profound film, admiring its unique filming techniques and original methods of plot unfolding, while the audience reviews suggest -------.

(A) otherwise
(B) in contrast
(C) instead
(D) on the contrary

130. Mr. Rogers ------- the proposals, but he has no other choice but to decline them due to the financial burden they will bring him.

(A) appeals
(B) focuses
(C) relates
(D) endorses

TEST 3 PART 5

GO ON TO THE NEXT PAGE

PART 6

Directions: Read the texts that follow. A word, phrase, or sentence is missing in parts of each text. Four answer choices for each question are given below the text. Select the best answer to complete the text. Then mark the letter (A), (B), (C), or (D) on your answer sheet.

Questions 131-134 refer to the following e-mail.

E-MAIL

From	williamr_thomas@abcsprts.com
To	jamesburns@kaum.net
Date	June 23
Subject	Scale barbecue grills

Dear Mr. Burns,

We have received your message and checked your record. It states that you ordered three barbecue grills (model no. SCT-250) through our TV home shopping channel on June 17 and they were scheduled to arrive June 22. We are sorry to hear that you have not yet received —**131**—. Usually it takes no more than three or four days to deliver items.

—**132**—. According to this information, your grills should arrive on June 23. If you do not receive your order by then, please —**133**— us.

We apologize for the inconvenience this has caused you. Obviously, it does not happen very often. I want to emphasize that this situation is very —**134**—.

Thank you.

William R. Thomas

ABC Sports International

131. (A) ones
(B) it
(C) some
(D) them

132. (A) Visit our store to purchase an additional item.
(B) Thank you for your feedback.
(C) We were able to track your order.
(D) Unfortunately, the items you ordered are not available at the moment.

133. (A) contacting
(B) contacted
(C) contact
(D) contacts

134. (A) interesting
(B) similar
(C) impossible
(D) unusual

Questions 135-138 refer to the following customer review.

I bought some fabrics at Trago's Textile Inc. last week. When I first called to ask some of the options they offered, the representative was very knowledgeable and helpful. So, I ordered some printed cotton and linen in bulk over the phone. Unfortunately, I probably —**135**— here for fabric anymore. The workers at the warehouse apparently didn't care about the —**136**— of the fabric they loaded onto my truck. Some of it was damaged and stained. —**137**—. They did let me replace some of the fabric there, but I had to return to their store with the damaged ones. Next time I will find a place that will let me —**138**— my own fabric. And I strongly recommend that you avoid doing business with Trago's Textile.

Mary T. Barra

135. (A) did not shop
(B) will not be shopping
(C) may not have shopped
(D) could not have shopped

136. (A) category
(B) width
(C) price
(D) quality

137. (A) There was a long line of waiting for a refund.
(B) I couldn't carry them by myself.
(C) They recommended a repair shop.
(D) About half of what I got looked used.

138. (A) design
(B) choose
(C) provide
(D) cut

GO ON TO THE NEXT PAGE

Questions 139-142 refer to the following letter.

Dear Henry's Fun

This letter is to serve as proof of your registration —**139**— confirm your participation in the 10th International Toy Fair, from July 10 to July 16. Since you participated in last year's fair, Henry's Fun will be offered —**140**— booths at a reduced rate. Please be aware that we have made small changes in regard to preparing your space. This year, all participants must have their booths ready by 9 P.M. on July 9. —**141**—. Tables and chairs needed will be provided by the organizer. On the day, you will need to visit our office next to the main entrance before you begin setting up your booths.

We appreciate your choosing to participate in our —**142**—.

Gregory Anderson, Coordinator

139. (A) rather than
(B) therefore
(C) and also
(D) in case

140. (A) rent
(B) rents
(C) renting
(D) rental

141. (A) The final schedule will be posted on our Web site.
(B) All trash and packing materials should also be removed by that time.
(C) The Rex Toy will be located next to our office.
(D) The number of participants has increased over the last ten years.

142. (A) contest
(B) event
(C) research
(D) course

Questions 143-146 refer to the following article.

Jackson City
Educational Committee Approved Funds

Special community programs with advanced technology —**143**— to the local residents of Jackson City. On Wednesday, the Jackson City Council announced that its "Local Hi-Tech Program" proposal was approved by the board of the City Education Committee. —**144**—.

Each community library in the city will be allotted $1,000,000 for the purchase of tablet computers. Library users will be allowed to take home the tablets —**145**— of the time for library programs, but they will be available only —**146**— its opening hours.

143. (A) came
(B) were coming
(C) are coming
(D) come

144. (A) Residents are looking forward to the final decision.
(B) The tablets will be donated by local businesses.
(C) The vote took place on Tuesday, August 10.
(D) Nevertheless, the programs will be the same as previous ones.

145. (A) none
(B) many
(C) all
(D) some

146. (A) at
(B) to
(C) for
(D) during

TEST 3 PART 6

GO ON TO THE NEXT PAGE

PART 7

Directions: In this part you will read a selection of texts, such as magazine and newspaper articles, e-mails, and instant messages. Each text or set of texts is followed by several questions. Select the best answer for each question and mark the letter (A), (B), (C), or (D) on your answer sheet.

Questions 147-148 refer to the following information.

Odessa Culinary Institute Guidelines for filling out a purchase order request

* List product codes if available, and describe the item or items in detail.
* Tick the box marked "No substitutes" if a specific brand is needed, and provide a clear reason in the vicinal space.
* Indicate the name of the supplier including the contact information or Web address.
* Order requests with no signature will not be processed, so submit the signed form to the purchasing department.
* Thoroughly look through your expense report.

Once the order has been filled, the expense of the purchase will be allocated to your divisional budget.

147. According to the information, what detail must be provided in every request?
(A) A signature
(B) A supplier's contact information
(C) A product code
(D) A reason for requesting a particular brand

148. What is suggested about the Odessa Culinary Institute's purchasing department?
(A) It has information on local suppliers.
(B) It requires budget reports from every division.
(C) It searches for less expensive items for divisions.
(D) It provides funding to each division's budget.

Questions 149-150 refer to the following notice.

Modern Beauty Apparel

※ Item Return Requests

- Within five days of purchase, customers may return clothes for store credit only. All returns must be accompanied by original receipts.
- Clothes must be in an unused and unworn condition with the attached tags when they are returned.
- Sales of clothes at reduced prices are final. Customer requests for returns or refunds will not be accepted.

149. What is the main reason the notice has been posted?
(A) To announce a sales event
(B) To inform customers of a policy
(C) To publicize a recent relocation
(D) To promote a new product

150. What is mentioned about products to be returned?
(A) No receipt is required for some clothes.
(B) Cash refunds may be given to some customers.
(C) The store resells them at discounted prices.
(D) They cannot be returned after a certain period.

GO ON TO THE NEXT PAGE

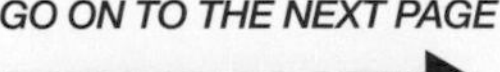

Questions 151-152 refers to the following article.

BERMONDSEY TOWN, August 11- The council of Bermondsey Town is currently looking through proposals from commercial property developers for establishing a business district on a 31,000-square-meter parcel of land to the north of town.

The business district is to be located in proximity to Highway R21, on the land where some Bermondsey Town companies once operated, such as Anerley Automobile Manufacturer, Charing Furniture, Inc., and Penge Appliance. The facilities will use integrated cutting-edge energy-efficient systems. The town also has a plan to build residential apartment complexes in the vicinity of the site within three years.

"We are excited about this chance to draw new businesses to our town," said town council member Virgil Valdez. "The business district will be in an excellent location, close to various dining establishments and accommodations, as well as a major transportation system. Once the intial stage of the design is done, space will be divided based on occupants' needs," he added. Since the region's train station, situated just fifteen kilometers away in Northolt, was expanded, most of the development plans in Bermondsey Town have been expedited.

151. What is indicated about the northern area of Bermondsey Town?

(A) There was once a train station there.
(B) It has been a residential district.
(C) Vehicles used to be produced there.
(D) An appliance business will start its operations there.

152. What aspect of the business district is NOT stated?

(A) The closest major transportation system
(B) Its vicinity to some dining businesses
(C) Its energy-saving building technology
(D) The total number of complexes to be constructed

Questions 153-154 refer to the following text message chain.

Clare Tamika 11:02 A.M.
One of the tenants from the apartment complex at 2642 Sudbury Hill called to inform me that she would like to move out at the beginning of June, but her lease is supposed to end at the end of July.

Lorene Miranda 11:03 A.M.
In that case, according to the lease agreement, tenants wanting to move out before the lease ends have to pay a penalty for the early leave. However, if they can find new tenants right away, occasionally some landlords may waive the penalty. Why don't you contact the landlord and ask whether they intend to grant an exemption?

Clare Tamika 11:04 A.M.
Since there are some people currently looking for rental properties in the town on our list, it could be worth trying that.

Lorene Miranda 11:05 A.M.
Absolutely, you shouldn't have difficulty finding new tenants as the Sudbury Hill apartment is a very popular one. Keep me informed of the progress.

Clare Tamika 11:07 A.M.
Okay. I will keep in touch.

153. What is the tenant most likely trying to do?
(A) Request a maintenance service
(B) Make the early termination of a lease
(C) Put a property on the market
(D) Move to a different apartment nearby

154. At 11:04 A.M., what does Ms. Tamika most likely mean when she writes, "It could be worth trying that"?
(A) She intends to contact the landlord.
(B) She is aware that a penalty should be charged.
(C) She wants to let the tenant know her responsibility.
(D) She will persuade the landlord to renovate the property.

GO ON TO THE NEXT PAGE

Questions 155-157 refer to the following e-mail.

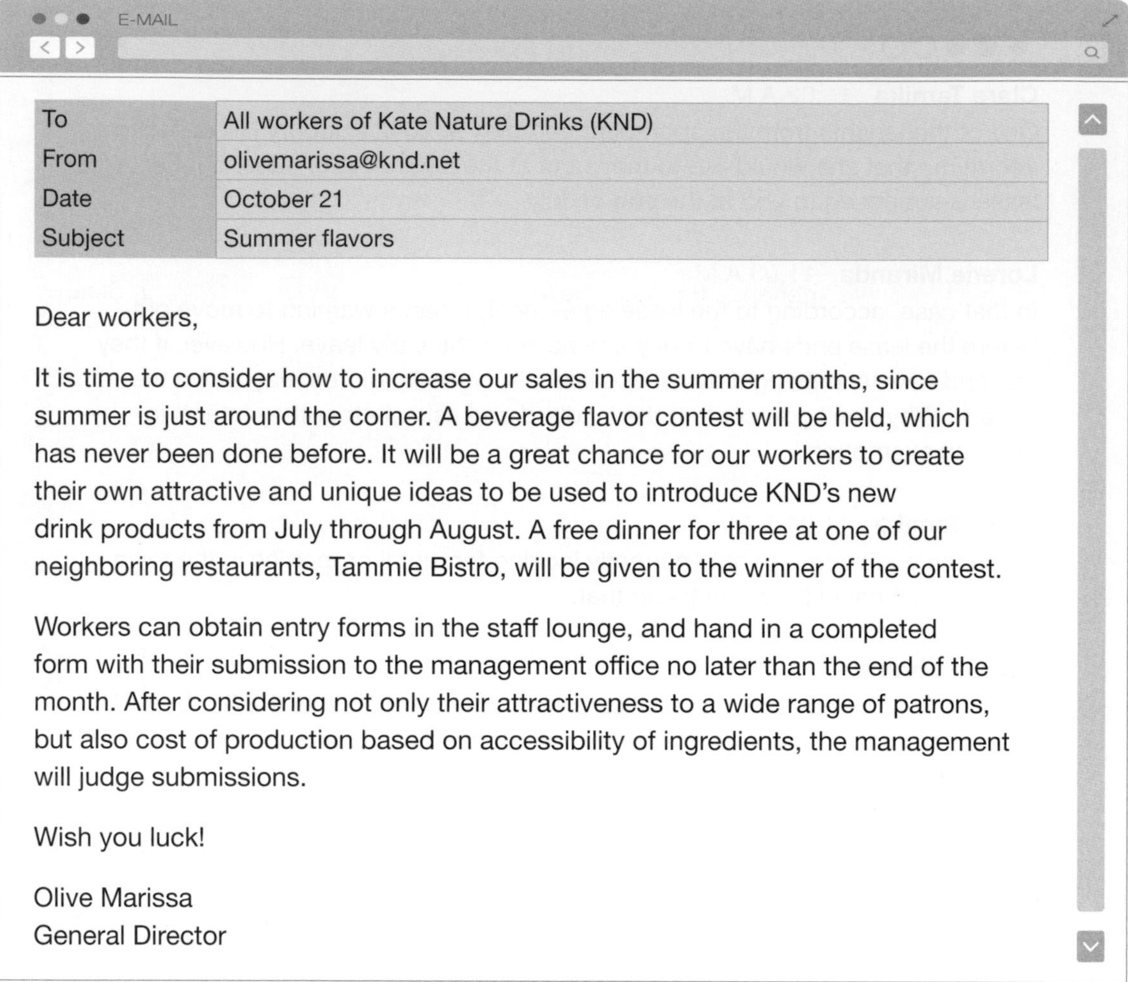

To	All workers of Kate Nature Drinks (KND)
From	olivemarissa@knd.net
Date	October 21
Subject	Summer flavors

Dear workers,

It is time to consider how to increase our sales in the summer months, since summer is just around the corner. A beverage flavor contest will be held, which has never been done before. It will be a great chance for our workers to create their own attractive and unique ideas to be used to introduce KND's new drink products from July through August. A free dinner for three at one of our neighboring restaurants, Tammie Bistro, will be given to the winner of the contest.

Workers can obtain entry forms in the staff lounge, and hand in a completed form with their submission to the management office no later than the end of the month. After considering not only their attractiveness to a wide range of patrons, but also cost of production based on accessibility of ingredients, the management will judge submissions.

Wish you luck!

Olive Marissa
General Director

155. What is the main purpose of the e-mail?
(A) To report a recent increase in drink sales
(B) To announce a new production policy
(C) To introduce a new competition
(D) To encourage employees to sample new beverage products

156. What is suggested about Tammie Bistro?
(A) It is only open during summer months.
(B) It is located relatively close to the drink company.
(C) It has recently introduced a new menu item.
(D) It uses seasonal ingredients for its menu.

157. What is NOT stated as a feature of great beverage products?
(A) They should have appealing packaging.
(B) They should be affordable to produce.
(C) They should use materials that are not difficult to acquire.
(D) They should be loved by a broad range of customers.

Questions 158-160 refer to the following flyer.

Could you use a holiday?

Come to Birds' Hill!

Several-time Winner of Travel Advice's
"Must-Visit Holiday Spot"

What Birds' Hill offers!

The beautiful nature! Experience the great views with plenty of wildlife throughout Sloane Forest. You can enjoy hiking and biking along approximately 20km of trails around the area. Our experienced guides can help you explore the beauty of the area's nature or you can wander on your own.

We also have indoor and outdoor sport facilities where you can play various sports such as football, baseball, tennis, and basketball. Come to our game room and enjoy chess and card games. By registering, you can rent a boat on the lake or experience a horse back ride when the weather is nice.

You can spend the evening reading and unwinding at our modern, relaxing library if you would like to have some quiet time. From the latest best sellers to classic literature, every visitor will be happy with our wide selection. A variety of movies are available, which you can check out and watch at your own place.

With the exception of guided tours, our daily package includes all services and activities provided at Birds' Hill. Please feel free to contact us for further price information.

158. What most likely is Birds' Hill?
(A) A sports facility
(B) A public park
(C) A wildlife preserve
(D) A holiday resort

159. What is suggested about Birds' Hill?
(A) It offers sport lessons for free.
(B) It is run by a nonprofit organization.
(C) It has received awards more than one time.
(D) It has recently opened a movie theater.

160. Why do the visitors probably pay an additional fee?
(A) To ride a horse
(B) To rent a bicycle
(C) To get a guide
(D) To use a boat

GO ON TO THE NEXT PAGE

Questions 161-163 refer to the following e-mail.

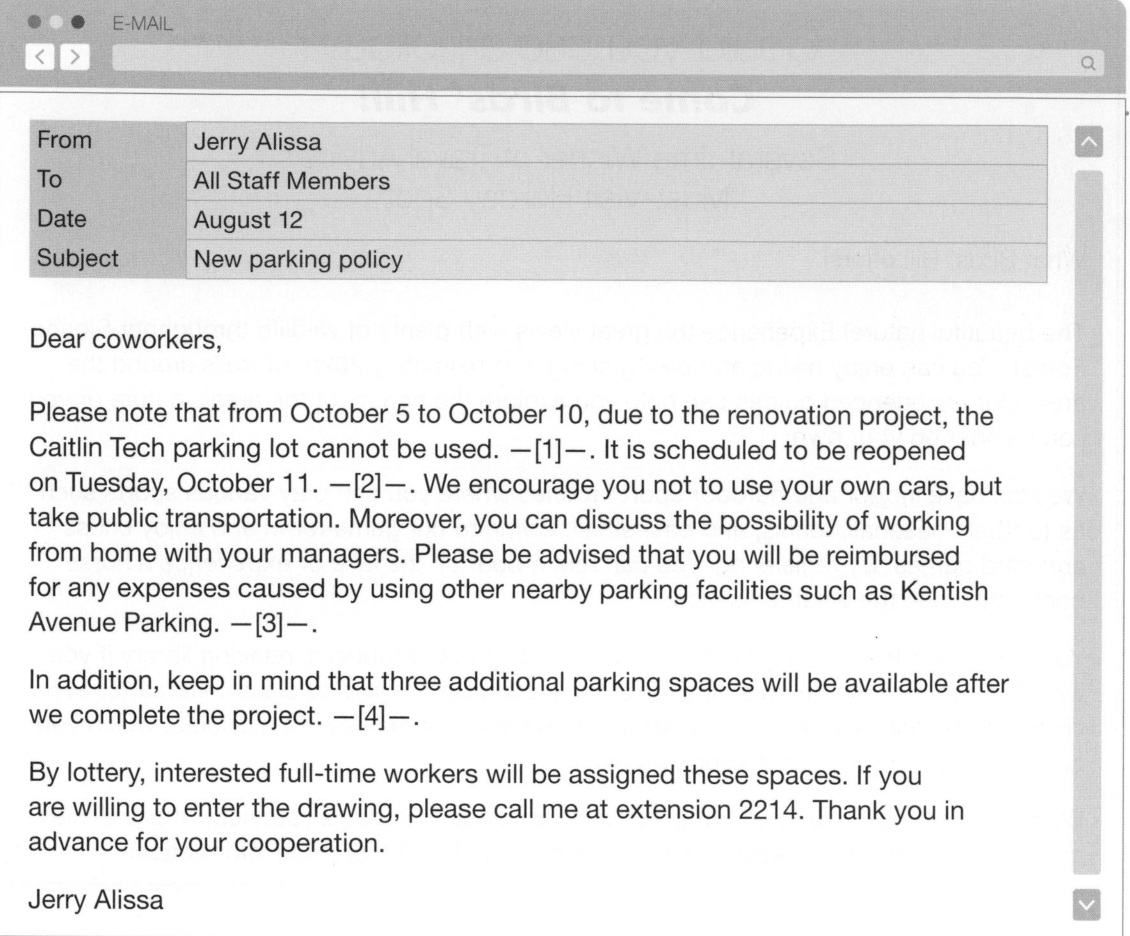

From	Jerry Alissa
To	All Staff Members
Date	August 12
Subject	New parking policy

Dear coworkers,

Please note that from October 5 to October 10, due to the renovation project, the Caitlin Tech parking lot cannot be used. —[1]—. It is scheduled to be reopened on Tuesday, October 11. —[2]—. We encourage you not to use your own cars, but take public transportation. Moreover, you can discuss the possibility of working from home with your managers. Please be advised that you will be reimbursed for any expenses caused by using other nearby parking facilities such as Kentish Avenue Parking. —[3]—.

In addition, keep in mind that three additional parking spaces will be available after we complete the project. —[4]—.

By lottery, interested full-time workers will be assigned these spaces. If you are willing to enter the drawing, please call me at extension 2214. Thank you in advance for your cooperation.

Jerry Alissa

161. According to the e-mail, what can workers talk about with their supervisors?
(A) The reimbursement for parking expenses
(B) Participating in a lottery drawing for a parking space
(C) The likelihood of telecommuting
(D) Finding nearby parking facilities

162. What is indicated about Kentish Avenue Parking?
(A) It is owned by Caitlin Tech.
(B) It will be reopened on October 11.
(C) It has lately been renovated.
(D) It is available for a fee.

163. In which of the positions marked [1], [2], [3], and [4] does the following sentence best belong?
"We plan to resurface and reseal the parking lot, and install a new fence."
(A) [1]
(B) [2]
(C) [3]
(D) [4]

Questions 164-167 refer to the following article.

The Communication Fair Plans Announced by Pauline

SOUTHFIELD (23. July)- Pauline, one of the leading conglomerates in the communication industry, announced yesterday that they are not going to introduce its newest mobile phone lines at this quarter's two-day-long Southfield Communication Fair in October. —[1]—.

The fair has been generally considered one of the most integral events of this quarter for the communication industry, in which the country's leading companies hold well-prepared presentations to boast about their latest collections. The fair has brought in much media attention and been popular among industry personnel. These days, however, interest of the general public has not been as strong as it used to be. —[2]—.

The CEO of Pauline, Rhonda Webb, clearly said at the press conference in the main office that the determination to skip this quarter's presentation at the fair does not reflect that Pauline will give up participating in the event. —[3]—. "We will have no public presentation, but there will be business-related meetings with our retail dealers and distribution partners," Webb added. "In order to publicize our latest mobile phones and services, we will intentionally expose the public to them not only through social media but also through our main Web site during the fair."

Ms. Webb replied, when asked about the new marketing strategy, that Pauline aims to increase interest in its new items and services through giving information to present users before launching them to the public. Moreover, by forgoing showing off its new items and services at the fair, Pauline will be able to avoid being rated by consumers in comparison to its competitors. "People will enjoy the new line of Pauline's products on its own merits." Webb insisted. —[4]—.

164. According to the article, what will Pauline do during the Communication Fair?
(A) Hold a press conference
(B) Film a presentation to post on its Web site
(C) Use the Internet to promote new products
(D) Collaborate with other companies in presentations

165. In the article, the word "integral" in paragraph 2, line 2, is closest in meaning to
(A) complete
(B) incorporated
(C) significant
(D) installed

166. What is the main reason Pauline intends to use the new strategy?
(A) It is looking for a site for the next quarter's fair.
(B) Its marketing budget has been cut.
(C) Its new products and services are not ready yet.
(D) It is reluctant to be evaluated against other companies.

167. In which of the positions marked [1], [2], [3], and [4] does the following sentence best belong?
"Professionals in the industry, hence, did not seem surprised at Pauline's announcement."
(A) [1]
(B) [2]
(C) [3]
(D) [4]

GO ON TO THE NEXT PAGE

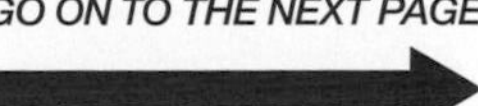

Questions 168-171 refer to the following information.

Amersham Communication, Ltd.
Weekly Discussion

In the business world, having a meeting with coworkers or clients can be a good approach to getting jobs properly done. However, it is important to use staff members' time in the most productive way. In order to help to find the most efficient way to accomplish that goal, here are a few questions to consider.

"What is the main reason for having a meeting?"
There must be a clear purpose of a meeting that could lead employees to reach an agreement on a common issue, to improve their business abilities, and to find out better ways to achieve their accomplishments. But holding a meeting only to address non-urgent updates should be avoided.

"When is the most appropriate time to meet?"
It is natural to put off a meeting when important data and figures are not ready or an essential person is not able to attend. However, the meeting should not be called off if doing so is not unavoidably necessary.

"Are there any other alternatives for how to reach the goal?"
E-mail can be an excellent way to be debriefed on information or report updates. If only a few team members are required to attend a meeting, it would be better to hold an informal small gathering at a location every member can easily access.

"What will occur if the meeting does not take place?"
Prior to calling off or rescheduling the meeting, it is important to think about what would happen. What could be missed? Would the cancellation provoke any issues among other participants or managers? You have to check whether there is enough information for members to have the task completed or find a better solution if they suggest that the meeting is not necessary.

168. What is the information about?

(A) What the best way to make a speech is
(B) How customer satisfaction can be increased
(C) Why more employees need to be hired
(D) How employees can work more efficiently

169. What is mentioned as an ideal reason to schedule a meeting?

(A) To deliver general information
(B) To help employees make a decision
(C) To hold a training session for new hires
(D) To promote positive relationships among employees

170. The word "essential", in paragraph 3, line 2, is closest in meaning to

(A) fundamental
(B) intrinsic
(C) critical
(D) simple

171. According to the information, how should information be reported?

(A) By contacting employees by telephone
(B) By e-mailing employees messages
(C) By sending letters to staff members
(D) By publishing a weekly newsletter

GO ON TO THE NEXT PAGE

Questions 172-175 refer to the following online chat discussion.

●●●○○

Jillian Araceli 1:12 P.M.
Good afternoon, everyone. Is there any news on the Fulham Community Park proposal we submitted last week?

Tammy Woods 1:13 P.M.
I contacted Ms. Fulham yesterday. She told me that the final decision was to be made by Tuesday, but I haven't heard from her yet.

Jillian Araceli 1:14 P.M.
That's sooner than expected. Although the soil has been prepared, unless the flowers and plants are ordered by today, they won't arrive in time for the deadline she asked.

Maggie Wilson 1:15 P.M.
We've already put in the order. We placed it this afternoon.

Jillian Araceli 1:15 P.M.
That's not really good. If we are not awarded the contract, we are required to pay for them even though they are not necessary any more. Do we have enough time to cancel the order before they are shipped to us?

Maggie Wilson 1:16 P.M.
I believe they may choose us again as they contracted us last year. Let me see.

Jillian Araceli 1:17 P.M.
Tammy, could you call Ms. Fulham and check how it is going?

Maggie Wilson 1:17 P.M.
No need to worry. We can call off the order by this evening with no cancellation fee.

Tammy Woods 1:18 P.M.
I think we should, Jillian. I just talked with Mr. Kim on the phone. He told me they closed the deal, but Ms. Fulham chose to work with Richmond Family.

Jillian Araceli 1:19 P.M.
That's a shame. But let's not be disappointed. There should be better jobs waiting for us.

172. What type of industry do the people most likely work in?
(A) News media
(B) Landscaping
(C) Business consulting
(D) Career development

173. At 1:16 P.M., what does Ms. Wilson mean she will do when she says, "Let me see"?
(A) Pay for shipment
(B) Draft an estimate
(C) Check a schedule
(D) Call off a delivery

174. Why did Mr. Kim contact Ms. woods?
(A) To order more supplies
(B) To notify her that another company won the contract
(C) To inform her that Ms. Fulham is not available
(D) To let her know about an extra fee

175. What will Ms. Wilson most likely do next?
(A) Revise a proposal
(B) Contact Ms. Fulham to thank her
(C) Withdraw an order
(D) Call a managerial meeting

GO ON TO THE NEXT PAGE

Questions 176-180 refer to the following e-mails.

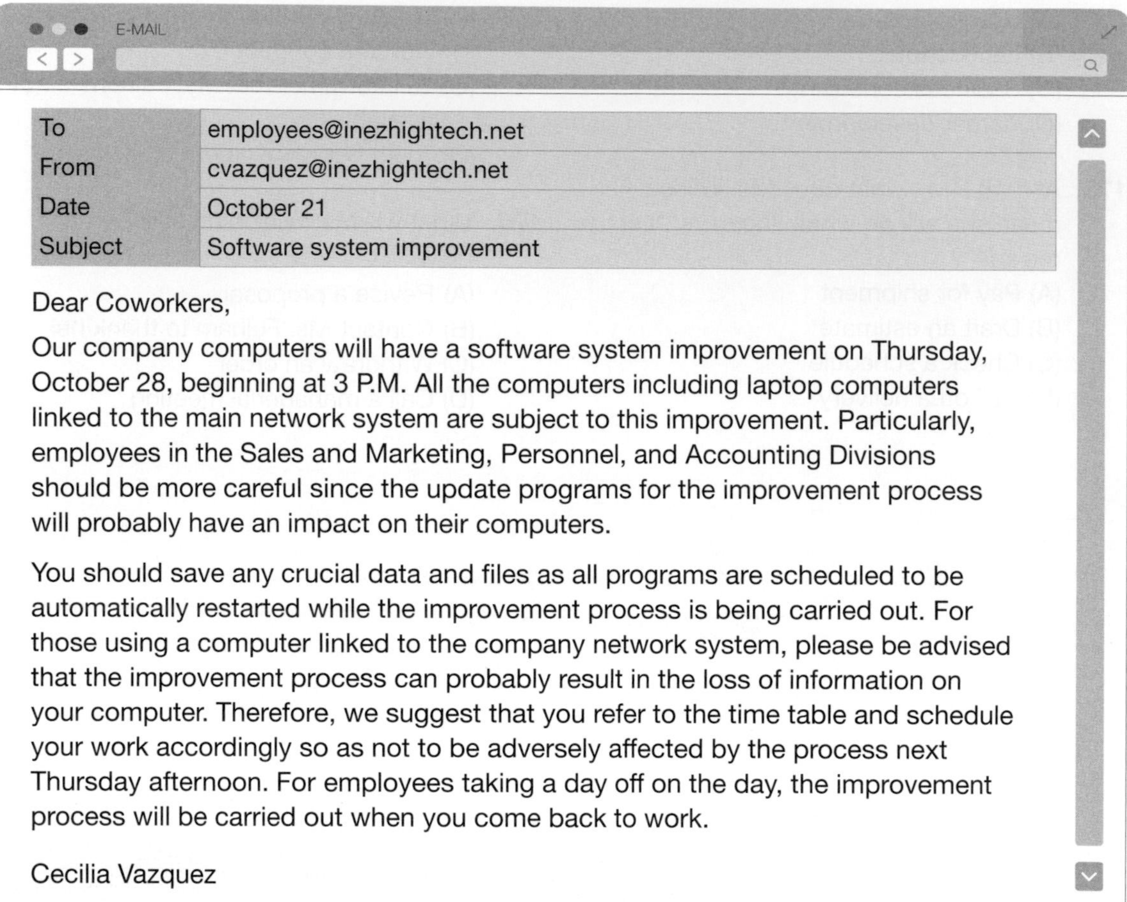

E-MAIL

To	employees@inezhightech.net
From	cvazquez@inezhightech.net
Date	October 21
Subject	Software system improvement

Dear Coworkers,

Our company computers will have a software system improvement on Thursday, October 28, beginning at 3 P.M. All the computers including laptop computers linked to the main network system are subject to this improvement. Particularly, employees in the Sales and Marketing, Personnel, and Accounting Divisions should be more careful since the update programs for the improvement process will probably have an impact on their computers.

You should save any crucial data and files as all programs are scheduled to be automatically restarted while the improvement process is being carried out. For those using a computer linked to the company network system, please be advised that the improvement process can probably result in the loss of information on your computer. Therefore, we suggest that you refer to the time table and schedule your work accordingly so as not to be adversely affected by the process next Thursday afternoon. For employees taking a day off on the day, the improvement process will be carried out when you come back to work.

Cecilia Vazquez

E-MAIL

To	jterry@inezhightech.net
From	avaughn@inezhightech.net
Date	October 22
Subject	Checks to vendors

Dear Ms. Terry,

This is to inform you about a potential issue sending next week's checks to our subcontractors. The process is normally scheduled to be carried out every Thursday. In consideration of Ms. Vazquez's e-mail I received yesterday, the time of issuing next week's checks is required to be adjusted for the process to be done smoothly. I am supposed to be away next Tuesday and Wednesday to participate in an accounting workshop. I will be able to do the task next Friday one day later than usual. Instead, it may be possible to do the task on Monday, October 25. Yet, some of the subcontractor payments will not be sent on time anyway. Please inform me of how I should proceed, and I will follow with your advice.

Shaun Vaughn

176. Why has the first e-mail been written?
(A) To prepare workers for a possible system performance problem
(B) To recommend that workers update their work
(C) To suggest a solution to a scheduling conflict
(D) To inform workers of a way to set up a software program

177. In what division does Ms. Vazquez most likely work?
(A) Sales and Marketing
(B) Accounting
(C) Tech support
(D) Personnel

178. What most likely is the reason Mr. Vaughn intends to reschedule a job?
(A) He wants to adjust the time of issuing checks.
(B) He received a prompt payment request from subcontractors.
(C) He wants to avoid losing data.
(D) His laptop is not working properly.

179. According to Mr. Vaughn, what could be an alternative date for the job to be rescheduled?
(A) October 21
(B) October 22
(C) October 28
(D) October 29

180. What is Mr. Vaughn planning to do on October 26?
(A) Attend a training session
(B) Issue a check to subcontractors
(C) Install a new software system
(D) Leave for his holiday

TEST 3 PART 7

GO ON TO THE NEXT PAGE

Questions 181-185 refer to the following e-mails.

E-MAIL

To	All our present customers
From	marketing@inezpublication.com.ca
Date	Friday, 21 October
Subject	Final Chance! These Copies Won't Be Printed Again!

Dear Valued Customer,

Here is surprising news for you! Once again it's time to hold our clearance sale on various collections of Inez Publication's books. All the copies in the sale will go out of print, so do not miss this great opportunity to acquire excellent books that can make your life more pleasant. Our Yearly Sale Pamphlet will soon be mailed to you, but by visiting our Web site, you can check out the list of collections on sale sooner. Placing an order through our Web site is recommended in order to purchase the copies you would like before they are out of stock. All purchases will be delivered for free until next week, and if more than four books are ordered, we will gift-wrap your books with no charge. Take advantage of this special chance!

Lauren Stone
Inez Publication Sales Director

Notice: This e-mail is being sent to you since you have purchased publications from Inez Publication. If our information about sales is not necessary for you anymore, just respond to this e-mail with the subject "No Subscription."

E-MAIL

Dear Mr. Schultz,

We appreciate your purchase. The below products will be delivered within 4-7 business days through the TRO Mail Service. Please be advised that no refund for any item will be issued.

Placed Order: 24 Oct 1:15 P.M.

Item No.	Quantity	Book title	Price per unit	Total
32118	1	Photo Shoot Text Book: With Various Skills	$11.50	$11.50
44312	1	Contemporary Photograph Collection	$9.00	$9.00
98031	1	The Photography Software for Amateurs	$15.50	$15.50
		Gift Packing		$6.00
		Delivery Fee		-
		Total		$42.00

181. What is the reason customers would use the online pamphlet rather than the print pamphlet?
(A) To be exempt from shipping fee
(B) To look through a wider range of books
(C) To search for books earlier
(D) To acquire a revised price list

182. What is suggested about Mr. Schultz?
(A) He is running his own business.
(B) He has collected a wide selection of photographs.
(C) He needed some books for his photography course.
(D) He has ordered some items from Inez Publication before.

183. What is most likely true about the items ordered?
(A) All of them are non-refundable.
(B) One of them will not be delivered in October.
(C) Some of them are rare books.
(D) Most of them will be available in an electronic version.

184. What should Mr. Schultz have done to get an additional benefit from the special offer?
(A) Use the online order system
(B) Obtain a student discount coupon
(C) Order more publications
(D) Submit his order before October

185. What is NOT suggested about Inez Publication?
(A) It can deliver books abroad.
(B) It holds a clearance sale each year.
(C) It keeps track of every customer's purchase record.
(D) It carries publications about photography.

GO ON TO THE NEXT PAGE

Questions 186-190 refer to the following notice, advertisement, and e-mail.

To	All LCG Fitness Trainers
From	Stacey Carroll
Date	September 18
Subject	Promotional offer

Dear Fitness trainers,

As mentioned earlier, we are planning to offer students the 30 percent summer discount on an annual basis if they register during the first two weeks of November since a lot of Loughton College students are expected to be in the city during the winter season. In addition, LCG Fitness is thinking about offering two different types of special rates to new members and those who want to continue their membership during the upcoming winter (From Nov 1 to Dec 1).

Before the final decision on the two possible offers is made, we are soliciting our staff's opinions. One would be a family discount option. If a current LCG member's family member (age over 17) registers for membership, they will be eligible for a 20 percent reduced rate.

The other option would be to let Diamond-level members' friends or acquaintances use LCG's facilities for free from 9 A.M. to 2 P.M. on Tuesdays and Wednesdays. They would be allowed to use the whole gym, including the swimming pool. But, the badminton courts would be restricted to our current members in order to avoid worsening the already long wait.

Please consider these possible options and reply by October 10 with the one which you believe could be more beneficial for our members as well as us.

Thanks for your assistance in advance.

Stacey Carroll
Head of Marketing
LCG Fitness Center

Winter Special Offers

Welcome Loughton College students!

Register between November 1 and December 10 to take advantage of a 30% discount on your winter membership at any level and receive a complimentary plastic water bottle.

Work out with a friend or an acquaintance every Tuesday and Wednesday:

Starting on November 1, all Diamond- and Crystal-level members are allowed to invite a friend or an acquaintance with no additional charge on Tuesdays and Wednesdays. In order to use LCG's facilities, they have to sign in and present their valid ID at the reception desk.

LCG Fitness Center

E-MAIL

To	Kerry Bush <kerrybush@lcgfitnesscenter.net>
From	Joann Bradley <joannbradley@lcgfitnesscenter.net>
Date	December 11
Subject	Re: The number of the new members

Kerry,

I appreciate you forwarding the report as usual. I was excited about the number of both Diamond- and Crystal-level members, which all rose by 13 percent after we had begun the winter promotion.

Most of them are from Loughton College and have registered for Diamond- memberships. This means that we should consider planning to launch another promotional offer for students when the spring semester starts. It is said that the gym in the college is scheduled to be refurbished during the following year. So, many students are going to search for alternative places to work out. Since other fitness facilities which can be deemed our competitors are several kilometers away from the college, if we provide shuttles for students to get to and from our center, they will be more likely to come to LCG Fitness Center.

I will keep you informed. Thank you.

Joann Bradley,
Sales Director
LCG Fitness Center

186. What is the main reason the notice has been written?
(A) To report a schedule change
(B) To recognize employees for their hard work
(C) To publicize a new discounted rate
(D) To ask employees for suggestions

187. What is indicated about the badminton courts?
(A) They are scheduled to be refurbished soon.
(B) They are located near the main building.
(C) They are in high demand in the center.
(D) They used to be a swimming pool.

188. What aspect of the promotional offer for the students has changed since September?
(A) The discount percentage for students has been reduced.
(B) The registration period for the promotional offer was lengthened.
(C) Students do not need to pay their membership fee monthly.
(D) Students can try the fitness facilities twice a month for free.

189. What is suggested about LCG Fitness Center?
(A) Fee discounts are available to every family member.
(B) It stays open late on Tuesdays and Wednesdays.
(C) Students are permitted to invite their friends and acquaintances.
(D) Crystal-level members can obtain plastic bottles when they sign up.

190. According to the e-mail, what will most likely happen at Loughton College?
(A) The community will be allowed to use its gym for a nominal fee.
(B) The fitness facility for students will be remodeled.
(C) Additional fitness trainers will be recruited.
(D) The new semester will start in the winter.

GO ON TO THE NEXT PAGE

Questions 191-195 refer to the following leaflet, course description, and phone message.

A new class at Renaissance Art Glass (RAG)
Creating Unique Colorful Stained Glass
Instructor: Barbara Brown
Price: £115

The class will be held for five successive Wednesday nights, from 7:00 P.M. to 10:00 P.M., beginning on September 9. It requires no previous experience, but registration is limited only to our current members of the community's arts associations.

Familiarize yourself with the basic level of making stained-glass artworks and take one of those you have made with you. Designing, glass-cutting, color selection, framing, and more will be included in the subjects of each class. You can design your own style or simply select from among a variety of sample patterns.

Those who registered for the class can buy materials for about £155 from RAG. Please be advised that they are available as required over the five-week period to make sure that attendees purchase the appropriate tools and supplies for each of their projects and also have the cost of the materials spread out. Similar tools and supplies are available elsewhere, but attendees should realize that quality is not the same. Using the best supplies makes the end outcome different.

Unique Colorful
Stained Glass

Subjects	Week	Tools and Supplies
Workroom Safety; Orientation and learning and practicing "glass-cutting" techniques and skills	1	glass cutter, cutting oil, protective goggles and industrial gloves, pliers, and ruler with metal edge
Designing patterns and glass or selecting from samples	2	glass, several pieces of thick paper, a pair of scissors, and color pens
Shaping your own style through grinding and cutting glass	3	industrial gloves, protective goggles
Applying enamel to glass panel according to the patterns you have created or chosen	4	enamel paint, enamel brushes, utility knife
Coating and framing	5	coating compound, frame

Please note that for students who need more time and an instructor's tips, the workroom at RAG is open on Friday from 11 A.M. to 5 P.M. In case you need time with an instructor after these hours, you are required to contact us in advance or be ready to work on your own in the workroom.

INCOMING MESSAGE

Received by: Alton Baldwin
Time: Tuesday, 1:00 P.M.
For: Barbara Brown

☐ Fax ☑ Telephone ☐ Office Visit

MESSAGE:

Brett Adams who is attending your class has called. He said he has his own brushes, so he is wondering whether the brushes are okay for the purpose of the class. I informed him that you would call him back to talk about it in detail. Please contact him at 233-5542.

191. What is indicated about the tools and supplies needed for RAG's new class?
(A) They are getting cheaper these days.
(B) They are not required to be brought all at once.
(C) They are not available in other supply stores.
(D) They will be distributed by the class instructor.

192. In the leaflet, the word "realize" in paragraph 3, line 5, is closest in meaning to
(A) sell
(B) cash
(C) know
(D) achieve

193. What does the course description imply?
(A) Attendees can leave their opinion after their class.
(B) RAG recently renovated its workroom.
(C) Attendees can get help even outside class hours.
(D) A class has been rescheduled to another day.

194. What is indicated about Mr. Adams?
(A) He has purchased all the tools and supplies.
(B) He is a member of a local association.
(C) He had to miss the orientation.
(D) He has supplied materials to RAG.

195. To which class session does the phone message most likely refer?
(A) Week 2
(B) Week 3
(C) Week 4
(D) Week 5

GO ON TO THE NEXT PAGE

Questions 196-200 refer to the following e-mails and quote.

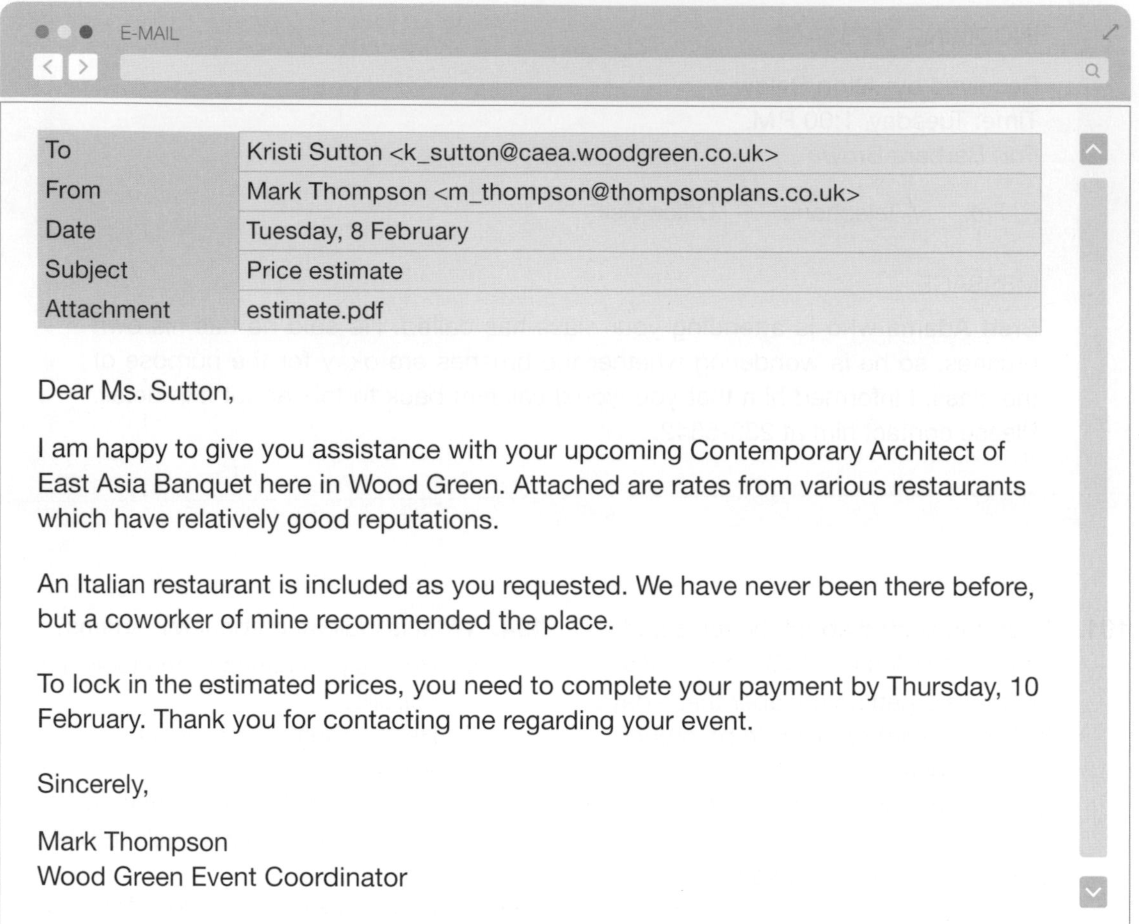

To	Kristi Sutton <k_sutton@caea.woodgreen.co.uk>
From	Mark Thompson <m_thompson@thompsonplans.co.uk>
Date	Tuesday, 8 February
Subject	Price estimate
Attachment	estimate.pdf

Dear Ms. Sutton,

I am happy to give you assistance with your upcoming Contemporary Architect of East Asia Banquet here in Wood Green. Attached are rates from various restaurants which have relatively good reputations.

An Italian restaurant is included as you requested. We have never been there before, but a coworker of mine recommended the place.

To lock in the estimated prices, you need to complete your payment by Thursday, 10 February. Thank you for contacting me regarding your event.

Sincerely,

Mark Thompson
Wood Green Event Coordinator

Rate Estimate for Dining Options

Banquet type: _Six courses_
Date of Event: _15 May_

Prepared for: _Contemporary Architect of East Asia Banquet_
Number of Diners: _30_

** All listed prices below include the meal, beverages, tax, and tips.*

Restaurant	Total cost	Price per diner	Type of Cuisine	Special features
Elm Cuisine	£660	£22	Chinese	Its outdoor patio seating area is available
Abbey House	£810	£27	Middle Eastern	Its catering menu is fully-customizable
Benessere Paranzo	£930	£31	Italian	Up to 35 seats available in its private banquet hall
Seafood Castle	£1,110	£37	Japanese	Provides live classic music
All Saints Table	£1,230	£41	Steak and Salad	Public transportation within walking distance

E-MAIL

To	Mark Thompson <m_thompson@thompsonplans.co.uk>
From	Kristi Sutton <k_sutton@caea.woodgreen.co.uk>
Date	Thursday, 10 February
Re	Payment

Dear Mr. Thompson,

We deeply appreciate your excellent help in arranging the banquet. Today, I have paid the full amount through your Web site. The fully-customizable menu is appealing, but we are more conscious about a location which should be conveniently accessible to the area's transportation.

Since the location has been decided, we now need your recommendation for a printer for the invitation. Also, the decorations have to be discussed, but we will be able to talk about them at the next meeting on 20 February. At the meeting, it will be really helpful if you give us advice on finalizing the design of the event and selecting an appropriate photographer.

Sincerely,
Kristi Sutton

196. What is suggested about Mr. Thompson?
(A) He is running his own travel agency.
(B) He is a restaurant manager.
(C) He used to have an Italian restaurant.
(D) He is involved in arranging a banquet.

197. What restaurant did Mr. Thompson list based on Ms. Sutton's request?
(A) Abbey House
(B) Elm Cuisine
(C) Benessere Paranzo
(D) Seafood Castle

198. What is indicated about Abbey House?
(A) Its price is the most affordable available.
(B) It can provide musical entertainment for free.
(C) Its menu items can be personalized.
(D) It has a separate dining area for a special event.

199. How much most likely has Ms. Sutton paid?
(A) £660
(B) £930
(C) £1,110
(D) £1,230

200. According to the second e-mail, what will Ms. Sutton most likely do next?
(A) Buy some office equipment
(B) Submit a print order
(C) Search for the photographers
(D) Create the design

Stop! This is the end of the test. If you finish before time is called, you may go back to Parts 5, 6, and 7 and check your work.

Answer Sheet

TOEIC TEST 1

LISTENING SECTION

1	2	3	4	5	6	7	8	9	10
Ⓐ Ⓑ Ⓒ Ⓓ	Ⓐ Ⓑ Ⓒ Ⓓ	Ⓐ Ⓑ Ⓒ Ⓓ	Ⓐ Ⓑ Ⓒ Ⓓ	Ⓐ Ⓑ Ⓒ Ⓓ	Ⓐ Ⓑ Ⓒ Ⓓ	Ⓐ Ⓑ Ⓒ Ⓓ	Ⓐ Ⓑ Ⓒ Ⓓ	Ⓐ Ⓑ Ⓒ Ⓓ	Ⓐ Ⓑ Ⓒ Ⓓ
11	12	13	14	15	16	17	18	19	20
Ⓐ Ⓑ Ⓒ Ⓓ	Ⓐ Ⓑ Ⓒ Ⓓ	Ⓐ Ⓑ Ⓒ Ⓓ	Ⓐ Ⓑ Ⓒ Ⓓ	Ⓐ Ⓑ Ⓒ Ⓓ	Ⓐ Ⓑ Ⓒ Ⓓ	Ⓐ Ⓑ Ⓒ Ⓓ	Ⓐ Ⓑ Ⓒ Ⓓ	Ⓐ Ⓑ Ⓒ Ⓓ	Ⓐ Ⓑ Ⓒ Ⓓ
21	22	23	24	25	26	27	28	29	30
Ⓐ Ⓑ Ⓒ Ⓓ	Ⓐ Ⓑ Ⓒ Ⓓ	Ⓐ Ⓑ Ⓒ Ⓓ	Ⓐ Ⓑ Ⓒ Ⓓ	Ⓐ Ⓑ Ⓒ Ⓓ	Ⓐ Ⓑ Ⓒ Ⓓ	Ⓐ Ⓑ Ⓒ Ⓓ	Ⓐ Ⓑ Ⓒ Ⓓ	Ⓐ Ⓑ Ⓒ Ⓓ	Ⓐ Ⓑ Ⓒ Ⓓ
31	32	33	34	35	36	37	38	39	40
Ⓐ Ⓑ Ⓒ Ⓓ	Ⓐ Ⓑ Ⓒ Ⓓ	Ⓐ Ⓑ Ⓒ Ⓓ	Ⓐ Ⓑ Ⓒ Ⓓ	Ⓐ Ⓑ Ⓒ Ⓓ	Ⓐ Ⓑ Ⓒ Ⓓ	Ⓐ Ⓑ Ⓒ Ⓓ	Ⓐ Ⓑ Ⓒ Ⓓ	Ⓐ Ⓑ Ⓒ Ⓓ	Ⓐ Ⓑ Ⓒ Ⓓ
41	42	43	44	45	46	47	48	49	50
Ⓐ Ⓑ Ⓒ Ⓓ	Ⓐ Ⓑ Ⓒ Ⓓ	Ⓐ Ⓑ Ⓒ Ⓓ	Ⓐ Ⓑ Ⓒ Ⓓ	Ⓐ Ⓑ Ⓒ Ⓓ	Ⓐ Ⓑ Ⓒ Ⓓ	Ⓐ Ⓑ Ⓒ Ⓓ	Ⓐ Ⓑ Ⓒ Ⓓ	Ⓐ Ⓑ Ⓒ Ⓓ	Ⓐ Ⓑ Ⓒ Ⓓ
51	52	53	54	55	56	57	58	59	60
Ⓐ Ⓑ Ⓒ Ⓓ	Ⓐ Ⓑ Ⓒ Ⓓ	Ⓐ Ⓑ Ⓒ Ⓓ	Ⓐ Ⓑ Ⓒ Ⓓ	Ⓐ Ⓑ Ⓒ Ⓓ	Ⓐ Ⓑ Ⓒ Ⓓ	Ⓐ Ⓑ Ⓒ Ⓓ	Ⓐ Ⓑ Ⓒ Ⓓ	Ⓐ Ⓑ Ⓒ Ⓓ	Ⓐ Ⓑ Ⓒ Ⓓ
61	62	63	64	65	66	67	68	69	70
Ⓐ Ⓑ Ⓒ Ⓓ	Ⓐ Ⓑ Ⓒ Ⓓ	Ⓐ Ⓑ Ⓒ Ⓓ	Ⓐ Ⓑ Ⓒ Ⓓ	Ⓐ Ⓑ Ⓒ Ⓓ	Ⓐ Ⓑ Ⓒ Ⓓ	Ⓐ Ⓑ Ⓒ Ⓓ	Ⓐ Ⓑ Ⓒ Ⓓ	Ⓐ Ⓑ Ⓒ Ⓓ	Ⓐ Ⓑ Ⓒ Ⓓ
71	72	73	74	75	76	77	78	79	80
Ⓐ Ⓑ Ⓒ Ⓓ	Ⓐ Ⓑ Ⓒ Ⓓ	Ⓐ Ⓑ Ⓒ Ⓓ	Ⓐ Ⓑ Ⓒ Ⓓ	Ⓐ Ⓑ Ⓒ Ⓓ	Ⓐ Ⓑ Ⓒ Ⓓ	Ⓐ Ⓑ Ⓒ Ⓓ	Ⓐ Ⓑ Ⓒ Ⓓ	Ⓐ Ⓑ Ⓒ Ⓓ	Ⓐ Ⓑ Ⓒ Ⓓ
81	82	83	84	85	86	87	88	89	90
Ⓐ Ⓑ Ⓒ Ⓓ	Ⓐ Ⓑ Ⓒ Ⓓ	Ⓐ Ⓑ Ⓒ Ⓓ	Ⓐ Ⓑ Ⓒ Ⓓ	Ⓐ Ⓑ Ⓒ Ⓓ	Ⓐ Ⓑ Ⓒ Ⓓ	Ⓐ Ⓑ Ⓒ Ⓓ	Ⓐ Ⓑ Ⓒ Ⓓ	Ⓐ Ⓑ Ⓒ Ⓓ	Ⓐ Ⓑ Ⓒ Ⓓ
91	92	93	94	95	96	97	98	99	100
Ⓐ Ⓑ Ⓒ Ⓓ	Ⓐ Ⓑ Ⓒ Ⓓ	Ⓐ Ⓑ Ⓒ Ⓓ	Ⓐ Ⓑ Ⓒ Ⓓ	Ⓐ Ⓑ Ⓒ Ⓓ	Ⓐ Ⓑ Ⓒ Ⓓ	Ⓐ Ⓑ Ⓒ Ⓓ	Ⓐ Ⓑ Ⓒ Ⓓ	Ⓐ Ⓑ Ⓒ Ⓓ	Ⓐ Ⓑ Ⓒ Ⓓ

READING SECTION

101	102	103	104	105	106	107	108	109	110
Ⓐ Ⓑ Ⓒ Ⓓ	Ⓐ Ⓑ Ⓒ Ⓓ	Ⓐ Ⓑ Ⓒ Ⓓ	Ⓐ Ⓑ Ⓒ Ⓓ	Ⓐ Ⓑ Ⓒ Ⓓ	Ⓐ Ⓑ Ⓒ Ⓓ	Ⓐ Ⓑ Ⓒ Ⓓ	Ⓐ Ⓑ Ⓒ Ⓓ	Ⓐ Ⓑ Ⓒ Ⓓ	Ⓐ Ⓑ Ⓒ Ⓓ
111	112	113	114	115	116	117	118	119	120
Ⓐ Ⓑ Ⓒ Ⓓ	Ⓐ Ⓑ Ⓒ Ⓓ	Ⓐ Ⓑ Ⓒ Ⓓ	Ⓐ Ⓑ Ⓒ Ⓓ	Ⓐ Ⓑ Ⓒ Ⓓ	Ⓐ Ⓑ Ⓒ Ⓓ	Ⓐ Ⓑ Ⓒ Ⓓ	Ⓐ Ⓑ Ⓒ Ⓓ	Ⓐ Ⓑ Ⓒ Ⓓ	Ⓐ Ⓑ Ⓒ Ⓓ
121	122	123	124	125	126	127	128	129	130
Ⓐ Ⓑ Ⓒ Ⓓ	Ⓐ Ⓑ Ⓒ Ⓓ	Ⓐ Ⓑ Ⓒ Ⓓ	Ⓐ Ⓑ Ⓒ Ⓓ	Ⓐ Ⓑ Ⓒ Ⓓ	Ⓐ Ⓑ Ⓒ Ⓓ	Ⓐ Ⓑ Ⓒ Ⓓ	Ⓐ Ⓑ Ⓒ Ⓓ	Ⓐ Ⓑ Ⓒ Ⓓ	Ⓐ Ⓑ Ⓒ Ⓓ
131	132	133	134	135	136	137	138	139	140
Ⓐ Ⓑ Ⓒ Ⓓ	Ⓐ Ⓑ Ⓒ Ⓓ	Ⓐ Ⓑ Ⓒ Ⓓ	Ⓐ Ⓑ Ⓒ Ⓓ	Ⓐ Ⓑ Ⓒ Ⓓ	Ⓐ Ⓑ Ⓒ Ⓓ	Ⓐ Ⓑ Ⓒ Ⓓ	Ⓐ Ⓑ Ⓒ Ⓓ	Ⓐ Ⓑ Ⓒ Ⓓ	Ⓐ Ⓑ Ⓒ Ⓓ
141	142	143	144	145	146	147	148	149	150
Ⓐ Ⓑ Ⓒ Ⓓ	Ⓐ Ⓑ Ⓒ Ⓓ	Ⓐ Ⓑ Ⓒ Ⓓ	Ⓐ Ⓑ Ⓒ Ⓓ	Ⓐ Ⓑ Ⓒ Ⓓ	Ⓐ Ⓑ Ⓒ Ⓓ	Ⓐ Ⓑ Ⓒ Ⓓ	Ⓐ Ⓑ Ⓒ Ⓓ	Ⓐ Ⓑ Ⓒ Ⓓ	Ⓐ Ⓑ Ⓒ Ⓓ
151	152	153	154	155	156	157	158	159	160
Ⓐ Ⓑ Ⓒ Ⓓ	Ⓐ Ⓑ Ⓒ Ⓓ	Ⓐ Ⓑ Ⓒ Ⓓ	Ⓐ Ⓑ Ⓒ Ⓓ	Ⓐ Ⓑ Ⓒ Ⓓ	Ⓐ Ⓑ Ⓒ Ⓓ	Ⓐ Ⓑ Ⓒ Ⓓ	Ⓐ Ⓑ Ⓒ Ⓓ	Ⓐ Ⓑ Ⓒ Ⓓ	Ⓐ Ⓑ Ⓒ Ⓓ
161	162	163	164	165	166	167	168	169	170
Ⓐ Ⓑ Ⓒ Ⓓ	Ⓐ Ⓑ Ⓒ Ⓓ	Ⓐ Ⓑ Ⓒ Ⓓ	Ⓐ Ⓑ Ⓒ Ⓓ	Ⓐ Ⓑ Ⓒ Ⓓ	Ⓐ Ⓑ Ⓒ Ⓓ	Ⓐ Ⓑ Ⓒ Ⓓ	Ⓐ Ⓑ Ⓒ Ⓓ	Ⓐ Ⓑ Ⓒ Ⓓ	Ⓐ Ⓑ Ⓒ Ⓓ
171	172	173	174	175	176	177	178	179	180
Ⓐ Ⓑ Ⓒ Ⓓ	Ⓐ Ⓑ Ⓒ Ⓓ	Ⓐ Ⓑ Ⓒ Ⓓ	Ⓐ Ⓑ Ⓒ Ⓓ	Ⓐ Ⓑ Ⓒ Ⓓ	Ⓐ Ⓑ Ⓒ Ⓓ	Ⓐ Ⓑ Ⓒ Ⓓ	Ⓐ Ⓑ Ⓒ Ⓓ	Ⓐ Ⓑ Ⓒ Ⓓ	Ⓐ Ⓑ Ⓒ Ⓓ
181	182	183	184	185	186	187	188	189	190
Ⓐ Ⓑ Ⓒ Ⓓ	Ⓐ Ⓑ Ⓒ Ⓓ	Ⓐ Ⓑ Ⓒ Ⓓ	Ⓐ Ⓑ Ⓒ Ⓓ	Ⓐ Ⓑ Ⓒ Ⓓ	Ⓐ Ⓑ Ⓒ Ⓓ	Ⓐ Ⓑ Ⓒ Ⓓ	Ⓐ Ⓑ Ⓒ Ⓓ	Ⓐ Ⓑ Ⓒ Ⓓ	Ⓐ Ⓑ Ⓒ Ⓓ
191	192	193	194	195	196	197	198	199	200
Ⓐ Ⓑ Ⓒ Ⓓ	Ⓐ Ⓑ Ⓒ Ⓓ	Ⓐ Ⓑ Ⓒ Ⓓ	Ⓐ Ⓑ Ⓒ Ⓓ	Ⓐ Ⓑ Ⓒ Ⓓ	Ⓐ Ⓑ Ⓒ Ⓓ	Ⓐ Ⓑ Ⓒ Ⓓ	Ⓐ Ⓑ Ⓒ Ⓓ	Ⓐ Ⓑ Ⓒ Ⓓ	Ⓐ Ⓑ Ⓒ Ⓓ

Answer Sheet

TOEIC TEST 2

LISTENING SECTION

1	Ⓐ Ⓑ Ⓒ Ⓓ
2	Ⓐ Ⓑ Ⓒ Ⓓ
3	Ⓐ Ⓑ Ⓒ Ⓓ
4	Ⓐ Ⓑ Ⓒ Ⓓ
5	Ⓐ Ⓑ Ⓒ Ⓓ
6	Ⓐ Ⓑ Ⓒ Ⓓ
7	Ⓐ Ⓑ Ⓒ Ⓓ
8	Ⓐ Ⓑ Ⓒ Ⓓ
9	Ⓐ Ⓑ Ⓒ Ⓓ
10	Ⓐ Ⓑ Ⓒ Ⓓ
11	Ⓐ Ⓑ Ⓒ Ⓓ
12	Ⓐ Ⓑ Ⓒ Ⓓ
13	Ⓐ Ⓑ Ⓒ Ⓓ
14	Ⓐ Ⓑ Ⓒ Ⓓ
15	Ⓐ Ⓑ Ⓒ Ⓓ
16	Ⓐ Ⓑ Ⓒ Ⓓ
17	Ⓐ Ⓑ Ⓒ Ⓓ
18	Ⓐ Ⓑ Ⓒ Ⓓ
19	Ⓐ Ⓑ Ⓒ Ⓓ
20	Ⓐ Ⓑ Ⓒ Ⓓ
21	Ⓐ Ⓑ Ⓒ Ⓓ
22	Ⓐ Ⓑ Ⓒ Ⓓ
23	Ⓐ Ⓑ Ⓒ Ⓓ
24	Ⓐ Ⓑ Ⓒ Ⓓ
25	Ⓐ Ⓑ Ⓒ Ⓓ
26	Ⓐ Ⓑ Ⓒ Ⓓ
27	Ⓐ Ⓑ Ⓒ Ⓓ
28	Ⓐ Ⓑ Ⓒ Ⓓ
29	Ⓐ Ⓑ Ⓒ Ⓓ
30	Ⓐ Ⓑ Ⓒ Ⓓ
31	Ⓐ Ⓑ Ⓒ Ⓓ
32	Ⓐ Ⓑ Ⓒ Ⓓ
33	Ⓐ Ⓑ Ⓒ Ⓓ
34	Ⓐ Ⓑ Ⓒ Ⓓ
35	Ⓐ Ⓑ Ⓒ Ⓓ
36	Ⓐ Ⓑ Ⓒ Ⓓ
37	Ⓐ Ⓑ Ⓒ Ⓓ
38	Ⓐ Ⓑ Ⓒ Ⓓ
39	Ⓐ Ⓑ Ⓒ Ⓓ
40	Ⓐ Ⓑ Ⓒ Ⓓ
41	Ⓐ Ⓑ Ⓒ Ⓓ
42	Ⓐ Ⓑ Ⓒ Ⓓ
43	Ⓐ Ⓑ Ⓒ Ⓓ
44	Ⓐ Ⓑ Ⓒ Ⓓ
45	Ⓐ Ⓑ Ⓒ Ⓓ
46	Ⓐ Ⓑ Ⓒ Ⓓ
47	Ⓐ Ⓑ Ⓒ Ⓓ
48	Ⓐ Ⓑ Ⓒ Ⓓ
49	Ⓐ Ⓑ Ⓒ Ⓓ
50	Ⓐ Ⓑ Ⓒ Ⓓ
51	Ⓐ Ⓑ Ⓒ Ⓓ
52	Ⓐ Ⓑ Ⓒ Ⓓ
53	Ⓐ Ⓑ Ⓒ Ⓓ
54	Ⓐ Ⓑ Ⓒ Ⓓ
55	Ⓐ Ⓑ Ⓒ Ⓓ
56	Ⓐ Ⓑ Ⓒ Ⓓ
57	Ⓐ Ⓑ Ⓒ Ⓓ
58	Ⓐ Ⓑ Ⓒ Ⓓ
59	Ⓐ Ⓑ Ⓒ Ⓓ
60	Ⓐ Ⓑ Ⓒ Ⓓ
61	Ⓐ Ⓑ Ⓒ Ⓓ
62	Ⓐ Ⓑ Ⓒ Ⓓ
63	Ⓐ Ⓑ Ⓒ Ⓓ
64	Ⓐ Ⓑ Ⓒ Ⓓ
65	Ⓐ Ⓑ Ⓒ Ⓓ
66	Ⓐ Ⓑ Ⓒ Ⓓ
67	Ⓐ Ⓑ Ⓒ Ⓓ
68	Ⓐ Ⓑ Ⓒ Ⓓ
69	Ⓐ Ⓑ Ⓒ Ⓓ
70	Ⓐ Ⓑ Ⓒ Ⓓ
71	Ⓐ Ⓑ Ⓒ Ⓓ
72	Ⓐ Ⓑ Ⓒ Ⓓ
73	Ⓐ Ⓑ Ⓒ Ⓓ
74	Ⓐ Ⓑ Ⓒ Ⓓ
75	Ⓐ Ⓑ Ⓒ Ⓓ
76	Ⓐ Ⓑ Ⓒ Ⓓ
77	Ⓐ Ⓑ Ⓒ Ⓓ
78	Ⓐ Ⓑ Ⓒ Ⓓ
79	Ⓐ Ⓑ Ⓒ Ⓓ
80	Ⓐ Ⓑ Ⓒ Ⓓ
81	Ⓐ Ⓑ Ⓒ Ⓓ
82	Ⓐ Ⓑ Ⓒ Ⓓ
83	Ⓐ Ⓑ Ⓒ Ⓓ
84	Ⓐ Ⓑ Ⓒ Ⓓ
85	Ⓐ Ⓑ Ⓒ Ⓓ
86	Ⓐ Ⓑ Ⓒ Ⓓ
87	Ⓐ Ⓑ Ⓒ Ⓓ
88	Ⓐ Ⓑ Ⓒ Ⓓ
89	Ⓐ Ⓑ Ⓒ Ⓓ
90	Ⓐ Ⓑ Ⓒ Ⓓ
91	Ⓐ Ⓑ Ⓒ Ⓓ
92	Ⓐ Ⓑ Ⓒ Ⓓ
93	Ⓐ Ⓑ Ⓒ Ⓓ
94	Ⓐ Ⓑ Ⓒ Ⓓ
95	Ⓐ Ⓑ Ⓒ Ⓓ
96	Ⓐ Ⓑ Ⓒ Ⓓ
97	Ⓐ Ⓑ Ⓒ Ⓓ
98	Ⓐ Ⓑ Ⓒ Ⓓ
99	Ⓐ Ⓑ Ⓒ Ⓓ
100	Ⓐ Ⓑ Ⓒ Ⓓ

READING SECTION

101	Ⓐ Ⓑ Ⓒ Ⓓ
102	Ⓐ Ⓑ Ⓒ Ⓓ
103	Ⓐ Ⓑ Ⓒ Ⓓ
104	Ⓐ Ⓑ Ⓒ Ⓓ
105	Ⓐ Ⓑ Ⓒ Ⓓ
106	Ⓐ Ⓑ Ⓒ Ⓓ
107	Ⓐ Ⓑ Ⓒ Ⓓ
108	Ⓐ Ⓑ Ⓒ Ⓓ
109	Ⓐ Ⓑ Ⓒ Ⓓ
110	Ⓐ Ⓑ Ⓒ Ⓓ
111	Ⓐ Ⓑ Ⓒ Ⓓ
112	Ⓐ Ⓑ Ⓒ Ⓓ
113	Ⓐ Ⓑ Ⓒ Ⓓ
114	Ⓐ Ⓑ Ⓒ Ⓓ
115	Ⓐ Ⓑ Ⓒ Ⓓ
116	Ⓐ Ⓑ Ⓒ Ⓓ
117	Ⓐ Ⓑ Ⓒ Ⓓ
118	Ⓐ Ⓑ Ⓒ Ⓓ
119	Ⓐ Ⓑ Ⓒ Ⓓ
120	Ⓐ Ⓑ Ⓒ Ⓓ
121	Ⓐ Ⓑ Ⓒ Ⓓ
122	Ⓐ Ⓑ Ⓒ Ⓓ
123	Ⓐ Ⓑ Ⓒ Ⓓ
124	Ⓐ Ⓑ Ⓒ Ⓓ
125	Ⓐ Ⓑ Ⓒ Ⓓ
126	Ⓐ Ⓑ Ⓒ Ⓓ
127	Ⓐ Ⓑ Ⓒ Ⓓ
128	Ⓐ Ⓑ Ⓒ Ⓓ
129	Ⓐ Ⓑ Ⓒ Ⓓ
130	Ⓐ Ⓑ Ⓒ Ⓓ
131	Ⓐ Ⓑ Ⓒ Ⓓ
132	Ⓐ Ⓑ Ⓒ Ⓓ
133	Ⓐ Ⓑ Ⓒ Ⓓ
134	Ⓐ Ⓑ Ⓒ Ⓓ
135	Ⓐ Ⓑ Ⓒ Ⓓ
136	Ⓐ Ⓑ Ⓒ Ⓓ
137	Ⓐ Ⓑ Ⓒ Ⓓ
138	Ⓐ Ⓑ Ⓒ Ⓓ
139	Ⓐ Ⓑ Ⓒ Ⓓ
140	Ⓐ Ⓑ Ⓒ Ⓓ
141	Ⓐ Ⓑ Ⓒ Ⓓ
142	Ⓐ Ⓑ Ⓒ Ⓓ
143	Ⓐ Ⓑ Ⓒ Ⓓ
144	Ⓐ Ⓑ Ⓒ Ⓓ
145	Ⓐ Ⓑ Ⓒ Ⓓ
146	Ⓐ Ⓑ Ⓒ Ⓓ
147	Ⓐ Ⓑ Ⓒ Ⓓ
148	Ⓐ Ⓑ Ⓒ Ⓓ
149	Ⓐ Ⓑ Ⓒ Ⓓ
150	Ⓐ Ⓑ Ⓒ Ⓓ
151	Ⓐ Ⓑ Ⓒ Ⓓ
152	Ⓐ Ⓑ Ⓒ Ⓓ
153	Ⓐ Ⓑ Ⓒ Ⓓ
154	Ⓐ Ⓑ Ⓒ Ⓓ
155	Ⓐ Ⓑ Ⓒ Ⓓ
156	Ⓐ Ⓑ Ⓒ Ⓓ
157	Ⓐ Ⓑ Ⓒ Ⓓ
158	Ⓐ Ⓑ Ⓒ Ⓓ
159	Ⓐ Ⓑ Ⓒ Ⓓ
160	Ⓐ Ⓑ Ⓒ Ⓓ
161	Ⓐ Ⓑ Ⓒ Ⓓ
162	Ⓐ Ⓑ Ⓒ Ⓓ
163	Ⓐ Ⓑ Ⓒ Ⓓ
164	Ⓐ Ⓑ Ⓒ Ⓓ
165	Ⓐ Ⓑ Ⓒ Ⓓ
166	Ⓐ Ⓑ Ⓒ Ⓓ
167	Ⓐ Ⓑ Ⓒ Ⓓ
168	Ⓐ Ⓑ Ⓒ Ⓓ
169	Ⓐ Ⓑ Ⓒ Ⓓ
170	Ⓐ Ⓑ Ⓒ Ⓓ
171	Ⓐ Ⓑ Ⓒ Ⓓ
172	Ⓐ Ⓑ Ⓒ Ⓓ
173	Ⓐ Ⓑ Ⓒ Ⓓ
174	Ⓐ Ⓑ Ⓒ Ⓓ
175	Ⓐ Ⓑ Ⓒ Ⓓ
176	Ⓐ Ⓑ Ⓒ Ⓓ
177	Ⓐ Ⓑ Ⓒ Ⓓ
178	Ⓐ Ⓑ Ⓒ Ⓓ
179	Ⓐ Ⓑ Ⓒ Ⓓ
180	Ⓐ Ⓑ Ⓒ Ⓓ
181	Ⓐ Ⓑ Ⓒ Ⓓ
182	Ⓐ Ⓑ Ⓒ Ⓓ
183	Ⓐ Ⓑ Ⓒ Ⓓ
184	Ⓐ Ⓑ Ⓒ Ⓓ
185	Ⓐ Ⓑ Ⓒ Ⓓ
186	Ⓐ Ⓑ Ⓒ Ⓓ
187	Ⓐ Ⓑ Ⓒ Ⓓ
188	Ⓐ Ⓑ Ⓒ Ⓓ
189	Ⓐ Ⓑ Ⓒ Ⓓ
190	Ⓐ Ⓑ Ⓒ Ⓓ
191	Ⓐ Ⓑ Ⓒ Ⓓ
192	Ⓐ Ⓑ Ⓒ Ⓓ
193	Ⓐ Ⓑ Ⓒ Ⓓ
194	Ⓐ Ⓑ Ⓒ Ⓓ
195	Ⓐ Ⓑ Ⓒ Ⓓ
196	Ⓐ Ⓑ Ⓒ Ⓓ
197	Ⓐ Ⓑ Ⓒ Ⓓ
198	Ⓐ Ⓑ Ⓒ Ⓓ
199	Ⓐ Ⓑ Ⓒ Ⓓ
200	Ⓐ Ⓑ Ⓒ Ⓓ

Answer Sheet

TOEIC TEST 3

LISTENING SECTION

1	Ⓐ Ⓑ Ⓒ Ⓓ	11	Ⓐ Ⓑ Ⓒ Ⓓ	21	Ⓐ Ⓑ Ⓒ Ⓓ	31	Ⓐ Ⓑ Ⓒ Ⓓ	41	Ⓐ Ⓑ Ⓒ Ⓓ	51	Ⓐ Ⓑ Ⓒ Ⓓ	61	Ⓐ Ⓑ Ⓒ Ⓓ	71	Ⓐ Ⓑ Ⓒ Ⓓ	81	Ⓐ Ⓑ Ⓒ Ⓓ	91	Ⓐ Ⓑ Ⓒ Ⓓ
2	Ⓐ Ⓑ Ⓒ Ⓓ	12	Ⓐ Ⓑ Ⓒ Ⓓ	22	Ⓐ Ⓑ Ⓒ Ⓓ	32	Ⓐ Ⓑ Ⓒ Ⓓ	42	Ⓐ Ⓑ Ⓒ Ⓓ	52	Ⓐ Ⓑ Ⓒ Ⓓ	62	Ⓐ Ⓑ Ⓒ Ⓓ	72	Ⓐ Ⓑ Ⓒ Ⓓ	82	Ⓐ Ⓑ Ⓒ Ⓓ	92	Ⓐ Ⓑ Ⓒ Ⓓ
3	Ⓐ Ⓑ Ⓒ Ⓓ	13	Ⓐ Ⓑ Ⓒ Ⓓ	23	Ⓐ Ⓑ Ⓒ Ⓓ	33	Ⓐ Ⓑ Ⓒ Ⓓ	43	Ⓐ Ⓑ Ⓒ Ⓓ	53	Ⓐ Ⓑ Ⓒ Ⓓ	63	Ⓐ Ⓑ Ⓒ Ⓓ	73	Ⓐ Ⓑ Ⓒ Ⓓ	83	Ⓐ Ⓑ Ⓒ Ⓓ	93	Ⓐ Ⓑ Ⓒ Ⓓ
4	Ⓐ Ⓑ Ⓒ Ⓓ	14	Ⓐ Ⓑ Ⓒ Ⓓ	24	Ⓐ Ⓑ Ⓒ Ⓓ	34	Ⓐ Ⓑ Ⓒ Ⓓ	44	Ⓐ Ⓑ Ⓒ Ⓓ	54	Ⓐ Ⓑ Ⓒ Ⓓ	64	Ⓐ Ⓑ Ⓒ Ⓓ	74	Ⓐ Ⓑ Ⓒ Ⓓ	84	Ⓐ Ⓑ Ⓒ Ⓓ	94	Ⓐ Ⓑ Ⓒ Ⓓ
5	Ⓐ Ⓑ Ⓒ Ⓓ	15	Ⓐ Ⓑ Ⓒ Ⓓ	25	Ⓐ Ⓑ Ⓒ Ⓓ	35	Ⓐ Ⓑ Ⓒ Ⓓ	45	Ⓐ Ⓑ Ⓒ Ⓓ	55	Ⓐ Ⓑ Ⓒ Ⓓ	65	Ⓐ Ⓑ Ⓒ Ⓓ	75	Ⓐ Ⓑ Ⓒ Ⓓ	85	Ⓐ Ⓑ Ⓒ Ⓓ	95	Ⓐ Ⓑ Ⓒ Ⓓ
6	Ⓐ Ⓑ Ⓒ Ⓓ	16	Ⓐ Ⓑ Ⓒ Ⓓ	26	Ⓐ Ⓑ Ⓒ Ⓓ	36	Ⓐ Ⓑ Ⓒ Ⓓ	46	Ⓐ Ⓑ Ⓒ Ⓓ	56	Ⓐ Ⓑ Ⓒ Ⓓ	66	Ⓐ Ⓑ Ⓒ Ⓓ	76	Ⓐ Ⓑ Ⓒ Ⓓ	86	Ⓐ Ⓑ Ⓒ Ⓓ	96	Ⓐ Ⓑ Ⓒ Ⓓ
7	Ⓐ Ⓑ Ⓒ Ⓓ	17	Ⓐ Ⓑ Ⓒ Ⓓ	27	Ⓐ Ⓑ Ⓒ Ⓓ	37	Ⓐ Ⓑ Ⓒ Ⓓ	47	Ⓐ Ⓑ Ⓒ Ⓓ	57	Ⓐ Ⓑ Ⓒ Ⓓ	67	Ⓐ Ⓑ Ⓒ Ⓓ	77	Ⓐ Ⓑ Ⓒ Ⓓ	87	Ⓐ Ⓑ Ⓒ Ⓓ	97	Ⓐ Ⓑ Ⓒ Ⓓ
8	Ⓐ Ⓑ Ⓒ Ⓓ	18	Ⓐ Ⓑ Ⓒ Ⓓ	28	Ⓐ Ⓑ Ⓒ Ⓓ	38	Ⓐ Ⓑ Ⓒ Ⓓ	48	Ⓐ Ⓑ Ⓒ Ⓓ	58	Ⓐ Ⓑ Ⓒ Ⓓ	68	Ⓐ Ⓑ Ⓒ Ⓓ	78	Ⓐ Ⓑ Ⓒ Ⓓ	88	Ⓐ Ⓑ Ⓒ Ⓓ	98	Ⓐ Ⓑ Ⓒ Ⓓ
9	Ⓐ Ⓑ Ⓒ Ⓓ	19	Ⓐ Ⓑ Ⓒ Ⓓ	29	Ⓐ Ⓑ Ⓒ Ⓓ	39	Ⓐ Ⓑ Ⓒ Ⓓ	49	Ⓐ Ⓑ Ⓒ Ⓓ	59	Ⓐ Ⓑ Ⓒ Ⓓ	69	Ⓐ Ⓑ Ⓒ Ⓓ	79	Ⓐ Ⓑ Ⓒ Ⓓ	89	Ⓐ Ⓑ Ⓒ Ⓓ	99	Ⓐ Ⓑ Ⓒ Ⓓ
10	Ⓐ Ⓑ Ⓒ Ⓓ	20	Ⓐ Ⓑ Ⓒ Ⓓ	30	Ⓐ Ⓑ Ⓒ Ⓓ	40	Ⓐ Ⓑ Ⓒ Ⓓ	50	Ⓐ Ⓑ Ⓒ Ⓓ	60	Ⓐ Ⓑ Ⓒ Ⓓ	70	Ⓐ Ⓑ Ⓒ Ⓓ	80	Ⓐ Ⓑ Ⓒ Ⓓ	90	Ⓐ Ⓑ Ⓒ Ⓓ	100	Ⓐ Ⓑ Ⓒ Ⓓ

READING SECTION

101	Ⓐ Ⓑ Ⓒ Ⓓ	111	Ⓐ Ⓑ Ⓒ Ⓓ	121	Ⓐ Ⓑ Ⓒ Ⓓ	131	Ⓐ Ⓑ Ⓒ Ⓓ	141	Ⓐ Ⓑ Ⓒ Ⓓ	151	Ⓐ Ⓑ Ⓒ Ⓓ	161	Ⓐ Ⓑ Ⓒ Ⓓ	171	Ⓐ Ⓑ Ⓒ Ⓓ	181	Ⓐ Ⓑ Ⓒ Ⓓ	191	Ⓐ Ⓑ Ⓒ Ⓓ
102	Ⓐ Ⓑ Ⓒ Ⓓ	112	Ⓐ Ⓑ Ⓒ Ⓓ	122	Ⓐ Ⓑ Ⓒ Ⓓ	132	Ⓐ Ⓑ Ⓒ Ⓓ	142	Ⓐ Ⓑ Ⓒ Ⓓ	152	Ⓐ Ⓑ Ⓒ Ⓓ	162	Ⓐ Ⓑ Ⓒ Ⓓ	172	Ⓐ Ⓑ Ⓒ Ⓓ	182	Ⓐ Ⓑ Ⓒ Ⓓ	192	Ⓐ Ⓑ Ⓒ Ⓓ
103	Ⓐ Ⓑ Ⓒ Ⓓ	113	Ⓐ Ⓑ Ⓒ Ⓓ	123	Ⓐ Ⓑ Ⓒ Ⓓ	133	Ⓐ Ⓑ Ⓒ Ⓓ	143	Ⓐ Ⓑ Ⓒ Ⓓ	153	Ⓐ Ⓑ Ⓒ Ⓓ	163	Ⓐ Ⓑ Ⓒ Ⓓ	173	Ⓐ Ⓑ Ⓒ Ⓓ	183	Ⓐ Ⓑ Ⓒ Ⓓ	193	Ⓐ Ⓑ Ⓒ Ⓓ
104	Ⓐ Ⓑ Ⓒ Ⓓ	114	Ⓐ Ⓑ Ⓒ Ⓓ	124	Ⓐ Ⓑ Ⓒ Ⓓ	134	Ⓐ Ⓑ Ⓒ Ⓓ	144	Ⓐ Ⓑ Ⓒ Ⓓ	154	Ⓐ Ⓑ Ⓒ Ⓓ	164	Ⓐ Ⓑ Ⓒ Ⓓ	174	Ⓐ Ⓑ Ⓒ Ⓓ	184	Ⓐ Ⓑ Ⓒ Ⓓ	194	Ⓐ Ⓑ Ⓒ Ⓓ
105	Ⓐ Ⓑ Ⓒ Ⓓ	115	Ⓐ Ⓑ Ⓒ Ⓓ	125	Ⓐ Ⓑ Ⓒ Ⓓ	135	Ⓐ Ⓑ Ⓒ Ⓓ	145	Ⓐ Ⓑ Ⓒ Ⓓ	155	Ⓐ Ⓑ Ⓒ Ⓓ	165	Ⓐ Ⓑ Ⓒ Ⓓ	175	Ⓐ Ⓑ Ⓒ Ⓓ	185	Ⓐ Ⓑ Ⓒ Ⓓ	195	Ⓐ Ⓑ Ⓒ Ⓓ
106	Ⓐ Ⓑ Ⓒ Ⓓ	116	Ⓐ Ⓑ Ⓒ Ⓓ	126	Ⓐ Ⓑ Ⓒ Ⓓ	136	Ⓐ Ⓑ Ⓒ Ⓓ	146	Ⓐ Ⓑ Ⓒ Ⓓ	156	Ⓐ Ⓑ Ⓒ Ⓓ	166	Ⓐ Ⓑ Ⓒ Ⓓ	176	Ⓐ Ⓑ Ⓒ Ⓓ	186	Ⓐ Ⓑ Ⓒ Ⓓ	196	Ⓐ Ⓑ Ⓒ Ⓓ
107	Ⓐ Ⓑ Ⓒ Ⓓ	117	Ⓐ Ⓑ Ⓒ Ⓓ	127	Ⓐ Ⓑ Ⓒ Ⓓ	137	Ⓐ Ⓑ Ⓒ Ⓓ	147	Ⓐ Ⓑ Ⓒ Ⓓ	157	Ⓐ Ⓑ Ⓒ Ⓓ	167	Ⓐ Ⓑ Ⓒ Ⓓ	177	Ⓐ Ⓑ Ⓒ Ⓓ	187	Ⓐ Ⓑ Ⓒ Ⓓ	197	Ⓐ Ⓑ Ⓒ Ⓓ
108	Ⓐ Ⓑ Ⓒ Ⓓ	118	Ⓐ Ⓑ Ⓒ Ⓓ	128	Ⓐ Ⓑ Ⓒ Ⓓ	138	Ⓐ Ⓑ Ⓒ Ⓓ	148	Ⓐ Ⓑ Ⓒ Ⓓ	158	Ⓐ Ⓑ Ⓒ Ⓓ	168	Ⓐ Ⓑ Ⓒ Ⓓ	178	Ⓐ Ⓑ Ⓒ Ⓓ	188	Ⓐ Ⓑ Ⓒ Ⓓ	198	Ⓐ Ⓑ Ⓒ Ⓓ
109	Ⓐ Ⓑ Ⓒ Ⓓ	119	Ⓐ Ⓑ Ⓒ Ⓓ	129	Ⓐ Ⓑ Ⓒ Ⓓ	139	Ⓐ Ⓑ Ⓒ Ⓓ	149	Ⓐ Ⓑ Ⓒ Ⓓ	159	Ⓐ Ⓑ Ⓒ Ⓓ	169	Ⓐ Ⓑ Ⓒ Ⓓ	179	Ⓐ Ⓑ Ⓒ Ⓓ	189	Ⓐ Ⓑ Ⓒ Ⓓ	199	Ⓐ Ⓑ Ⓒ Ⓓ
110	Ⓐ Ⓑ Ⓒ Ⓓ	120	Ⓐ Ⓑ Ⓒ Ⓓ	130	Ⓐ Ⓑ Ⓒ Ⓓ	140	Ⓐ Ⓑ Ⓒ Ⓓ	150	Ⓐ Ⓑ Ⓒ Ⓓ	160	Ⓐ Ⓑ Ⓒ Ⓓ	170	Ⓐ Ⓑ Ⓒ Ⓓ	180	Ⓐ Ⓑ Ⓒ Ⓓ	190	Ⓐ Ⓑ Ⓒ Ⓓ	200	Ⓐ Ⓑ Ⓒ Ⓓ

NEW TOEIC終極奪高分祕笈，
詳盡掌握解題竅門，一舉奪得金色證書950！

新制多益實戰模擬試題精闢出題，
完美破解新制多益考題趨勢，助你勇奪新高分！

本書為目標考取 950 分以上高分的考生，彙整多益測驗中反覆出現的高難度題型，試題著重在難度較高的 10%，精選出完整 3 回聽力／閱讀實戰試題，每題皆詳盡解說解題步驟與秘技，幫助讀者熟習頻出字彙與重要文法。考生可運用本書精確掌握解題脈絡，密集訓練難度較高的考題，習得破題要領，勇奪新制多益超高分！

精闢分析新制多益命題趨勢與比重

針對新制多益命題趨勢，依各大題考試重點分析出題動向及題型比重，提供一目瞭然的圖表資訊，迅速掌握新制考題命題方向。

3 回實戰模擬試題，題題緊扣新制多益考題動向

名師統整考場實戰經驗精心出題，模擬試題完全仿照新制多益命題趨勢，出題精準全面，直指新制考點核心！

模擬題附中譯解析，逐題詳盡剖析破題步驟與要點

模擬試題附有中譯與詳盡解析，由名師逐題一步步親授破題技巧，藉由畫重點的方式，明確標出題目中關鍵句及各選項正誤處。先提點第一步答題技巧，再依照答題邏輯，按部就班、逐題詳解題目與解題邏輯，扎實打穩應試實力！

重要頻出字彙與文法重點

解析部分同時選出題目中關鍵字彙與重要文法，有助考前熟習新制多益的頻出詞彙與文法觀念，最短時間一次背齊關鍵重點，穩奪高分！

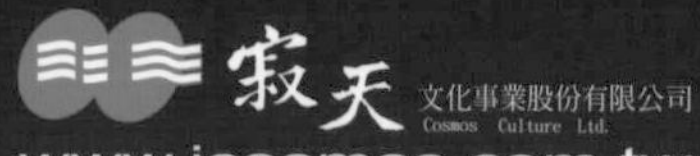

www.icosmos.com.tw C1372-1614

勇奪新制多益950

完整3回實戰演練＋試題完全解密攻略

中譯解析本

Yoo, su-youn——著

關亭薇／沈家淩
蔡裴驊／蘇裕承——譯

勇奪新制多益950

完整3回實戰演練＋試題完全解密攻略

中譯解析本

MP3

Yoo, su-youn——著

關亭薇／沈家淩
蔡裴驊／蘇裕承——譯

目錄

TEST 1
解析

解答 TEST 1

1. (B)	**2.** (D)	**3.** (D)	**4.** (A)	**5.** (A)	**6.** (B)	**7.** (A)	**8.** (A)	**9.** (A)	**10.** (A)
11. (B)	**12.** (B)	**13.** (C)	**14.** (B)	**15.** (C)	**16.** (B)	**17.** (C)	**18.** (C)	**19.** (C)	**20.** (A)
21. (B)	**22.** (B)	**23.** (B)	**24.** (B)	**25.** (A)	**26.** (B)	**27.** (B)	**28.** (A)	**29.** (B)	**30.** (C)
31. (C)	**32.** (B)	**33.** (B)	**34.** (C)	**35.** (D)	**36.** (C)	**37.** (A)	**38.** (B)	**39.** (C)	**40.** (C)
41. (C)	**42.** (D)	**43.** (A)	**44.** (B)	**45.** (D)	**46.** (A)	**47.** (C)	**48.** (C)	**49.** (B)	**50.** (A)
51. (C)	**52.** (A)	**53.** (C)	**54.** (A)	**55.** (D)	**56.** (C)	**57.** (C)	**58.** (A)	**59.** (B)	**60.** (D)
61. (C)	**62.** (B)	**63.** (D)	**64.** (A)	**65.** (D)	**66.** (D)	**67.** (C)	**68.** (A)	**69.** (C)	**70.** (C)
71. (B)	**72.** (B)	**73.** (B)	**74.** (D)	**75.** (A)	**76.** (D)	**77.** (C)	**78.** (A)	**79.** (B)	**80.** (C)
81. (B)	**82.** (C)	**83.** (B)	**84.** (D)	**85.** (C)	**86.** (C)	**87.** (C)	**88.** (A)	**89.** (A)	**90.** (A)
91. (B)	**92.** (D)	**93.** (B)	**94.** (B)	**95.** (B)	**96.** (C)	**97.** (D)	**98.** (C)	**99.** (B)	**100.** (C)
101. (B)	**102.** (A)	**103.** (C)	**104.** (A)	**105.** (A)	**106.** (D)	**107.** (B)	**108.** (A)	**109.** (D)	**110.** (D)
111. (D)	**112.** (D)	**113.** (C)	**114.** (B)	**115.** (B)	**116.** (A)	**117.** (D)	**118.** (A)	**119.** (D)	**120.** (A)
121. (A)	**122.** (B)	**123.** (A)	**124.** (D)	**125.** (D)	**126.** (A)	**127.** (C)	**128.** (B)	**129.** (D)	**130.** (C)
131. (A)	**132.** (D)	**133.** (C)	**134.** (C)	**135.** (A)	**136.** (B)	**137.** (D)	**138.** (C)	**139.** (A)	**140.** (C)
141. (A)	**142.** (D)	**143.** (D)	**144.** (B)	**145.** (B)	**146.** (A)	**147.** (B)	**148.** (C)	**149.** (C)	**150.** (A)
151. (B)	**152.** (B)	**153.** (B)	**154.** (C)	**155.** (A)	**156.** (C)	**157.** (B)	**158.** (D)	**159.** (D)	**160.** (D)
161. (A)	**162.** (C)	**163.** (C)	**164.** (B)	**165.** (D)	**166.** (C)	**167.** (B)	**168.** (C)	**169.** (B)	**170.** (C)
171. (B)	**172.** (A)	**173.** (C)	**174.** (D)	**175.** (C)	**176.** (B)	**177.** (C)	**178.** (B)	**179.** (C)	**180.** (B)
181. (C)	**182.** (D)	**183.** (D)	**184.** (C)	**185.** (B)	**186.** (C)	**187.** (C)	**188.** (D)	**189.** (C)	**190.** (C)
191. (B)	**192.** (C)	**193.** (B)	**194.** (C)	**195.** (D)	**196.** (C)	**197.** (C)	**198.** (B)	**199.** (D)	**200.** (B)

PART 1

1

(A) A woman is stocking some sandwiches.
(B) A woman is shopping for some merchandise.
(C) A woman is labeling each item.
(D) A woman is trying to tie her hair.

(A) 女子正將三明治補貨上架。
(B) 女子正在購物。
(C) 女子正為每件物品逐一貼上標籤。
(D) 女子正試著紮起頭髮。

字彙 stock 為……備貨　merchandise 商品　tie 紮

01 答案會採較為籠統的描述方式。

PART 1 中，答案會使用涵蓋範圍較廣的單字，不會使用過於明確、單指某項物品的單字。

STEP 1 照片分析

❶ 單人照片　❷ 看著商品　❸ 商品陳列在架上

STEP 2 聽到照片中未呈現的單字時，請立即刪去該選項。

(A) A woman is ~~stocking~~ some sandwiches.
▶女子並未做將三明治上架的動作。

(B) A woman is shopping for some merchandise. ▶ 答案

(C) A woman is ~~labeling~~ each item.
▶女子並未做貼標籤的動作。

(D) A woman is ~~trying to tie~~ her hair.
▶女子並未做綁頭髮的動作。

STEP 3 較為籠統的描述 POINT

1. 使用涵蓋範圍較廣的名詞選項通常會是答案，並不會使用較為明確、單指某樣東西的名詞。

限定某樣東西的單字	涵蓋範圍較廣的單字
copy machine / copier 複印機／影印機	equipment / machine 設備／機器
tomato 番茄 vegetable 蔬菜 necklace 項鍊	merchandise / item 商品／項目 goods / produce 商品／農產品 jewelry 珠寶
map 地圖　magazine 雜誌　notepad 記事本	document / paper 文件／紙
bulldozer 推土機　forklift 堆高機	heavy machine 重型機械

2. 使用涵蓋範圍較廣的動作動詞選項通常會是答案，並不會使用較為明確、單指某個動作的動詞。

限定某個動作的單字	涵蓋範圍較廣的單字
sweep 打掃 mop 用拖把拖洗 scrub / wipe 擦洗／擦拭	clean / clear 打掃／清理
make a presentation 發表演說 listen to the presentation 聆聽簡報	have a meeting 開會
shake hands 握手	greet each other 互相問候

2

(A) Flags are hanging from the windows of the building.
(B) A billboard is being taken away from the wall.
(C) A woman is putting some towels into a bag.
(D) A variety of items are being displayed outdoors.

(A) 旗幟從大樓的窗戶懸掛而下。
(B) 廣告看板正從牆上被移走。
(C) 女子正把一些毛巾裝進袋子裡。
(D) 各式各樣的物品正在戶外展示。

字彙 flag 旗幟　billboard （路旁的）大型廣告看板　take away 移走
display 陳列、展示　outdoors 在戶外

02 be being displayed 可以作為無人照片的答案。

進行被動式 be being displayed 的意思為「陳列」，照片中不一定要有人物，也不用呈現出此動作，因此該用法可以作為無人照片的答案。

STEP 1 照片分析

❶ 照片為〈人＋物〉　❷ 旗子放在戶外展示
❸ 人們正在看東西　❹ 後方有大樓

STEP 2 聽到照片中未呈現的單字時，請立即刪去該選項。

(A) Flags are ~~hanging from the windows~~ of the building.
▶ 旗子沒有掛在大樓的窗戶上。

(B) A billboard is ~~being taken away~~ from the wall.
▶ 照片中沒有人在移除廣告看板。

(C) A woman is ~~putting~~ some towels into a bag.
▶ 女子並未做出把毛巾放進袋子的動作。

(D) A variety of items are being displayed outdoors. ▶ 答案

STEP 3 答案為 being p.p. 的情況，與照片中的人物無關。

(1) 物品陳列的狀態、或出現在背景中：

display（陳列、展示）、decorate（裝飾）、exhibit（展出）、cast（投射）、occupy（占據）等動詞。

例 Some shadows are being cast on a balcony.
幾道陰影被投射在陽臺上。

(2) 物品依靠機器自動產生動作的情況：

move（移動）、transport（運送）等動詞。

例 Luggage is being moved on the conveyer belt.
行李由傳輸帶輸送。

3

(A) Some flowers are being planted. (A) 花叢正被栽植而下。
(B) Some trees are being trimmed. (B) 樹木正進行修整。
(C) A path is being resurfaced. (C) 小徑正被重新鋪設。
(D) A wheelbarrow is being pushed. (D) 手推車正被推著走。

字彙 plant 栽種　trim 修剪　path 小徑　resurface 為……鋪設新表面
wheelbarrow （花園中的）手推車

03 照片為〈人物＋事物〉時，若選項以事物作為主詞，後方通常會使用 be being p.p.。

「事物主詞＋ be being p.p.」＝「人物正在對事物做某個動作」

STEP 1 照片分析

❶ 照片為〈人＋物〉　❷ 男子推著手推車
❸ 花為綻放的狀態　❹ 照片中有樹木

STEP 2 聽到照片中未呈現的單字時，請立即刪去該選項。

(A) Some flowers are ~~being planted~~.
▶照片中沒有人在種花。

(B) Some trees are ~~being trimmed~~.
▶照片中沒有人在修剪樹木。

(C) A path is ~~being resurfaced~~.
▶照片中沒有人在鋪路。

(D) A wheelbarrow is being pushed. ▶ 答案

STEP 3 照片中同時出現人物和事物的 POINT

1. 判斷人物和背景的比例各占多少。
2. 確認照片中的地點，以及周遭事物的位置與狀態。
3. 請務必熟記與照片中的事物特徵有關的單字。
4. 請特別留意，錯誤選項中可能會出現與人物動作不相干的動詞。
5. 請特別留意，錯誤選項中可能會提到照片中沒有的事物。

4

(A) Some of the tables have been set.
(B) Some lighting fixtures are being installed on a ceiling.
(C) Some food is being served to customers.
(D) A seating area has been placed outdoors.

(A) 某些餐桌已被布置好。
(B) 天花板上正在裝設照明設備。
(C) 某些食物正被端上桌供應給客人。
(D) 戶外設有一個座位區。

字彙 lighting fixture 照明設備　serve 供應　place 放置

04 熟記無人照片的兩大重點。

STEP 1 照片分析

❶ 照片中沒有人，只有物品。
❷ 擺著數張桌子。
❸ 窗戶處於開啟的狀態。
❹ 照片中出現一些燈具。

STEP 2 聽到照片中未呈現的單字時，請立即刪去該選項。

(A) Some of the tables have been set. ▶ 答案

(B) Some lighting fixtures are ~~being installed~~ on a ceiling.
▶照片中並未出現裝設燈具的人。

(C) Some food is ~~being served~~ to customers.
▶照片中並未出現送餐的人，也沒有客人。

(D) A seating area has been placed ~~outdoors~~.
▶照片呈現的是室內的座位。

STEP 3 物品照刪去法 POINT

(1) 請確認主要事物的位置和狀態、以及周遭事物和背景畫面。

❶ 確認主要事物的位置和狀態。
❷ 確認周遭事物。
❸ 確認地點和背景畫面。
❹ 若題目為無人照片，選項卻出現人物名詞時，屬於錯誤描述，請立即刪去該選項。
❺ 請特別留意，錯誤選項中可能會提及照片中未出現的事物。

(2)「be being p.p.」不能作為答案。

- 「事物主詞＋ be being p.p.」表示「某人針對某物做某個動作」，因此此用法不適用於無人照片，屬於錯誤的敘述。
- 〔例外〕display（陳列）表示一種持續的狀態，因此即使照片中沒有人，仍可以使用進行被動式。

例 Some items are being displayed.
某些物品正在展示中。

5

(A) A man is loading some clothes into a machine.
(B) A man is pouring a detergent into a container.
(C) A man is bending over a bathtub.
(D) A man is closing the machine door.

(A) 男子正把一些衣物裝進機器裡。
(B) 男子正把洗衣粉倒進容器中。
(C) 男子正俯身靠向浴缸。
(D) 男子正蓋上機器的門。

字彙 machine 機器　pour 倒　detergent 洗衣粉　container 容器　bend over 彎腰　bathtub 浴缸

05 單人照片的重點為人物動作和外觀。

STEP 1 照片分析

❶ 照片中出現一個人。
❷ 男子把手伸進洗衣機裡。
❸ 男子看向洗衣機內部。
❹ 地板上有一些衣服。
❺ 洗衣機的門開著。

STEP 2 聽到照片中未呈現的單字時，請立即刪去該選項。

(A) A man is loading some clothes into a machine. ▶ 答案

(B) A man is ~~pouring~~ a detergent into a container.
▶ 男子並未把洗衣粉倒入容器中。

(C) A man is ~~bending over~~ a bathtub.
▶ 男子並未在浴缸前做出彎腰的動作，照片中也沒有浴缸。

(D) A man is ~~closing~~ the machine door.
▶ 男子並未關上機器的門。

STEP 3 單人照片的 POINT

1. 請特別留意針對動作或狀態的描寫。

2. 最新出題趨勢：請依序觀察人物的「手→眼睛→服裝」。

照片類型	答案類型
人物上半身入鏡	❶ 詳細描述動作 ↓ ❷ 描述符合人物身處地點或情境的行為 ↓ ❸ 針對外貌、外型進行描述 ↓ ❹ 描述周遭（地點）的狀況或物品
人物全身皆入鏡	❶ 描述符合情境的行為 ↓ ❷ 詳細描述動作 ↓ ❸ 針對外貌、外型進行描述 ↓ ❹ 描述周遭（地點）的狀況或物品

6

(A) A hallway has been deserted.
(B) Columns have been erected along a walkway.
(C) All of the people are walking in the same direction.
(D) Some people are resting on some stairs

(A) 走廊空無一人。
(B) 石柱沿著走道豎立。
(C) 所有的人都朝著同一方向行進。
(D) 有些人在階梯上休息。

字彙 hallway 走廊　desert 遺棄　column 石柱　erect 豎立　walkway 走道　direction 方向　stair 階梯

06 照片聚焦於全景時，即使當中有人，也請特別留意描述事物狀態的選項。

在後半段照片題中，照片中同時出現人和物時，針對兩者的描述會平均分配。

STEP 1 照片分析

❶ 人和背景畫面。
❷ 照片中有一排柱子。
❸ 有一些人在走路。

STEP 2 聽到照片中未呈現的單字時，請立即刪去該選項。

(A) A hallway has been ~~deserted~~.
▶走廊上有人。

(B) Columns have been erected along a walkway. ▶ 答案

(C) All of the people are walking in the ~~same direction~~.
▶照片中的人並未往同一個方向走。

(D) Some people are resting on some ~~stairs~~.
▶照片中沒有出現階梯。

STEP 3 照片中有人並不代表答案一定是針對人物的描述。

雖然有時針對照片中最顯眼的行為描述選項即為正確答案，但是有時答案反而是針對意想不到的部分進行描述的選項。

假設照片中有個人坐在椅子上看著報紙，請特別留意答案可能不是針對他的行為或動作進行描述，而是描述他身旁事物的位置或狀態。

描述行為或動作	描述身旁事物的位置或狀態
A man is reading a newspaper. 男子正在看報紙。	There is a bench next to the grassy area. 草地旁有一張長椅。
A man is holding a piece of paper. 男子手中拿著一張紙。	
A man is sitting on a bench. 男子正坐在長椅上。	

PART 2

07. How do I get to the restaurant you told me about?

(A) There's a map on their Web site. ▶ 間接回答
(B) I really ~~enjoyed~~ the ~~dinner~~. ▶ 時態 x | 相關單字 x
(C) ~~But~~ you should take a taxi. ▶ but 有誤 x

07. 我該如何才能前往你跟我提過的餐廳呢？
(A) 他們的官網上有地圖。
(B) 晚餐真的讓我吃得很盡興。
(C) 但你應該搭計程車去。

08. Are you having problems with logging on to your computer, too?

(A) Actually, everyone has the same issue today.
(B) Yes, I ~~did~~ it. ▶ 時態 x
(C) Too much is not always a ~~problem~~. ▶ 相同單字 x

08. 你在登入電腦時，是否也有問題？
(A) 事實上，今天每個人都碰到相同的問題。
(B) 沒錯，是我做的。
(C) 過剩並不總會構成問題。

09. Do we have any more brochures or pamphlets?

(A) They are usually in the closet in the basement. ▶ 間接回答
(B) Yes. John ~~will~~ design them. ▶ 時態有誤
(C) ~~For the promotional event~~. ▶ 適用 Why 問句

09. 我們有沒有多餘的廣告手冊或是宣傳單？
(A) 它們通常會在地下室的儲藏室裡。
(B) 沒錯，約翰將進行設計。
(C) 是為了宣傳活動。

10. Where's the best place to get more chairs for our conference room?

(A) Human resources just bought some. ▶ 對象、來源
(B) We can get a ride to the ~~conference~~ center. ▶ 相同單字 x
(C) ~~You~~ should stay at the nearest hotel. ▶ 主詞有誤

10. 何處能找到更多的椅子搬進會議室？
(A) 人力資源部才剛買進一些椅子。
(B) 我們可以搭車前往會議中心。
(C) 你應該入住最近的飯店。

11. When will the main entrance of our store be repaired?

(A) ~~We~~ will open our new store next week. ▶ 主詞有誤
(B) Some parts were just ordered. ▶ 間接回答
(C) Actually, we can ~~store~~ them in the warehouse. ▶ 相同單字 | 適用 where 問句

11. 我們商店的大門何時會修理？
(A) 我們的新商店將在下個星期開幕。
(B) 才剛訂購了一些零件。
(C) 事實上，我們可以把它們儲存在倉庫裡。

12. How do you plan to market your new service? ▶ 手段、方法

(A) I usually go to the local ~~market~~. ▶ 相同單字
(B) Mostly with advertisements. ▶ 手段
(C) We will get ~~there by car~~. ▶ 適用 How . . . get to . . . ?

12. 你計劃如何推銷你的新服務？
(A) 我通常都會去本地市場。
(B) 主要會靠廣告。
(C) 我們會搭車去。

13. Hasn't the budget for the new project been approved yet?

(A) That seems ~~promising~~. ▶ 適用 How is . . . ?
(B) More ~~financial support~~. ▶ 相關單字 x
(C) The director just received it. ▶ 間接回答——解釋

13. 新計畫的預算還沒核准嗎？
(A) 看來似乎很有希望。
(B) 更多的金援。
(C) 主管才剛收到計畫預算。

14. I am thinking of buying a new dining table and chairs from Home Office Furniture.

(A) That's a great place to work. ▶相關單字 x | 適用 How is . . . ?

(B) You can find a discount coupon on their Web site. ▶告知下一步的行動

(C) For more than six sets. ▶適用 How many 問句

14. 我正考慮要從家居辦公家具公司買新的餐桌椅。

(A) 那是個工作的好地方。

(B) 你可以在他們的官方網站上找到折價券。

(C) 要買超過六組。

15. Who should I contact about the travel reimbursement form?

(A) The payroll department is busy. ▶適用 How is . . . ?

(B) Mr. Troeger is working for the travel agency. ▶適用 Where 問句

(C) I have an e-mail with the information.

15. 我該聯繫誰才能拿到差旅費報支單呢？

(A) 薪資部門業務繁忙。

(B) 特洛格爾先生正任職於旅行社。

(C) 我有一封電子郵件內有相關資訊。

16. Is there any nice place for lunch within walking distance?

(A) No, we haven't been there. ▶相同單字 x

(B) Most people here usually bring food from home. ▶非正面答覆——間接說明

(C) Just some chips for me. ▶相關單字 x

16. 這附近有沒有步行可到的午餐推薦用餐地點呢？

(A) 不，我們沒去過那裡。

(B) 這裡大多數的人通常都從家裡自帶食物。

(C) 給我幾片洋芋片就好。

17. Why don't you attend the national business conference next month? ▶建議

(A) The market trend of online shopping. ▶相關單字 x

(B) Well, the conference was rather boring. ▶時態有誤

(C) I'm waiting to find out who the speakers will be. ▶間接回答

17. 你何不參加下個月舉辦的全國商務會議呢？

(A) 網路購物的市場趨勢。

(B) 唔，那場會議頗為無趣。

(C) 我正等著查明會議講者是誰。

18. Excuse me. Where should I put these projectors?

(A) They should be here by noon. ▶適用 When 問句

(B) I put them in the storage this morning. ▶時態有誤

(C) Marco is in charge of all the equipment. ▶等同於 I don't know

18. 請問一下，我應該把這些投影機放在何處？

(A) 它們應該中午前就會到了。

(B) 今天早上我把它們放進倉庫裡了。

(C) 馬可負責管理所有設備。

19. You have already been to the new amusement park, haven't you?

(A) Right, I need a parking lot. ▶發音相似 | 時態有誤

(B) The park offers an entertaining tour as well. ▶相關單字 x

(C) I'd go there again with you. ▶間接回答

19. 你已經去過新的遊樂園了，不是嗎？

(A) 沒錯，我需要一個停車位。

(B) 遊樂園也有提供有趣的遊覽行程。

(C) 我可以跟你再去一次。

20. The board of directors called an emergency meeting this afternoon.

(A) But I have to check my schedule first.
▶ 補充說明

(B) The ~~chairman~~ wants to retire soon.
▶ 相關單字 x

(C) They are in the ~~meeting~~ room. ▶ 相同單字 x

20. 董事會今天下午召開緊急會議。
(A) 但我得先確認一下我的行程。
(B) 董事長想盡快退休。
(C) 他們正在會議室裡。

21. When is this plane supposed to take off? ▶ 未來

(A) At the ~~airport~~.
▶ 相關單字 x | 適用 Where 問句

(B) Isn't it listed on the itinerary? ▶ 反問

(C) Flying back to ~~Orlando~~. ▶ 適用 Where 問句

21. 這架班機預計何時起飛？
(A) 在機場。
(B) 不是列在班機行程表上了嗎？
(C) 飛回奧蘭多。

22. Should we take a train or a bus to the convention center? ▶ 選擇

(A) **Neither** ~~was~~ finished. ▶ 時態有誤

(B) It's right on the train route. ▶ 間接回答

(C) At the earliest ~~time~~. ▶ 適用 When 問句

22. 我們應該要搭火車還是巴士前往會議中心？
(A) 兩個都沒完工。
(B) 它就位在火車行經的路線上。
(C) 要搭最早的班次。

23. Our company will announce the release of our new product next week. ▶ 未來

(A) The response to the product ~~was~~ very positive.
▶ 時態有誤

(B) Is there any promotional event? ▶ 反問

(C) ~~I~~ was there, too. ▶ 主詞有誤

23. 本公司將於下週宣布新產品上市。
(A) 產品的市場反應非常好。
(B) 會有任何促銷活動嗎？
(C) 我當時也在場。

24. Why don't you register for the staff health and safety training? ▶ 建議

(A) ~~No~~. I will get there on time. ▶ 適用附加問句

(B) I already attended that two weeks ago.
▶ 間接回答

(C) There were ~~100 people~~ present.
▶ 相關單字 x | 適用 How many 問句

24. 你何不報名參加員工的衛生與安全培訓呢？
(A) 不，我會準時到的。
(B) 兩個星期前我已經參加過了。
(C) 當時有一百個人在場。

25. How many of our branches achieved record sales this year?

(A) The report's coming out this Friday.
▶ 間接回答

(B) ~~Yes~~, we are expecting a sales increase.
▶ 不能以 Yes 或 No 回答

(C) Our ~~revenue~~ is rather high.
▶ 相關單字 x | 適用 How much 問句

25. 今年我們有幾家分店的銷售紀錄創新高？
(A) 這個星期五報表會出來。
(B) 沒錯，我們預計銷量會增加。
(C) 我們的收益頗高。

26. Have you talked to Sylvia Hanson about the contract yet?

(A) Yes, ~~they~~ are doing well. ▶ 主詞有誤

(B) She'll be back from vacation tomorrow.

▶ 間接回答——解釋

(C) John didn't have much ~~contact~~ with me.

▶ 發音相似 x

26. 你跟席薇亞．韓森談過合約了嗎？

(A) 是的，他們做得很好。

(B) 她明天會收假歸隊。

(C) 約翰沒有經常與我聯繫。

---

27. Let's place an order for more experimental equipment. ▶ 勸說或建議

(A) A couple of ~~projectors~~.

▶ 相關單字 x ∣ 適用 How many 問句

(B) Isn't the project being postponed? ▶ 反問

(C) Okay, that looks ~~heavy~~.

▶ 相關單字 x ∣ 適用 Could you help me . . . ?

27. 我們再多訂購一些實驗設備吧。

(A) 幾台投影機。

(B) 這計畫不是延期了嗎？

(C) 好啊，看起來是很重。

---

28. How often do you go to the gym these days?

▶ 頻率、次數

(A) It's been under renovation for a month.

▶ 間接回答

(B) ~~Two days ago.~~ ▶ 時間——適用 When 問句

(C) You can use my ~~membership~~. ▶ 相關單字 x

28. 最近你多久去一次健身房？

(A) 它已整修一個月了。

(B) 兩天前。

(C) 你可以使用我的會員資格。

---

29. Your car doesn't seem to have enough space for those boxes.

(A) I left them ~~on your desk~~. ▶ 適用 Where 問句

(B) We're renting a bus. ▶ 提出替代方案

(C) ~~At the stationery store~~. ▶ 適用 Where 問句

29. 你的車似乎沒有足夠的空間放下那些箱子。

(A) 我把它們放在你的桌上。

(B) 我們要租一台巴士。

(C) 在文具店。

---

30. I can assist you with the travel arrangements, if you want. ▶ 勸說或建議

(A) No, ~~it's~~ not mine. ▶ 適用 Is it . . . ? 問句

(B) Just a few, if you can ~~lend~~ me one. ▶ 相關單字 x

(C) I don't think that will be necessary.

▶ 高頻率回答方式

30. 如果你需要的話，我可以幫你安排旅遊行程。

(A) 不，不是我的。

(B) 只需要一些，如果你可以借給我的話。

(C) 我不覺得有這個必要。

---

31. How did Mr. Lewis like the report? ▶ 看法

(A) From the ~~library~~. ▶ 適用 Where 問句

(B) ~~I~~ gave that to him. ▶ 主詞有誤

(C) He spoke to the director about it. ▶ 間接回答

31. 路易士先生覺得報告怎麼樣？

(A) 從圖書館。

(B) 我給他了。

(C) 他跟主管談過這件事了。

07 針對 Wh- 問句的間接回答——「請確認……」。

題目分析 **How do I get to the restaurant you told me about?**

「How do I get to ＋地點？」詢問的是前往特定地點的方法。

選項分析

(A) There's a map on their Web site. ▶ 答案

在新制測驗中，較少出現直接回答某種手段或方法，反而會使用 by、through 等介系詞，採間接回答的方式，請對方透過「地圖、廣告、公告」確認。

(B) I really enjoyed the dinner. ❺ 時態有誤

問句為現在式，不能使用過去式回答。動詞 enjoy 和 like 用來表達看法，因此回答問句「How was ＋主詞 . . . ?」較為適當。

(C) But you should take a taxi. ❷ 適用其他問句

新制測驗中出現以 but 回答的選項，通常用來回答助動詞開頭的問句，不適用於 Wh- 問句。先以 Yes 或 No 回答事實與否，再以 but 補充說明內容。本選項適合回答問句如「Should I take a bus?（我該搭公車嗎？）」。

08 以 Actually 回答助動詞開頭的問句，不使用 Yes 或 No 回答。

題目分析 **Are you having problems with logging on to your computer, too?**

「Are you having problems with . . . ?」表示是否有問題，用來詢問對方的狀況。

選項分析

(A) Actually, everyone has the same issue today. ▶ 答案

表示除了我（I）和你（You）之外，每個人（everyone）都遭遇相同的問題，針對全體一次說明完畢，因此可以作為答案。

(B) Yes, I did it. ❺ 時態有誤

問句為現在式，不能使用過去式回答。該選項適用過去式問句「Did you . . . ?」。

※若選項回答包含副詞「already（已經）」或「just（剛剛）」，通常會是正確答案，無關問句的類型為何。

(C) Too much is not always a problem. ❹ 相同單字陷阱

重複使用題目句中的 problem，為陷阱選項，與題目內容無關。

09 選擇疑問句經常採間接回答的方式。

題目分析 **Do we have any more brochures or pamphlets?**

針對問句「我們有……嗎？」，通常會回答有或無。

選項分析

(A) They are usually in the closet in the basement. ▶ 答案

in the basement（在地下室）回答的是地點，通常會搭配 where 開頭的問句。但是本題問句中的手冊（brochures）或小冊子（pamphlets），這兩樣東西皆可被放在地下室的儲藏室裡，因此該選項可以視為間接回答。這類回答方式屬於高難度的回答。

(B) Yes. John will design them. ❺ 時態有誤

題目句問的是現在的狀態。此選項為未來式，答道「John 將會設計」，代表現在還沒有手冊或小冊子，但選項卻答 Yes，因此不正確。

(C) For the promotional event. ❷ 適用其他問句

故意使用與 pamphlets（小冊子）有關的詞 promotional event（宣傳活動），屬於陷阱選項。應搭配以 Why 開頭的問句較為適當，回答「原因」。

10 Where 問句：不回答地點，而是告知消息來源或對象。

題目分析 **Where's the best place to get more chairs for our conference room?**

「Where's the best place . . . ?」詢問的是地點。

選項分析

(A) Human resources just bought some. ▶ 答案

一般會以地點回答 Where 開頭的問句，但是在新制測驗中，不太會直接回答地點，而是告知消息來源或對象，像是人物、報紙、廣告或新聞。舉例來說：問句為「Where is the book?」（書在哪裡？），答案可能為「John took it.」（在 John 手上。）本題則回答部門名稱 Human resources（人力資源部）作為答案。

(B) We can get a ride to the conference center. ❹ 相同單字陷阱

重複使用題目句中 conference room 的 conference，屬於陷阱選項。

(C) You should stay at the nearest hotel. ❸ 主詞有誤

題目句中沒有選項中 you 對應的對象，因此不能作為答案。

11 即使答句和問句的時態不同，只要當中出現特定副詞，仍可作為正確答案。

題目分析 **When will the main entrance of our store be repaired?**

以 When 開頭的未來式疑問句。

選項分析

(A) We will open our new store next week. ❸ 主詞有誤

題目句中並未出現 We 對應的名詞，且重複使用題目句中的單字 store（商店），屬於陷阱選項。此回答適合作為問句「When will you do . . . ?」（你何時要……？）的答案。

(B) Some parts were just ordered. ▶ 答案

若選項中包含 just（剛剛）、already（已經）、still（仍然）或 yet（尚未）等副詞，可以得知事情是否正在進行或者是否已完成，因此無關答句的時態，大多可作為正確答案。此選項中 just 的意思為事情處於「剛做好……」的狀態，表示已經完成的概念，因此雖然時態和問句不同，仍可作為正確答案。

(C) Actually, we can store them in the warehouse. ❹ 相同單字陷阱

若選項中出現 Actually，有極高的機率為正解。欲詳細說明某件事情時，會使用副詞 Actually（事實上……）。通常會以 Actually 代替 Yes 或 No，回答以 Do 動詞、Be 動詞、或其他助動詞開頭的問句，向對方詳細說明內容。而本題的題目句並未出現選項中 them 所對應的名詞，又重複使用單字 store，屬於陷阱選項。

12 問句為「How ＋助動詞」時，要回答方法或手段。

題目分析 **How do you plan to market your new service?**

「How do you plan . . . ?」問句中，How 後方連接動詞，詢問手段或方法。

選項分析

(A) I usually go to the local market. ❺ 時態有誤

題目句問的是往後的計畫，要回答未來式。但是此選項為現在式，時態不正確，因此不能作為答案。

(B) Mostly with advertisements. ▶ 答案

問句為「How ＋助動詞 . . . ?」時，會使用表示「手段或方法」的介系詞，回答做某件事的手段或方法。此處以介系詞 with 加上 advertisement（廣告），表示以該手段銷售新的服務，故為正確答案。

(C) We will get there by car. ❷ 適用其他問句

雖然此處以介系詞 by 表示方式，但前方的副詞 there 表示地點，與題目內容無關。此選項適合回答問句「How . . . get to ＋地點？」（如何前往……？）。

13 否定疑問句或附加問句的答案不會出現 Yes 或 No，而是採解釋方式答覆。

題目分析 **Hasn't the budget for the new project been approved yet?**

否定疑問句「Hasn't . . . p.p.?」的答案通常不會出現 Yes 或 No。

選項分析

(A) That seems promising. ❷ 適用其他問句

形容詞 promising（有望的）表示的是一種狀態，這類表示狀態的形容詞或副詞，用來表達自身的想法，因此適合搭配問句「How is . . . ?」（……如何？）。

(B) More financial support. ❹ 相關單字陷阱

此處的 financial support（財務支援）與題目句中的 budget（預算）有所關聯，屬於陷阱選項，不能作為答案。

(C) The director just received it. ▶ 答案

新制測驗中，否定疑問句或附加問句的答案，不太會用 Yes 或 No 直接回答某行為或事實的有無。反而會以相關說明或告知下一步的行動，代替 Yes 或 No。本題句子詢問批准與否，此處回答「主管剛收到」，等同於回答 No 的概念，間接表示尚未被批准，屬於「解釋型」的回答。

否定疑問句的答案敘述通常會是❶變更事項 ❷不知情 ❸解釋 ❹尚未完成，代替回答 No 的概念。

14 直述句的回答：告知下一步的行動。

題目分析 **I am thinking of buying a new dining table and chairs from Home Office Furniture.**

「I am thinking . . .」（我正考慮……）表示說話者的想法，答案通常是告知對方下一步的行動、或是提出替代方案。

選項分析

(A) That's a great place to work. ❹ 相關單字陷阱

改以「That's a good idea.」（這個點子不錯。）回答本題的直述句較為適當。「a great place to work」（很適合工作的地方）表達的是自己的想法，應搭配詢問對方想法的問句「How do you like your new job?」（你覺得新工作如何？）較為適當。另外，選項使用 place，與題目句中的 Office 有所關聯，屬於陷阱選項。

(B) You can find a discount coupon on their Web site. ▶ 答案

直述句沒有提出任何問題，所以也沒有規定一定要回答什麼內容才行，但是通常會以表示同意或不同意對方所說的話作為答覆。新制測驗中，經常出現的答案為說明同意的原因、或是補充說明其他內容，較少出現「So do I.」（我也是）或「I think so.」（我也這麼認為）這類過於簡單的答覆。本題題目句表示想要購買傢俱，該選項請對方查看網站上的優惠，等同於間接表示同意對方的想法，並補充說明購買的方式。

(C) For more than six sets. ❷ 適用其他問句

選項中包含數字 six，應搭配以 How many（有多少數量？）開頭的問句較為適當。

15 以代名詞回答 Who 問句。

題目分析 **Who should I contact about the travel reimbursement form?**

開頭四個字為「Who should I contact」，詢問「我該和誰聯絡」。

選項分析

(A) The payroll department is busy. ❷ 適用其他問句

一般會以人名、部門名稱、公司名稱或職稱回答以 Who 開頭的問句，但是偶爾會出現難度較高的考題，像是加上動詞或修飾語，故意把句子變得很長；或是有兩個選項分別提到人名和職稱。雖然該選項提到部門名稱（payroll department），但是後方連接形容詞（busy），表示該部門處於忙碌的「狀態」，應搭配以「How is . . . ?」（……如何？）開頭的問句較為適當。

(B) Mr. Troeger is working for the travel agency. ❷ 適用其他問句

選項中提到第三者時，通常可以作為 Who 問句的正確答案。但是該選項後半段為 working for the travel agency（在旅行社工作），指的是此人在什麼公司工作，並非題目中提到的負責退款（reimbursement）事宜的人。因此該選項應搭配以 where 開頭，詢問在哪裡工作的問句較為適當。另外，該選項可能會被解釋成和「在旅行社工作的 Troeger 先生」聯絡，但是題目中提到退款表格（reimbursement form），也許是由同公司不同部門的人員提問，不能單憑在旅行社工作的回答當作答案。

(C) I have an e-mail with the information. ▶ 答案

一般來說，Who 問句的答案要回答人名或是職稱，但是在難度較高的考題中，答案會以代名詞來回答，例如回答當事者 I（回答者本人）、You（對方）、或第三者 Someone、Anyone、Everyone 等不特定的對象。尤其在近幾年測驗中，經常以 I 回答，並在後方補充說明內容。該選項 (C) 說明本人知道相關資訊，間接表示請對方交給本人（I），因此可以作為正確答案。

16 非正面答覆——間接說明情況。

題目分析 **Is there any nice place for lunch within walking distance?**

本題的解題關鍵為「Is there any nice place」，詢問「是否有不錯的地方」。

選項分析

(A) No, we haven't been there. ❹ 相同單字陷阱

雖然能以 Yes 或 No 回答 Be 動詞開頭的問句，但是本題題目句中的副詞 there 指的是「什麼樣的地方」，而該選項中的 there 指的是「那裡」，請分清楚兩者的差異。選項中的 there 僅重複使用題目句中的單字，不能作為答案。

(B) Most people here usually bring food from home. ▶ 答案

回答 Be 動詞或助動詞開頭的問句時，若選項已經明確表達出肯定或否定的概念，則會省略 Yes 或 No。過往測驗中，通常會先回答 Yes 或 No，表明肯定或否定後，再告知對方資訊、或表達自己想說的話；但在新制測驗中，會以完整的句子表達肯定或否定的概念，因此一定要聽完整句話，才能找出答案。與過往的考題相比，難度略為提升。本題詢問適合用餐的地點，該選項回答大多數的人都是從家裡帶食物來吃，間接表示為 No 的概念，並說明實際情況，故為正確答案。

(C) Just some chips for me. ❹ 相關單字陷阱

該選項故意使用 chips，與題目句中的 for lunch 有所關聯，屬於陷阱選項。另外，雖然 just 為答案中常見的副詞，但是此處並非表示動作完成與否，因此不能作為答案。

17 「勸說或建議」最常出現的回答是：反問或是等待中。

題目分析 **Why don't you attend the national business conference next month?**

本題的解題關鍵為「Why don't you attend」，建議對方「何不參加會議？」。

選項分析

(A) The market trend of online shopping. ❹ 相關單字陷阱

應搭配以 What 開頭的問句較為適當，像是「What was the conference about?」（會議的重點是什麼？）。選項內容與題目句中的 conference（會議）有所關聯，為常見的陷阱選項。

(B) Well, the conference was rather boring. ❺ 時態有誤

勸說或建議的問句屬於針對未來的提問，答案通常是未來式。但是若以副詞 already（已經）、或 almost（幾乎）來回答，表示「已經完成」或是「快完成了」，答案便可以使用過去式。雖然該選項為過去式，但是表達的是對會議的想法，並非表示動作完成的概念，因此不能作為答案。

(C) I'm waiting to find out who the speakers will be. ▶ 答案

問句為勸說或建議時，常見的回答有以「Sure.」（沒問題）或「Okay.」（好）表示同意；以「I'm sorry.（對不起）」或「No thanks.」（沒關係，謝謝）拒絕對方。但是在新制測驗中，答案經常採間接回答的方式，像是「我確認一下」或「還不確定」。本題建議對方參加會議，而該選項回答要確認講者是誰，間接表示「我還不確定」，故為正確答案。若句子表達的是「還不確定」的概念，等同於視情況而定，歸類於「I don't know」的回答方式。

18 間接表示自己不太清楚——請你問一下 John（Ask John.）。

題目分析 **Excuse me. Where should I put these projectors?**

本題的解題關鍵為「Where should I put」，詢問「要把……放在哪裡？」。

選項分析

(A) They should be here by noon. ❷ 適用其他問句

該選項提到確切的時間點（by noon），若回答時間，應搭配以 When 開頭的問句較為適當。

(B) I put them in the storage this morning. ❺ 時態有誤

一般會以地點來回答 Where 開頭的問句。該選項的 in the storage 為表示地點的名詞，因此可能會被誤會是正確答案。但是本題問的是現在放在此處的投影機，之後要放在哪裡，屬於未來的概念。而該選項使用過去式（put），因此不能作為答案。題目句中的 put 位於助動詞 should 的後方，為現在式動詞；選項則使用過去式，表示過去的動作。選項與題目句使用相同的單字，故為陷阱選項。

(C) Marco is in charge of all the equipment. ▶ 答案

雖然一般會以地點來回答 Where 開頭的問句，但是若選項中出現「我還沒收到」、「我不太清楚」、「請你問一下……」這幾種回答時，通常一定是答案。該選項回答「由 Marco 負責」，間接表示「我不太清楚，請向第三者詢問或確認」的概念，故為正確答案。新制測驗中，這類回答方式極為常見，因此請務必熟記。

19 不以 Yes 或 No 回答否定疑問句和附加問句的情況：(1) 告知往後的行動 (2) 補充相關說明 (3) 回答已包含 Yes 或 No 的概念在內。

題目分析 **You have already been to the new amusement park, haven't you?**

本題為附加問句，「You have already been . . .」表示向對方確認事實、或徵求對方同意。

選項分析

(A) Right, I need a parking lot. ❺ 時態有誤

雖然回答 Right 帶有肯定的概念，但是本題附加問句的時態為完成式，回答也要使用相同的時態才行。而選項內容為現在式，因此不能作為答案。同時，parking 與題目句中 park 的發音相似，屬於陷阱選項。

(B) The park offers an entertaining tour as well. ❹ 相關單字陷阱

選項使用與題目句相同的單字 park，還用了 an entertaining tour，與 new amusement park 有所關聯，屬於陷阱選項。另外，選項中用到副詞 as well（也），表示「追加」的概念，因此題目句中要提到遊樂園提供的設施，該選項才能作為答案。但是題目問的是對方的經驗，因此該選項並不適用。

(C) I'd go there again with you. ▶ 答案

新制測驗中，附加問句的答案不會出現 Yes 或 No，而是以完整的句子來表達 Yes 或 No 的概念。題目句問對方是否去過遊樂園，該選項回答「go there again（再去一次）」，間接表示自己已經去過，等同於回答 Yes，同時建議下次一同前往，告知對方往後的行動。

20 以 but 表示轉折加上補充說明。

題目分析 **The board of directors called an emergency meeting this afternoon.**

本題為直述句，由「The board . . . called」傳達一項事實。

選項分析

(A) But I have to check my schedule first. ▶ 答案

PART 2 中，最新出現的回答方式為使用 but 回答，表示「補充說明」或「否定對方，但換個角度來說有好處」，屬於「轉折」的概念。題目句向對方傳達召開緊急會議一事，而該選項使用 but 回答「我知道，但是我得先確認一下我的時間」，間接表示自己不確定是否會參加，屬於「I don't know」的回答方式，因此答案為 (A)。

(B) The chairman wants to retire soon. ❹ 相關單字陷阱

該選項使用 chairman（董事長），與題目句中的 directors（理事）有所關聯，屬於陷阱選項。又此答覆表示「原因」，應搭配以 Why 開頭的問句較為適當。

(C) They are in the meeting room. ❹ 相同單字陷阱

該選項故意使用與題目句相同的單字 meeting，屬於陷阱選項。此答覆應搭配以 Where 開頭的問句較為適當，例如：「Where are the directors?」（請問理事們在哪裡？）。

21 When 問句的特殊回答方式——提及來源或地點反問對方。

題目分析 **When is this plane supposed to take off?**

本題關鍵字為「when、plane、take off」，「is supposed to（預計要……）」詢問對方往後的計畫。

選項分析

(A) At the airport. ❹ 相關單字陷阱

airport 與題目句中的 plane 有所關聯，屬於陷阱選項。又 At the airport 表示地點，應該配以 Where 開頭的問句較為適當。When 問句題的選項中，至少會出現一個回答地點的錯誤選項。

(B) Isn't it listed on the itinerary? ▶ 答案

When 問句的答案通常會使用時間副詞，回答特定的時間、或是動作發生的時間點等。但是新制測驗中，常使用高難度的回答方式：提及地點或來源。例如問句為「When will . . . arrive?」（何時抵達……？），正確答案為「It's delayed at the airport.」（被耽擱在機場）。雖然回答中出現地點名詞 airport，但是因為加上動詞 delay（耽擱），具有時間的概念，等同於間接回答「尚未抵達」，故為正確答案。而該選項回答 on the itinerary，乍看之下像是回答地點，但是名詞 itinerary（行程表）與時間有關，因此該選項可以作為答案。聆聽題目時，請務必聽清楚 Where 或 When 問句後方連接的動詞，以便找出正確答案。

(C) Flying back to Orlando. ❷ 適用其他問句

flying 與題目句中 take off（起飛）有所關聯，屬於陷阱選項，應搭配以 Where 開頭的問句較為適當。

22 改寫題目句中的單字、或採間接回答的方式。

題目分析 **Should we take a train or a bus to the convention center?**

本題為選擇疑問句，解題關鍵為「Should we take」、「train or bus」，請對方從兩種交通方式中選出一種，時態為未來式。

選項分析

(A) Neither was finished. ❺ 時態有誤

選擇疑問句常見的回答有：❶二擇一：A / B / either ❷兩者都可以：both / whichever / It doesn't matter. ❸兩者皆非：neither / I'm fine. thanks.。雖然 (A) 回答 neither，看似為正確答案，但是題目句為未來式（should），該選項卻使用過去式 was finished，時態不正確，因此不能作為答案。

(B) It's right on the train route. ▶ 答案

回答選擇疑問句時，通常會重複提到 A 或 B 其中一個選擇，但在新制測驗中，則會改寫為相關單字回答。像該選項的 train route 間接表示選擇 train，故為正確答案。

(C) At the earliest time. ❷ 適用其他問句

at the earliest time（盡可能愈早愈好）表示時間概念，應搭配以 When 開頭的問句較為適當。

23 提出與直述句相關的問題。

題目分析 **Our company will announce the release of our new product next week.**

本題為直述句，解題關鍵為「Our company will announce the release」，題目使用未來式（will）。

選項分析

(A) The response to the product was very positive. ❺ 時態有誤

題目使用未來式，表示新產品即將上市，但該選項卻以過去式回答產品獲得了正面的評價，因此不能作為答案。形容詞 positive（正面的）表達的是一種狀態，應搭配以 How was 開頭的問句較為適當。

(B) Is there any promotional event? ▶ 答案

直述句帶有向對方徵求同意或確認的概念，回答方式有❶同意、附和對方並補充說明 ❷不同意 ❸告知往後的行動 ❹反問對方額外的資訊。該選項針對新產品上市（the release of our new product）一事反問對方是否有宣傳活動，等同於附和對方並額外提問，故為正確答案。

(C) I was there, too. ❸ 主詞有誤

根據題目句，無從得知該選項的 there 指的地點為何，因此不能作為答案。該回答適合搭配「John was at the conference.（John 剛參加了會議）」，表示同意、附和的概念。

24 【勸說、建議、請求】聽到選項出現 almost/already/still，就是答案。

題目分析 **Why don't you register for the staff health and safety training?**

本題的解題關鍵為「why don't you」和「register for」，表示勸說或建議的概念。

選項分析

(A) No, I will get there on time. ❷ 適用其他問句

該選項適合用來回答向對方確認的附加問句，如「You won't be late for you doctor's appointment, will you?」（你不會超過約診時間才到吧？）。通常不會以 No 來拒絕勸說、建議或請求的問句。

(B) I already attended that two weeks ago. ▶ 答案

問句表示勸說或建議時，常見回答方式有❶同意：Sure / Of course ❷拒絕：I'm sorry but . . .。但在新制測驗中，則會使用較婉轉的方式表達同意或拒絕。該選項回答「我兩週前就參加過了」，委婉拒絕對方的建議，故為正確答案。already（已經）/ actually（實際上）/ just（剛剛）皆為答案中常見的副詞，請務必熟記。

(C) There were 100 people present. ❹ 相關單字陷阱

100 people（一百人）與題目句中的 register for（報名）有所關聯，屬於陷阱選項。該選項回答的是數字，應搭配以 How many（有多少數量）開頭的問句較為適當。

25 婉轉的回答方式——結果還沒出來。

題目分析 **How many of our branches achieved record sales this year?**

本題關鍵字為「How many」、「achieved」和「sales」，詢問數量。

選項分析

(A) The report's coming out this Friday. ▶ 答案

本題詢問「有幾間分公司」，該選項回答「相關報告要等到週五才會出爐」，間接表示「結果還沒出來，所以不太清楚」的概念。PART 2 中，最常出現的回答方式之一為「I don't know」（我不知道）。

❶ 我不知道（I don't know）
❷ 請向其他人詢問（Ask Mark）
❸ 我確認一下（Let me check）
❹ 尚未決定（It's not decided yet）
❺ 我沒印象（I don't remember）
❻ 我沒聽說過這件事（I haven't heard anything）
❼ 沒有人知道這件事（Who knows）

以上皆屬於「我不知道」的回答方式。一般會使用動詞「check」（確認）表達「請你確認看看」，但是有時候也會使用名詞 manual（手冊）、instructions（說明書）、report（報告）來表達同樣的概念。

(B) Yes, we are expecting a sales increase. ❶ 不能以 Yes 或 No 回答

Wh- 問句不會使用 Yes 或 No 來回答。

(C) Our revenue is rather high. ❹ 相關單字陷阱

revenue 與題目句中的 sales 有所關聯，屬於陷阱選項。該選項應搭配以 How much 開頭，詢問「價格」或「分量」的問句較為適當。

26 不以 Yes 或 No 回答助動詞問句的情況：①告知往後的行動 ②間接說明狀況

題目分析 **Have you talked to Sylvia Hanson about the contract yet?**

本題的解題關鍵為「Have you talked」。

選項分析

(A) Yes, they are doing well. ❸ 主詞有誤

題目詢問的是 you，選項卻回答 they，因此不能作為答案。

(B) She'll be back from vacation tomorrow. ▶ 答案

回答助動詞開頭的問句時，若採間接回答的方式，告知或解釋沒有做的原因，就會省略掉 No。該選項回答「她明天才會回來（所以尚未跟她說）」，間接解釋為何自己還沒說的原因。

(C) John didn't have much contact with me. ❹ 發音相似陷阱

contact 和題目句中 contract 的發音相似，為陷阱選項。回答人名（John）應搭配以 Who 開頭的問句、或是以 Where 開頭詢問來源或對象的問句較為適當。

27 以反問方式確認對方建議的事項。

題目分析 **Let's place an order for more experimental equipment.**

本題為表示勸說或建議訂購的直述句，解題關鍵為「Let's place an order」。

選項分析

(A) A couple of projectors. ❹ 相關單字陷阱

projectors（投影機）與題目句中的 equipment（設備）有所關聯，屬於陷阱選項。且該選項使用 a couple of，表示數量的概念，應搭配以 How many（有多少數量）開頭的問句較為適當。

(B) Isn't the project being postponed? ▶ 答案

Let's 用於表示建議或勸說的句子當中。一般會直接回答同意或拒絕，像是「I'm sorry」（對不起）。但在新制測驗中，則會以一整句話表達同意或拒絕與否。本題建議訂購實驗設備，該選項反問對方計畫不是延期了嗎，間接表達拒絕對方的概念，因此答案為 (B)。

(C) Okay, that looks heavy. ❹ 相關單字陷阱

乍看之下 okay 像是同意對方的建議，但後方使用 heavy（重的），僅與題目句中的 equipment 有所關聯，不能作為答案。該選項應搭配「Could you help me . . . ?」（方便幫我……嗎？）請求對方幫忙的問句較為適當。

28 間接回答——間接告知狀況。

題目分析 **How often do you go to the gym these days?**

本題為以 How often 開頭的問句，關鍵字為「How often、go、gym」，答案應回答頻率或次數。

選項分析

(A) It's been under renovation for a month. ▶ 答案

回答 How often 問句時，通常會提到頻率或次數，像是 once a week（一週一次）。但是若為高難度的回答方式，則會像該選項一樣，回答 gym（體育館）正在維修（under renovation），間接說明現在的狀況沒辦法去。

(B) Two days ago. ❷ 適用其他問句

two days ago（兩天前）表示時間，應搭配以 when 開頭的問句較為適當。

(C) You can use my membership. ❹ 相關單字陷阱

membership 僅與題目句中的 gym 有所關聯，不能作為答案。該選項應搭配以 How can 開頭，詢問方法的問句較為適當。

29 針對問題提出解決方案。

題目分析 **Your car doesn't seem to have enough space for those boxes.**

本題為直述句，關鍵字為「car、doesn't、enough space」。

選項分析

(A) I left them on your desk. ❷ 適用其他問句

on your desk（在你的桌上）使用表示地點的副詞，應搭配以 Where 開頭的問句較為適當。

(B) We're renting a bus. ▶ 答案

本題提出「空間不足」的問題，而該選項提出解決方案為「租巴士」，故為正確答案。bus（巴士）和 car（汽車）同屬於車子類，請熟記此種回答方式。

(C) At the stationery store. ❷ 適用其他問句

At the stationery store（文具店）表示地點，應搭配以 Where 開頭的問句較為適當。

30 針對對方的建議，可以回答「我自己來就行了」。

題目分析 **I can assist you with the travel arrangements, if you want.**

本題句子表示勸説或建議，關鍵字為「I can、assist、you」。

選項分析

(A) No, it's not mine. ❷ 適用其他問句

該選項適用 be 動詞開頭的問句，像是「Is it . . . ?」。

(B) Just a few, if you can lend me one. ❹ 相關單字陷阱

lend（借）僅與題目句中的 assist（幫忙）有所關聯，不能作為答案。該選項應搭配問句「Do you want . . . ?」較為適當。

(C) I don't think that will be necessary. ▶ 答案

該選項回答「我想應該不需要」，拒絕對方的建議，故為正確答案。針對表示勸説或建議的句子，除了回答接受或拒絕之外，也可以表示「我自己來就行了」的概念作為答案。

31 委婉表示「我不知道」。

題目分析 **How did Mr. Lewis like the report?**

本題關鍵字為「How、Mr. Lewis like、report」，詢問 Lewis 的想法。

選項分析

(A) From the library. ❷ 適用其他問句

the library（圖書館）為地點，應搭配以 Where 開頭的問句較為適當。

(B) I gave that to him. ❸ 主詞有誤

題目詢問 Mr. Lewis 的想法，回答時主詞要用 Mr. Lewis，但該選項使用 I，因此不能作為答案。

(C) He spoke to the director about it. ▶ 答案

「他跟主管談論過這件事了」，提到第三者，間接表示自己「不知道」，因此答案為 (C)。請特別熟記，若選項中提及題目中未出現的第三者姓名或職稱，並使用過去式動詞回答，等同於間接表示「請向那個人詢問」。

PART 3

Questions 32-34 refer to the following conversation.

W	Excuse me, my name is Jennifer. My colleague made a reservation for our meeting here at Crown Hotel and he told me the receptionist will let us know where to go when we get here.	32-D 32-A 32-C
M	Ma'am. Do you have the reservation number?	
W	Hmm . . 32 I am afraid not, but I didn't think I would need it.	
M 33	Oh, well . . . my shift just started. I haven't checked the list for this afternoon yet. What time are you going to start the meeting?	
W	We are supposed to start at 7 P.M. and we need a conference room for ten. Why don't you check the record on your computer? It should be booked under our company name, Huston Consulting.	
M 34	Sorry, I don't see any reservation under that name. Let me give my supervisor a call. He should know. Could you wait in the lounge? It will take no more than five minutes.	34-D 34-A

32. What problem is the woman having?
(A) She doesn't know ~~where the hotel~~ is.
(B) She doesn't know the reservation number.
(C) She is ~~late~~ for the meeting.
(D) She ~~wants to make a reservation~~ for a meeting room.

女／問題／前
→ 注意表示否定的句子。

33. What does the man imply when he says, "My shift just started"?
(A) He is a ~~new employee~~.
(B) He cannot answer her question.
(C) He ~~lacks experience~~.
(D) He could not find any reservation.

掌握說話者意圖／中
→ 指定句前後對白。

34. What is the woman asked to do?
(A) Call a supervisor (B) Come back later
(C) Stay in the hotel (D) Check the reservation record

男／要求事項／後／要求女子的事
→ 男子的對白／後半段

第 32-34 題 對話

女：打擾一下，我叫珍妮佛。我的同事在皇冠飯店這裡訂了一間會議室，他告訴我當我們抵達時，接待人員會告知我們會議室地點。

男：您好，女士。您有預約號碼嗎？

女：唔，恐怕沒有，我不覺得我會需要用到預約號碼。

男：喔，嗯……我才剛開始當班，所以還沒檢視今天下午的預訂清單。你們的會議將於何時開始？

女：我們應該會在晚間七點開始，且我們需要一間十人的會議室。你何不檢視電腦上的紀錄？應該是以我們的公司名稱預約的，休士頓顧問公司。

男：抱歉，我沒看到以這個公司名稱所做的預約。請讓我打個電話給我的主管，他應該知情。能否請您在大廳稍作等待？不會超過五分鐘。

32. 女子有何問題？
(A) 她不知道飯店在何處。
(B) 她不知道預約號碼。
(C) 她開會遲到了。
(D) 她想要預訂一間會議室。

33. 當男子說「我才剛開始當班」，他有何暗示？
(A) 他是新進員工。
(B) 他無法回答她的問題。
(C) 他缺乏經驗。
(D) 他找不到任何預定資料。

34. 女子被要求做何事？
(A) 打給主管 (B) 稍後再回來
(C) 待在飯店內 (D) 檢視預約紀錄

32 若題目詢問問題為何，答案通常會出現在第一和第二段對白中。

STEP 1 **說話者會在對話開頭直接提出問題，或者由第一個說話者先提出問題後，再由第二個說話者反應問題所在，因此通常可以在第一段或第二段對白中找出答案。**

本題詢問女子碰到什麼問題。男子問女子「Do you have the reservation number?」，接著女子回答「I am afraid not.」，提到預約號碼，因此答案為 (B)。

STEP 2 **陷阱選項和錯誤選項**

(A) She doesn't know where the hotel is.

▶「here at Crown Hotel」中提到飯店，因此該選項有誤。

(B) She doesn't know the reservation number. ▶ 答案

(C) She is late for the meeting. ▶ 雖然對話中提到 meeting，但是無法得知「late」與否。

(D) She wants to make a reservation for a meeting room. ▶ 預約的人應為「my colleague」。

33 請先刪除與引號內字面意思相同的選項。▶ my shift just started

STEP 1 **若選項使用與內相同的單字、或是字面意思相同的敘述，來表達說話者意圖時，通常不會是正確答案。**

指定句後方說道：「I haven't checked the list for this afternoon yet.」，由此可以得知男子剛交班完畢，尚未確認下午的工作清單，這表示他無法回答女子的問題，因此答案為 (B)。

STEP 2 **陷阱選項和錯誤選項**

(A) He is a new employee.

▶「new employee」僅與對話中的「just started」有所關聯，不能作為答案。

(B) He cannot answer her question. ▶ 答案

(C) He lacks of experience.

▶「lack of experience」僅與對話中的「just started」有所關聯，不能作為答案。

(D) He could not find any reservation.

34 題目使用被動語態時，答案會出現在另一方以 You 開頭的對白中。

STEP 1 **若題目使用被動語態時，請仔細聆聽表示「勸說、建議或要求」的對白，以便找出答案。「What is the woman asked to do?」指的是「她被男子要求什麼事情？」，因此請從男子的對白中找出答案。**

後半段對話中，男子說道：「Could you wait in the lounge?」，請女子待在休息室等候。而前半段對話中提到地點：「here at Crown Hotel」，表示這段話指的是飯店休息室，因此答案為 (C)。

STEP 2 陷阱選項和錯誤選項

(A) Call a supervisor ▶ 指男子下一步動作，並非答案。
(B) Come back later
(C) Stay in the hotel ▶ 答案
(D) Check the reservation record
▶ 由「I don't see」得知為男子負責的事，因此不能作為答案。

字彙 **colleague** 同事 **make a reservation** 預訂 **receptionist** 接待員 **shift** 輪班工作時間 **be supposed to V** 應該 **conference room** 會議室 **book** 預訂 **supervisor** 管理者；主管

Questions 35-37 refer to the following conversation.

M	Hi, 35 I found an advertisement for your hotel in the newspaper, and I'm interested in staying there for my vacation next month. Could you tell me more about it?	35-A 35-C
W 36	I would be happy to. We are a five-star commercial hotel with a European architectural style, elegant decoration and top quality facilities, as well as professional services. The best thing is our hotel is located in the heart of London downtown, where there are few other hotels. You have direct access to many city attractions.	36-A 36-D
M 37	Great, I'm actually planning to visit the Historical Museum and some famous old buildings such as cinemas and restaurants. It sounds like the perfect place for me.	37-C 37-B

35. How did the man hear about the hotel?
(A) From an ~~online~~ advertisement
(B) From a coworker
(C) From a newspaper ~~article~~
(D) From a media commercial

男子／關鍵字 hotel／前
→ 以過去式提及資訊來源。

36. According to the woman, how is the hotel different from its competitors?
(A) It offers a high-quality ~~service~~.
(B) It has a great reputation.
(C) It has proximity to local attractions.
(D) It has ~~many locations~~.

女子／hotel 的特色／中
→ 注意形容詞最高級。

37. What will the man do in London?
(A) Go sightseeing
(B) Watch ~~movies~~
(C) Visit an ~~exhibition~~
(D) Work in city renovation

男子／未來／關鍵字 London／後
→ I will . . . ／ I am planning

第 35-37 題 對話

男：嗨，我在報紙上發現了你們飯店的廣告，我有意在下個月前往度假。妳能否告知我更多的相關資訊？

女：樂意之至。我們是一家五星級的商務飯店，擁有歐式的建築風格、雅致的裝潢及頂級的設施，更有專業的服務。最棒的是本飯店坐落於倫敦市中心，少有其他飯店比鄰。您可由此直達許多市區的景點。

男：太好了，事實上我正打算參觀歷史博物館以及其他著名的古蹟建築，諸如電影院及餐廳。聽起來，這裡完全適合我。

35. 男子如何得知飯店的相關資訊？
(A) 從網路廣告得知
(B) 從同事那裡得知
(C) 從報紙上的一篇文章得知
(D) 從媒體廣告得知

36. 根據女子所言，此飯店與其競爭業者的區別在於？
(A) 它提供優質的服務。
(B) 它頗負盛名。
(C) 它鄰近當地景點。
(D) 它有許多連鎖分店。

37. 男子將在倫敦從事何事？
(A) 觀光旅遊　(B) 看電影
(C) 參觀展覽　(D) 進行市容改造

35 答案會出現在關鍵字 hotel 的前後句當中。

STEP 1 **當題目詢問特定關鍵字時，通常會先聽到關鍵字，再聽到答案的內容，但在新制測驗中，有時反而會先聽到答案的內容，之後才聽到關鍵字。**

本題詢問男子如何得知這家 hotel，因此請仔細聆聽男子的第一句對白，從 hotel 前後方找出答案。由「I found an advertisement . . . newspaper」可知得知男子透過報紙上廣告得知 hotel，因此答案為 (D)「透過媒體廣告」。

STEP 2 **陷阱選項和錯誤選項**

(A) From an online advertisement
▶ 由「an advertisement . . . newspaper」可以得知該敘述有誤。

(B) From a coworker

(C) From a newspaper article ▶ 未提及 article。

(D) From a media commercial ▶ 答案

36 題目中出現 different 或 special 等類似單字時，指的是對話中提及的特色或差異。

STEP 1 **若題目詢問特色或差異時，可以對應至對話中的形容詞最高級或 best。**

「The best thing is our hotel is located . . .」提到飯店位置，後方又提到「You have direct access to many city attractions」，表示飯店位置的特色為鄰近許多觀光景點，因此答案為 (C)。

STEP 2 **陷阱選項和錯誤選項**

(A) It offers a high-quality service.
▶ 由「five-star」可能會聯想到「high quality」，但是對話中並未提到「service」的特色。

(B) It has a great reputation.

(C) It has proximity to local attractions. ▶ 答案

(D) It has many locations. ▶「location」僅與「located」有所關聯，不能作為答案。

37 後半段對話中，未來資訊的答案會出現在「I'll . . .」或「I'm . . .」後方。

STEP 1 大部分的對話會以「過去→未來」的順序進行，因此若題目的問題與未來相關，答案會出現在後半段對話中。

後半段對話中，男子說道：「I'm actually planning to visit the Historical Museum and some famous old buildings」，此段話表示男子打算去觀光。

→ 選項會將對話中的詳細內容，改寫成較為廣義的敘述。
visit Historical Museum、famous old buildings → (A) Go sightseeing

STEP 2 陷阱選項和錯誤選項

(A) Go sightseeing ▶ 答案
(B) Watch movies ▶ 聽到 cinema 可能會聯想到 movie。
(C) Visit an exhibition ▶ 聽到 museum 可能會聯想到 exhibition。
(D) Work in city renovation

字彙 advertisement 廣告 commercial 商業的；商務的 architectural 有關建築的 attraction 有吸引力的事物；景點 reputation 名聲 proximity 鄰近

Questions 38-40 refer to the following conversation with three speakers.

M1	38 I need to buy a new dishwasher. My old one is broken. It's the third time this month. Bella, Patrick, can you recommend any brand? I have no idea where to buy appliances or electronics here.	38-C
W 39	Have you heard of a brand called Varelle? I recently bought a refrigerator from Varelle, and it's great. Much more energy efficient than other refrigerators of similar price.	38-D
M2	I second this suggestion. Actually, I recently got an e-mail with a 50% discount coupon and other online special offers. If you buy any item from Ocean Appliances, you will get a voucher for dinnerware.	40-D
M1 40	That's unbelievable! Will you forward me the e-mail with that offer, Patrick?	
M2	Sure, as soon as I get back to my office, I will do that for you.	40-A

38. What are the speakers discussing?
(A) Cooking recipes　**(B) Home appliances**
(C) Electronics ~~stores~~　(D) Brand ~~logos~~

三人對話／主旨／前
→ 前半段對話

39. What does the woman like about the product she bought?
(A) It is fully functional.　(B) It is ~~inexpensive~~.
(C) It is energy efficient.　(D) It comes in various colors.

單人說話者——女子／關鍵字 product
→ 女子的對白、product 優點

40. What does Patrick agree to do?
(A) ~~Visit~~ an office　(B) Call a store
(C) Forward a message　(D) Apply a ~~discount~~

Patrick／同意／後
→ 對前一句話的反應

第 38-40 題 三人對話

男1：我需要買一台新的洗碗機，舊的洗碗機壞了，這是這個月第三次了。貝拉、派翠克，你們有沒有推薦的品牌？我不知道這附近哪裡可以買到家用電器或是電子設備。

女：你有聽過瓦勒爾這個牌子嗎？我最近才剛買了一台該牌的冰箱，非常好用。它比同價位的他牌冰箱更節能省電。

男2：我附議。事實上，我最近收到一封電子郵件，提供了五折的折價券及其他的線上購物優惠。如果你向大洋家用電器購買產品，便可獲得餐具組的禮券。

男1：真令人難以置信！你能轉寄給我這封提供禮券的電子郵件嗎，派翠克？

男2：當然，我一回到辦公室，就馬上轉寄給你。

38. 談話者正在討論何事？
(A) 烹飪食譜 (B) 家用電器
(C) 電器商場 (D) 品牌商標

39. 關於女子所購入的產品，女子喜歡何特點？
(A) 功能齊全。 (B) 價錢低廉。
(C) 節能省電。 (D) 有多種顏色可選。

40. 派翠克同意做何事？
(A) 參訪辦公室 (B) 去電商家
(C) 轉寄訊息 (D) 使用折扣

38 三人對話題組的第一題，通常會詢問三人的職業或對話主旨。

STEP 1 **有別於雙人對話，三人對話題組會針對三人的共同點或差異提問。第一題會詢問說話者的職業或整篇對話的主旨，等同於詢問三人的共同點。而主旨題的解題方式則與雙人對話相同，請先看完選項，再聆聽前半段對話內容，並從中找出答案。**

「I need to buy a new dishwasher. My old one is broken.」當中提到洗碗機（dishwasher），因此答案為 (B) Home appliances。

→ 選項會將對話中的詳細內容，改寫成較為廣義的敘述。
dishwasher（洗碗機）→ (B) Home appliances（家用電器）

STEP 2 **陷阱選項和錯誤選項**

(A) Cooking recipes ▶ 聽到 dishwasher 可能會聯想到 cooking。
(B) Home appliances ▶ 答案
(C) Electronics stores ▶ 聽到 refrigerator 可能會聯想到 electronics，但對話中並未提及 stores。
(D) Brand logos ▶ 雖然對話中有提到品牌，但並未談到標誌。

39 第二題通常會指定某個人，並針對此人提問。

STEP 1 三人對話題組中，題目會用 the woman/man 或人名來指定某個說話者，並針對此人提出問題。

本題詢問該篇三人對話中，女子喜歡產品的哪一部份。第一名男子提到 brand，請對方推薦品牌。接著女子回答 Varelle，並說道「it's great. Much more energy efficient」，稱讚該品牌並提出產品優點，因此答案為 (C)。

STEP 2 陷阱選項和錯誤選項

(A) It is fully functional.
(B) It is inexpensive. ▶ 聽到 similar price 可能會誤會為價格。
(C) It is energy efficient. ▶ 答案
(D) It comes in various colors. ▶ 對話中並未提到顏色。

40 「同意」指肯定前一句話的內容。

STEP 1 題目的「同意」指以 Sure、Of course 等話語回應前一句要求或建議，因此聆聽重點並非題目句主詞所說的話，請從前一個人的對白中找出答案。

本題詢問 Patrick 同意的事情，因此答案會出現在 Patrick 回答的前一句對白中。Patrick 前一句話說道：「Will you forward me the e-mail with that offer, Patrick?」，接著他以 Sure 表示同意寄送郵件的要求，因此答案為 (C)。

STEP 2 陷阱選項和錯誤選項

(A) Visit an office ▶ 對話中有提到 office，但沒有提到 visit，因此不能作為答案。
(B) Call a store
(C) Forward a message ▶ 答案
(D) Apply a discount ▶ 重複使用對話中的 discount，與該題無關。

字彙 dishwasher 洗碗機　broken 損壞的　recommend 推薦　appliances 家用電器
electronics 電子設備　recently 近來　efficient 效率高的　similar 相似的
dinnerware 餐具組　forward 轉寄（信件或電子郵件）　as soon as 一……就……

Questions 41-43 refer to the following conversation.

W 41	Derrick, did you have any chance to look over the charts and figures for our meeting tomorrow?	
M	Oh yes, I did. I have reviewed all the materials. You did a good job and have nothing to worry about. All the information is very well organized.	41-B 41-A
W 42	Okay, then we are all set for the conference. By the way, what time are you going to leave tomorrow? I'm going to book a train now. How about a ten o'clock train?	
M 43	I am so sorry to say this, but some important new clients plan to visit and I might have lunch with them, so I might not be able to go to the meeting. You might have to give the presentation by yourself.	42-B 42-C
W	But as you know, I don't have enough experience to handle such an important meeting.	43-B 43-D
M	Don't worry. You are all prepared for this job. Everything will be fine.	

41. What did the woman ask the man to do?

(A) ~~Organize~~ a meeting
(B) Review ~~her application~~
(C) Check some data
(D) Submit some documents

女子／要求／前
→ 題目順序＝對話先後順序

42. What does the woman plan to do today?

(A) Reserve a table
(B) ~~Meet a client~~
(C) ~~Give a presentation~~
(D) Book a train

女子／計畫／關鍵字 **today**
→ 未來式和相關動詞用法

43. Why does the woman say, "I don't have enough experience to handle such an important meeting"?

(A) To express concern about working alone
(B) To give an ~~excuse for a delay~~
(C) To get feedback from the man
(D) To ask the man for some ~~advice~~

掌握說話者意圖／女子
→ 指定句前後對白

第 41-43 題 對話

女：德瑞克，有沒有可能請你檢視一下明天開會要用的圖表及數據？

男：喔，我看過了，所有的資料我都再檢查過了。妳做得很好，不需要擔心，所有的資料都整理得井井有條。

女：好，那明天的會議我們就都預備好了。順便問一下，明天你何時會離開？我現在要預訂火車票，十點的火車如何？

男：我得說聲抱歉，有幾個重要的新客戶預計會來拜訪我，我應該會與他們共進午餐，所以我有可能無法參加明天的會議，妳也許得獨自做簡報了。

女：但你是知道的，我沒有足夠的經驗應付如此重要的會議。

男：別擔心，妳已經做好萬全的準備了，一切都會沒事的。

41. 女子要求男子做何事？
(A) 籌辦會議
(B) 審查她的書面申請
(C) 核查數據資料
(D) 繳交文件

42. 女子今日預計做何事？
(A) 預訂餐廳
(B) 會見客戶
(C) 做簡報
(D) 訂火車票

43. 為何女子會說：「我沒有足夠的經驗應付如此重要的會議」？
(A) 對獨自作業表示擔憂
(B) 為延誤工作推託
(C) 取得男子的意見回饋
(D) 尋求男子的建議

41 題目順序和對話先後順序一致。

STEP 1 **本題詢問女子要求男子事情，這類題型的答案通常會出現在後半段對話中。但是該題放在題組第一題，因此解題時，請務必考量到題目順序會符合對話先後順序這點。**

女子第一句話說道：「did you have any chance to look over the charts and figures for our meeting tomorrow?」，詢問男子是否確認過資料內容，因此答案為 (C)。

→ 選項會將對話中的詳細內容，改寫成較為廣義的敘述。
look over the charts and figures → (C) check some data

STEP 2 **陷阱選項和錯誤選項**

(A) Organize a meeting ▶ 聽到 organized 可能會聯想成該選項。
(B) Review her application ▶ 對話中並未提及「her application」。
(C) Check some data ▶ 答案
(D) Submit some documents

42 對話中會以 I'll . . . 或 I'm planning/going to 等未來式用法表達未來的資訊。

STEP 1 對話中會以未來式和相關動詞用法表達未來的資訊。本題詢問女子的計畫，因此請從女子所說的話中，確認使用未來式的內容。

「I'm going to book a train now.」表示她要預訂火車票，因此答案為 (D)。

STEP 2 陷阱選項和錯誤選項

(A) Reserve a table
(B) Meet a client ▶ 為男子所說的話。
(C) Give a presentation ▶ 為男子告知女子明天要做的事情，並非答案。
(D) Book a train ▶ 答案

43 題目詢問引號內的說話者意圖時，請確認指定句前方的連接詞。

STEP 1 本題詢問指定句在對話中代表的意思，因此請確認前後對白的內容，並找出最符合的答案。

男子說道：「可能要由妳負責報告（You might have to give the presentation by yourself.）」。接著女子回答 but 以及「I don't have enough experience to handle such an important meeting」（但是我的經驗不足，無法應付如此重要的會議），表示她擔心無法獨立進行報告，因此答案為 (A)。

STEP 2 陷阱選項和錯誤選項

(A) To express concern about working alone ▶ 答案
(B) To give an excuse for a delay ▶ 聽到 but 可能會聯想到此類負面內容。
(C) To get feedback from the man
(D) To ask the man for some advice
▶ 聽到「don't have enough experience」可能會聯想成 advice。

字彙 look over（快速）檢查　all set 準備好　handle 處理　application 申請（書）
reserve 預訂　express 表達　concern 擔憂；顧慮　excuse 藉口

Questions 44-46 refer to the following conversation.

M	Hello, Jennifer. I was about to call you. Did you want to see me?	
W 44	Yes, Mr. Becker. The Transportation Authority called yesterday and said they wanted an update on the new rail terminal construction. How's the work going? Any delays?	44-A
M 45	I thought there might be some delays, but in fact we're ahead of schedule. They will be able to open the terminal one month earlier than planned.	
W	Oh! I wasn't expecting that. You know it is nice not to rush to meet the deadline.	45-B 45-C
M	I'm pleased about it, too. But is there anything else we should check? I just want to make sure before I call them.	
W 46	Well, why don't you wait for our subcontractors? They are handling some minor details, so things depend on their progress. They should be sending me a status report tomorrow.	46-B

44. What are the speakers mainly discussing?
(A) A road ~~repair~~
(B) A construction project
(C) A train delay
(D) Public transportation options

主旨／前
→ 注意對話開頭的內容。

45. What does the woman imply when she says, "Oh! I wasn't expecting that"?
(A) She has not prepared for a meeting.
(B) She ~~has forgotten~~ the deadline.
(C) She was not informed of the change.
(D) She is happy to hear some news.

掌握說話者意圖／女子
→ 女子對男子的話的反應。

46. What will the woman receive soon?
(A) A progress report
(B) A signed ~~contract~~
(C) A construction invoice
(D) A traveler's check

女子／未來／後
→ 注意未來式或助動詞 would/should 用法。

第 44-46 題 對話

男：嗨，珍妮佛。我才剛想要打電話給妳，妳找我？

女：是的，貝克先生。交通局昨天來電詢問新火車站的施工進度。工作進行的如何？有任何延誤嗎？

男：我原也以為應該會有些延誤，但實際上我們的進度超前。他們將能比計畫提前一個月啟用新的火車站。

女：喔！真沒想到。很高興不需倉促加工趕最後交期。

男：這情形我也很樂見，但是否有其他需要我們進行確認之處？在回電給他們之前，我只是想再確認一下。

女：唔，你何不再等等承包商？他們正在處理一些小細節，所以事情還需取決於他們的進度，他們明天應該就會寄進度報告過來給我。

44. 對話者主要討論何事？
(A) 道路維修 (B) 營建計畫
(C) 火車誤點 (D) 大眾運輸選項

45. 當女子說：「喔！真沒想到」，她暗指什麼？
(A) 她沒準備好要開會討論。
(B) 她忘了最後期限。
(C) 她未被告知有變動。
(D) 某些消息令她喜聞樂見。

46. 女子即將收到何物？
(A) 進度報告
(B) 簽署好的合約
(C) 工程費用請款單
(D) 旅行支票

44 若題目為主旨題，答案通常會出現在第一和第二段對白中。

STEP 1 題目詢問主旨或目的時，答案有 90% 的機率會出現在對話開頭部分。

「an update on the new rail terminal construction」和「How's the work going?」表示內容與 construction 有關。

→ 選項會將對話中的詳細內容，改寫成較為廣義的敘述。
a new rail terminal construction → (B) a construction project

STEP 2 陷阱選項和錯誤選項

(A) A road repair ▶「a new rail terminal」為新建工程，但 repair 指「修理」，不能作為答案。
(B) A construction project ▶ 答案
(C) A train delay
(D) Public transportation options

45 題目詢問說話者意圖時，請以該「指定句」為基準，確認前後連接的句子。

STEP 1 說話者意圖題通常考的是對前一人說的話的答覆或反應，因此若選項包含前一人對白中的「特定單字」或相關敘述，就是正確答案。

指定句前方男子說道：「They will be able to open the terminal one month earlier than planned.」，表示「會比預定計畫提早開通」。接著女子回答：「Oh! I wasn't expecting that.」並補充說道「太好了，這樣就不用倉促加工趕最後期限了（it is nice not to rush to meet the deadline）」，表示她對於男子所說的話感到開心，因此答案為 (D)。

STEP 2 陷阱選項和錯誤選項

(A) She has not prepared for a meeting.

(B) She has forgotten the deadline.

▶ 重複使用「deadline」，且「forgotten」（忘記）有誤，不能作為答案。

(C) She was not ~~informed~~ of the change.

▶ 重複使用指定句中「not」的概念，且該敘述有誤，不能作為答案。

(D) She is happy to hear some news. ▶ 答案

46 題目詢問建議、要求或未來計畫時，答案會出現在後半段對話中。

STEP 1 一般來說，未來計畫的答案會出現在最後一段對白中。

本題詢問女子將會收到什麼東西，因此請特別留意女子提到「I'll receive . . .」或「They will send me . . .」，等同於其他人會寄東西給女子。後半段對話中，女子說道「They should be sending me a status report tomorrow.」，表示她將收到報告書，因此答案為 (A)。

STEP 2 陷阱選項和錯誤選項

(A) A progress report ▶ 答案

(B) A signed contract ▶ 聽到「subcontractors」可能會聯想成該選項。

(C) A construction invoice

(D) A traveler's check

字彙 **be about to V** 剛要…… **update** 新資訊；更新 **construction** 建設 **delay** 延誤 **rush** 倉促行事 **meet the deadline** 趕上截止期限 **subcontractor** 轉包商；承攬商 **progress** 進展；進度 **invoice** （供之後支付的）費用清單

Questions 47-49 refer to the following conversation.

M	Hi, Mary, 47 I'd like to discuss the sales report on our medical chairs.	47-C 47-B
W	Sure, anything wrong on the report?	
M	Well . . . . Actually, 48 the figures were rather disappointing. The effect of our recent advertising campaign with actors was not as good as we expected.	47-A 48-A
W	Hmm . . . I think we'll need to change our strategies and use different advertising methods.	49-A
M	49 I was thinking we could try using social network services for the rest of the year. Social media is becoming one of the most effective ways of spreading the word about something.	
W	That's a good idea. We can offer some promotions to customers who post their picture with one of our chairs.	49-C

47. What type of company do the speakers most likely work for?
(A) An ~~advertising~~ company
(B) An ~~office~~ furniture store
(C) A medical equipment manufacturer
(D) A digital camera store

職業 / 前
→ our / your / this / here

48. Why is the man disappointed?
(A) An actor did not appear.
(B) A ~~medical~~ center was unavailable.
(C) Sales figures did not meet expectations.
(D) Some products were defective.

男子／問題
→ 女子的提問、男子的答覆

49. What does the man suggest doing?
(A) ~~Replacing~~ an agency
(B) Advertising through social media
(C) ~~Offering~~ additional discounts
(D) Improving the product quality

男子／建議／後
→ 男子的對白、we could . . .

第 47-49 題 對話

男：嗨，瑪莉，我想討論一下公司醫療椅的銷售報告。

女：沒問題，報告有何問題？

男：嗯，事實上，數字頗令人失望。我們最近商請演員參與的宣傳活動，效果不如預期。

女：嗯……我想我們需要改變策略，運用不同的宣傳手法。

男：我在想我們能否在今年剩餘的時間裡，試著使用社群服務。社群媒體已日益成為最有效的宣傳方式之一。

女：好主意。對於願意在網路上張貼與本公司按摩椅合照的顧客，我們可以提供些許優惠。

47. 對話者最有可能任職於何種類型的公司？
(A) 廣告公司 (B) 辦公家具行
(C) 醫療設備製造商 (D) 數位相機店

48. 男子為何失望？
(A) 一名演員並未現身。
(B) 預約不到醫療中心的服務。
(C) 銷售數字不如預期。
(D) 出現瑕疵商品。

49. 男子提議從事何事？
(A) 換一家經銷商
(B) 透過社群媒體做行銷
(C) 提供額外折扣
(D) 改善產品品質

47 前半段對話中會談到職業。

STEP 1 **答案會出現在前兩句話中，以 our/your/this/here 加上表示地點或職業的名詞。**

對話說道：「I'd like to discuss the sales report on our medical chairs.」，當中的 our 為答題關鍵。由此段話可以得知說話者們任職於生產醫療用椅的公司，因此答案為 (C)。

→ 選項會將對話中的詳細內容，改寫成較為廣義的敘述。
medical chairs → (C) medical equipment

STEP 2 **陷阱選項和錯誤選項**

(A) An advertising company ▶ 聽到「advertising」可能會聯想成該選項。
(B) An office furniture store
▶ 對話中提到「chairs」，但是並未提及「office」，應改成「medical」。
(C) A medical equipment manufacturer ▶ 答案
(D) A digital camera store

48 直接由本人口中說出問題和擔憂的地方。

STEP 1 **若題目使用 concern、worry、problem 等單字詢問問題為何時，該問題通常會出現在對話開頭處。由說話者直接說出問題；或者由第一名說話者提出問題，再由第二名說話者的回答帶出問題所在。**

女子說道：「anything wrong on the report?」，男子對此回答：「the figures were rather disappointing.」，此話顯示男子對數字感到失望。the figures 指的是前方提過的 the sales report，因此答案為 (C)。

STEP 2 **陷阱選項和錯誤選項**

(A) An actor did not appear. ▶ 雖然對話中有提到「actors」，但無從得知「appear」與否。
(B) A medical center was unavailable. ▶ 故意使用「medical」的陷阱選項。
(C) Sales figures did not meet expectations. ▶ 答案
(D) Some products were defective.

49 題目詢問要求或建議時，解題關鍵在後半段對話中，以 You/We 開頭說明。

STEP 1 **除了直接建議對方之外，還可以使用直述句，間接表示勸說或建議。請務必熟記以下常見的用法：You should / must / can / need to / had better . . .**

女子表示要使用其他廣告方式，接著男子回覆：「we could try using social network services.」。「we could . . .」為解題關鍵，且當中提到「social network services」，因此答案為 (B)。

STEP 2 陷阱選項和錯誤選項

(A) Replacing an agency ▶ 聽到「need to change」可能會聯想到「replace」。
(B) Advertising through social media ▶ 答案
(C) Offering additional discounts ▶ 故意使用「can offer」的陷阱選項。
(D) Improving the product quality

字彙 discuss 討論　sales report 銷售報告　figures 數字　effect 效果
advertising 廣告（業）　manufacturer 製造商　disappoint （使）失望
unavailable 無法取得的　defective 有缺陷的；有瑕疵的　agency 經銷商

Questions 50-52 refer to the following conversation.

M	Jennifer, I was told in the department meeting that you need more workers in the factory. 50 51	51-D
W	Yes, since our business is rapidly growing, I'm afraid we can't process all the orders we have. Actually, all workers had to work over the weekends last month.	50-B 51-A
M	52 All right, I'll send you a form for the job description. Just update it with current job requirements and send it back to me. Then, I'll post it on our Web site.	52-B

50. Which part of the company does the woman most likely manage?
(A) The factory
(B) The ~~store~~
(C) The mail room
(D) The warehouse

女子／職業、地點／前
→ 前半段對話

51. What are the speakers mainly talking about?
(A) ~~Placing~~ an order
(B) Inspecting workstations
(C) Recruiting new employees
(D) ~~Preparing~~ a meeting

說話者／主旨／前
→ 分布比例 2：1

52. What does the man ask the woman to do?
(A) Update a document
(B) ~~Complete~~ a daily task
(C) Contact an agency
(D) Research some prices

男子／要求／後
→ 後半段對話、表示要求的句型

第 50-52 題 對話

男：珍妮佛，我從部門會議上得知工廠需要更多的工人。

女：沒錯，由於公司的業績成長迅速，我擔心我們無法處理所有的訂單。事實上，上個月所有的工人週末都在加班。

男：好吧，我會寄給妳職務說明書的填寫表格。妳只要更新現在的職務需求，再把它寄回給我就可以了，然後我會把它張貼在我們的官網上。

50. 女子最有可能管理公司何處？
(A) 工廠　(B) 賣場
(C) 收發室　(D) 倉庫

51. 對話者主要在討論何事？
(A) 下訂單　(B) 視察個人工作區
(C) 招聘新員工　(D) 籌備會議

52. 男子要求女子做何事？
(A) 更新文件資料　(B) 完成日常任務
(C) 聯絡經銷處　(D) 進行市場價格調查

50 前半段對話中會談到職業或地點。

STEP 1 由男子（女子）的對白，可以得知男子（女子）的職業或公司地點。

男子說道：「I was told . . . that you need more workers in the factory.」，提到女子負責管理的部門。此段話表示女子任職的工廠需要更多的員工，因此答案為 (A)。

STEP 2 陷阱選項和錯誤選項

(A) The factory ▶ 答案
(B) The store ▶ 聽到「orders」可能會聯想到「store」。
(C) The mail room
(D) The warehouse

51 若題目詢問主旨或目的，答案會出現在開頭前兩句話。

STEP 1 在 PART 3 中，題目的答案會以 1：1：1（前：中：後）的比例分布於對話中，但有些時候答案會集中出現在某段對話中。假設兩題的答案都出現在前半段對話中，答案的分布比例會變成 2：1。

題組第一題詢問女子負責管理的地方（職業）；第二題詢問本篇對話的主旨。職業和主旨通常會出現在前半段對話中，因此本篇題目答案的分布比例即為 2：1，等於事先就能猜到前半段對話中將會出現本題的答案。男子說道：「you need more workers in the factory.」，表示工廠需要更多的員工，因此對話的主旨為 (C) Recruiting new employees。

STEP 2 陷阱選項和錯誤選項

(A) ~~Placing~~ an order ▶ 雖然對話中有提到「orders」，但談論的內容與訂單無關，因此不能作為答案。
(B) Inspecting workstations
(C) Recruiting new employees ▶ 答案
(D) Preparing a meeting ▶ 對話中只有提到「meeting」，沒有提到「prepare」，因此有誤。

52 答案會以祈使句表示向對方（you）要求或建議的內容。

STEP 1 由後半段對話確認是否出現表示要求或建議的常見句型。

本題詢問男子要求的事情。後半段對話中，男子說道：「I'll send you a form . . . Just update it」，請對方更新文件，因此答案為 (A)。

STEP 2 陷阱選項和錯誤選項

(A) Update a document ▶ 答案
(B) Complete a daily task ▶ 聽到「job description」可能會聯想到「daily task」。
(C) Contact an agency
(D) Research some prices

字彙 rapidly 迅速地 process 處理 description 描述 current 當前的
requirement 要求；需求 inspect 視察 workstation 個人工作區 recruit 招聘

Questions 53-55 refer to the following conversation with three speakers.

M1	Hi, Julie and Peter. Do you know where Kate is today? I haven't seen her all morning.	
W 53	I think she is out of town for a press conference today. But I have her phone number. Do you need it?	53-B
M1 54	No, that's OK. I heard Kate speaks Chinese, and I got an e-mail from a client in China. I'll just wait until tomorrow to get it translated.	54-B
W	Hey, Peter! You lived in China for about six years, right? 55	55-C 55-A
M2	Yeah, I will be available after 4 P.M. if you'd like me to work on it.	

53. What does the woman offer to do?
(A) Review a document
(B) Confirm a ~~timetable~~
(C) Provide contact information
(D) Reserve a meeting room

女子／提出解決方式／前
→「由我來做」句型

54. What is Kate needed for?
(A) Translating an e-mail
(B) Contacting a keynote ~~speaker~~
(C) Preparing a contract
(D) Writing an article

關鍵字 Kate／需要的東西
→ 提到 Kate 的前後對白

55. Why does the woman say, "You lived in China for about six years"?
(A) She ~~corrects some information~~.
(B) She suggests her colleague for a position.
(C) She needs some ~~travel tips~~.
(D) She wants to help her colleague.

掌握說話者意圖／女子
→ 確認前後文意。

第 53-55 題 三人對話

男1：嗨，茱莉、彼得，你們知不知道凱特今日人在何處？我一整個上午都沒見到她。

女：我想她今天是出去參加新聞記者會了。但我有她的手機號碼，你需要嗎？

男1：不用，沒關係。我聽說凱特會說中文，而我收到一封中國客戶寄來的電子郵件，我等到明天再請她翻譯好了。

女：嘿，彼得，你之前在中國住了六年左右，對吧？

男2：是啊，我下午四點之後會有空，如果你需要我翻譯的話。

53. 女子主動提議做何事？
(A) 審核文件 (B) 確認時間表
(C) 提供聯絡資訊 (D) 預訂會議室

54. 為何需要凱特？
(A) 翻譯一封電子郵件 (B) 聯繫主講人
(C) 準備合約 (D) 撰寫文章

55. 為何女子會說：「你之前在中國住了六年左右」？
(A) 她更正某些資訊。
(B) 她為同事引薦職缺。
(C) 她需要一些旅遊情報。
(D) 她想要幫助同事。

53 針對對方的問題提出解決方式。

STEP 1 **除了詢問要求或建議之外，還有一種題型為 offer question。此類題型的解題關鍵句不會使用 you，而是以 I will / Let me / Do you want me to do 等句型表示「由我來……」。**

男子 1 正在尋找 Kate，對此女子回答：「But I have her phone number. Do you need it?」，表示女子可以提供 Kate 的聯絡方式，因此答案為 (C)。

→ 選項會將對話中的詳細內容，改寫成較為廣義的敘述。
phone number → (C) contact information

STEP 2 **陷阱選項和錯誤選項**

(A) Review a document
(B) Confirm a timetable ▶ 聽到「she is out of town」可能會聯想到「timetable」。
(C) Provide contact information ▶ 答案
(D) Reserve a meeting room

54 答案位在關鍵字所在之處的前後對白中。

STEP 1 **請特別留意新制測驗中，答案不太會出現在關鍵字後方，而是出現在下一個人的對白裡。關鍵字會被改成代名詞（it/he/she/they 等）再提及答題線索。**

「I heard Kate speaks Chinese . . . I'll just wait until tomorrow to get it translated.」，提到他想拜託 Kate 翻譯郵件，因此答案為 (A)。

STEP 2 **陷阱選項和錯誤選項**

(A) Translating an e-mail ▶ 答案
(B) Contacting a keynote ~~speaker~~ ▶「speaker」與對話中「speak」的發音相似，為陷阱選項。
(C) Preparing a contract
(D) Writing an article

55 請先刪除與引號內字面意思相同的選項。

STEP 1 **題目詢問說話者意圖時，答案不會是引號內指定句字面上的意思，請務必確認前後文意，以便找出答案。**

男子 1 表示明天再請 Kate 翻譯（I'll just wait until tomorrow to get it translated），接著女子叫 Peter，並跟他說「You lived in China for about six years, right?」。由此段話可以得知她認為同事 Peter 可以幫男子 1 的忙，因此答案為 (D)。

STEP 2 **陷阱選項和錯誤選項**

(A) She corrects some information. ▶ 副詞「right」表示補充說明的概念，並非形容詞「正確的」；而此處使用同義動詞「correct」作為陷阱選項。

(B) She suggests her colleague for a position.

(C) She needs some ~~travel tips~~. ▶ 聽到「lived in China」可能會聯想到該選項的內容。

(D) She wants to help her colleague. ▶ 答案

字彙 all morning 整個上午　be out of town 不在城內；出城　press conference 新聞記者會　available 有空的　confirm 確認　reserve 預訂　contract 契約　position 職務

Questions 56-58 refer to the following conversation with three speakers.

M 56	Jeannie, it's great that our real estate company is growing so fast. But it's been hard for all of our employees to communicate with each other.	56-D
W1	That's true. Maybe we should set up a page on our internal Web site so people can share information and ideas. 57	
W2	You are right. Also employees can link interesting articles they want to share.	57-D
M	We need someone to coordinate everything to set it up.	
W1 58	Lucy, your team has done several similar projects before. Why doesn't your team take over this project?	58-B
M	I agree with Jeannie. If you want, I can talk to your supervisor regarding this project.	58-C

56. What is the conversation mainly about?
(A) Advertising approaches
(B) Internet providers
(C) Employee communication
(D) ~~Real estate properties~~

主旨／前
→ 前半段對話／注意 however 或 but 後方的內容。

57. What does Jeannie suggest?
(A) Buying some supplies
(B) Comparing some results
(C) Using a Web site
(D) Reading an ~~article~~

關鍵字 Jeannie ／建議
→ Jeannie 的對白中使用句型 we should 表示建議

58. What will the man ask Lucy to do?
(A) Coordinate a project
(B) Organize a ~~business trip~~
(C) ~~Talk to the supervisor~~
(D) Interview job candidates

男子／要求／ Lucy ／後
→ Why don't you . . . ?

第 56-58 題 三人對話

男　：珍妮，我們的房地產開發公司能發展得如此迅速，真的是太棒了！可是員工之間的溝通交流一直以來總是不便。

女1 ：真的，也許我們應該在公司內部網站設立一個頁面，以供資訊及意見的交流。

女2 ：說得對，員工也可以提供網路連結，分享有趣的文章。

男　：我們需要有人居中協調設立網頁。

女1 ：露西，妳的團隊之前完成了幾個類似的專案，何不由妳的團隊接手此次的計畫？

男　：我同意珍妮的提議。如果妳願意的話，我可以跟妳的主管提。

56. 談話的內容主要與什麼有關？
(A) 廣告手法
(B) 網路服務提供業者
(C) 員工溝通
(D) 房地產

57. 珍妮有何建議？
(A) 購買一些日用品
(B) 對照成效
(C) 使用網站
(D) 閱讀文章

58. 男子將要求露西做何事？
(A) 協調專案　(B) 安排出差
(C) 與主管討論　(D) 面試求職者

56 However 和 But 後方會出現答題的關鍵線索。

STEP 1 **對話中出現 but、however、actually 這類表示轉折語氣的連接詞或副詞時，多用來表示極為重要的內容，後方常會一併帶出答案。因此確認對話中的轉折詞為取得高分的技巧之一。**

本題詢問對話的主旨，聆聽前半段對話時，可以從 But 後方找到答題線索。「But it's been hard for all of our employees to communicate with each other.」當中提到員工之間的溝通（communicate），因此答案為 (C) Employee communication。

STEP 2 **陷阱選項和錯誤選項**

(A) Advertising approaches
(B) Internet providers
(C) Employee communication ▶ 答案
(D) Real estate properties ▶ 聽到「real estate company」可能會聯想到該選項。

57 三人對話題組的第二題通常會針對某個人提問。▶ Jeannie

STEP 1 **題目可能詢問某名說話者或特定人士碰到的問題、擔憂的事或建議為何。對話中經常使用 you 向對方要求或建議某事，因此請務必熟記以下常見句型：Please . . .、Let's . . .、You / We should / must / can / need to / had better . . .，此類表示要求或建議的句型正是答題關鍵。**

男子叫了「Jeannie」這個名字，接著 Jeannie 本人回答「That's true. Maybe we should set up a page on our internal Web site」，表示 Jeannie 建議增設網頁，因此答案為 (C) Using a Web site。

STEP 2 **陷阱選項和錯誤選項**

(A) Buying some supplies
(B) Comparing some results
(C) Using a Web site ▶ 答案
(D) Reading an article ▶ 重複使用對話中的單字，與本題內容無關。

58 題目詢問要求或建議時，解題關鍵在後半段對話中，以 You 說明。

STEP 1 **題目詢問建議、要求或未來計畫時，答案會出現在後半段對話中。**

後半段對話中說道：「Lucy, . . . Why doesn't your team take over this project?」，表示 Jeannie 建議 Lucy 負責這個計畫，接著男子附和：「I agree with Jeannie」，表示男子也建議由 Lucy 負責，因此答案為 (A)。

STEP 2 陷阱選項和錯誤選項

(A) Coordinate a project ▶ 答案

(B) Organize a business trip ▶ 對話中未提到「business trip」。

(C) Talk to the supervisor ▶ 為男子要做的事情。

(D) Interview job candidates

字彙 real estate 房地產 communicate 溝通 set up 建立 internal 內部的 link 提供連結 coordinate 協調 take over 接手

Questions 59-61 refer to the following conversation and a table.

W Martin, how is the preparation of our workshop going? 59-D 59-C

M Well . . . I think it's almost done. I found a great place and Maria gave

59 me the final budget for the expenses this morning. So we can finalize everything.

W Wow, that's great.

M Now, the most important thing will be the seminar room at the Wellington Hotel. I've used Phoenix in the past and it's nice. But we're

60 expecting more than 30 people. So we'll need the largest room. 60-C

W That's right. Oh . . . did you make arrangements for the ride? If not, I'll

61 be happy to arrange a bus from the office to the hotel. 61-D

Wellington Seminar Room	
Name	Capacity
Bonnie	20
Lakeside	25
Phoenix	30
Jackson	40

59. What information did the man receive this morning?

(A) The number of participants

(B) The budgeted money

(C) The ~~topics of a seminar~~

(D) The ~~preferred~~ menus

男子／關鍵字 this morning／前
→ 前半段對話

60. Look at the graphic. Which room will the speakers choose?

(A) Bonnie

(B) Lakeside

(C) ~~Phoenix~~

(D) Jackson

圖表資訊／ which room
→ 表格中的 Capacity 部分、注意最高級和表示數量的用法。

61. What does the woman offer to do?

(A) Consult her supervisor

(B) Revise a budget report

(C) Arrange transportation for employees

(D) ~~Reserve a seminar room~~ in a hotel

女子／建議／後
→ 女子的對白、I'll . . .

第 59-61 題 對話與圖表

女：馬丁，研討會準備得如何？

男：嗯……我想應該差不多了。我找到一個絕佳的地點，而今天早上瑪麗亞也已給我經費的最終預算了。所以，每件事都可以定案了。

女：哇，太好了。

男：現在，最重要的事是威靈頓飯店的會議廳。我曾使用過鳳凰廳，很不錯。但這次預計會有超過三十名的與會人士，所以我們需要最大的會議廳。

女：沒錯。對了……你安排好接駁車了嗎？如果沒有，我很樂意安排從公司到飯店的接駁巴士。

威靈頓飯店會議廳	
名稱	可容納人數
邦尼廳	20 人
湖濱廳	25 人
鳳凰廳	30 人
傑克森廳	40 人

59. 男子今天早上收到什麼資料？
(A) 與會人數　(B) 預算金額
(C) 研討會議題　(D) 首選菜單

60. 請見圖表，對話者將選擇哪一間會議廳？
(A) 邦尼廳　(B) 湖濱廳
(C) 鳳凰廳　(D) 傑克森廳

61. 女子主動提議做何事？
(A) 徵詢主管意見
(B) 修訂預算報告
(C) 為員工安排交通工具
(D) 預訂飯店的會議廳

59 題目中出現關鍵字時，答案會在該關鍵字前後的句子。

STEP 1 題目中出現特定的時間點或數字時，對話中勢必會出現該關鍵字，因此請務必在該關鍵字附近找出答案。值得留意的是，通常會先聽到關鍵字，再聽到答案的內容，但在新制測驗中，有時反而會先聽到答案的內容，之後才聽到關鍵字。

男子說道：「Maria gave me the final budget for the expenses this morning」，由關鍵字 this morning 可以得知他收到了 final budget（最終版本預算），因此答案為 (B)。

STEP 2 陷阱選項和錯誤選項

(A) The number of participants
(B) The budgeted money ▶ 答案
(C) The topics of a seminar ▶ 聽到「workshop」可能會聯想到「topics of a seminar」。
(D) The ~~preferred~~ menus ▶ 聽到「preparation」可能會聯想到發音相似的單字「preferred」。

60 圖表資訊 ▶ 答案不會是對話中提到的選項。

STEP 1 **圖表題要整合對話和圖表的內容後，才能選出答案。請特別留意圖表中的排序、最高級、數量。**

對話中說道：「we'll need the largest room」，提到需要最大的一間，因此答案為 (D)，可以容納最多的人數。

STEP 2 **陷阱選項和錯誤選項**

(A) Bonnie
(B) Lakeside
(C) Phoenix ▶ 雖然對話中提到「30 people」，但是並非僅 30 人，而是 30 人以上。
(D) Jackson ▶ 答案

61 題目詢問建議、要求或未來計畫時，答案會出現在後半段對話中。

STEP 1 **除了詢問要求或建議之外，還有一種題型為 offer question。此類題型的解題關鍵句不會使用 you，而是以 I will / Let me / Do you want me to do 等句型表示「由我來……」。**

女子說道：「I'll be happy to arrange a bus from the office to the hotel」，提到她將安排接駁的公車，因此答案為 (C)。

→ 選項會將對話中的詳細內容，改寫成較為廣義的敘述。
a bus → (C) transportation

STEP 2 **陷阱選項和錯誤選項**

(A) Consult her supervisor
(B) Revise a budget report
(C) Arrange transportation for employees ▶ 答案
(D) Reserve a seminar room in a hotel
▶ 雖然對話中提到「hotel」，但並未提到「reserve a seminar room」，因此不能作為答案。

字彙 preparation 準備工作　budget 預算　expense 開銷　finalize 最後確定
expect 預料　arrangement 安排　make arrangements for 為……作準備
arrange 安排　capacity 容量

TEST 1 PART 3 中譯&解析

Questions 62-64 refer to the following conversation and a poster.

W Gail, there will be a jazz concert this month. I know you are a big fan of jazz. Are you interested in going? 62

M Well, the concert is actually intended for kids. Next month though, there's an orchestra concert that I was thinking of going to. 62-C

W 63 Oh, really? I didn't realize that. Then I'll skip the jazz concert. And I can't go to the concert next month because I will be attending a trade show in Akron on that day. 63-B

M 64 Too bad. But don't worry. They're scheduled to perform on the following week at the Perrel Art Center. If you want, I'll buy tickets for you. 64-B

Perrel Art Center Events	
4 September	International Toy Expo
9 October	Kids Jazz Concert
17 November	Aston City Orchestra
25 December	Christmas Traditions

62. Look at the graphic. When does the conversation take place?
(A) In September **(B) In October**
(C) In November (D) In December

圖表資訊／前
→ 前半段對話、this month

63. Why is the woman unable to go to the orchestra's concert?
(A) She will be visiting some clients.
(B) She will be preparing a presentation.
(C) She will be on vacation.
(D) She will be participating in a trade show.

女子／發生問題的原因
→ 女子的對白、because . . .

64. What does the man offer to do?
(A) Purchase a ticket (B) Revise a schedule
(C) Attend a conference (D) Research for a project

男子／建議／後
→ 男子的對白、I'll . . .

第 62-64 題 對話與海報

女：蓋爾，這個月將有一場爵士音樂會。我知道你是爵士樂的超級粉絲，有興趣去聽嗎？

男：嗯，那場音樂會其實是為兒童所舉辦的。不過，下個月會有一場交響音樂會，我有考慮要去。

女：哦，真的嗎？我沒注意到。那，我就不去爵士音樂會了。而我也無法去聽下個月的音樂會，因為當天我將在阿克倫市參加貿易展覽會。

男：真可惜。但別擔心，他們預計會在接下來的那個星期，在佩雷爾藝術中心進行表演。如果妳有想去的話，我可以幫妳買票。

佩雷爾藝術中心展演訊息	
9 月 4 日	國際玩具博覽會
10 月 9 日	兒童爵士音樂會
11 月 17 日	奧斯頓市立管絃樂團
12 月 25 日	聖誕節傳統節慶活動

62. 請見圖表，對話發生於何時？
(A) 九月 (B) 十月
(C) 十一月 (D) 十二月

63. 為何女子無法參加交響音樂會？
(A) 她將拜訪客戶。
(B) 她將準備做一場簡報。
(C) 她將去度假。
(D) 她將參加商展。

64. 男子主動提議做何事？
(A) 買票 (B) 修改行程安排
(C) 參加會議 (D) 進行專案研究

62 圖表資訊 ▶ 對話中與圖表相符的內容即是答案。

STEP 1 **對話會按照題目順序依序談論相關內容，因此請留意前半段對話，確認與圖表相符的答題線索。**

「there will be a jazz concert this month」，提到這個月將舉辦爵士演場會，表示進行本篇對話的時間和舉辦爵士演唱會的時間同為十月，因此答案為 (B)。

STEP 2 **陷阱選項和錯誤選項**

(A) In September
(B) In October ▶ 答案
(C) In November ▶ 對話中提到「orchestra concert」將於下個月舉行。
(D) In December

63 直接由本人口中說出問題和擔憂的地方。

STEP 1 **經常用來表示造成問題和擔憂的原因有：遲到（late）、延後（delayed）、忙碌（busy）、缺乏（lack）、故障（out of order）等。**

男子說道：「Next month though, there's an orchestra concert」，而後女子回答：「I can't go to the concert next month because I will be attending a trade show」，表示她得參加貿易博覽會，因而無法去下月舉行的交響樂演奏會，因此答案為 (D)。

STEP 2 **陷阱選項和錯誤選項**

(A) She will be visiting some clients.
(B) She will be preparing a presentation. ▶ 聽到「show」可能會聯想到「presentation」。
(C) She will be on vacation.
(D) She will be participating in a trade show. ▶ 答案

64 請特別留意以下提出建議（offer）的句型：I/We will、Let me、I can . . . for you

STEP 1 **require 指的是要求對方，因此會向對方說「你（you）應該……」；offer 指的則是自己提供，因此會說「由我（I）來做……」**

男子說道：「I'll buy tickets for you.」，表示他會負責買票，因此答案為 (A)。

STEP 2 **陷阱選項和錯誤選項**

(A) Purchase a ticket ▶ 答案
(B) Revise a schedule ▶ 聽到「scheduled」可能會選錯，為陷阱選項。
(C) Attend a conference ▶ 對話中女子提到「attending」，該選項故意使用前半段的「attend」。
(D) Research for a project

字彙 big fan 超級粉絲　intend for 為……而準備　realize 領悟；發覺　skip 省略；跳過
trade show 貿易展覽會　be scheduled to V 計劃做……事

Questions 65-67 refer to the following excerpt from a meeting and a chart.

M	Hi, Jessie. Could you take a look at this chart? As you know, I have a meeting this afternoon regarding the new store opening project.	66-B
W 65	Actually I have reviewed that already. And I think the beverage that got the least votes should be discounted by 30 percent for promotion.	
M 66	I agree with you. Due to last week's promotion, the sales of americano have really increased. It was Jason's idea. I should thank him.	66-A 66-C
W 67	Then, you should speak of that at the meeting. If you need my opinion regarding this project, you can ask me anytime.	67-A 67-D 67-B

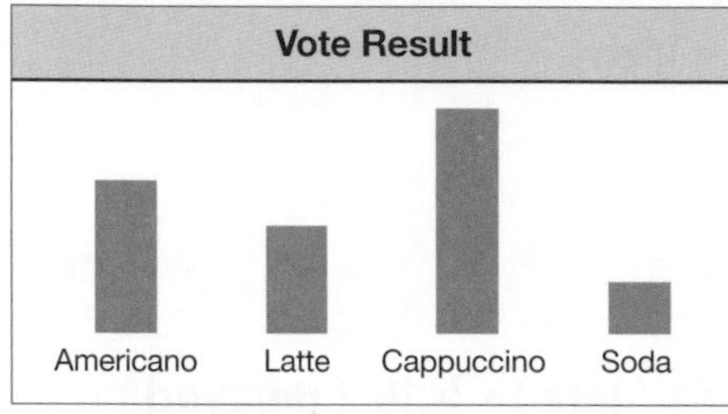

65. Look at the graphic. Which beverage will be discounted this week?

(A) Americano (B) Latte
(C) Cappuccino **(D) Soda**

66. What does the man thank Jason for?

(A) ~~Developing~~ a new beverage
(B) Organizing a ~~chart~~
(C) Sharing helpful ~~information~~
(D) Suggesting a sales promotion

67. What does the woman remind the man to do?

(A) ~~Talk to~~ other colleagues (B) Join the project
(C) Ask for advice (D) ~~Make~~ some suggestions

圖表資訊／前

→ 題目排序＝對話先後次序、表格——最高級用法

男子／ thank ／關鍵字 Jason

→ 關鍵字 Jason 前後的句子

女子／要求／後

→ you can . . .

第 65-67 題 會議摘錄與圖表

男：嗨，潔西。妳能不能看一下這張圖表？妳知道的，今天下午我有個會議要開，是關於新分店的開幕計畫。

女：事實上，我已經檢視過了。我覺得得票數最低的飲料應該打七折促銷。

男：我同意。由於上個星期的促銷活動，美式咖啡的銷售量真的有成長。這是傑森的點子，我應該感謝他。

女：那麼，你應該在會議中提及。如果你需要我為這個計畫出謀劃策，可以隨時問我。

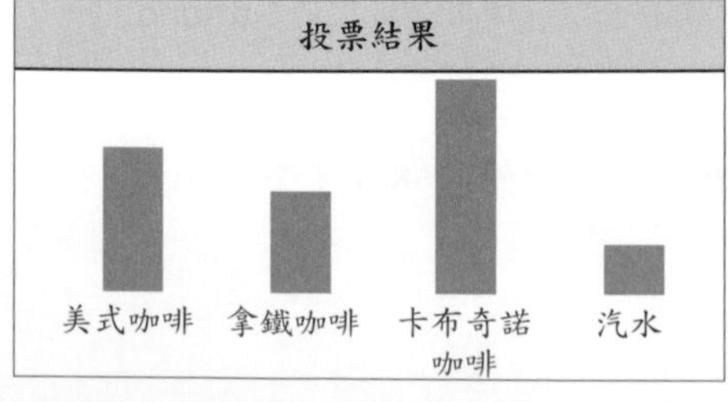

65. 請見圖表，哪一款飲料會在本週做折扣？

(A) 美式咖啡 (B) 拿鐵咖啡
(C) 卡布奇諾咖啡 (D) 汽水

66. 男子為何要感謝傑森？

(A) 開發新款飲品
(B) 整理圖表
(C) 分享有用的資訊
(D) 提議做促銷活動

67. 女子提醒男子做何事？

(A) 與其他同事討論
(B) 參與專案計畫
(C) 尋求建議
(D) 提出建言

65 圖表資訊 ▶ 若對話中提到圖表（Graph / Bar / Pie）的排序、最高級或數量時，就是答案所在之處。

STEP 1 圖表的作用為「比較」，因此請從排序、最高級、數量等用法確認答案。

對話中說道：「the beverage that got the least votes should be discounted」，表示以獲得最少票數的飲料進行優惠，因此答案為 (D)。

STEP 2 陷阱選項和錯誤選項

(A) Americano ▶ 對話中只有提到「the sales of americano」，並非給予「discount」的飲料。
(B) Latte
(C) Cappuccino
(D) Soda ▶ 答案

66 題目中出現關鍵字時，答案會在該關鍵字前後的句子。

STEP 1 若題目中出現特定的關鍵字，聆聽對話時，勢必會於該關鍵字前後聽到答案。一般來說會先聽到關鍵字，再聽到答案的內容，但在新制測驗中，有時反而會先聽到答案的內容，之後才聽到關鍵字。

本題的關鍵字為 Jason，該關鍵字前後說道：「Due to last week's promotion」和「It was Jason's idea. I should thank him.」。這兩句話表示男子要感謝 Jason 提出促銷的概念，因此答案為 (D)。

STEP 2 陷阱選項和錯誤選項

(A) Developing a new beverage ▶ 雖然對話中有提到「americano」，但並沒有說到研發出它。
(B) Organizing a chart ▶ 重複使用對話中的單字，與本題內容無關。
(C) Sharing helpful ~~information~~ ▶ 聽到「idea」可能會聯想到「information」。
(D) Suggesting a sales promotion ▶ 答案

67 題目詢問男子該做的事情時，答案會出現在女子以 You 開頭的對白當中。

STEP 1 表達「義務」的概念時，可以使用 You should . . . / Please . . . 開頭的句型來要求或建議對方。

女子說道：「If you need my opinion regarding this project, you can ask me anytime.」，表示對方隨時都可以來請教自己，因此答案為 (C)。

STEP 2 陷阱選項和錯誤選項

(A) Talk to other colleagues ▶ 聽到「speak」可能會聯想到「talk to」。
(B) ~~Join~~ the project ▶ 雖然對話中有提到「project」，但並未要求對方參加。
(C) Ask for advice ▶ 答案
(D) Make some suggestions ▶ 雖然對話中有提到「opinion」，但並非請男子提出建議，而是告知男子可以尋求女子的建議，因此該敘述有誤。

字彙 regarding 關於　review 審查；檢視　promotion 促銷　organize 整理

Questions 68-70 refer to the following telephone message and identification badge.

M	Hi, 68 I am here to see the head security officer Cathy Miller. My name is Derek Moreno and I'm a new employee starting today.	68-C
W	Ms. Miller is out of the office. Did you make an appointment today?	
M	Actually I was supposed to be here this morning. But today's training fell behind. I could not come earlier.	
W	She will not be available this afternoon. Do you want me to leave a message?	70-A
M 69	Thanks, I was issued a parking permit and an employee ID badge at the orientation. But when I was back at my office, I realized the office number on my badge isn't correct. Everything else on the badge looks okay.	
W	I can help you with that. Could you show me your badge?	70-B
M	Sure. Here it is. 70	

Name: Derek Moreno
Office ID: 124034
Department Code: 3111
Office number: 422
Phone number: 243-8876

68. Where is the conversation most likely taking place?

(A) At the security office
(B) At the maintenance department
(C) At the ~~training center~~
(D) At the human resources department

地點／前
→ 前半段對話、here

69. Look at the graphic. What employee information does the man say is incorrect?

(A) 124034 (B) 3111 **(C) 422** (D) 243-8876

圖表資訊／男子／問題
→ 對話中不會直接提到選項內容。

70. What does the woman ask the man to do?

(A) ~~Leave a message~~
(B) ~~Change~~ a badge
(C) Present an employee ID
(D) Return the call

女子／要求／後
→ Could you . . . ?

第 68-70 題　電話留言與識別證

男：嗨，我想見安全管理處主任凱西・米勒。我叫德瑞克・莫雷諾，是今天到職的新進員工。

女：米勒小姐不在辦公室，你今天有預約嗎？

男：事實上，我應該今天早上就來報到的。但是今天的培訓耽擱了，所以我沒辦法提早過來。

女：她今天下午沒空，需要我幫你留言嗎？

男：謝了，我參加培訓的時候，取得了一張停車證以及員工識別證，但當我回到辦公室時，我發現我識別證上的辦公室編號不正確，其他的資訊倒都還好。

女：我可以幫你處理這件事，可以借看一下你的員工識別證嗎？

男：當然，請看。

	姓名：德瑞克・莫雷諾 辦公室識別碼：124034 部門代碼：3111 辦公室編號：422 電話號碼：243-8876

68. 對話最有可能發生在何處？
(A) 安全管理處
(B) 維修部
(C) 培訓中心
(D) 人力資源部

69. 請見圖表，男子提到哪項員工資訊不正確？
(A) 124034
(B) 3111
(C) 422
(D) 243-8876

70. 女子要求男子做何事？
(A) 留言
(B) 換個識別證
(C) 出示員工識別證
(D) 回電

68 前半段對話中會談到地點或職業。

STEP 1 前兩句話會聽到 our / your / this / here 加上表示地點或職業的名詞。

對話開頭說道：「I am here to see the head security officer Cathy Miller.」，表示他來這裡見安全管理處主任，因此答案為 (A)。

STEP 2 陷阱選項和錯誤選項

(A) At the security office ▶ 答案
(B) At the maintenance department
(C) At the training center ▶ 聽到「new employee」可能會聯想到該選項的內容。
(D) At the human resources department

69 圖表資訊 ▶ 對話中不會提到圖表上的詳細內容。

STEP 1 圖表題的選項不會直接出現在對話當中，因此要綜合對話和圖表的內容，才能找出答案。

男子說道：「the office number on my badge isn't correct.」，提到 office number 有誤，對照圖表的 office number 後，可以發現答案為 (C)。

STEP 2 陷阱選項和錯誤選項

(A) 124034
(B) 3111
(C) 422 ▶ 答案
(D) 243-8876

TEST 1 PART 3 中譯&解析

70 題目詢問要求或建議時，解題關鍵在後半段對話中，以 You 說明。

STEP 1 **要求、建議、未來計畫的答案會出現在後半段對話中。除了直接勸說、建議、要求、請求對方之外，還可以使用直述句，間接表示勸說或建議。**

最後一段對話中，女子說道：「Could you show me your badge?」，要求對方出示證件，因此答案為 (C) Present an employee ID。

STEP 2 **陷阱選項和錯誤選項**

(A) Leave a message ▶ 重複使用對話中的內容，與本題無關。
(B) Change a badge ▶ 雖然對話中有提到「badge」，但並未提到「change」，因此該敘述有誤。
(C) Present an employee ID ▶ 答案
(D) Return the call

字彙 **be out of the office** 不在辦公室 **appointment** 約會；會面 **fall behind** 落後 **available** 有空的 **issue** 頒發；配給 **parking permit** 停車證 **realize** 意識到；發現 **maintenance** 維護；維修

PART 4

Questions 71-73 refer to the following advertisement.

71	Are you looking for speakers? If you want a whole-home music system, STS Home is the single best music-streaming device you can buy. It's inexpensive, easy to use, and guaranteed to perform to your satisfaction. STS Home is unique because, unlike other speakers, it allows comprehensive integrating of all sound devices	71-C 72-A 72-C
72	with customizable play back design in more ways than any of our competitors' products. It allows live music streaming to your system and access to a high number of playlists from the Internet. The sound is so great that you will feel like you're in a movie theatre. Still not convinced? Then visit our Web site at STSHomeaudio.com today and	
73	you can try out the system for one month at no cost.	73-D

71. What product is being advertised?
(A) An Internet provider **(B) Some audio equipment**
(C) A musical ~~performance~~ (D) A magazine subscription

廣告產品／前
→ Are you interested / looking for . . . ?

72. What does the speaker say is unique to the product?
(A) It is the ~~cheapest~~ on the market.
(B) It has a variety of functions.
(C) It has the ~~longest~~ warranty.
(D) It has received the best reviews.

產品特色
→ 使用最高級、形容詞的句子

73. What can listeners do at a Web site?
(A) Read customer reviews **(B) Sign up for a free trial**
(C) Download a ~~coupon~~ (D) Listen to some samples

聽者／能做的事／後
→ 祈使句

TEST 1 PART 4 中譯&解析

第 71-73 題 廣告

您正在尋找揚聲器嗎？如果您想要一組家庭環繞式音響系統，STS Home 音樂串流器將會是您的最佳選擇。它價格平實、使用方便，保證能滿足您所有期待。有別於他牌的揚聲器，STS Home 音樂串流器的獨特之處在於，它能整合所有的音響設備，多樣化的客製播放設計選項，遠勝於其他的競爭產品。它能從網路上讀取大量的音樂播放清單，讓您使用音響系統即可收聽線上音樂。絕佳的音質更會讓您恍若置身電影院。還在猶豫嗎？今天就瀏覽我們的官方網站 STSHomeaudio.com，可以讓您免費試用一個月哦。

71. 何項產品在做廣告？
(A) 網際網路服務
(B) 音響設備
(C) 音樂表演
(D) 雜誌訂閱

72. 根據講者所言，該產品的獨特之處為何？
(A) 它是市面上最便宜的。
(B) 它擁有多樣化功能。
(C) 它的保固期最長。
(D) 它最獲好評。

73. 聽眾可以在官方網站上做何事？
(A) 閱讀顧客評論
(B) 報名參加免費試用
(C) 下載優惠券
(D) 試聽

71 廣告主旨為宣傳產品或服務。

STEP 1 **廣告中，由「Are you interested . . . ? / Are you looking for . . . ?」告知產品或服務。**

第一句說道：「Are you looking for speakers?」，表示本文廣告的是 (B) Some audio equipment。

STEP 2 **陷阱選項和錯誤選項**

(A) An Internet provider
(B) Some audio equipment ▶ 答案
(C) A musical performance ▶ 聽到「music」可能會聯想到「musical」。
(D) A magazine subscription

72 請特別留意形容詞 special、unique、good、excellent。

STEP 1 **題目詢問廣告產品的功能或特色時，會使用單字 advantage、special、feature，答案可以對應至獨白中提及 different、famous、special、最高級（best）的地方。**

獨白中提到 unique，請特別留意後方連接的內容：「有別於其他喇叭（unique because unlike other speakers）」。後方接著說道：「it allows comprehensive integrating of all sound devices . . . from the Internet.」，提到它可以整合所有的音訊裝置，並透過網路提供播放清單和即時音樂串流服務。這表示它具備多樣的功能，因此答案為 (B)。

→ **雖然獨白提到明確的資訊，但是選項通常會改寫成較為廣義的敘述。**
「unique because, . . . theatre」→ (B) functions（功能）

STEP 2 **陷阱選項和錯誤選項**

(A) It is the cheapest on the market.
▶「inexpensive（價格低廉的）」不等同於「cheapest（最便宜的）」。
(B) It has a variety of functions. ▶ 答案
(C) It has the longest warranty. ▶ 聽到「guaranteed」可能會聯想到「warranty」。
(D) It has received the best reviews.

73 聆聽後半段獨白時，請聽清楚關鍵字 Web site 前後的內容，確認聽者可以於網站上做的事。

STEP 1 **題目詢問廣告中要求或建議聽者的事情，因此請由後半段獨白中的祈使句找出答案。**

後半段獨白說道：「Then visit our Web site at STSHomeaudio.com today and you can try out the system for one month at no cost.」，提到進入網站後，可以獲得一個月免費體驗的機會。這表示說話者建議聽者 (B) Sign up for a free trial。

→ **雖然獨白提到明確的資訊，但是選項通常會改寫成較為廣義的敘述。**
try out the the system for one month at no cost → (B) a free trial

STEP 2 陷阱選項和錯誤選項

(A) Read customer reviews
(B) Sign up for a free trial ▶ 答案
(C) Download a coupon
(D) Listen to some samples ▶ 聽到「try out the system」可能會誤選該選項。

字彙 streaming 串流 guarantee 擔保 perform 執行 satisfaction 滿意 comprehensive 全面的 integrate （使）成為一體；整合 access 讀取（電腦文檔） convince 使信服

Questions 74-76 refer to the following announcement.

74 Before you start your factory shift, I have some information to share. Thanks to all of your hard work, the Spanish client's order for a new design textile was successfully met. Since the automated spinning and weaving machinery is old, new ones need to be installed. So I'm pleased to announce that management has decided to replace it with XQ-1000. With XQ-1000, the weaving work will be processed more
75 quickly and more efficiently. In order to avoid work interruption, it will be installed this Saturday morning. So all of you are asked to clean
76 the floor and do not leave your personal belongings in the workroom. Thank you.

74-B
75-D
75-B
76-C

74. Where most likely do the listeners work?
(A) At a restaurant
(B) At a design company
(C) At an employment agency
(D) At a textile factory

聽者職業／前
→ 注意聆聽第一句以 you 開頭的話。

75. What is suggested about XQ-1000?
(A) It can save more time.
(B) It improves product quality.
(C) It is easily operated.
(D) It is safer than the old model.

關鍵字／XQ-1000
→ 注意聆聽關鍵字前後的內容。

76. What are the listeners asked to do?
(A) Sign up for a seminar
(B) Attend a safety training session
(C) Clean the lounge room
(D) Take their belongings with them

聽者／要求／後
→ 注意聆聽 please / you should . . . / 祈使句。

第 74-76 題 宣告

在各位開始上工之前，我有些事情要宣布。由於大家辛勤工作，我們順利完成了西班牙客戶所預訂的新款織品設計訂單。因為紡織機器已經老舊，所以必須安裝新的設備。因此，我很高興在此宣布，管理階層決定用 XQ-1000 型號設備來替換老舊機器。有了 XQ-1000，紡織作業將會更快、更有效率。而為了避免中斷工作，新的設備將在這個星期六早上進行安裝。所以請諸位將地板清理乾淨，勿把私人物品遺留在工作間，感謝大家的配合。

74. 聽眾最有可能在何處工作？
(A) 在餐廳 (B) 在設計公司
(C) 在職業介紹所 (D) 在紡織廠

75. 關於XQ-1000，發言者有何暗示？
(A) 它能節省更多時間。
(B) 它改善產品的品質。
(C) 它容易操作。
(D) 它比舊款的型號設備更安全。

76. 聽眾被要求做何事？
(A) 報名參加研討會
(B) 參加安全訓練講習
(C) 清理會客室
(D) 帶走自己的私人物品

74 前兩句話會以代名詞（I / You / We）或地方副詞（here / this ＋地點名詞）告知職業或地點。▶ 聽者工作的地點

STEP 1 獨白會按照主題，採固定方式表達職業或地點，請務必熟記。前兩句話會聽到 our / your / this / here 加上表示地點或職業的名詞。

本題詢問聽者工作的地點。獨白中說道：「Before you start your factory shift」以及「the Spanish client's order for a new design textile was successfully met.」，這兩句話表示聽者在紡織工廠工作，因此答案為 (D) At a textile factory。

STEP 2 陷阱選項和錯誤選項

(A) At a restaurant
(B) At a design company ▶ 聽到「design textile」可能會誤選該選項。
(C) At an employment agency
(D) At a textile factory ▶ 答案

75 題目中出現關鍵字時，答案會在該關鍵字前後的句子。▶ XQ-1000

STEP 1 若題目中出現特定的關鍵字，聆聽獨白時，勢必會於該關鍵字前後聽到答案。

獨白中說道：「With XQ-1000, the weaving work will be processed more quickly and more efficiently.」，提到使用該產品將能提升工作速度和效率。這表示將能省下更多時間，因此答案為 (A)。

→ 雖然獨白提到明確的資訊，但是選項通常會改寫成較為廣義的敘述。
be processed more quickly and more efficiently → (A) can save more time

STEP 2 陷阱選項和錯誤選項

(A) It can save more time. ▶ 答案
(B) It improves product quality. ▶ 聽到「efficiently」可能會聯想到「improve quality」。
(C) It is easily operated.
(D) It is safer than the old model. ▶ 獨白中並未提到「safer」。

76 題目出現被動語態時，請注意聆聽表示勸說或建議的句子。

STEP 1 題目出現被動語態時，通常是詢問說話者向聽者要求或建議的事情，因此獨白中會使用 You will . . . 或祈使句以告知聽者。

獨白中說道：「So all of you are asked to clean the floor and do not leave your personal belongings in the workroom.」，要求聽者將地板清潔乾淨，並帶走個人隨身物品。選項將獨白中的 not leave 改寫成 Take their belongings with them，因此答案為 (D)。

STEP 2 陷阱選項和錯誤選項

(A) Sign up for a seminar
(B) Attend a safety training session ▶ 聽到「factory shift」可能會聯想到「safety training」。
(C) Clean the lounge room ▶ 雖然獨白中有提到「clean」，但是並未要求打掃會客室。
(D) Take their belongings with them ▶ 答案

字彙 shift 輪班　thanks to 由於　textile 織物　meet 完成；達成　automated 自動化的
spinning and weaving machinery 紡織機器　management 管理階層
replace A with B 以 B 取代 A　process 處理　avoid 避免　interruption 打斷
belongings 擁有物　workroom 工作間

Questions 77-79 refer to the following talk.

Hello, My name is Norman. And I will be your server tonight. This is the menu for today's dinner. We've recently added a few more Asian dishes to our menu. You might want to check them before you order. **77-A**
Today's Specials include a Japanese dish and a Chinese dish for Asian food lovers. We choose only the best ingredients, all of which
77 come from our very own local farm. Our fresh produce is grown by
78 the restaurant's owner, Stewart, who is a talented farmer. Now, tonight **78-D**
we have a very special deal for you. All appetizers will be served at **77-B**
half-price. Today's entrée is pan-fried, cornmeal-crusted oysters. I eat **77-D**
79 them all the time. Let me take your beverage orders first while you browse our menu. **79-A** **79-D**

77. According to the speaker, what is special about the restaurant?
(A) It ~~serves many~~ dishes.　(B) It has ~~original~~ appetizers.
(C) It owns a local farm.　(D) It ~~offers low prices~~.

78. Who is Stewart?
(A) A business owner　(B) A famous chef
(C) A server　(D) A ~~talented~~ actor

79. Why does the speaker say, "I eat them all the time"?
(A) To ~~complain~~ about a ~~menu~~　**(B) To recommend a dish**
(C) To explain a ~~waiting~~ time　(D) To clarify a ~~menu~~ item

說話者／restaurant 的特色
→ 注意使用最高級，形容詞的句子。

關鍵字 Stewart／職業
→ 注意聆聽關鍵字前後的句子。

掌握說話者意圖
→ 注意指定句前後的內容。

第 77-79 題 談話

嗨，我叫諾曼，今晚將由我來為您服務。這是本日的晚餐菜單。本餐廳近來新增了幾道亞洲料理，或許您在點餐之前，會想要先參考看看。針對喜愛品嚐亞洲料理的顧客，本日特餐包含一道日式料理以及一道中華料理。本餐廳只選用最佳的食材，全部產自餐廳自有的地方農場。我們的新鮮農產品，皆由農藝高超的餐廳老闆史都華所親手栽種。本餐廳今晚為您提供特別優惠，所有的開胃菜半價優待。今晚的主菜是香煎脆皮牡蠣，我自己也常常吃這道料理。在您瀏覽菜單的時候，讓我先幫您點杯飲料。

77. 根據發言者所言，餐廳的特色為何？
(A) 它提供多種菜色。
(B) 它有獨創的開胃菜。
(C) 它擁有專屬的地方農場。
(D) 它的價位低廉。

78. 史都華是何人？
(A) 企業主 (B) 知名主廚
(C) 服務生 (D) 有天賦的演員

79. 為何發言者會說：「我自己也常常吃這道料理」？
(A) 抱怨菜單 (B) 推薦菜色
(C) 說明上菜時間 (D) 解釋菜色

77 請特別留意形容詞 special、unique、good、excellent。

STEP 1 通常會使用最高級形容詞表示特色或優點。

本題為第一題，因此請將注意力放在前半段獨白中，並仔細聆聽當中是否出現選項中的單字或相關單字。本題詢問餐廳的特色，因此請找出提及特色的句子。獨白中出現 only、best、our very own 這些單字，可以得知餐廳精選最棒的食材。整句話提到食材都是來自餐廳自有的地方農場（We choose only the best ingredients, all of which come from our very own local farm），因此餐廳的特色為 (C) It owns a local farm。

STEP 2 陷阱選項和錯誤選項

(A) It serves many dishes. ▶ 當中僅提到最近加入了新菜色，無從得知菜色選擇是否多樣。
(B) It has original appetizers. ▶ 餐廳特色片段中並未提及這一點。
(C) It owns a local farm. ▶ 答案
(D) It offers low prices. ▶ 聽到「All appetizers will be served at half-price.」，可能會誤選該選項，但是獨白中並未提到所有品項價格都很低廉。

78 題目中出現關鍵字時，答案會在該關鍵字前後的句子。▶ Stewart

STEP 1 若題目中出現特定的關鍵字，聆聽獨白時，勢必會於該關鍵字前後聽到答案。

第二題中出現人名關鍵字。當題目出現專有名詞，詢問職業或公司時，請務必聽清楚關鍵字前後的內容。獨白中說道：「the restaurant's owner, Stewart」，因此答案為企業老闆 (A)。

→ 雖然獨白提到明確的資訊，但是選項通常會改寫成較為廣義的敘述。
the restaurant's owner → (A) A business owner

STEP 2 陷阱選項和錯誤選項

(A) A business owner ▶ 答案
(B) A famous chef ▶ 聽到「restaurant」可能會誤選該選項。
(C) A server
(D) A talented actor ▶ 重複使用獨白中「talented farmer」的「talented」。

79 題目中出現指定句詢問說話者意圖時，答案會是說明較為籠統的選項。

STEP 1 指定句主要作為承先啟後的角色，表達說話者的意圖，因此要先確認前後文的意思，才能理解指定句真正的意思和說話者的意圖。

前方介紹完主餐後，提到自己也常吃這道料理（I eat them all the time.）。由此可知說話者提出此句話的原因，為的是推薦料理，因此答案為 (B) To recommend a dish。

STEP 2 陷阱選項和錯誤選項

(A) To complain about a menu ▶ 不滿意菜單的人應為客人。
(B) To recommend a dish ▶ 答案
(C) To explain a waiting time ▶ 與說話者的身分「waiter」的發音相似。
(D) To clarify a menu item
▶ 聽到指定句前方說道：「Today's entrée is . . .」，可能會誤選該選項，但本題詢問的是說話者提出「我也常吃這道料理」的意圖；前方句子已經介紹過菜單。

字彙 special 特製菜餚；特餐　ingredient （食品的）成分；食材
talented 有才能的；有才華的　produce 農產品　entrée 主菜　beverage 飲料
browse 瀏覽

Questions 80-82 refer to the following broadcast.

	Hello everyone. Thanks for listening to *More In Business World*. I	80-A
	am your host William, and today we have a very special guest, Gail	80-D
80	Nelson, the CEO of Homeland Dining Chains. She has been in the	
	restaurant industry for more than 30 years. She will share some	
	quick tips on improving your local restaurant. Today's topic is online	
	promotion. Running an online promotion can be expensive these	
81	days, but online promotions can bring more potential clients to	82-A
	your store. Plus, there are social media networks for reaching out	82-B
82	to your target audiences. She will tell you three tips for a successful	
	promotion strategy.	

80. What is indicated about Gail Nelson?
(A) She is running an ~~online~~ business.
(B) She is well known in her field.
(C) She has many years of work experience.
(D) She owns a ~~small~~ restaurant.

關鍵字 Gail Nelson／前
→ 注意聆聽提及代名詞的句子。

81. Why does the speaker say, "Running an online promotion can be expensive these days"?
(A) To reduce the marketing ~~expenses~~
(B) To acknowledge a common opinion
(C) To suggest ~~alternative~~ promotional methods
(D) To contradict the marketing ~~expert's~~ claim

掌握說話者意圖／中
→ 注意指定句前後方的文意。

82. What will the guest most likely do next?
(A) ~~Promote~~ her restaurant　(B) Talk to the ~~audience~~
(C) Give detailed suggestions　(D) Prepare a speech

第三者／未來／後
→ 注意使用代名詞和未來式的句子。

第 80-82 題 廣播

哈囉，大家好。歡迎收聽「商業世界面面觀」。我是你們的主持人威廉，今天我們邀請到的特別來賓，是家園餐飲連鎖公司的執行長，蓋兒·尼爾森。她在餐飲業已有三十年以上的資歷，將分享一些改善地方餐廳業績的速成訣竅。今日的主題是網路行銷。如今，網路行銷可能所費不貲，但卻可以為你帶來更多的潛在顧客。此外，還有社群媒體能幫助你打進目標客群。她將與諸位分享成功行銷的三個訣竅。

80. 關於蓋兒·尼爾森，提到了什麼？
(A) 她經營一家電子商務公司。
(B) 她在業界非常知名。
(C) 她擁有多年工作經歷。
(D) 她擁有一家小餐館。

81. 為何發言者會說：「如今，網路行銷可能所費不貲」？
(A) 欲縮減行銷經費
(B) 欲認同普遍共識
(C) 欲提議替代的行銷手法
(D) 欲反駁行銷專家的主張

82. 來賓接下來最有可能做何事？
(A) 推銷她的餐廳 (B) 與聽眾對話
(C) 給予詳細的建議 (D) 準備演講

80 題目中出現關鍵字時，答案會在該關鍵字前後的句子。▶ Gail Nelson

STEP 1 若題目中出現特定的關鍵字，聆聽獨白時，勢必會於該關鍵字前後聽到答案。在新制測驗中，答案不會直接出現在關鍵字後方，而是在下一句對白中使用代名詞（it / they / he / she）帶出答案。

獨白將關鍵字「Gail Nelson」換成 she，以「for more than 30 years」帶出她的工作經歷，因此答案為較為廣義的說明 (C) She has many years of work experience。

STEP 2 陷阱選項和錯誤選項

(A) She is running an ~~online~~ business. ▶ 獨白中並未提到「online」。
(B) She is well known in her field.
(C) She has many years of work experience. ▶ 答案
(D) She owns a small restaurant.
▶ 應改成「Homeland Dining Chains」，而非「small restaurant」。

81 請先刪除與引號內字面意思相同的選項。

STEP 1 聆聽題目中的指定句，搭配前後方句子，確認文意後，便能找出答案。

「Running an online promotion can be expensive these days」，後方說道：「but online promotions can bring more potential clients to your store.」。由此可知指定句表達的是說話者認同普遍的看法，因此答案為 (B) To acknowledge a common opinion。

STEP 2 陷阱選項和錯誤選項

(A) To reduce the marketing ~~expenses~~ ▶ 與「expensive」的發音相似。
(B) To acknowledge a common opinion ▶ 答案
(C) To suggest alternative promotional methods ▶ 聽到「online」可能會聯想到「alternative」。
(D) To contradict the marketing ~~expert's~~ claim ▶ 並未提到「expert」。

82 最後一句話出現Let's、next、from now等類似用法時，表示說明往後計畫。

STEP 1 **題目使用 next 詢問未來資訊時，請留意以 I / you / she / he will 開頭的最後一句話。**

獨白最後說道：「She will tell you three tips」，以此句話表示建議，因此答案為 (C) Give detailed suggestions。

→ 雖然獨白提到明確的資訊，但是選項通常會改寫成較為廣義的敘述。
three tips → (C) detailed suggestions

STEP 2 **陷阱選項和錯誤選項**

(A) Promote her restaurant ▶ 並未宣傳自己的餐廳。
(B) Talk to the audience ▶ 獨白和選項所指的「audiences」不同。
(C) Give detailed suggestions ▶ 答案
(D) Prepare a speech

字彙 **promotion** 推廣；行銷 **share** 分享 **expensive** 昂貴的 **potential** 潛在的 **reach out to** 接觸 **acknowledge** 承認；認同 **contradict** 反駁

Questions 83-85 refer to the following telephone message.

83 Hello, Alice. This is Federico from Fedex Express Delivery. Today, I'm scheduled to deliver office furniture to several offices in Birmingham.	83-A 83-D
84 Right now I'm looking for one of the addresses on the list I was given. There should be an office at 102 Lancaster Drive. Well, I drove up and 85 down the whole road, and all I see are houses. I'll deliver the furniture to the other offices on my list but while I'm doing that, could you please check the list and call me back with the correct address?	84-B 85-A

83. Where does the speaker most likely work?
(A) At a doctor's office
(B) At a delivery company
(C) At a construction firm
(D) At a ~~furniture~~ store

說話者／職業／前
→ 由「This is 說話者 from . . .」帶出說話者工作地點。

84. What problem does the speaker mention?
(A) ~~Damaged~~ office furniture
(B) Road ~~conditions~~
(C) A missing ~~check~~
(D) A wrong address

說話者／問題
→ 請和第一題一併聆聽。

85. What does the speaker imply when she says, "All I see are houses"?
(A) She is very impressed with the ~~houses~~.
(B) She is confused with ~~all~~ the addresses.
(C) She claims a mistake has been made.
(D) She thinks there are too many ~~buildings~~.

掌握說話者意圖／後
→ 聆聽時，請確認指定句前後文意。

第 83-85 題 電話留言

喂，愛麗絲。我是聯邦快遞的費德里柯。我預定今天運送辦公家具到伯明罕的幾處辦公室。我現在正在找派送清單上的其中一處位址，應該有一家公司位於蘭卡斯特路 102 號，不過我開著車沿著整條路來來回回地尋找，看到的都是一般民宅。我會繼續將家具送往清單上的其他公司，但與此同時，可否請妳核對一下派送清單，再回電告知我正確的地址？

83. 說話者最有可能在何處任職？
(A) 診所　(B) 貨運公司
(C) 營建公司　(D) 家具行

84. 說話者提到有何問題？
(A) 受損的辦公家具
(B) 路況
(C) 支票遺失
(D) 地址誤植

85. 當說話者提到：「看到的都是一般民宅」時，她有何暗示？
(A) 她對住宅區的房子印象深刻。
(B) 她把所有的地址都弄混了。
(C) 她聲稱有個地方出錯。
(D) 她認為建築物太多了。

83 前兩句話會以代名詞（I / You / We）或地方副詞（here / this ＋地點名詞）告知職業或地點。▶ 說話者的職業

STEP 1 獨白會按照主題，採固定方式表達職業或地點，請務必熟記。

電話留言 → 說話者的職業：This is 說話者 from . . .；聽者的職業：This is for 聽者。

本題詢問說話者的職業。開頭說道：「This is Federico from Fedex Express Delivery.」，由此話可知說話者任職於快遞公司，因此答案為 (B) At a delivery company。

STEP 2 陷阱選項和錯誤選項

(A) At a doctor's office ▶ 聽到「office furniture」可能會誤選該選項。
(B) At a delivery company ▶ 答案
(C) At a construction firm
(D) At a furniture store ▶ 聽到「office furniture」可能會誤選該選項。

84 連兩題針對問題點或職業等詢問時，答案的分布比例會變成 2：1。▶ 說話者的問題

STEP 1 連兩題詢問地點、職業、主旨或問題點時，獨白中的答案分布比例會變成 2：1。這類題型的第一題會詢問說話者的職業、第二題則會詢問問題為何，因此請從前半段獨白中，找出這兩個問題的答題線索。

獨白中說道：「I'm looking for one of the addresses on the list I was given. There should be an office . . . all I see are houses.」，表示住址有誤，因此答案為 (D) A wrong address。

STEP 2 陷阱選項和錯誤選項

(A) Damaged office furniture ▶ 位於獨白中第二句，並非答題線索所在之處。
(B) Road conditions ▶ 獨白中說道「the whole road」，提到「road」，但是並未提到「conditions」。
(C) A missing check ▶ 聽到「looking for」可能會聯想到「missing」。
(D) A wrong address ▶ 答案

85 題目詢問說話者說出指定句的意圖時，請務必搭配指定句前後文找出答案。

STEP 1 題目詢問說話者意圖時，務必要確認指定句前後的文意。

指定句前方説道：「there should be an office」，加上指定句表示：「All I see are houses」，提到應該要有辦公室，但他只有看到房子。以指定句表達他碰上了一些問題，因此答案為 (C) He claims a mistake has been made。

STEP 2 陷阱選項和錯誤選項

(A) He is very impressed with the houses. ▶ 重複使用指定句中的「houses」。
(B) He is confused with all the addresses. ▶ 只有其中一個，並非所有的住址。
(C) He claims a mistake has been made. ▶ 答案
(D) He thinks there are too many buildings. ▶ 聽到「houses」可能會聯想到「buildings」。

字彙 furniture 家具　address 地址　up and down 來回地　check 核對　construction 建造　damaged 受損的　confuse 使困惑　claim 聲稱

Questions 86-88 refer to the following excerpt from a meeting.

Thanks for attending today's meeting. Before we get started, I want
86 to let you know we appreciate your hard work and the extra hours each of you put in getting our new line of designer clothes ready for market. Thanks to your willingness to work overtime, all of our new
87 products will be ready in time for the Global Apparel Show coming up next week in Ontario. As you know, that's in addition to the clothing
88 we usually display, but we should not worry. This time we reserved three booths in the middle of the exhibition hall, and it's a large space.

86-A
87-A 87-B

86. Why does the speaker thank the listeners?
(A) For attending the exhibition
(B) For designing a Web site
(C) For working overtime
(D) For being punctual

說話者／thank 的原因／前
→ 注意聆聽表達感謝的句子和後方的內容。

87. According to the speaker, what is scheduled for next week?
(A) A clothing release　(B) A trade show
(C) An apparel show　(D) A car exhibition

關鍵字 next week
→ 注意聆聽關鍵字前後的句子。

88. What does the speaker imply when she says, "It's a large space"?
(A) There is room to display new merchandise.
(B) The building is much bigger.
(C) The number of companies participating this time has increased.
(D) High attendance is anticipated.

掌握說話者意圖
→ 務必要確認連接詞。

TEST 1 PART 4 中譯&解析

第 86-88 題 會議摘錄

感謝各位出席今日的會議。在會議開始之前，我想要先表達的是，公司感謝大家為了新一系列品牌服裝的上市，辛勤工作、超時加班。也多虧諸位願意加班，公司所有的新產品將能及時在下週、於安大略舉辦的全球服飾展中展出。如眾所知，這次公司較以往展出更多的服飾，但我們無需擔心，因為我們已在展覽館中央預訂了三個攤位，空間很大。

86. 發言者為何感謝聽眾？
(A) 感謝他們參加展覽
(B) 感謝他們設計官方網站
(C) 感謝他們超時工作
(D) 感謝他們準時

87. 根據發言者所言，下一週排定何事？
(A) 新裝上市 (B) 貿易展
(C) 服飾展 (D) 車展

88. 當發言者提到「空間很大」，她暗示何事？
(A) 有空間展示新的商品。
(B) 該幢建築大得多。
(C) 此次參展的公司數目有所增加。
(D) 預計將有眾多民眾參觀展覽。

86 題目以 why 詢問時，獨白會重複使用題目句的內容並於後方提及原因。

STEP 1 聆聽獨白時，請仔細聆聽 why 後方的關鍵字，其後方將會出現答案。

why 後方的關鍵字為 thank，因此本題詢問的是感謝的原因。獨白中說道：「we appreciate your hard work and the extra hours each of you . . .」，感謝各位超時工作，因此答案為 (C) For working overtime。

STEP 2 陷阱選項和錯誤選項

(A) For attending the exhibition ▶ 聽到「attending today's meeting」可能會誤選該選項。
(B) For designing a Web site ▶ 聽到「designer」可能會誤選該選項。
(C) For working overtime ▶ 答案
(D) For being punctual ▶ 聽到「hours」可能會誤選該選項。

87 題目中出現關鍵字時，答案會在該關鍵字前後的句子。▶ next week

STEP 1 若題目中出現特定的關鍵字，聆聽獨白時，勢必會於該關鍵字前後聽到答案。

一般來說會先聽到關鍵字，再聽到答案的內容，但在新制測驗中，有時反而會先聽到答案的內容，之後才聽到關鍵字，請特別留意。而本題同樣適用這個原則，關鍵字 next week 前方提到：「Apparel show」，因此答案為 (C) An apparel show。

STEP 2 陷阱選項和錯誤選項

(A) A clothing release ▶ 聽到「apparel」可能會聯想到 clothing，但是並未提到推出。
(B) A trade show ▶ 重複使用獨白中的單字「show」。
(C) An apparel show ▶ 答案
(D) A car exhibition

88 題目詢問引號內的說話者意圖時，請確認指定句前後方的連接詞。

STEP 1 題目詢問說話者意圖時，請務必確認指定句前後的連接詞。

指定句前方說道：「that's in addition to the clothing we usually display」，提到將展示更多的衣服。接著又提到這次預訂了三個攤位（This time we reserved three booths）。這表示指定句指的是有足夠的空間展示產品，因此答案為 (A)。

STEP 2 陷阱選項和錯誤選項

→ 若選項出現指定句中的單字、或是意思相同的單字時，便不是答案。

(A) There is room to display new merchandise. ▶ 答案

(B) The building is much bigger. ▶「building / bigger」等同於「large space」的意思。

(C) The number of companies participating this time has ~~increased~~.
▶ 聽到「large」可能會聯想到「increase」。

(D) High attendance is anticipated. ▶ 聽到「large」可能會聯想到「high attendance」。

字彙 attend 出席　appreciate 感激　get A ready 準備好 A　willingness 自願　overtime 超時　display 陳列　exhibition 展覽（會）

Questions 89-91 refer to the following telephone message and conference schedule.

Hello, this is Vanessa Romero from Pioneer Natural Resources Company. Last month I attended your impressive presentation at the international management workshop and I had a chance to speak to you after about my small firm. The reason why I'm calling is in regard
89 to your consulting service. I'd like to hire you to discuss ways to make
90 my company's operating system more efficient. I know your company specializes in this type of work, and I'm hoping you'll be interested in
91 this project. Could you please contact me with a list of your consultant fees? My number is 932-858-7721. Thank you.

89-B 89-C 91-A 91-D

The International Management Workshop	
9:00 A.M.	Business Operating Systems, Mitchel Kim
11:00 A.M.	Human Resources, Vanessa Romero
1:00 P.M.	Small Business, Sung Park
2:00 P.M.	How to Start a Business, Kelly Scott
4:00 P.M.	Q&A

89. What is the purpose of the call?
(A) To make a job offer
(B) To ~~attend~~ the workshop
(C) To ~~give~~ a presentation
(D) To arrange for a meeting

來電目的／前
→ 注意聆聽前半段獨白中以 I'm calling . . . / I'd like to . . . 開頭的句子。

TEST 1 PART 4 中譯&解析

90. Look at the graphic. Who is the speaker calling?
(A) **Mitchel Kim**
(B) Vanessa Romero
(C) Sung Park
(D) Kelly Scott

圖表資訊／聽者
→ 注意代名詞和時間表

91. What does the speaker ask the listener to do?
(A) Consult the report
(B) **Provide some information**
(C) ~~Work more~~ efficiently
(D) Get a discount

說話者／對聽者的要求／後
→ 注意聆聽疑問句和祈使句。

第 89-91 題 電話留言與會議時程

您好，我是先鋒自然資源公司的凡妮莎・羅米洛。上個月我參加了國際管理研討會，您的簡報令我印象深刻，便在會後找機會與您談了一下敝公司。我今天來電的目的是洽詢您的顧問諮詢服務。我想向您諮詢改善敝公司作業系統效率的方法。我知道貴公司專門從事這類型的工作，希望您能對這個專案感興趣。不知能否提供貴公司的顧問諮詢收費標準？我的電話是 932-858-7721，謝謝。

國際管理研討會	
上午 9:00	主題：業務操作系統 主講人：米契爾・金
上午 11:00	主題：人力資源管理 主講人：凡妮莎・羅米洛
下午 1:00	主題：小型企業 主講人：桑・帕克
下午 2:00	主題：如何創業 主講人：凱利・史考特
下午 4:00	問答時間

89. 此通來電的目的為何？
(A) 提供工作機會
(B) 參加研討會
(C) 做簡報
(D) 籌辦會議

90. 請見圖表，來電者電洽何人？
(A) 米契爾・金
(B) 凡妮莎・羅米洛
(C) 桑・帕克
(D) 凱利・史考特

91. 來電者要求受話者做何事？
(A) 查閱報告
(B) 提供資訊
(C) 工作更有效率
(D) 取得折扣

89 通常會使用「I'm calling . . .」表示電話留言的目的。

STEP 1 獨白前兩句話通常會提及目的；但是當目的為要求事項時，則會出現在後半段獨白中。

「I'm calling . . .」或「I'd like to . . .」用來表示電話留言的目的。獨白中說道：「The reason why I'm calling is in regard to your consulting service. I'd like to hire you . . .」，表示要提供對方工作機會，因此答案為 (A)。

→ 雖然獨白提到明確的資訊，但是選項通常會改寫成較為廣義的敘述。
I'd like to hire you →改寫成較為廣義的說法：(A) make a job offer

STEP 2 陷阱選項和錯誤選項

(A) To make a job offer ▶ 答案
(B) To attend the workshop ▶ 雖然獨白中有提到「attend」和「workshop」，但與來電目的無關。
(C) To give a presentation ▶ 雖然獨白中有提到「presentation」，但與來電目的無關。
(D) To arrange for a meeting

90 圖表資訊 ▶ 圖表題的選項不會直接出現在獨白當中。

STEP 1 請先看過題目和表格，以確認獨白中會出現哪些答題線索。

題目選項列出演講者的姓名，因此可以預先猜到答題線索為表格中的時間和研討會名稱。獨白中提到：「make my company's operating system more efficient」和「I know your company specializes in this type of work」，表示聽者 you 的專業為 operating system，因此答案為 (A) Mitchel Kim。

STEP 2 陷阱選項和錯誤選項

(A) Mitchel Kim ▶ 答案
(B) Vanessa Romero ▶ 打電話的人。
(C) Sung Park ▶ 聽到獨白中的「my small firm」，可能會連結至表格中的「small business」。
(D) Kelly Scott

91 題目詢問要求或建議時，答案會位在後半段獨白中，並以 please 告知。

STEP 1 PART 4 中詢問要求或建議時，指的是說話者（speaker）向聽者（listeners）要求的事情，因此答題線索會出現在後半段獨白中。

後半段獨白中說道：「Could you please contact me with a list of your consultant fees?」，詢問聽者可否聯絡自己，並告知收費方式。這表示說話者要求聽者 (B) Provide some information。

→ 雖然獨白提到明確的資訊，但是選項通常會改寫成較為廣義的敘述。
a list of . . . fees → (B) some information

STEP 2 陷阱選項和錯誤選項

(A) Consult the report ▶ 聽到「consultant fees」可能會誤選該選項。
(B) Provide some information ▶ 答案
(C) Work more efficiently ▶ 聽到「more efficient」可能會誤選該選項。
(D) Get a discount ▶ 聽到「fee」可能會聯想到「discount」。

字彙 impressive 令人印象深刻的 management 管理 in regard to 關於 hire 僱用 specialize in 專門從事

Questions 92-94 refer to the following broadcast and map.

You are listening to your Queens local news report and this is today's
92 weather. The typhoon passed through our city last night. Due to severe
93 damage caused by the heavy winds, this morning the intersection at the corner of Cliffton Street and Peterson Avenue is closed. All of the traffic lights there have been out of order, and road crews have just started arriving to repair them. According to the weather forecast, the repairs should be finished by 7 P.M., so drivers are asked to detour to the
94 south. However, this repair work will not have any impact on tomorrow's marathon along Cliffton Street, so if you are planning to participate in the event, stick to your plans. We'll have more details about tomorrow's event after this commercial break.

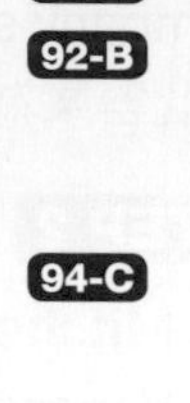

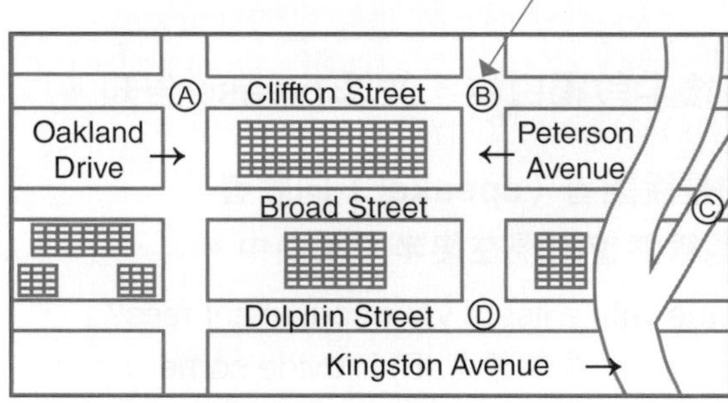

92. What caused a problem?
(A) A broken-down car
(B) An incorrect road sign
(C) Road construction
(D) Bad weather

93. Look at the graphic. Which location is the speaker describing?
(A) Location A
(B) Location B
(C) Location C
(D) Location D

94. What does the speaker say will take place tomorrow?
(A) A city tour
(B) An outdoor event
(C) Repair work
(D) A special election

問題原因／前
→ 注意聆聽開頭前兩句話。

圖表資訊／地點
→ 圖表為地圖時，請注意聆聽表示地點的介系詞。

關鍵字 tomorrow／後
→ 注意聆聽關鍵字前後的句子。

第 92-94 題　廣播與地圖

您現在正在收聽的是皇后區地方新聞，以下是今日天氣概況。颱風昨夜過境本市，強風造成嚴重損害，導致克里夫頓街與皮特森大道的交叉路口於今晨進行封閉。該處所有的交通號誌都已故障，道路維修團隊才剛抵達進行搶修。根據氣象預測，道路維修會於晚間七點以前修繕完畢，所以請駕駛向南繞道而行。此次的道路維修工作，將不會對明日在克里夫頓街舉辦的馬拉松賽造成任何影響；如果您打算參加馬拉松，可按原定計畫進行。廣告之後，會有更多明日活動的相關資訊。

92. 何事造成問題？
(A) 汽車故障　(B) 交通號誌出錯
(C) 道路施工　(D) 惡劣的天氣

93. 請見圖表，發言者所形容的位置為何？
(A) A 處　(B) B 處
(C) C 處　(D) D 處

94. 根據發言者所言，何事將於明日舉辦？
(A) 市區觀光　(B) 戶外活動
(C) 維修工作　(D) 特別選舉

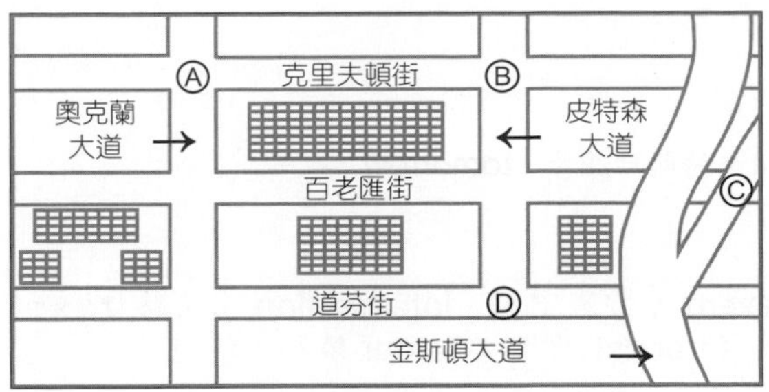

92 開頭前兩句話會談到「原因」。

STEP 1 獨白中會同時提到原因和問題。

獨白說道：「The typhoon passed through our city last night. Due to severe damage caused by the heavy winds, . . . is closed」，提到颱風過後，強風造成了嚴重的災害、道路封閉，因此答案為 (D)。

→ 雖然獨白提到明確的資訊，但是選項通常會改寫成較為廣義的敘述。
typhoon、heavy winds → (D) Bad weather

STEP 2 陷阱選項和錯誤選項

(A) A broken-down car
(B) An incorrect road ~~sign~~ ▶ 聽到「traffic lights」可能會聯想到「sign」。
(C) Road construction ▶ 聽到「Peterson Avenue」可能會聯想到「road」。
(D) Bad weather ▶ 答案

93 圖表資訊 ▶ 圖表題為地圖時，請由表示地點的介系詞確認位置。

STEP 1 請檢視地圖中的地點名詞，並用表示地點的介系詞找出答案。

獨白中提到「at the corner」，後方連接著答題線索。當中提到目前「Cliffton Street」和「Peterson Avenue」的交叉口已被封閉（the intersection at the corner of Cliffton Street and Peterson Avenue is closed），由此可知說話者描述的地點為 (B) Location B。

94 題目中出現關鍵字時，答案會在該關鍵字前後的句子。▶ tomorrow

STEP 1 若題目中出現特定的關鍵字，聆聽獨白時，勢必會於該關鍵字前後聽到答案。

關鍵字「tomorrow」後方提到「marathon」，表示明天將舉辦馬拉松，因此答案為 (B) An outdoor event。

→ 雖然獨白提到明確的資訊，但是選項通常會改寫成較為廣義的敘述。
marathon → (B) An outdoor event

STEP 2 陷阱選項和錯誤選項

(A) A city tour

(B) An outdoor event ▶ 答案

(C) Repair work ▶ 現在正在進行「repair work」，時間點並非「tomorrow」。

(D) A special election

字彙 typhoon 颱風　pass through 經過　severe 非常嚴重的　intersection 交叉路口
out of order 故障　crew 全體工作人員　forecast 預報　detour 繞行；繞道
stick to 堅守；固守

Questions 95-97 refer to the following excerpt from a meeting and pie chart.

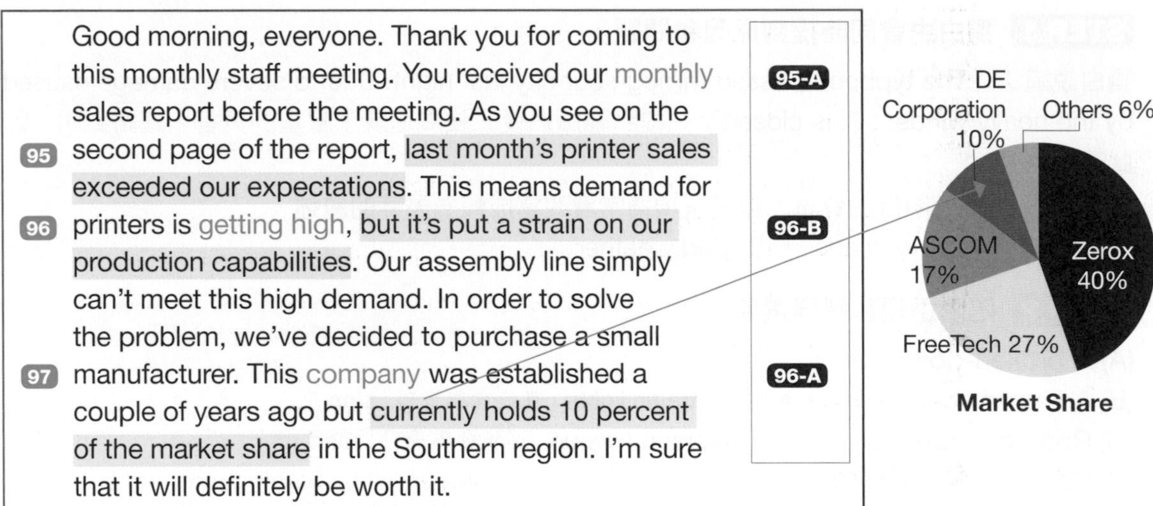

Good morning, everyone. Thank you for coming to this monthly staff meeting. You received our monthly sales report before the meeting. As you see on the
95 second page of the report, last month's printer sales exceeded our expectations. This means demand for
96 printers is getting high, but it's put a strain on our production capabilities. Our assembly line simply can't meet this high demand. In order to solve the problem, we've decided to purchase a small
97 manufacturer. This company was established a couple of years ago but currently holds 10 percent of the market share in the Southern region. I'm sure that it will definitely be worth it.
95-A
96-B
96-A
DE Corporation 10%
Others 6%
ASCOM 17%
Zerox 40%
FreeTech 27%
Market Share

95. What does the speaker point out on the report?

(A) A team has been nominated for a monthly ~~award~~.

(B) Sales are higher than expected.

(C) A new ~~executive~~ has been hired.

(D) A business will be ~~merged~~.

說話者／關鍵字 report
→ 注意聆聽過去式句子。

96. Why is the speaker concerned?

(A) The company seems to have lost its competitive edge.

(B) The operating costs have ~~increased~~.

(C) The production capacity is limited.

(D) Numerous complaints have been received.

說話者／問題點
→ 注意聆聽表示轉折的連接詞 But 後方的內容。

97. Look at the graphic. Which company may be acquired?

(A) Zerox　(B) FreeTech

(C) ASCOM　**(D) DE Corporation**

圖表資訊／公司／後
→ 注意聆聽數字。

第 95-97 題 會議摘錄與圓餅圖

各位早安，感謝諸位出席本次的員工月會。相信大家在開會前，都已收到本月的銷售報告。如同各位可在報告的第二頁中所見，上個月的印表機銷售量超出預期。這表示印表機的需求日益提升，但同時也對公司的生產能力造成了壓力。我們的生產線根本無法滿足如此高的需求。為了解決這個問題，公司決定併購一家小型製造業者。這家公司在幾年前創立，如今在南部地區擁有一成的市占率，相信這筆交易絕對值得。

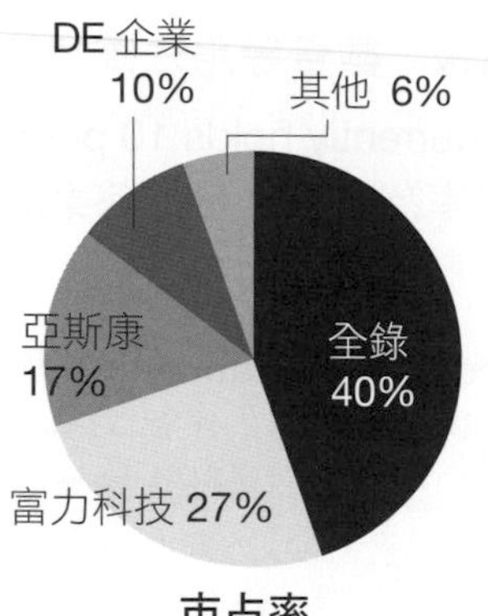

市占率

95. 發言者指出報告中的什麼？
(A) 一工作團隊榮獲本月最佳表現提名。
(B) 銷售量超出預期。
(C) 公司僱用一位新主管。
(D) 將有企業併購。

96. 發言者為何擔憂？
(A) 公司似乎失去競爭力。
(B) 營運支出增加。
(C) 生產力受限。
(D) 收到大量客訴。

97. 請見圖表，哪一家公司將被併購？
(A) 全錄 (B) 富力科技
(C) 亞斯康 (D) DE 企業

95 題目中出現關鍵字時，答案會在該關鍵字前後的句子。▶ report

STEP 1 若題目中出現特定的關鍵字，聆聽獨白時，勢必會於該關鍵字前後聽到答案。

「As you see on the second page of the report」後方說道：「last month's printer sales exceeded our expectations」，使用過去式表示上個月印表機銷售量比預期的好，因此答案為 (B)。

→ 雖然獨白提到明確的資訊，但是選項通常會改寫成較為廣義的敘述。
exceeded → (B) higher than

STEP 2 陷阱選項和錯誤選項

(A) A team has been nominated for a monthly ~~award~~. ▶ 獨白中並未提到「award」。
(B) Sales are higher than expected. ▶ 答案
(C) A new executive has been hired. ▶ 與「exceeded」的發音相似。
(D) A business will be merged.

96 But / However 後方會告知問題點。

STEP 1 獨白中出現 But、However 或 Actually 等表示轉折語氣的連接詞時，後方通常會帶出正確答案。

but 為表示轉折語氣的連接詞，前方提到印表機的需求增加，接著說道：「but it's put a strain on our production capabilities」，表示說話者擔心依照目前的生產能力，似乎不堪負荷，因此答案為 (C)。

STEP 2 陷阱選項和錯誤選項

(A) The company seems to have lost its competitive edge.
▶ 重複使用獨白中的「company」。

(B) The operating costs have increased. ▶ 聽到「getting high」可能會聯想到「increased」。

(C) The production capacity is limited. ▶ 答案

(D) Numerous complaints have been received.

97 圖表資訊 ▶ 提到圖表中的數量時，即為正確答案。

STEP 1 圖表的作用為「比較」，因此請從排序、最高級、數量等用法確認答案。

後半段獨白說道：「purchase a small manufacturer」和「currently holds 10 percent of the market share」，提到收購小型製造業者，而該公司的市占率為 10%，因此答案為 (D) DE Corporation。

字彙 staff meeting 員工會議　sales report 銷售報告　exceed expectations 超出預期　demand 需求　put a strain on 對……施加壓力　assembly line 生產作業線　meet 滿足　manufacturer 製造商　market share 市場占有率　region 區域

Questions 98-100 refer to the following telephone message and route options.

Hi, Kevin. This is Julie. I'm really excited to attend the **conference** at
98 McLean **this Friday**. You know, it is my first time joining an international 98-A
conference since I started working here at JML Fashion. Anyway, I 100-D
checked the directions this morning. The shortest route only takes 50
99 minutes, but unfortunately, it costs a lot — there are three tolls on the
way. So I think we'd better take another route. It will **take** approximately
70 minutes. It's a little longer, but I think it's the most economical and
fastest way for us since it has only **one toll**. Oh, and **would you mind**
100 **checking the schedule** to see what time the conference ends? I left
mine at my office, and I have to reschedule my doctor's appointment on 100-A, B
that day.

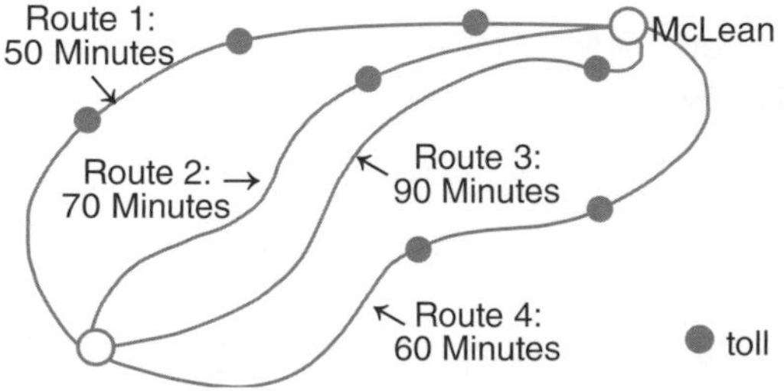

98. According to the speaker, what type of event is being held?
(A) An international ~~fashion show~~
(B) An annual picnic
(C) An industrial conference
(D) A job fair

主旨（活動類型）／前
→ 注意聆聽開頭前兩句話。

99. Look at the graphic. Which route does the speaker recommend taking?
(A) Route 1　　(B) Route 2
(C) Route 3　　(D) Route 4

圖表資訊／推薦路線
→ 注意聆聽表示轉折的連接詞 But。

100. What is the listener asked to do?
(A) Reschedule an appointment
(B) Confirm a reservation
(C) Check a timetable
(D) Sign up for an event

聽者／要求／後
→ 注意聆聽表示勸說或建議的句子。

第 98-100 題 電話留言與路線選擇

嗨，凱文，我是茱莉。一想到要參加這個星期五在麥克林舉辦的會議，就讓我非常興奮。你知道，這是自我開始任職於 JML 時尚公司以來，首次參加的國際會議。總之，我今早查看了一下交通路線，最短的路線只需要花 50 分鐘，可惜的是，因為要經過三個收費站，所以車資很貴。所以我覺得我們最好換一條路線。這個路線預計會花 70 分鐘，有一點久，但我覺得這是對我們來說最快速、經濟的方式，因為只需要經過一個收費站。喔，對了，你是否介意幫我查看一下會議日程，看看會議何時結束？我把我的日程表留在辦公室了，我得和我的醫生把那天的門診改期。

98. 根據來電者，即將舉辦何種活動？
(A) 國際時裝秀　　(B) 年度野餐聚會
(C) 產業會議　　(D) 就業博覽會

99. 請見圖表，來電者建議取道哪條路線？
(A) 路線一　　(B) 路線二
(C) 路線三　　(D) 路線四

100. 受話者被要求做何事？
(A)約會改期
(B)確認預約
(C) 查看會議日程
(D)報名參加活動

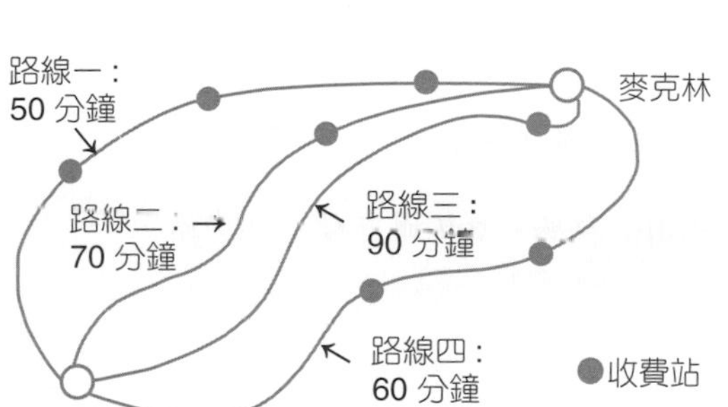

98 獨白中會依序出現答案線索。

STEP 1 本題詢問活動的類型，答案位在開頭前兩句話當中。

獨白中說道：「attend the conference at McLean this Friday, international conference」和「JML Fashion」，表示說話者要參加本週五舉行的時尚產業會議，因此答案為 (C) An industrial conference。

STEP 2 陷阱選項和錯誤選項

(A) An international fashion show
▶ 雖然獨白中有提到「international」，但是後方連接的對象不同。

(B) An annual picnic

(C) An industrial conference ▶ 答案

(D) A job fair

TEST 1 PART 4 中譯&解析

99 圖表資訊 ▶ 圖表題的選項不會直接出現在獨白當中。

STEP 1 **選項列出了路線，因此聆聽獨白時，請確認圖表中路線以外的資訊。也就是說，當中提及選項未列出的時間、或收取過路費的次數時，請務必仔細聆聽。**

獨白說道：「we'd better take another route. It will take approximately 70 minutes」和「since it has only one toll」，提到花費 70 分鐘，而且只要收取一次過路費，因此答案為 (B)。

→ 請特別留意，「**But / However**」等表示轉折語氣的單字後方，會出現關鍵的答題線索。

100 題目出現被動語態時，請注意聆聽表示勸說或建議的句子。

STEP 1 **題目出現被動語態時，通常是詢問說話者向聽者要求或建議的事情，因此獨白中會使用 You will . . .、祈使句、或是表示請求的問句以告知聽者。**

後半段獨白中說道：「would you mind checking the schedule to see what time the conference ends?」，請對方看一下日程表確認會議結束的時間，因此說話者要求聽者做的事為 (C) Check a timetable。

→ 雖然獨白提到明確的資訊，但是選項通常會改寫成較為廣義的敘述。
schedule → (C) timetable

STEP 2 **陷阱選項和錯誤選項**

(A) Reschedule an appointment ▶ 為說話者下一步的動作，並非答案。
(B) Confirm a reservation ▶ 聽到「**appointment**」可能會誤選該選項。
(C) Check a timetable ▶ 答案
(D) Sign up for an ~~event~~ ▶ 聽到「**conference**」可能會誤選該選項。

字彙 conference 會議 direction 指示路徑 route 路線 toll 通行費；收費站
approximately 大約 economical 省錢的；有經濟效益的

PART 5

101 (Before taking on a managerial position), you / must have / enough experience
介系詞片語 主詞 1 動詞 1
and qualifications / and / understand / how / --------- aspect (of your company) / runs.
受詞 連接詞 動詞 2 連接詞 主詞 3 動詞 3

請確認數量形容詞和名詞是否符合單複數一致性。
-------- aspect (of your company) + runs

STEP 1 空格要填入形容詞，修飾名詞 aspect。

名詞 aspect 為單數可數名詞，因此前方要使用限定詞，扮演形容詞的角色。而 (C) whole 和 (D) complete 皆為一般形容詞，因此不能作為答案。

STEP 2 each 後方要連接單數可數名詞；all 後方要連接複數可數名詞。

因此，答案為 (B) each。

STEP 3 請確認以下數量形容詞和名詞單複數的一致性。

❶ each / one / another ＋單數可數名詞
❷ many / a few / numerous ＋複數可數名詞
❸ much / a little / an amount of ＋不可數名詞

句子翻譯 在接任管理職務之前，你必須有足夠的經驗與資歷，並要懂得公司各面向的運作流程。
字彙 qualification 資歷　run 經營
答案 (B) each

102 Elizabeth Zane's teaspoons, / (in varying decorative shapes and sizes and
主詞 介系詞片語
approximately between $25 and $45,) / can be sold / (as a collection) / or / (-------).
動詞（完整句） 介系詞片語 對等連接詞

對等連接詞兩邊要連接性質相同的對象。
as a collection + or + --------

STEP 1 請由對等連接詞 or 前後方連接的單字來確認答案。

若連接的單字有重複的部分，可以省略。or 前方為介系詞片語 as a collection，因此空格會出現以下兩種可能性：

❶ 一種是省略重複的部分 as a，僅保留名詞 separation。
❷ 另一種是將 as a collection 視為副詞片語，空格要填入副詞。

空格要表達的是販售物品的單位，❶ as a separation 表示「分離」的概念，並不適當。答案應為副詞 (A) separately（個別地），填入後表示販售單位為整組合賣或「單賣」。

STEP 2 完整句後方要連接副詞。

「Elizabeth . . . can be sold」為結構完整的句子，後方應連接副詞。而後方本來要以副詞 collectively 代替 as a collection，變成「副詞 or 副詞」的結構。但是，collectively 的意思為「全體地」，不適用於表達「整組」合售的概念，因此才會使用 as a collection 代替。又 separately 用於表達單位時，意思為「個別地、分開地」，符合完整句要連接的詞性，因此可以填入空格當中。

STEP 3 對等連接詞兩邊要連接性質相同的單字、片語、或子句。

請確認連接對象的詞性是否符合「名詞 and 名詞」或「動詞 or 動詞」的規則。

對等連接詞	→不能放在句首。 →可以省略重複的部分，僅保留「片語和片語」或「單字和單字」。 （只有 so 的前後方都要連接完整句。）

句子翻譯 伊莉莎白贊恩的茶匙有各種形狀和大小的設計，售價約在 25 元至 45 元之間，可成套購買、也可單買。
字彙 decorative 裝飾性的
答案 (A) separately

103 The elevator / could carry / --------- of five thousand kilos (per day), / which /
主詞 1 動詞 1 受詞 1 副詞片語 代替句子的連接詞
means / it / could deliver / over a million kilos of material (per year). 兼主詞 2
動詞 2 主詞 3 動詞 3 受詞 3 副詞片語

請分清楚可數名詞 vs 不可數名詞。
及物動詞 carry + -------- of + 數字名詞

STEP 1 空格位在及物動詞 carry 的受詞位置，應填入名詞。

選項中，(A) loaded 為過去分詞（p.p.），因此不能作為答案。

STEP 2 (B) load 和 (D) loader 皆為可數名詞，前方要加上冠詞才行，因此不能作為答案。

綜合上述，答案為 (C) loads。再補充一點，a load of / loads of 的意思為「許多的、一車的」，請特別熟記。

STEP 3 a ＋名詞＋ of ＝形容詞

- a number of / a variety of / a series of + 複數名詞
- a load of = loads of = a lot of = lots of + 複數／不可數名詞

句子翻譯 這台電梯每日可乘載五千公斤的重量，也就是說每年可運輸上百萬公斤的乘載量。
字彙 material 原料；材料
答案 (C) loads

104 The Committee / was not / --------- convinced (of the need)
主詞 動詞 補語 介系詞片語
(to establish an additional facility and branches) (in Vietnam.)
形容詞片語修飾名詞 need 介系詞片語

題目為副詞詞彙題時，請一併確認被修飾的對象。
was not + -------- + 補語 (convinced)

STEP 1 空格修飾補語 convinced，應填入副詞。

選項皆為副詞，因此請按照句子的意思和結構，找出最適當的答案。(B) enough 要放在形容詞或副詞後方作修飾，因此不能作為答案。

STEP 2 請找出可以搭配否定副詞 not 一起使用的副詞。

首先，(D) surely 的用法為 surely not，因此不能作為答案；(C) almost 帶有「not completely（不完整的）」概念，因此不會加上 not 使用，而是用來修飾數字或是已完成的動作動詞。再補充一點，not 可以搭配 all 和 always 使用，表示部分否定的概念，請特別留意。綜合上述，答案應為 (A) fully，意思為「完整地、完全地」，填入後表示「不完整地、不完全地」。

STEP 3 以副詞修飾不同的對象

❶ very/extremely ＋形容詞／副詞：非常……
❷ 形容詞／副詞＋ enough：夠……
❸ much ＋形容詞／副詞的比較級：……得多

句子翻譯 委員會沒有完全信服有必要在越南新建額外的設備與分所。
字彙 committee 委員會 convinced 信服的 facility 設備
答案 (A) fully

105 (These days), (for brands) (that / want to provide / ---------
social customer service), it / is / more important /
(than ever) to establish close relationships with their customers.

(These days)：副詞片語；(for brands)：介系詞片語；that：關係代名詞（主格）；want to provide：動詞 1；social customer service：受詞 1；it：虛主詞；is：動詞；more important：補語；(than ever)：副詞；to establish close relationships with their customers：to 不定詞（真主詞）

副詞＋狀態形容詞（good、bad）＋名詞 vs. 形容詞＋分類形容詞（economic）＋名詞
及物動詞 provide + -------- + 分類形容詞 social + 名詞 customer service

STEP 1 空格要用來修飾 provide 的受詞 social customer service。

修飾的對象中出現形容詞，因此前方不會再連接其他名詞。而 (C) personality 和 (D) personalization 皆為名詞，因此不能作為答案。

STEP 2 不能使用副詞修飾分類形容詞。

形容詞分成❶表示名詞的性質或狀態的一般形容詞和❷表示名詞種類的分類形容詞。副詞可以修飾性質或狀態，卻不能修飾種類，請特別留意這一點。social customer service（社群客戶服務）中的 social 屬於分類形容詞，不能使用副詞修飾，因此空格要填入另一個形容詞，來修飾名詞 customer service。綜合上述，答案為形容詞 (A) personalized（個人化），填入後表示「客製化的社群客戶服務」。

句子翻譯 現今，想要提供客製化社群客戶服務的品牌，與顧客建立起緊密的關係比以往都還要來得重要。
字彙 than ever 比以前更…… personality 人格 personalization 個性化
答案 (A) personalized

106 (In order to connect to the Internet), you / will need to put in / the
user name and password / (that / was given / to you)
(when / you / set up / your account (--------- the Internet Service Provider).

(In order to connect to the Internet)：副詞片語；you：主詞 1；will need to put in：動詞 1；the user name and password：受詞 1；that：關係代名詞（主格）；was given：動詞 2；(to you)：介系詞片語；when：從屬連接詞；you：主詞 3；set up：動詞 3；your account：受詞 3；(--------- the Internet Service Provider)：介系詞片語

介系詞 with 帶有伴隨或責任的概念。
完整句 + -------- + 名詞（公司名稱）

STEP 1 確認後方名詞，選出適當的介系詞。

空格後方名詞 the Internet Service Provider 為公司名稱，而選項中的介系詞皆可以連接該名詞，因此請再確認空格前方的內容。

STEP 2 若選項中介系詞的意思都很接近時，不能光憑中文解釋選出答案。

(A) 填入 of 後，解釋為「公司的帳戶」。雖然看似沒有問題，但是 of 表示「所有、所屬或組成要素」，個人帳戶不應該屬於該公司所有；(B) 填入 at 後，表示地點的概念，搭配前方句子，可以

解釋為「在此處開設帳戶」；但是 password that was given to you（提供給您的密碼）表示負責管理的公司才可以提供 password，因此空格並不適合填入 at；(D) with 帶有伴隨或一起的概念，也可以用來表示「主管、責任、管理」，因此答案為 (D) with，表示「由該公司負責管理的帳戶」。

STEP 3 介系詞 at 和 on 用來表示時間和地點。

❶ at ＋時間名詞／地點名詞（地址或電話）
❷ on ＋星期、日期名詞／距離、樓層

除此之外，at 還可以連接表示距離、速度、或價格的名詞；on 還有另一個意思為「關於……」，與 about 的意思相同，表示主旨的概念，請務必熟記。

句子翻譯 若欲連上網路，您將需要輸入當初與網路服務業者申辦帳戶時所用的使用者姓名與密碼。
字彙 put in 提交　set up one's account 開立帳號
答案 (D) with

107 --------- / our marketing team / had expected / the GLOBE Innovation Expo / to be a success, the reviews (from the attendees) (still) / overwhelmed / all of us.

（主詞 1：our marketing team；動詞 1：had expected；受詞 1：the GLOBE Innovation Expo；受詞補語：to be a success；主詞 2：the reviews；介系詞片語：(from the attendees)；副詞：(still)；動詞 2：overwhelmed；受詞 2：all of us）

由副詞子句的連接詞確認句子間的關係。
------- + 完整句 , 完整句

STEP 1 空格後方連接兩個句子，因此要填入連接詞。

選項中，(C) Even so 為副詞，因此不能作為答案。

STEP 2 副詞子句的連接詞可以用來表示時間的先後順序。

空格後方的 had expected 為過去完成式，而主要子句中的 overwhelmed 為過去式，若填入 (A) Whenever（無論什麼時候），前後時態應該要一致，因此不適合填入該選項；(D) Because 表示原因或理由，雖然適用「後發生＋ because ＋先發生」的句型結構，但是主要子句中用到副詞 still，表示「儘管如此」，而前後內容分別為「期待的事＋______＋驚訝或事情不符合期待」，因此不適合作為答案。綜合上述，答案應為 (B) Although，表示與期待相反或兩者相互對照的概念。

句子翻譯 儘管行銷團隊預期能在全球創新大展有良好的表現，但與會者的評論仍讓我們所有人不知所措。
字彙 attendee 出席者　overwhelm 使不知所措
答案 (B) Although

108 FedEx / makes / three --------- / to deliver a package, and (following the third one), the undeliverable package / will be held (at our local office) and available (for pick-up for seven days).

（主詞 1：FedEx；動詞 1：makes；受詞：three ---------；形容詞片語修飾空格內名詞：to deliver a package；連接詞：and；介系詞片語：(following the third one)；主詞 2：the undeliverable package；動詞 2：will be held；介系詞片語：(at our local office)；補語：available；介系詞片語：(for pick-up for seven days)）

搭配動詞 make 一起使用的名詞
makes + -------- + to 不定詞

STEP 1　空格為 makes 的受詞，且受到 to 不定詞的修飾，因此要填入名詞。

make 的意思為「做出」，主要會搭配 effort（努力）、decision（決定）、mistake（錯誤）等名詞一起使用。本題的答案為名詞 (A) attempts，受到 to 不定詞的修飾，填入後表示「嘗試做」。

STEP 2　(B) purposes 和 (C) goals 分別表示目的和目標，通常會搭配動詞 achieve 一起使用，意思為「達成」。

另外，(D) experiences 的意思為經驗，要搭配動詞 have 一起使用。

「名詞＋ to 不定詞」搭配 to 不定詞使用的名詞：

ability to V 有能力去做……	effort to V 盡力去做……
incentive to V 有動力去做……	plan to V 計劃去做……
right to V 有權去做……	way to V 有方法做……
chance to V 有機會去做……	attempt to V 嘗試去做……

句子翻譯　聯邦快遞在嘗試三次投件未果後，會將無法投遞的包裹暫置在當地營業所，並開放七天的領取時間。

字彙　following 在……之後　undeliverable 無法送達的　pick-up 提取

答案　(A) attempts

109　The tasks / (involved in maintaining this apartment) --------- (within the responsibilities)
主詞 1　形容詞片語　介系詞片語
(of our on-site maintenance personnel) who / are (always) / happy (to assist you).
介系詞片語　關係代名詞（主格）動詞 2　補語　副詞片語

題目為動詞詞彙題時，務必先確認各動詞為及物還是不及物動詞，以及其意思。
主詞 (The tasks) + -------- + 介系詞 (within) + 名詞

STEP 1　空格後方連接介系詞 within，且選項的動詞為主動語態，因此空格要填入不及物動詞。

(A) have 和 (C) present 皆為及物動詞，因此不能作為答案。(B) cover 當作及物動詞使用時，意思為「包含」；當作不及物動詞使用時，意思則為「代替」，會搭配介系詞 for 一起使用。

STEP 2　確認主詞和動詞後方連接對象兩者間的關係。

名詞 responsibility 所涵蓋的範圍較廣，而名詞 task 屬於當中的一部分，因此答案為 (D) fall，意思為「屬於……」。主詞包含連接對象在內時，才會使用 (A) have 或 (B) cover。

STEP 3　fall 當作不及物動詞時，可以搭配各種不同的介系詞一起使用。

❶ 表示往下移動，意思為「落下、跌落、減弱」，會搭配副詞 down 或介系詞 from / to 一起使用。
❷ 等同於 become 的意思，例如 fall in love（墜入愛河）。
❸ 表示「屬於」某個群體，會搭配 into / within / under 一起使用。
❹ 表示所屬、責任、範圍、類型等。

句子翻譯　有關這間公寓的修繕任務，係由我們現場的修繕管理人員負責，他們將竭誠為您服務。

字彙　on-site 在現場的　personnel 人員　assist 協助

答案　(D) fall

110 If / --------- of these products / are / available (at a store) where /
連接詞 主詞 1 動詞 1 補語 形容詞子句 連接詞
you / (normally) shop, (then) visit / our Web site / and / place / an order.
主詞 2 動詞 2 動詞 3 受詞 3 連接詞 動詞 4 受詞 4

學會分辨表示否定意義的副詞、形容詞和代名詞。
連接詞 + -------- + of + 複數名詞 + 複數動詞 (are)

STEP 1 空格為 If 子句的主詞，受到介系詞 of 後方內容的修飾，因此要填入名詞。

選項中，(A) no 為形容詞、(B) not 為副詞，皆不能作為答案。雖然 (C) nothing 為名詞，但是不能被介系詞片語修飾，因此也不適合填入。綜合上述，答案應為 (D) none。

STEP 2 代名詞 no one vs. none vs. nothing

代名詞	no one	none	nothing
代替的對象	人物	人物、事物、不可數、可數	事物
可否被 of 介系詞片語修飾	x	o	x

句子翻譯 若您無法在平時購買的商店購得這些商品，請上我們的官網訂購。
字彙 available 可獲得的 place an order 訂購
答案 (D) none

111 (Only when stepping back) --------- analyze / a complicated situation (from various
分詞構句＝副詞片語 原形動詞 受詞 1 介系詞片語
aspects), so that / we / can handle / any kind of problems (related to our job).
連接詞 主詞 2 動詞 2 受詞 2 分詞構句＝形容詞片語

倒裝句：將 only 放到句首時，主詞和動詞要交換位置。
only 分詞構句 (Only when stepping back) + -------- + 原形動詞

STEP 1 「連接詞＋副詞」的句型結構中，計算主要動詞的數量時，分詞也要包含在內。

請先確認「連接詞＋ 1 ＝動詞的數量」。句中有 when 和 so that 兩個連接詞，等於要有三個主要動詞才對，因此空格要填入動詞，連接原形動詞 analyze。雖然 (C) in order to 後方可連接原形動詞，但是形成分詞構句後，並未出現主要動詞，因此不能作為答案；(B) our ability 為名詞，因此也不適合填入。選項中，只有 (A) is able to 和 (D) are we able to 有包含動詞。

STEP 2 句子中沒有出現主詞時，要使用分詞、或是原形動詞開頭的祈使句。

若填入 (A) is able to，前方沒有從事該動作的主詞，因此並不適當。be able to V 表示具備從事該動作的能力，因此答案為 (D) are we able to。倒裝句的結構為「be 動詞＋主詞＋形容詞＋ to 不定詞」。

STEP 3 將副詞 only 放到句首，表示強調時，主要子句的動詞要移到主詞前方倒裝。

原本的句子為「We are able to analyze . . . only when stepping back.」。

句子翻譯 唯有退一步思考，我們才能從各角度來分析複雜的狀況，進而解決與我們工作相關的各種難題。
字彙 step back 退一步（考慮問題） aspect 方面 related to 與……有關
答案 (D) are we able to

112 These proposals, (some of ---------) / have already been accepted (by the government), include / the reform (of fuel policies) / and / the expansion (of social safety net coverage).

主詞 1 / 主詞 2 / 動詞 2 / 介系詞片語 / 動詞 1 / 受詞 1 / 連接詞 / 受詞 2

主要動詞的數量＝連接詞數量＋ 1
主詞 , + (some of -------- +), + 動詞

STEP 1 「連接詞＋ 1 ＝動詞的數量」

句中有 have been accepted 和 include 兩個主要動詞，因此空格要填入連接詞，用來連接兩個動詞，並當作介系詞 of 的受詞。而 (A) them 和 (C) those 皆為代名詞，因此不能作為答案。

STEP 2 「數量詞、不定／數量代名詞＋ of」後方連接關係代名詞時，只能連接 which 或 whom。

根據本句的結構，空格要填入關係代名詞，代替先行詞 proposals，因此可以選擇 (B) that 或 (D) which 作為答案。但是，關係代名詞 that 不能放在介系詞後方，因此答案要選 (D) which。

❶ 先行詞為人物＋ all/most/half . . . of whom ＋不完整句
❷ 先行詞為事物＋ all/most/half . . . of which ＋不完整句

句子翻譯 這些提案包括石油政策改革與社會安全網絡的擴張，有部分已獲得政府的批准。
字彙 reform 改革　safety net 安全網　coverage （保險）範圍
答案 (D) which

113 The latest reports / suggest / that / Samsung's next mobile phone / will be / its most expensive / ---------, (exceeding the $1,000 mark for the first time).

主詞 1 / 動詞 1 / 連接詞 / 主詞 2 / 動詞 2 / 補語 / 分詞構句＝副詞片語

副詞放在最高級後方作修飾。
主詞 + will be + 最高級 (its most expensive) + --------

STEP 1 空格前方為完整句「主詞＋ be ＋補語」，因此空格要填入副詞。

空格要填入副詞，強調前方的最高級 its most expensive。
(A) just 為強調原級 as—as 的副詞；(B) later 為表示時間或順序的副詞，意思為「以後」，並不適當。

STEP 2 副詞修飾最高級時放置的位置

(D) very 用於強調最高級時，要放在最高級前方，用法為「the very ＋最高級」，因此不能填入空格中。綜合上述，答案應選 (C)，yet 放在最高級的後方表示強調。

修飾比較級和最高級的副詞

❶修飾比較級的副詞	❷修飾最高級的副詞	❸修飾比較級和最高級
much / (by) far / even / still / a lot	much / (by) far / the very	yet + 比較級 / the 最高級 + yet

句子翻譯 最近的報導指出，三星的下一支手機將會是有史以來最為昂貴的一款，首次突破 1,000 美元。
字彙 suggest 暗示；指出　exceed 超出　mark 標線
答案 (C) yet

114 This versatile table, (model no. 2301), / is designed to fit / (compactly) (for daily use) /
主詞 1 同位語名詞 動詞 1 副詞 介系詞片語
and / (conveniently) --------- / to seat a big party of ten (for special occasions).
連接詞 副詞 動詞 2 副詞片語 介系詞片語

句中使用對等連接詞時，後方可以省略相同的部分。
主詞 (This versatile table) + 動詞 (is designed)+ and + --------

STEP 1 空格前方連接對等連接詞 and，因此請填入適當的動詞。

and 前方的動詞為 is designed，而空格前方省略主詞 This versatile table，因此答案要選單數動詞 (B) expands。

STEP 2 分析錯誤選項

主詞為複數時，才能使用 (A) expand；(C) expanded 為過去式，句中並未出現表示過去的時間副詞，因此並不適合填入該選項；(D) be expanded，be 通常會放在助動詞後方，因此不能作為答案。

句子翻譯 這款多功能桌（型號 2301）特別為日常使用所設計，特殊場合最大可延展至供 10 人就座。
字彙 versatile 萬用的 compactly 緊密地 seat 容納……人
答案 (B) expands

115 Lake Front Towers, / (located in the heart of Toronto), / has / one hundred rooms,
主詞 分詞構句（插入句） 動詞 受詞
--------- (with a view of the city).
介系詞片語

省略不定代名詞和關係代名詞。
完整句 + -------- +（介系詞片語）

STEP 1 請先確認句子中省略了哪些字詞。

原本的句子為 _____（of which are）with a view of the city，當中省略了關係代名詞和 be 動詞，因此空格中要填入不定代名詞，代替先行詞 rooms。而 (C) almost 為副詞、(D) such 為形容詞，皆不能作為答案。

★表達部分關係〈數詞／代名詞／數量形容詞＋ of which/whom〉
all（全部）、half（一半）、most（大部分）、both（兩者）、many（很多）、some（一些）＋ of ＋ whom/which

STEP 2 rooms 為可數名詞，可以使用代名詞 (B) most 來代替。

(A) much 為代名詞，用來代替不可數名詞，因此不能作為答案。

★ most 的四大出題重點
❶ the most ＋形容詞／副詞：最高級
❷ the most ＋名詞：many、much 的最高級
❸ 不定代名詞：most ＋ of ＋特定名詞
❹ 一般形容詞：most ＋名詞「大多數的」

句子翻譯 湖前塔飯店位於多倫多市中心，內有 100 間客房，其中大多都能欣賞到城市景觀。
字彙 in the heart of 在……中央 view of the city 城市景觀
答案 (B) most

名詞子句連接詞

116 Please note / that / employees / are not able to take / paid annual leave --------- they /
動詞 1 主詞 2 動詞 2 受詞 2 主詞 3
have completed / (at least) one year's continuous service
動詞 3 受詞 3
(from the date of employment).
介系詞片語

狀態持續＋ until ＋時間點 vs. 一次性動作／動作完成＋ by the time ＋時間點
完整句 + -------- + 主詞 + 動詞

STEP 1 空格連接 that 子句後方的兩個完整句，因此要填入從屬連接詞。

雖然選項皆為從屬連接詞，但是單憑套入中文意思，仍無法確認答案。

STEP 2 請確認表時間的從屬連接詞各自搭配的時態和動詞。

「狀態持續＋ until ＋時間點」vs.「動作完成＋ by the time ＋時間點」

空格後方使用動詞 complete，表示一次性動作或動作已完成，而主要子句 not able to take paid annual leave 指的是不能使用年假，因此答案要選 (A) until。請務必熟記「not . . . until」，意思為「直到……才」。

STEP 3 確認錯誤選項。

若填入 (C) when，主要子句和副詞子句的動詞時態要一致才行。但是至少要經過一年的時間（at least one year's . . .），才能請年假，因此不適合填入該選項。

句子翻譯 請注意，員工須自受雇日起連續工作至少一年以上，才能請帶薪年假。
字彙 note 注意到 paid annual leave 帶薪年假 continuous 持續的
答案 (A) until

117 (In most cases), all outdoor activities for students / --------- (when /school/
介系詞片語 主詞 1 動詞 1 連接詞 主詞 2
has been closed (all day) / or / closed early).
動詞 2 副詞 連接詞 副詞

請確認從屬連接詞前後的時間順序。
主詞 + -------- + when + 主詞 + has been p.p.

STEP 1 題目考動詞時態時，請依序確認動詞的單複數→時態。

空格為主要動詞的位置，要填入及物動詞 cancel。空格後方沒有連接受詞，因此要使用被動語態才行。而 (B) have canceled 為主動語態，因此不能作為答案。

STEP 2 由時間副詞或從屬子句中的動詞，確認填入空格的動詞時態。

句中並未出現搭配動詞的時間副詞，因此請確認從屬子句中動詞的時態。when 子句中的動詞為現在完成式，請找出適合搭配使用的動詞。表示時間的副詞子句可以使用現在式代替未來式，空格可以填入現在式或未來式動詞，因此答案要選 (D) will be canceled。值得留意的是，(C) would have been canceled 中的 would have p.p. 屬於假設語氣中的過去完成式用法。

★表示時間的副詞子句中，會以現在式代替未來式、以現在完成式代替未來完成式

從屬子句	主要子句
表示時間／條件的從屬連接詞＋動詞（現在式） when / while / as / before / after / if	主詞＋動詞（未來式） will ＋原形動詞

句子翻譯 在大多數情況下，如果學校整日或提前關閉，所有的學生戶外活動都將取消。
字彙 outdoor activities 戶外活動　all day 一整天
答案 (D) will be canceled

118 Our new gift package (with --------- health-care products) / will be released /
主詞　介系詞片語　動詞
(next month) (so as to meet the needs of current or potential customers).
副詞　副詞片語：為了⋯⋯（目的）

請先確認形容詞修飾的名詞類型。
with -------- health-care products

STEP 1 products 屬於事物名詞，請選出適合修飾該名詞的形容詞。

(B) comparable 的意思為「可比較的」，用於比較兩個大小或品質（quality）相似的東西；(D) raised 指的是數值、數量、品質「上升或改善」，也可以指「提出」questions 或 concerns，並不會搭配 products 一起使用。

STEP 2 「valuable ＋人物／事物／抽象名詞」vs.「worthy ＋人物」

(A) valuable 可以用來表示物品（product）在使用上為「有用的、有價值的」；(C) worthy 放在名詞前方使用時，指的是受到人們尊重，不適合用來修飾 products，因此答案要選 (A) valuable。再補充一點，worthy 還有一個用法為「be worthy of ＋人物／事物」。

句子翻譯 我們的醫療保健禮盒組將於下個月上市，以滿足當前顧客與潛在顧客的需求。
字彙 health-care 醫療保健　be released 發行；上市　meet 滿足　current 當前的　potential 潛在的
答案 (A) valuable

119 One of the reasons (Mr. Hicks / is widely respected (--------- so many people)) /
主詞 1　主詞 2　動詞 2　介系詞片語
is / his great insight and a wealth of understanding of consumer behaviour.
動詞 1　補語 1

被動語態（be p.p.）中以介系詞連接動作執行者。
is respected + -------- + so many people

STEP 1 一般會省略關係副詞 why。

原本的句子為「the reason (why) ＋完整句」，省略 why 後則變成「One of the reason is . . .」。

STEP 2 被動語態（be p.p.）後方連接介系詞 by 再加上動作執行者。

be respected 動作的執行者為 so many people，因此空格要填入介系詞。答案要選 (D) by 帶出動作執行者，指受到 so many people 的尊敬。(A) plus 的用法為「A plus B」，不適合填入空格中；(B) from 指的是來源或出身，適合搭配的動詞有 receive、get、obtain 等；(C) in 用於表示時間或地點。

句子翻譯 希克斯先生備受大家尊敬的其中一個原因，是他出色的洞察力和對消費者行為的廣泛理解。
字彙 insight 洞察力　consumer 消費者
答案 (D) by

120 Our new customers / --------- receive / a ten percent discount (on their first order at
主詞 1　動詞 1　受詞 1　副詞片語
the site by entering their membership number and password).

以現在式搭配頻率副詞陳述一件事實
主詞 + -------- + 動詞

STEP 1 請找出適當的副詞，修飾現在式動詞 receive。

句中並未出現時間副詞，以現在式（receive）陳述一項事實：「新會員首購可享九折的優惠」。(A) customarily（習慣上、通常）為頻率副詞，可以用來描述事實，故為正確答案。

頻率副詞的位置： ❶ 放在助動詞和主要動詞之間。
❷ 放在 be/have 動詞和過去分詞之間。
❸ 放在 be 動詞後方、一般動詞前方。

usually 和 often 可以放在句首，也可以放在句尾，而 always 通常不會放在句首。
表否定的頻率副詞（not、hardly、never、seldom）一定要放在動詞前方。

* **週期**：hourly 每小時、daily 每天、monthly 每月、yearly/annually 每年
* **次數**：once 一次、twice 兩次、three times 三次
* **頻率**：regularly 經常、always 總是、frequently/often 常常、sometimes 偶爾、usually 經常

STEP 2 分析錯誤選項

(B) exactly 的意思為「確切地、正好地」，指數字或數量剛好符合、或者用於強調與對象正好相同或不同時，屬於表示強調的副詞；而 receive 表示動作，兩者不適合一起使用。

(C) repeatedly 的意思為「不停地」，與句中的 first order 相抵觸，因此不能作為答案。

(D) almost 的意思為「幾乎」，表示不完整的狀態，通常會用來修飾數字或動作完成。

句子翻譯 我們的顧客在網站首次下單時，輸入會員帳號與密碼即可獲得 9 折優惠。
字彙 password 密碼
答案 (A) customarily

121 (In order to --------- a refund request), a customer / should contact /
副詞片語（目的）　主詞　動詞
the Internet service provider (directly) (as set forth in the applicable policy).
受詞　副詞　分詞構句

請確認動詞為及物動詞還是不及物動詞，並確認該動詞適合連接哪一類名詞。
-------- + 要求退款 (a refund request)

STEP 1 挑出可以連接受詞的及物動詞。

空格連接受詞 a refund request，因此要填入適當的及物動詞。而 (C) proceed（進行）為不及物動詞，因此不能作為答案。

STEP 2 確認及物動詞後方要連接的受詞為人物還是事物。

(B) appoint 的用法為「appoint ＋人物＋ to (do) sth」，意思為「指派、任命……」，受詞要使用人物名詞，因此該選項並不適合；(D) ask 和後方名詞 request 的意思相同，也不適合填入空格中。綜合上述，答案要選 (A) initiate（開始實施、創始）。

★重要的 S+V+O 句型及物動詞：連接人物作為受詞

通報／告知類動詞	指派、任命類動詞
advise（建議）、inform（通知）、remind（提醒）、notify（通知）、assure（使確信）、brief（簡報）	appoint（任命）、nominate（提名）

句子翻譯 如欲提出退款要求，顧客須依政策中的說明，直接與網路服務業者聯絡。
字彙 set forth 闡明　applicable policy 適用政策
答案 (A) initiate

---

122 (During the military parade), motorists / were stuck / (in traffic for two hours)
介系詞片語　主詞 1　動詞 1　介系詞片語
(on a five-kilometer --------- of road) (between Lancaster City and Hamilton).
介系詞片語（地點）　介系詞片語

分辨名詞後方要連接一段時間或距離。
on a five-kilometer -------- of road

STEP 1 **five-kilometer / road 可以指長度（length）或距離（distance）。**

(B) stretch 為可數名詞，前方可以加上表示長度或距離的形容詞作修飾，意思為「綿延……長的地區、區間」。另外，stretch 也可以用來表示持續的一段時間，請特別熟記。例如：a stretch of two weeks（為期兩個星期左右）。

STEP 2 名詞表示一段時間時，不能搭配表示物理長度的單字一起使用。

(A) journey（可數／旅程）；(C) duration（不可數／持續一段時間）；(D) period（可數／期間），三者皆表示一段時間，而 kilometer 和 road 指的是距離，因此不適合搭配在一起使用。

句子翻譯 在閱兵遊行期間，機車騎士在蘭開斯特市與漢密爾頓之間約五公里的路程，塞了兩個小時之久。
字彙 military parade 閱兵　be stuck in traffic 塞車
答案 (B) stretch

---

123 Southwestern Energy Company / is hosting / its 10th Annual Convention
主詞 1　動詞 1　受詞 1
(next month) (where / all of our employees / will experience / a ---------
副詞片語　形容詞子句　主詞 2　動詞 2
range of expert presentations, seminars, and hands-on demonstrations).
受詞 2

務必要分清楚意思相似的單字。
a -------- range of expert presentations

STEP 1 空格用來修飾後方的單數名詞 range，因此要填入形容詞。

(C) few 用來修飾複數可數名詞，不能修飾單數名詞 range。several 和 few 的意思相似，也曾出現在題目中作為陷阱選項。

STEP 2 請分辨意思同為「多樣的」diverse vs. various vs. assorted。

range 可以指範圍（年齡、距離）、幅度或商品，但通常會使用 a range of 表示「很多的（a number of）」。若要解釋得更為明確，a range of 指的是彼此雖然不一樣，但是屬於同一個類型（type）。(B) various 指的是屬於不同的類型（type），因此不能作為答案；(D) assorted 也是指屬於不同的類型，因此也不適當；(A) diverse 指的是彼此相異（very different from each other），但都屬於同一個類型（type），故為正確答案。

再補充一點，請一併熟記其他意思相似的用法「a variety / range / series of ＋複數名詞」。

> 句子翻譯 西南能源公司將在下個月舉辦第十屆年度大會，所有員工將可參加各式各樣的專家演講、工作坊與實作訓練。
>
> 字彙 host 主辦 range 一系列 expert 專家 hands-on 實際動手做的
>
> 答案 (A) diverse

124 Many options / are being --------- / as / the city / discusses / the future of the old
主詞 1 動詞 1 連接詞 主詞 2 動詞 2 受詞 2
church, (the historic brick building) (which / was constructed (two hundred years ago)).
the old church 的同位語 關係代名詞（主格） 動詞 3 時間副詞片語

表達情感／認知／所有的狀態動詞不能使用進行式。
Many options are being -------- + 副詞子句

STEP 1 空格位在被動進行式 be being p.p. 的位置，因此空格要填入 p.p.。

按照句型結構，空格要填入過去分詞，而 (B) famous 為形容詞，因此不能作為答案。

STEP 2 表達情感／認知／所有的狀態動詞不能使用進行式。

首先，請將被動語態句型改寫成主動語態，方能加速理解句意。

這表示現在句子中的主詞 Many options 會變成受詞，因此請確認適合搭配該受詞的動詞為何。find、know、consider 後方皆可以連接事物名詞 many options，但是動詞 (A) found 和 (C) known 指的是心裡的認知，不能使用（現在）進行式，因此答案為 (D) considered。

> 句子翻譯 這座城市正在討論這座古老教堂的未來，該教堂約在 200 年前所興建，是極具歷史意義的磚砌建築，有許多選項皆被納入考慮。
>
> 字彙 option 選項 historic 有歷史意義的
>
> 答案 (D) considered

125 Ford Family / has sold / more than 100 million albums (worldwide), (making them one of
主詞 1 動詞 1 受詞 1 副詞
the most successful bands), (------- only The Philips in record sales).
形容詞片語修飾名詞 albums 副詞片語

務必要熟悉介系詞的正確用法。
完整句 , -------- + 名詞

STEP 1 behind 除了指物理位置之外，還可以指成果／進展／成功上「落後」。

空格前方提到「Ford Family 在全世界的專輯銷量超過一億張，為最成功的樂團之一」。但是在唱片銷量上，僅次於 The Philips，因此答案為 (D) behind。

STEP 2 **確認介系詞的正確用法。**

(A) except 的用法為「全體對象＋ except ＋排除對象」；(C) among 要連接複數名詞，因此不能作為答案；(B) over 適合搭配表示一段時間的名詞，表示「在……期間」，也可以用來表示比起比較對象更好，但是本題指的是比不上 The Philips，因此並不適合填入空格中。

> 句子翻譯 福特家族在全世界的專輯銷量已超過一億張，為史上最成功的樂團之一，其唱片銷量僅在飛利浦樂團之後。
>
> 字彙 record sales 唱片銷售
>
> 答案 (D) behind

126 Please notify / your customers / that / air or hotel --------- (made through a third-party payment account or online travel agency) / will not be refunded.

動詞 1（notify）　受詞 1（your customers）　連接詞（that）　主詞 2（air or hotel ---------）　形容詞片語（made through a third-party payment account or online travel agency）　動詞 2（will not be refunded）

> purchase 可以連接可數名詞或不可數名詞。
> **air or hotel -------- + made + 介系詞 + 名詞 + 動詞**

STEP 1 **that 子句的主要動詞為 will not be refunded。**

空格後方為動詞 made 開頭的分詞構句，修飾 that 子句的名詞主詞。

STEP 2 **空格要填入名詞時，名詞選項優於動名詞選項。**

句子的主要動詞為 will not be refunded，空格受到分詞 made 的修飾，為主詞的位置，因此要填入名詞。若選項同時出現名詞和動名詞時，選擇名詞選項優於動名詞選項，因此不能選擇 (C) purchasing 作為答案。(D) purchaser（買方）為人物名詞，且為可數名詞。使用單數時，前方要加上冠詞；使用複數時，後方要加上 s，因此不能填入該選項。

STEP 3 **確認名詞為可數或不可數名詞。**

purchase 指購買行為時，為不可數名詞；指購買的東西時，為可數名詞。本句話提到無法退款一事，指的是購買的東西，因此答案為可數名詞複數形 (A) purchases。還有一個用法為 make a purchase（購買），請一併熟記。

> 句子翻譯 請告知顧客，透過第三方付款帳戶或線上旅行社所訂購的機票或飯店住宿，將不予以退款。
>
> 字彙 third-party 第三方　refund 退款
>
> 答案 (A) purchases

127 The tenth International Movie Festival / is held (this weekend,) / but / the celebration / was held (one week ---------).

主詞 1（The tenth International Movie Festival）　動詞 1（is held）　連接詞（but）　主詞 2（the celebration）　動詞 2（was held）　副詞片語（one week ---------）

> 搭配「數量詞＋時間名詞」一起使用的副詞
> **活動 + was held + one week --------**

STEP 1 **確認完整句中的「數字＋時間單位＋副詞」。**

完整句後方連接 one week，為「數量詞＋時間名詞」。選項中，只有副詞 (C) earlier 可以放在數量詞後方使用。(B) following（在……以後）當作介系詞使用時，用法為「following ＋名詞」；

(D) previously（之前）為常見的時間副詞，前方不會再加上時間名詞；(A) advanced 為形容詞，意思為「先進的、進步的」，不能作為答案。

STEP 2 搭配數字＋時間單位一起使用的副詞。

one week after/before（＋名詞／子句）：在……一週前／後
one week ago/early(earlier)/later：一週之前／一週前／一週後

> 句子翻譯 第十屆國際電影節將在本週末舉行，但慶祝活動已在一週前舉辦完畢。
> 字彙 be held 舉行　celebration 慶祝活動
> 答案 (C) earlier

128 Should / emergency assistance / be required (--------- our regular business hours),
助動詞　主詞 1　動詞 1　介系詞片語
you / can contact / our emergency office number (at 062-343-4111).
主詞 2　動詞 2　受詞 2　介系詞片語

> 以介系詞 outside 連接時間名詞。
> **完整句 + -------- + 時間名詞**

STEP 1 本題要選出介系詞，修飾後方的時間名詞（business hours）。

本句為倒裝句，省略 if 後，主詞和助動詞交換位置，should 便移至句首。(B) outside 可以作為副詞或介系詞使用。一般會想到的用法為搭配地方名詞，表示「在外面、外部」，但 outside 也可以指超越某種範圍或限制，請一併熟記這兩種用法。

★ outside 的用法：

❶ outside ＋地方名詞：在……之外　例 outside the town
❷ outside ＋界線／限制：超出……　例 outside my experience

STEP 2 分辨介系詞要連接的是一段時間還是時間點。

複數名詞 business hours 表示一段時間，而 (A) at 要連接時間點，因此不能作為答案；(C) next to（在……旁邊）為介系詞，但是後方要連接地方名詞，因此也不是答案；(D) off 為副詞，不能作為答案。綜合上述，答案要選 (B) outside。

> 句子翻譯 若您在我們上班時間以外時需要緊急救助，請致電我們的緊急狀況辦公室 062-343-4111。
> 字彙 be required 有必要；有需要　business hours 上班時間
> 答案 (B) outside

129 (After much --------- by the judges), the finalists / have been selected
介系詞片語　主詞 1　動詞 1
(in all five categories of the World Music Awards).
介系詞片語

> 確認 much 的詞性和用法。
> **介系詞 + much ---- + 介系詞 + 名詞 (by the judges)**

STEP 1 形容詞 much 用來修飾不可數名詞。

空格位在介系詞 after 的受詞位置，受到形容詞 much 的修飾，因此要填入名詞。而選項中，只有 (D) deliberation（深思熟慮）為名詞。

STEP 2 副詞 much 主要用來修飾形容詞比較級。

介系詞片語 by judges 指動作執行者，因此可能會認為空格要填入過去分詞 (B) deliberated，而此處的 much 便會視為副詞，用來修飾 p.p.。但是 much 作為副詞使用時，通常會放在形容詞比較級前方。若要修飾動詞，要使用 so / too / very + much 放在句尾。

句子翻譯 經過評審團的深思熟慮後，最終入圍者入圍了世界音樂獎的所有五個類別。

字彙 deliberation 深思熟慮　finalist 入圍決賽者

答案 (D) deliberation

130 Private investors (for this project) / will receive / financial benefits, (such as dividends, right issues, or warrants,) --------- / they / had invested in / a company's ordinary shares.

（主詞 1：Private investors；動詞 1：will receive；受詞 1：financial benefits；介系詞片語：such as dividends, right issues, or warrants；主詞 2：they；動詞 2：had invested in；受詞 2：a company's ordinary shares）

選擇連接詞時，務必要先確認兩個句子間的關係。
完整句 + -------- + 主詞 + 動詞

STEP 1 「主要動詞的數量＝連接詞數量＋ 1」

空格前後各連接一個子句，因此要填入連接詞。而 (A) otherwise 為副詞，因此不能作為答案。

STEP 2 選擇連接詞時，務必要先確認兩個句子間的關係。

(B) unless 的意思為「除非……」，表示條件。副詞子句要使用現在式、主要子句要使用未來式，因此不適合填入空格中。

(D) so that 表示目的或結果，為副詞子句的連接詞。用法為「先發生的事＋ so that ＋後發生的事」，而本題的句型結構為「未來＋ -------- ＋過去完成」，因此不適合作為答案。答案要選 (C) as if，表示「就像……一樣」。

句子翻譯 該項目的個人投資者將獲得如股息、股票認購權與認股權證等財務收益，就如同投資公司的一般股票。

字彙 dividend 股息　right issue 權利股發行　ordinary share 普通股（票）

答案 (C) as if

PART 6

Questions 131-134 refer to the following information.

Call for Volunteers
Fall Bio Blitz

The Office of Sustainability is looking for 20 volunteers to help run our Fall Bio Blitz event on Sunday, February 10 next year. Volunteers will assist with registration, escort Bio Blitz participants out to join hikes, and will also be welcomed to participate in all event activities. We want **you** to **encourage** event **participants** and **help to facilitate** a positive experience for them. **— 131 —**.

What is Bio Blitz? Spend the day with us identifying plants and animal species on the Niagara-on-the-Lake Campus. Expert scientists lead citizen scientists like **— 132 —** on hikes around the property **— 133 —** identifying and cataloging the bugs, birds, amphibians, mammals, and plants. Niagara College is hosting the Fall Bio Blitz on Sunday, February 10 from 2:00 P.M. to 9:00 P.M. at the entrance to the Wetland Ridge Trail. Students, staff, and community members **— 134 —** to this free event and help 活動尚未舉行 nation that can inform our species inventory of the campus!

If you are interested in volunteering for this event, please e-mail Amber Schmucker, Sustainability Engagement Officer, by Monday, December 27 at aschmucker@niagaracollege.ca.

131. **(A) However, any issues and incidents should be reported to the volunteer coordinator directly.**
(B) For more information on our ~~campus schedule~~, please visit the event page on our Web site.
(C) Furthermore, attendance on ~~all four days~~ is preferred.
(D) In addition, volunteers are asked to attend ~~this~~ orientation one day before the event.

132. (A) them
(B) ours
(C) himself
(D) us

133. (A) that
(B) during ▶ ＋一段時間
(C) while ▶ ＋ ing「當……的時候」→分詞構句
(D) on ▶ ＋ ing「一……就」→先後順序

134. (A) have invited
(B) are invited
(C) will be invited
(D) would have been invited

句子插入題
→ 確認空格前後方的內容。

代名詞
→ 題目考的是代名詞時，請留意要與前方提過的對象一致。

介系詞 vs. 連接詞
→ 確認介系詞後方的名詞。

動詞時態
→ 確認其他動詞的時態。

第 131-134 題 資訊

招募志工

秋日生態快閃活動

生態永續發展推動辦公室正尋求二十名志工，協助我們在明年二月十日星期日舉辦秋日生態快閃活動。志工將協助處理報到程序，陪同參加活動的民眾徒步健行，同時也可參與所有的細項活動。我們需要志工激勵參加的民眾，助他們有個美好的活動體驗。不過，倘若發生任何問題或是事故，皆必須向志工統籌人員直接彙報。

什麼是生態快閃活動呢？跟著我們用一整天的時間，一起在濱湖尼亞加拉校區辨識各種動植物物種。專家學者會帶領像我們一樣的公民科學家徒步繞行校區，就昆蟲、鳥類、兩棲動物、哺乳動物以及植物等進行辨識，並記錄編目。尼亞加拉學院將於二月十日星期日下午二時至九時，在濕地嶺步道的入口處，舉辦一場秋日生態快閃活動。敬邀學生、教職員以及社區居民來參與這個免費的活動，協助蒐集資料，增添本校的物種目錄！

如果您有興趣擔任本活動的志工，敬請於十二月二十七日星期一以前，寄電子郵件至 aschmucker@niagaracollege.ca，永續工作推動專員安柏．施慕克收。

字彙 sustainability 永續性　volunteer 志工　assist 協助　registration 登記
escort 陪同　hike 徒步旅行　be welcomed 歡迎　facilitate 促進
property 地產　identify 識別　catalog 為……編目　amphibian 兩棲動物
mammal 哺乳動物　collect 採集　inform 通知　species 物種　inventory 財產目錄

131 句子插入

題目為句子插入題時，請由空格前後方內容確認答題關鍵字。

STEP 1 前一句話提到志工所扮演的角色。

本篇文章的主旨為招募志工，空格前方的句子提到志工要負責的工作，因此空格要填入擔任志工的工作內容。

STEP 2 請確認選項中的關鍵字。

(A) 不過，倘若發生任何問題或是事故，皆必須向志工統籌人員直接彙報。
→負責做的事情／扮演的角色。

(B) 欲進一步了解本校校園活動時間表，請瀏覽本校官網的校園活動頁面。
→前方並未提到校區日程表（campus schedule），因此不能作為答案。

(C) 此外，優先錄取參加全程四日活動的民眾。
→活動只有一天，並非為期四天（four days），因此不能作為答案。

(D) 除此之外，志工需在活動的前一天參加此培訓。
→句中提到 this orientation，但是前方並未出現 this 所指的內容，因此不能作為答案。

答案要選 (A)，表示志工的工作內容。

字彙 incident 事件　report 報告　furthermore 此外　attendance 出席

132 連接單詞——代名詞
題目考的是代名詞時，請確認它指的是空格前方的哪一個對象。

STEP 1 代名詞用來代替前方出現過的名詞，因此請從空格前方找出重複提及的對象。

STEP 2 空格要填入介系詞 like 的受詞。

選項的代名詞皆能放在介系詞後方，而本題的答案要選 (D) us（我們），放在 like 後方表示「像我們一樣的市民科學家」。若填入 (A) them（他們），表示「向他們一樣的市民科學家」，則會變成 expert scientists = citizen scientists，並不合理；(B) ours（我們的）為所有格代名詞，前方並未出現它能代替的對象；(C) 為 himself（他自己），而前方同樣未出現 he 相對應的對象。

133 連接單詞——連接詞
連接詞後方要連接 S+V；介系詞後方要連接名詞。

STEP 1 務必要先確認句中的主要動詞和連接詞。

選項有連接詞 (A) that（那）和 (C) while（當……的時候）、介系詞 (B) during（在……的整個期間）和 (D) on（一……就），因此請先確認句中主要動詞和連接詞的數量。空格所在句子中只有一個主要動詞 lead，卻沒有任何連接詞，因此可以判斷空格應該要填入介系詞。

STEP 2 選出適合搭配後方名詞的介系詞。

介系詞 during 表示「在……期間」，後方要連接表示一段特定時間的名詞，不適合連接動作 identifying，因此不能作為答案；on 加上 V-ing 表示先後順序，指「一……就」，也不適合填入空格中。本題答案要選 (C) while 加上 V-ing 為分詞構句，表示「當……的時候」。while 作為副詞子句連接詞時，後方可以直接連接動詞的 -ing / p.p.，將子句變成分詞構句，請務必熟記。

134 動詞時態
題目為動詞時態題時，請確認其他動詞的時態。

STEP 1 題目為動詞時態題時，請依照單複數→語態→時態的順序逐一確認。

空格要填入動詞，而 invite 為及物動詞，後方要連接人物名詞作為受詞。但是空格後方連接介系詞，表示要填入被動語態。而 (A) have invited 為主動語態，因此不能作為答案。

STEP 2 請由前後句子的時態來確認動詞時態。

由前方句子可以得知活動尚未發生，因此答案要選未來式 (C) will be invited（將受邀）。(D) would have been invited（本來會受邀）為與過去事實相反的假設語氣；(B) are invited（受邀）指的是現在發生的一般事實，請特別熟記。

Questions 135-138 refer to the following advertisement.

Mars Office
Renovation Experts

與供應家具有關的內容

MORE creates a new atmosphere and interior to suit every single office, no matter the size. Most office designs are uninspired. Therefore, work environments create uninspired and stressful employees. Things like lack of privacy, poor lighting, poor ventilation, poor temperature control, or inadequate sanitary facilities can create a stressful work environment. So just let us do our job! **Our designs** have **— 135 —** small traditional **offices** as well as large-scale projects commissioned by architects and property developers. **— 136 —**. However, **no** single **supplier** can offer office **furniture** for all spaces and sizes. That is why MORE has developed close relationships with many professional furniture manufacturers **— 137 —** to provide us with the **custom designs** we need. **Such resources** give **us** the variety necessary **to complete** any **— 138 —**. In summary, we can bring you the most ideal office you've ever dreamed of.

135. **(A) transformed**
(B) related
(C) associated
(D) assembled

動詞詞彙
→ 確認受詞。

136. (A) ~~A work environment~~ is one of the most important issues you should consider.
(B) For most projects, we use furniture from our own factories.
(C) Some furniture needs ~~special care~~.
(D) Under normal conditions, our furniture is ~~guaranteed~~ for one year.

句子插入題
→ 確認空格前後的句子。

137. (A) readily
(B) readier
(C) readiest
(D) ready

名詞＋形容詞
→ 在名詞後方放置副詞或形容詞。

138. (A) research
(B) form
(C) order
(D) agreement

名詞詞彙
→ 確認相關的動詞、介系詞、形容詞。

第 135-138 題 廣告

火星辦公室
翻修專家

「火星辦公室翻修專家」為每一間不同的辦公室，量身打造出專屬的全新氛圍及內部裝潢，無論空間大小皆能翻修。多數的辦公室設計總是枯燥乏味。而這樣的辦公環境，激發不出員工的創意，反徒增員工的壓力。諸如缺乏隱私、照明不足、通風不良、室內空調不佳或是衛生設備不足等情形，都有可能打造出讓人備感壓力的工作環境。那麼，就讓行家出手吧！我們的設計不僅讓小型的傳統辦公室面目一新，也能改造建築師及土地開發商所委任的大型計畫。其中大多數的計畫，皆使用我們自有工廠所產的家具。然而，沒有一家供應商能為所有不同規模大小的空間，提供合適的辦公家具。這也是為何本公司會與多家專業的家具製造業者，發展出密切的合作關係，以便提供我們所需要的客製化設計。如此多樣化的資源，讓我們足以完成任何的訂單需求。綜上所述，我們可以為您帶來夢想中的理想辦公室。

字彙 atmosphere 氣氛　suit 適合　uninspired 無創意的　stressful 緊張的
lack of ……短缺　lighting 照明設備　ventilation 通風　inadequate 不充分的
sanitary 公共衛生的　large-scale 大規模的　commission 委任　close 密切的
custom 按顧客要求專門……的；客製的　in summary 總的來說　ideal 理想的

135 動詞詞彙

題目為動詞詞彙題時，請確認連接的受詞。

STEP 1 題目為動詞詞彙題時，請先確認及物或不及物動詞搭配的介系詞。

related 指「有關聯的」，用法為 relate A to B，(C) associated 指「聯想、結交」，用法為 associate A with B，請務必熟記。

STEP 2 請務必確認及物動詞可以連接的受詞。

選項皆為及物動詞，但是 (D) assembled 的意思為「組裝」，不適合連接 offices 當作受詞，因此不能作為答案。本篇文章為廣告，針對設計宣傳的部分，表示「我們的設計將能改造辦公室」較為適當，因此答案要選 (A) transformed，意思為「使變化、煥然一新」。

字彙 transform 使改變；改造

136 句子插入
題目為句子插入題時，請由空格前後方內容確認答題關鍵字。

STEP 1 「______」＋ However ＋單一業者無法提供所有家具。

由後方連接的句子「然而，沒有一家供應商能為所有不同規模大小的空間，提供合適的辦公家具。」，由此可知得知前面要填入與此句話意思相反的句子。

STEP 2 請確認選項中的關鍵字。

(A) 工作環境是你該考慮的幾個重要問題之一。
→與後方提及供應家具的內容無關，因此不能作為答案。

(B) 其中大多數的計畫，皆使用我們自有工廠所產的家具。
→表示大部分是使用自家工廠生產的家具，故為正確答案。

(C) 有些家具需要特殊維護。→後方並未提到維護的內容，因此不能作為答案。

(D) 在正常情況下，我們的家具保固期是一年。→後方並未提到保固的內容，因此不能作為答案。

綜合上述，答案為 (B)。

字彙 under normal conditions 在正常情況下　guarantee 擔保

137 形容詞
在名詞後方放置副詞或形容詞。

STEP 1 空格前方為完整句，因此空格通常會填入副詞。

STEP 2 句尾的副詞要用來修飾句中的動詞。

若將 (A) readily 填入空格中，意思為「容易發展」，不符合文意。因此答案要選 (D) ready，修飾前方名詞 manufacturers，連接後方 to 不定詞，表示「專業的家具業者準備好提供客製化的家具給我們」。

字彙 readily 容易地　ready to V 準備好去做……

138 名詞詞彙
題目為名詞詞彙題時，請確認相關的動詞、介系詞、形容詞。

STEP 1 由選項內容可以得知本題為名詞詞彙題。

題目為名詞詞彙題時，請確認相關的動詞、介系詞、形容詞。

STEP 2 請選出適合作為及物動詞 complete 受詞的名詞。

句中的 such resources（這樣的資源）指的是前句話中的 custom designs，因此答案要選 (C) order，填入後表示「提供客製化的設計讓我們能順利完成任何訂單」。

字彙 research 研究　form 表格　agreement 協議

Questions 139-142 refer to the following e-mail.

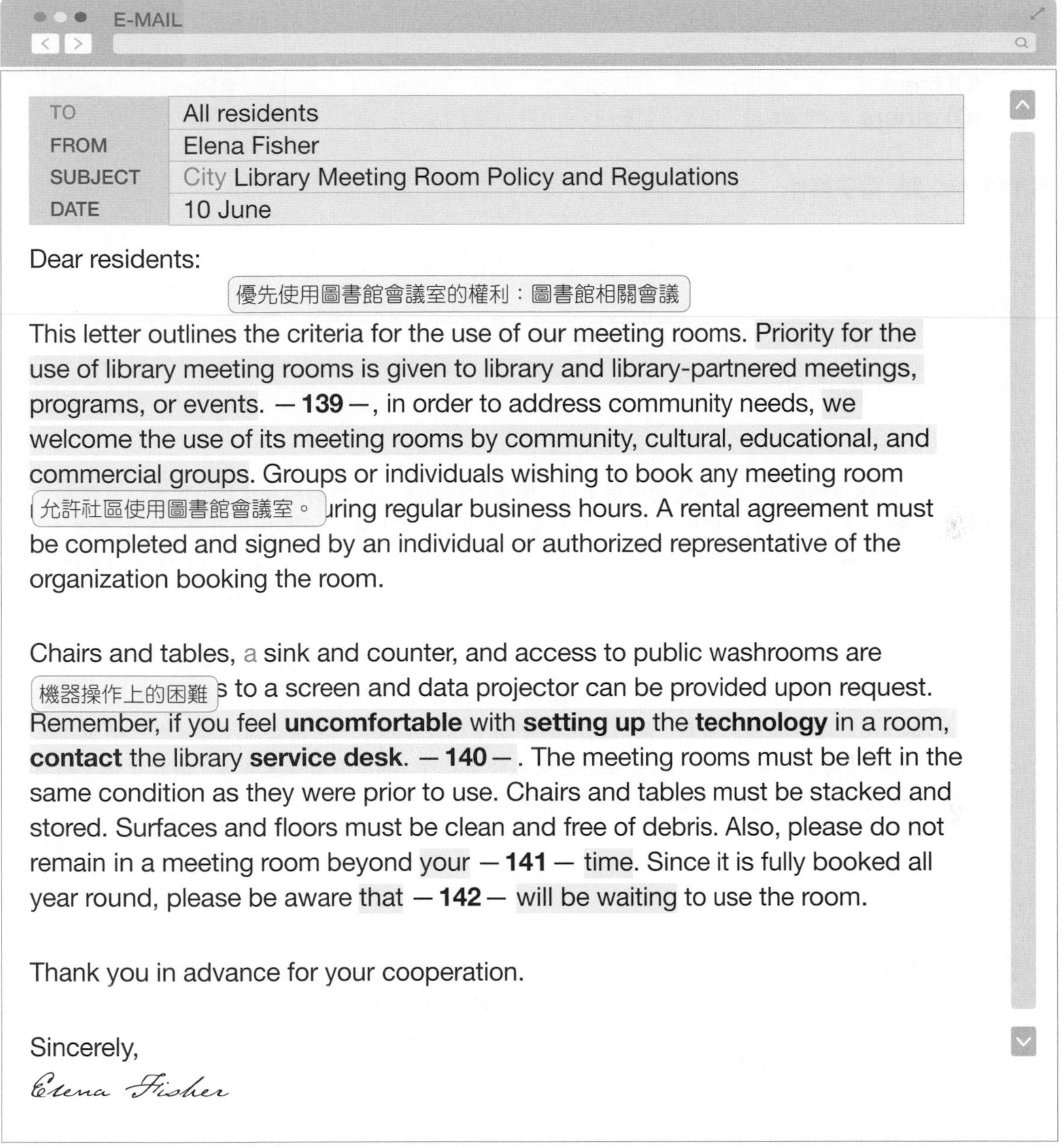

E-MAIL

TO	All residents
FROM	Elena Fisher
SUBJECT	City Library Meeting Room Policy and Regulations
DATE	10 June

Dear residents:

優先使用圖書館會議室的權利：圖書館相關會議

This letter outlines the criteria for the use of our meeting rooms. Priority for the use of library meeting rooms is given to library and library-partnered meetings, programs, or events. — **139** —, in order to address community needs, we welcome the use of its meeting rooms by community, cultural, educational, and commercial groups. Groups or individuals wishing to book any meeting room 允許社區使用圖書館會議室。 uring regular business hours. A rental agreement must be completed and signed by an individual or authorized representative of the organization booking the room.

Chairs and tables, a sink and counter, and access to public washrooms are 機器操作上的困難 s to a screen and data projector can be provided upon request. Remember, if you feel **uncomfortable** with **setting up** the **technology** in a room, **contact** the library **service desk**. — **140** — . The meeting rooms must be left in the same condition as they were prior to use. Chairs and tables must be stacked and stored. Surfaces and floors must be clean and free of debris. Also, please do not remain in a meeting room beyond your — **141** — time. Since it is fully booked all year round, please be aware that — **142** — will be waiting to use the room.

Thank you in advance for your cooperation.

Sincerely,

Elena Fisher

139. **(A) However** (B) Therefore
(C) Whereas (D) So that

140. (A) Access to ~~library data~~ can be approved within five business days of your request.
(B) Only ~~groups~~ larger than twelve will be eligible for meeting rooms.
(C) One of our technicians will be on-site for you prior to your meeting.
(D) Ms. Fisher is able to make an exception in ~~such cases~~.

連接副詞
→ 確認前後句子的關係。

句子插入題
→ 確認空格前後的句子。

141. **(A) allotted** (B) allotting
(C) allotment (D) allot

所有格____名詞
→ 空格要填入形容詞。

142. (A) it
(B) some
(C) there
(D) others ▶ others 前方提及的對象之外不定代名詞

代名詞
→ others 代替不特定的名詞。

第 139-142 題 電子郵件

收件者	全體居民
寄件者	艾琳娜．費雪
主旨	市立圖書館會議室使用政策規章
寄件日期	6 月 10 日

敬啟者：

本函將簡略說明圖書館會議室的使用準則。圖書館或圖書館協辦的相關會議、計畫以及活動，將享有圖書館會議室的優先使用權。然而，為因應地方需求，圖書館歡迎各地方社團、文化團體、教育團體及商業團體商借使用會議室。計劃預訂會議室的個人或團體，可於正常的上班時間辦理預約登記。辦理預約的個人或是團體代表，須填妥會議室租用同意書，並完成簽署。

租借會議室，桌椅、洗手台及公眾廁所皆可供使用。螢幕及數據投影機亦可申請提供。請謹記，倘若您對會議設備的架設有所疑慮，可洽圖書館服務台提供協助。在您的會議開始之前，本館將派一位技術人員在現場為您服務。使用過後的會議室應恢復原狀。桌椅必須堆疊放好。桌面及地面必須清理乾淨、勿留碎屑。同時，請勿在您的規定時間之外，繼續在會議室逗留。由於會議室的商借預約常年額滿，請謹記尚有其他人靜待使用會議室。

在此感謝您的配合。

艾琳娜．費雪 謹致

字彙 **outline** 概述 **criteria** 準則（criterion 的名詞複數） **priority** 優先考慮的事
address 應付；滿足 **agreement** 協定 **representative** 代表
access to 有權使用 **upon request** 經要求 **stack** 把……堆疊
debris 碎片 **all year round** 一整年

139 連接副詞
確認空格前後句子的關係，便能找出連接副詞的答案。

STEP 1 **選項中的連接詞有 whereas 和 so that。**

請先確認句中主要動詞和連接詞的數量。本句話中只有一個主要動詞 welcome，因此連接詞 (C) whereas 和 (D) so that 皆不適合作為答案。

STEP 2 **句首的連接副詞用來說明前後句子的關係。**

空格前的句子提到圖書館主辦或協辦的會議，有優先使用會議室的權利，後方的句子則提到 community 可以使用，表示前後句為相互對比的關係。(B) therefore 為「因此」，表示結果，不適合作為答案。因此答案要選 (A) However，意思為「然而」，表示前後為相反的概念。

字彙 whereas 儘管　so that 以便

140 句子插入
題目為句子插入題時，請由空格前後方內容確認答題關鍵字。

STEP 1 **if uncomfortable / contact / service desk**

空格前方的句子提到，如果對於會議室的機器操作上有困難，請聯絡服務櫃檯。因此，空格填入的句子要談到聯絡服務櫃檯後，提供的處理方式。

STEP 2 **請確認選項中的關鍵字。**

(A) 圖書館資料的使用申請，會於提出申請後的五個工作天之內核准完成。
→並未提及 library data，因此不能作為答案。

(B) 只有超過十二人以上的團體才得使用會議室。
→並未提到人數，因此 (B) 也不能作為答案。

(C) 在您的會議開始之前，本館將派一位技術人員在現場為您服務。

(D) 在這種請況下，費雪女士可以破例通融。
→雖然當中提到特定人士，但是前方並未提到 such cases（這樣的情況），因此不能作為答案。

綜合上述，(C) 提到由技術人員（technicians）解決問題，故為正確答案。

字彙 approve 批准　eligible 有資格的　on-site 現場的　prior to 在……之前
make an exception 作為例外；破例

141 分詞形容詞

受到修飾的名詞為受詞時，使用 p.p.；受到修飾的名詞為主詞時，使用 V-ing。

STEP 1 空格位在所有格和名詞之間，要填入形容詞。

STEP 2 請務必確認分詞和被修飾名詞之間的關係。

(C) allotment 為名詞、(D) allot 為動詞，因此皆不能作為答案。其餘兩個選項為分詞，因此請留意被修飾名詞是分詞的受詞還是主詞。句末的 time 是 allot（分配）的受詞，因此答案為過去分詞 (A) allotted。allotting 的用法為「名詞＋ allotting ＋名詞」，請特別留意。

字彙 allot 分配給……

142 代名詞

代名詞用來代替前方出現過的名詞。

STEP 1 空格要填入動詞 will be waiting 的主詞。

空格為主詞的位置，要填入名詞，而 (A) it 和 (C) there 皆不適合作為正在「等待」的對象。

STEP 2 請務必熟記 others 用來代替不特定的名詞。

since 連接的句子提到「整年的預約很滿，尚有等待使用會議室的人。」(B) some 的意思為「一些」，代替前方提及對象的其中一部分，不適合填入本句話中。(D) others 的意思為「其他人（其他東西）」，為不定代名詞，可以用來代替不特定的名詞，請特別熟記。

Questions 143-146 refer to the following article.

A spokesperson for NYC University — **143** — **that Shepherd Nolan**, a local entrepreneur, **made** a sizeable **donation** toward the expansion of the Fairland campus. "Without his generous support," said Stacy Mckinney, director of facility management, "our school would have been limited in our renovation plans going forward."

如果沒有他的捐款，翻修計畫將受到限制。

— **144** —. **Now**, a couple of **new wings** will be constructed on the south end of the — **145** — main campus building, as well as on the northeast corner of Lloyd Research Center. Additionally, **a new fitness center** will be located — **146** — the current student **lounge**. During the construction period, the closest entrance to the west side of the main campus building will be at the north end of the West Wing. These changes will be in effect for the duration of the construction period for the fitness center, which is scheduled to continue until the winter of next year.

將進行翻修計畫

143. (A) will confirm
(B) confirmation
(C) will be confirming
(D) has confirmed

動詞時態
→ 確認其他動詞的時態。

144. (A) Ms. Mckinney's ~~performance~~ at Lloyd Research Center was outstanding.
(B) The renovation plan had been delayed because of budget cuts.
(C) The number of research projects has decreased over the past ten years.
(D) The original ~~fitness center~~ is being converted into the on-site laboratory for students.

句子插入題。
→ 確認空格前後的句子。

145. (A) temporary
(B) existing
(C) located
(D) proposed

形容詞詞彙
→ 確認空格後方的名詞。

146. **(A) adjacent to** ▶ +地方名詞
(B) although ▶ 連接詞
(C) instead of ▶ +代替的對象
(D) besides ▶ +補充

介系詞詞彙
→ 確認句中的答題關鍵詞。

第 143-146 題 文章

紐約大學的發言人已證實，本地企業家雪佛·諾蘭捐贈大筆資金擴建紐約大學斐爾蘭校區。設備管理主任史黛西·麥堅尼說道：「若非他的慷慨解囊，本校的改建計畫將無法持續推行。」

過去由於預算縮減，導致改建計畫延宕。現如今，在現有的校園主建築南端，以及洛伊德研究中心的東北角處，將增建幾幢側翼建築。此外，新的健身中心也將與現有的學生交誼廳毗鄰而居。在工程期間，校區主建築西側最近的出入口將改在建築西翼的北端。此調整將於健身中心的建築工程期間生效，預計將持續至明年冬季。

字彙 spokesperson 發言人　entrepreneur 企業家　make a donation 捐款
sizeable 相當大的　expansion 擴展　generous 大方的；慷慨的
go forward 進行　wing（增建的）建築翼部　be located 坐落於
be in effect 生效

143 動詞時態

題目為動詞時態題時，請確認其他動詞的時態。

STEP 1 空格要填入動詞。

空格後方有連接詞 that 和主要動詞 made，而 A spokesperson 後方沒有動詞，因此空格要填入動詞才行。(B) confirmation 為名詞，因此不能作為答案。

STEP 2 若句中沒有表示特定時間的副詞，請根據其他動詞的時態來判斷空格要填入的動詞時態。

that 子句後方連接過去式 made，選項中 (A) will confirm 和 (C) will be confirming 皆為未來式，因此不能作為答案。本題答案要選 (D) has confirmed，以現在完成式表示確認（confirm）過去的事實「地方企業家捐款一事」。

144 句子插入

題目為句子插入題時，請由空格前後方內容確認答題關鍵字。

STEP 1 空格要填入與捐款和 renovation plan 有關的內容。

空格前方的句子提到特定企業家捐款一事，若沒有那位企業家的捐款（donation），renovation plan（翻新計畫）將受到限制，空格後方的句子則提到「現在（now）將建設（will be constructed）新的側翼建築」。因此，答案要選 (B)，表示「過去因為預算刪減，延誤了翻新計畫（renovation plan）。」

STEP 2 請確認選項中的關鍵字。

(A) 麥堅尼女士在洛伊德研究中心的表現非常出色。
→前方並未提到特定人物的表現（performance），因此不能作為答案。

(B) 過去由於預算縮減，導致改建計畫延宕。

(C) 過去十年來，研究計畫的數量有所減少。
→前方並未提及研究計畫的數量（the number of research projects）減少。

(D) 原有的健身中心將改建為學生的校園實驗室。
→本句話提到 fitness center，與前方句子毫無關係。

字彙 performance 工作表現　outstanding 卓越的　delay （使）延誤　budget cut 預算削減　the number of ……的數目　decrease 減少　convert （使）轉變

145 形容詞詞彙
題目為形容詞詞彙題時，請確認相關的名詞。

STEP 1 空格要填入適當的形容詞，修飾名詞 main campus building。

前方提到要在行政大樓南方興建 new wings（新的側翼建築），因此答案要選 (B) existing「現存的」，填入後表示「在目前的行政大樓增設新的側翼建築」。

字彙 temporary 暫時的　proposed 被提議的

146 介系詞
介系詞後方會連接名詞。

STEP 1 空格要填入介系詞，放在完整句和地點名詞之間。

空格後方連接表示地點的名詞 lounge，選項中 (B) although 為連接詞，因此不能作為答案。請從其餘選項中，選出適合搭配名詞 lounge 的介系詞。

STEP 2 請確認介系詞的意思，以及該介系詞如何表示兩個名詞間的關係。

使用形容詞 adjacent 表示「a new fitness center 鄰近 lounge」，並搭配表示位置的介系詞 to 最為適當，因此答案為 (A) adjacent to（靠近）。

(C) instead of（取而代之）的用法為 A instead of B，句中要提到代替和被代替的對象，因此不適合作為答案。

(D) besides 的意思為「此外」，為補充說明的介系詞，請務必熟記。

Questions 147-148 refer to the following e-mail.

E-MAIL

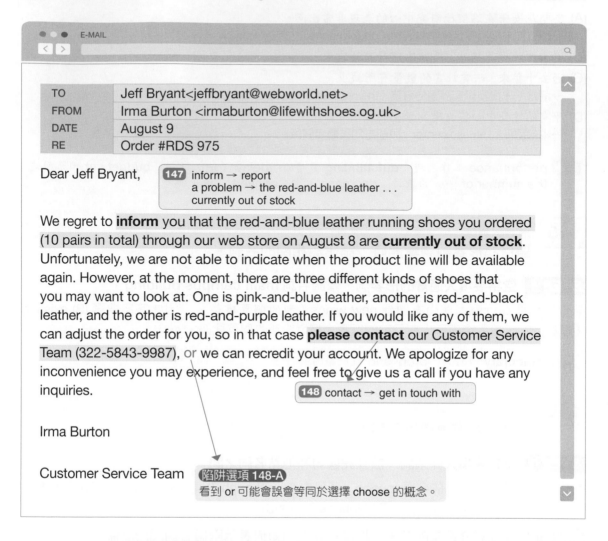

TO	Jeff Bryant<jeffbryant@webworld.net>
FROM	Irma Burton <irmaburton@lifewithshoes.og.uk>
DATE	August 9
RE	Order #RDS 975

Dear Jeff Bryant,

147 inform → report
a problem → the red-and-blue leather . . . currently out of stock

We regret to **inform** you that the red-and-blue leather running shoes you ordered (10 pairs in total) through our web store on August 8 are **currently out of stock**. Unfortunately, we are not able to indicate when the product line will be available again. However, at the moment, there are three different kinds of shoes that you may want to look at. One is pink-and-blue leather, another is red-and-black leather, and the other is red-and-purple leather. If you would like any of them, we can adjust the order for you, so in that case **please contact** our Customer Service Team (322-5843-9987), or we can recredit your account. We apologize for any inconvenience you may experience, and feel free to give us a call if you have any inquiries.

148 contact → get in touch with

Irma Burton

Customer Service Team

陷阱選項 148-A
看到 or 可能會誤會等同於選擇 choose 的概念。

147. What is the main reason the e-mail has been written?
(A) To schedule a ~~return~~ of a product
(B) To report a problem with an order
(C) To confirm a shipping date and time
(D) To reply to a customer

目的／前
→ 採籠統的敘述表示主旨或目的。

文中對象：You

148. What is Mr. Bryant encouraged to do?
(A) Choose a ~~shipping option~~
(B) Return the shoes and get a ~~refund~~
(C) Get in touch with a certain department
(D) ~~Cancel~~ the order and make a new purchase

收件人／要求／後
→ 寄件人要求的事項會使用祈使句或 you should 開頭的句子。

第 147-148 題 電子郵件

收件者	傑夫・布萊恩 <jeffbryant@webworld.net>
寄件者	伊瑪・波頓 <irmaburton@lifewithshoes.og.uk>
寄件日期	8 月 9 日
主旨	RDS 975 號訂單

親愛的傑夫‧布萊恩：

很遺憾必須通知您，您在八月八日透過本公司官網所訂購的紅藍相間皮革慢跑鞋（一共十雙），目前缺貨。很遺憾，我們也無法明確指出這系列的產品何時會再有貨。不過，我們目前有其他三種不同的鞋款，您或許會想要參考看看。一款是粉藍相間皮革，另一款是紅黑相間皮革，再一款是紅紫相間皮革。如果您有意願選購其中任一鞋款，我們可以幫您調整訂單，請撥打我們的客服部電話：322-5843-9987；若否，則我們可以退款至您的帳戶。抱歉增添您的困擾，若您有任何疑問，請隨時與我們聯繫。

伊瑪‧波頓
顧客服務部

字彙 regret 遺憾　leather 皮革　currently 現在　out of stock 無庫存
indicate 指出　adjust 調整　(re)credit（再度）把錢存進銀行戶頭
apologize 道歉　feel free to V 儘管去做……　inquiry 詢問

147. 此封電子郵件的主要撰寫原因為何？

(A) 安排退貨
(B) 回報訂單問題
(C) 確認貨物的運送時間
(D) 答覆顧客

STEP 1 題目詢問目的時，答案有 90% 的機率會出現在開頭前兩句話。

本題詢問撰寫電子郵件的原因。第一句話寫道：「We regret to inform you」，表示要告知對方一件不好的狀況。由「you ordered」和「are currently out of stock」指出對方訂購的商品缺貨中，因此答案為 (B)。

STEP 2 分析錯誤選項

看到文中的 shoes 可能會聯想至 (A) product，但是文中並未提及安排 return（換貨）的時間，因此不能作為答案。另外，當中沒有提到送貨的內容，且此封電子郵件為首封寫給顧客的郵件，因此 (C) 和 (D) 都不是答案。

148. 來函鼓勵布萊恩先生做何事？

(A) 選擇運輸選項

(B) 寄回鞋子並取得退款

(C) 與某部門聯繫

(D) 取消訂單並重新選購

STEP 1 後半段文章中，會出現要求事項的答案。

本題詢問要求收件人 Bryant 的事項，答案會出現在後半段文章中，使用「please 開頭的祈使句／ you should ／ we want you ／ if you would like ／祈使句」其中一種句型帶出答案。後半段文章寫道：「please contact our Customer Service Team」，要求對方聯絡客服部門，因此答案為 (C)。

STEP 2 分析錯誤選項

(A) 看到 or 可能會誤會等同 choose，表示選擇的概念，但是文中並未提到 shipping option，因此不能作為答案；(B) 雖然前半段文中有提到 shoes，但是並未出現 return 或 refund，因此 (B) 也不是答案。

Questions 149-151 refer to the following leaflet.

Pop & Jazz
Concert

The Canonbury [150 free of charge → No admission fee] ...e seasonal music event, Pop & Jazz concert, **free of charge** this coming weekend. This concert is held every summer for Canonbury citizens. As many public places CCC is running, **this city park** provides a place for citizens to gather for citywide festivals and public events. However, the CCC is largely dependent on donations [149 this city park → public facility] outdoor events such as this concert. We are gratefully accepting donations either at the event site, the Canonbury City Park, or online at www.canonburycity.org/donate.

Become one of our CCC members, by signing up online at www.canonburycity.org/membership or visiting our information desk. **CCC members** receive various **benefits** including a **bimonthly newsletter** covering current and upcoming exhibitions, a yearly city **calendar highlighting our major events**, and **free invitations** to every exhibition. Members are required to make a minimum financial contribution of £50 yearly.

151-A a bimonthly newsletter → periodic publications
151-C free invitations → invitations are sent to members
151-A calender . . . events → a copy of a schedule . . . events

陷阱選項 150-D
針對 CCC members 的內容，並非針對 Pop & Jazz concert。

149. Where would the leaflet most likely be given out?
(A) In a community ~~center~~
(B) In an art school
(C) In a public facility
(D) In a concert hall

文章的出處／前
→ 請由前半段文章確認本文的出處或地點。

150. What is mentioned about the Pop & Jazz concert?
(A) No admission fee is required
(B) Famous musicians participate every summer.
(C) It will take place only at the city park.
(D) A minimum financial contribution of £50 is required.

請先整理出題目和選項的關鍵字後，再觀看文章，找出相符的敘述。

151. What is NOT stated as an advantage of members?
(A) Members receive periodic publications.
(B) Members' donations are listed on a Web site.
(C) Members are invited to some activities.
(D) A copy of a schedule covering some events is sent to members.

找出不符合 member 好處的敘述。
→ 請先刪去好處。

第 149-151 題 傳單

流行爵士音樂會

卡農伯里市社區中心(以下簡稱「卡市社」),將於這個週末舉辦一場免費的季節性音樂活動——流行爵士音樂會。這個音樂會在每年夏季都會為全卡農伯里市居民舉辦。正如同「卡市社」所經管的許多其他公眾空間一樣,這個市立公園為市民提供一個可以參與全市盛會及公開活動的場地。然而,「卡市社」所籌辦的戶外活動,諸如此次的音樂會,大部分皆仰賴民眾的捐款。我們熱切歡迎大家於活動場地、卡農伯里市公園,或是登入卡農伯里市社區組織的官方網站 www.canonburycity.org/donate,進行捐款。

若想成為「卡市社」的一員,您可登入卡農伯里市社區中心官網的會員專區 www.canonburycity.org/membership,進行線上註冊;或是逕洽我們的服務檯。「卡市社」的會員擁有多項福利,包括每兩個月出刊一次、刊載當期與近期展覽活動的新聞電子報,標註本市重大活動的城市年曆,以及可免費參加每場展覽活動的邀請函。本社的會員每年需要貢獻至少五十英鎊的捐款。

字彙 seasonal 季節性的　citywide 全市的　largely 主要地;大部分地
coordinate 協調　site 地點　bimonthly 兩月一次的　financial contribution 捐款

149. 此傳單最有可能於何處發放?

(A) 在社區活動中心

(B) 在藝術學校

(C) 在公共場所

(D) 在音樂廳

STEP 1 題目詢問文章出處或地點時,請確認前半段文章中有所關聯的單字。

本題詢問發放本篇傳單的地點。文中寫道:「this city park provides a place for citizens to gather for citywide festivals and public events」,提到「this city park」,由此可以得知發放傳單的地點為 (C) 公共場所。

STEP 2 請特別留意故意使用相同單字的陷阱選項。

(D) 本文僅告知舉辦 concert 的消息,並未提及 concert hall。

150. 關於流行爵士音樂會，本文提到何事？

(A) 可免費入場。

(B) 每年夏季皆有知名音樂家共襄盛舉。

(C) 只會在市立公園舉辦。

(D) 至少需要捐款五十英鎊才得參加。

STEP 1 請先整理出題目和選項的關鍵字後，再觀看文章，找出相符的敘述。

請從文中找出與關鍵字 Pop & Jazz concert 有關的內容並和選項對照。文中寫道：「Pop & Jazz concert, free of charge this coming weekend」，表示可以免費參加 Pop & Jazz 演唱會，因此答案為 (A)。

STEP 2 當題目的關鍵字極為明確時，文中會直接提及該關鍵字。

(B) 文中並未提到知名音樂家每年夏季都會參加。
(C) 文中並未提到往後舉辦的地點。
(D) 並非針對 Pop & Jazz concert 的內容，而是與加入 CCC 會員有關。

151. 關於會員福利，沒有提到下列何者？

(A) 會員將定期收到出版品。

(B) 會員的捐款將羅列於官網上。

(C) 會員會受邀參加活動。

(D) 將寄送給會員刊載某些活動的時間表。

STEP 1 看到 NOT Question 時，請善用刪去法。

請從文中找出與關鍵字 advantage of members 有關的內容並和選項對照。後半段文章中提及 member，並使用 benefits 列出加入會員的好處，因此請逐一刪去符合好處的選項。

(A) a bimonthly newsletter → periodic publications：定期刊物
(C) free invitations → are invited to some activltles：活動邀請
(D) a yearly city calender . . . events
→ a copy of a schedule covering some events：活動日程表

綜上所述，本題答案為 (B)。

Questions 152-155 refer to the following e-mail.

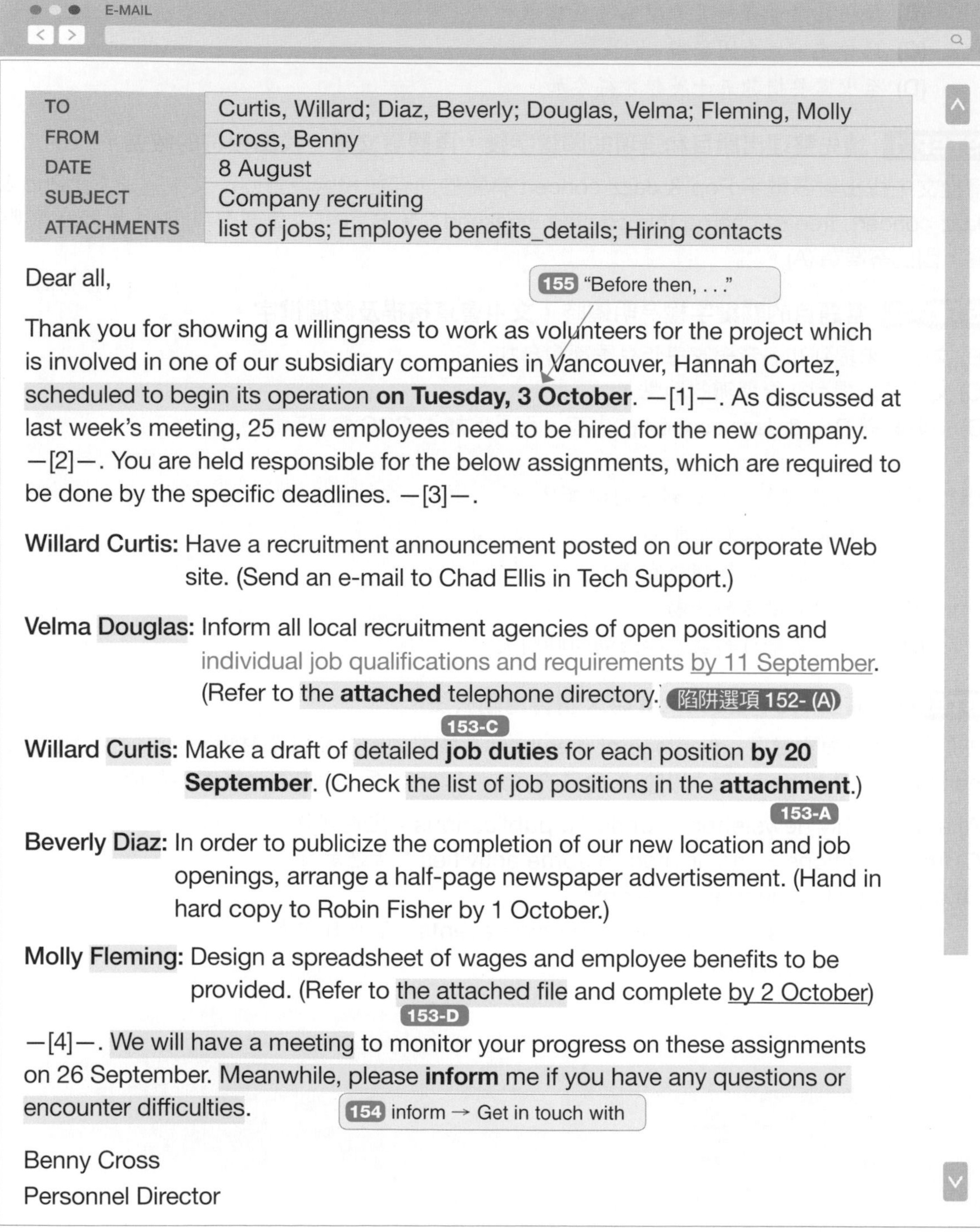

TO	Curtis, Willard; Diaz, Beverly; Douglas, Velma; Fleming, Molly
FROM	Cross, Benny
DATE	8 August
SUBJECT	Company recruiting
ATTACHMENTS	list of jobs; Employee benefits_details; Hiring contacts

Dear all,

155 "Before then, . . ."

Thank you for showing a willingness to work as volunteers for the project which is involved in one of our subsidiary companies in Vancouver, Hannah Cortez, scheduled to begin its operation **on Tuesday, 3 October**. —[1]—. As discussed at last week's meeting, 25 new employees need to be hired for the new company. —[2]—. You are held responsible for the below assignments, which are required to be done by the specific deadlines. —[3]—.

Willard Curtis: Have a recruitment announcement posted on our corporate Web site. (Send an e-mail to Chad Ellis in Tech Support.)

Velma Douglas: Inform all local recruitment agencies of open positions and individual job qualifications and requirements by 11 September. (Refer to the **attached** telephone directory.) 陷阱選項 152- (A)

153-C

Willard Curtis: Make a draft of detailed **job duties** for each position **by 20 September**. (Check the list of job positions in the **attachment**.)

153-A

Beverly Diaz: In order to publicize the completion of our new location and job openings, arrange a half-page newspaper advertisement. (Hand in hard copy to Robin Fisher by 1 October.)

Molly Fleming: Design a spreadsheet of wages and employee benefits to be provided. (Refer to the attached file and complete by 2 October)

153-D

—[4]—. We will have a meeting to monitor your progress on these assignments on 26 September. Meanwhile, please **inform** me if you have any questions or encounter difficulties.

154 inform → Get in touch with

Benny Cross
Personnel Director

152. When is the draft of detailed job responsibilities due?

(A) September 11 **(B) September 20**

(C) October 1 (D) October 2

關鍵字／**job responsibilities**／前

→ 找出關鍵字。

153. According to the e-mail, who will NOT use one of the e-mail attachments?

(A) Mr. Curtis **(B) Ms. Diaz**

(C) Ms. Douglas (D) Ms. Fleming

NOT／關鍵字 **e-mail attachments**

→ 找出未提到關鍵字的人

Mr. Cross →寄件人：I

154. What does Mr. Cross ask the recipients to do before they meet?

(A) Send him their completed work

(B) Visit the subsidiary company

(C) Get in touch with him as needed

(D) Cooperate with each other on assignments

寄件人的要求事項／關鍵字 **before they meet**／後

→ 一般會使用祈使句或 you should . . . 表示要求或建議。

155. In which of the positions marked [1], [2], [3], and [4] does the following sentence best belong?

"Before then, there is a lot of work to do."

(A) [1] (B) [2]

(C) [3] (D) [4]

句子插入題／關鍵字 **before then**

→ 找出後方適合連接 then 的句子。

第 152-155 題 電子郵件

收件者	威勒・柯提斯；比佛利・狄亞茲；薇瑪・道格拉斯；莫莉・弗萊明
寄件者	班尼・克洛斯
寄件日期	8 月 8 日
主旨	公司招募
附件	職缺明細；員工福利__細節；人事顧問公司聯繫資料

大家好！

感謝諸位願意義務協助溫哥華子公司的籌備專案。這家名為「漢納・寇帝茲」的子公司，預計將於 10 月 3 日星期二開始營運。在那之間，還有很多工作要做。根據我們上星期的會議討論結果，新公司將需聘請 25 名員工。諸位被分派的負責任務如下，必須於特定期限內完成。

威勒・柯提斯：負責於公司官方網站張貼徵才公告。（請寄送電子郵件給技術支援部的查德・艾利斯。）

薇瑪・道格拉斯：負責在 9 月 11 日以前，將本公司的職缺訊息、個別職缺的應徵資格及要求，知會本地所有的人事顧問公司。（請參照附件內的電話簿。）

威勒・柯提斯：負責在 9 月 20 日以前，為每一項職缺研擬出一份詳細的職責草案。（請檢視附件內的職缺明細。）

比佛利．狄亞茲：負責刊登半頁的報紙廣告，宣傳公司新位址的竣工以及相關職缺。（請於10月1日以前將紙本資料送交羅賓．費雪。）

莫莉．弗萊明：負責設計薪資及員工福利試算表，以供使用。（請參照附件檔案，並於10月2日以前完成。）

我們將在9月26日再度召開會議，以檢視各位的工作進展。同時，如果各位有任何疑問或遇到任何困難，請讓我知道。

班尼．克洛斯
人事主管

字彙 willingness 自願　be involved in 涉及　subsidiary 隸屬的　operation 營運
be held responsible for 為……負責　assignment （分派的）任務
specific 特定的　corporate 公司的　recruitment agency 招募公司
job qualification 職缺資格條件　requirement 必要條件
telephone directory 電話簿　make a draft of 起草　publicize 宣傳；廣告
spreadsheet 試算表　employee benefits 員工福利
encounter 遇到（困難、危險等）

152. 詳細的工作職責草案該於何時完成？

(A) 9月11日　(B) 9月20日
(C) 10月1日　(D) 10月2日

STEP 1 答案會出現在期間、星期或數字等關鍵字旁。

請先抓出題目的關鍵字為 detailed job responsibilities。文中提到 Willard Curtis 的工作為「Make a draft of detailed job duties for each position by 20 September.」，表示在9月20日以前要初步列出各職缺的工作職責，因此答案為 (B)。

STEP 2 分析錯誤選項

(A) September 11 為通知人事顧問公司的時間，並非答案；(C) October 1 為半頁報紙廣告的紙本資料繳交截止日；(D) October 2 為完成電子試算表設計的期限。

153. 根據該封電子郵件，誰將不會使用到電郵的附件？

(A) 柯提斯先生　(B) 狄亞茲女士
(C) 道格拉斯女士　(D) 弗萊明女士

STEP 1 看到 NOT Question 時，請善用刪去法。

本題詢問不會用到電子郵件附件的人。請抓出題目的關鍵字 e-mail attachment，並刪去相符的選項。Willard Curtis 可以對應至文中的「Make a draft of . . . job positions in the attachment」；Velma Douglas 可以對應至文中的「Inform all local recruitment agencies . . . Refer to the attached telephone directory」；Molly Fleming 可以對應至文中的「Refer to the attached file」，表示這三個人都要確認附件，因此答案為 (B)。

154. 克洛斯先生要求收件者在下一次開會前做何事？

(A) 把完成的工作寄給他

(B) 參訪子公司

(C) 倘有需要，可以與他聯繫

(D) 相互合作以完成任務

STEP 1 **後半段文章中，會出現要求事項的答案。**

本題詢問 Cross 先生要求收件人在會議前做的事，請由後半段文章進行確認。文中寫道：「We will have a meeting」，提出要一起開會。後方還寫道「Meanwhile, please inform me if you have any questions . . . difficulties」，以祈使句表達如有任何疑問或困難之處，請跟他聯絡，因此答案為 (C)。

155. 下列句子最適合擺在 [1]、[2]、[3]、[4] 哪一個標註處？

「在那之前，還有很多工作要做。」

(A) [1] (B) [2]

(C) [3] (D) [4]

STEP 1 **句子插入題可以根據指示形容詞、指示代名詞或副詞選出答案。**

句子插入題要根據上下文意，將題目的指定句插入最適當的空格中，因此請確認題目列出的指定句內容。指定句 Before then 當中的 then 為時間副詞，適合放在提及時間的句子後方。文中「Tuesday, 3 October」提到明確的時間，因此指定句要放在 [1]。

Questions 156-159 refer to the following text message chain.

●●●○○

Nellie Bishop 11:29 A.M.
Hello, everyone. Does anyone know Karla is working today?

Randy Bennett 11:30 A.M.
I am pretty sure she is on duty today. What's the matter?

Nellie Bishop 11:30 A.M. 156 meeting rooms / this floor → conference center
I just checked the **meeting rooms** and found out that one of **our speakers seems defective**. It makes a crackling sound.

Randy Bennett 11:31 A.M.
Oh, no way. When is the marketing forum supposed to begin?

157 對前一句話的反應

Nellie Bishop 11:32 A.M.
At noon. Some people have already arrived, and more than 100 are expected.

Naomi Brewer 11:33 A.M. 158 → She takes the initiative.
I am just calling the maintenance department. Give me a second. Well, there aren't any spare speakers in the storage room. **Nellie**, we have only about 30 minutes left, and we haven't finished setting up the microphones and the projector. **Could you drive** over to the nearest **audio shop** and borrow or buy some?

159 drive → Go
audio shop → a local store

Randy Bennett 11:34 A.M.
That's a good idea. Nellie, **while you are away**, we will check **this floor**. I think I saw one around the corner on my way **here** this morning.

Nellie Bishop 11:35 A.M.
Alright. I can do that for you.

陷阱選項 159-A
只有提到 drive over，並非前往 her office。

156. Where most likely is Ms. Bishop?
(A) In her office
(B) At a storage room
(C) At a conference center
(D) In a maintenance department

Bishop 所在的地點
→ 找出指定人物提到的地點。

157. At 11:31 A.M., why does Mr. Bennett most likely write, "Oh, no way"?
(A) A coworker ~~has not come to work~~.
(B) Some equipment is not working properly.
(C) ~~They don't know~~ how to get a new speaker.
(D) ~~Attendance~~ is more than expected.

掌握說話者意圖
→ 確認指定句前後的文意。

158. What is suggested about Ms. Brewer?
(A) She is going to quit her current position.
(B) She was recently recruited.
(C) She agreed to go with Randy's idea.
(D) She takes the initiative.

Brewer 的詳細資訊
→ 看完選項後，再從指定人物的對白中找出答案。

159. What will Ms. Bishop most likely do next?
(A) Drive over ~~to her office~~
(B) Try to find Karla
(C) ~~Repair~~ some equipment
(D) Go to a local store

Bishop 稍後要做的事
→ 確認後半段文章。

第 156-159 題 訊息串

娜莉・畢夏 上午 11:29
嗨，大家。有人知道卡拉今天有上班嗎？

蘭迪・班奈特 上午 11:30
我很確定她今天有來上班，怎麼了嗎？

娜莉・畢夏 上午 11:30
我剛看了一下會議室，發現其中一台喇叭好像有點問題，它會發出雜音。

蘭迪・班奈特 上午 11:31
喔，不會吧。行銷座談會預計何時開始？

娜莉・畢夏 上午 11:32
中午。有一些人已經到了，預計會有一百多個人。

娜歐米・布魯爾 上午 11:33
給我一點時間，讓我打電話給維修部。唉，儲藏室裡沒有多餘的喇叭。娜莉，我們只剩下三十分鐘了，但麥克風和投影機都還沒架設好。能不能請妳開車去最近的一家音響店，去商借或是購買幾台過來？

蘭迪・班奈特 上午 11:34
好主意。娜莉，當妳不在的時候，我們也會在這層樓找一找。我記得今天早上我來這裡的時候，曾在角落看到過一台。

娜莉・畢夏 上午 11:35
好吧，我可以幫這個忙。

字彙 **on duty** 當值　**defective** 有缺陷的　**crackling** 劈啪作響的聲音
spare 多餘的　**storage** 儲藏　**set up** 使（器械、機器等）準備使用

156. 畢夏女士最有可能在何處？

(A) 在她的辦公室

(B) 在儲藏室

(C) 在會議中心

(D) 在維修部

STEP 1 文章為線上聊天或文字簡訊時，請先掌握登場人物間的關聯性。

→登場人物有三人：

Nellie Bishop：告知問題者。

Randy Bennett & Naomi Brewer：尋找並提出解決方案者。

本題詢問 Bishop 現在在哪裡。Bishop 的訊息寫道：「I just checked . . . defective」，告知對方會議室的喇叭有點問題。接著 Randy Bennett 問她行銷座談會開始的時間，由此可以得知 Bishop 提出的是 conference 的相關狀況，而她所在的地點為 (C) conference center。另外，Randy Bennett 在最後的訊息寫道：「在妳外出期間，我們會負責檢查這層樓的狀況（this floor）」，由此句話可以再次確認 Ms. Bishop 現在在 conference center。

STEP 2 分析錯誤選項

由 Naomi 提出 (B) storage 和 (D) maintenance，並非答案。

157. 班奈特先生在上午 **11:31** 寫下「喔，不會吧」，最有可能的原因為何？

(A) 一名同事沒來上班。

(B) 某個設備功能異常。

(C) 他們不知如何取得一台新喇叭。

(D) 出席率超過預期。

STEP 1 線上聊天文中出現詢問「意圖」的考題時，請確認指定句前後的轉折詞，並選擇較為籠統的敘述作為答案。

指定句前方的訊息寫道：「. . . found out that one of our speakers seems defective」，提出喇叭有點問題，接著便出現指定句「Oh, no way」，由此可以得知這句話是針對設備故障的反應，因此答案為 (B)。

STEP 2 熟記常見的答覆方式。

no way 指「怎麼可能、絕對不行」，用於對前一句話表示強烈的疑問時，請務必熟記。

158. 關於布魯爾女士，本文有何暗示？

(A) 她將辭去現有職務。

(B) 她最近才就職。

(C) 她同意採取蘭迪的建議。

(D) 她主動採取行動。

STEP 1 人名通常會是重要的關鍵字。

本題的關鍵字為 Ms. Brewer，要從文章中找出相關內容，並和選項相互對照。文中寫道：「I am just calling the maintenance department. Give me a second」和「Could you drive over to the nearest audio shop and borrow or buy some?」，提到她聯絡了維修部門，嘗試解決設備的問題，但是維修部門也沒有多餘的設備。接著她向 Nellie 提出其他解決方式，因此答案為 (D) 表示她「主動採取行動」。

159. 畢夏女士接下來最有可能做何事？

(A) 開車前往辦公室

(B) 試圖找到卡拉

(C) 修理某項設備

(D) 前往本地商場

STEP 1 題目詢問未來計畫時，答案通常會出現在另一個人的對白中，以勸說或建議的方式帶出答案。

本題詢問 Bishop 下一步要做的事情。Bishop 在最後的訊息寫道：「I can do that for you.」，表示她同意前一個人的提議。而前方為 Naomi 的提議：「Could you drive over to the nearest audio shop and borrow or buy some?」，請她到附近店家租借或購買，因此答案為 (D)。

STEP 2 分析錯誤選項

(A) 訊息中有提到 drive，但前往的地方應為 shop 才對。

(C) speakers 可以改寫成 equipment，但是訊息中並未提到修理。

Questions 160-163 refer to the following letter.

RTCQ Australia
983 Gunnersbury Avenue
Melbourne, VIC X7R 3R1

21 October

Mr. Julius Shelton
214 Sloane Road
Sydney, NSW R3A 5T2

160-B half-year → duration
160-A Products Development Team → division
160-C your supervisor → manager

Dear Mr. Shelton 收件人：You

We are happy that you have accepted our **half-year paid internship** position with the **Products Development Team** at RTCQ Australia. —[1]—. The first day of your internship will be on Wednesday, 5 December. You may have other scheduled commitments in the beginning of December, so if necessary, the starting date can be adjusted. This can be discussed further in November when your schedule becomes clearer. —[2]—.

第三者

Your supervisor will be Mr. Martin Soto, our head of Quality Control, who specializes in improving products' durability using eco-friendly materials. **Mr. Soto** said to me that **he happened to find your report** in the magazine *Life with Nature* last year, which impressed him. —[3]—.

163 "..., he was certain ..."

161 he happened to find your report → He read a report written by Mr. Shelton

Please find the enclosed contract and review it thoroughly. If there are no concerns or questions about the terms of the contract, **you can sign and send it back** to us at the address above by 29 October. As soon as the signed contract arrives, our personnel department will get in touch with you to prepare a staff ID badge, an e-mail account, and a parking space. —[4]—.

陷阱選項 162-D
開設 e-mail 帳戶為人事部門（personnel department）要做的事。

162 send it back → Mail a signed document

Janie Terry 寄件人：I
Managing Director of Personnel

160. What is NOT mentioned about Mr. Shelton's internship?
(A) The division he will be working in 收件人：You
(B) The duration he will work
(C) The manager he will report to
(D) The wage he will receive

關鍵字 internship ／ NOT question
→ 刪去正確的選項。

第三者——your supervisor / he

161. What is suggested about Mr. Soto?
(A) He read a report written by Mr. Shelton.
(B) ~~Mr. Terry~~ is working under his supervision.
(C) He is a ~~well-known~~ specialist in a field.
(D) Mr. Shelton was interviewed by him.

162. What will Mr. Shelton probably do next?
(A) Arrange a meeting with Mr. Soto
(B) Discuss a starting date
(C) Mail a signed document
(D) ~~Open~~ an e-mail account

163. In which of the positions marked [1], [2], [3], and [4] does the following sentence best belong?
"Not to mention, he was certain that you will be a great addition to his team."
(A) [1] (B) [2] **(C) [3]** (D) [4]

關鍵字 Mr. Soto
→ 在文中找到關鍵字後，選出內容相符的選項。

收件人：You
Shelton／未來計畫／後
→ 下一步計畫會出現在後半部文章中。

句子插入題
→ 確認文中出現的指示代名詞、轉折詞。

第 160-163 題 信件

澳大利亞 RTCQ 公司
澳洲墨爾本市根拿士貝利大道 983 號 VIC X7R 3R1

十月二十一日

此致：
尤利烏什・謝爾頓先生
雪梨斯隆路 214 號 NSW R3A 5T2

謝爾頓先生，您好，

很高興您接受澳洲 RTCQ 公司產品研發部門為期半年的支薪實習工作。您的實習工作將於十二月五日星期三開始。也許您在十二月初已排定其他的預定工作，若有需要，實習起始日可以再做調整。待十一月您的行程更確定之時，屆時我們可以再細談。

督導您的人將會是我們的品管部門主管，馬丁・索托先生，他專門研究使用環保素材以延長產品的耐用性。索托先生跟我談到，他去年恰巧在《與自然相伴》這本雜誌上讀到您的報告，印象十分深刻。更不用說，他非常確信你的加入將為他的團隊增添優勢。

隨信所附的實習合約，請您詳細檢視。倘若您對於合約條款無任何疑慮，請在簽名後，於十月二十九日前，依信封上的地址將合約寄回。公司收到簽名完成的合約當下，人事部便會與您聯繫，以便為您準備員工識別證、設立電子郵件帳號，以及安排停車位。

賈尼・泰瑞
人事部總經理

字彙 **scheduled** 預定的 **commitment** 承諾的工作 **adjust** 調整 **specialize in** 專攻 **durability** 耐久性 **happen to V** 碰巧 **thoroughly** 仔細地 **terms of the contract** 合約條款 **get in touch with** 與⋯⋯取得聯繫

160. 關於謝爾頓先生的實習工作，文中未提及何事？

(A) 他將任職的部門

(B) 他將任職的期間

(C) 他該向其匯報的經理

(D) 他將得到的薪酬

STEP 1 **看到 NOT Question 時，請善用刪去法。**

題目出現 Not 時，請由題目關鍵字 internship 找出相關內容，並刪去與文章內容相符的選項。看到「you have accepted our half-year paid internship position with the Products Development Team」，可以得知 (A) 產品開發部和 (B) 工作時間為六個月；下一段提到：「Your supervisor will be Mr. Martin Soto」，表示 (C) 他的主管為 Soto，因此答案要選 (D)。

161. 關於索托先生，本文有何暗示？

(A) 他讀了謝爾頓先生寫的一篇報告。

(B) 泰瑞先生在他監督下工作。

(C) 他是某領域的知名專家。

(D) 謝爾頓先生是他面試進來的。

STEP 1 **答案通常會出現在關鍵字旁。**

本題的關鍵字為 Mr. Soto，屬於第三人，文中以 he 代稱，因此請找出內容相符的選項。文中寫道：「he happened to find your report in the Magazine *Life with Nature* last year」，提到 Soto 看過雜誌上刊登 Shelton 所寫的報導，因此答案為 (A)。

STEP 2 **分析錯誤選項。**

(B) Terry 為寄件人，文中僅提到 Soto 為 Shelton 的 supervisor，無從得知該選項的內容是否正確；(C) 文中無法得知 Soto 是否為知名的專家。

162. 謝爾頓先生接下來可能會做何事？

(A) 安排與索托先生開會

(B) 討論就職的日期

(C) 寄回簽名完成的合約

(D) 開立一個電子郵件帳號

STEP 1 文章為信件時，請查看後半段文章，由表示建議、命令或勸說的句子確認未來計畫。

本題詢問 Shelton 之後要做的事。Shelton 為本封信的收件人，因此要從對方提及的建議、勸說或命令中找出答案。文中寫道：「Please find the enclosed contract . . . you can sign and send it back」，請他在合約書上簽名並寄回，因此答案為 (C)。

STEP 2 信件中的 you 指收件人，I 或 we 指寄件人。

(D) 由「our personnel department will . . . prepare a staff ID badge, an e-mail account」可以得知開設 e-mail 帳戶為寄件人所屬部門負責的事情，因此並非答案。

163. 下列句子最適合擺在 [1]、[2]、[3]、[4] 哪一個標註處？

「更不用說，他非常確信你的加入將為他的團隊增添優勢。」

(A) [1]

(B) [2]

(C) [3]

(D) [4]

STEP 1 句子插入題可以根據指示形容詞、指示代名詞、或副詞選出答案。

要插入的句子中使用人稱代名詞 he，表示前一句話中有提到第三者，因此答案為 [3]。前方寫道：「Mr. Soto . . . which impressed him」，Soto 看到雜誌上刊登 Shelton 所寫的報導，令他印象深刻。接著填入 Soto 想僱用 Shelton 加入團隊符合文意，因此答案為 (C)。

Questions 164-166 refer to the following contract.

Renewal Contract for Maintenance Service
Tooting Vehicle
We appreciate your loyalty to Tooting Vehicle!

164 renewal contract → (B) contracted before

Client Name: Jamie Crawford **Address:** 432 Fulham Broadway, London, UK **Post Code:** RC12 5Q3 **Telephone:** 345-3215-4432	**Client Signature:** Jamie Crawford **Amount Due on Acceptance:** £ 99.00

Basic Plan: £ 99.00

This six-month service plan includes cleaning of your vehicle as well as conducting regular inspection.

Advantages provided:

- **Verifying** the **engine** for the best function
- **Inspecting** the overall **tires**
- Securing connecting components
- **Sanitizing cooling and heating systems**
- Filling cooling water

165 (A) Inspecting tires → Checking tires
(B) Verifying engine → Inspecting engines
(C) Sanitizing cooling and heating systems → Cleaning cooling and heating systems

Super Plan: £ 149.00

Subscribers with this twelve-month service plan are offered relief-care service. On top of the basic cleaning and inspection of your vehicle, subscribers are provided **with night and weekend services at no additional fee**.

166 night and weekend services at no additional fee → Servicing after operating hours

Inspection: Subscribers are able to use the inspection service during usu[al opening hours, Monday] through Friday, 9 A[...]	**Service Request Calls:** Except for Super Plan holders, an extra £ 25.00 fee will be charged to the client account when a request is ordered during nights and weekends.

陷阱選項 164-D
Crawford 加入 Basic Plan → 使用週末服務要負擔額外的費用

164. What is suggested about Ms. Crawford?
(A) She got a car ~~insurance quote~~.
(B) She has contracted Tooting Vehicle before.
(C) She will have her tires changed immediately.
(D) She will be ~~exempted~~ from the extra service fee for weekends.

關鍵字 Crawford
→ 整理出各選項的關鍵字後，再查看文章，找出相符的選項。

165. What is NOT part of the Basic Plan?
(A) Checking car tires
(B) Inspecting the engines
(C) Cleaning cooling and heating systems
(D) Changing engine oil

NOT ／關鍵字 Basic Plan
→ 刪去和文章內容相符的選項。

166. What additional advantage is included in the fee of the Super Plan?

(A) Cooling water supplement
(B) ~~Replacement~~ of components at no charge
(C) Servicing after operating hours
(D) Inspection service ~~every month~~

關鍵字 Super Plan／額外的優勢

→ 查看後半段文章，由關鍵字所在之處確認額外的服務。

第 164-166 題 合約

圖汀汽車維修服務續約
感謝您對圖汀汽車的長期愛用！

客戶姓名：潔米・克勞馥 住址：英國倫敦富勒姆大道 432 號 郵遞區號：RC12 5Q3 電話：345-3215-4432	客戶簽名處：潔米・克勞馥 應收金額：英鎊 99 元

基礎方案：英鎊 99 元

此六個月的服務方案包含車輛清潔以及車輛的例行檢查。

內容包括：
– 檢驗引擎性能
– 徹底檢查所有輪胎
– 加固連接零件
– 清潔汽車冷暖空調系統
– 加滿冷卻水

特優方案：英鎊 149 元

訂購十二個月服務方案的用戶，將享有緊急救援維修服務。除了基本的車輛清潔及檢驗服務之外，本方案用戶還可享有免費的夜間及週末服務。

檢驗部分：	救援服務需求：
用戶可於平常營業時間，星期一至星期五上午九時至下午六時，使用車輛檢驗服務。	除了特優方案的用戶之外，其餘用戶的夜間及週末服務需求，都將額外收取 25 英鎊的服務費。

字彙 renewal 更新　loyalty 忠誠　amount due 應付款項　conduct 進行　verify 檢驗
secure 緊固　component 零件　sanitize 使清潔　subscriber 訂購者
on top of 除……之外（還）　holder 持有者

164. 關於克勞馥女士，本文有何暗示？

(A) 她收到一張汽車保險報價單。

(B) 她之前與圖汀汽車簽有合約。

(C) 她想將她的輪胎立刻換掉。

(D) 她將不需支付額外服務費即可享週末服務。

STEP 1 題目要求找出相符的「事實」時，請先整理出各選項的關鍵字，再查看文章內容。

題目中的 Crawford 為合約中的簽約人，表示要由整篇文章確認與此人相符的事實。因此請先整理出各選項的關鍵字，再選出符合文章內容的選項。由開頭「Renewal Contract」當中的「Renewal」可以得知她先前就曾經和 Tooting Vehicle 簽過合約，因此答案為 (B)。

STEP 2 由各選項的關鍵字找出相對應的內容，並刪去有錯誤之處的選項。

(C) 文中寫道：「Inspecting the overall tires」，提到 tires，但是並未提到 changed。
(D) 加入 Super Plan 的人才不用負擔額外的服務費用。由「Amount Due on Acceptance: £99.00」表示 Crawford 要加入的是 Basic Plan: £99.00，因此該選項並非答案。

165. 下列何者沒有包含在基礎方案內？

(A) 檢視車輛輪胎

(B) 檢查引擎

(C) 清潔汽車冷暖空調系統

(D) 更換機油

STEP 1 看到 NOT Question 時，請善用刪去法。

題目中出現 Not，因此請由題目關鍵字 Basic Plan 找出相關說明，並刪去與文章內容相符的選項。「Inspecting the overall tires」檢查輪胎屬於 (A)；「Verifying the engine」檢查引擎屬於 (B)；「Sanitizing cooling and heating systems」消毒冷暖氣屬於 (C)，因此答案要選 (D)。

166. 特優方案的費用中包含哪一項額外福利？

(A) 補充冷卻水

(B) 免費替換零件

(C) 營業時間過後的服務

(D) 每個月的檢驗服務

STEP 1 題目要求找出相符的「事實」時，請先整理出各選項的關鍵字，再查看文章內容。

題目的關鍵字為 additional advantage 和 Super Plan。一般會先提到基本項目，再告知額外附加的服務項目。Super Plan 的說明為「On top of the basic cleaning and inspection of your vehicle, subscribers are provided with night and weekend services at no additional fee.」，提到除了基本服務之外，還有提供週末和夜間的免費服務，因此答案為 (C)。

Questions 167-169 refer to the following letter.

Dear Editor, 收件人：You

It is always a great pleasure to read your thoughtful articles. I am writing to discuss your recent article "*Inviting Arenas for Music* – The 167 discuss, point out → correct wrong information was put in the June edition of *Life with Music Magazine*. The ... read about such a splendid place that I am familiar with and the photos in it were really great. It contained one thing I'd like to point out, though. –[1]–.

In the article, Cindy Walters was introduced as the founder of the Imperial Concert Hall; ac 169 "She" → Cindy Walters, "wasn't stable" → initial stage ged in the initial stage of the business, she was just one of ... cia Warner who was the actual owner of the arena. I happened to learn about this since I had several opportunities to perform at the arena with my band, which naturally gave us chances to interact with Ms. Warner sometimes. –[3]–. 168 perform . . . with my band → musician

I think who the owner of the business is was not the focus of the article, but still it is, I believe, an essential part of the story of the Imperial Concert Hall. Ms. Warner tried to give many new gifted local musicians more chances to perform through her business. In spite of that, she is hardly recognized enough for her contributions. –[4]–. In order to avoid doing her a disservice, she should be given her due.

Sincerely,

Ricky Webb 寄件人：I

Ricky Webb

167. Why has the letter been written?
(A) To ~~review~~ a concert hall
(B) To correct wrong information
(C) To publicize ~~upcoming~~ events
(D) To recognize a ~~performer's~~ accomplishment

目的／前
→ 找出 I'm writing 開頭的句子。

168. Who most likely is Mr. Webb? 寄件人：I
(A) An editor
(B) A ~~reporter~~
(C) A musician
(D) An entrepreneur

Webb 的職業／寄件人／I
→ 確認與 I 一併被提及的職業。

169. In which of the positions marked [1], [2], [3], and [4] does the following sentence best belong?
"She didn't want to be co-owner when the business wasn't stable."
(A) [1] **(B) [2]** (C) [3] (D) [4]

句子插入題
→ 前一句話要能對應指定句中的 she 和 business。

TEST 1 PART 7 中譯&解析

第 167-169 題 信件

編輯您好：

拜讀您所編輯的深度文章，一直是一種享受。我此次來信，是想討論《音樂生活》雜誌六月號所刊登的一篇文章：「迷人的音樂聖地——皇家音樂廳」。很開心能讀到一篇文章是關於我所熟知的華麗處所，文章所附的照片真的拍得很棒。不過，文中所提的一點，我仍想特別指出。

根據該篇文章所述，辛蒂．華特斯是皇家音樂廳的創辦人。事實上，雖然她參與了音樂廳的初始創建階段，她不過只是其中一位投資者。而當音樂廳營運狀況不穩定時，她也不想成為合夥人。艾莉西亞．華納才是音樂廳的真正創辦人。因為我有多次機會與我的樂團在這個場地表演，自然偶爾會與華納女士有所接觸，所以我碰巧知道這件事情。

我知道該篇文章的重點不在於音樂廳的創辦人是誰；不過，我相信它仍是這個關於皇家音樂廳的故事中，不可或缺的一部分。華納女士嘗試透過她的音樂廳，為許多本地的新秀音樂家提供更多的演出機會。儘管如此，她所做的貢獻仍是鮮為人知。為了避免對她造成不公，還是應該給她應得的認可。

瑞奇．韋伯 謹上

字彙 thoughtful 富有思想的　inviting 吸引人的　arena 場地　splendid 華麗的
be familiar with 對……熟悉　point out 指出　founder 創始人
engage in 參加；參與　initial 最初的　investor 投資者
interact with 與……相互配合　essential 必要的　gifted 有天賦的
contribution 貢獻　disservice 有害行為　give somebody one's due 給某人應得的

167. 此封信的撰寫目的為何？

(A) 回顧音樂廳　(B) 更正錯誤資訊
(C) 宣傳近期活動　(D) 認可表演者的成就

STEP 1 開頭前兩句話有 90% 的機率會出現文章的目的。

文章中第二句話寫道：「I am writing to discuss your recent article」，表達他想要和對方討論一下最近的報導。後方又寫道：「It contained one thing I'd like to point out, though」，提到他想指出某個部分的問題，這表示他寫這封信的目的是希望對方修正報導中的錯誤之處，因此答案為 (B)。

STEP 2 分析錯誤選項

recent article 與 (C) upcoming 不符，因此該選項並非答案。文中並未提及其他選項的內容。

168. 韋伯先生最有可能是何人？

(A) 編輯
(B) 記者
(C) 音樂家
(D) 企業家

STEP 1 確認 I ／ You ／第三者的職業為何。

信件文章中，人名有可能是寄件人、收件人或第三者，請特別留意。而人名 Webb 出現在文章的最後，位在 Sincerely 後方，表示為寄件人，因此可從文中提及 I 的句子來掌握 Webb 的身分。「I had several opportunities to perform at the arena with my band」提到他曾和自己的樂團一同表演，因此答案要選 (C)。

169. 下列句子最適合擺在 [1]、[2]、[3]、[4] 哪一個標註處？

「而當音樂廳營運狀況不穩定時，她也不想成為合夥人。」

(A) [1]

(B) [2]

(C) [3]

(D) [4]

STEP 1 句子插入題可以根據指示形容詞、指示代名詞或副詞選出答案。

題目指定句中出現 she 和 wasn't stable，表示前方句子有提到 she 所對應的女子，請由此關鍵找出答案。[2] 和 [3] 前方分別提到 Cindy Walters 和 Ms. Warner，而 [2] 前方的句子中還提到 initial stage，指的就是事業尚處於不穩定的狀態（not stable），因此答案要選 (B) [2]。

Questions 170-171 refer to the following e-mail.

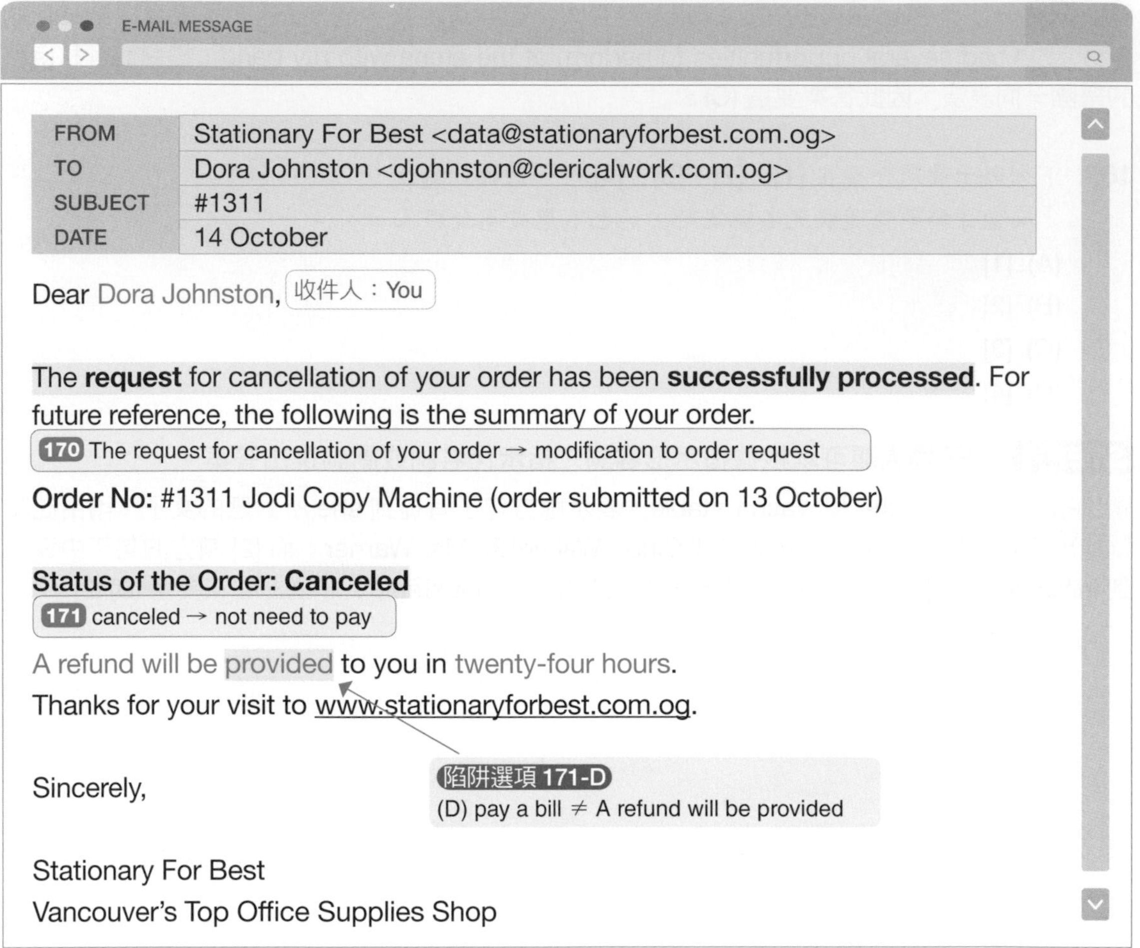
E-MAIL MESSAGE

FROM	Stationary For Best <data@stationaryforbest.com.og>
TO	Dora Johnston <djohnston@clericalwork.com.og>
SUBJECT	#1311
DATE	14 October

Dear Dora Johnston, 收件人：You

The **request** for cancellation of your order has been **successfully processed**. For future reference, the following is the summary of your order.

170 The request for cancellation of your order → modification to order request

Order No: #1311 Jodi Copy Machine (order submitted on 13 October)

Status of the Order: **Canceled**

171 canceled → not need to pay

A refund will be provided to you in twenty-four hours.

Thanks for your visit to www.stationaryforbest.com.og.

Sincerely,

陷阱選項 171-D
(D) pay a bill ≠ A refund will be provided

Stationary For Best
Vancouver's Top Office Supplies Shop

170. What is the reason the e-mail has been sent?
(A) To announce a new policy
(B) To inquire about an item's availability
(C) To confirm a modification to an order request
(D) To apologize for a delay in delivery

目的／前
→ 確認開頭前兩句話。

171. What information is given to Ms. Johnston about payment?
(A) She should already have got a refund.
(B) She does not need to pay for the product.
(C) She has paid for the order in full.
(D) She will pay a bill in twenty-four hours.

關鍵字 Johnston／payment
→ 從文章中找出關鍵字，並選出內容相符的選項。

第 170-171 題 電子郵件

寄件者	永佳公司 <data@stationaryforbest.com.og>
收件者	朵拉・約翰斯頓 <djohnston@clericalwork.com.og>
主旨	#1311 號訂單
寄件日期	10 月 14 日

朵拉・約翰斯頓女士您好：

您取消訂單的要求業已處理完成。以下是您的訂單摘要，供您參考。

訂單編號：#1311 號訂單 茱迪影印機（訂單日期：十月十三日）

訂單狀態：取消

您將於二十四小時之內收到退款。

感謝您造訪本公司官方網站 www.stationaryforbest.com.og.

溫哥華頂尖辦公用品專賣店 永佳公司 謹上

字彙 process 處理 for future reference 備查

170. 寄發此封電子郵件的原因為何？

(A) 宣布一項新政策
(B) 詢問一項商品是否有貨
(C) 確認訂單的修改要求
(D) 為延遲交貨道歉

STEP 1 開頭前兩句話有 90% 的機率會出現文章的目的。

開頭寫道：「The request for cancellation of your order has been successfully processed」，提到訂單取消成功，這表示本封電子郵件的撰寫目的，是為針對對方修改訂單的要求進行確認，因此答案為 (C)。

171. 關於支付的全額，約翰斯頓女士收到何資訊？

(A) 她應該已經收到退款了。
(B) 她不需要支付產品的費用。
(C) 訂單金額她已支付全額。
(D) 她將於二十四小時內付款。

STEP 1 答案通常會採換句話說的方式。

一般來說，英文會避免重複使用相同的字句，因此選項不太會使用和內文相同的單字，而是以意思相近的單字進行改寫。

本題要選出與關鍵字 payment 有關的內容相符的選項。文中並未直接提到 payment，而是採用更為明確的單字 cancellation 和 refund，因此請由相關敘述選出內容相符的選項。「Status of the Order: Canceled」表示訂單已經取消，不再需要付款，因此答案為 (B)。

STEP 2 分析錯誤選項。

「A refund will be provided to you」表示會退款給對方，而 (A) 指的是已經收到退款，並不正確。文中提到 refund 代表對方已經付款，但是無從得知是否為 in full（全額），因此不能選 (C) 作為答案。

Questions 172-175 refer to the following letter and agreement.

Kilburn Gold Electric Inc. **1**
661 Neasden, Kingsbury Road, London

23 April

Dear Mr. Allen 收件人：You

This letter is to **offer you the position of Customer Service Representative, starting Thursday, 24 May**, at the initial salary of ￡31,000 per year. In compliance with company policy, you will work for six months on a probationary basis, and at the last month of the period, we will make a decision as to whether to offer you a permanent position with our company.

172-B inform → Get in touch with

Please **inform** us of acceptance of the job offer **by Wednesday, 9 May**, by either sending an **e-mail to our Personnel Division**, pd@kgei.com, or making a phone call at 21-3346-2211. If there are any circumstances keeping you from taking on your responsibilities on the date stated, please let us know at your earliest convenience in order for us to accommodate you. However, be advised that a new starting day cannot be accepted no later than Tuesday, 5 June.

You are required to report to the Personnel Division **on your starting date**. Please note that you need to bring a copy of this letter with you to let the head of personnel sign and date it. Moreover, you have to show **official documents** like your driving license or passport, and bank account number.

172-C your driving license or passport → proof of identification

172-D a senior employee → an experienced coworker

To help new staff members adjust to our organization, we implement a traditional practice that **pairs a new comer with a senior employee in the department**. Hence, Mr. Alton Baldwin has been assigned to answer any questions you probably have such as your responsibilities and department's ambience. You can reach him by calling at 31-3342-4495, or sending an e-mail at a_baldwin@kgei.com. Keep in mind that the new employee orientation you are required to attend has been scheduled for Friday, 25 May. At that time, we will let you know about employee benefits and company policies. Lastly, thank you for joining Kilburn Gold Electric Inc., and we hope you will be our invaluable asset.

Sincerely,
Ruby Morales 寄件人：I
Head of Personnel Division

173 該公司按照慣例會將新進員工和資深員工配成一組
→負責 Allen 的資深員工為 Alton Baldwin
→ Allen 被分派到的部門＝ Customer Service Department
＝ Alton Baldwin 任職的部門

Agreement on Employment Conditions and Terms

2

I have hereby accepted employment with Kilburn Gold Electric Inc. under the conditions and terms specified.

Signature: *Scott Allen*

Name: Scott Allen

Starting Date: 1 June

172. What is a new staff member NOT required to do?

(A) Hand in a copy of their degree certificate

(B) Get in touch with the personnel division prior to their first day

(C) Present proof of identification on the first day

(D) Work with an experienced coworker

173. What is indicated about Mr. Baldwin? 第三者 : he

(A) He is a ~~personnel~~ officer.

(B) He has worked for Kilburn Gold Electric Inc. ~~since its founding~~.

(C) He is working in the customer service division.

(D) He will direct Mr. Allen to the ~~personnel division~~.

不屬於要求的事項

→ 整理出各選項的關鍵字後，再查看文章，刪去相符的選項。

Baldwin ／相關細節

→ 查看文章確認關鍵字所在之處，並選出與內容相符的選項。

1

Kilburn Gold Electric Inc.
661 Neasden, Kingsbury Road, London

23 April

Dear Mr. Allen,

> **175** 原本建議的上班日期：5 月 24 日
> 下方 Allen 簽名的合約中，正式開始上班日期＝ 6 月 1 日
> →上班時間有所變動

This letter is to offer you the position of Customer Service Representative, **starting Thursday, 24 May**, at the initial salary of £31,000 per year. In compliance with company policy, you will work for six months on a probationary basis, and at the last month of the period, we will make a decision as to whether to offer you a permanent position with our company.

To help new staff members adjust to our organization, we implement a traditional practice that pairs a new comer with a senior employee in the department. Hence, Mr. Alton Baldwin has been assigned to answer any questions you probably have such as your responsibilities and department's ambience. You can reach him by calling at 31-3342-4495, or sending an e-mail at a_baldwin@kgei.com. Keep in mind that the new employee orientation you are required to attend has been scheduled for **Friday**, 25 May. At that time, we will let you **know about employee benefits and company policies**. Lastly, thank you for joining Kilburn Gold Electric Inc., and we hope you will be our invaluable asset.

> **174** employee orientation and company polices
> → organizations rules

Sincerely,

Ruby Morales
Head of Personnel Division

2

Agreement on Employment Conditions and Terms

I have hereby accepted employment with Kilburn Gold Electric Inc. under the conditions and terms specified.

Signature: Scott Allen
Name: Scott Allen
Starting Date: 1 June

收件人：You

174. When will Mr. Allen officially be notified of the organization's rules?

(A) On Tuesday (B) On Wednesday
(C) On Thursday **(D) On Friday**

收件人／未來計畫／後

→ 找出 rules 替換成什麼單字。

175. What is indicated about Mr. Allen?

(A) He will ~~get a raise~~ after his probationary period.
(B) He will ~~not~~ be eligible for ~~employee benefits~~ for a half year.
(C) He postponed his starting date.
(D) He will be working with an experienced employee ~~for the first six months~~.

關鍵字 Allen ／相關細節

→ 查看文章確認關鍵字所在之處，並選出與內容相符的選項。

第 172-175 題 信件與同意書

1

基爾伯恩金電公司
倫敦金斯柏瑞路尼斯登村 661 號
四月二十三日

艾倫先生您好：

本公司特此予以通知，公司預計提供給您的客服代表職務，將始於五月二十四日星期四，基本工資為年薪三萬一千英鎊。依照公司政策規定，您將有六個月的試用期，試用期的最後一個月，公司會決定是否給予您正式的職位。

請於五月九日星期三以前，寄送電子郵件至人事部門電子信箱 pd@kgei.com，或是來電至 21-3346-2211，回覆本公司是否願意接受此項職務。若您因故無法於上述日期就職，請盡早告知，俾便本公司予以配合。不過請注意，您的就職日期將不得晚於六月五日星期二。

您必須向人事部門報備您的就職日期。請注意務必攜帶此通知書，俾便人事主管簽署並標註日期。此外，您也須出示您的官方證件，諸如駕駛執照、護照以及您的銀行帳號。

為有助新進員工加速適應，公司的傳統作法是將新進員工與部門內一名資深職員配對分組。因此，公司指派阿爾頓·鮑德溫先生答覆您可能產生的任何疑問，例如您的工作職責以及部門環境等。您可以撥打他的電話專線 31-3342-4495，或是寄送電子郵件至他的信箱 a_baldwin@kgei.com。請記住，新進員工須參加的培訓，日期謹訂於五月二十五日星期五。屆時，公司將會告知您員工福利及公司政策規定。最後，感謝您加入基爾伯恩金電公司，期待您能成為本公司的重要資產。

人事部門主管
露比·莫拉雷斯 謹上

2

聘僱條款 同意書

本人特此聲明接受基爾伯恩金電公司之聘僱條款。

簽名處．史考特·艾倫
姓名：史考特·艾倫
就職日期：六月一日

字彙 initial salary 基本工資 in compliance with 依照 on a probationary basis 試用期 permanent position 正式的職位 circumstances 情況 responsibilities 職責 at your earliest convenience 儘快 accommodate 通融 adjust 適應 implement 實施 hence 因此 ambience 環境 invaluable 寶貴的 asset 資產 specify 具體說明

172. 新進員工不需做何事？

(A) 繳交學歷證件影本

(B) 在就職日之前，聯繫人事部門

(C) 在就職日當天出示身分證件

(D) 與資深同僚共事

STEP 1 **看到 NOT Question 時，請善用刪去法。**

文章第一句話寫道：「This letter is to offer you the position . . . starting Thursday, 24 May」，表示這封信寄給 5 月 24 日開始上班的新進員工，而本題要刪去與文中要求事項相符的選項。

「inform us of acceptance of the job offer by Wednesday, 9 May, by either sending an e-mail to our Personnel Division」表示在正式上班日之前要聯絡人事部門，因此請刪去 (B)；「you have to show official documents like your driving license or passport, and bank account number」，等同於 (C) 繳交身分證明文件；「traditional practice that that pairs a new comer with a senior employee in the department」表示會將新進員工和資深員工分配在一起工作，與 (D) 的敘述相符，綜合上述，只有 (A) 不屬於要求事項。

173. 關於鮑德溫先生，本文有何暗示？

(A) 他是一名人事專員。

(B) 自基爾伯恩金電公司創辦以來，他即任職於該公司。

(C) 他在客服部門工作。

(D) 他將指示艾倫先生前往人事部門。

STEP 1 **確認 I／You／第三者各自的職業。**

本封信件中， Allen 為收件人、Morales 為寄件人、Baldwin 則是第三者，因此請從文章中找出關鍵字 Baldwin 所在之處，並選出與內文相符的選項。Mr. Alton Baldwin 正前方寫道：「we implement a traditional practice that pairs a new comer with a senior employee in the department」，提到新進員工會和同個部門的資深員工一起工作，而 Baldwin 正是要和收件人一起工作的資深員工。又文章開頭第一句話寫道：「offer you the the position of Customer Service Representative」，表示收件人將於客服部門工作，Baldwin 也任職於相同部門，因此答案要選 (C)。

174. 艾倫先生何時才會被正式告知公司的政策規定？

(A) 星期二

(B) 星期三

(C) 星期四

(D) 星期五

STEP 1 答案會出現在期間、星期或數字等關鍵字旁。

題目關鍵字為 rules，請由後半段文章來確認往後計畫。後半段寫道：「Friday, 25 May. At that time, we will let you know about employee benefits and company policies」，表示週五將告知對方公司的規定，因此答案為 (D)。

175. 關於艾倫先生，本文有何暗示？
(A) 試用期過後，他將獲得加薪。
(B) 在這半年期間，他將無法享有員工福利。
(C) 他延遲了就職日期。
(D) 他在前六個月將與一名資深員工一起工作。

STEP 1 題目要求找出相符的「事實」時，請先整理出各選項的關鍵字，再查看文章內容。

題目提到本封信的收件人 Allen，請查看文章，找出人名以及選項關鍵字。第一句話寫道：「the position of Customer Service Representative, starting Thursday, 24 May」，提到原本建議的上班日期為 5 月 24 日。但下方的合約書中寫道：「Starting Date: 1 June」，表示開始上班日延至 6 月 1 日，因此答案要選 (C)。

Questions 176-180 refer to the following information and form.

Enjoying the Watford Contemporary Photo Archive (WCPA) 1

The Watford Contemporary Photo Archive (WCPA) boasts not only various digital photos and prints but also a wide range of periodicals, books of paintings, and genuine materials acquired from many accomplished photographers and private collectors. Our invaluable collections are displayed throughout the whole ground floor of the building; the rare collections are exhibited on the first floor.

All visitors are required to follow the below guidelines to keep WCPA's possessions safely preserved.

176 要求事項和注意事項

176 fill out a membership → apply for membership

- Upon each visitor's first visit, they need to **fill out a membership application form** at the reception office. In order to obtain membership cards, every member must provide credit card information and a photo ID.
- The entire materials we have collec[...] looking through them, please keep in mind [...] main as arranged. If you find any of them is **missing or out of place**, please inform one of our employees; **do not make any effort to correct errors yourself**.

177 missing or out of place → misplaced
correct errors → arranging

- Our archive possessions should be handled in ways that avoid any damage, so do not leave any traces or marks during usage. Any damage may result in members paying a fine.
- Copy machines are accessible throughout the ground floor.
- Each material from any archive section has to be returned by 5:00 P.M.

Please comply [...] through the rare collections.

180 文章2→1
文章2中，material 的數量為 5 項，
在文章1中寫道：「no more than four materials at once」，因此答案為 (B)。

- Through a ra[...] can be requested from one of our employees. Each visitor is allowed to view no more than four materials at once. The materials need to be returned to the reference office when a visitor requests more than four.
- Visitors are permitted to examine these items only in the rare collection area.
- All personal belongings such as jackets, laptops, and bags must be kept in a cabinet before getting into the rare collection area. For **taking notes, writing materials can be provided upon request**.

178 provided → distributed

- Visitors are not able to request rare collection item after 4:30 P.M.

Watford Contemporary Photo Archive (WCPA)
Request Form for Rare Collections 2

Name: Jeff Bryant **Membership No.:** 9321
Date: February 22
E-mail: jeffbryant@y-young.com **Telephone:** 321-8872-8723

To help us locate the materials you would like to view, please complete the two sections below.

	Item Number	Brief Account
Material 1	TO 822210	Original flyer: Museum show of Henry Carter's artwork 179
Material 2	TR 474382	Henry Carter's work of art (India, 1941)
Material 3	JU 008331	Henry Carter's personal exhibition (Indonesia, 1943)
Material 4	CV 103469	Latimer Monthly News (published May, 1942)
Material 5	RO 339201	Henry Carter's family photo (New York, 1944)
Material 6		

176. What is suggested about the WCPA?
(A) Its opening hours differ from day to day.
(B) It is imperative for visitors to apply for its membership.
(C) It allows ~~only local residents~~ to access the first floor.
(D) Its items are kept in ~~several~~ buildings.

關鍵字 WCPA
→ 整理出各選項的關鍵字後，再查看文章，找出相符的選項。

177. According to the information, what are visitors prohibited from doing?
(A) Touching delicate materials
(B) Leaving personal belongings ~~at a desk~~
(C) Arranging misplaced materials
(D) ~~Reserving~~ items before their visit

visitors ／ prohibit ／訪問者的注意事項
→ 會以 do not 或 you should not 告知注意事項。

178. How can visitors to the rare collection area take personal notes?
(A) By borrowing digital recording equipment
(B) By using writing tools distributed by the WCPA
(C) By asking for photocopies for notes
(D) By using one of the WCPA's tablet PCs

visitors ／方法／ take notes
→ 極有可能以 if you 句型告知 take notes 的方法。

179. What most likely is Mr. Bryant's research about?
(A) A collection of rare ~~photographs~~
(B) ~~Belongings~~ of a specific individual
(C) The works of a certain artist
(D) The preservation of historical ~~photos~~

Bryant 的研究主題
→ 確認 Bryant 所寫的表格。

180. What does Mr. Bryant's request for materials indicate?
(A) He has to return materials before 5:00 P.M.
(B) He cannot view all his requested materials at once.
(C) He has never been to the WCPA.
(D) He needs to ~~pay a fee~~ to request some items.

Bryant 表格／列出的內容
→ 將文章二 Bryant 表格的內容對照文章一的 information 進行確認。

第 176-180 題 資訊與表格

1

歡迎參觀沃特福德當代影像資料館

沃特福德當代影像資料館擁有豐富的館藏，除了形形色色的數位照片及數位圖像之外，還包括多樣廣泛的期刊、繪畫書籍，以及從知名攝影大師及私人收藏家所蒐羅而來的原始真跡。本館館藏於本大樓的一樓展出，二樓則展示本館的珍稀館藏。

所有參觀的民眾須遵守下列的行為準則，以維護本館的珍貴資產：

- 每位首度參訪的民眾，皆須於接待處填妥會員申請表。每名會員必須提供信用卡資料以及身分證照，以便取得會員資格證。
- 本館所有館藏資料皆可開放供會員查閱。翻閱館藏時，請記得資料的排放位置應維持原樣。倘發現有資料遺失或是錯置，請告知本館員工；請勿嘗試自行歸位。
- 請避免對本館館藏造成任何損害，使用期間請勿遺留任何痕跡或標記。任何損傷都將可能導致罰款。
- 一樓各處設有影印機可供使用。
- 出借的檔案資料須於下午五點前歸還。

借閱珍稀館藏時，尤須遵守以下特別規定：

- 填妥珍稀館藏借閱表格、並遞交給本館任一員工，便可借閱珍稀館藏。每位參訪者一次不得借閱超過四件館藏。當借閱館藏超過四項時，參訪者須將所借資料直接歸還至資料參考室。
- 參訪者只可在珍稀館藏展區內檢視所借資料。
- 所有的私人物品，包含外套、筆記型電腦以及手提包，都需寄放在置物櫃，始得進入珍稀館藏展區。若有筆記需求，本館可提供紙筆。
- 下午四點三十分之後，珍稀館藏不得借閱。

2

沃特福德當代影像資料館
珍稀館藏借閱表格

姓名：傑夫・布萊恩　　**會員編號：**9321
申請日期：2 月 22 日
電子信箱：jeffbryant@y-young.com　　**聯絡電話：**321-8872-8723

請填妥下列兩處，俾便本館找出您欲檢視的館藏資料。

	項目編號	簡述
資料 1	TO 822210	亨利・卡特藝術品博物館展覽之原版宣傳單張
資料 2	TR 474382	亨利・卡特藝術作品（印度，1941）
資料 3	JU 008331	亨利・卡特個展（印尼，1943）
資料 4	CV 103469	拉蒂莫月刊（1942 年 5 月號）
資料 5	RO 339201	亨利・卡特全家福照片（攝於 1944 年紐約）
資料 6		

字彙 contemporary 當代的 archive 檔案館 boast 以有……而自豪
periodical 期刊 genuine 真跡的 invaluable 無價的 ground floor 一樓
first floor 二樓 possession 財產 obtain 獲得 order 次序 trace 痕跡
mark 標記 fine 罰款 comply with 遵守 at once 同時 examine 細查
personal belongings 個人物品 upon request 根據申請 locate 確定……的地點

176. 關於沃特福德當代影像資料館，本文有何暗示？
(A) 它的開放時間每日有別。
(B) 參訪者必須申請加入會員。
(C) 它的二樓展廳只允許當地居民參觀。
(D) 它的館藏分別藏於幾幢不同的建築物內。

STEP 1 題目要求找出相符的「事實」時，請先整理出各選項的關鍵字，再查看文章內容。

題目關鍵字 WCPA 出現在第一篇文章中，因此請由第一篇文章來確認。各選項的關鍵字分別為 (A) open hours、(B) membership、(C) first floor、(D) several buildings，請在文章中找尋這些關鍵字。文中寫道：「Upon each visitor's first visit, they need to fill out a membership application form」，表示首次來訪時需要加入會員，因此答案為 (B)。

STEP 2 分析錯誤選項

文中並未提到 (A) open hours；「the rare collections are exhibited on the first floor」並未限制只有 residents 可以進入，因此 (C) 並非答案；文中沒有提到 (D) several buildings，因此也不是答案。

177. 根據本文，參訪者禁止做何事？
(A) 觸碰易碎資料
(B) 將私人物品遺留在桌上
(C) 歸整錯置的資料
(D) 在參訪前先寄放物品

STEP 1 題目詢問要求或請求時，請找出以 please、I need you to、if you 開頭的句型。

題目提到 visitors，屬於不特定的某些人，指觀看資訊者，因此請從第一篇文章中找出答案。題目使用 prohibited，在文章中會以否定祈使句帶出答案，因此請找出「do not . . .」所在之處。文中寫道：「If you find any of them is missing . . . do not make any effort to correct errors yourself」，指「千萬不要親自動手調整」。(C) 將 out of place 改寫成 misplaced，故為正確答案。

178. 珍稀館藏區的參觀民眾如何才能記錄個人筆記？
(A) 租借數位記錄設備
(B) 使用當代影像資料館分發的書寫工具
(C) 索取資料影本作為筆記
(D) 使用當代影像資料館的平板電腦

STEP 1 後半段文章中會提到與方法有關的內容。

題目出現明確的關鍵字 take notes，詢問的對象為 visitors，因此請從第一篇文章的後半段找出關鍵字。文中寫道：「For taking notes, writing materials can be provided upon request.」，表示只要提出要求，就會提供作筆記的用具，代表會由 WCPA 提供筆記用具，因此答案為 (B)。

179. 布萊恩先生的研究最有可能關於？

(A) 珍稀照片系列收藏
(B) 特定人士的私有物
(C) 某位藝術家的藝術作品
(D) 歷史照片的保存

STEP 1 看到題目便能得知答案在哪一篇文章中。

題目關鍵字為 Bryant，明確告知人名，因此可以推測出答案會出現在第二篇文章中。本題詢問研究主題，而第二篇文章為要求提供資料的表格，查看各項資料的說明，便能推測出研究主題。表格中的 Brief account 欄位都有提到同一個人名 Henry Carter，當中只有一項有提到 photo，因此 (A) 和 (D) 不適合作為答案。另外 Henry Carter 的個人物品也不足以涵蓋所有資料，因此答案要選 (C)，表示 Henry Carter's artwork。

180. 從布萊恩先生要求借閱的資料中，可以看出何事？

(A) 他必須於下午五點之前歸還借閱資料。
(B) 他無法同時檢閱所有他想借閱的資料。
(C) 他從沒去過當代影像資料館。
(D) 他必須付費才得以要求檢閱資料。

STEP 1 五道題中，至少會有一題必須同時查看兩篇文章的內容，才能選出答案。

題目關鍵字和選項內容分別屬於不同文章時，請同時查看兩篇文章。

雖然題目是針對第二篇文章出題，但是只要看到選項內容，便能得知要同時確認兩篇文章的內容。從第二篇要求 rare collection 的表格中，無法得知他是否曾去過 WCPA，因此 (C) 不能作為答案；(D) 寫到 fee，但兩篇文章中都沒有提到，因此也不能作為答案；看到「Each material from any archive section has to be returned by 5:00 P.M.」可能會選擇 (A) 作為答案，但是稀有收藏品並不適用這項規定，不能作為答案；第二篇文章中，要求的資料為五項，而第一篇文章中 rare collections 的 guidelines 寫道：「Each visitor is allowed to view no more than four materials at once.」，這表示他無法一次取得所有的資料，因此答案為 (B)。

Questions 181-185 refer to the following agenda and letter.

Finsbury Business College

1

181 One-day event at Golders Hotel Headquarters (GHH)

Tuesday, March 21, 10:15 A.M. to 3:30 P.M.

Timetable

陷阱選項 181
注意 (B) 和 (D) 皆提到 students。

10:15 A.M. Finsbury students and their instructor come to the security office to get access cards

10:30 A.M. Lect 181 What an Internship Is Required to Do for Operations

11:10 A.M. Lecture: Qualifications for an Internship in Public Relations

11:50 A.M. Lecture: Possible Difficulties in Administration

12:30 P.M. Lunch after a guided tour of the office building

183

2:00 P.M. Lecture: How Things Are Going as an Intern in Sales and Marketing

2:45 P.M. Open discussion including Q & A and Closing

If you are interested in this event, you must register in advance or on-site. If you register in advance, you'll only need to pick up your name tag and other materials on-site.

2

April 23

Mr. Corey Gardner
Finsbury Business College
754 Stanmore Avenue
Croxley, RW 43 1Q4

Dear Mr. Gardner, 收件人：You

陷阱選項 185-(C)
並未提到見過 students。

About a month ago when I visited Golders Hotel Headquarters (GHH) with the schoolfellows from Finsbury Business College, I was lucky to have an opportunity to converse with you right after your seminar. You and your coworkers' presentations were very impressive, particularly Dana Frazier's speech about her operation management responsibilities and Clark George's wider perspective on his duties publicizing GHH's services and products.

Considering my goal to be a GHH's intern, however, your talk was the most relevant one among them. It was fascinating to **hear** about your managerial duties and your previous experience 185 as an intern. It seems like the path you have come along is **almost the same** as the one I am planning to follow. Therefore, if you could give me some guidelines regarding what skills and knowledge you needed to fulfill your daily duties as an 182 intern in sales and marketing at Golders Hotel, it would be greatly appreciated. Any advice I could have from you will definitely help me secure the skills and knowledge that I am going to need. 184

Thank you for your help in advance and I hope to meet you again. It would be great for me to have a chance to work with you in the near future.

Sincerely,

Delbert Acosta 寄件人：I

181. What was most likely the purpose of the event?

(A) To inform the ~~employees~~ of the seminars

(B) To publicize ~~a new training program~~ to students

(C) To encourage students to participate in an internship

(D) To help business school students to complete their ~~project~~

由第一篇文章確認活動的目的。

→ 找出 Timetable 主題的共通點。

182. In what field is Mr. Acosta most likely majoring? 2的寄件人：I

(A) ~~Operations management~~

(B) ~~Public relations~~

(C) Hotel management

(D) Sales and marketing

Acosta 主修的領域

→ 由第二篇文章確認。

183. When did Mr. Gardner most likely deliver his speech?

(A) At 10:30 A.M. 2的收件人：You

(B) At 11:10 A.M.

(C) At 11:50 A.M.

(D) At 2:00 P.M.

Gardner／演講時間

→ 第二篇文章提到 Gardner；第一篇文章提到時間。

184. In the letter, the word "secure" in paragraph 2, line 7, is closest in meaning to

(A) keep

(B) safe

(C) acquire

(D) purchase

同義詞題

→ 確認指定單字前後方的句子。

185. What is indicated about Mr. Gardner?

(A) He ~~signed up~~ for the seminars.

(B) He worked as an intern.

(C) He met ~~business school students~~ after the event.

(D) He is working at the Golders Hotel Headquarters.

關鍵字 Gardner

→ 由第二篇文章確認。

第 181-185 題 議程與信件

1

芬斯伯里商學院

活動名稱：格德斯飯店總部一日遊

時間：三月二十一日星期二，上午 10 點 15 分至下午 3 點 30 分

時間表

上午 10:15　芬斯伯里商學院師生前往安全管理處取得出入許可證
上午 10:30　專題演講：企業對實習生有何要求
上午 11:10　專題演講：公關部門的實習資格
上午 11:50　專題演講：管理實習生的潛在困難
下午 12:30　辦公大樓巡禮之後，享用午餐
下午 2:00　專題演講：市場銷售部的實習情況
下午 2:45　開放討論，包含 QA 問答以及閉幕式

如果您有興趣參加本次活動，您可提前報名或是在現場報名。若您預先報名，您到現場只需直接領取名牌及其他書面資料。

2

四月二十三日

克諾斯萊區斯丹摩大道 754 號 RW 43 1Q4

芬斯伯里商學院

柯瑞・加德納先生收

加德納先生您好：

大約一個月以前，我與芬斯伯里商學院同學一同參觀格德斯飯店總部時，很幸運地在您的演說結束之後，有機會與您交談。您與您同事的演說都讓人印象非常深刻，尤其是達娜・弗拉澤爾談到她在營運管理方面的職責，以及克拉克・喬治對於自己在宣傳格德斯飯店總部的服務及產品時，較為宏觀的工作理念。

不過，考量到我的目標是成為格德斯飯店總部的實習生，所以您的演說是在這其中與我的目標最相關的。聽您談及您的管理職責以及過去的實習經驗，真的非常的引人入勝。您一路走來的經歷與我計劃想追尋的目標，看來幾乎完全一致。因此，如果您能給我一些指導，關於您在格德斯飯店市場銷售部實習時，完成日常職責所需要的知識與技能，我會非常地感激您。您的任何一項建議，絕對有助於我習得我所需要的知識及技能。

在此先感謝您的協助，希望能再與您見面。如果能在不久的將來有機會與您共事，對我來說那就真的太棒了。

誠摯地

戴伯特・阿考斯塔　敬上

字彙 headquarters 總部　instructor 大學講師　operations 企業
public relations 公共關係　administration 管理　open discussion 自由討論
on-site 現場的；當場　schoolfellow 同學　converse 交談
operation management 經營管理　perspective 觀點　publicize 宣傳
considering 考慮到　relevant 有關的　daily duty 日常工作職責　appreciate 感激

181. 此活動最有可能的目的是？

(A) 通知員工有關研討會的訊息

(B) 向學生宣傳新的訓練課程

(C) 鼓勵學生參加實習

(D) 幫助商學院學生完成他們的專題研究

STEP 1 請善用題目所提供的線索和文章內有關答案的資訊。

題目提到活動，表示要查看第一篇文章的時間表。請從時間表列出的內容中找尋共通點，即為活動的目的所在。當中寫道：「10:30 A.M. Lecture: What an Internship」與「11:10 A.M. Lecture: Qualifications for an Internship」，表示目的為 internship，因此答案要選 (C)。

STEP 2 分析錯誤選項

雖然文章開頭有出現 (B) 和 (D) 當中的 students，但是並未提到 (B) new training program 和 (D) project，因此不能作為答案。

182. 阿考斯塔先生的主修專業最有可能在哪個領域？

(A) 經營管理

(B) 公共關係

(C) 飯店管理

(D) 市場銷售

STEP 1 人名為最重要的關鍵字。

本題詢問寄件人 Acosta 主修的領域，從第二篇文章的信件可以確認 Acosta 的相關資訊。文中寫道：「the path you have come along is almost the same as the one I am planning to follow」，表示對方所走的路正是自己想要追隨的道路。接著寫道：「skills and knowledge you needed to fulfill your daily duties as an intern in sales and marketing at Golders Hotel」，向對方請教在 sales and marketing 領域實習時，每天在執行工作上所需的知識和技巧，由此可以得知寄件人主修的領域也是 (D) Sales and marketing，因此答案為 (D)。

STEP 2 分析錯誤選項。

(A) 出現在「Dana Frazier's speech about her operation management responsibilities」；(B) 出現在「Clark George's wider perspective on his duties publicizing GHH's services . . .」，但皆與題目無關，因此不能作為答案。

183. 加德納先生最有可能在何時發表演說？

(A) 上午 10:30
(B) 上午 11:10
(C) 上午 11:50
(D) 下午 2:00

STEP 1 整合圖表資訊和文章內容後，才能選出答案。

本題詢問 Gardener 先前演講的時間，此人為第二篇文章的收件人，當中會以 you 提及相關內容。而選項列出明確的時間，因此要再由第一篇文章來確認答案。

第二篇文章中寫道：「your talk was the most relevant one among them. It was fascinating to hear about your managerial duties and your previous experience as an intern」，提到演講的主題。對照第一篇文章後，會發現為下午兩點的演講「2:00 P.M. Lecture: How Things Are Going as an Intern in Sales and Marketing」，因此答案為 (D)。

184. 信函中第二段、第七行的「secure」意思最接近

(A) 保有
(B) 安全的
(C) 取得
(D) 購買

STEP 1 題目考同義詞時，要根據前後文意，選出最適合替換的單字。

除了確認題目所列出的單字之外，還要掌握該單字在句中所使用的意思，以便找出意思相同的單字作為答案。該單字所在的句子為「secure the skills and knowledge」，表示「獲得技巧和知識」。選項中 (C) 表示「取得」，兩者的意思相同。

185. 關於加德納先生，本文有何暗示？

(A) 他報名參加研討會。
(B) 他曾經實習過。
(C) 他在活動結束後與商學院學生見面。
(D) 他正任職於格德斯飯店總部。

STEP 1 確認 I ／ You ／第三者以及各自的職業為何。

本題關鍵字為 Mr. Gardner，要找出符合此人的敘述。第二篇文章中，會以 you 提及相關內容，請相互對照並選出內容相符的選項。

文中寫道：「your previous experience as an intern」，提到 Gardner 過去曾做過實習工作，因此答案為 (B)。

文中還寫道：「I was lucky to have an opportunity to converse with you right after your seminar」，表示研討會結束後，很幸運有機會和你談話。乍看之下會以為 (C) 的敘述正確，但是此處的 I 指的是 Acosta，並非和 business school students 見面，因此為錯誤的敘述；(D) 根據文章可以得知 Gardner 曾在飯店實習過，但是並未提到他現在的工作地點為飯店總部（headquarters），因此該選項不能作為答案。

Questions 186-190 refer to the following e-mails and press release.

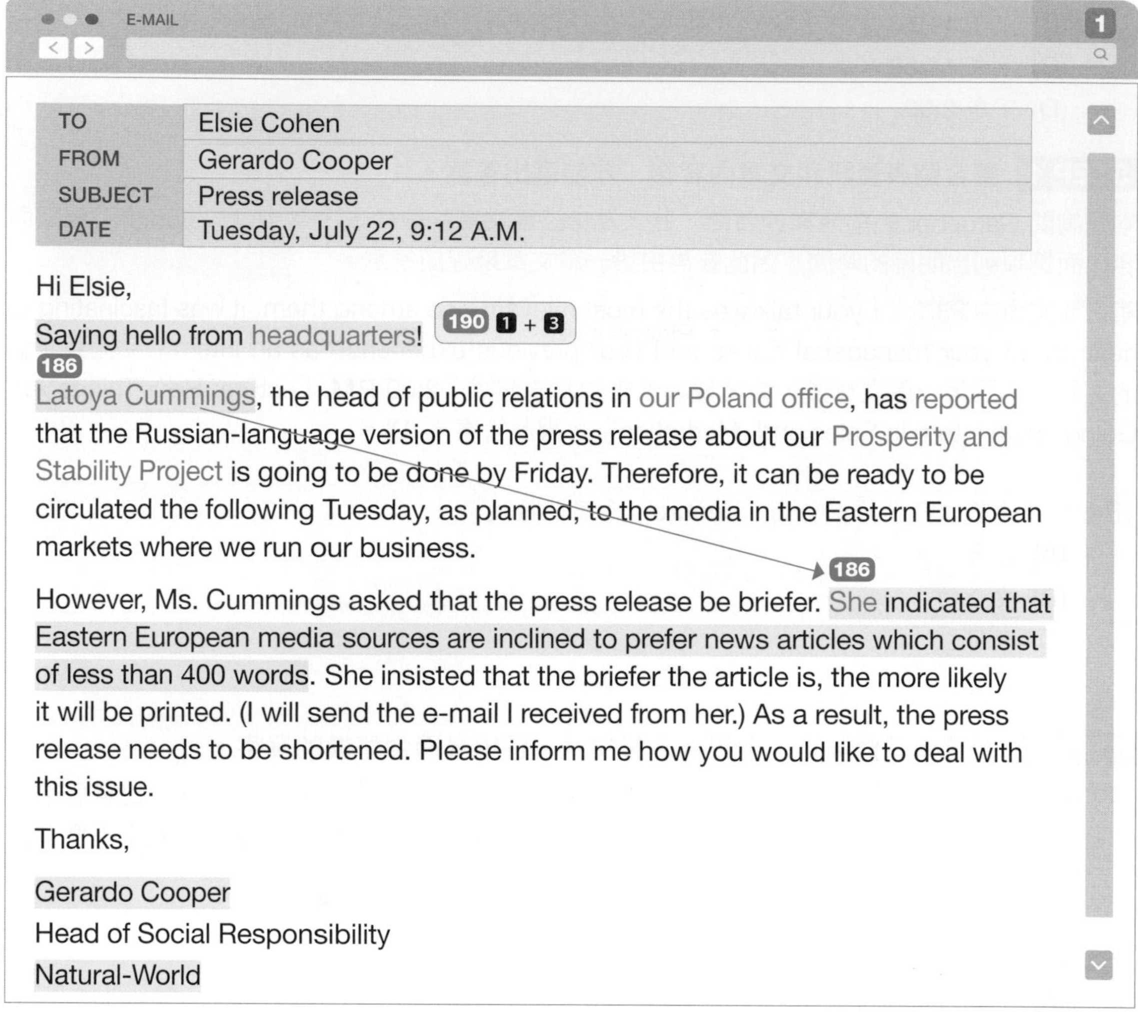
E-MAIL

TO	Elsie Cohen
FROM	Gerardo Cooper
SUBJECT	Press release
DATE	Tuesday, July 22, 9:12 A.M.

Hi Elsie,

Saying hello from headquarters! 190 1 + 3

186

Latoya Cummings, the head of public relations in our Poland office, has reported that the Russian-language version of the press release about our Prosperity and Stability Project is going to be done by Friday. Therefore, it can be ready to be circulated the following Tuesday, as planned, to the media in the Eastern European markets where we run our business.

186

However, Ms. Cummings asked that the press release be briefer. She indicated that Eastern European media sources are inclined to prefer news articles which consist of less than 400 words. She insisted that the briefer the article is, the more likely it will be printed. (I will send the e-mail I received from her.) As a result, the press release needs to be shortened. Please inform me how you would like to deal with this issue.

Thanks,

Gerardo Cooper
Head of Social Responsibility
Natural-World

第三者：she

186. What is suggested about Ms. Cummings?

(A) She has approved the Prosperity and Stability Project.
(B) She has met Mr. Cooper in person.
(C) She is knowledgeable about news formats in Eastern Europe.
(D) She has recently transferred to the Poland office.

Cummings：文章1

→ 文中會以 he/she 提及第三者，請從相關敘述找出答案。

E-MAIL 2

TO	Gerardo Cooper
FROM	Elsie Cohen 第二篇文的寄件人：I
SUBJECT	Press release
DATE	Tuesday, July 22, 11:43 A.M.
ATTACHMENT	Important Project.doc

Hello Gerardo, 187 made some correction → revised

All of our team members have shared the e-mail you sent me earlier today. We have made some corrections to the press release according to Ms. Cummings' recommendation and attached it. Please look through it to make sure that the information does not have any mistake. Then, you can send it to her as soon as you can in order for her to translate it into Russian. In addition, could you remind her to contact all related social media to have it posted?

Thanks,

陷阱選項 187-(D)
要求對方的事項

Elsie Cohen
Head of Communication
Natural-World

第二篇文的寄件人：I

187. What did Ms. Cohen do recently?
(A) She translated a press release ~~herself~~.
(B) She visited the Poland branch.
(C) She revised a publicity material.
(D) She has information posted on social media.

Cohen ／ do recently：文章2
→ 過去的資訊出現在前半段文章中。

3

Official Announcement for Natural-World Announces Important Project

Natural-World is pleased to announce its Prosperity and Stability Project. Over the next four years, the firm will put a minimum investment of $600 million throughout (188) all the nations where it runs its business to enhance availability of educational reading materials, which are very important for children in need. In cooperation with national and global child welfare associations, educational publications and programs will be provided to educators and professionals in the childcare industry. Furthermore, schools and local childcare institutions will offer a wide range of educational materials to children while nursery schools will offer educational toys and storybooks. Check out more information about the project by visiting www.naturalworld.net/project.

190 1 + 3

189
(Natural-World is a publishing company based in Canada, which also boasts its presence in Poland, Romania, Russia, and Ukraine.)

188. What is the main reason the project will be carried out?
(A) To promote the education industry
(B) To encourage teachers to make educational materials
(C) To establish more childcare institutions
(D) To offer children better educational items

project／執行原因：文章3
→ 詢問執行計畫的原因等同於詢問目的。

189. What is stated in the press release?
(A) The location in which the materials are produced
(B) The number of Natural-World's international branches
(C) The industry where Natural-World operates
(D) The annual profit Natural-World earns

從文章中找出選項的關鍵字：文章3

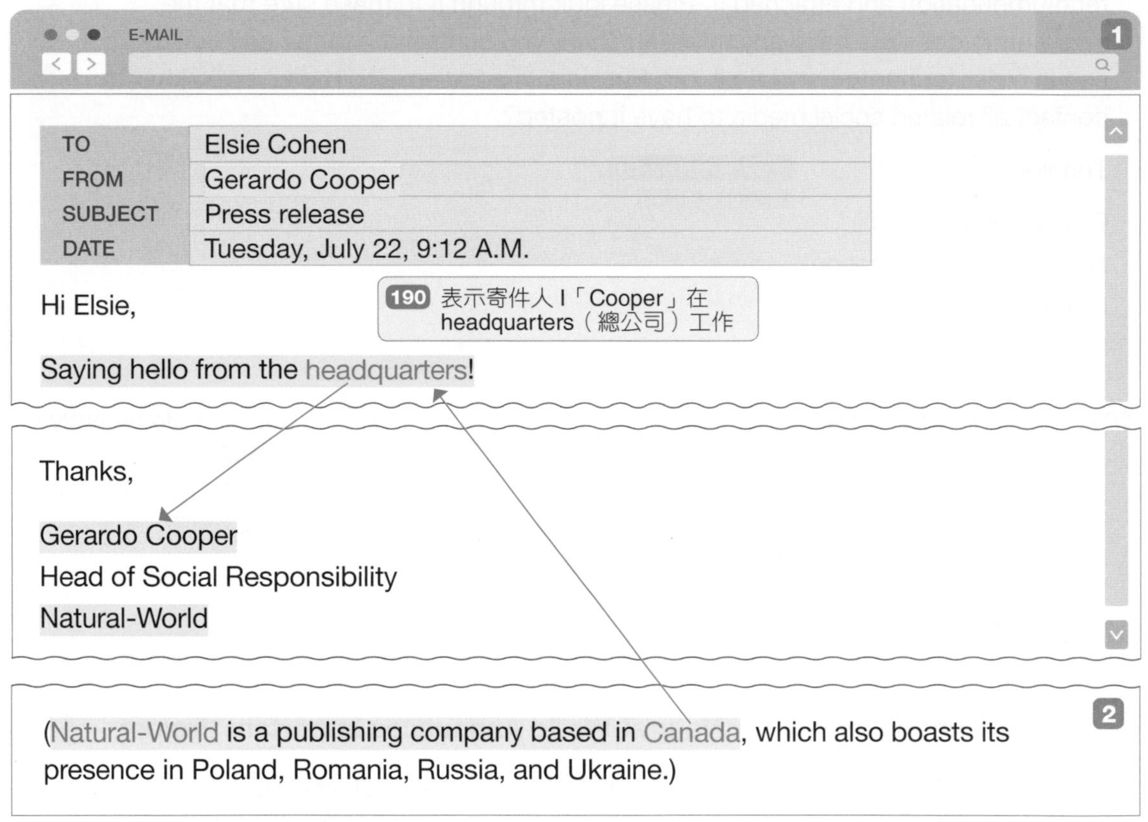
E-MAIL 1

TO	Elsie Cohen
FROM	Gerardo Cooper
SUBJECT	Press release
DATE	Tuesday, July 22, 9:12 A.M.

Hi Elsie,

190 表示寄件人 I「Cooper」在 headquarters（總公司）工作

Saying hello from the headquarters!

Thanks,

Gerardo Cooper
Head of Social Responsibility
Natural-World

2

(Natural-World is a publishing company based in Canada, which also boasts its presence in Poland, Romania, Russia, and Ukraine.)

1的寄件人：I

190. Where does Mr. Cooper most likely work?
(A) In Poland
(B) In Romania
(C) In Canada
(D) In Ukraine

Cooper／工作地點：文章1、3
→ 確認 Cooper 信中提及的資訊後，再查看別篇文章找出相關內容。

第 186-190 題 兩封電子郵件與新聞稿

1

收件者	艾希・柯恩
寄件者	赫拉多・庫柏
主旨	新聞稿
寄件日期	7 月 22 日星期二，上午 9:12

嗨，艾希，

我在總部跟妳問好！

根據波蘭分處公關部主任拉托亞・卡明斯的彙報，公司「穩定繁榮計畫」的俄文版新聞稿在星期五以前可以完成。因此，我們可以按照事前的規畫，在下星期二將新聞稿分發給公司主要經營市場——東歐市場的媒體。

不過，卡明斯女士要求新聞稿能簡短些。她表示，東歐的媒體偏好少於四百字的新聞報導。她強調文章越短，越有可能刊登。（我會把她寄來的電子郵件轉給妳看。）因此，新聞稿必須再做刪減。請讓我知曉妳會如何處理此事。

謝了。

自然世界公司 社會責任部主任 赫拉多・庫柏

2

收件者	赫拉多・庫柏
寄件者	艾希・柯恩
主旨	回覆：新聞稿
寄件日期	7 月 22 日星期二，上午 11:43
附件	重要計畫 .doc

哈囉，赫拉多，

今天稍早前你寄來的電子郵件，我已經轉給我們所有的組員了。我們已依照卡明斯女士的建議，對新聞稿做了些修改，隨信附上。請瀏覽一下新聞稿，確認其中資訊沒有出錯，然後你便可以盡快轉寄給她翻成俄文。此外，你能不能提醒她記得聯繫所有相關社群媒體以便刊載新聞稿？

謝了。

自然世界公司 傳播部主任 艾希・柯恩

自然世界公司重要計畫官方聲明 3

「自然世界公司」很榮幸在此宣布，本公司即將展開「穩定繁榮計畫」。本公司預計在接下來的四年之內，在公司經營業務的所有國家，挹注至少六億美元的資金，以增加教育性閱讀素材的供應，這對貧童來說尤為重要。本公司將與國際級以及當地國家的兒童福利聯盟合作，為兒童保育業教育工作者及專業人員提供教育出版品及教育方案。此外，學校及當地的幼保機構也會提供兒童各式各樣的教材，而幼兒園則會提供益智玩具及故事書。請瀏覽我們的官方網站 www.naturalworld.net/project，以了解更多計畫相關訊息。

(「自然世界」是一家加拿大出版公司，在波蘭、羅馬尼亞、俄羅斯及烏克蘭皆設有辦事處。)

字彙 press release 新聞稿　headquarters 總部　public relations 公關活動
circulate （使）散布　brief 簡短的　indicate 指出　media source 媒體資料來源
be inclined to V 傾向於……的　shorten （使）縮短　deal with 處理
look through 瀏覽　official announcement 官方聲明　minimum 最低限度
throughout 在各處　availability 可得性　in need 在窮困中的
in cooperation with 與……合作　welfare association 福利聯盟
institution 機構　a wide range of 範圍廣泛的　nursery school 托兒所
boast 以有……而自豪　presence 存在

186. 關於卡明斯女士，本文有何暗示？

(A) 她核准了「穩定繁榮計畫」。　(B) 她親自面見庫柏先生。
(C) 她熟知東歐媒體偏好的新聞稿格式。　(D) 她最近才被調往波蘭分處。

STEP 1 題目要求找出相符的「事實」時，請先整理出各選項的關鍵字，再查看文章內容。

題目關鍵字為 Cummings，出現在第一篇文章中。請先整理出各選項的關鍵字，再選出與內文相符的選項。第一篇文章的收件人為 Elsie、寄件人為 Cooper，而 Cummings 為第三者，因此文中會以代名詞 she 或 he 代稱，請由此確認相關敘述。文中寫道：「She indicated that Eastern European media sources are inclined to prefer news articles which consist of less than 400 words」，表示她相當了解東歐的報導格式，因此答案為 (C)。

STEP 2 分析錯誤選項

(A)「Latoya Cummings . . . reported . . . the press release about our Prosperity the Stability Project」不等同 approve 的概念，因此不能作為答案。

(B) 從文章無法得知她是否親自和 Cooper 見過面。

(D) 從文章無法得知她最近是否調職。

187. 柯恩女士最近做了何事？

(A) 她自己翻譯新聞稿。　(B) 她參訪波蘭分處。
(C) 她修改了一份文宣資料。　(D) 她在社群媒體上刊登訊息。

STEP 1 前半段文章會提出問題或過去的資訊。

題目關鍵字為 Cohen 和 do recently，而第二篇文章的寄件人為 Cohen，因此請從中找出答案。過去的資訊會出現在前半段文章中，因此請確認前半段的內文。當中寫道：「We have made some corrections to the press release」，提到他修改了報導，因此答案為 (C)。

STEP 2 分析錯誤選項

(A) 開頭寫道「all of our team members have shared the e-mail you sent」，僅提到團隊共享郵件的內容，並未提到翻譯一事，因此不是答案；(D) 後半段寫道：「could you remind her to contact all related social media to have it posted?」，向對方提出要求，因此也不是答案。

188. 執行該計畫的主因為何？

(A) 為了推廣教育事業　　(B) 鼓勵教師製作教材

(C) 開設更多幼保機構　　(D) 提供兒童更好的讀物

STEP 1 請務必從文中找出關鍵字 project。

第一篇文章提到與該計畫由關的執行狀況；第三篇文章則為介紹該計畫的報導。執行 project 的原因出現在第三篇文章的前半段，當中以 to 不定詞帶出目的「to enhance availability of educational reading materials, which are very important for children in need」，表示將會提供更多的教育刊物給有需要的孩子，因此答案要選 (D)。

STEP 2 分析錯誤選項

文中寫道：「educational publications and programs will be provided to educators and professionals」，當中提到 teachers，千萬別因此誤選 (B)。

189. 新聞稿所述內容為何？

(A) 教材的製造地點　　(B) 自然世界公司國際分處的數量

(C) 自然世界公司的經營領域　　(D) 自然世界公司的年營收

STEP 1 內文會告知明確的資訊，但是答案會採較為籠統的方式敘述。

題目中出現 press release，表示要從第三篇文章中找出相關的內容。選項列出較為籠統的內容，請從文中找出相對應的詳細資訊。「Natural-World is a publishing company based in Canada」，指出該公司屬於出版業，因此答案為 (C)。雖然 (A) 也提到地點，但是文中並未提到生產 materials 的地點；(B) 文中僅提及海外分公司的地點，並未明確告知數量。

190. 庫柏先生最有可能任職何處？

(A) 波蘭　　(B) 羅馬尼亞

(C) 加拿大　　(D) 烏克蘭

STEP 1 選項皆為地點、時間或人名時，請務必查看所有的文章。

本題詢問 Cooper 工作的地點。第一篇文章的寄件人為 Cooper，因此請先由內文確認他的身分。當中寫道：「Saying hello from headquarters!」，表示傳達來自總公司的問候。且文章最後寫道：「Natural-World」，表示他在此工作。第三篇文章中提到 Natural-World 的總公司：「Natural-World is a publishing company based in Canada」，由此句話可以得知他在加拿大工作，因此答案為 (C)。

Questions 191-195 refer to the following e-mail, advertisement, and article.

TO	marionfernandez@manitobastation.com
FROM	cedricfitzgerald@albertasteel.org
DATE	11 August
SUBJECT	September Appointment

Dear Ms. Fernandez,

191

This is to confirm that an Alberta Steel representative, Jacquelyn Cross, is scheduled to visit Manitoba Station on the afternoon of 25 September. In order to have the evaluation process expedited, please sort out your **scrap metal**. At that time, the terms and conditions of the contract will be negotiated.

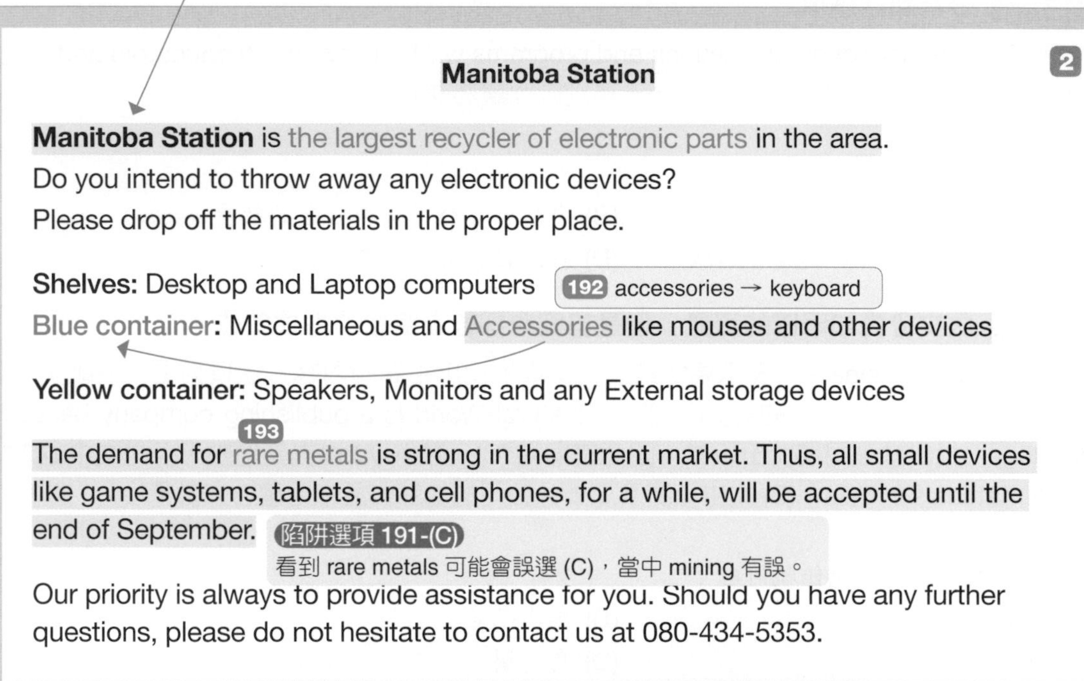

Manitoba Station

Manitoba Station is the largest recycler of electronic parts in the area.
Do you intend to throw away any electronic devices?
Please drop off the materials in the proper place.

Shelves: Desktop and Laptop computers 192 accessories → keyboard

Blue container: Miscellaneous and Accessories like mouses and other devices

Yellow container: Speakers, Monitors and any External storage devices

193

The demand for rare metals is strong in the current market. Thus, all small devices like game systems, tablets, and cell phones, for a while, will be accepted until the end of September. 陷阱選項 191-(C) 看到 rare metals 可能會誤選 (C)，當中 mining 有誤。

Our priority is always to provide assistance for you. Should you have any further questions, please do not hesitate to contact us at 080-434-5353.

收件人：You

191. What field does Ms. Fernandez most likely specialize in?

(A) ~~Developing~~ computers
(B) Recycling electronics
(C) ~~Mining~~ for rare metals
(D) ~~Producing~~ computer parts

192. According to the advertisement, where should a small item like a keyboard be put?

(A) On the shelves
(B) In the yellow container
(C) In the blue container
(D) At the service desk

Fernandez／專攻領域：文章1、2
→ 確認內文中提及 Fernandez 的部分。

keyboard／放置地點：文章2
→ 找出與 keyboard 有關的關鍵字 accessories。

193. Why did Manitoba Station ask that the rare items be dropped off through September?
(A) Because the ~~prices~~ for items ~~will decrease~~.
(B) Because the market condition for the items is good.
(C) Because it will relocate to another region.
(D) Because its ownership will change soon.

廣告／rare items／September：文章2
→ 查看文章找出關鍵字所在之處。

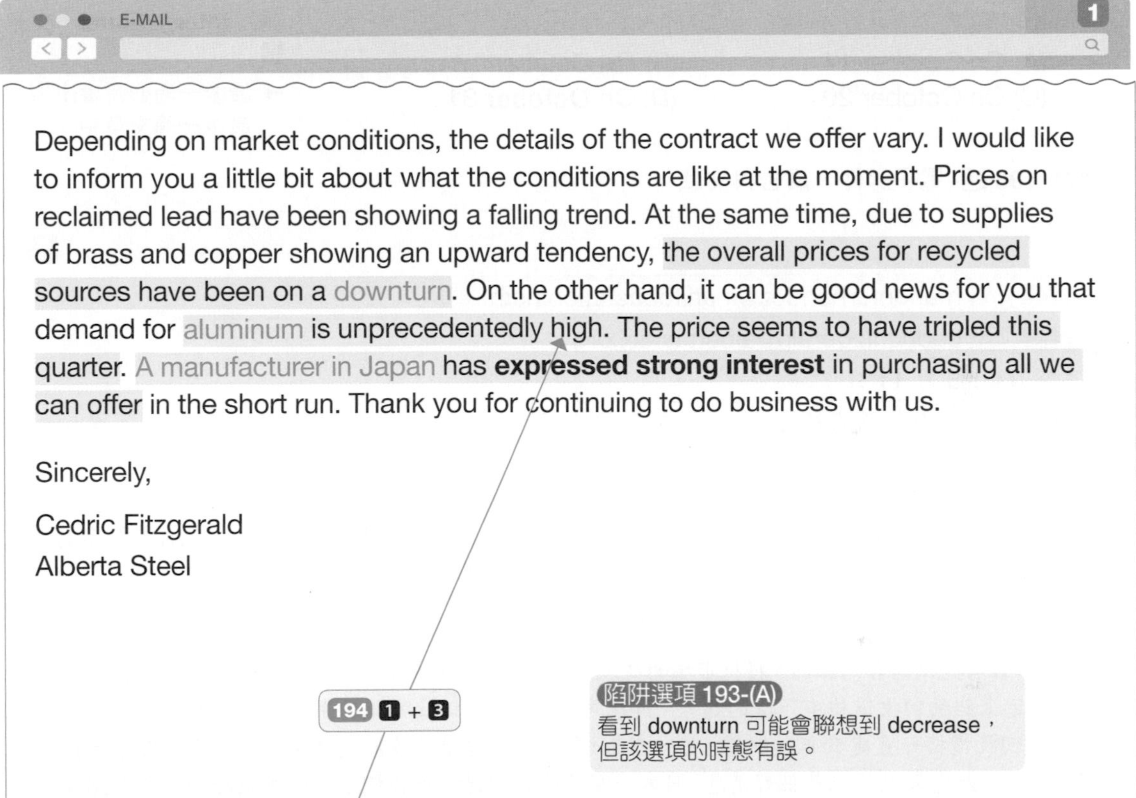
E-MAIL 1

Depending on market conditions, the details of the contract we offer vary. I would like to inform you a little bit about what the conditions are like at the moment. Prices on reclaimed lead have been showing a falling trend. At the same time, due to supplies of brass and copper showing an upward tendency, the overall prices for recycled sources have been on a downturn. On the other hand, it can be good news for you that demand for aluminum is unprecedentedly high. The price seems to have tripled this quarter. A manufacturer in Japan has **expressed strong interest** in purchasing all we can offer in the short run. Thank you for continuing to do business with us.

Sincerely,

Cedric Fitzgerald
Alberta Steel

194 1 + 3

陷阱選項 193-(A)
看到 downturn 可能會聯想到 decrease，但該選項的時態有誤。

3

TOKYO (14 Oct.) - Dixon Appliances announced yesterday the earliest launch of its newest tablet PC, the R2Q-1000. The new tablet will be the most affordable as well as the lightest and fastest one in its class. The use of newly created capacitors made these high-quality devices possible. In addition, the R2Q is one of the first mass-manufactured tablet PCs using up to 60 percent recycled material, most of which is taken out of outdated electronic products. The Japanese firm's flagship shop in Tokyo will begin selling the R2Q models to a limited number of customers starting next week. Dixon is going to make the device available at outlets across Japan by 20 Oct., even though consumers abroad need to wait until 31 Oct.

195 abroad → international

194. What is Dixon Appliances most likely using in its new tablet PC?

(A) Lead　(B) Brass
(C) Aluminum　(D) Copper

Dixon Appliances ／ using ／ new tablet PC：文章1、3
→ 由關鍵字前後的內容確認答案。

195. When will the new tablet PC be available on the international market?

(A) On October 14　(B) On October 17
(C) On October 20　**(D) On October 31**

new tablet PC ／上市日期／ international：文章3
→ 最後一題通常會出現在最後一篇文章中。

第 191-195 題 電子郵件、廣告與文章

1

收件者	marionfernandez@manitobastation.com
寄件者	cedricfitzgerald@albertasteel.org
寄件日期	8 月 11 日
主旨	九月的正式拜會

費南德茲女士您好，

本函是與您確認亞伯達鋼鐵公司的代表賈桂琳·克羅斯，預計將於九月二十五日下午參訪曼尼托巴回收站。為了加速評估過程的進行，請將貴公司的廢五金挑揀出來。屆時，雙方也將就合約的條款及條件，進行協商。

本公司提供的合約細節，將視市場的情況而有所調整。我想藉此讓您了解一下現階段的市場現況。近來鉛的回收價格有下降的趨勢。與此同時，由於黃銅及紅銅的供給呈現上升趨勢，所以銅的整體回收價格一直處於低迷狀態。另一方面，鋁的市場需求已達歷史新高，回收價格在這一季翻了三倍，這對您來說可能是個好消息。日本一家製造業者對收購我們短期內所能提供的所有鋁資源，表示出了強烈的興趣。感謝貴公司與本公司持續合作。

亞伯達鋼鐵公司 塞德里克·費茲傑羅 謹上

2

曼尼托巴回收站

曼尼托巴回收站是本地最大的電子零件回收業者。
您想要丟棄任何電子設備嗎？
請將丟棄的材料棄置於適當的位置。

貨架上：桌上型電腦及筆記型電腦
藍色集裝箱：各式五花八門的配備，如滑鼠等其他器材
黃色集裝箱：喇叭、螢幕以及任何外接式儲存裝置

目前市場對稀有金屬的需求強烈。因此，自現在起至九月底這段時間內，本站將集中回收所有的小型器材，例如遊戲配備、平板電腦以及手機等。

顧客至上向來是本公司的一貫宗旨。若您有任何疑問，請直接撥打 080-434-5353，隨時與我們聯繫。

3

（10 月 14 日，東京報導）狄克森電器公司昨日宣布，該公司最新的平板電腦 R2Q-1000 首發上市。該平板電腦將會是同等級中，最輕、處理效率最快，且最為經濟實惠的一款機型。如此高品質的設備得以面世，要歸功於全新研發的電容器。此外，R2Q 平板電腦是第一款使用 60% 以上的回收材料所製、並大量生產的平板機種。其中大部分的材料都是回收過時的電子產品所取得。該公司在東京的旗艦店將於下個星期開始，有限度地開放少量 R2Q 平板機種進行銷售；而全日本各地的經銷處則可望在 10 月 20 日之前可以開始銷售 R2Q；至於國外的消費者，則必須等到 10 月 31 日才可以購得。

字彙 representative 代表　evaluation process 評估過程　expedite 加快
sort out 挑出　scrap metal 廢五金　terms and conditions 條款
negotiate 就……談判　market condition 市場情況　vary （使）呈現差異
reclaimed 回收的　upward 向上的　tendency 趨勢　downturn 下降
unprecedentedly 空前地　triple 增至三倍　quarter 季度　manufacturer 製造業者
in the short run 在短期內　intend to V 打算（做）……　throw away 扔掉
miscellaneous 各種各樣的　external device 外接裝置　priority 優先考慮的事
assistance 援助　hesitate 躊躇　affordable 買得起的；負擔得起的
capacitor 電容器　outdated 舊式的　flagship shop 旗艦店

191. 費南德茲女士最有可能專精哪個領域？

(A) 研發電腦
(B) 回收電器
(C) 開採稀有金屬
(D) 生產電腦零件

STEP 1 關鍵字旁未出現答案時，請確認是否還有其他解題線索。

本題關鍵字 Fernandez 為第一篇文章的收件人，但是第一篇文章中並未直接提到她從事的領域。當中寫道：「This is to confirm that an Alberta Steel representative, Jacquelyn Cross, is scheduled to visit Manitoba Station」，向 Fernandez 確認 Jacquelyn Cross 將至 Manitoba Station 拜訪的行程，由此可以得知 Fernandez 是 Manitoba Station 公司的人。

而第二篇文章為 Manitoba Station 的廣告，第一句話寫道：「Manitoba Station is the largest recycler of electronic parts in the area.」，指出為回收電子零件的公司，因此答案要選 (B)。

192. 根據告示，鍵盤這類的小型物件該置於何處？

(A) 放在貨架上
(B) 放進黃色集貨箱
(C) 放進藍色集貨箱
(D) 放在服務檯上

STEP 1 答案通常會採換句話說的方式。

題目關鍵字為 keyboard，為意思極為明確的單字。但值得留意的是，文章中通常會使用較為廣義的單字來代替。第二篇文章中寫道：「Blue container: Miscellaneous and Accessories like mouses and other devices」，keyboard 屬於 Accessories（飾品、配件），因此可以得知鍵盤要放在 (C)。

193. 為何曼尼托巴回收站會要求在九月份回收稀有物品？

(A) 因為這些物品的回收價格將下跌。
(B) 因為這些物品的市場行情看漲。
(C) 因為它將搬遷至另一個地區。
(D) 因為它即將易主。

STEP 1 答案通常會出現在關鍵字旁。

從第二篇文章中找出 September 所在的句子為：「The demand for rare metals . . . until the end of September」，提到由於稀有金屬的需求增加，因此預計將回收到九月底。這代表稀有金屬在市場的行情極佳，答案要選 (B)。

194. 狄克森電器最有可能使用何物來製造其新款平板電腦？

(A) 鉛

(B) 黃銅

(C) 鋁

(D) 紅銅

STEP 1 五道題中，至少會有一題必須同時查看兩篇文章的內容，才能選出答案。

題目關鍵字為 Dixon Appliances，而選項列出製作 PC 所使用的材料，兩者分別出現在第三篇文章和第一篇文章中，因此請整合這兩篇文章的內容，以便找出答案。

第三篇文章為十月份的報導，當中寫道：「tablet PC using up to 60 percent recycled material, most of which is taken out of outdated electronic products. The Japanese firm's flagship shop in Tokyo」，提到日本一家公司將舊的電子產品加以利用製作平板電腦。

第一篇文章為八月份所寫的郵件，當中寫道：「it can be good news for you that demand for aluminum is unprecedentedly high. The price seems to have tripled this quarter. A manufacturer in Japan has expressed strong interest in purchasing all we can offer」，提到鋁的價格上升以及有家日本公司有意購買鋁。由此可以得知應為日本公司 Dixon Appliances 有意購買鋁來生產新型平板電腦，因此答案為 (C)。

195. 新款平板電腦將於何時在國際市場上市？

(A) 10 月 14 日

(B) 10 月 17 日

(C) 10 月 20 日

(D) 10 月 31 日

STEP 1 答案通常會採換句話說的方式。

題目關鍵字為 tablet PC 和 international market，前者出現在第三篇文章中。另外，題目詢問的是未來的狀況，因此可以由後半段文章中找出答案。當中寫道：「consumers abroad need to wait until 31 Oct」，將題目中的 international 改寫成 abroad，因此答案要選 (D) On October 31。

Questions 196-200 refer to the following e-mails and meeting minutes.

E-MAIL **1**

TO	Sherri Wade
FROM	Glen Tran
DATE	Wednesday, September 11
SUBJECT	Guidelines: Writing meeting minutes

Hi Sherri,

I was informed that you will stand in for me to take notes at the department meeting tomorrow. Since it is the first time for you to do this, I would like to offer you some guidelines you should follow.

Make sure to make a list and note anyone who is not present. Meeting notes need to be saved in the department folder, but we forward the notes and any material given out at the meeting to people who are not able to come. My handout has already been scanned and saved **196** in the department folder, so you can use it. The agenda for tomorrow's meeting will also be there in case you would like to access it for reference when you take minutes.

197

Although we will be talking about many topics, you need to be able to include only integral decisions and information that influence our department. Keep the notes brief in order for the members of our department to go through them readily. Abbreviating names of organizations and departments and using bullet points can be helpful to do so. Only referring to people by their last name is also recommended. Feel free to ask any questions. See you tomorrow morning!

Glen

196. What is indicated about Mr. Tran? 寄件人：I

(A) He had to ~~miss~~ the department meeting.

(B) He ~~distributed~~ handout materials at the department meeting.

(C) He will keep the meeting agenda in the department folder.

(D) He will have to visit ~~Sydney~~ to participate in an event.

關鍵字 Tran／文章1

→ 由第一篇文章確認寄件人 Tran 的相關內容。

197. In the first e-mail, the word "include" in paragraph 3, line 1, is closest in meaning to

(A) back up

(B) memorize

(C) capture

(D) review

同義詞題 include／文章 

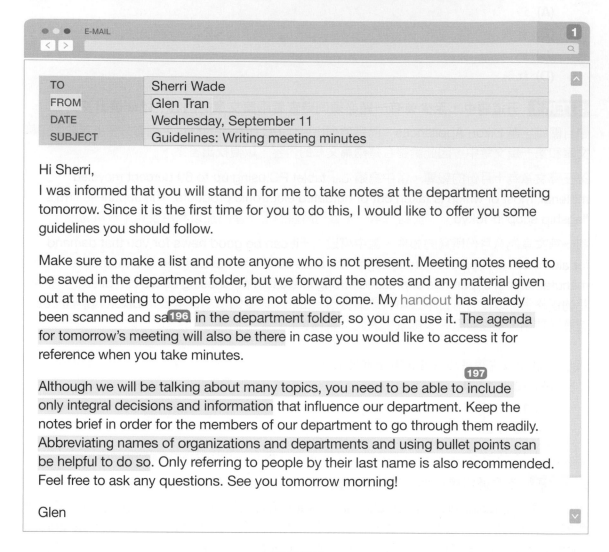

→ 找出該單字前後連接的單字。

Accounting Services Department Meeting Minutes

2

On September 12
2:00-3:30 P.M.

Absent: Ana Stephens, Willie Walters

Attended: Kay Schneider, Ella Romero, Ella Rilay, Roy Reed, Eleanor Porter, Sherri Wade, Glen Tran, Celia Sharp

- Romero noted that RX has been experiencing data-loss issues with its accounting software program. Since Tran is handling the same problem with another client, he will take care of that inquiry.

199

- Reed and Porter attended the Accounting Symposium in Sydney from September 7 to 8 and were asked to deliver a talk at next year's symposium in Washington.
- The department's outing will take place at St. James Park on Friday, October 2. As Schneider will be temporarily helping the New York branch this fall, Rilay will be held accountable for this year's outing arrangements.
- Tran reported that his team is about to review the budget for monthly operating costs. He reminded staff members to avoid making excessive printouts and copies.

Minutes Taken by Sherri Wade

this year's outing arrangements
→ preparing a yearly social event

198. What task is Mr. Schneider usually in charge of?
(A) Dealing with client complaints
(B) Preparing a yearly social event
(C) Handling the monthly budget
(D) Taking notes at every meeting

Schneider 的工作／usually／文章2
→ 確認關鍵字連接的資訊。

第三者：he

199. What has Mr. Reed recently done?
(A) He has visited a branch office.
(B) He has contacted Royal X-oriental Inc.
(C) He has given a talk at an event.
(D) He has been to Sydney.

Reed／最近做的事／文章2
→ 找出文中提及關鍵字 Reed 的片段，並選出相符的選項。

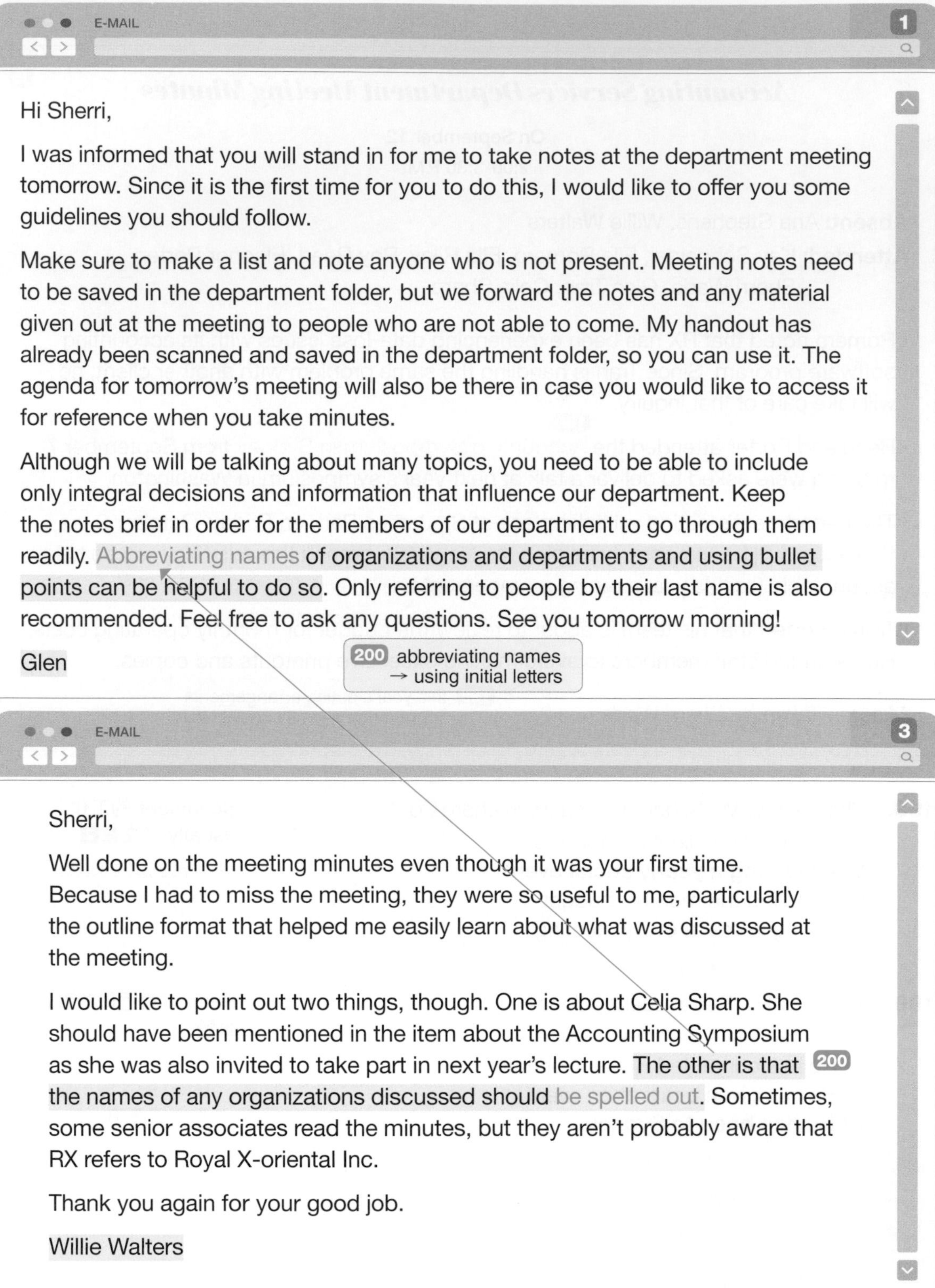

E-MAIL 1

Hi Sherri,

I was informed that you will stand in for me to take notes at the department meeting tomorrow. Since it is the first time for you to do this, I would like to offer you some guidelines you should follow.

Make sure to make a list and note anyone who is not present. Meeting notes need to be saved in the department folder, but we forward the notes and any material given out at the meeting to people who are not able to come. My handout has already been scanned and saved in the department folder, so you can use it. The agenda for tomorrow's meeting will also be there in case you would like to access it for reference when you take minutes.

Although we will be talking about many topics, you need to be able to include only integral decisions and information that influence our department. Keep the notes brief in order for the members of our department to go through them readily. Abbreviating names of organizations and departments and using bullet points can be helpful to do so. Only referring to people by their last name is also recommended. Feel free to ask any questions. See you tomorrow morning!

Glen

200 abbreviating names → using initial letters

E-MAIL 3

Sherri,

Well done on the meeting minutes even though it was your first time. Because I had to miss the meeting, they were so useful to me, particularly the outline format that helped me easily learn about what was discussed at the meeting.

I would like to point out two things, though. One is about Celia Sharp. She should have been mentioned in the item about the Accounting Symposium as she was also invited to take part in next year's lecture. The other is that 200 the names of any organizations discussed should be spelled out. Sometimes, some senior associates read the minutes, but they aren't probably aware that RX refers to Royal X-oriental Inc.

Thank you again for your good job.

Willie Walters

200. What suggestion for taking minutes do Mr. Tran and Mr. Walters disagree on?

(A) Only recording members' last names
(B) Using initial letters of organizations' names
(C) Checking who is present or absent
(D) Entering information into a computer

Tran／Walters／disagree／文章2、3

→ 從文中找出各選項的關鍵字，並選出與內文相符的選項。

第 196-200 題 兩封電子郵件與會議紀錄

1

收件者	雪莉・韋德
寄件者	格林・陳
日期	9 月 11 日，星期三
主旨	會議紀錄的撰寫原則

嗨，雪莉：

我被告知妳將在明天的部門會議中，代替我做會議紀錄。因為這是妳第一次做會議紀錄，所以我想指導妳一些原則，讓妳有個依循的方向。

請確保做一張出席列表，並記下缺席會議者的姓名。會議記錄必須存檔在部門資料夾，但我們會將會議紀錄以及會議中所分發的任何資料，轉寄給無法出席會議的人。我已經將我收到的會議資料掃瞄好，存進部門資料夾裡了，妳可以拿去用。資料夾裡也會有明天會議的議程，當妳在做會議紀錄時，或許會想要拿來參考。

雖然會議中會論及許多議題，但妳只需要能記下會影響我們部門的必要決議及資訊即可。簡要紀錄，好讓我們的部門成員能快速檢閱。縮短機構與部門的名稱，以及運用項目符號，都可以有助紀錄簡要。同時也建議妳，提到人名時，稱呼姓氏即可。有何問題儘管問我。明早見！

格林

2

會計服務部會議紀錄
九月十二日，下午 2 點至 3 點 30 分

缺席者：安娜・史帝芬斯、威利・華德士
出席者：凱・施耐德、艾拉・羅米洛、愛菈・雷利、羅伊・里德、伊蓮諾・波特、雪莉・韋德、格林・陳、塞莉亞・夏普

- 羅米洛提到 RX 公司的會計軟體近來有資料遺失的現象。既然陳也正在幫另一名客戶處理同樣的問題，就讓他來研究這個議題。
- 里德跟波特兩人，出席了九月七日至八日在雪梨召開的會計研討會，獲邀於明年在華盛頓召開的研討會上發表演說。
- 部門遠足預定於十月二日星期五，地點在聖詹姆士公園。由於施耐德將在秋季暫時支援紐約分處，所以雷利將負責籌辦今年的遠足活動。
- 陳報告說他的團隊即將開始審查每個月的營運成本預算。他提醒同仁避免過多的電腦列印及複印。

會議記錄・雪莉・韋德

3

收件者	雪莉．韋德
寄件者	威利．華德士
日期	9 月 13 日，星期五
主旨	妳的會議紀錄

雪莉：

會議紀錄做得很好，儘管這是妳第一次做。由於我因故缺席，所以會議紀錄對我來說非常有幫助，特別是提綱格式，讓我能輕鬆了解會議的討論內容。

不過，我仍想要提出兩點。一是關於塞莉亞．夏普。在會計研討會的那一點，她應該也要被提及，因為她也同時獲邀於明年會議上發表演說。另一點則是，任何在會議中被論及的機構名稱，都應該要以全名拼出。有時，某些高級股東在閱讀會議紀錄時，有可能會不清楚 RX 公司指的是 Royal X-oriental 公司。

妳的會議紀錄做得很好，再次感謝。

威利．華德士

字彙 meeting minutes 會議記錄　stand in for 代替某人　take notes 記筆記
present 出席的　forward 發送　material 資料　give out 分發　agenda 會議議程
for reference 僅供參考　integral 不可或缺的　readily 很快地　abbreviate 縮寫
bullet point 項目符號　issue 問題　inquiry 探究　symposium 研討會
outing 遠足　temporarily 暫時地　be held accountable for 對……負責
arrangement 籌畫　be about to V 剛要……　operating cost 營運成本
excessive 過度的　outline format 提綱格式　spell out 闡明
senior associate 高級股東

196. 關於陳先生，本文有何暗示？

(A) 他不得不在會議中缺席。

(B) 他在會議中分發會議資料。

(C) 他將把會議議程存在部門資料夾中。

(D) 他將必須前往雪梨參加一場活動。

STEP 1 請善用題目所提供的線索和文章內有關答案的資訊。

題目關鍵字為 Mr. Tran，而 Tran 為第一篇文章中的寄件人，因此請從中找出答案。文中寫道：「The agenda for tomorrow's meeting will also be there」，表示他將保管選項中提及的 agenda。且句中 there 所指的是前方的 in the department folder，因此答案要選 (C)。

STEP 2 分析錯誤選項

文中寫道：「My handout has already been scanned and saved」，當中提到 (B) 的 handout，但是並未提到分配，因此並非答案；(D) 文中並未提到有人要訪問雪梨，因此也不是答案。

197. 在第一封電子郵件中，第三段、第一行中的「include」一字，意思最接近於

(A) 補充 (B) 記住

(C) 留存 (D) 審查

STEP 1 題目考同義詞時，要根據前後文意，選出最適合替換的單字。

請務必要確認該單字在句中所使用的意思，以便找出相符的選項。「Although we will be talking about many topics, you need to be able to include only integral decisions and information」，提到雖然會談論到很多個主題，但是紀錄中只需包含必要的決定和資訊。該單字的意思和 capture（留存）相似，因此答案為 (C)。

198. 施耐德先生通常負責何項工作？

(A) 處理顧客投訴 (B) 籌備年度社交活動

(C) 處理每月預算 (D) 在每場會議中做紀錄

STEP 1 確認特定名詞所指的對象。

題目關鍵字為 Mr. Schneider，出現在第二篇文章中。當中寫道：「As Schneider will be temporarily helping . . . Rilay will be held accountable for this year's outing arrangements」，提到 Schneider 暫時要負責其他工作，他原本的工作改由 Rilay 代替。而 Schneider 平常的工作為 outing arrangements，指準備活動，因此答案要選 (B)。

199. 里德先生最近做了何事？

(A) 他參訪了分處。 (B) 他聯繫了 Royal X-oriental 公司。

(C) 他在一個活動中發表演說。 (D) 他去了雪梨。

STEP 1 確認特定名詞所指的對象。

Reed 出現在第二篇文章中。當中寫道：「Reed and Porter attended the Accounting Symposium in Sydney」，提到他參加了在雪梨舉辦的座談會，因此答案為 (D)。

200. 在製作會議紀錄的建議上，陳先生與華德士先生兩人的分歧之處為何？

(A) 只需要記錄員工的姓氏

(B) 使用機構名稱的開頭縮寫

(C) 查核出、缺席者身分

(D) 將資料輸入電腦

STEP 1 五道題中，至少會有一題必須同時查看兩篇文章的內容，才能選出答案。

題目中的 Tran 和 Walters 皆為電子郵件的寄件人，請從兩篇文章中找出提及撰寫會議記錄的部分，並選出兩方想法不一致的內容。

第三篇文章中寫道：「the names of any organizations discussed should be spelled out」，Walters 提到要完整寫下所有被討論到的公司的名稱。而第一篇文章中則寫道：「Abbreviating names of organizations and departments and using bullet points can be helpful to do so.（建議寫下公司名稱的縮寫）」。由這兩段話可以得知兩人對於公司名稱寫法的想法並不一致，因此答案為 (B)。

TEST 2

解析

解答 TEST 2

01. (B)	**02.** (D)	**03.** (C)	**04.** (A)	**05.** (A)	**06.** (B)	**07.** (C)	**08.** (C)	**09.** (C)	**10.** (A)
11. (C)	**12.** (C)	**13.** (C)	**14.** (B)	**15.** (B)	**16.** (A)	**17.** (C)	**18.** (A)	**19.** (A)	**20.** (A)
21. (A)	**22.** (C)	**23.** (B)	**24.** (A)	**25.** (B)	**26.** (A)	**27.** (B)	**28.** (C)	**29.** (B)	**30.** (B)
31. (B)	**32.** (B)	**33.** (A)	**34.** (A)	**35.** (B)	**36.** (B)	**37.** (A)	**38.** (C)	**39.** (A)	**40.** (D)
41. (C)	**42.** (B)	**43.** (D)	**44.** (C)	**45.** (B)	**46.** (A)	**47.** (D)	**48.** (D)	**49.** (A)	**50.** (B)
51. (B)	**52.** (D)	**53.** (A)	**54.** (D)	**55.** (A)	**56.** (A)	**57.** (D)	**58.** (B)	**59.** (B)	**60.** (C)
61. (A)	**62.** (D)	**63.** (A)	**64.** (B)	**65.** (A)	**66.** (C)	**67.** (C)	**68.** (C)	**69.** (C)	**70.** (A)
71. (C)	**72.** (C)	**73.** (A)	**74.** (B)	**75.** (C)	**76.** (A)	**77.** (B)	**78.** (D)	**79.** (D)	**80.** (A)
81. (C)	**82.** (A)	**83.** (D)	**84.** (A)	**85.** (D)	**86.** (D)	**87.** (B)	**88.** (A)	**89.** (D)	**90.** (D)
91. (D)	**92.** (C)	**93.** (C)	**94.** (B)	**95.** (B)	**96.** (D)	**97.** (D)	**98.** (C)	**99.** (B)	**100.** (B)
101. (A)	**102.** (B)	**103.** (D)	**104.** (A)	**105.** (D)	**106.** (B)	**107.** (D)	**108.** (D)	**109.** (A)	**110.** (D)
111. (C)	**112.** (C)	**113.** (C)	**114.** (D)	**115.** (D)	**116.** (A)	**117.** (D)	**118.** (A)	**119.** (A)	**120.** (D)
121. (C)	**122.** (B)	**123.** (C)	**124.** (C)	**125.** (A)	**126.** (C)	**127.** (A)	**128.** (A)	**129.** (B)	**130.** (C)
131. (B)	**132.** (B)	**133.** (A)	**134.** (A)	**135.** (D)	**136.** (A)	**137.** (C)	**138.** (B)	**139.** (D)	**140.** (B)
141. (D)	**142.** (C)	**143.** (B)	**144.** (B)	**145.** (D)	**146.** (D)	**147.** (C)	**148.** (C)	**149.** (C)	**150.** (D)
151. (C)	**152.** (B)	**153.** (B)	**154.** (C)	**155.** (C)	**156.** (C)	**157.** (B)	**158.** (C)	**159.** (B)	**160.** (A)
161. (C)	**162.** (B)	**163.** (D)	**164.** (C)	**165.** (B)	**166.** (B)	**167.** (C)	**168.** (A)	**169.** (B)	**170.** (C)
171. (B)	**172.** (A)	**173.** (A)	**174.** (C)	**175.** (B)	**176.** (B)	**177.** (B)	**178.** (B)	**179.** (C)	**180.** (B)
181. (C)	**182.** (B)	**183.** (A)	**184.** (B)	**185.** (D)	**186.** (C)	**187.** (C)	**188.** (D)	**189.** (B)	**190.** (A)
191. (B)	**192.** (D)	**193.** (A)	**194.** (B)	**195.** (B)	**196.** (A)	**197.** (B)	**198.** (C)	**199.** (D)	**200.** (B)

PART 1

1

(A) A woman is wearing a safety helmet.
(B) A woman is resting both of her hands on the desk.
(C) A woman is talking to a customer to discuss a plan.
(D) A woman is bending over to pick up her tumbler.

(A) 女子戴著安全帽。
(B) 女子的兩隻手都靠在桌上。
(C) 女子正和客戶討論一項計畫。
(D) 女子正彎身拿起她的保溫瓶。

字彙 safety helmet 安全帽　rest 擱在、倚靠　pick up 拿起、撿起　tumbler 保溫瓶

01 先刪去錯誤選項，再找出正確答案。

作答 PART 1 時，如果聽到選項中出現照片中沒有的名詞或動詞，就不能作為答案。刪去法指的就是先刪去與照片不相符的錯誤描述，再選擇剩下的選項作為答案。

STEP 1 照片分析

❶ 單人照片
❷ 女子正在講電話
❸ 女子手中拿著筆
❹ 桌上放著安全帽和保溫瓶

STEP 2 聽到照片中未呈現的單字時，請立即刪去該選項。

(A) A woman is ~~wearing~~ a safety helmet.
▶安全帽放在桌子上。

(B) A woman is resting both of her hands on the desk. ▶ 答案

(C) A woman is talking to ~~a customer~~ to discuss a plan.
▶照片中並未出現客戶。

(D) A woman is bending over to ~~pick up~~ her tumbler.
▶女子並未俯身拿取保溫瓶。

STEP 3 刪去法 POINT

❶ 若聽到照片中未出現的名詞或動詞，皆為錯誤的描述。
❷ 單人照片→選項通常會使用同樣的主詞，因此請專心聽寫動詞和後半段描述。
❸ 多人照片→請確認主詞的單複數是否搭配適當的動詞。
❹ 若選項以物品開頭作為主詞，並使用完成式表示「**處於……的狀態**」，通常就是答案。
❺ 若照片為無人照片，聽到進行被動式 be being p.p.，即為錯誤的選項。

2

(A) A woman is taking a measurement with a measuring tape.
(B) A man is removing some wooden panels from the wall.
(C) They're talking on the stair.
(D) They're kneeling down on the floor.

(A) 女子正拿量尺在測量。
(B) 男子正從牆上拆下一些木鑲板。
(C) 他們正在樓梯上講話。
(D) 他們正跪在地板上。

字彙 **measurement** 測量 **measuring tape** 量尺 **panel** 鑲板 **kneel down** 跪（下）、跪著

02 照片出現兩人或兩人以上時，答案會是共同動作或全體的狀態。

▶ 請特別留意，兩人或兩人以上的照片有別於單人照片，請務必要掌握每個人的動作和狀態、以及物品的狀況。

▶ 聽到不同的主詞時，要把焦點集中在不同的對象，因此需要培養臨場反應的能力。

STEP 1 照片分析

❶ 雙人照片
❷ 兩人呈現跪著的姿勢
❸ 男子指著某樣東西
❹ 女子盯著男子看
❺ 地上放著工具

STEP 2 聽到照片中未呈現的單字時，請立即刪去該選項。

(A) A woman is taking a ~~measurement with a measuring tape~~.
　▶女子並未使用量尺測量。

(B) A man is ~~removing~~ some wooden panels from the wall.
　▶男子並未拆下任何東西。

(C) They're talking on the stair.
　▶樓梯上沒有人。

(D) They're kneeling down on the floor. ▶ 答案

STEP 3 雙人照片的 POINT

❶ 照片為雙人照片時，請依序觀察人物的「共同之處→個別細節」。
❷ 觀看照片的方向請由左方看至右方。
❸ 若選項以雙方拿著或給對方的物品作為主詞時，通常會使用進行被動式的用法。
❹ 主詞為物品時，請由周遭事物的狀態判斷答案。

照片類型	出題頻率前五高的正確答案
雙人照片的情況	❶ 描寫兩人的共同動作或狀況
	❷ 描寫單人或兩人的動作細節
	❸ 描寫人物的外貌、外型等
	❹ 描寫兩人身旁物品的動向或狀態
	❺ 描寫周遭（地點）的狀況或物品狀況

3

(A) A row of lampposts is being installed.
(B) Some cars are traveling in opposite directions.
(C) There's a walkway over a street.
(D) Cars are being parked along the curb.

(A) 正在裝設一排路燈燈柱。
(B) 一些車輛正朝相反的方向行駛。
(C) 街道上方有天橋。
(D) 車輛正沿著人行道停放。

字彙 lamppost 路燈柱　install 安裝、設置　travel 行駛、往來
walkway （尤指有篷或高架的）走道、人行道　curb 人行道的路緣

03 請由句末的「介系詞＋名詞」確認物品的位置。

介系詞片語「介系詞＋名詞」可以用來表示地點。而在 PART 1 中，介系詞片語會放在句末，因此即便聽到正確的名詞，也請務必聽到最後，確認是否為正確描述。

STEP 1 照片分析

❶ 道路的照片
❷ 路上有車輛在移動
❸ 照片中有出現天橋

STEP 2 聽到照片中未呈現的單字時，請立即刪去該選項。

(A) A row of lampposts is ~~being~~ installed.
▶ 照片中沒有裝設路燈的人。

(B) Some cars are traveling in ~~opposite directions~~.
▶ 所有的車都往同樣的方向行駛。

(C) There's a walkway over a street. ▶ 答案

(D) Cars are ~~being parked~~ along the curb.

▶由照片無法得知是否在停車。

STEP 3 物品照的刪去 POINT

1. 請確認主要事物的位置和狀態、以及周遭事物和背景畫面。
   1. 確認主要事物的位置和狀態。
   2. 確認周遭事物。
   3. 確認地點和背景畫面。
   4. 若題目為無人照片，選項卻出現人物名詞時，屬於錯誤描述，請立即刪去該選項。
   5. 請特別留意，錯誤選項中可能會提及照片中未出現的事物。

2. be being p.p. 不能作為答案。
   - 「事物主詞＋ be being p.p.」表示「某人針對某物做某個動作」，因此此用法不適用於無人照片，屬於錯誤的敘述。
   - 〔例外〕display（陳列）表示一種持續的狀態，因此即使照片中沒有人，仍可以使用進行被動式。

     例 Some items are being displayed.（一些商品正在陳列中。）

4

(A) One of the men is pointing to a sheet of paper.

(B) Some men are examining a document with a surveying instrument.

(C) They're putting on some protective gear.

(D) Some scaffolds are being erected on the construction site.

(A) 其中一名男子正指著一張紙。

(B) 有些男子正用測量儀器檢查一份文件。

(C) 他們正穿上防護裝備。

(D) 工地裡正在搭鷹架。

字彙 point to 指向　document 文件　surveying instrument 測量儀器　put on 穿上、戴上　protective gear 防護裝備　scaffold 鷹架　erect 豎立

04 照片出現兩人以上時，若聽到單數主詞開頭的選項，請仔細觀察該人物主詞的狀況。

▶多人照片的選項通常會提到共同動作或所處地點。

▶新制測驗的多人照片題，答案經常描述其中特定一人的動作或狀態。

STEP 1 照片分析

❶ 多人照片
❷ 三人都戴著安全帽，並穿著安全背心
❸ 其中一名男子帶著眼鏡，並用手指著紙張
❹ 其中一名男子正在使用測量用的機器

STEP 2 **聽到照片中未呈現的單字時，請立即刪去該選項。**

(A) **One of the men is pointing to a sheet of paper.** ▶ 答案

(B) ~~Some men~~ are examining a document with a surveying instrument.
▶ 使用機器和看資料的人並非同一名男子。

(C) They're ~~putting on~~ some protective gear.
▶ 背心已經穿在他們身上了。

(D) Some scaffolds are ~~being erected~~ on the construction site.
▶ 照片中沒有人在搭設鷹架。

STEP 3 多人照片的 POINT

1. 若提到其中特定一人，會使用 One of the men 描寫某個不一樣的動作或狀態。
2. 若使用 Some people 或 They 描寫共同動作或狀態時，為正確答案。

照片類型	答案類型
多人照片的情況	❶ 描寫共同動作或狀況
	❷ 描寫其中特定一人的動作
	❸ 描寫人物周遭的狀況

5

(A) Some flowers are suspended in the air.
(B) Containers have been filled with earth.
(C) Flower arrangements have been made on the table.
(D) Some dishes have been placed on the roof of the greenhouse.

(A) 有些花懸掛在空中。
(B) 容器裡裝滿土。
(C) 桌上裝飾著插花作品。
(D) 溫室的屋頂上放著一些盤子。

字彙 **suspend** 懸掛、懸浮 **flower arrangement** 插花 **greenhouse** 溫室

05 掌握表示事物位置或狀態的動詞。

STEP 1 照片分析

❶ 無人物品照
❷ 地上擺著花盆容器
❸ 上方懸掛著一些花

STEP 2 聽到照片中未呈現的單字時，請立即刪去該選項。

(A) Some flowers are suspended in the air. ▶ 答案

(B) Containers have ~~been filled with earth~~.
▶ 照片中的容器並未裝滿泥土。

(C) Flower arrangements have been made ~~on the table~~.
▶ 照片中沒有桌子，也沒有插著花。

(D) Some dishes have been placed ~~on the roof~~ of the greenhouse.
▶ 沒有盤子放在屋頂上。

STEP 3 以地點位置出題的 POINT

物品照一般會以「位於……」表示位置，可以使用現在式或過去式表示。
請熟記以下表示「位於……」的基本用法，便能輕鬆聽懂描述。

be placed 放置、安置	**be situated** 位於
be left 遺留、遺忘	**be put** 放在
be arranged 排列、布置	**be hung** 掛在
be set up 擺放或豎起某物	**There is/are** 有（單數／複數）

6

(A) Some ingredients are being chopped on the board.
(B) The table has been illuminated by lighting fixtures.
(C) People are helping themselves to the food.
(D) Some food is being cooked in a kitchen.

(A) 正在砧板上切食材。
(B) 燈具照亮了桌子。
(C) 人們正自行取用食物。
(D) 廚房裡正在烹煮食物。

字彙 **ingredient** 食品的成分、材料 **chop** 切、剁 **illuminate** 照亮、照射
lighting fixture 固定燈具 **help** 盛（飯菜）、斟（酒）
help oneself to 隨意取用（飲料、食品）

06 描寫照明、燈光、水、路等自然現象或狀態。

STEP 1 照片分析

❶ 無人物品照
❷ 準備了一些食物
❸ 燈光照向桌子
❹ 桌上擺了一些盤子

STEP 2 聽到照片中未呈現的單字時，請立即刪去該選項。

(A) Some ingredients ~~are being chopped~~ on the board.
▶ 照片中並未出現切食材的人。

(B) The table has been illuminated by lighting fixtures. ▶ 答案

(C) ~~People~~ are helping themselves to the food.
▶ 照片中沒有出現任何人。

(D) Some food is ~~being cooked~~ in a kitchen.
▶ 照片中沒有看到有人在烹煮食物。

STEP 3 描寫自然現象或狀態的用法

- Buildings overlook a forest. 建築物俯瞰著森林。
- Waves are breaking along the shore. 波浪打到岸邊而破碎。
- Mountains are reflected in the water. 山脈倒映在水中。
- Water is flowing down the mountain. 水從山上流下來。
- A path leads to the building. 一條通往建築物的小徑。
- There are clouds in the sky. 空中有雲朵。

PART 2

07. Where's the printer in this office?

(A) Five ~~pages~~ long.
▶ 相關單字 x ❙ 適用 How many 問句

(B) I thought it was ~~on Monday~~. ▶ 適用 When 問句

(C) Ours is broken. ▶ 間接回答

07. 這間辦公室的印表機在哪裡？

(A) 共有五頁。

(B) 我以為是在星期一。

(C) 我們的印表機故障了。

---

08. Whose turn is it to clean the staff lounge today?

(A) It is ~~on the second floor~~.
▶ 適用 Where 問句

(B) For all our ~~staff~~ members. ▶ 相同單字 x

(C) I already took care of it.
▶ 使用 already 回答的選項，無須考量題目句時態

08. 今天輪到誰打掃員工休息室？

(A) 在二樓。

(B) 開放給所有員工。

(C) 我已經打掃了。

---

09. Would you like to join Jake and me for lunch?

(A) He doesn't really ~~like~~ it.
▶ 主詞有誤 ❙ 相同單字 x

(B) It ~~was~~ very ~~delicious~~.
▶ 適用 How 問句、時態有誤

(C) I have a meeting soon.
▶ 以「我很忙」拒絕對方的建議

09. 你要跟傑克和我去吃午餐嗎？

(A) 他其實沒有很喜歡。

(B) 非常美味。

(C) 我馬上就要去開會了。

---

10. When will the concert begin tonight?

(A) Sorry, I don't work here. ▶ 以地點表示「我不知道」

(B) In the ~~concert~~ hall. ▶ 適用 Where 問句

(C) I ~~enjoyed~~ the music a lot. ▶ 時態有誤

10. 今晚的音樂會幾點開始？

(A) 抱歉，我不是這裡的員工。

(B) 在音樂廳。

(C) 我非常喜歡這音樂。

---

11. What brand of smartphone do you use?

(A) A local electronic store. ▶ 適用 Where 問句

(B) There is ~~a call~~ for you. ▶ 相關單字 x

(C) Are you thinking of buying one?
▶ 詢問對方往後的行動

11. 你的手機是哪個廠牌？

(A) 一家本地的電子用品商店。

(B) 有你的電話。

(C) 你想買一支嗎？

---

12. Most of our customers buy their clothes online.

(A) Yes, they like our ~~new clothing line~~.
▶ 相同單字 x ❙ 相似單字 x

(B) We will extend our assembly ~~line~~. ▶ 相似單字 x

(C) But some still prefer trying them on in the store.
▶ 使用 but 補充說明

12. 我們大部分的顧客都上網買衣服。

(A) 是的，他們喜歡我們的新系列服飾。

(B) 我們會擴大生產線。

(C) 但是，有些顧客還是偏好來店裡試穿。

---

13. Didn't you go out for the concert yesterday?

(A) Yes, ~~she~~ is a huge fan of jazz. ▶ 主詞有誤

(B) Yes, I ~~am leaving~~ at midnight. ▶ 時態有誤

(C) I had to work late.
▶ 省略 Yes 或 No，採解釋方式回答

13. 你昨天不是去聽音樂會了嗎？

(A) 是的，她超級喜歡爵士樂。

(B) 是的，我要在午夜時離開。

(C) 我加班到很晚。

14. I can't find the schedule for this year.

(A) I'll have it, ~~too~~.

▶直述句為肯定句時，too 用來表示同意

(B) I'll send you that by e-mail. ▶表示「由我來做」

(C) $50. ▶適用問句 How much is it?

14. 我找不到今年的進度表。

(A) 我也要一份。

(B) 我會用電子郵件寄給你。

(C) 50 元。

---

15. How many samples should I send to the headquarters?

(A) Every third quarter.

▶適用 How often 問句｜相似單字 x

(B) Simpson already dispatched them.

▶使用 already 回答的選項，無須考量題目句時態

(C) Not ~~many~~ of them attended. ▶相同單字 x

15. 我應該寄多少份樣本給總公司？

(A) 每年第三季。

(B) 辛普森已經寄了。

(C) 他們沒有很多人出席。

---

16. Wasn't the annual sales report due yesterday?

(A) It's taking longer than expected.

▶表示「尚未完成」

(B) Earlier this year. ▶相關單字 x

(C) No, it should be ~~reported~~ monthly.

▶相同單字 x

16. 年度銷售報告不是應該昨天交嗎？

(A) 花的時間比原先預期的長。

(B) 今年稍早。

(C) 不，應該每個月報告。

---

17. Do you want me to bring today's agenda for the meeting or email it to everyone in advance?

(A) ~~He~~ reviewed it. ▶主詞有誤

(B) That will be great, thank you.

▶回答勸說或建議

(C) Everyone there will have a laptop.

▶間接回答，用 laptop 代替 email

17. 你要我把今天會議的議程拿來，還是先用電子郵件寄給大家？

(A) 他審閱過了。

(B) 那就太好了，謝謝你。

(C) 那裡的每個人都會有筆記型電腦。

---

18. The sales conference is going to start at 2, isn't it?

(A) Let's look at the invitation. ▶表示「我不知道」

(B) In Room ~~2~~. ▶適用 Where 問句｜相同單字 x

(C) Yes, it ~~won~~ several awards.

▶時態有誤

18. 銷售會議兩點開始，不是嗎？

(A) 我們來看一下邀請函吧。

(B) 在第二會議室。

(C) 是的，得了好幾個獎。

---

19. The deadline for registration is extended to the end of this week.

(A) Where did you hear that? ▶以反問方式答覆

(B) Five-digit codes. ▶適用問句 What do I need . . . ?

(C) Yes, I'd like to. ▶回答勸說或建議

19. 註冊登記的截止日期延長到這星期。

(A) 你從哪裡聽來的？

(B) 五位數的密碼。

(C) 是的，我想要。

20. How are we going to review all these applications today?

(A) David will help us. ▶提出解決方式

(B) They are on the Web site. ▶適用 Where 問句

(C) Right, press the ~~application~~ button. ▶相同單字 x

20. 我們今天要怎麼審核完這些申請書？

(A) 大衛會幫我們。

(B) 它們在網站上。

(C) 對，按下申請鍵。

---

21. Why don't we discuss the proposed budget this afternoon?

(A) We can do it first thing tomorrow instead.
▶使用 instead（作為替代）間接表示同意

(B) ~~No~~, not that I know of.
▶不能用 No 回答表示勸說或建議的問句

(C) Does ~~he~~ work on the proposal, too? ▶主詞有誤

21. 我們何不今天下午討論預算案？

(A) 我們可以明天一早再討論。

(B) 不，據我所知不是。

(C) 他也參與這個提案嗎？

---

22. Your assistant sent the invoice to the supplier, didn't he?

(A) It was a wrong ~~address~~. ▶相關單字 x

(B) No, he ~~is~~ not. ▶時態不一致

(C) Hasn't the payment arrived yet?
▶以反問方式確認

22. 你的助理把帳單明細寄給供應商了，不是嗎？

(A) 地址錯了。

(B) 不，他不是。

(C) 還沒收到款項嗎？

---

23. Here are twenty copies of the agenda you asked for.

(A) The meeting ~~was~~ in Room 102.
▶時態不一致

(B) Adams is joining us, too.
▶使用第三人作為答覆

(C) I already ordered ~~coffee~~. ▶發音相似 x

23. 這裡是 20 份你要的議程表。

(A) 會議在 102 室。

(B) 亞當也會和我們一起。

(C) 我已經點了咖啡。

---

24. Who's going with me to the international trade show?

(A) The department budget allows only one person this time. ▶以 one person 代替名字回答

(B) ~~No~~, none of them. ▶不能使用 Yes 或 No 回答

(C) I believe it was in Sydney. ▶適用 Where 問句

24. 誰要和我一起去國際貿易展？

(A) 部門預算這次只夠一個人去。

(B) 不，他們都不是。

(C) 我想是在雪梨。

---

25. How do I contact a local dealer in this area?

(A) An authorized car ~~dealer~~.
▶相同單字 x | 適用 What 問句

(B) I left the business card on your desk.
▶採間接回答方式，請對方「確認名片或公告」

(C) In a couple of days. ▶適用 When 問句

25. 我要怎麼聯絡這一區的經銷商？

(A) 一位授權汽車經銷商。

(B) 我把名片放在你桌上了。

(C) 幾天之內。

26. Should I talk to the manager about the pay increase or will you?

(A) Actually, I'm not sure that's a good idea.
▶屬於選擇疑問句中「我不知道」回答方式

(B) Yes, we ~~talked~~ to everyone.
▶時態不一致｜相同單字 x

(C) Sure, I agree with that.
▶不能使用 Yes 或 No 回答

26. 要我去和經理談加薪的事，還是你要去？

(A) 其實，我不確定這是個好主意。

(B) 是的，我們和每個人都談過了。

(C) 當然，我同意。

---

27. Aren't you going to travel somewhere during your vacation?

(A) Just one round-trip ~~ticket~~. ▶相關單字 x

(B) I'm planning to tend my garden. ▶回答行程

(C) ~~Okay~~, I will follow up on the request.
▶適用表示勸說或建議的問句

27. 你休假時，不去哪裡玩嗎？

(A) 只是一張來回票。

(B) 我打算整理我的花園。

(C) 好的，我會關注要求事項的後續發展。

---

28. Where's the manual for the new security system?

(A) ~~Yes~~, ID card needed. ▶不能使用 Yes 或 No 回答

(B) ~~To~~ the maintenance department.
▶適用以 Where 詢問目的地或方向的問句

(C) Ms. Smith can help you.
▶採間接回答方式「請向第三人確認」

28. 新保全系統的使用手冊在哪裡？

(A) 是的，需要身分證件。

(B) 去維修部門。

(C) 史密斯女士可以幫你。

---

29. Why didn't you leave for the client meeting?

(A) ~~It~~ was not working well. ▶主詞有誤

(B) The schedule was changed. ▶解釋原因

(C) I thought you ~~were~~. ▶與題目句的助動詞不一致

29. 你為什麼沒去和客戶開會？

(A) 運作得不太順。

(B) 時間改了。

(C) 我以為你是。

---

30. I don't see an invoice in this package.

(A) You will see that, ~~too~~. ▶適用表示肯定的直述句

(B) They must have forgotten to include it.
▶解釋型回答

(C) The total is $500. ▶適用 How much 問句

30. 我在這個包裹裡沒看到帳單明細。

(A) 你也會看到那個。

(B) 他們一定是忘記放進去了。

(C) 總金額是 500 元。

---

31. Let's have a meeting this afternoon to discuss the promotional events.

(A) About ten spots. ▶適用 How many 問句

(B) Theresa's not back yet, though.
▶針對建議的間接答覆

(C) They ~~were~~ very successful. ▶時態不一致

31. 我們今天下午來開個會討論促銷活動吧。

(A) 大約有 10 個點。

(B) 但是，泰瑞莎還沒回來。

(C) 活動非常成功。

07 針對 Wh- 問句的間接回答──「已經取消了、臨時有更動、壞掉了」。

題目分析 **Where's the printer in this office?**

本題以「Where's the printer」詢問東西的位置。

選項分析

(A) Five pages long. ❷ 適用其他問句

回答數字，應搭配以 How many 開頭的問句較為適當。且當中使用 page，與題目句中的 printer 有所關聯，屬於陷阱選項。

(B) I thought it was on Monday. ❷ 適用其他問句

回答時間，適合搭配問句「When was the concert . . . ?」。Where 問句題最常出現此類型的陷阱選項。

(C) Ours is broken. ▶ 答案

本題以「在哪裡」詢問東西的位置。該選項回答「我們的印表機故障了」，等同於間接表示「現在無法使用」，此類回答方式為新制測驗的命題趨勢。

08 即使答句和問句的時態不同，只要當中出現特定副詞，仍可作為正確答案。

題目分析 **Whose turn is it to clean the staff lounge today?**

開頭兩個字「Whose turn」等同於 who 的概念，詢問「輪到誰負責」。

選項分析

(A) It is on the second floor. ❷ 適用其他問句

使用副詞片語表示地點，應搭配以 Where 開頭的問句較為適當。

(B) For all our staff members. ❷ 適用其他問句

雖然當中提到 members，乍看之下像是針對 Who 問句的回答，但是由於開頭為介系詞 for，表示「為了……」，因此不能作為 Whose turn 問句的答案。且該選項重複使用題目句中的 staff，屬於陷阱選項。

(C) I already took care of it. ▶ 答案

「我已經做過這件事」表示「是由我負責」的概念，故為正確答案。值得留意的是，雖然答句的時態通常要和題目句一致，但若選項中出現 already，帶有「已經」的概念在內，則不一定要與題目句的時態一致。

09 通常會以「我已經有約了」或「我自己來就行了」回絕對方的勸說或建議。

題目分析 **Would you like to join Jake and me for lunch?**

本題為表示勸說或建議的問句，詢問對方「要不要一起吃午餐」。

選項分析

(A) He doesn't really like it. ❸ 主詞有誤

題目句中提到特定人士時，才能用 He 或 She 回答。例如：「How did Mr. Kim like . . . ?」。

(B) It was very delicious. ❷ 適用其他問句

以形容詞回答，應搭配以 How was 開頭，詢問狀態或想法的問句較為適當。且本題問句指的是未來發生的事情，因此不該使用過去式回答。

(C) I have a meeting soon. ▶ 答案

舊制測驗中，通常會使用「I'm sorry」或「I'm afraid」委婉拒絕對方，但在新制測驗中，則較常使用「我很忙」或「我有約了」等間接回答的方式。

10 新制測驗中會以地點回答 When 問句。

題目分析 **When will the concert begin tonight?**

題目為「音樂會何時開始」，詢問未來的時間點。

選項分析

(A) Sorry, I don't work here. ▶ 答案

題目以「音樂會何時開始」詢問未來的時間點。而該選項使用地方副詞「我不在這裡工作」，間接表示「我不知道」。

(B) In the concert hall. ❷ 適用其他問句

該選項應搭配以「Where will . . . ?」開頭、詢問地點的問句較為適當。

(C) I enjoyed the music a lot. ❺ 時態有誤

題目句為未來式，因此不該使用過去式回答。該選項應搭配詢問想法的問句「How was the concert?」較為適當。

11 請特別留意反問對方往後的行動或方法的選項。

題目分析 **What brand of smartphone do you use?**

答題關鍵為 What 後方連接的名詞，因此若選項中提到 brand 的種類，通常就是答案。

選項分析

(A) A local electronic store. ❷ 適用其他問句

當中提到 store，僅與題目句中的 smartphone 有所關聯。該選項應搭配問句「Where do you buy . . . ?」較為適當。

(B) There is a call for you. ❹ 相關單字陷阱

當中提到 call，僅與題目句中的 phone 有所關聯，屬於陷阱選項。值得留意的是，選項使用 There is/are 來回答時，可以搭配 Where 問句，為難度較高的回答方式。

(C) Are you thinking of buying one? ▶ 答案

聽完問題後，回答可以針對往後行動提出疑問、或是進一步反問對方以釐清現況。本題詢問「現在使用哪個廠牌」，而該選項回答「你想要買一支嗎？」是針對對方往後的行動提出疑問。當中以代名詞 one 代替 smartphone，請特別留意。

12 以 but 補充說明回答事實與否。

題目分析 **Most of our customers buy their clothes online.**

本題為直述句，意在向對方確認事實或尋求同意。請務必要聽清楚關鍵字 customers、buy 和 online。

選項分析

(A) Yes, they like our new clothing line. ❹ 相似單字陷阱

當中使用 clothing，與題目句中 clothes 的發音相似，屬於陷阱選項。若題目以動詞 like，詢問對方是否同意「喜歡」這個想法時，該選項才能作為答案。但是本題的關鍵字為 buy 和 online，對此回答「他們喜歡我們的新系列服飾」並不適當。

(B) We will extend our assembly line. ❹ 相似單字陷阱

當中使用 line，重複使用題目句中 online 的字尾，屬於陷阱選項。該選項應搭配以「What will you . . . ?」開頭、詢問往後計畫的問句較為適當。

(C) But some still prefer trying them on in the store. ▶ 答案

新制測驗中，若題目為確認事實與否或尋求同意的直述句時，答案可以使用 but 來回答。該選項回答「但是仍有一些客人喜歡在店內試穿」，補充說明內容，故為正確答案。

13 否定疑問句或附加問句的答案不會出現 Yes 或 No，而是採解釋方式答覆。

題目分析 **Didn't you go out for the concert yesterday?**

否定疑問句中的 not 並非否定概念，而是強調自己的想法。因此請先拿掉 not，視為一般問句「主詞……是否做……」來判斷答案。本題的解題關鍵為「Didn't you go」。

選項分析

(A) Yes, she is a huge fan of jazz. ❸ 主詞有誤

題目句中提到特定人士時，才能用 he 或 she 回答。該選項應搭配問句「Will Margaret go . . . ?」較為適當。

(B) Yes, I am leaving at midnight. ❺ 時態有誤

時態與題目句不一致，不能作為答案。題目句為過去式，因此不該使用現在式來回答。該選項應搭配問句「Are you going to . . . ?」較為適當。

(C) I had to work late. ▶ 答案

本題針對過去提問「你有去嗎？」，而該選項解釋自己「當時工作到很晚」，故為正確答案。請記住，在新制測驗中，否定疑問句的答案經常會省略 Yes 或 No，以 ❶ 變更事項 ❷ 不知情 ❸ 解釋 ❹ 尚未完成等作為答覆。

14 題目以直述句提出問題時，可以回答解決方法或替代方案。

題目分析 **I can't find the schedule for this year.**

本題為直述句，以「I can't find . . .」提出問題所在。

選項分析

(A) I'll have it, too. ❷ 適用其他問句

too 的意思為「而且、也」，經常用來表示同意直述句的內容，但前提是直述句為肯定句才能適用。而本題的句子為否定句，因此並不適當。若題目改成「I received a book.（我收到書了）」，該選項才能作為答案。

(B) I'll send you that by e-mail. ▶ 答案

題目表示「我找不到」，而該選項回答「我寄給你」，提出解決方法，故為正確答案。請記得，題目為直述句時，答案經常使用句型「I'll . . .」回答解決方法或替代方案。

(C) $50. ❷ 適用其他問句

回答金額，應搭配問句「How much is it?」較為適當。

15 即使答句和問句的時態不同，只要當中出現特定副詞，仍可作為正確答案。

題目分析 **How many samples should I send to the headquarters?**

本題為 How many 開頭的問句，詢問數量「有多少」。

選項分析

(A) Every third quarter. ❷ 適用其他問句、❹ 相似單字陷阱

應搭配 How often 開頭，詢問頻率的問句較為適當。且句中的 quarter 與題目句中的 headquarters 發音相似，屬於陷阱選項。

(B) Simpson already dispatched them. ▶ 答案

若選項中包含 just（剛剛）、already（已經）、still（仍然）或 yet（尚未）等副詞，可以得知事情是否正在進行或者是否已完成，因此不管時態是否與問句一致，通常可以作為正確答案。例如：just 的意思為事情處於「剛做好……」的狀態，表示已經完成的概念，因此即便答句和問句的時態不同，仍可作為正確答案。

(C) Not many of them attended. ❹ 相同單字陷阱

重複使用題目句中的 many，為陷阱選項。另外，答句的時態通常要和問句相同，本題問句詢問未來的事情，但該選項卻使用過去式，因此不能作為答案。「參加的人不多」應搭配詢問狀態或想法的問句「How was the meeting?（開會的狀況如何？）」較為適當。

16 否定疑問句或附加問句的答案不會出現 Yes 或 No，而是採解釋方式答覆。

題目分析 **Wasn't the annual sales report due yesterday?**

本題的解題關鍵為「Wasn't . . . due」，詢問「不是昨天就截止了嗎？」

選項分析

(A) It's taking longer than expected. ▶ 答案

否定疑問句的答案敘述通常會省略 No，回答後方其一：❶ 變更事項 ❷ 不知情 ❸ 解釋 ❹ 尚未完成。該選項省略 No，解釋「比原訂時間延後」，故為正確答案。

(B) Earlier this year. ❹ 相關單字陷阱

this year 與題目句中的 annual 有所關聯，屬於陷阱選項。

(C) No, it should be reported monthly. ❹ 相同單字陷阱

重複使用題目中的名詞 report，為陷阱選項。該選項應搭配以「Can I report . . . ?」開頭的問句較為適當。

17 【選擇疑問句】改寫題目句中的單字、或採間接回答的方式。

題目分析 **Do you want me to bring today's agenda for the meeting or email it to everyone in advance?**

本題的解題關鍵為「me to bring . . . or email it」。

選項分析

(A) He reviewed it. ❸ 主詞有誤

題目的主詞為 you，而該選項以第三人稱代名詞 He 回答，因此不能作為答案。應搭配以「Did Mr. Kim . . . ?」開頭的問句較為適當。

(B) That will be great, thank you. ❷ 適用其他問句

該選項適用於回答表勸説或建議的問句。選擇疑問句為二選一的概念，因此並不適當。

(C) Everyone there will have a laptop. ▶ 答案

該選項屬於間接回答，「每個人都會有筆記型電腦」暗示對方採寄送郵件的方式。

18 若選項表示「我不知道」，通常就是正確答案。

題目分析 **The sales conference is going to start at 2, isn't it?**

本題的解題關鍵為「conference is going to start」，確認「會議開始的時間」。

選項分析

(A) Let's look at the invitation. ▶ 答案

除了「I don't know」之外，「我確認一下」或「我問問看」皆屬於表明「我不知道」的回答方式，為正確答案的機率極高。本題詢問會議是否為兩點開始，而該選項回答「確認邀請函的內容」，等同於「我確認一下」，故為正確答案。

(B) In Room 2. ❷ 適用其他問句

該選項應搭配以 Where 開頭，詢問地點的問句較為適當，像是「Where is the conference . . . ?」。另外，選項中重複使用題目句中的 two，屬於答題陷阱。

(C) Yes, it won several awards. ❺ 時態有誤

答句的時態要和問句一致，該選項應搭配問句「Was ABC company given . . . ?」較為適當。

19 【直述句】反問對方消息來源。

題目分析 **The deadline for registration is extended to the end of this week.**

本題為直述句，向對方確認、尋求對方的同意。解題關鍵為「deadline」和「is extended」。常見的回答方式為表示同意與否，另外還有一種回答方式為提出建議並反問對方。

選項分析

(A) Where did you hear that? ▶ 答案

回答「你從哪裡聽來的？」反問對方消息來源。欲提供對方建議、或向對方再次確認時，通常會使用「反問」的回答方式。

(B) Five-digit codes. ❷ 適用其他問句

回答名詞，應搭配以 What 開頭的問句較為適當，像是「What do I need . . . ?」。

(C) Yes, I'd like to. ❷ 適用其他問句

該選項適用於回答表勸說或建議的問句，表示同意的概念。適合搭配的問句為「Would you go . . . ?」。

20 若選項中提到第三人，也可以作為正確答案。

題目分析 **How are we going to review all these applications today?**

本題詢問「該如何檢視」，為詢問方法或想法的問句。

選項分析

(A) David will help us. ▶ 答案

回答「大衛會幫我們」，等同提出解決方式，故為正確答案。另外，考題中經常會以「How do you like . . . ?」詢問想法，請特別熟記。

(B) They are on the Web site. ❷ 適用其他問句

乍看之下 Web site 像是一種解決方法，但是 on the Web site 表示的是東西的位置，應搭配以「Where are . . . ?」開頭的問句較為適當。

(C) Right, press the application button. ❹ 相同單字陷阱

重複使用題目句中的 application，屬於答題陷阱。該選項應搭配以「Can I . . . ?」開頭，尋求對方答應或認可的問句。

21 間接表示同意對方建議

題目分析 **Why don't we discuss the proposed budget this afternoon?**

「Why don't we」表示勸說或建議，為極具代表性的句型，請務必要聽清楚後方連接的動詞為何。而本題的解題關鍵為「Why don't we discuss」。

選項分析

(A) We can do it first thing tomorrow instead. ▶ 答案

常見的回答為同意或拒絕建議，但是在新制測驗中，則會使用間接同意的方式回答「改成下次再進行」或「改由其他人做」。

(B) No, not that I know of. ❶ 不能使用 Yes 或 No 回答

若表示「我不知道」，通常會是答案。但是若以 No 回答表示勸說或建議的問句，則為錯誤的回答方式，不能作為答案。請特別熟記，一般會以「I'm sorry」或「I'm afraid」開頭，委婉拒絕對方的勸說或建議。

(C) Does he work on the proposal, too? ❸ 主詞有誤

雖然採反問的方式極有可能是答案，但題目中並未出現對應 he 的特定人士，因此該選項不能作為答案。

22 反問否定疑問句或附加問句，以確認事實與否。

題目分析 **Your assistant sent the invoice to the supplier, didn't he?**

請特別注意，聽到否定疑問句或附加問句時，只要確認動詞即可。本題的解題關鍵為「your assistant sent」。

選項分析

(A) It was a wrong address. ❹ 相關單字陷阱

address 與題目句中的 sent 有所關聯，為答題陷阱。該選項應搭配以 Why didn't 開頭，詢問原因或指責對方的問句較為適當。

(B) No, he is not. ❺ 時態有誤

答句的時態要和問句一致才行。本題題目句為過去式，而該選項卻使用現在式，因此不能作為答案。

(C) Hasn't the payment arrived yet? ▶ 答案

回答「還沒收到款項嗎？」，以反問方式向對方確認某項事實。反問的回答方式通常會出現一到兩題，屬於出題比重較高的用法，主要分為以下四種反問方式：

❶ 以 Wh- 問句詢問相關細節

❷ 以反問方式確認某事是否屬實

❸ 提出疑問以釐清狀況

❹ 詢問方法

23 【直述句】提及未來情況告知對方往後的行動

題目分析 **Here are twenty copies of the agenda you asked for.**

本題為直述句，提到「這裡有二十份」，由此可以預先想到回答可能會以 Thanks 或 But 表示認同或反對。

選項分析

(A) The meeting was in Room 102. ❺ 時態有誤

題目句表達的是現況，但該選項使用過去式回答，因此不能作為答案。當中使用副詞片語表示地點，應搭配以 Where 開頭的問句較為適當。

(B) Adams is joining us, too. ▶ 答案

題目提及「有二十份」，該選項回答「Adams 也會和我們一起」，間接表示「We need more copies.」，故為正確答案。

(C) I already ordered coffee. ❹ 相似發音陷阱

選項若使用副詞 already，表示就算時態和問句不一致，仍可作為答案。但是當中還用了 coffee，和題目句中 copies 的發音相似，屬於答題陷阱，請特別留意。

24 選項中出現 he/she/they 時，通常不會是答案。

題目分析 **Who's going with me to the international trade show?**

本題為 Who 開頭的問句，詢問「誰會一起去」。

選項分析

(A) The department budget allows only one person this time. ▶ 答案

本題為 Who 開頭的問句，該選項回答「因為部門預算有限，只夠一個人去」，間接表示「不會有其他人一起」。在新制測驗中，難度較高的考題不會直接回答人名，而是採換句話說的方式表示「one person」。

(B) No, none of them. ❶ 不能使用 Yes 或 No 回答

若題目中提到特定人士，像是 the manager(s) 時，答案才能出現第三人稱代名詞 he、she、they。而在本題中，問句並未提到與 them 相對應的人物，因此不能作為答案。

(C) I believe it was in Sydney. ❷ 適用其他問句

副詞片語 in Sydney 表示地點，應搭配以 Where 開頭的問句較為適當。

25 以 How 詢問手段或方法的高難度題型

題目分析 **How do I contact a local dealer in this area?**

本題問句為「如何聯絡」，詢問手段或方法。

選項分析

(A) An authorized car dealer. ❹ 相同單字陷阱、❷ 適用其他問句

重複使用題目句中的 dealer，屬於答題陷阱。且回答名詞，應搭配以 Who 開頭的問句，請特別留意。

(B) I left the business card on your desk. ▶ 答案

新制測驗中，不太會直接回答方法，而是使用 by 或 through 等介系詞，暗示對方確認「名片或公告」。

(C) In a couple of days. ❷ 適用其他問句

若問句以 How long 開頭，詢問為期多久，經常會以該選項回答，請務必熟記。

26 以 Actually 回答選擇疑問句，不使用 Yes 或 No 回答。

題目分析 **Should I talk to the manager about the pay increase or will you?**

本題為選擇疑問句，詢問「該由我、還是由你來說」。

選項分析

(A) Actually, I'm not sure that's a good idea. ▶ 答案

該選項表示「不知道」，不選擇任何一個選項，故為正確答案。若選項未使用 Yes 或 No，明確表示同意或否定，而是改用 actually 回答時，通常就是正確答案。

(B) Yes, we talked to everyone. ❺ 時態有誤

答句的時態要和問句一致才行。另外，請留意到該選項重複使用問句中的 talk，屬於陷阱選項。

(C) Sure, I agree with that. ❶ 不能使用 Yes 或 No 回答

選擇疑問句不能使用 Yes 或 No 來回答。另外，值得留意的是，sure 可以用來回答表示建議的問句，但不適用於選擇疑問句。

27 聽到否定疑問句或附加問句時，只要確認動詞即可。

題目分析 **Aren't you going to travel somewhere during your vacation?**

本題詢問對方的行程，解題關鍵為「Aren't you going」。

選項分析

(A) Just one round-trip ticket. ❹ 相關單字陷阱

ticket 與題目句中的 travel 有所關聯，為答題陷阱。該選項回答名詞，應搭配以 what 開頭的問句較為適當。

(B) I'm planning to tend my garden. ▶ 答案

回答「我打算整理我的花園」，確切告知行程，故為正確答案。當問句為否定疑問句或附加問句，回答中卻未出現 Yes 或 No 時，通常會重複提及題目句中的內容。但值得注意的是，當中不會使用與題目相同的單字。

(C) Okay, I will follow up on the request. ❷ 適用其他問句

Okay 表示同意的概念，用於回答表示勸説或建議的問句，不會用來回答否定疑問句或附加問句。

28 【Where 問句】回答人名、新聞、報紙、廣告、Web site 等來源。

題目分析 **Where's the manual for the new security system?**

本題為以 Where 開頭的問句，詢問使用手冊的位置，解題關鍵為「Where's the manual」。

選項分析

(A) Yes, ID card needed. ❶ 不能使用 Yes 或 No 回答

Wh- 問句不能使用 Yes 或 No 來回答。該選項應搭配以「Do I have to . . . ?」開頭的問句較為適當。

(B) To the maintenance department. ❷ 適用其他問法的問句

當中提到地點，可以用來作為 Where 問句的答案。但是前方加上介系詞 to，表示移動方向或動線的概念，因此應搭配以 Where 加上動詞開頭的問句較為適當，像是「Where do I go . . . ?」動詞帶有移動的概念。

(C) Ms. Smith can help you. ▶ 答案

本題詢問「使用手冊在哪裡」，常見的回答為部門名稱。但在新制測驗中，若為難度較高的考題，則會以人名、新聞、報紙、廣告、Web site 等來源作為答案，請特別留意。

29 以「Why didn't you . . . ?」問句指責或詢問對方原因。

題目分析 **Why didn't you leave for the client meeting?**

本題為「why . . . not . . . ?」問句，詢問對方「沒有去」的原因。

選項分析

(A) It was not working well. ❸ 主詞有誤

題目句的主詞為 you，回答要使用 I 或 We，因此該選項不能作為答案。選項中出現副詞或形容詞時，應搭配以「How was . . . ?」開頭，詢問狀態或想法的問句較為適當。

(B) The schedule was changed. ▶ 答案

題目問「為什麼沒有去……？」略帶有指責意味。新制測驗中，經常出現「行程有異動」或「和預定行程撞期」等，採解釋原因的回答方式。

(C) I thought you were. ❷ 適用其他疑問詞或助動詞問句

問句和答句的時態、助動詞都必須一致才行。題目中助動詞為 did，回答中也要使用同樣的助動詞 did，而該選項使用 you were，因此不能作為答案。

30 【表否定的直述句】以理由或解釋來回答。

題目分析 **I don't see an invoice in this package.**

本題的直述句為否定句，表示「我沒看見」，解題關鍵為「I don't see」。表否定的直述句通常是希望指出對方的錯誤、或是想到知道原因，因此會告知理由或解釋。

選項分析

(A) You will see that, too. ❹ 相同單字陷阱

重複使用題目句中的 see，屬於答題陷阱。too 的意思為「而且、也」，只要回答中提到 too，有極高的機率為正確答案。但是本題直述句為否定句，表示同意時，要使用「not . . . either」或「neither」才行，因此該選項不能作為答案。

(B) They must have forgotten to include it. ▶ 答案

題目句欲得知「沒看見東西」的原因，該選項解釋「一定是他們忘記了」，故為正確答案。解釋或說明理由時，經常使用「must have p.p.」，表示「一定是……」。

(C) The total is $500. ❷ 適用其他問句

該選項應搭配問句「How much is it?」較為適當。

31 婉轉回答對方的建議。

題目分析 **Let's have a meeting this afternoon to discuss the promotional events.**

本題的解題關鍵為「Let's have a meeting」，請務必仔細聽清楚關鍵字。

選項分析

(A) About ten spots. ❷ 適用其他問句

若回答為數字，通常會搭配以「How many . . . ?」開頭的問句。

(B) Theresa's not back yet, though. ▶ 答案

回答「但是，泰瑞莎還沒回來」，間接表示下午可能沒辦法開會。新制測驗中，經常用 though 代替 but，請特別留意這個用法。

(C) They were very successful. ❺ 時態有誤

題目句的時態為現在式，但該選項卻使用過去式回答，因此不能作為答案。選項中出現形容詞或副詞時，應搭配以「How was . . . ?」開頭，詢問現況、狀態、想法的問句。

PART 3

Questions 32-34 refer to the following conversation.

W	Thanks for calling Mondiago City Library. How may I help you?	32-D
M	Hello, I went to your library this morning and after returning home,	
32	I found my notebook missing. I was in the Social Science Room on the second floor.	32-A
W	Actually, we haven't had any missing articles for now, but it is time to	
33	clean the facility, I'll let the cleaning staff know. Can you tell me your seat number?	
M	Yes, it was 16E. I sat next to the window.	
W	Okay. I'll ask the staff to locate the item you're missing, and I'll call	
34	you right after they check for it. Can I have your phone number?	34-D

32. What was the man missing?
(A) A ~~computer~~ **(B) A notebook**
(C) A pencil case (D) A ~~book~~

男子／過去／ missing／前
→ 注意聆聽過去式。

33. Why does the woman say, "I'll let the cleaning staff know"?
(A) To ask for some help
(B) To complain about a service
(C) To correct some mistaken ~~information~~
(D) To inform them of a ~~schedule change~~

女子／掌握說話者意圖
→ 指定句前後對白

34. What will the man do next?
(A) Give her his contact information
(B) ~~Locate some items~~
(C) ~~Contact the staff~~
(D) Check ~~a floor plan~~

男子／未來／後
→ 注意聆聽後半段對話。

第 32-34 題 對話

女：謝謝您致電蒙迪亞哥市立圖書館，有什麼需要服務的地方？

男：哈囉，我今天早上去你們圖書館，回家後發現我的筆記本不見了，我當時待在二樓的社會科學室。

女：事實上，我們到現在都沒有收到遺失的物品，但現在是館內的打掃時間，我會告訴清潔人員。您可以告訴我，您的座位號碼嗎？

男：好，是16E，我坐在靠窗邊。

女：好，我會請員工去找您遺失的物品。他們一找到相符的物品，我就會打電話給您。您可以告訴我電話號碼嗎？

32. 男子遺失了什麼？
(A) 一台電腦
(B) 一本筆記本
(C) 一個鉛筆盒
(D) 一本書

33. 女子為什麼說：「我會告訴清潔人員」？
(A) 為了請求協助
(B) 為了客訴一項服務
(C) 為了改正一項錯誤的資訊
(D) 為了通知他們時程表更動

34. 男子接下來會做什麼？
(A) 給她他的聯絡資訊
(B) 找出某些物品
(C) 聯絡員工
(D) 核對樓層平面圖

32 直接由本人口中說出問題和擔憂的地方。

STEP 1 若題目詢問問題為何，答案通常會出現在第一和第二段對白中。

男子直接談及他碰到的問題，因此請仔細聆聽男子所說的話。對話中說道：「I found my notebook missing.」，提到他弄丟了筆記本，因此答案為 (B) A notebook。

STEP 2 陷阱選項和錯誤選項

(A) A computer ▶ 聽到「notebook」可能會誤選該選項。
(B) A notebook ▶ 答案
(C) A pencil case
(D) A book ▶ 聽到「library」可能會誤選該選項。

33 請先刪除與引號內字面意思相同的選項。

STEP 1 題目詢問說話者意圖時，答案不會是引號內指定句字面上的意思。而且若選項使用與引號內相同的單字、或是字面意思相同的敘述，來表達說話者意圖時，通常不會是正確答案。

雖然引號中的 let / know 和 (D) inform 的意思相同，但是對話中並未提到 schedule change 或是要修改 information，因此 (C) 也不能作為答案。對話中說道：「Actually we haven't had any missing articles for now.」，表示沒有拾獲任何物品。接著說道：「but it is time to clean the facility.」，提到現在是打掃時間，會告知打掃人員此事。表示女子會請打掃人員協助，因此答案為 (A)。

STEP 2 陷阱選項和錯誤選項

(A) To ask for some help ▶ 答案
(B) To complain about a service
(C) To correct some mistaken information
▶ 聽到「let . . . know」可能會聯想到「information」。
(D) To inform them of a schedule change
▶ 雖然「let . . . know」和「inform」的意思相同，但該選項並非答案。

34 題目使用 next 詢問某人的未來資訊時，答案會出現在對方建議或要求此人的句子當中，屬於高難度考題。

STEP 1 題目詢問某人的下一步動作（未來資訊）時，答案通常會出現在當事人所說的話當中；但是若為難度較高的考題，則會採同意對方建議或要求的方式來表達（等同於此人的下一步動作），因此請務必聽清楚對方建議或要求的內容為何。

雖然本題詢問的是男子下一步的動作，但是本篇對話中，最後說話的人為女子，因此得由該名女子要求男子的內容，推測出男子下一步的動作為何。對話最後，女子說道：「Can I have your phone number?」，請男子留下聯絡方式，因此答案為 (A) Give her his contact information。選項將對話中的 phone number 改寫成涵蓋範圍較廣的 contact information。

STEP 2 陷阱選項和錯誤選項

(A) Give her his contact information ▶ 答案
(B) Locate some items ▶ 向 cleaning staff 要求的事情，並未向男子提出此要求。
(C) Contact the staff ▶ 為女子要做的事，並非男子該做的事。
(D) Check a floor plan ▶ 對話中並未提及 floor plan。

字彙 city library 市立圖書館　notebook 筆記本　social science 社會科學
missing articles 遺失物　for now 現在、目前　facility 設施、場所
cleaning staff 清潔人員　seat number 座位號碼　locate 找出

Questions 35-37 refer to the following conversation.

W 35	Excuse me. I'm a keynote speaker for the journalism conference today. I'm wondering where the conference will be held.	35-A
M 36	Welcome to Victoria Hotel. It will be held in the Sapphire Hall on the second floor. And I think you must be Margaret Pearson, right? I was asked to escort you to the waiting room for the conference. Wait a second. Please follow me.	35-D
W 37	Oh, thank you. Wow, it's kind of spacious. It's 10 o'clock now, so I have enough time to prepare for my presentation. I'd like to make a few more copies of my handouts. Where can I do that?	36-D 36-C
M	There's a business center upstairs. It's in front of the elevator.	
W	It may take some time to copy them, so I'll grab a bite.	37-B

35. Why is the woman at a hotel?
(A) To ~~organize~~ a conference
(B) To make a presentation
(C) To stay for her business trip
(D) To ~~visit~~ a hotel guest

女子／待在 hotel 的原因／前
→ 注意聆聽第一句話。

36. What was the man asked to do?
(A) Offer her free refreshments
(B) Guide her to the site
(C) ~~Make copies~~ for her
(D) ~~Prepare for the presentation~~

男子／被要求的事
→ 注意男子是否提及 should 或 ask。

37. What is available upstairs?
(A) A copy machine
(B) A ~~restaurant~~
(C) A microphone
(D) A gift shop

關鍵字／ upstairs ／後
→ 注意是否出現 please 或 you should。

第 35-37 題 對話

女：不好意思，我是今天新聞研討會的專題主講人，請問研討會在哪裡舉行？

男：歡迎光臨維多利亞飯店。研討會在二樓的藍寶石廳舉行。我想，妳一定是瑪格麗特．皮爾森吧？他們請我送妳到研討會的等候休息區。請稍等。請跟我來。

女：噢，謝謝你。哇，這裡有點大。現在是十點，所以，我有充足的時間準備我的演講。我想要多印幾份我的講義，我可以去哪裡印？

男：樓上有個商務中心，在電梯前面。

女：影印可能要花點時間，那麼我先去吃點東西。

35. 女子為什麼去飯店？
(A) 為了籌備一場研討會
(B) 為了發表演說
(C) 為了出差住宿
(D) 為了拜訪飯店的房客

36. 男子被要求做什麼？
(A) 提供她免費點心　(B) 引導她到現場
(C) 幫她影印　(D) 準備演講

37. 樓上有什麼？
(A) 一台影印機　(B) 一家餐廳
(C) 一支麥克風　(D) 一間禮品店

35 前半段對話中會談到職業或地點。

STEP 1 女子會談到待在飯店的原因為何。

女子在第一句説道：「I'm a keynote speaker for the journalism conference today.」，表示女子為會議的演講者。接著男子説道：「Welcome to Victoria Hotel.」，由此句話可以得知對話地點在飯店，表示女子為了發表演説才會待在飯店，因此答案為 (B)。

STEP 2 陷阱選項和錯誤選項

(A) To organize a conference ▶ 雖然對話中有提到「conference」，但是並非籌備會議。
(B) To make a presentation ▶ 答案
(C) To stay for her business trip
(D) To visit a hotel guest ▶ 雖然對話中有提到「hotel」，但並未提到「guest」。

36 直接由本人口中說出被要求的事情。

STEP 1 題目詢問男子被要求的事情，答案會在男子所說的話當中。

男子説道：「I was asked to escort you to the waiting room for the conference.」，提到男子被要求帶女子前往等候室，因此答案為 (B)。選項將對話中的 escort 改寫成 guide。

STEP 2 陷阱選項和錯誤選項

(A) Offer her free refreshments ▶ 聽到「hotel」可能會誤選該選項。
(B) Guide her to the site ▶ 答案
(C) Make copies for her ▶ 女子要做的事。
(D) Prepare for the presentation ▶ 女子要做的事。

37 題目中出現關鍵字時，答案會在該關鍵字前後的句子。▶ upstairs

STEP 1 若題目中出現特定的關鍵字，聆聽對話時，勢必會於該關鍵字前後聽到答案。一般來說會先聽到關鍵字，再聽到答案的內容，但在新制測驗中，有時反而會先聽到答案的內容，之後才聽到關鍵字。

女子道：「I'd like to make a few copies of my handouts」，接著男子回答：「There's a business center upstairs.」，由此段話可以得知樓上的商務中心可以影印，因此樓上可供使用的東西為 (A) A copy machine。

STEP 2 陷阱選項和錯誤選項

(A) A copy machine ▶ 答案

(B) A restaurant

▶ 聽到「grab a bite」可能會誤選該選項。

(C) A microphone

▶ 聽到「presentation」可能會聯想到「microphone」。

(D) A gift shop

字彙 **keynote speaker** 專題演講主講人 **journalism** 新聞業、新聞寫作 **conference** 研討會 **escort** 護送 **spacious** 寬敞的 **make a copy of** 影印 **handout** 講義、傳單 **upstairs** 樓上 **take some time** 花點時間 **grab a bite** 簡單吃點東西

TEST 2 PART 3 中譯&解析

Questions 38-40 refer to the following conversation with three speakers.

M1 Hello, welcome to Philgram Advertising. May I help you? 38-A

W Hi, yes. My name is Molly Hong from Hong's Organic Beverage. I have a meeting here at 2 o'clock.

M1 Let me see. All right. You are going to meet with Mr. Gallahan, the Personnel Manager. His office is on the 14th floor. I'll inform his secretary of your arrival. (38)

W Thank you. By the way, is there any place that I can use a computer? I have to check my urgent e-mails.

M1 I'm sorry but visitors are not allowed to use our computers in the office. There should be some computers you can use in the café. Patrick, can you pass her the floor map of this building? 39-D

M2 Sure, here you are. The café is located on the basement floor and its pastry and muffins are so delicious. (39) 39-C

W Oh, thank you. I'll stop by to check my e-mails (40) before meeting Mr. Gallahan. 40-B

38. Who is Mr. Gallahan?

(A) ~~A receptionist~~
(B) An owner
(C) A manager
(D) A sales representative

關鍵字／Mr. Gallahan／職業／前
→ 注意聆聽提到 Mr. Gallahan 的片段。

39. According to Patrick, what is suggested about the café?

(A) Its food quality is good.
(B) It is located on the ~~rooftop~~.
(C) It offers ~~a morning set~~.
(D) It is restricted to ~~building visitors~~.

Patrick／關鍵字 café
→ 注意聆聽 Patrick 提到 café 的片段。

40. What will the woman do next?

(A) ~~Install~~ a new computer ~~program~~
(B) ~~Check her schedule~~
(C) ~~Meet Mr. Gallahan~~
(D) Go to the café

女子／未來／後
→ 注意女子提到 I'll . . . 的對白。

第 38-40 題 三人對話

男1：哈囉，歡迎來到菲爾格蘭廣告公司，有什麼需要服務的地方？

女：嗨，有的。我是洪氏有機飲料的莫莉・洪。我約了2點要來開會。

男1：我看看。對，妳和人事經理葛拉漢先生有約。他的辦公室在14樓。我會通知他的秘書妳到了。

女：謝謝你。順便問一下，有什麼地方可以借我電腦用嗎？我必須查看緊急的電子郵件。

男1：抱歉，訪客不能使用我們辦公室裡的電腦。咖啡館應該有電腦可用。派崔克，你可以把大樓的平面圖給她看嗎？

男2：當然可以，來，給妳。咖啡館在地下室，那裡的糕點和瑪芬蛋糕很好吃。

女：噢，謝謝你。我會在見葛拉漢先生之前，先過去查看我的電子郵件。

38. 葛拉漢先生是誰？
(A) 櫃檯接待人員
(B) 老闆
(C) 經理
(D) 業務代表

39. 根據派崔克的說法，可得知咖啡館的什麼？
(A) 它的食物品質很好。
(B) 它位在屋頂。
(C) 它供應早餐套餐。
(D) 它限大樓用戶消費。

40. 女子接下來會做什麼？
(A) 安裝新的電腦軟體
(B) 查看她的時程表
(C) 和葛拉漢先生碰面
(D) 到咖啡館去

38 三人對話題組的第一題，通常會詢問三人的職業或對話主旨。

STEP 1 本題詢問第三者 Gallahan 的職業，請由開頭對話中的名詞確認職業和對話地點。

對話說道：「You are going meet with Mr. Gallahan, the Personnel Manager.」，提到他是人事部經理，因此答案為 (C) A manager。

STEP 2 陷阱選項和錯誤選項

(A) A receptionist ▶ 第一名男子的職業。
(B) An owner
(C) A manager ▶ 答案
(D) A sales representative

39 三人對話題組的第二題，通常會指定某個人，並針對此人提問。

STEP 1 若題目中出現特定人物的名字，聆聽對話時，請特別留意此人為哪一名說話者。

男子 1 説道：「There should be some computers you can use in the café. Patrick, can you pass her the floor map of this building?」，提到咖啡館內有幾台電腦可供使用，並請 Patrick 提供女子樓層簡介圖。而後男子 2 回答：「The café is located on the basement floor and its pastry and muffins are so delicious.」，提到咖啡館的位置，並告知咖啡館內販售美味的食物。由此段話可以確認男子 2 為 Patrick，因此答案為 (A)。

STEP 2 陷阱選項和錯誤選項

(A) Its food quality is good. ▶ 答案
(B) It is located on the rooftop. ▶ 對話中並未提到「rooftop」。
(C) It offers a morning set. ▶ 聽到「pastry and muffins」可能會聯想到「morning set」。
(D) It is restricted to building visitors. ▶ 僅談到訪客不能使用辦公室內的電腦，與 café 無關。

40 三人對話群組最後一題，通常會詢問未來計畫或建議。

STEP 1 題目詢問往後將發生的事情時，答案為 I'll . . . / Let's . . . 後方連接的第一個動詞。

後半段對話中，女子提到下一步動作。女子説道：「I'll stop by to check my e-mails.」，提到她將前往此處確認郵件。而前方男子 2 介紹了 café 的特色，由此可知女子要去的地方為咖啡館，因此答案為 (D)。

STEP 2 陷阱選項和錯誤選項

(A) Install a new computer program ▶ 聽到「computers」可能會聯想到「install program」。
(B) Check her schedule
(C) Meet Mr. Gallahan ▶ 為女子 Molly Hong 要做的事，但並非她要做的第一件事。
(D) Go to the café ▶ 答案

字彙 organic 有機的　beverage 飲料　personnel manager 人事經理
inform A of B 通知 A 關於 B　secretary 秘書　arrival 到達
basement floor 地下室、地下層　stop by 順路造訪

Questions 41-43 refer to the following conversation with three speakers.

W1	Betty, you mentioned in the staff meeting that we need two more people to work in the gallery because our business is growing significantly. 41 42	42-A 41-B
W2	Yes, that's right.	
W1	But the only problem is that we have spent most of our budget 42 assigned for this year. Why don't we add only one more person?	42-C
W2	Hmm, that would be better for us financially. Kevin, as soon as management approves the additional budget planning for that, can you post the job opening on our Web site? I'll send you the job description I have on file.	42-D
M	43 Now that our personnel management policy has been changed, the current job requirements need to be revised. I'll update and post them on the Web site too.	43-C

41. Where do the speakers most likely work?

(A) At a warehouse (B) At a museum
(C) At a gallery (D) At a factory

42. What is the main topic of the conversation?

(A) Making an ~~exhibition~~
(B) Hiring a new employee
(C) ~~Increasing~~ the budget
(D) Planning ~~another schedule~~

43. According to the man, what has been changed?

(A) A display (B) A class
(C) ~~A Web site~~ **(D) A policy**

說話者們的職業／前
→ 注意聆聽第一句話。

主旨
→ 注意聆聽對話中的同義單字。

男子／變更事項／changed
→ 注意聆聽過去式、現在完成式。

第 41-43 題 三人對話

女1：貝蒂，妳在員工會議時提到，因為我們的業務大幅成長，藝廊需要再多加兩個人。

女2：是的，沒錯。

女1：不過，唯一的問題是，我們今年的預算大部分都分配好了。我們何不再多加一個人就好？

女2：嗯，那樣對我們的財務方面會比較好。凱文，等管理部門一核准這項額外的預算，你可以在我們的網站貼出職缺需求嗎？我會把我檔案裡的職務說明寄給你。

男 ：既然我們的人事管理方針已經改變，目前的職務條件要求需要修改。我會在更新後一起貼在網站上。

41. 說話者最可能在哪裡工作？

(A) 在倉庫 (B) 在博物館
(C) 在藝廊 (D) 在工廠

42. 這段對話的主題是什麼？

(A) 策劃展覽
(B) 僱用新員工
(C) 增加預算
(D) 安排另一個時程表

43. 根據男子的說法，什麼東西已經改變？

(A) 一項展覽 (B) 一個類別
(C) 一個網站 (D) 一項規定

41 前半段對話中會談到地點或職業。

STEP 1 前兩句話會聽到 our / your / this / here 加上表示地點或職業的名詞。

本題詢問説話者們任職的地點。開頭説道：「we need two more people to work in the gallery」，提到畫廊需要再僱用員工，因此説話者們工作的地方為 (C) At a gallery。

STEP 2 陷阱選項和錯誤選項

(A) At a warehouse

(B) At a museum ▶ 聽到「gallery」可能會誤選該選項。

(C) At a gallery ▶ 答案

(D) At a factory

42 若題目詢問主旨或目的，答案會出現在開頭前兩句話。

STEP 1 題目詢問對話主旨時，聽完第一句話後，通常就能順利解題。千萬不要從頭到尾默默聽完整篇對話後，才開始選答案。務必要先看完選項內容，如此一來只要聆聽前半段對話，便能找出答案。

女子 1 説道：「we need two more people to work in the gallery」，接著女子 2 回答：「That's right.」，此段對話表示她們在談論僱用新員工一事，因此對話主旨為 (B) Hiring a new employee。

STEP 2 陷阱選項和錯誤選項

(A) Making an exhibition ▶ 聽到「gallery」可能會聯想到「exhibition」。

(B) Hiring a new employee ▶ 答案

(C) Increasing the budget ▶ 對話中提到已經花完既有預算，因此該選項並不適當。

(D) Planning another schedule

▶ 雖然對話中有提到「planning」，但並未提到「another schedule」。

43 題目中提到男子和關鍵字時，請從男子的對白和關鍵字前後方找出答案。

STEP 1 請仔細聆聽男子提到什麼東西被更改。

男子説道：「Now that our personnel management policy has been changed」，提到政策已修改，因此答案為 (D) A policy。

STEP 2 陷阱選項和錯誤選項

(A) A display

(B) A class

(C) A Web site

▶「web site」為刊登徵人資訊的地方，並未有所更動。

(D) A policy ▶ 答案

字彙 staff meeting 員工會議　significantly 顯著地、相當數量地　budget 預算
assign 分配、指派　management 管理　approve 同意　additional 額外的
job opening 職缺　post 貼出（布告等）　job description 職務說明
now that 既然、由於　personnel management 人事管理　policy 政策、方針
job requirement 職務條件要求　revise 修改

Questions 44-46 refer to the following conversation with three speakers.

M1 44	Hi, Daniel and Akiko. The manager from Humston Manufacturing called me yesterday and asked how the preparations for their 10th anniversary are going.	45-D
W	Almost everything is going smoothly. I visited the Plaza Hotel and booked the Crystal Ballroom which can accommodate up to 200 people. In addition, Kelly Flowers has taken on the job of making centerpieces for the tables.	44-D 46-D
M2 45	Akiko, you mean the store which we hired for the Magnet Food's event last month? They did an excellent job. Everyone liked those decorations.	
W	Exactly. One thing we have to do is to arrange the catering service. Daniel, do you have any ideas for who to call?	
M2	How about Palcon Catering Company? One of my friends used that service for his company's event and all of his employees were satisfied with its quality food. If you want, I'll ask him for the contact number.	
W 46	That's great. I also heard that company has a good reputation. Once you give me the number, I'll call and reserve the service.	46-B

44. Why did someone from Humston Manufacturing call?
(A) To inquire about the ~~prices~~
(B) To ~~make a reservation~~
(C) To check the status of the event
(D) To ~~visit the hotel~~

關鍵字／**Humston／Manufacturing**／來電原因／前
→ 注意聆聽第一句話。

45. What is mentioned about Kelly Flowers?
(A) Its quality was not good.
(B) It was used by the company last month.
(C) Its style was imitated by other stores.
(D) It was owned by ~~Humston Manufacturing~~.

關鍵字／**Kelly Flowers**
→ 注意聆聽關鍵字前後句。

46. What will the woman do next?
(A) Call a business
(B) ~~Provide contact information~~
(C) Check customer reviews
(D) ~~Reserve a hotel~~

女子／未來／後
→ 注意女子提到 I'll . . . 的對白。

第 44-46 題 三人對話

男1：嗨，丹尼爾和明子。漢斯頓工業的經理昨天打電話給我，問他們公司十週年慶的活動準備得如何了。

女：絕大部分都進行得很順利。我去廣場大飯店訂了水晶廳，那裡最多可以容納200人。此外，凱莉花藝接下了餐桌中心擺飾的工作。

男2：明子，妳是指上個月邁格奈食品的活動時，我們找的那間花藝店嗎？他們的表現很出色，大家都很喜歡那些裝飾。

女：就是他們，我們要做的就是安排外燴服務。丹尼爾，你知道要找誰嗎？

男2：找派肯外燴公司如何？我的一個朋友找他們去辦他公司的活動，所有的員工都很滿意食物的品質。如果妳要，我可以去問他聯絡電話。

女：太好了，我也聽說那家公司聲譽很好。等你給我電話號碼，我就打去預訂。

44. 漢斯頓工業的人為什麼來電？
(A) 為了詢問價格
(B) 為了預訂
(C) 為了確認活動的狀況
(D) 為了造訪飯店

45. 關於凱莉花藝，對話中提到什麼？
(A) 它的品質不太好。
(B) 這家公司上個月僱用過它。
(C) 其他店家模仿它的風格。
(D) 為漢斯頓工業所屬。

46. 明子接下來會做什麼？
(A) 打電話給一家公司
(B) 提供聯絡資訊
(C) 查看顧客的評論
(D) 預訂飯店

44 題目中出現關鍵字時，答案會在該關鍵字前後的句子。
▶ Humston Manufacturing

STEP 1 **若題目中出現特定的關鍵字，聆聽對話時，勢必會於該關鍵字前後聽到答案。一般來說會先聽到關鍵字，再聽到答案的內容，但在新制測驗中，有時反而會先聽到答案的內容，之後才聽到關鍵字。**

本題的關鍵字為 Humston Manufacturing。對話中說道：「The manager from Humston Manufacturing . . . asked how the preparations for their 10th anniversary are going on.」，提到經理來電確認十週年活動準備的狀況，因此答案為 (C) To check the status of the event。

STEP 2 **陷阱選項和錯誤選項**

(A) To inquire about the prices ▶ 對話中詢問準備狀況，並未詢問價格。
(B) To make a reservation ▶ Akiko 做的事。
(C) To check the status of the event ▶ 答案
(D) To visit the hotel ▶ Akiko 做過的事。

45 題目中出現關鍵字時，答案會在該關鍵字前後的句子。▶ Kelly Flowers

STEP 1 若題目中出現特定的關鍵字，聆聽對話時，勢必會於該關鍵字前後聽到答案。一般來說會先聽到關鍵字，再聽到答案的內容，但在新制測驗中，有時反而會先聽到答案的內容，之後才聽到關鍵字。

本題的關鍵字為 Kelly Flowers。女子說道：「the store which we hired for the Magnet Food's event last month? They did an excellent job」，稱讚上個月負責 Magnet Food 公司活動的店家 Kelly Flowers，認為他們做的很棒，因此答案為 (B)。

STEP 2 陷阱選項和錯誤選項

(A) Its quality was not good.
(B) It was used by the company last month. ▶ 答案
(C) Its style was imitated by other stores.
(D) It was owned by Humston Manufacturing. ▶ 並非所屬於「Humston Manufacturing」。

46 若題目詢問往後將發生的事情，答案為 I'll . . . 或 Let's . . . 後方連接的第一個動詞。

STEP 1 本題詢問女子下一步動作，答案會出現在後半段女子的對白中。

女子提到自己的下一步動作：「Once you give me the number, I'll call and reserve the service.」，表示向 Daniel 取得聯絡方式後，她會負責預約外燴服務，因此答案為 (A) Call a business。

STEP 2 陷阱選項和錯誤選項

(A) Call a business ▶ 答案
(B) Provide contact information ▶ Daniel 要做的事。
(C) Check customer reviews
(D) ~~Reserve a hotel~~ ▶ Akiko 做過的事。

字彙 manufacturing 製造業、工業　preparation 準備　anniversary 週年紀念
smoothly 順利地　accommodate 容納　up to 最多
centerpiece（正式宴會擺放在餐桌上的）中央裝飾品　decoration 裝飾、裝飾品
catering service 承辦宴席的服務；外燴服務　be satisfied with 對……感到滿意
reputation 聲譽、名聲

Questions 47-49 refer to the following conversation.

W	Good afternoon. My name is Polly Wayne and I have an appointment with Dr. Parker at 2.	
M 47	Hello, Ms. Wayne. I'll check you into the system. Well, I'm sorry but due to unexpected circumstances, the doctor will be delayed for 30 minutes. Could you wait for him?	47-B
W	Well, I wish I could, but I have a meeting with a client at 3 P.M.	
M	Then, can I reschedule your appointment?	48-C
W 48	No, I won't be here until next month because of a business trip, so it will be hard to schedule another appointment. I'm just here to have a regular checkup, so I think it will be okay to see another doctor right now.	48-A
M 49	Okay, then I'm going to put you into Dr. Olson's office right now. In the meantime, why don't you take a seat in the waiting room? It won't take long.	

47. What does the man explain to the woman?
(A) Some unexpected ~~weather~~ is coming.
(B) A computer system is ~~not working properly~~.
(C) She should come back ~~tomorrow~~.
(D) She needs to wait for some time.

男子的說明／前
→ 注意聆聽男子第一句對白。

48. What does the woman want to do?
(A) Attend the conference
(B) Meet ~~Dr. Parker~~
(C) ~~Reschedule an appointment~~
(D) See a doctor immediately

女子／想做的事
→ 注意聆聽後半段女子的對白。

49. What does the man tell the woman to do?
(A) Sit in a waiting room
(B) Fill out a form
(C) ~~Return~~ later today
(D) ~~Postpone~~ a meeting

男子／要求或建議／後
→ 男子的要求／注意聆聽表示建議的句型。

第 47-49 題 對話

女：午安，我是波莉．韋恩，我和派克醫師預約兩點。

男：哈囉，韋恩女士。我來把妳登入系統。嗯，抱歉，由於發生突發狀況，醫生會晚半個小時。妳可以等他嗎？

女：嗯，我希望可以，但我下午三點要和客戶開會。

男：那，我可以重排妳的約診嗎？

女：沒辦法，因為我要出差，下個月才會回來，所以很難安排約診。我只是來做定期檢查，所以，我想，現在可以先看另一個醫生，沒關係的。

男：好，那我現在就把妳排給歐森醫師。在這期間，妳何不到等候室坐坐？不會等太久的。

47. 男子對女子解釋什麼事？
(A) 有突發的天氣狀況。
(B) 電腦系統無法正確運作。
(C) 她應該明天再來。
(D) 她必須等一段時間。

48. 女子想要做什麼？
(A) 參加研討會　(B) 見派克醫師
(C) 重新安排約診　(D) 馬上看醫生

49. 男子告訴女子做什麼？
(A) 到等候室坐坐　(B) 填寫一份表格
(C) 今天稍晚再來　(D) 延後會議

47 題目中提及男子，因此答案會出現在男子的對白中。

STEP 1 一般來說，若題目針對男子提問，答案會在男子的對白中；若針對女子提問，答案則會在女子的對白中。

本題詢問男子向女子說明的內容，因此請注意聆聽男子所說的話。男子說道：「I'm sorry but due to unexpected circumstances, the doctor will be delayed for 30 minutes.」，提到由於發生意外的狀況，醫生會晚點到，請對方稍待片刻，因此答案為 (D)。

STEP 2 陷阱選項和錯誤選項

(A) Some unexpected weather is coming.
▶ 雖然對話中有提到「unexpected」，但是並未提到「weather」，因此不能作為答案。

(B) A computer system is not working properly. ▶ 男子已確認過「computer system」。

(C) She should come back tomorrow. ▶ 女子預約的日期為當天。

(D) She needs to wait for some time. ▶ 答案

48 直接由女子口中說出她本人想要做的事。

STEP 1 本題詢問女子想做的事，因此請確認後半段女子的對白。

本題詢問女子想做什麼事，因此請務必從女子的對白中確認答案。女子說道：「I think it will be okay to see another doctor right now.」，表示她不一定要指定 Parker 醫生，願意改看其他醫生，因此答案為 (D) See a doctor immediately。

STEP 2 陷阱選項和錯誤選項

(A) Attend the conference ▶ 聽到「business trip」可能會聯想到「conference」。

(B) Meet Dr. Parker ▶ 對話中提到當前無法給 Parker 醫生看診。

(C) Reschedule an appointment ▶ 雖然對話中有提到，但是女子要去出差，無法配合。

(D) See a doctor immediately ▶ 答案

49 題目詢問要求或建議時，解題關鍵在後半段對話中，以 You 說明。

STEP 1 請由男子的最後一段話確認男子的要求。

最後一段對白中，出現男子要求對方的內容：「why don't you take a seat in the waiting room?」，請女子先在等候室稍坐一下，因此答案為 (A)。

STEP 2 陷阱選項和錯誤選項

(A) Sit in a waiting room ▶ 答案

(B) Fill out a form

(C) Return later today
▶ 對話中並未提到此內容。

(D) Postpone a meeting
▶ 雖然對話中有提到「meeting」，但是並未提到延後。

字彙 appointment 約會、預約
unexpected 意外的、突如其來的
delay 延緩、延誤
client 客戶　business trip 出差
regular checkup 定期檢查
office 辦公室、（醫師或牙醫）診所
take a seat 請坐、坐下

Questions 50-52 refer to the following conversation.

M	Michelle, as you know, a new system has been put in place in Detroit and Denver plants. In accordance with the new system, we need to have a safety training session for their employees. [50]	50-A 50-D
W	You're right. If we train them together, we can save a lot of money.	
M	That sounds good. In which city should we hold the training? I think the number of employees in each plant is almost the same. [51]	52-A
W	It costs a lot to travel to Denver at this time of year.	51-A 51-D
M	That's true. I'll talk to the training coordinator to see what she thinks. [52]	

50. What are the speakers discussing?
(A) ~~Replacing~~ an old system
(B) Planning a training session
(C) Assigning a budget
(D) ~~Operating~~ a factory

主旨／前
→ 注意聆聽第一句話。

51. Why does the woman say, "It costs a lot to travel to Denver at this time of year"?
(A) Another option for the transportation will be needed.
(B) A different location should be chosen.
(C) She doesn't want to transfer to ~~Denver~~.
(D) She needs to take her ~~vacation~~.

女子／掌握說話者意圖
→ 確認指定句前後對白。

52. What will the man do next?
(A) Review the task
(B) Postpone the event
(C) Send ~~another director~~
(D) Contact his colleague

男子／未來／後
→ 注意男子提到 I'll . . . 的對白。

第 50-52 題 對話

男：蜜雪兒，妳知道的，底特律和丹佛的工廠裝了一套新系統。依照這套新系統，我們必須給那裡的員工上安全訓練課程。

女：你說得對。如果，我們讓他們一起訓練，可以省下大筆費用。

男：聽起來很棒。我們要在哪個城市舉行訓練？我想，兩間工廠的員工數量差不多一樣。

女：每年這個時間去丹佛的旅費都很貴。

男：的確如此，我會找訓練協調員談談，聽聽她的想法。

50. 說話者在討論什麼？
(A) 換掉舊系統 (B) 規劃訓練課程
(C) 分配預算 (D) 經營工廠

51. 女子為什麼說：「每年這個時間去丹佛的旅費都很貴」？
(A) 需要選擇另一種交通工具。
(B) 應該選另一個地點。
(C) 她不想調去丹佛。
(D) 她需要休假。

52. 男子接下來會做什麼？
(A) 檢視任務內容
(B) 延後活動
(C) 派另一位主管
(D) 和同事聯絡

TEST 2 PART 3 中譯&解析

50 若題目詢問主旨或目的，答案會出現在開頭前兩句話。

STEP 1 **題目詢問對話主旨時，聽完第一句話後，通常就能順利解題。千萬不要從頭到尾默默聽完整篇對話後，才開始選答案。務必要先看完選項內容，如此一來只要聆聽前半段對話，便能找出答案。**

男子說道：「In accordance with the new system, we need to have a safety training session for their employees.」，提到導入新系統後，必須安排員工接受安全教育訓練，因此答案為 (B) Planning a training session。

STEP 2 **陷阱選項和錯誤選項**

(A) Replacing an old system ▶ 已換掉舊系統，因此時態不正確。

(B) Planning a training session ▶ 答案

(C) Assigning a budget

(D) Operating a factory ▶ 雖然對話中有提到「plant」，但並未提到「operating」。

51 題目中出現指定句詢問說話者意圖時，答案會是說明較為籠統的選項。

STEP 1 **指定句主要作為承先啟後的角色，表達說話者的意圖，因此要先確認前後文的意思，才能理解指定句真正的意思和說話者的意圖。**

男子第一句話說道：「a new system has been put in place in Detroit and Denver . . . we need to have a safety training session for their employees.」，提到由於 Detroit and Denver 工廠安裝了新系統，因此必須安排員工們接受安全教育訓練。

男子在下一段對話又說道：「In which city should we hold the training? I think the number of employees in each plant is almost the same.」，提到兩間工廠的員工人數差不多，詢問女子應該安排在哪個地區進行訓練。而後女子回答近期前往 Denver 得花費一筆可觀的費用，表示她認為應該選擇 Denver 以外的區域，因此答案為 (B)。

STEP 2 **陷阱選項和錯誤選項**

(A) Another option for the transportation will be needed.
▶ 聽到「travel」可能會聯想到「transportation」。

(B) A different location should be chosen. ▶ 答案

(C) She doesn't want to transfer to ~~Denver~~. ▶ 對話中並未提到調派一事。

(D) She needs to take her ~~vacation~~. ▶ 聽到「travel」可能會聯想到「vacation」。

52 若題目詢問往後將發生的事情，答案為 I'll . . . 或 Let's . . . 後方連接的第一個動詞。

STEP 1 本題詢問男子下一步動作，答案會出現在後半段男子的對白中。

最後一段對話中，男子説道：「I'll talk to the training coordinator to see what she thinks.」，表示他會告知負責訓練的人，並詢問她的想法，因此答案為 (D)「聯絡他的同事」。

STEP 2 陷阱選項和錯誤選項

(A) Review the task ▶ 聽到「**hold the training**」可能會聯想到「**review**」。
(B) Postpone the event
(C) Send another director
(D) Contact his colleague ▶ 答案

字彙 **plant** 工廠 **in accordance with** 依照 **safety training** 安全訓練
the number of ……的數量 **coordinator** 協調者

Questions 53-55 refer to the following conversation.

M 53	Jane, our winter sportswear sales were low in November. They were not what we had expected, were they?	
W 54	Well, I heard that a new promotional event will start soon. So, we should wait and see what will happen in a few weeks.	53-B 54-C
M	Yeah. I know, but it's toward the end of the season.	
W	You're right. This time of the year should be busy with a number of orders.	
M	I've got an idea. Why don't we try to contact some resorts and hotels about displaying our showcases and offering special discounts to their guests?	53-C 55-D 55-B 55-C
W	That sounds good. I'll make a list of hotels and resorts. 55	

53. What kind of business do the speakers most likely work for?
(A) A clothing store
(B) An advertising firm
(C) A ~~resort~~
(D) A travel agency

職業、地點／前
→ 注意聆聽第一句話。

54. What does the man imply when he says, "It's toward the end of the season"?
(A) He wants to encourage staff members to cheer up.
(B) His team will ~~finish~~ a project soon.
(C) A clearance sale ~~should be held.~~
(D) The promotion will begin too late.

男子／掌握說話者意圖
→ 確認指定句前後文意。

55. What does the woman offer to do? **(A) Compile a list** (B) Send ~~some vouchers~~ to guests (C) ~~Select some items~~ for discounts (D) Make a reservation	女子／建議／後 → 注意聆聽後半段女子提到的勸說或建議。

第 53-55 題 對話

男：珍，我們的冬季運動服飾，11月的業績很差。這跟我們的預期不同，不是嗎？

女：嗯，我聽說很快會有新的促銷活動。所以，我們應該等看看幾個星期後的情況。

男：是，我知道，但已經要季末了。

女：你說得對，每年這個時候應該要忙著處理很多訂單。

男：我有個主意。我們為何不試著聯絡一些度假中心和飯店，談談陳列我們的展示櫃，並提供他們的房客優惠價格？

女：聽起來很棒。我來列一張飯店和度假中心的清單。

53. 說話者最可能在哪種公司工作？
(A) 服飾店 (B) 廣告公司
(C) 度假中心 (D) 旅行社

54. 男子說：「已經要季末了」，意味著什麼？
(A) 他想要鼓舞員工振作起來。
(B) 他的團隊很快會完成一項專案。
(C) 應該舉辦出清特賣。
(D) 促銷活動會太晚才開始。

55. 女子提議要做什麼？
(A) 編輯一份清單
(B) 寄一些兌換券給客人
(C) 選一些品項打折
(D) 預訂

53 前半段對話中會談到地點或職業。

STEP 1 前兩句話會聽到 our / your / this / here 加上表示地點或職業的名詞。

本題詢問說話者們任職的公司。開頭說道：「our winter sportswear sales were low in November.」，表示他們公司有販售冬天的運動服，因此說話者們工作的地方為 (A) A clothing store。

STEP 2 陷阱選項和錯誤選項

(A) A clothing store ▶ 答案
(B) An advertising firm ▶ 聽到「promotional event」可能會誤選該選項。
(C) A resort ▶ 雖然後半段對話中有提到，但是出現在解決方式中，與工作地點無關。
(D) A travel agency

54 題目詢問引號內的說話者意圖時，請確認指定句前方的連接詞。

STEP 1 **題目詢問說話者意圖時，指定句通常是對前一人說的話的答覆或反應，因此若選項包含前一人對白中的「特定單字」或相關敘述，就是正確答案。另外，若指定句前方有連接詞時，請務必分清楚答案應表達正面還是負面的意涵。**

指定句前方說道：「a new promotional event will start . . . will happen in a few weeks.」，提到宣傳活動馬上就要開始了，要過幾週後才能判定結果如何。而且該指定句前方出現連接詞 but，屬於轉折語氣，表示指定句表達的想法與前方句子為相反的概念，因此答案為 (D)。

STEP 2 **陷阱選項和錯誤選項**

(A) He wants to encourage staff members to cheer up.
(B) His team will finish a project soon. ▶「finish」和「end」的意思相同，因此請刪去該選項。
(C) A clearance sale should be held. ▶ 聽到「promotional event」可能會聯想到「sale」。
(D) The promotion will begin too late. ▶ 答案

55 題目詢問建議、要求或未來計畫時，答案會出現在後半段對話中。

STEP 1 **除了詢問要求或建議之外，還有一種題型為 offer question。此類題型的解題關鍵句不會使用 you，而是以「I will . . .」或「Let me . . .」等句型表示「由我來⋯⋯」。**

女子告知自己的下一步動作：「I'll make a list of hotels and resorts.」，提到她會列出飯店和度假村的清單，這表示她待會要做的事為 (A) Compile a list。選項將對話中的 make a list 改寫成 compile a list，故為正確答案。

STEP 2 **陷阱選項和錯誤選項**

(A) Compile a list ▶ 答案
(B) Send some vouchers to guests
▶ 對話中提到要提供顧客「special discounts」，並非「vouchers」。
(C) Select some items for discounts
▶ 雖然對話中有提到「discounts」，但並未提到「select some items」。
(D) Make a reservation ▶ 聽到「hotels」和「resorts」，可能會誤選該選項。

字彙 sportswear 運動服 sales 銷售（額） promotional 促銷的 a number of 一些 display 陳列

Questions 56-58 refer to the following conversation.

M	Hi, Adeline. Did you see the contract I left on your desk? The board of directors decided to start the project next year, so we need to revise the	56-B 57-C
56	terms and conditions.	
W	Oh, I didn't know that. Actually, I'm leaving for a meeting now and will	
57	be back around noon. I think it will be better if you stop by my office and tell me everything in detail. Can you do that for me?	
M	Sorry, but I have an appointment with a client early this afternoon, 58 Why don't you ask Lorraine? She was in the board meeting, so she knows more than I do.	58-C
W	All right. I'd better call her now.	

56. What is the main topic of the conversation?
(A) Revising a document
(B) Seeing a ~~contractor~~
(C) Finishing a report
(D) Meeting a client

主旨／前
→ 注意聆聽第一句話出現的同義詞。

57. Why does the woman say, "I'm leaving for a meeting now"?
(A) ~~She~~'s asking the ~~man~~ to ~~extend a deadline~~.
(B) She is not able to ~~attend the meeting~~.
(C) She ~~has already prepared for~~ the project.
(D) She does not have time to look at a document.

女子／掌握說話者意圖
→ 確認指定句前後的文意和連接詞。

58. What does the man say he will do this afternoon?
(A) ~~Attend~~ the board meeting
(B) Meet with a client
(C) ~~Contact a colleague~~
(D) Prepare a budget

男子／未來／ this afternoon ／後
→ 注意聆聽後半段男子使用 I'll . . . 或談及未來的句子。

第 56-58 題 對話

男：嗨，艾德琳。妳看了我放在妳桌上的合約嗎？董事會決定明年開始執行企畫，因此，我們需要修改條款與條件。

女：噢，我不知道這件事。事實上，我現在要出門去開會，大約中午回來。我想，如果你順道來我辦公室，把一切細節告訴我會比較好。你可以幫我這個忙嗎？

男：抱歉，但過了中午我和客戶有約。妳為何不問問洛琳？她有參加董事會，所以，她比我清楚。

女：好的，我最好現在打給她。

56. 這段對話的主題是什麼？
(A) 修改一份文件　(B) 見一個承包商
(C) 完成一份報告　(D) 見一位客戶

57. 女子為什麼說：「我現在要出門去開會」？
(A) 她要求男子延長截止期限。
(B) 她無法參加會議。
(C) 她已經為專案作好準備。
(D) 她沒有時間仔細看文件。

58. 男子說他今天下午要做什麼？
(A) 參加董事會。
(B) 見一位客戶。
(C) 聯絡一位同事。
(D) 準備預算案。

56 若題目詢問主旨或目的，答案會出現在開頭前兩句話。

STEP 1 題目詢問對話主旨時，聽完第一句話後，通常就能順利解題。千萬不要從頭到尾默默聽完整篇對話後，才開始選答案。務必要先看完選項內容，如此一來只要聆聽前半段對話，便能找出答案。

男子說道：「The board of directors decided to start the project next year, so we need to revise the terms and conditions.」，提到董事會決議後，需要修改企畫的簽約條件，因此對話主旨為 (A) Revising a document。

STEP 2 陷阱選項和錯誤選項

(A) Revising a document ▶ 答案
(B) Seeing a contractor ▶ 聽到「contract」可能會誤選該選項。
(C) Finishing a report
(D) Meeting a client ▶ 為男子要做的事。

57 請先刪除與引號內字面意思相同的選項。

STEP 1 題目詢問說話者意圖時，答案不會是引號內指定句字面上的意思。而且若選項使用與引號內相同的單字、或是字面意思相同的敘述，來表達說話者意圖時，通常不會是正確答案。

指定句前方說道：「we need to revise the terms and conditions.」，提到需要修改合約書的條件。而後女子回答：「I didn't know that.」表達自己並不知情，再說出指定句。接著又說道：「and will be back around noon.」，表示她要去開會，沒空看合約書，因此答案為 (D)。

STEP 2 陷阱選項和錯誤選項

(A) She's asking the man to extend a deadline. ▶ 男子請女子修改條件，因此該選項有誤。
(B) She is not able to attend the meeting. ▶ 使用指定句字面上的意思，不能作為答案。
(C) She has already prepared for the project.
▶ 雖然對話中有提到「project」，但應為未來的計畫。
(D) She does not have time to look at a document. ▶ 答案

58 題目中出現關鍵字時，答案會在該關鍵字前後的句子。▶ this afternoon

STEP 1 若題目中出現特定的關鍵字，聆聽對話時，勢必會於該關鍵字前後聽到答案。一般來說會先聽到關鍵字，再聽到答案的內容，但在新制測驗中，有時反而會先聽到答案的內容，之後才聽到關鍵字。

男子說道：「I have an appointment with a client early this afternoon.」，提到今天下午和客戶有約。表示男子今天下午要做的事為 (B) Meet with a client。

STEP 2 陷阱選項和錯誤選項

(A) Attend the board meeting ▶ 已經開過董事會，因此該敘述不正確。
(B) Meet with a client ▶ 答案
(C) Contact a colleague ▶ 為女子要做的事。
(D) Prepare a budget

字彙 contract 合約 board of director 董事會 revise 修改
terms and conditions 條款與條件 stop by 順道拜訪 in detail 詳細地

Questions 59-61 refer to the following conversation and Web page.

M Okay, we've set up all the equipment made for the premieres we're hosting tonight. Do you want me to do anything else? 59-A 59-C

W Not really, it looks perfect to me. The movie starts at 8 o'clock, so we should wait till then. 59

M Sure. What do you think about taking a break with a cup of coffee and some cake? There are some nice cafés downtown. ARRIS Coffee is the closest and they have great dessert as well.

W 60 Not this time. We always go there whenever we are here. Let's try someplace new. How about this one? It's only two kilometers away.

M 61 I have heard about that place a lot. You know, one of my coworkers, Kate, she really fancies their drip coffee. I will call her and ask what the best dessert there is.

W Okay, then I will see you guys in the lobby in five minutes.

Cafés Near Me

Café	Distance
ARRIS Coffee	0.5 km
Towers Break	1 km
Hasbro's House	2 km
Adobe's Café	2.5 km

1 2 3 4

59. What will happen at 8:00?
(A) Some equipment ~~will be delivered~~.
(B) A film will be premiered.
(C) ~~A tour~~ will be held.
(D) A presentation will start.

關鍵字 8:00／未來／前
→ 注意聆聽第一句話中的未來式。

60. Look at the graphic. Which café do the speakers decide on?
(A) ~~ARRIS Coffee~~
(B) Towers Break
(C) Hasbro's House
(D) Adobe's Café

圖表資訊
→ 確認選項以外的圖表資訊。

61. What will the man do next?
(A) Get a recommendation
(B) Pay a parking ~~fee~~
(C) Give some instructions
(D) Make a reservation

男子／未來／後
→ 注意聆聽後半段男子的對白。

第 59-61 題 對話與網頁

男：好了，我們已經裝設好今晚我們主辦首映會所需的設備了。妳還有其他事要我做的嗎？

女：沒有，在我看來很完美了。電影八點開始，所以，在那之前我們就等吧。

男：當然。妳覺得休息一下，喝杯咖啡、吃點蛋糕怎麼樣？市區有些不錯的咖啡館。艾瑞斯咖啡最近，他們的甜點也很棒。

女：這次不要，每次我們來這邊都去那裡。我們試試新的地方，這一家怎麼樣？只有兩公里遠。

男：我聽很多人提過。妳知道嗎？我的一個同事，凱特真的很迷他們的手沖滴濾咖啡。我來打給她，問問那裡最好的甜點是什麼。

女：好，那五分鐘後大廳見。

59. 八點時會發生什麼事？
(A) 要運送一些設備。
(B) 電影要首映。
(C) 要進行導覽。
(D) 演講要開始。

60. 請見圖表，說話者決定去哪一家咖啡館？
(A) 艾瑞斯咖啡
(B) 淘兒休息站
(C) 哈斯堡之家
(D) 阿多比咖啡

61. 男子接下來會做什麼？
(A) 聽取推薦　(B) 付停車費
(C) 給出指示　(D) 預訂

在我附近的咖啡館	
咖啡館	距離
艾瑞斯咖啡	0.5 公里
淘兒休息站	1 公里
哈斯堡之家	2 公里
阿多比咖啡	2.5 公里

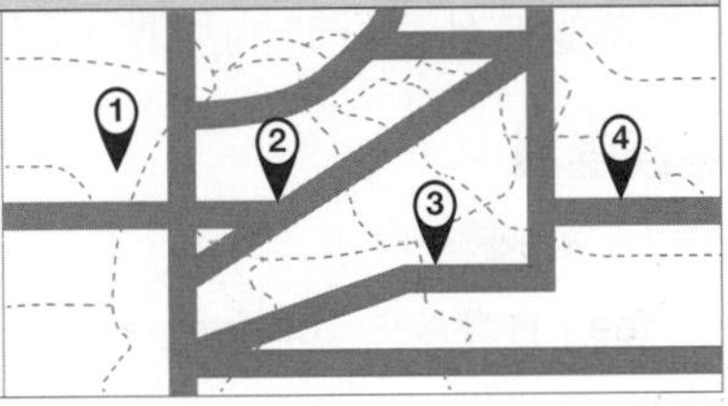

59 題目中出現關鍵字時，答案會在該關鍵字前後的句子。▶ at 8:00

STEP 1 **若題目中出現特定的關鍵字，聆聽對話時，勢必會於該關鍵字前後聽到答案。一般來說會先聽到關鍵字，再聽到答案的內容，但在新制測驗中，有時反而會先聽到答案的內容，之後才聽到關鍵字。**

女子說道：「The movie starts at 8 o'clock, so we should wait till then.」，提到電影八點開演，因此答案為 (B)。值得留意的是，選項將對話中的 start 改寫成 be premiered。

STEP 2 **陷阱選項和錯誤選項**

(A) Some equipment ~~will be delivered~~
▶ 雖然對話中有提到「equipment」，但已經完成安裝，因此該選項有誤。

(B) A film will be premiered. ▶ 答案

(C) A tour will be held. ▶「hold」與對話中「host」的發音相似。

(D) A presentation will start.

60 答案不會是對話中提到的選項內容。

STEP 1 **選項列出咖啡廳名稱，因此聆聽對話時，請確認圖表中的其他資訊。由圖表可以得知將聽到與距離有關的單字。**

選項列出咖啡廳名稱，所以聆聽對話時，請將注意力放在咖啡廳名稱以外的資訊上。男子說道：「ARRIS Coffee is the closest and they have great dessert as well.」，提議前往 ARRIS Coffee。但是女子回答：「Not this time.」拒絕男子的提議，並說道：「Let's try someplace new. How about this one? It's only two kilometers away.」，提議前往距離兩公里遠的另一家咖啡廳。確認圖表資訊後，會發現距離兩公里遠的地方為 (C) Hasbro's House，故為正確答案。

61 後半段對話中，未來資訊的答案會出現在「I'll . . .」後方。

STEP 1 **題目詢問下一步動作（未來資訊）時，答案通常會出現在當事人所說的話當中。**

男子提到自己的下一步動作：「I will call her and ask what the best dessert there is.」，提到他會打電話給同事，向對方確認有什麼好吃的甜點，因此答案為 (A) Get a recommendation。

STEP 2 **陷阱選項和錯誤選項**

(A) Get a recommendation ▶ 答案
(B) Pay a parking fee ▶「fee」與對話中「coffee」的發音相似。
(C) Give some instructions
(D) Make a reservation ▶ 聽到「that place」可能會誤選該選項。

字彙 set up 擺放、設置　equipment 設備　premiere 首映　host 主辦　till then 直到那時
take a break 休息　downtown 城市的商業區、鬧區　whenever 每當、無論什麼時候
someplace 在某處、到某處　away 隔開……遠　fancy 愛好　coworker 同事

Questions 62-64 refer to the following conversation and signs.

M	Welcome to McComic Food, Mary. Congratulations on being a new employee in our company.	
W	Nice to meet you. I'm so excited to start the orientation today.	
M	Before beginning, I'd like to brief you on the schedule. First, we're going to give you a tour of the laboratory where you'll work. As the sign indicates, you'll need to keep all of your belongings in a locker next to the entrance of the laboratory.	62-C
W	Does that include my cell phone?	63-D
M	Yes. Everything you see inside should be kept confidential, so phones aren't allowed.	
W	I understand. By the way, I received a call yesterday saying that I should bring three recommendation letters and my portfolio. 63	
M	That's right. You should submit them to the Human Resources	
64	Department after we're done. And after the tour of the laboratory, I'll introduce you to your supervisor, Matthew, in the cafeteria on the first floor.	64-D

1 Sign up at the information desk	**2** Enter a dustproof room
3 Wear protective garments	**4** Leave all items

62. Look at the graphic. Which sign does the man refer to?
(A) Sign 1
(B) ~~Sign 2~~
(C) ~~Sign 3~~
(D) Sign 4

男子／前
→ 確認前半段男子的對白和圖表資訊。

63. What did the woman bring today?
(A) A collection of documents
(B) A signed contract
(C) A journal
(D) ~~A cell phone~~

女子／ **bring** ／ **today**
→ 注意聆聽女子的對白：以 I 開頭的現在式或過去式句子。

64. What will the man do at the end of the tour?
(A) ~~Submit some documents~~
(B) Meet her supervisor
(C) ~~Fill out a form~~ on the first floor
(D) Receive a ~~souvenir~~

男子／未來／ **at the end of the tour**
→ 注意聆聽後半段男子的對白：未來式句子。

第 62-64 題 對話與標示

男：歡迎來到麥克米食品，瑪麗。恭喜妳成為我們公司的新員工。

女：很高興認識你，我迫不急待要開始今天的新進人員訓練。

男：開始之前，我想跟妳簡報流程。首先，我們要帶妳參觀妳要工作的實驗室。正如標示牌上顯示的，妳必須把妳的所有物品放在實驗室入口的置物櫃裡。

女：包括我的手機嗎？

男：是的。妳在裡面看到的所有事物都應該要保密，所以不能帶手機。

女：我了解。對了，我接到電話說，我必須帶三封推薦信和我的作品集來。

男：沒錯。在我們這邊結束後，妳必須把那些交到人事部去。在參觀完實驗室後，我會帶妳到一樓的餐廳，把妳介紹給妳的主管馬修。

1. 在服務台簽到	2. 進入無塵室
3. 穿上防護衣	4. 拿出所有物品寄放

62. 請見圖表，男子指的是哪個標示牌？
(A) 第一個標示牌
(B) 第二個標示牌
(C) 第三個標示牌
(D) 第四個標示牌

63. 女子今天帶了什麼來？
(A) 一些文件
(B) 一份簽了名的合約
(C) 一本日誌
(D) 一支手機

64. 參觀完後，男子會做什麼？
(A) 交出一些文件。
(B) 和她的主管碰面。
(C) 到一樓填寫一份表格。
(D) 獲得一份紀念品。

62 請一邊預測答案出現的位置，一邊觀看選項。

STEP 1 對話會依序出現答案線索，因此千萬不要默默聽完整篇對話後，才開始選答案。務必要按照題目順序，將注意力放在該題目列出的選項上，並仔細聆聽對話中是否提及選項中的單字或相關單字。

本題詢問男子提到的內容屬於圖表中的哪一項。對話會依序出現答案，因此請仔細聆聽前半段男子所說的話，確認是否出現圖表中的部分內容或相關單字。男子說道：「you'll need to keep all of your belongings in a locker.」，請對方將隨身物品放在置物櫃裡，因此答案為(D)。

→ 選項會將對話中的詳細內容，改寫成較為廣義的敘述。
all of your belongings → all items

STEP 2 陷阱選項和錯誤選項

(A) Sign 1
(B) Sign 2
(C) Sign 3 ▶ 聽到「laboratory」可能會聯想到「protective garments」。
(D) Sign 4 ▶ 答案

63 題目中提及女子，因此答案會出現在女子的對白中。

STEP 1 本題針對女子提問，因此答案會出現在女子的對白中。

本題詢問女子今天帶來什麼東西。女子說道：「I received a call yesterday saying that I should bring three recommendation letters and my portfolio」，提到昨天接到電話告知她要帶推薦信和作品集，因此女子今天帶來的東西為 (A)。

→ 選項會將對話中的詳細內容，改寫成較為廣義的敘述。
three recommendation letters and my portfolio → (A) A collection of documents

STEP 2 陷阱選項和錯誤選項

(A) A collection of documents ▶ 答案
(B) A signed contract
(C) A journal
(D) A cell phone ▶ 重複使用對話中的「cell phone」。

64 後半段對話中，未來資訊的答案會出現在「I'll . . .」後方。

STEP 1 請確認題目關鍵字 at the end of the tour。

請由最後一段男子的對白，確認男子往後要做的事。男子說道：「after the tour of the laboratory, I'll introduce you to your supervisor, Matthew, in the cafeteria on the first floor.」，提到參觀完實驗室後，要帶女子到一樓的員工餐廳，介紹女子的主管給她認識。這表示男子會和女子的主管見面，因此答案為 (B)。

STEP 2 陷阱選項和錯誤選項

(A) Submit some documents ▶ 為新員工培訓結束後要做的事。
(B) Meet her supervisor ▶ 答案
(C) Fill out a form on the first floor ▶ 雖然對話中有提到「first floor」，但是並未提到要填寫資料。
(D) Receive a souvenir ▶ 聽到「tour」可能會聯想到「souvenir」。

字彙 brief 簡報　laboratory 實驗室　belongings 攜帶物品、財產
confidential 機密的　submit 呈遞　dustproof 防塵的　garment 衣服

Questions 65-67 refer to the following conversation and invitation.

M	Hello, this is Clark Peters from Marcus Marketing Firm. I've just received the sample invitation, and you did great work.	
W 65	Hi, Clark. I'm glad you like it. Once you finish checking the information on the sample, I'll have the printing department print the invitations out right away. Does everything look okay?	65-C 65-D
M 66	Well, I think it seems perfect. Wait, I found an error! We originally reserved the Emerald Hall for 100 people, but the number of participants is expected to be higher than last year, so management decided to reserve the Diamond Hall instead, which can accommodate about 200 people.	
W	Okay, got it. Anything else?	
M	That's all.	
W	Sounds good. Your invoice said that you'd like to receive some copies of the invitation at your office, right?	
M	Yes, when will they be delivered?	
W 67	The printing work will be completed by Thursday and we will be shipping them by overnight delivery, so you should receive them the next day.	

You're Invited to the 10th Anniversary of Marcus Marketing Firm!

Friday, November 21, 6:00 P.M.
Emerald Hall, Montreal Boutique Hotel
RSVP to Cindy Wong 532-4661

65. What did the woman ask the man to do?
(A) Review some work (B) Send an e-mail
(C) Check a ~~reservation~~ (D) ~~Visit~~ a printing shop

女子／前／要求的事
→ 注意聆聽第一段女子的對白。

66. Look at the graphic. What should be changed?
(A) The title (B) The date
(C) The place (D) The phone number

圖表資訊／需要變更的事項
→ 將對話中提出的問題和圖表資訊相互連結。

67. When will the man probably receive the delivery?
(A) On Wednesday (B) On ~~Thursday~~
(C) On Friday (D) On Saturday

男子／未來／收到的時間點
→ 注意聆聽後半段男子的對白：未來式。

第 65-67 題 對話與邀請函

男：哈囉，我是馬科斯行銷公司的克拉克·彼得斯。我剛剛收到邀請函的樣本，你們做得很棒。

女：嗨，克拉克，很高興你喜歡。等你檢查完樣本上的資訊後，我就馬上請印刷部門把邀請函印出來。看起來都沒錯嗎？

男：嗯，我覺得看起來很完美。等等，我發現一個錯誤！我們原本預訂了可容納100人的翡翠廳，但預期參加人數會比去年多，所以管理部門決定改訂鑽石廳，那裡可以容納200人。

女：好，知道了。還有其他的嗎？

男：就這樣。

女：聽起來很好。你在出貨單上寫說，你們辦公室想要一些邀請函，是嗎？

男：是的，什麼時候會寄送？

女：印刷工作會在星期四完成，我們會用隔夜送達服務寄出，所以，你應該會在隔天收到。

邀請您參加馬科斯行銷公司的十週年慶祝會！ 11 月 21 日星期五 晚上六時 蒙特婁精品酒店 翡翠廳 請回覆給辛蒂·黃 532-4661

65. 女子要求男子做什麼？
(A) 再檢查一項工作
(B) 寄一封電子郵件
(C) 核對預訂
(D) 去列印店

66. 請見圖表，哪部分應該要修改？
(A) 標題
(B) 日期
(C) 地點
(D) 電話號碼

67. 男子最可能何時收到貨品？
(A) 星期三
(B) 星期四
(C) 星期五
(D) 星期六

65 題目針對過去提問時，答題線索會出現在前半段對話中；針對未來提問時，答題線索則會出現在後半段對話中。

STEP 1 對話會依序出現答題線索，因此聆聽對話時，請按照題目順序，將注意力放在選項上。

本題詢問女子要求男子的事情，請確認第一段女子的對白。第一名男子說道：「I've just received the sample invitation, and you did great work.」，表示他收到女子製作的樣品。

而後女子說道：「Once you finish checking the information on the sample, I'll have the printing department print the invitations out right away. Does everything look okay?」，告訴男子待他確認完畢後，就會拿到印刷部門列印，詢問男子樣品是否沒問題。此段話表示女子要求男子確認製作物是否沒問題，因此答案為 (A)。

STEP 2 陷阱選項和錯誤選項

(A) Review some work ▶ 答案

(B) Send an e-mail

(C) Check a reservation

▶ 對話中並未提到 reservation。

(D) Visit a printing shop

▶「have the printing department print the invitations out」為未來將做的事，因此不能作為答案。

66 找出 Brochure 或 Coupon 當中有誤的部分。

STEP 1 **圖表中包含眾多資訊，因此請逐一確認聆聽的內容和表格羅列的資訊是否一致。**

對話中男子先提出問題，再告知需要更動的地方。男子說道：「I found an error!」提出問題，接著說道：「We originally reserved the Emerald Hall.」，提到原本預約的地方為 Emerald Hall。之後又說：「but the number of . . . higher」，表示由於人數增加，必須更改地點，因此答案為 (C) A place。

67 題目使用 next 詢問未來資訊時，請留意以「I / We will . . .」開頭的最後一句對白！

STEP 1 **題目詢問某人的下一步動作（未來資訊）時，答案通常會出現在當事人所說的話當中。但是若為難度較高的考題，則會採同意對方建議或要求的方式來表達（等同於此人的下一步動作），因此請務必聽清楚對方建議或要求的內容為何。**

雖然本題詢問的是男子的下一步動作，但是最後一句話為女子的對白，因此可以推測出女子將於對話最後向男子提出要求或建議。

男子說道：「when will they be delivered?」，而後女子回答：「The printing work will be completed by Thursday」，提到印刷工作將於週四完成，接著說道：「and we will be shipping them by overnight delivery.」，表示會使用隔日快遞，並補充：「so you should receive them the next day.」。由此段話可以得知男子會在隔天收到，因此答案為週五 (C)。

STEP 2 **陷阱選項和錯誤選項**

(A) On Wednesday
(B) On Thursday ▶ 為印刷完成日，送達日為隔天。
(C) On Friday ▶ 答案
(D) On Saturday

字彙 **print out** 列印出來 **accommodate** 容納 **invoice** 出貨單
deliver 遞送 **overnight delivery** 隔夜送達

Questions 68-70 refer to the following conversation and graph.

W	Mohamad, thanks for meeting me today. I had a meeting with some	**68-A**
68	clients all morning, so this was the only time I was available.	
M	That's okay. I have finished reviewing the report you sent me yesterday.	**69-D**
	Last quarter's sales were very impressive! We introduced new menu	
	items for autumn and expected sales to be higher than the previous	
69	quarter's, but we recorded the highest volume of sales in 2016.	
W	You're right. The board of directors were all satisfied with the results. Our	
	success was due to your great ideas, so I want you to develop the new	**70-C**
	menu for the next season. Have you thought about it at all?	
M	How about chocolate chip and orange scones? This year, orange crop	
70	yields have increased greatly, so I think we can make a profit by using	**70-B**
	oranges.	

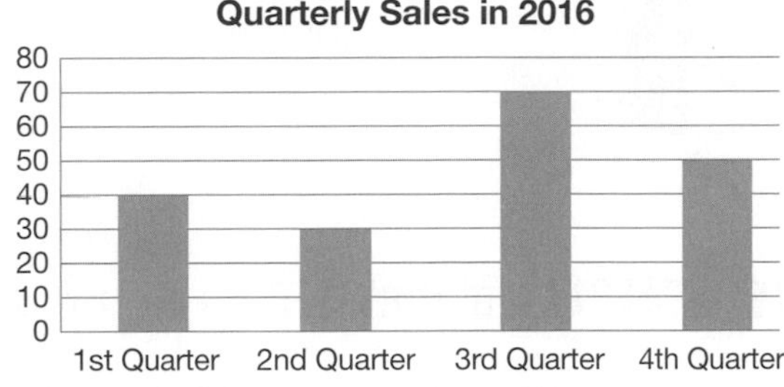

68. What did the woman do in the morning?

(A) ~~Called~~ some clients
(B) ~~Wrote~~ a report
(C) Attended a meeting
(D) ~~Sent~~ a manual

女子／前／ in the morning

→ 注意聆聽女子對白中的過去式。

69. Look at the graphic. Which quarter is being discussed?

(A) Quarter 1
(B) Quarter 2
(C) Quarter 3
(D) Quarter 4

圖表資訊／討論的季度

→ 注意對話中的最高級、排序，並對照圖表。

70. What does the man suggest?

(A) Using some fruit
(B) ~~Increasing~~ prices
(C) Launching promotional events
(D) Opening new branches

男子／建議

→ 注意聆聽後半段男子提議的內容。

第 68-70 題 對話與圖表

女：穆罕默德，謝謝你今天和我碰面。我整個早上都在和客戶開會，所以，這是我唯一有空的時間。

男：沒關係。我已經看過妳昨天寄給我的報告。上一季的業績表現非常令人印象深刻！我們推出秋天的新菜色，預期銷售額會比前一季高，但是，我們創下了2016年的最高銷售額。

女：你說得沒錯，董事會全都對成果很滿意。我們的成功都歸功於你的絕佳點子，因此，我想要你開發下一季的新菜單。你有開始想了嗎？

男：巧克力脆片和柑橘司康如何？今年的柑橘產量大增，所以，我想我們選用柑橘會有利潤。

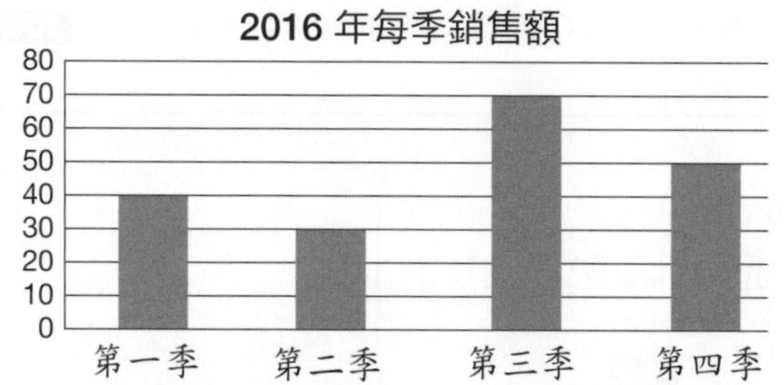

68. 女子早上做了什麼？
(A) 打電話給一些客戶。
(B) 寫一份報告。
(C) 參加會議。
(D) 寄送一份手冊。

69. 請見圖表，對話中討論的是哪一季？
(A) 第一季。
(B) 第二季。
(C) 第三季。
(D) 第四季。

70. 男子建議什麼？
(A) 使用某種水果。
(B) 提高價格。
(C) 推出促銷活動。
(D) 開新分店。

68 題目中出現關鍵字時，答案會在該關鍵字前後的句子。▶ in the morning

STEP 1 **若題目中出現特定的關鍵字，聆聽對話時，勢必會於該關鍵字前後聽到答案。一般來說會先聽到關鍵字，再聽到答案的內容，但在新制測驗中，有時反而會先聽到答案的內容，之後才聽到關鍵字。**

請確認關鍵字 woman 和 in the morning。女子說道：「I had a meeting with some clients all morning.」，提到她和客戶開了整個上午的會，因此答案為 (C) 參加會議。有時答案會出現在關鍵字前方，請特別留意。

STEP 2 **陷阱選項和錯誤選項**

(A) Called some clients ▶ 雖然對話中有提到「clients」，但無從得知是否通過電話。
(B) Wrote a report ▶ 重複使用對話中的「report」。
(C) Attended a meeting ▶ 答案
(D) Sent a manual ▶ 重複使用對話中的「sent」。

69 若對話中提到圖表（Graph / Bar / Pie）的排序、最高級或數量時，就是答案所在之處。

STEP 1 **圖表的作用為「比較」，因此請從排序、最高級、數量等用法確認答案。**

男子說道：「but we recorded the highest volume of sales in 2016.」，提到創下 2016 年最佳銷售量的紀錄。確認長條圖後，可以發現數量最多的為 (C) Quarter 3，故為正確答案。

70 題目詢問建議、要求或未來計畫時，答案會出現在後半段對話中。

STEP 1 **除了直接勸說、建議、要求、請求對方之外，還可以使用直述句，間接表示勸說或建議。**

最後一段對話，男子說道：「How about chocolate chip and orange scones?」，提到新菜單中可以使用橘子，這表示他建議使用水果。

STEP 2 **陷阱選項和錯誤選項**

(A) Using some fruits ▶ 答案
(B) Increasing prices ▶ 對話中提到成本因而降低，因此該選項不正確。
(C) Launching promotional events ▶ 聽到「great ideas」可能會誤選該選項。
(D) Opening new branches

字彙 impressive 令人印象深刻　autumn 秋天　be satisfied with 對……感到滿意
crops 作物　yield 產量　make a profit 獲利

PART 4

Questions 71-73 refer to the following broadcast.

Welcome back to Mina's Morning Today. I'm your host Mina Kang. The
city council has recently approved the proposed construction for the new 71-B
71 shopping complex which will open next March. Most of our residents
expect that there will be great benefits to our city. However, some issues
have been raised among residents. Because two of the four lanes are 72-B
closed due to the construction, the traffic around the site seems to have 72-D
gotten worse. To alleviate this problem, the city council will introduce the
Two-Shift System which will require residents to only use their cars every
72 other day. Since this is our big decision to the city, the city will hold a
public hearing this Saturday earlier than scheduled. If you are interested
73 in attending, please visit the city's Web site, www.HamingtonCity.go.kr 73-D
and leave your contact information.

71. What will happen next March?
(A) A proposal ~~will be accepted~~.
(B) A ~~construction site~~ will open.
(C) A new building will open.
(D) A shopping mall will be ~~closed~~.

關鍵字 next March／前
→ 注意聆聽未來式句子。

72. According to the speaker, what has changed?
(A) The construction ~~site~~
(B) The road ~~expansion~~
(C) The public hearing date
(D) The ~~transportation~~ system

關鍵字 changed
→ 注意聆聽提及 originally 或 scheduled 的句子。

73. Why does the speaker ask the listeners to visit the Web site?
(A) To sign up to participate
(B) To ~~raise~~ some ~~questions~~
(C) To ~~take a survey~~
(D) To ~~check residents' opinions~~

要求／ Web site ／後
→ 注意聆聽提及 please 或 you should 的句子。

第 71-73 題 廣播

歡迎繼續收聽米娜的早安今日節目，我是主持人米娜·姜。市議會最近通過了將在明年三月開幕的新購物中心工程建案。大部分的市民都期待，這會讓本市受惠良多。然而，市民也提出一些問題。由於四線道的馬路因為工程而封閉兩線，工地附近的交通似乎更糟了。為了減輕這個問題，市議會將引進兩班制系統，要求市民每隔一天才開車。既然這是本市的重大決定，市政府將在本週六召開公聽會，這比預定時間早些。如果您有興趣參加，請上市政府網站：www.HamingtonCity.gov.kr，留下您的聯絡資料。

71. 明年三月會發生什麼事？
(A) 有個提案會通過。
(B) 有個建築工地會動工。
(C) 一棟新的建築物將啟用。
(D) 一間購物商場將關閉。

72. 根據說話者，什麼事情改變了？
(A) 建築工地
(B) 道路拓寬
(C) 公聽會的日期
(D) 運輸系統

73. 說話者為什麼要求聽眾造訪網站？
(A) 為了報名參加活動。
(B) 為了提出一些問題。
(C) 為了參加調查。
(D) 為了查看市民的意見。

71 題目中出現關鍵字時，答案會在該關鍵字前後的句子。▶ next March

STEP 1 若題目中出現特定的關鍵字，聆聽獨白時，勢必會於該關鍵字前後聽到答案。一般來說會先聽到關鍵字，再聽到答案的內容，但在新制測驗中，有時反而會先聽到答案的內容，之後才聽到關鍵字。

獨白說道：「the new shopping complex which will open next March」，提到新的購物中心將於明年三月開幕。

→ 雖然獨白提到明確的資訊，但是選項通常會改寫成較為廣義的敘述。
new shopping complex → (C) new building

STEP 2 陷阱選項和錯誤選項

(A) A proposal will be accepted. ▶ 提案書早已通過，因此該敘述不正確。

(B) A construction site will open. ▶ 主詞應改成「shopping complex」。

(C) A new building will open. ▶ 答案

(D) A shopping mall will be ~~closed~~. ▶ 獨白中並未提及「closed」。

72 題目詢問變動事項時，答案通常會出現在 earlier 或 originally 前後。

STEP 1 請注意表達變動事項的單字：earlier / scheduled / originally。

獨白中說道：「the city will hold a public hearing this Saturday earlier than scheduled」，由「earlier than scheduled」可以得知時間有所變動，因此答案為 (C) The public hearing date。

STEP 2 陷阱選項和錯誤選項

(A) The construction site ▶ 雖然獨白中有提到「construction」，但是並未提到「site」。

(B) The road expansion
▶「road」僅與獨白中「lane」的意思相似，且當中並未提到「expansion」。

(C) The public hearing date ▶ 答案

(D) The transportation system ▶ 聽到「traffic」可能會聯想到「transportation system」。

73 題目詢問要求或建議時，答案會位在後半段獨白中，並以 please 告知。

STEP 1 PART 4 中詢問要求或建議時，指的是說話者（speaker）向聽者（listeners）要求的事情，因此會有固定的提問和回答模式，而答題線索會出現在後半段獨白中。當中經常會使用 If you 或 please 來表達建議的內容，請務必熟記。

獨白中說道：「the city will hold a public hearing this Saturday earlier than scheduled. If you are interested in attending, please visit the city's Web site.」，提到城市預計舉辦公聽會，如有興趣參與，請上網站申請，因此答案為 (A) To sign up to participate。

STEP 2 陷阱選項和錯誤選項

(A) To sign up to participate ▶ 答案
(B) To raise some questions ▶ 聽到「discuss」可能會誤選該選項。
(C) To take a survey
(D) To check residents' opinions ▶ 聽到「visit the city's Web site」可能會誤選該選項。

字彙 host 主持人　city council 市議會　approve 同意、批准　propose 提議
complex 建築群　resident 居民　benefit 得益、受惠　issue 問題、爭議
raise 提出、發出　among 在……之間　site 地點、場所　get worse 變糟
alleviate 減輕　two-shift 二班制　every other day 每隔一天　public hearing 公聽會
contact information 聯絡資料

Questions 74-76 refer to the following telephone message.

74 Hi, Mr. Leed. This is Dante's Sporting Goods Store. I'm calling to give you an update on your orders. You ordered one flat bench and two ten-pound dumbbells. According to the invoice, it looks like the bench
75 is going to be delivered this afternoon but the dumbbells you ordered will not arrive yet. In addition, we've received news that a snowstorm is approaching tonight. Due to the weather, it is expected that most of the roads which our delivery trucks usually use will be blocked. To
76 apologize for this delay, all of your shipping charges will be refunded.

74-A
75-B 74-C
76-C 76-D

74. What type of business does the speaker work for?
(A) A ~~fitness center~~
(B) A sporting goods store
(C) A ~~newspaper~~ company
(D) An automotive repair shop

職業／說話者／前
→ 請由 This is 開頭的句子確認。

75. What does the speaker say about Mr. Leed's order?
(A) Some of the items are no longer available.
(B) It was mistakenly ~~canceled~~.
(C) It will be delayed.
(D) All of his order has been ~~delivered already~~.

關鍵字 **Mr. Leed's order**
→ 注意聆聽表示原因的介系詞或連接詞。

76. What will the speaker offer the listener?
(A) A free delivery
(B) A beverage voucher
(C) A shipping service ~~upgrade~~
(D) A discount

建議／後
→ 注意聆聽表示未來或建議的句子。

第 74-76 題 電話留言

嗨，里德先生，這裡是丹堤運動用品店，我打來告訴你關於你訂單的最新進度。你訂了一張平臥椅和兩個十磅重啞鈴。根據出貨單，看起來平臥椅今天下午會出貨，但你訂的啞鈴還沒來。此外，我們接到消息，今天晚上有暴風雪。由於天氣的關係，預期我們的貨運卡車平常行駛的大部分道路會封閉。為了表達延遲出貨的歉意，我們將會退還你全部的運費。

74. 說話者在什麼公司上班？
(A) 健身中心 (B) 運動用品店
(C) 報社 (D) 修車廠

75. 關於里德先生的訂單，說話者說了什麼？
(A) 有些品項已經斷貨。
(B) 訂單不小心被取消。
(C) 會延後出貨。
(D) 他所有訂的貨都已經送出。

76. 說話者提議給聽話者什麼？
(A) 免費運送 (B) 一張飲料優惠券
(C) 運送服務升級 (D) 折扣

74 前兩句話會以代名詞（I / You / We）或地方副詞（here / this ＋地點名詞）告知職業或地點。

STEP 1 前兩句話會聽到 our / your / this / here 加上表示地點或職業的名詞。

第一句話說道：「This is Dante's Sporting Goods Store」，由此可知說話者在運動用品店工作，因此答案為 (B)。

STEP 2 陷阱選項和錯誤選項

(A) A fitness center ▶ 聽到「sporting」可能會聯想到「fitness center」。
(B) A sporting goods store ▶ 答案
(C) A newspaper company ▶ 聽到「news」可能會聯想到「newspaper」。
(D) An automotive repair shop

75 題目中出現關鍵字時，答案會在該關鍵字前後的句子。▶ Lead's order

STEP 1 若題目中出現特定的關鍵字，聆聽獨白時，勢必會於該關鍵字前後聽到答案。一般來說會先聽到關鍵字，再聽到答案的內容，但在新制測驗中，有時反而會先聽到答案的內容，之後才聽到關鍵字。

首先，務必要知道的是 order 可以替換成同義詞 invoice。獨白中說道：「According to the invoice, . . . but the dumbbells you ordered will not arrived yet」，說話者告知訂購的商品尚未送達，指出配送延遲的狀況，因此答案為 (C)。

STEP 2 陷阱選項和錯誤選項

(A) Some of the items are no longer available.
(B) It was mistakenly canceled. ▶ 聽到「not arrived」可能會聯想到「canceled」。
(C) It will be delayed. ▶ 答案
(D) All of his order has been delivered already.
▶ 其中一項預計今天下午送達，另一項則延遲送達，因此該敘述有誤。

76 題目詢問建議、要求或未來計畫時，答案會出現在後半段獨白中。

STEP 1 題目詢問要求或建議時，有固定的提問和回答模式，而答題線索會出現在後半段獨白中。

後半段獨白說道：「all of your shipping charges will be refunded」，提到將會退還運費，因此答案為 (A)。

STEP 2 陷阱選項和錯誤選項

(A) A free delivery ▶ 答案
(B) A beverage voucher
(C) A shipping service upgrade
▶ 雖然獨白中有提到「shipping」，但是並未提到「upgrade」。
(D) A discount ▶ 聽到「charges」可能會聯想到「discount」。

字彙 according to 根據　invoice 出貨單　snowstorm 暴風雪
approach 接近、即將到達　block 封鎖　shipping charge 運費

Questions 77-79 refer to the following telephone message.

	Hello, Marc. This is Meredith. I was glad at seeing you at the hotel &	77-A
77	hospitality industry seminar last Saturday. I was sorry that we didn't have	77-D
	enough time to speak with each other after my presentation. Anyway, I	
	was told that you asked some of the presenters for advice on where to	
	hire some skilled receptionists for your new hotel branch. In my case,	77-C
	I use Morgan Employment Agency. They offer a special program which	
78	can connect a company with an employee by using detailed analysis.	
	Actually, I have hired five receptionists through the agency until now.	78-C
79	I'll be out of the office through this Thursday, so if you want to talk about	79-C
	this further, please give me a call this Friday.	

77. What did the speaker do last Saturday?
(A) She ~~stayed~~ at the hotel.
(B) She gave a presentation.
(C) She participated in the ~~reception~~.
(D) She went to a ~~hospital~~.

關鍵字 last Saturday ／前
→ 注意聆聽提及 I was 或 did 的過去式句子。

78. What does the speaker mean when she says, "I have hired five receptionists through the agency"?
(A) Her business was successful.
(B) She couldn't complete the work.
(C) She had ~~authority to hire workers~~.
(D) She wants to make a recommendation.

掌握說話者意圖
→ 注意指定句前後的文意。

79. When will the speaker return to the office?
(A) On Tuesday　(B) On Wednesday
(C) On ~~Thursday~~　**(D) On Friday**

關鍵字 return to the office ／未來／後
→ 注意聆聽 I'll . . . 開頭的未來式句子。

第 77-79 題 電話留言

哈囉，馬克，我是梅瑞迪斯，很高興上星期六在飯店與餐旅業研討會見到你。很抱歉，在我演講後，我們沒有時間彼此聊聊。對了，我得知你詢問了一些講者，要去哪裡為你的新飯店分館召募熟練的櫃檯接待人員。以我來說，我會選擇摩根人力仲介公司。他們提供一套特別的軟體，透過詳細分析後，可以連結公司端和員工端。事實上，到目前為止，我透過這家仲介公司，已經僱用了五位接待人員。這個星期四之前我都不在辦公室，因此，如果你想進一步聊聊這件事，請在這個星期五打電話給我。

77. 說話者上星期六做了什麼？
(A) 她住在飯店。 (B) 她發表了演講。
(C) 她參加了歡迎會。 (D) 她去了醫院。

78. 當說話者說：「我透過這家仲介公司，已經僱用了五位接待人員」，意指什麼？
(A) 她的生意很成功。
(B) 她無法完成工作。
(C) 她獲授權僱用員工。
(D) 她想要推薦。

79. 說話者何時會回到辦公室？
(A) 星期二 (B) 星期三
(C) 星期四 (D) 星期五

77 題目中出現關鍵字時，答案會在該關鍵字前後的句子。▶ last Saturday

STEP 1 **若題目中出現特定的關鍵字，聆聽獨白時，勢必會於該關鍵字前後聽到答案。一般來說會先聽到關鍵字，再聽到答案的內容，但在新制測驗中，有時反而會先聽到答案的內容，之後才聽到關鍵字。**

關鍵字 last Saturday 的前後說道：「I was glad at seeing you . . . last Saturday. I was sorry that we didn't have enough time . . . after my presentation」，提到雖然上週六有見到面，但在自己的演講過後，沒有充分的時間聊天。這表示說話者於上週六進行演講，因此答案為 (B)。

STEP 2 **陷阱選項和錯誤選項**

(A) She stayed at the hotel. ▶ 雖然獨白中有提到「hotel」，但並沒有入住。
(B) She gave a presentation. ▶ 答案
(C) She participated in the reception. ▶ 聽到「receptionist」可能會誤選該選項。
(D) She went to a hospital. ▶ 聽到發音相似的單字「hospitality」，可能會誤選該選項。

78 題目中出現指定句詢問說話者意圖時，答案會是說明較為籠統的選項。

STEP 1 **指定句主要作為承先啟後的角色，表達說話者的意圖，因此要先確認前後文的意思，才能理解指定句真正的意思和說話者的意圖。**

指定句前方說道：「I use Morgan Employment Agency. They offer a special program . . . by using detailed analysis」，提到自己利用人力仲介公司，並談到其優點。而後提到透過人力仲介公司「僱用了五名接待人員」，表示說話者想要推薦此間人力仲介公司，因此答案為 (D)。

STEP 2 **陷阱選項和錯誤選項**

(A) Her business was successful.
(B) She couldn't complete the work.
(C) She had authority to hire workers. ▶ 重複使用獨白中的「hire」。
(D) She wants to make a recommendation. ▶ 答案

79 後半段對話中，未來資訊的答案會出現在「I'll . . .」後方。

STEP 1 題目詢問某人的下一步動作時，請留意後半段獨白中以 I will 開頭的句子。

獨白中說道：「I'll be out of the office through this Thursday」，提及直到週四他都不會在辦公室，表示說話者回辦公室的時間為週五，因此答案為 (D)。

STEP 2 陷阱選項和錯誤選項

(A) On Tuesday
(B) On Wednesday
(C) On Thursday
▶ 雖然獨白中提到「Thursday」，但指的是他出差到週四，所以這段期間都不在辦公室。
(D) On Friday ▶ 答案

字彙 **hospitality industry** 餐旅業 **connect** 連結 **skilled** 熟練的、有技能的
receptionist 接待員 **in my case** 以我來說、以我為例 **analysis** 分析
employment agency 職業介紹所、人力仲介 **detailed** 詳細的
be out of the office 不在辦公室

Questions 80-82 refer to the following broadcast.

Thanks for your news report, Carol. Now for the weekday weather
update for Lexington. Local residents will be excited to hear
that spring-like weather is coming. The sky will be clear and the
80 temperature warm with a light breeze until Thursday. With this 82-B
81 beautiful weather, you could enjoy the annual music festival in
Lexington Park on Wednesday evening. Unfortunately, a heavy
snow is expected on Friday morning and conditions will remain cold 80-D
throughout Saturday. After that, the temperature will drop suddenly
below zero. Some of the roads in the city will likely be icy, so be 81-A 82-D
82 careful when driving. Lexington road crews will work around the clock
in order to keep the roads clear so that next Monday's traffic will not
be affected. Your sports update is up next. 81-B

80. What will the weather conditions be like until Thursday?
(A) Warm (B) Rainy
(C) Humid (D) ~~Snowy~~

81. What will be held in the park?
(A) A road ~~repair~~ (B) A sports event
(C) Musical performances (D) Some exhibitions

82. What does the speaker imply when he says, "Lexington road crews will work around the clock"?
(A) There will be no traffic congestion next week.
(B) The temperature ~~will be higher~~ than expected.
(C) Some roads will be closed for clearing.
(D) Some of the residents ~~will take a detour~~.

關鍵字 Thursday／天氣／前
→ 確認前半段提及天氣的片段。

關鍵字 in the park／未來
→ 注意聆聽關鍵字前後方內容。

掌握說話者意圖
→ 注意指定句前後的文意。

第 80-82 題 廣播

謝謝妳的新聞報導，卡蘿。現在是萊辛頓的最新週間天氣預報。本地居民會很高興聽到春日般的天氣即將來臨。星期四之前天空晴朗，氣候溫暖，微微有風。在這樣美好的天氣裡，你可以好好享受星期三晚上在萊辛頓公園舉行的年度音樂節。可惜，星期五早上預期會下大雪，而且寒冷的天氣會持續星期六整天。之後，氣溫會驟降到零度以下。市內有些道路可能會結冰，因此要小心開車。萊辛頓道路工程人員會二十四小時工作，以確保道路無障礙，如此，星期一早上的交通才不會受影響。接下來是最新的體育新聞。

80. 星期四之前的天氣狀況如何？
(A) 溫暖　(B) 下雨
(C) 潮濕　(D) 下雪

81. 公園裡會舉行什麼活動？
(A) 修補道路。　(B) 體育活動。
(C) 音樂表演。　(D) 一些展覽。

82. 當說話者說：「萊辛頓道路工程人員會二十四小時工作」，意指什麼？
(A) 下星期的交通不會受阻。
(B) 氣溫會比預期高。
(C) 有些道路會封閉進行清理。
(D) 有些居民要繞道而行。

80 獨白主題為天氣預報時，題目會針對特定日的天氣提問。▶ until Thursday

STEP 1 天氣預報會按照現在 ⇨ 不久的未來報導天氣。

請先確認本題的關鍵字為 until Thursday。獨白中說道：「The sky will be clear and the temperature warm with a light breeze until Thursday.」，答案出現在關鍵字 until Thursday 的前方，請特別留意。由此話可以得知到週四的溫度都很暖和，因此答案為 (A)。

STEP 2 陷阱選項和錯誤選項

(A) Warm ▶ 答案　(B) Rainy
(C) Humid　(D) Snowy ▶ 週五早上才會下雪，因此該選項不正確。

81 雖然聽到的是明確的資訊，但是答案會改寫成較為廣義的敘述。▶ in the park

STEP 1 請確認本題的關鍵字為 in the park。

獨白中說道：「you could enjoy the annual music festival in Lexington Park」，提到你可以在公園享受年度音樂慶典，因此答案為 (C)。

→ 雖然獨白提到明確的資訊，但是選項通常會改寫成較為廣義的敘述。
the annual music festival → (C) musical performances

STEP 2 陷阱選項和錯誤選項

(A) A road repair ▶ 雖然獨白中有提到「road」，但與本題無關。
(B) A sports event ▶ 出現在最後一行，與本題無關。
(C) Musical performances ▶ 答案
(D) Some exhibitions

TEST 2 PART 4 中譯 & 解析

82 請先刪除與引號內字面意思相同的選項。

STEP 1 若選項使用與引號內相同的單字、或是字面意思相同的敘述時，通常不會是正確答案。

指定句前方說道：「Some of the roads in the city will likely be icy」，提到部分路段的地面結冰。而後又說道：「next Monday's traffic will not be affected」，提到不會影響到下週一的交通路況。由這兩段話可知指定句指的是會持續進行剷雪工作，不會影響到路況，因此答案為 (A) 不會導致交通壅塞。

STEP 2 陷阱選項和錯誤選項

(A) There will be no traffic congestion next week. ▶ 答案
(B) The temperature will be higher than expected. ▶ 聽到前半段的「warm」可能會誤選該選項。
(C) Some roads will be closed for clearing. ▶ 與指定句字面上的意思相同。
(D) Some of the residents will take a detour. ▶ 聽到「roads . . . be icy」可能會誤選該選項。

字彙 **news report** 新聞報導 **resident** 居民 **breeze** 微風 **annual** 年度、每年的 **unfortunately** 可惜、不幸 **heavy snow** 大雪 **remain** 繼續存在 **throughout** 從頭到尾 **road crew** 道路維修人員 **around the clock** 24 小時、日以繼夜 **affect** 影響

Questions 83-85 refer to the following excerpt from a meeting.

	All right. The last agenda item for the manager's monthly meeting is	84-D 83-A
83	the result of the marketing survey which was conducted last week.	83-B 83-C
	As summer is coming, it's time to introduce new ice cream flavors.	
	We recently developed yogurt ice cream with lime and asked a focus	
	group to review this new flavor. As you can see from this chart,	84-B
84	the result was generally favorable. We still need to add some more	
	sweetness to match the local tastes. Let's use the rest of the meeting	
	to come up with some ideas about new ingredients. However, this	
85	meeting room is reserved for the new-employee training in an hour, so	85-A 85-B
	we'll only be able to discuss this briefly.	

83. What happened last week?
(A) A summer ~~event~~ was discussed.
(B) A marketing ~~presentation~~ was made.
(C) A ~~performance evaluation~~ was conducted.
(D) Certain research was undertaken.

關鍵字 last week／前
→ 注意聆聽關鍵字和過去式句子。

84. What information is the speaker showing?
(A) Feedback from a focus group
(B) ~~Details~~ of a new ~~contract~~
(C) Reviews of the new ~~packaging~~
(D) ~~Updates~~ on ~~safety guidelines~~

說話者提供的資訊
→ 注意聆聽提到 As you see 或 This 的句子。

85. Why does the speaker say, "this meeting room is reserved for the new-employee training in an hour"? (A) To encourage employees to ~~attend the next meeting~~ (B) To ask for ~~permission to extend~~ the meeting (C) To require people to ~~leave the room~~ **(D) To ask for understanding**	**掌握說話者的意圖** → 注意聆聽指定句前後的文意。

第 83-85 題 會議摘錄

好，經理級月會的最後一個待議事項是上星期進行的行銷調查結果。由於夏季即將來臨，該推出新的冰淇淋口味了。我們最近研發出加了萊姆的優格冰淇淋，並找了焦點團體品評這種新口味。正如你們從這張曲線圖所見，結果是普遍受到喜愛。但我們仍需要再增加甜度，以符合本地口味。讓我們利用會議剩下的時間來想出一些新食材的點子。不過，這間會議室預定一小時後要進行新進人員訓練，所以，我們只能簡短討論。

83. 上星期發生了什麼事？
(A) 討論夏季的活動。
(B) 做了行銷簡報。
(C) 進行績效評估。
(D) 進行某項研究。

84. 說話者展示出什麼資料？
(A) 焦點團體的反應意見
(B) 一份新合約的細節
(C) 對新包裝的評論
(D) 安全指南的更新

85. 說話者為什麼說：「這間會議室預定一小時後要進行新進人員訓練」？
(A) 鼓勵員工參加下一場會議
(B) 請求准予延長會議
(C) 要求大家離開會議室
(D) 要求理解

83 題目針對過去提問時，答案會出現在前半段對話中。

STEP 1 **關鍵字 last week 指的是過去，因此請注意聆聽前半段獨白中的過去式句子。**

獨白中說道：「the marketing survey which was conducted last week」，提到上週完成了市場調查，因此答案為 (D)。

→ 雖然獨白提到明確的資訊，但是選項通常會改寫成較為廣義的敘述。
marketing survey → (D) certain research

STEP 2 **陷阱選項和錯誤選項**

(A) A summer event was discussed. ▶ 聽到「meeting」可能會聯想到「event」。
(B) A marketing presentation was made. ▶ 重複使用獨白中的「marketing」。
(C) A performance evaluation was conducted. ▶ 重複使用獨白中的「conduct」。
(D) Certain research was undertaken. ▶ 答案

84 雖然聽到的是明確的資訊，但是答案會改寫成較為廣義的敘述。

STEP 1 例如選項可能會將意思明確的單字 a report，改寫成較為廣義的通稱 document。

獨白中說道：「asked a focus group to review this new flavor. As you can see from this chart, . . . 」，提到要求特定群體給予評價，並告知結果為何。這表示說話者想要提供的資訊為針對特定群體的調查結果，因此答案為 (A)。

→ 雖然獨白提到明確的資訊，但是選項通常會改寫成較為廣義的敘述。
review this new ice cream → (A) feedback

STEP 2 陷阱選項和錯誤選項

(A) Feedback from a focus group ▶ 答案
(B) Details of a new contract ▶ 聽到「review」可能會聯想到「details」。
(C) Reviews of the new packaging ▶ 並非針對「new packaging」的評論。
(D) Updates on safety guidelines ▶ 聽到「agenda」可能會聯想到「guidelines」。

85 題目詢問引號內的說話者意圖時，請確認指定句前後方的連接詞。

STEP 1 題目詢問說話者意圖時，請務必確認指定句前後的連接詞。

題目詢問說話者意圖時，請確認指定句前後的文意，並找出答案。指定句前方說道：「Let's use the rest of the meeting to come up with some ideas about new ingredients.」，提到大家利用剩下的會議時間，想想新食材的點子。

指定句後方則說道：「so we'll only be able to discuss this briefly」，提到只能簡單討論一下。而指定句前方出現 however 表示轉折語氣，會連接意思相反的句子，所以指定句指的是請大家多多包涵一下，因此答案為 (D)。

STEP 2 陷阱選項和錯誤選項

(A) To encourage employees to attend the next meeting ▶ 重複使用獨白中的「meeting」。
(B) To ask for permission to extend the meeting ▶ 重複使用獨白中的「meeting」。
(C) To require people to leave the room ▶ 要求的事情為「discuss this briefly」。
(D) To ask for understanding ▶ 答案

字彙 survey 調查　conduct 進行　flavor 味道　favorable 討人喜歡的、贊同的
sweetness 甜味　come up with 想出、提供　ingredient 成份、材料
employee training 員工訓練　briefly 簡短地、短暫地

Questions 86-88 refer to the following introduction.

86 Welcome to the summer session of the Maxim Business Owners Program. I'm Patrick Marcus, the coordinator of this program. Our educational organization has been widely known for providing support, such as valuable advice and financial assistance to small business owners. Through today's program, you will have an opportunity to participate in social gatherings for small business owners and share some knowhow related to starting a business with other owners. Today, Katherine Cooper, who was one of the
87 recipients of our support last year, will make a presentation on how to market your business when facing fierce competition. Due to the time
88 limit, she will receive questions after her presentation. Now, let's give her a warm round of applause.

87-D

88-B 88-C

86. What is the purpose of the introduction?

(A) To ~~review~~ a series of lectures
(B) To introduce new machinery
(C) To request donations
(D) To describe a support program

介紹的目的／前
→ 前半段會提到目的或主旨。

87. According to the speaker, what is suggested about Ms. Cooper?

(A) She was given an ~~award~~ for her success.
(B) She has participated in the program before.
(C) She is one of the well-known authors.
(D) She ~~recently opened~~ her own business.

關鍵字 **Ms. Cooper**
→ 注意聆聽 she 開頭的句子。

88. Why does the speaker say, "She will receive questions after her presentation"?

(A) Not to interrupt during her talk
(B) Not to send her questions by e-mail
(C) To ask questions at any time
(D) To leave a question in advance

掌握說話者意圖
→ 注意聆聽指定句前後的文意。

TEST 2 PART 4 中譯&解析

第 86-88 題 介紹

歡迎參加梅克辛企業主課程夏季班。我是課程協調員派崔克·馬科斯。我們這家教育機構以對小企業主提供支援、如有用的建議和財務協助而廣為人知。透過今天的課程，你們有機會參加小企業主的社交聚會，並和其他企業主分享創業的實用知識與技能。今天，我們去年援助的受助者之一，凱薩琳·庫柏要簡報如何在面對激烈競爭下行銷你的企業。由於時間有限，她會在簡報後接受提問。現在，讓我們以熱烈的掌聲歡迎她。

86. 這段介紹的目的是什麼？
(A) 評論一系列的課程 (B) 介紹新的機械裝置
(C) 要求捐款 (D) 描述一個支援課程

87. 根據說話者，我們可以得知庫柏女士的什麼事？
(A) 她因為她的成就而獲獎。
(B) 她以前參加過這個課程。
(C) 她是一位知名作家。
(D) 她最近自己創業。

88. 說話者為什麼說：「她會在簡報後接受提問」？
(A) 不要打斷她的談話
(B) 不要以電子郵件寄問題給她
(C) 隨時可以問問題
(D) 事先提出問題

86 開頭前兩句話通常會提到主旨或目的。

STEP 1 **獨白中可能會出現「welcome＋特定活動」或「I'd like to＋獨白主旨」。**

獨白中說道：「Welcome to . . . Maxim Business Owners Program」和「Our educational organization has been widely known for providing support . . . to small business owners」，提到將舉行協助小型企業主的課程活動，因此答案為 (D)。動詞 describe 的意思為「描述、敘述」，請務必熟記。

STEP 2 **陷阱選項和錯誤選項**

(A) To review a series of lectures ▶ 並非給予課程評價。
(B) To introduce new machinery ▶ 並非介紹新的機器。
(C) To request donations
(D) To describe a support program ▶ 答案

87 獨白中提及討論會或研討會時，會在人名後方介紹職業和經歷。
▶ Ms. Cooper

STEP 1 **若題目中出現特定的關鍵字，聆聽獨白時，勢必會於該關鍵字前後聽到答案。**

本題的關鍵字為 Ms. Cooper。獨白中說道：「Katherine Cooper, who was one of the recipients fo our support last year, will make a presentation」，提到接下來要演講的女子為去年獲得支援的人之一，因此答案為 (B)。

STEP 2 **陷阱選項和錯誤選項**

(A) She was given an award for her success. ▶ 並未提到她得過獎。
(B) She has participated in the program before. ▶ 答案
(C) She is one of the well-known authors.
(D) She recently opened her own business. ▶ 並未提到她最近展開了新事業。

88 請先刪除與引號內字面意思相同的選項。

STEP 1 **若選項使用與引號內相同的單字、或是字面意思相同的敘述時，通常不會是正確答案。**

指定句前方說道：「Due to the time limit」，提到原因為時間有限，由此可推測出後方指定句想表達的是不希望演講中途被打斷，因此答案為 (A)。

STEP 2 **陷阱選項和錯誤選項**

(A) Not to interrupt during her talk ▶ 答案
(B) Not to send her questions by email
▶「send her questions」與「receive questions」的意思相同。
(C) To ask questions at any time ▶「ask questions」與「receive questions」的意思相同。
(D) To leave a question in advance

字彙 summer session 夏季班　coordinator 協調人　valuable 有用的、有價值的
financial assistance 財務協助　social gatherings 社交聚會
knowhow 實用的知識與技能　recipient 接受者　market 行銷　fierce 激烈的
due to 由於　applause 鼓掌

Questions 89-91 refer to the following news report and weather forecast.

89 Welcome back! Next is the latest update about the Fifth Annual Easy Home Cook-Off. We've been waiting since last year for this event, which will be held outside at the national park. The Cook-Off always attracts a lot of participants. All of the competitors are asked to bring a single homemade dish. A panel of famous chefs will select the winner based on taste, presentation, and uniqueness. This is a great opportunity to spend time with your children. You can bring the whole family, and entry and
90 food samples are free. For those interested in participating, the contest registration form is available on the community Web site. We're expecting
91 rain the day before, but you won't need an umbrella on the day of. I hope to see all of you there.

89-C 89-B 90-C 90-A 90-B

Saturday	Sunday	Monday	Tuesday
Partly Sunny	Cloudy	Rain	Sunny

89. What event is being described?
(A) A technology fair　(B) A national festival
(C) A cooking show　**(D) A food contest**

主旨／前
→ 開頭前兩句話通常會提到主旨。

90. According to the speaker, what can the listeners find on the Web site?
(A) A schedule for the contest　(B) A weather report
(C) A food sample　**(D) An entry form**

關鍵字 Web site
→ 注意聆聽關鍵字前後的句子。

91. Look at the graphic. Which day is the event being held?
(A) Saturday　(B) Sunday
(C) Monday　**(D) Tuesday**

圖表資訊／星期／後
→ 注意聆聽表示轉折語氣的 But 和 However。

第 89-91 題　新聞報導與氣象預報

歡迎回來！接下來是第五屆年度輕鬆家庭烹飪比賽的最新消息。我們從去年就在等待的這個活動，將在國家公園外舉行。這個烹飪比賽總是吸引許多人參加，所有的參賽者都要帶一道自製的菜餚來。由知名主廚組成的評審小組將根據味道、外觀和獨特性選出優勝者。這是一個和你的孩子相處的好機會。你可以把全家人都帶來，報名及試吃都免費。有興趣參加的人，社區網站上有比賽的報名表。我們預料前一天會下雨，但當天不需要帶傘。我希望可以在那裡見到你們大家。

星期六	星期日	星期一	星期二
晴時多雲	多雲	雨	晴

89. 獨白中描述的是什麼活動？
(A) 科技展　(B) 國定假日
(C) 烹飪節目　(D) 料理比賽

90. 根據說話者，聽眾可以在網站上找到什麼？
(A) 比賽的時程表　(B) 氣象報告
(C) 試吃品　(D) 報名表

91. 請見圖表，活動在哪一天舉行？
(A) 星期六　(B) 星期日
(C) 星期一　(D) 星期二

89 前半段獨白中，會提到廣播的主題。

STEP 1 第一句話的 about 後方會帶出主旨，請特別注意。

獨白中說道：「 . . . the latest update about the Fifth Annual Easy Home Cook-Off」，後方提到「competitors」，表示談論的內容與料理大賽有關，因此答案為 (D)。

STEP 2 陷阱選項和錯誤選項

(A) A new technology fair
(B) A national festival ▶ 聽到「national park」可能會誤選該選項，但是並非 festival。
(C) A cooking show ▶ 重複使用獨白中的「cook」。由「competitors」可以得知該選項有誤。
(D) A food contest ▶ 答案

90 題目中出現關鍵字時，答案會在該關鍵字前後的句子。▶ Web site

STEP 1 題目針對 Web site 提問時，後半段獨白中，通常會出現表示原因或方法的句子。

由「contest registration form / available / Web site」可以得知報名方式，因此答案為 (D)。
→ 雖然獨白提到明確的資訊，但是選項通常會改寫成較為廣義的敘述。
contest registration form → (D) An entry form

STEP 2 陷阱選項和錯誤選項

(A) A schedule for the contest ▶ 獨白中並未提到「schedule」。
(B) A weather report ▶ 聽到「umbrella」可能會聯想到「weather」。
(C) A food sample ▶ 雖然獨白中有提到，但與本題內容無關。
(D) An entry form ▶ 答案

91 圖表題選項 (A)–(D) 的內容不會直接出現在獨白當中。

STEP 1 選項列出星期，因此聆聽獨白時，請確認圖表中星期以外的內容。

請聽清楚表示天氣的單字。獨白中說道：「 . . . rain the day before, but you won't need an umbrella on the day of」，提到前一天下雨，而下過雨的隔天為 (D) Tuesday，故為正確答案。But / However 為表示轉折語氣的單字，後方會出現關鍵的答題線索，請特別留意！

字彙 **attract** 吸引 **participant** 參加者 **uniqueness** 獨特性 **entry** 進入、參加 **registration** 登記、註冊 **expect** 預料、預期

Questions 92-94 refer to the following advertisement and list.

Tidlis Furniture is celebrating its 10th anniversary and we are having a big sale. All kinds of chairs are on sale for up to 30% off the original price. Plus, if you sign up for membership, you can get an additional 10% off for items manufactured by **Duke**. Don't worry about complicated furniture assembly. All our customers are satisfied with that we can deliver it as a finished product to your home and office. To place an order and get a list of our various products, visit our Web site at www.tidlisfurniture.com. This amazing offer lasts until October 24.

92 (price. Plus, if you sign up for membership…) 93 (that we can deliver it…) 94 (To place an order…)

93-A 94-A 93-B 93-D 94-C

Item name	Manufacturer
Kids chair	Jerry
Home chair	Kahn
Office chair	Duke
Premium office chair	Raon

92. Look at the graphic. If you are a member, what chair can you purchase at an additional discounted price?
(A) Kids chair
(B) Home chair
(C) Office chair
(D) Premium office chair

圖表資訊／member／additional discounted／前
→ 注意聆聽第一句話和提到 you 的句子。

93. According to the speaker, why do customers like Tidlis Furniture?
(A) It offers reasonable prices.
(B) Its products ~~are easy to assemble~~.
(C) It provides a complete product.
(D) There is no delivery ~~charge~~.

關鍵字 customers／like
→ 注意聆聽關鍵字的前後方。

94. What can be found on the Web site?
(A) A special offer
(B) A list of products
(C) A coupon
(D) Contact information

關鍵字 Web site／後
→ 注意聆聽關鍵字前後方的內容。

第 92-94 題 廣告與表單

堤得里斯家具慶祝十週年舉行大拍賣。所有的椅子廉價出售，最高折扣為原價的七折。此外，若加入會員，杜克的全品項產品還可以再打九折。別擔心複雜的家具組裝問題。我們所有的顧客都相當滿意，因為我們可以把組裝好的成品送到您的家中和辦公室。想要訂購並檢視我們各種產品的清單，請上我們的網站：www.tidlisfurniture.com。這項令人驚喜的優惠價格將持續到 10 月 24 日。

產品名稱	製造商
童椅	傑瑞
家居椅	卡恩
辦公椅	杜克
優質辦公椅	隆恩

92. 請見圖表，如果你是會員，哪種椅子買了可以再打折？

(A) 兒童椅 (B) 家居椅
(C) 辦公椅 (D) 優質辦公椅

93. 根據說話者，消費者為什麼喜歡堤得里斯家具？

(A) 價格合理。 (B) 產品容易組裝。
(C) 供應成品。 (D) 不收運費。

94. 在網站上可以找到什麼？

(A) 特別優惠 (B) 產品清單
(C) 優惠券 (D) 聯絡資料

92 圖表題選項 (A)–(D) 的內容不會直接出現在獨白當中。

STEP 1 選項列出產品，因此聆聽獨白時，請確認圖表中產品以外的內容，也就是注意提及製造業者的片段。

獨白中說道：「if you sign up for membership, you can get an additional 10% off for items manufactured by Duke」，提到如果加入會員，購買 Duke 公司產品，就能額外獲得九折的優惠，因此答案為 Duke 公司製造的產品 (C) Office chair。

93 題目以 why 詢問時，獨白會重複使用題目句的內容並於後方提及原因。

STEP 1 聆聽獨白時，請仔細聆聽 why 後方的關鍵字，其後方將會出現答案。若題目以關鍵字詢問原因或理由時，該關鍵字指的通常是結果，因此請確認獨白中是否出現選項列出的原因。

本題的關鍵字為 customers，獨白中說道：「our customers are satisfied」，表示客人都很滿意。後方又說道：「we can deliver it as a finished product to your home and office」，提到可以將成品運送至家中或辦公室，因此答案為 (C)。選項將獨白中的 finished product 改寫成 complete product。

STEP 2 陷阱選項和錯誤選項

(A) It offers reasonable prices. ▶ 聽到「big sale」可能會誤選該選項。

(B) Its products are easy to assemble.

▶ 雖然獨白中有提到「assembly」，但是該敘述並不符合「we can deliver it as a finished product」，因此不能作為答案。聽到「deliver」可能會聯想到「delivery」。

(C) It provides a complete product. ▶ 答案

(D) There is no delivery charge. ▶

94 題目中出現關鍵字時，答案會在該關鍵字前後的句子。▶ Web site

STEP 1 **後半段獨白中，Web site 通常會和表示目的或方法的句子一同出現。**

關鍵字 Web site 前方說道：「To place . . . product」，提到進入 Web site 的目的，由 Web site 可以找出答案為 (B)。

STEP 2 **陷阱選項和錯誤選項**

(A) A special offer ▶ 聽到「big sale」可能會誤選該選項。

(B) A list of products ▶ 答案

(C) A coupon ▶ 聽到「Web site」可能會誤選該選項。

(D) Contact information

字彙 celebrate 慶祝　anniversary 週年紀念（日）　up to 接近於、最多
original 最初的、本來的　manufacture 製造　complicated 複雜的　assembly 組裝
be satisfied with 對……感到滿意　place an order 訂購　various 各種各樣的、不同的
last 持續

Questions 95-97 refer to the following talk and diagram.

Welcome to Del Bone China. I'm Paul Sanders from Public Relations. I'll be leading your tour today and show you how we produce Del Bone China's dishware. Before entering the factory, you'll watch a video which shows the basic production process which includes choosing soils, working the clay, making various figurations, and drying the pottery. Then, you'll visit the factory and watch the remainder of the process. This will also give you an opportunity to experience ceramic making firsthand. You can draw your own design, then we will bake and glaze them, and you'll receive them at the end of the tour as souvenirs. Because all areas contain some proprietary information, photography is prohibited, so please turn off your mobile phones. Now, let's move to the Audiovisual Room to watch the video.

95 (line 3) 96 (line 9) 97 (line 10)

95-D

97-A, C

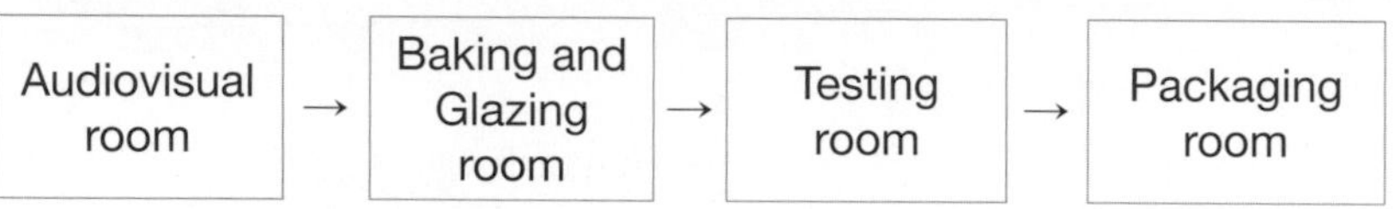

95. Where is the talk taking place?
(A) At an art museum **(B) At a factory**
(C) At a retail store (D) At a ~~travel agency~~

96. Look at the graphic. Where will the listeners get souvenirs?
(A) Audiovisual room (B) Baking and Glazing room
(C) Testing room **(D) Packaging room**

97. Why should the listeners turn off their mobile phone?
(A) They will likely ~~break~~.
(B) The system is likely to be affected.
(C) The area needs to stay ~~silent~~.
(D) Some information needs to be kept confidential.

地點／前
→ 第一句話通常會談到職業或地點。

圖表資訊／關鍵字 souvenirs
→ 注意聆聽關鍵字前後的內容。

要求／後／關鍵字 mobile phone
→ 注意聆聽後半段提及 please 或 you should 的句子。

第 95-97 題 談話與圖表

歡迎來到德爾骨瓷，我是公關部的保羅·桑德斯。今天由我帶各位參觀，並展示我們如何製作德爾骨瓷的餐具。在進入工廠之前，你們會先觀看一段影片，播放基本的製作過程，包括選擇土壤、黏土塑形、做出不同形狀，然後燒乾陶器。然後，你們會參觀工廠，觀看剩下的過程。這也帶給你們第一手體驗瓷器製作的機會。你們可以畫出自己的設計圖，然後我們會把它們燒乾並上釉，你們會在導覽結束時，拿到它們當紀念品。因為所有的區域都含有機密資訊，因此禁止拍照，所以，請關閉你們的行動電話。現在，讓我們前往視聽室觀賞影片。

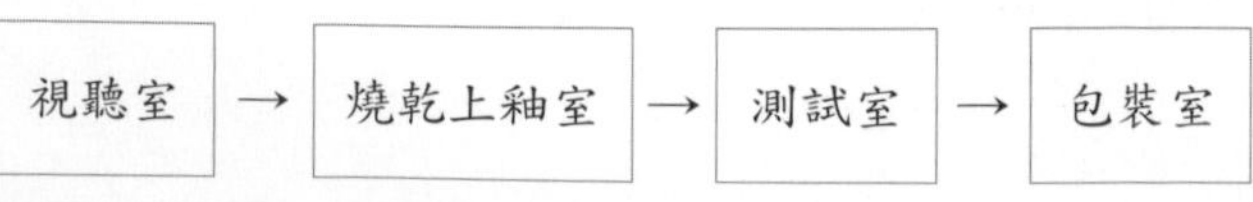

95. 這段話發生在哪裡？
(A) 在美術館 (B) 在工廠
(C) 在零售商店 (D) 在旅行社

96. 請見圖表，聽眾會在哪裡拿到紀念品？
(A) 視聽室 (B) 燒乾上釉室
(C) 測試室 (D) 包裝室

97. 為什麼聽眾應該關閉他們的行動電話？
(A) 他們很可能會弄壞。
(B) 系統可能會受影響。
(C) 廠區必須保持安靜。
(D) 有些資訊必須保密。

95 前兩句話會以代名詞（I / You / We）或地方副詞（here / this＋地點名詞）告知職業或地點。▶ 獨白地點

STEP 1 **獨白會按照主題，採固定方式表達職業或地點，請務必熟記。前兩句話會聽到 our / your / this / here 加上表示地點或職業的名詞。**

本題詢問本篇獨白發生的地點，因此請務必確認第一句話。獨白中說道：「Welcome to Del Bone China」，提到公司名稱。而後說道：「I'll be leading your tour today」，表示今天將由我為各位解說。後方又說道：「Before entering the factory」，表示本篇獨白與參觀工廠有關，因此地點在工廠 (B) At a factory。

STEP 2 **陷阱選項和錯誤選項**

(A) At an art museum
(B) At a factory ▶ 答案
(C) At a retail store
(D) At a travel agency ▶ 聽到「tour」可能會聯想到「travel」。

96 圖表題選項 (A)–(D) 的內容不會直接出現在獨白當中。

STEP 1 **圖表題詢問地點時，務必要聽清楚介系詞。**

說明「tour」時，有提到「souvenirs」。獨白中說道：「you'll receive them at the end of the tour as souvenirs」，可以對應至圖表的參觀順序。表示聽者會歷經畫畫、燒窯、上釉的過程，接著在最後（at the end of the tour）會收到陶瓷品作為紀念品，因此答案為最後一個地方 (D) Packaging room。

97 題目以 why 詢問時，獨白會重複使用題目句的內容並於後方提及原因。

STEP 1 **聆聽獨白時，請仔細聆聽 why 後方的關鍵字，其後方將會出現答案。**

Why 後方的關鍵字為 turn off 和 mobile phone，表示本題詢問的是禁止使用手機的原因。獨白中說道：「Because all areas contain some proprietary information, photography is prohibited」，提到特定產品牽涉到專利問題，禁止拍攝照片，因此答案為 (D)。

→ 雖然獨白提到明確的資訊，但是選項通常會改寫成較為廣義的敘述。
proprietary → (D) confidential

STEP 2 **陷阱選項和錯誤選項**

(A) They will likely break. ▶ 聽到「mobile phone」可能會誤選該選項。
(B) The system is likely to be affected.
(C) The area needs to stay silent. ▶ 聽到「mobile phone」可能會誤選該選項。
(D) The information needs to be kept confidential. ▶ 答案

字彙 bone china 骨瓷　public relations 公共關係　dishware 餐具　soil 土壤
work the clay 黏土塑形　figuration 形狀　remainder 剩餘部分
firsthand 第一手的、直接的　glaze 給……上釉　souvenir 紀念品　proprietary 專有的
photography 拍照　prohibit 禁止　audiovisual room 視聽室

Questions 98-100 refer to the following instructions and floor plan.

As you may know, we've received some complaints from the Sales
98 Department. They want to expedite the order process, especially
during weekends, so, today, we'll discuss the reorganization of our
warehouse. As usual, each of you spends eight minutes locating
and packing the goods you need. But if we add some shelving units
99 between the order station and employee lounge, I think we'll be
able to save some time, and that's what everyone has requested.
Now, I'd like to ask some of you to work a few extra hours today. If
100 you're willing to volunteer for this, please come by my office after this
meeting.

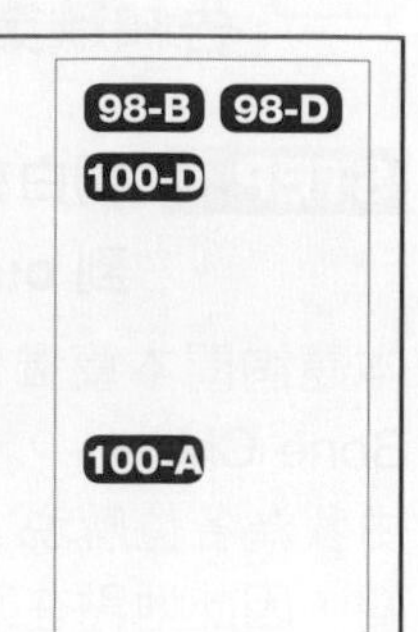

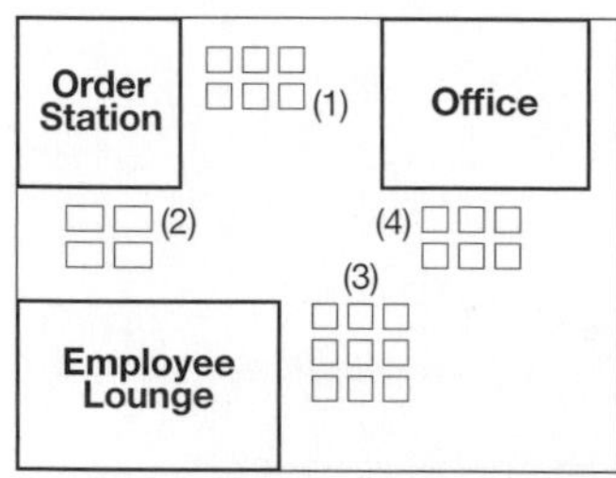

98. Why is the change being made?
(A) To address complaints ~~from customers~~
(B) To get more ~~feedback~~
(C) To improve the order fulfillment process
(D) To check for ~~errors~~

變動事項／前
→ 注意聆聽前半段的現在式句子。

99. Look at the graphic. Where is the place being described?
(A) Area 1
(B) Area 2
(C) Area 3
(D) Area 4

圖表資訊／ the place
→ 注意聆聽圖表中選項以外的資訊。

100. Where should the interested listeners go?
(A) To the ~~employee lounge~~
(B) To the office
(C) To the meeting room
(D) To the ~~Sales Department~~

interested 聽者／要求／後／地點
→ 注意聆聽後半段提及 please 或 you should 的句子。

第 98-100 題 指示與樓層平面圖

你們可能已經知道，我們收到業務部的抱怨。他們想要加快訂貨的流程，尤其是在週末的時候，因此，我們今天要討論倉儲區的改造。依照慣例，你們每個人會花八分鐘找出你們所需的商品裝箱。但是，如果我們在訂購台和員工休息區中間加一些層架，我想，我們就能節省一些時間，而那就是大家的要求。現在，我想要求你們一些人今天加班幾個小時。如果你們願意自願加班，請在會議後到我辦公室來。

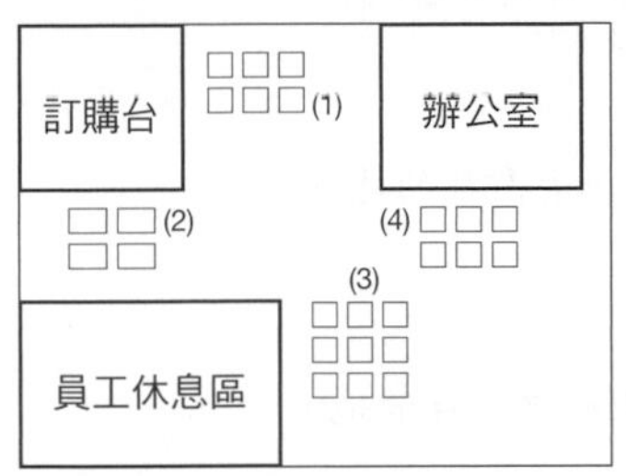

98. 為什麼要做改變？
(A) 為了處理顧客的投訴
(B) 為了得到更多意見回饋
(C) 為了改善完成訂單的流程
(D) 為了檢查錯誤

99. 請見圖表，文中描述的是哪個地方？
(A) 第一區　(B) 第二區
(C) 第三區　(D) 第四區

100. 感興趣的聽眾要到哪裡去？
(A) 員工休息區　(B) 辦公室
(C) 會議室　(D) 業務部

98 題目詢問變動事項時，請注意聆聽前半段獨白中的過去式句子。

STEP 1 前半段獨白的過去式句子，會帶出問題點和變動的原因。

本題詢問產生變動的原因。獨白中說道：「we've received some complaints from the Sales Department. They want to expedite the order process」，提到收到業務部門抱怨訂單處理速度不夠迅速。又說道：「we'll discuss the reorganization of our warehouse」，表示將討論重新整頓倉庫一事，以解決此問題。由此可知為了加快訂單處理速度，才會產生變動，因此答案為 (C) To improve the order fulfillment process。

STEP 2 陷阱選項和錯誤選項

(A) To address complaints from customers ▶「complaints」並非主旨。
(B) To get more feedback ▶ 聽到「complaints」可能會聯想到「feedbacks」。
(C) To improve the order fulfillment process ▶ 答案
(D) To check for errors ▶ 聽到「complaints」可能會聯想到「errors」。

99 圖表題選項 (A)–(D) 的內容不會直接出現在獨白當中。

STEP 1 獨白中不會提及選項列出的區域，因此請確認其他部分來找出答案，也就是要聆聽確切的地點或修飾語。

獨白中說道：「if we add some shelving units between the order station and employee lounge」，提到為了解決問題，要在訂購區和員工休息室之間裝設架子，因此答案為 (B)。

→ But / However 為表示轉折語氣的單字，後方會出現關鍵的答題線索，請特別留意！

100 題目詢問要求或建議時，答案會位在後半段獨白中，並以 please 告知。

STEP 1 **PART 4 中詢問要求或建議時，指的是說話者（speaker）向聽者（listeners）要求的事情，因此答題線索會出現在後半段獨白中。當中經常會使用 If you 或 please 來表達建議的內容，請務必熟記。**

後半段獨白中說道：「If you're willing to volunteer for this, please come by my office」，請願意協助的人到說話者的辦公室，因此請聽者去的地方為 (B) To the office。

STEP 2 **陷阱選項和錯誤選項**

(A) To the employee lounge ▶ 雖然獨白中有提到，但並非說話者要求聽者前往的地方。
(B) To the office ▶ 答案
(C) To the meeting room
(D) To the Sales Department ▶ 雖然獨白中有提到，但並非說話者要求聽者前往的地方。

字彙 complaint 抱怨、投訴　sales department 業務部　expedite 加快、促進
reorganization 改造、重新安排　warehouse 倉庫　as usual 照常、按慣例
locate 找出……的位置　goods 商品　shelving unit 層架　order station 訂購站
employee lounge 員工休息區　volunteer 自願做……　come by 拜訪

PART 5

101 HSBC Bank / is not / responsible (for any ---------) (arising out of the use of a local
主詞 動詞 補語 介系詞片語 (分詞：修飾空格)
Internet service provider or caused by any browser software) (during an online
(介系詞片語)
transaction or electronic transfer).

介系詞後方要連接名詞。
for any + --------

STEP 1 **空格為介系詞 for 的受詞，且受到形容詞 any 的修飾，因此要填入名詞。**

選項中，(C) lose 為動詞、(D) lost 為分詞，因此皆不能作為答案。

STEP 2 **原則上會以原本的詞性為優先：名詞 > 動名詞（V-ing）**

空格要填入名詞，而選項同時出現動名詞和名詞時，原則上會以原本詞性為優先，因此要選名詞作為答案 (A) losses（損失）。

STEP 3 **例外情形：要選擇 V-ing 作為答案的題型**

由名詞加上 ing 變成動名詞（視為名詞）	一般動名詞（現在分詞）（保留動名詞的特色）
❶ 本身沒有名詞，以動名詞代替名詞。	❶ 動詞連接動名詞作為受詞 例 consider（考量）、avoid（避免）
❷ 名詞本身為 ing 形態 例 planning（計畫）、pricing（定價）	❷「介系詞＋動名詞」的慣用語 例 be committed to V-ing（致力於……）
❸ 複合名詞 例 accounting department（會計部門）	❸ 表示一個動作，並非指人事物等對象。

句子翻譯 匯豐銀行對於在進行線上交易或電子金融轉帳時，因使用當地網路服務所引發、或任何瀏覽器所造成的損失，概不負責。

字彙 be responsible for 對……負責 electronic transfer 電子金融轉帳

答案 (A) losses

102 --------- / is retiring (at the end of the year), / so / the chance (that a position will open)
主詞 1 動詞 1 連接詞 主詞 2（以名詞子句作為同位語）
/ is minimal.
動詞 2

確認填入主詞位置的名詞和後方動詞是否符合單複數的一致性。
-------- + is retiring

STEP 1 **確認填入主詞位置的名詞和後方動詞是否符合單複數的一致性。**

(C) Any other 為形容詞，不能作為答案。動詞 is 為單數，而 (A) Few 要連接複數動詞，因此也不適合填入空格中。

STEP 2 **anyone 用於肯定句時，意思為「無論哪個人」。**

(B) No one 和 (D) Anyone 皆為單數，若根據文法規則，皆能填入空格中。但是要注意的是 No one 要用於否定句，Anyone 則會用於肯定句，因此請找出適合搭配 so 後方內容的選項。「所以空出新職缺的機率很低」當中使用 minimal，搭配「沒有人要退休」較為適當，因此要選表示否定的 (B) No one。

句子翻譯 年底沒有人退休，因此，有職缺的機會極微小。
字彙 retire 退休 minimal 極微的、最小的
答案 (B) No one

103 Only qualified researchers / will be granted / --------- (for the use of secondary data) (obtained from the National Health Service).
主詞 / 動詞 / 受詞 / 介系詞片語
（分詞：修飾名詞 data）

授與動詞的被動語態後方可以連接另一個受詞。
will be granted + -------- + （介系詞片語）

STEP 1 請務必記下「主要動詞的數量＝連接詞數量＋ 1」這道公式。

選項中，(A) 和 (B) 都屬於主要動詞，因此請先確認本句話中主要動詞和連接詞的數量。句中有主要動詞 will be granted，但並未出現連接詞，因此 (A) permit 和 (B) is permitted 皆不能作為答案。

STEP 2 考題中會出現的授與動詞有「給予」動詞、award 和 grant。

動詞 grant 屬於授與動詞，其被動語態有以下兩種用法：

★「grant ＋人物（researchers）＋事物（permission）」的被動語態

❶ 人物（researchers）＋ will be granted ＋事物（permission）

❷ 事物（permission）＋ will be granted ＋人物（researchers）

本句的主詞為人物，因此 will be granted 後方要連接表示事物的名詞，答案為 (D) permission。

句子翻譯 只有符合資格的研究人員，才會獲准使用取自國民保健制度的次級資料。
字彙 qualified 有資格的、合格的 obtain 獲得
答案 (D) permission

104 A bunch of customers / have complained / that / there is / an --------- rattling noise (coming from the front driver's side) / once / the window / is down.
主詞 1 / 動詞 1 / 連接詞 / 動詞 2 / 主詞 2
形容詞片語 / 連接詞 / 主詞 3 / 動詞 3

不能使用副詞修飾分類形容詞。
an -------- rattling noise

STEP 1 冠詞＋副詞＋一般形容詞＋名詞 vs. 冠詞＋形容詞＋分類形容詞＋名詞

空格位在冠詞和名詞之間，而 (D) annoy 為原形動詞，不適合填入空格中。一般來說，會把副詞加在形容詞前方，但是 rattling 這個形容詞指的是 noise（噪音）的類型，「rattling noise」可以當作複合名詞，指汽車發出的聲響。這表示空格修飾的對象並非 rattling，而是要填入形容詞，修飾名詞 noise。

STEP 2 情緒動詞以過去分詞修飾人物、以現在分詞（V-ing）修飾事物。

annoy 為情緒動詞，根據修飾對象的不同，要搭配不同的分詞。而本題空格修飾的名詞 noise 為事物，因此答案要選 (A) annoying。

STEP 3 情緒動詞必背 list

please/delight 使高興 amuse 逗……高興 satisfy 使滿意 disappoint 使失望 depress 使沮喪	excite/interest 使興奮 charm 使陶醉 fascinate/attract 迷住、有吸引力 exhaust 使精疲力盡 confuse 使困惑

句子翻譯 一群顧客抱怨，窗戶一降下來，前排駕駛座側邊就傳出惱人的嘎嘎聲。

字彙 a bunch of 一群　window is down 窗戶降下來

答案 (A) annoying

105 Women / account for / half of the world's population / and / represent /
主詞 1　動詞 1　受詞 1　連接詞 1　動詞 2
the --------- purchasing decision makers, / so / even cosmetic brands
受詞 2　連接詞 2　主詞 3
(for men) / need to appeal to / both the targeted men and their wives.
動詞 3　受詞 3

the 後方不會連接數量形容詞。
冠詞 (the) + -------- + 名詞 (purchasing decision makers)

STEP 1 冠詞和名詞之間要填入形容詞。

空格用來修飾名詞 purchasing decision makers（購買決策者），因此要填入形容詞。而 (B) plenty 為名詞，因此不能作為答案；(A) most 為數量形容詞，雖然後方可以連接複數名詞，但是不能放在冠詞後方，因此也不適合填入空格中；(C) certain 放在名詞前方作修飾時，指可以確信的人事物，前方不能加上定冠詞 the。綜合上述，答案要選 (D) primary（首要、主要的）。

STEP 2 most 的四大出題重點

❶ the most ＋形容詞／副詞：最高級
❷ the most ＋名詞：many、much 的最高級
❸ 不定代名詞：most of ＋特定名詞
❹ 一般形容詞：most ＋名詞「大多數的」

句子翻譯 女性佔世界人口的一半，而且是主要的購物決策者，因此，即使是男性化妝品品牌，也需要吸引所針對的男性顧客及他們的太太。

字彙 account for （在數量上）佔　appeal to 對……有吸引力、受……歡迎

答案 (D) primary

106 (--------- her consistent efforts, achievements, and a higher-educational background),
介系詞片語
Jade / will rapidly move up / (from an entry-level position to the marketing manager
主詞　動詞　介系詞片語
within five years).

由後方連接的名詞選出適當的介系詞。　**-------- her consistent efforts**

STEP 1 由後方連接的名詞選出適當的介系詞。

空格要填入適當的介系詞，搭配後方名詞，並扮演副詞的角色。請特別留意，要由介系詞後方的名詞來判斷適合搭配的介系詞，而空格後方的名詞為 efforts。

STEP 2

(A) Since 為介系詞，要搭配表示過去時間點的名詞；(C) Among 要連接複數名詞；(D) Upon 的意思為「在……後立即」，表示時間的概念，因此不適合作為答案。本題答案要選 (B) Given，意思為「考慮到……」。看到 given 時，很容易把它當成過去分詞，但是它也可以作為介系詞和連接詞，請務必熟記。

STEP 3 值得留意的分詞介系詞

• following 在……以後 • including 包括 • excluding 除……之外	• notwithstanding 儘管 • regarding/concerning 關於 • barring 除……之外	• pending 在……期間 • given/considering 考慮到 • beginning/starting 開始

句子翻譯 考量到她的不斷努力、成就和較高的學歷背景，潔德會在 5 年內，很快從基層的職位升到行銷部經理。

字彙 consistent 一貫的、始終如一的 move up 晉升 entry-level 入門的、初級的

答案 (B) Given

107 (--------- found in his field), Chester Guzman's vast knowledge (of international trade) / gives / him / a unique perspective and a great reputation.

分詞構句 / 主詞 / 形容詞片語 / 動詞 / 間接受詞 / 直接受詞

分詞構句前方可以放置連接詞或副詞。

-------- + p.p. (found) + 介系詞片語 (in his field), + 完整句

STEP 1 分詞構句前方可以放置從屬連接詞或副詞。

空格後方連接以過去分詞 found 開頭的分詞構句，因此空格可以填入從屬連接詞或副詞。(A) Less 適合搭配形容詞或副詞，表示比較級，因此不能作為答案；(B) Enough 當作副詞使用時，要放在形容詞或副詞的後方作修飾，因此也不適合作為答案；(C) Apart 為副詞，意思為「分開、相隔地」，會放在句尾或是動詞後方，因此也不正確。綜合上述，答案要選 (D) Seldom。

STEP 2 頻率副詞要放在助動詞後方、主要動詞前方。

原本的句子為「連接詞＋ it was ＋ seldom ＋ found in his field」，再改寫成分詞構句，因此請確認頻率副詞擺放的位置。

句子翻譯 切斯特．古茲曼擁有在他的領域裡少有的淵博國際貿易知識，使他擁有獨特的觀點和極佳的聲譽。

字彙 seldom found 很少發現 vast 龐大的 perspective 觀點、看法

答案 (D) Seldom

108 --------- / the following location / not work best (for you), notify / one of our managers / so / alternative arrangements / can be made.

主詞 1 / 動詞 1 / 介系詞片語 / 動詞 2 / 受詞 / 連接詞 / 主詞 3 / 動詞 3

連接詞後方要連接主詞＋動詞。

-------- + 名詞 + not + 原形動詞

STEP 1 「主要動詞的數量＝連接詞數量＋ 1」

若選項中出現連接詞時，請先確認句中主要動詞和連接詞的數量。本句話中有三個主要動詞 work、notify、can be made 和一個連接詞 so，因此空格要再填入一個連接詞。

STEP 2 單數主詞＋原形動詞 -s / -es。

主詞 location 為單數，後方要連接「原形動詞 -s / -es」，但是請注意到後方連接的是原形動詞 work，這表示空格不能填入 (A) When 和 (B) If 這兩個連接詞。

STEP 3 使用假設語氣，表示對未來的懷疑時，若省略 if，句子的結構會變成「should ＋名詞＋原形動詞」。

原本的句子為「If the following location should not work best for you」，屬於假設語氣中對未來的懷疑。若省略 if，則會形成倒裝句，因此答案為 (D) Should。(C) As well as 不能放在句首。

★省略 if 後倒裝

對未來的懷疑：If ＋主詞＋ should ＋原形動詞→ Should ＋主詞＋原形動詞
與現在事實相反：If ＋主詞＋過去動詞→ Did ＋主詞＋原形動詞
與過去事實相反：If ＋主詞＋ had p.p. → Had ＋主詞＋ p.p.

句子翻譯 萬一以下的地點對你都不方便，請通知我們的任一位經理，好另做其他安排。
字彙 work 適用、行得通　notify 告知　alternative arrangement 替代安排
答案 (D) Should

109 Southland / will host / the Global Trading Forum (next year), / although /
主詞 1　動詞 1　受詞　時間副詞片語　連接詞
it / has --------- alternated (between Otago and Cantebury).
主詞 2　動詞 2　介系詞片語

以 although 表達與期待相反的事。
完整句 , although + 主詞 + has -------- + alternated

STEP 1 題目為副詞詞彙題時，請先確認副詞後方修飾的對象。

選項皆為副詞，且空格後方為 alternated，因此要選出適合修飾它的副詞。(C) nearly 要修飾「完整的、已完成的對象」，因此不適合作為答案。

STEP 2 句中出現 although 表示與期待相反的事，因此請先確認後方連接的子句。

連接詞 although 的意思為「儘管……」，表示主要子句和從屬子句兩者為相反或對比的關係。主要子句為「特定區域＋ will host」，而 although 後方連接詞的子句為「has alternated ＋特定地點」，因此這句話要表達的是「雖然現在在特定地點舉行，但是之後將換到其他地點」。這表示空格要填入副詞，描述到目前為止發生的事。選項中只有 (A) traditionally 符合，意思為「傳統上」。

STEP 3 意思相反的副詞組合

positively（正面地）vs. negatively（負面地）
exceptionally（例外地）vs. generally（一般地）

句子翻譯 雖然傳統上一直由奧塔哥和坎特伯里兩地輪流主辦，但明年的全球貿易論壇將換由塞斯蘭主辦。
字彙 alternate 交替、輪流
答案 (A) traditionally

110 Holiday Inn / has --------- / (from a single motel to a multi-national hotel franchise)
主詞 動詞 介系詞片語
(with well over 400 locations in operation worldwide).
介系詞片語

has p.p. 為主動語態。
has + -------- + 介系詞片語

STEP 1 不及物動詞＋介系詞片語

空格位在主動語態 has p.p. 的位置，且後方直接連接介系詞片語，因此要選出不及物動詞作為答案。選項中，(A) planned、(B) established 和 (C) furthered 皆為及物動詞，皆不能作為答案，因此答案要選不及物動詞 (D) evolved。

STEP 2 值得留意的不及物動詞

merge 合併	register、sign up 註冊、登記
proceed 繼續進行	emerge 出現、顯露
reply、respond 回覆、回應	comply（對要求、命令等）依從

句子翻譯 假日飯店從一家汽車旅館，逐步發展為在全世界超過 400 個地方營運的跨國連鎖飯店。
字彙 multi-national 跨國的 in operation 營運 plan 計劃、規劃 further 進一步
evolve 逐步形成、發展
答案 (D) evolved

111 Now that / our technical support team / has taken / all the necessary steps, we /
連接詞 1 主詞 1 動詞 1 受詞 1 主詞 2
-------- / that / there will be / no more technical issues (preventing our customers
動詞 2 連接詞 2 動詞 3 主詞 3 形容詞片語
from shopping online).

以 expect 表示客觀的「期待」。
主詞 (we) + -------- + 受詞子句 (that there will be . . .)

STEP 1 題目為動詞詞彙題時，請確認空格後方是否連接受詞。

題目為動詞詞彙題時，可以由空格後方是否連接受詞，來確認空格要填入及物動詞、還是不及物動詞。空格後方連接 that 開頭的名詞子句，因此要填入及物動詞。而選項皆為及物動詞，因此無法由此判斷出答案。

STEP 2 務必熟記句型「now that ＋原因 , 結果」。

now that 為引導原因的連接詞。本句話中，以表示原因的 now that 子句提到「已採取所有必要的措施」，提出客觀的依據，而主要子句應表示結果為「期待」不會再發生問題，因此答案為 (C) expect。(B) estimate 的意思為「估計」，指估算價值、大小、速度、費用等，不適合作為答案；另外，本句話中有提出根據，因此不能使用 (A) suppose（推測）和 (D) guess（猜測）。

句子翻譯 既然我們的技術支援小組已經採取一切必要措施，我們預料不會再有技術問題妨礙我們的顧客線上購物了。
字彙 take 採取 step 步驟、措施 prevent A from B 阻止 A 做 B
答案 (C) expect

112 --------- two factories (in London) and one (in Sydney) / have been closed,
主詞 1 動詞 1
the Melbourne facility / will remain / open.
主詞 2 動詞 2 補語

以從屬連接詞連接兩個完整句。
-------- + 完整句 , 完整句

STEP 1 「主要動詞的數量＝連接詞數量＋ 1」。

選項出現連接詞時，請先確認句中主要動詞和連接詞的數量。本句話中有兩個主要動詞 have been closed 和 will remain，因此空格要填入連接詞。而 (A) Besides 只能作為介系詞或副詞，因此不能作為答案；(B) Rather than 為對等連接詞，不能放在句首。

STEP 2 選出連接詞之前，請先確認動詞發生的順序。

本句話的結構為「______＋主詞＋ have p.p., 主詞＋ will 原形動詞」，不能填入 (D) Before，因此答案要選 (C) Although。

STEP 3 動詞發生的順序取決於連接詞

主要子句	連接詞	從屬子句
先發生的事	before	後發生的事
後發生的事	after	先發生的事

句子翻譯 雖然倫敦有二家、雪梨也有一家工廠已關閉，但墨爾本的廠會繼續運作。
字彙 facility 設施、場所
答案 (C) Although

113 --------- (among the reasons) (BAP World / is / the premier operating system available)
介系詞片語 （形容詞子句省略關係副詞 why：主詞 1 ＋動詞 1 ＋補語 1）
is / the fact (that it's open-source software),
動詞 2 主詞 2（名詞子句：主詞 3 ＋動詞 3 ＋補語 3）
(meaning that / anyone / can change or modify / the source code).
副詞片語：連接詞 主詞 4 動詞 4 受詞 4

將補語移至句首加強語氣時，會形成倒裝句。
-------- + 動詞 (is) + 主詞 (the fact)

STEP 1 many 當作名詞使用時，屬於複數名詞。

看到空格位在句首時，第一個會聯想到要填入名詞作為主詞。但是選項列出的單字皆為形容詞，因此請再重新檢視本句話的句型結構。雖然選項中 many 和 chief 也可以作為名詞使用，但是 many 屬於複數，後方不能連接單數 is；而 chief 作為名詞使用時，表示人物，若用單數要搭配冠詞一起使用才行，因此兩者若作為名詞皆不能作為答案。

STEP 2 將補語移至句首加強語氣時，主詞和動詞要交換位置。

綜合上述，空格應該要填入形容詞。因此本句話為倒裝句，強調形容詞補語，才符合句首為形容詞的結構。本句話中，第一個 is 為 BAP World 的動詞，第二個 is 才是空格搭配的動詞。among 為介系詞，表示「在……之中」，因此答案要選 (C) Chief，意思為「主要的」。

句子翻譯 BAP 世界之所以是現有的最佳作業系統，主要是因為它是開放原始碼軟體，這表示任何人都可以更改或修改原始碼。

字彙 premier 首要的 modify 修改

答案 (C) Chief

114 (According to the recent marketing research), (only) half (of U.S. households)
介系詞片語 主詞
/ read / --------- of their advertising mail.
動詞 受詞

all of the ＋複數／不可數名詞
-------- of their + 不可數名詞 (mail)

STEP 1 請由 of 後方單字的單複數，判斷出適合搭配的不定代名詞。

of 後方連接不可數名詞 mail，而選項中，(A) each 和 (B) few 都要連接複數名詞，因此不能作為答案；(C) everything 不能連接後方以 of 開頭的介系詞片語，因此答案要選 (D) all。

STEP 2 不定代名詞的出題模式

❶ one/each of the+ 複數名詞 + 單數動詞
❷ some/all of the+ 複數名詞／不可數名詞
❸ few/several/many+ 複數名詞 + 複數動詞
❹ little/much+ 不可數名詞 + 單數動詞

句子翻譯 根據近期的行銷研究顯示，美國家庭中只有一半會把他們的廣告郵件全都看過。

字彙 household 家庭、戶

答案 (D) all

115 Jeffrey Lambert / --------- / the weekly sales meeting (this morning), but
主詞 1 受詞 1 時間副詞片語 連接詞
he / had / a scheduling conflict.
主詞 2 動詞 2 受詞 2

would have p.p. 表示與過去事實相反。
主詞 + -------- + 受詞 (the weekly sales meeting)

STEP 1 確認時態為一致。

空格位在主詞 Jeffrey Lambert 後方，要填入動詞，且空格後方連接受詞，因此空格要填入主動語態。句中除了 this morning 之外，並未出現其他時間副詞，因此請由 but 後方的動詞 had 確認空格的時態。空格要和 had 的時態一致，而 (C) wants to attend 為現在式、(A) should attend 表示未來，因此皆不能作為答案。

STEP 2 請務必熟記「助動詞＋ have p.p.」的意思。

★「助動詞＋ have p.p.」有以下幾種意思：
❶ should+have p.p.（表示對過去感到遺憾或後悔）
❷ must+have p.p.（表示對過去事實的強烈推測）
❸ would+have p.p.（表示與過去事實相反）

but 表示轉折語氣，因此前後要連接概念相對的子句。後方連接 scheduling conflict（撞期），表示前方內容應使用假設語氣「應該要出席，但時間上有衝突」，因此答案為 (D) would have attended。

句子翻譯 傑佛瑞・蘭伯特今天早上原本要參加業務週會，但他的行程撞期。
字彙 weekly 每週的、一週一次的 scheduling 將……列入時程表 conflict 衝突
答案 (D) would have attended

116 The board of directors / will not move / (to the next stage of the project)
主詞 1 動詞 1 介系詞片語
--------- those (opposing it) / number / more than 100 shareholders.
主詞 2（形容詞片語） 動詞 2 受詞 2

以從屬連接詞連接兩個完整句。
完整句 + -------- + 完整句

STEP 1 空格連接兩個完整句時，要填入副詞子句連接詞。

(D) depending on 為介系詞，因此不能作為答案；(C) whether 為引導名詞子句的連接詞，因此也不能作為答案。

STEP 2 表時間或條件的副詞子句中，會以現在式代替未來式。

主要子句 will not move 的時態為未來式，副詞子句 number 的時態為現在式，因此答案要選 (A) if，為表示條件的從屬連接詞。

★表示時間或條件的副詞子句中，會以現在式代替未來式、以現在完成式代替未來完成式

從屬子句	主要子句
表示時間或條件的從屬連接詞＋主詞＋動詞（現在式） when/while/as/before/after/if	主詞＋動詞（未來式） will+ 原形動詞

句子翻譯 如果反對專案的股東人數超過 100 人，董事會就不會進入專案的下一個階段。
字彙 oppose 反對 number 共計 shareholder 股東
答案 (A) if

117 (In a competitive insurance market), most customers / are more ---------
介系詞片語 主詞 動詞（比較級）
(in which services they choose and which company they would like to purchase
A and B 結構
those products or solutions from.)

題目考的是將形容詞填入補語位置時，請先確認主詞。
most customers are + more --------

STEP 1 請找出適合搭配人物名詞使用的形容詞。

空格要填入適合搭配人物主詞 customers 使用的形容詞。選項中，(C) rigorous 指的是系統、過程、或考試相當嚴格，因此不適合作為答案；(B) punctual（準時的＝ on time），表達的是時間概念，因此也不能作為答案。

TEST 2 PART 5 中譯&解析

STEP 2 再確認可以搭配空格後方介系詞 in 的形容詞。

本句話要表達的是「大多數顧客在選擇上（choose）更加⋯⋯」，因此答案為 (D) selective，意思為「（選擇、購買上等）慎重、挑剔的」，可以描述人物的取向，又能搭配介系詞 in 一起使用。(A) dominant 指佔優勢的，並不適合用來指顧客的行為。

句子翻譯 在競爭激烈的保險市場裡，大部分的顧客對他們要選哪一種服務，以及他們要跟哪個公司購買那些產品或方案，有較多的選擇性。

字彙 competitive 競爭的　selective 有選擇性的

答案 (D)selective

---

118 The new capital city / was --------- (by chief architect Andrew Evans)
主詞　動詞　介系詞＋名詞 1
(educated at Cornell University), (/ and / his assistant Rudy Ferguson).
形容詞片語　連接詞　名詞 2

題目考的是動詞的被動語態時，請先確認主詞和動詞間的關係。
主詞 (The new capital city)＋was -------- + by + 人物 (chief architect Andrew Evans)

STEP 1 不及物動詞沒有被動語態，因此不能作為答案。

本句話改成主動語態為「Chief architect Andrew Evans ______ the new capital city」，而 (B) proceeded 為不及物動詞，因此不能作為答案。

STEP 2 確認動詞的用法。

空格後方使用 by 加上動作執行者，表示由建築師規劃都市，因此答案為 (A) planned。(C) involved 的用法為「involve ＋ doing sth」或「involve 人物 in (doing) sth」，若改寫成被動語態，主詞要為人物才行，因此該選項不能作為答案；(D) supposed 為及物動詞，意思為「（雖然不太確定，但是我）認為應該是」，表示推測的概念，後方通常會連接（that）子句。還有一個用法為「be supposed to do」，表示預計要做的事。

句子翻譯 新首都是由曾就讀於康乃爾大學的首席建築師安德魯‧伊文斯，和他的助理魯迪‧佛格森所規劃。

字彙 assistant 助理、助手　proceed 進行、開始、繼續做下去　involve 涉及　suppose 猜想、認為應該

答案 (A) planned

---

119 Lloyd's Distance Learning Course / is / (by far) the most --------- (we / have seen)
主詞 1　動詞 1　補語 1　（主詞 2／動詞 2）
and / offers / innovative e-learning classes and degree programs
連接詞　動詞 3　受詞 3
(through a digital learning platform).
介系詞片語

最高級後方的名詞可以省略。
主詞 + be 動詞 + the most 形容詞（名詞）

STEP 1 最高級後方的名詞與主詞為「同格」關係時，會省略名詞 course。

根據本句的句型結構，空格應填入形容詞，但是若將選項中的名詞 (B) detail 或 (C) details 填入空格時，和主詞 course 會變成同格的關係，因此並不適合填入空格中。也就是說，最高級後方應省略名詞，填入形容詞。

STEP 2 過去分詞形容詞 vs. 現在分詞形容詞

若要將及物動詞改成分詞形容詞，放在名詞後方修飾時，答案有九成以上會是過去分詞形容詞，請特別熟記這點。另外，若答案為現在分詞形容詞時，通常會使用不及物動詞或 V-ing 形態。(A) detailed 為過去分詞，作為形容詞使用時，指涵蓋詳細的內容，故為正確答案。(D) detailing 為不可數名詞，意思與 decorations 相同，不適合作為答案。

★常考的分詞形容詞

finished 完成的	designated 指定的	accomplished 已實現的	complicated 複雜的
damaged 受損的	talented 有才能的	dedicated 專注的	existing 現存的
detailed 詳細的	estimated 估計的	unbiased 無偏見的、公正的	missing 失蹤的、丟失的
limited 有限的	opposing 反對的、對面的	demanding 費時費力的、高要求的	challenging 具挑戰性的

句子翻譯 洛伊遠距學習課程是目前我們見過最詳細的課程，其透過數位學習平台，提供創新的數位學習課程和學位課程。

字彙 distance learning 遠距學習、函授學習　by far 到目前為止　innovative 創新的

答案 (A) detailed

120 Our Richmond office / is located / (slightly) (--------- the Golden Cinema on 23 Winspear Avenue).
主詞　動詞　副詞　副詞片語

由後方連接的名詞選出適當的介系詞。
is located + -------- + 表示地點的名詞

STEP 1 空格後方連接的名詞為地點，因此空格要填入可以搭配地點使用的介系詞。

(B) over 要連接表示一段時間的名詞，意思為「在……期間」，因此不適合作為答案。

STEP 2 地方介系詞 past / across / opposite ＋表示地點的名詞

(A) across 和 (C) opposite 的意思為「在……對面」，兩者都可以連接表示地點的名詞，但是空格前方為 slightly（稍微地）表示程度上的差異，並不適合搭配這兩個介系詞。綜合上述，答案要選 (D) past，意思為「經過」。

句子翻譯 我們的里奇蒙營業處位於溫斯皮爾大道 23 號，就在黃金劇院再過去一點。

字彙 slightly 稍微地

答案 (D) past

121 The agenda (of this meeting) / is / to discuss / what / we / need to know about
主詞 1　介系詞片語　動詞 1　補語　名詞子句連接詞　主詞 2　動詞 2
(--------- to promote the new product) (on social media).
about 的受詞　介系詞片語

介系詞 about 後方要連接名詞／名詞片語／名詞子句。
about + -------- + to 不定詞片語

STEP 1 介系詞 about 後方要連接名詞／名詞片語／名詞子句。

選項中，(A) decision 為可數名詞，若要填入單數形態，前方要加上冠詞才行，因此不能作為答案；(B) try 為動詞，不能連接在介系詞後方。由剩下的兩個選項，可以得知空格要填入連接詞。(D) after 為引導副詞子句的連接詞，不能連接 to 不定詞片語，因此答案要選 (C) how。

STEP 2 以連接詞引導名詞子句時，若後方沒有主詞，可以連接 to 不定詞。

how / when / where 為名詞子句連接詞，後方可以連接 to 不定詞，結合成名詞片語，請特別熟記。how to do 表示「做……的方法」。

句子翻譯　這次會議的議程，是要討論我們在社交媒體上促銷新產品所需知道的事項。
字彙　agenda 議程
答案　(C) how

122 (During the summer), we / ship / packages (with frozen gel packs)
介系詞片語　主詞　動詞　受詞　介系詞片語
(to prevent dairy and meat products / and / other --------- items (from deteriorating).)
副詞用法：修飾動詞　prevent 的受詞　連接詞　prevent 的受詞　介系詞片語

動詞 prevent + 名詞 1（dairy and meat products）and 名詞 2（other -------- items）

STEP 1 本題要選出形容詞，來修飾及物動詞 prevent（阻止）的名詞受詞。

空格位在 prevent A from B（阻止 A 做 B）當中，要選出適當的形容詞，修飾名詞受詞 item。prevent 後方連接的第一個受詞為「乳製品和肉製品」，因此適合選擇形容詞 (B) perishable 來修飾 items，意思為「容易腐壞的」。(A) plentiful 的意思為「數量豐富的、多的」，並不符合句意；(C) spoiled 要修飾人物，意思為「被寵壞的」，也不適合填入空格中；(D) adverse 的意思為「不利的、敵對的」，不適合搭配 from deteriorating 一起使用。

句子翻譯　夏季時，我們會在包裹裡放入冷凍凝膠包一起運送，以防止乳製品和肉製品及其他易腐敗物品變壞。
字彙　frozen gel pack 冷凍凝膠包　dairy 牛奶製的　deteriorate 惡化、變壞
答案　(B) perishable

123 If / you / can schedule / a meeting (--------- 9:00 tomorrow morning),
連接詞　主詞 1　動詞 1　受詞 1　介系詞片語
our director / will rearrange / his flight (to be in attendance).
主詞 2　動詞 2　受詞 2　to 不定詞的副詞用法

根據慣用語選出適當的介系詞。
schedule A (a meeting) -------- B (9:00 tomorrow morning)

STEP 1 **由後方連接的名詞選出適當的介系詞。**

空格後方連接 9:00 tomorrow morning，為表示時間概念的名詞，而 (D) in 要連接月分或年度，因此不適合作為答案；(B) to 後方連接時間名詞時，用法為 from A to B，因此並不適合填入本題的空格中。

STEP 2 **分辨介系詞 at 和 for 的差異。**

時間名詞通常會搭配 (A) at 一起使用，但是若填入該選項，表示正在安排明天上午九點的會議，與主要子句的內容有所衝突。但若填入 (C) for，搭配動詞 schedule，為 schedule A for B（將 A 安排至 B）的用法，表示將會議時間安排在九點，故為正確答案，因此答案要選 (C) for。

★動詞＋受詞＋介系詞

acquaint A with B	使 A 了解 B	include A with B	B 包含 A
attribute A to B	把 A 歸因於 B	brief A on B	向 A 簡報 B
replace A with B	用 B 取代 A	compare A with B	把 A 和 B 相比
prevent A from B	阻止 A 做 B	transfer A to B	將 A 轉移到 B

句子翻譯　如果你能把會議排在明天早上九點，我們經理會重新安排他的班機以便出席。

字彙　**rearrange** 重新安排　**be in attendance** 到場、出席

答案　**(C) for**

124 CIBC Bank / offers / more sophisticated online banking systems
主詞　動詞　受詞
(to help / our clients / run their businesses more ---------).
動詞　受詞　受詞補語（to 不定詞的副詞用法）

副詞可以修飾名詞以外的其他詞性。
run their businesses + more --------

STEP 1 **題目為副詞詞彙題時，請確認空格修飾的對象。**

空格要填入副詞，修飾 run their business（經營事業）。

STEP 2 **請將副詞分類，並熟記適合修飾的動詞。**

(A) broadly 的意思為「大體上」，用於概括範圍較大的內容時；(B) greatly 為表示程度的副詞，會搭配表示增減的動詞使用，不適合用於本題的句子中；填入 (D) potentially（潛在地）並不符合句意。綜合前述，答案要選 (C) efficiently 較為適當，表示「有效率地」經營。

句子翻譯　CIBC 銀行提供更成熟的線上金融系統，以幫助我們的客戶更有效地經營生意。

字彙　**sophisticated** 精密的、高度發展的

答案　**(C) efficiently**

125 The decision (about whether the factory / can reopen) / will be ---------
主詞 1 介系詞 名詞子句連接詞 主詞 2 動詞 2 動詞 1
(until / the Ministry / has carried out / a thorough investigation of this risk).
副詞子句連接詞 主詞 3 動詞 3 受詞 3

題目考動詞的被動語態時，請先確認主詞和動詞間的關係。
(The decision) + will be --------

STEP 1 題目考動詞的被動語態時，請優先確認主詞。

主詞為 The decision，表示主動語態的句子為 will _____ + the decision，而 (C) informed 後方要連接人物名詞作為受詞、(D) agreed 為不及物動詞，兩者皆不能作為答案。另外，請特別留意 (B) resolved 要連接 issues、problems 等「問題」作為受詞，因此答案要選 (A) deferred。

STEP 2 連接人物名詞作為受詞的及物動詞

★「通報／告知＋人物受詞」

advise 勸告	assure 擔保、使放心
inform 通知	warn 警告
remind 提醒	convince 使確信
notify 通知	persuade 說服

句子翻譯 等到該部對這次風險進行過徹底的調查後，才能決定工廠是否能重新開工。
字彙 carry out 執行 thorough 徹底的 investigation 調查 defer 推遲
答案 (A) deferred

126 (At Molson Coors Brewing Company), we / do --------- (we can)
介系詞片語 主詞 1 動詞 1 形容詞子句
(to help / our employees / achieve their full potential).
to 不定詞 help 的受詞 受詞補語

及物動詞後方要連接受詞。
do + -------- + we can

STEP 1 空格位在及物動詞 do 的後方，為受詞的位置，要填入名詞。

本句話的主要動詞為 do，空格後方的 we can 為形容詞子句，用來修飾填入空格的名詞。值得留意的是，形容詞子句省略了關係代名詞受格 that，因此本句話不需要再填入其他主要動詞或連接詞。而 (A) so 和 (D) whichever 皆為連接詞，因此不能作為答案。

STEP 2 代名詞 those 用來代替前方所提過的名詞。

(B) those 為代名詞，用來代替前方所提過的複數名詞。然而，空格前方並未出現複數名詞，因此該選項不能作為答案。綜合前述，答案要選 (C) everything。

句子翻譯 在摩森酷爾斯啤酒釀造公司，我們會盡一切所能幫助我們的員工充分發揮他們的潛力。
字彙 brewing company 啤酒釀造公司 potential 潛在的
答案 (C) everything

127 Debra Mason, (a widely recognized --------- (on Northwestern Asian cultural history and art)), / was / a curator of the Toronto Museum.
主詞 與主詞同格 介系詞片語 動詞 補語

請熟記「冠詞＋副詞＋形容詞＋名詞」的句型結構。
a widely recognized + --------

STEP 1 冠詞後方要以名詞作結。

空格要填入適合搭配冠詞 a 的名詞，而 (B) authoritative 為形容詞、(C) authorizing 為動狀詞，皆不適合作為答案。

STEP 2 人物名詞和事物名詞

(A) authority 指「當權者」，屬於人物名詞；(D) authorization 的意思為「認可」，屬於事物名詞，因此請根據前後方內容判斷空格適合填入的名詞。空格的名詞和主詞 Debra Mason 屬於「同格」關係，表示對人物名詞進一步說明，因此答案要選 (A) authority。

句子翻譯 大家公認的西北亞文化歷史與藝術權威戴博拉·曼森，是多倫多博物館的策展人。
字彙 recognized 確認的 Northwestern 西北部的
答案 (A) authority

128 --------- member / is assigned / a task / depends on / the speciality (required for a project.)
主詞 1 動詞 2
連接詞（名詞子句作為主詞 2） 受詞 1 動詞 2 受詞 2
修飾語

主要動詞的數量＝連接詞數量＋ 1
-------- 名詞 is assigned . . . / depends on . . .

STEP 1 選項出現連接詞時，請先確認「主要動詞的數量＝連接詞數量＋ 1」。

本句話有兩個主要動詞 is 和 depends，卻沒有連接詞，因此空格要填入連接詞。(A) Which 為疑問形容詞，可以引導名詞子句，作為主要動詞 depends 的主詞，同時修飾空格後方的名詞。請特別留意，(B) Each、(C) Any 和 (D) Some 可以作為形容詞使用，但是不能扮演連接詞的角色。

STEP 2 疑問形容詞 which / what ＋（沒有加上所有格或冠詞的）名詞

❶「疑問形容詞＋（沒有加上所有格或冠詞的）名詞＋動詞⋯⋯」：
which / what 作為疑問形容詞使用時，修飾名詞開頭的完整句。

❷「疑問形容詞＋（沒有加上所有格或冠詞的）名詞＋ to 不定詞」

❸ 疑問形容詞後方不能連接所有格、冠詞、代名詞。

句子翻譯 任務要分派給哪個成員，要依照專案所需的專長而定。
字彙 assign 分派、指定 specialty 專長
答案 (A) Which

129 Recent studies (from the University of California) / indicate / that / the ---------
主詞 1 介系詞片語 動詞 1 從屬連接詞 主詞 2
(of visual aids) to a presentation / can provide / the presenter (with a lot of advantages).
介系詞片語 動詞 2 受詞 2 介系詞片語

題目為名詞詞彙題時，請確認該名詞搭配的動詞。
the -------- . . . to a presentation can provide

STEP 1 題目為名詞詞彙題時，請確認該名詞搭配的動詞或介系詞。

本題要選出適當的名詞，作為 provide（提供）的主詞，且適合搭配 to a presentation 一起使用。根據句意，應填入 (B) addition「附加」，表示「在發表中加入視覺輔助資料，能為發表者帶來很多好處。」(A) feature（特色）可以作為 can provide 的主詞，但是和 advantages 的意思相似，不太適合作為答案；而 (C) pictures 和 (D) tool 皆與 visual aids 的概念雷同，因此也不適合作為答案。

句子翻譯 加州大學的近期研究顯示，簡報時額外使用視覺輔助設備，能帶給演講者許多好處。
字彙 indicate 指出、表明　visual aid 視覺輔助設備
答案 (B) addition

130 (--------- poorly / the customer / may be treating / them), customer service
副詞 主詞 1 動詞 1 受詞 主詞 2
representatives / are required to treat / customers (with professionalism).
動詞 2 受詞 2 介系詞片語

However ＋形容詞／副詞＋主詞＋動詞
-------- + 副詞 + 主詞 + 動詞

STEP 1 選項出現一個以上的連接詞時，請先確認「主要動詞的數量＝連接詞數量＋ 1」。

本句話有兩個主要動詞 may be treating 和 are required，卻沒有連接詞，因此空格要填入連接詞。而 (B) Seldom 和 (D) Rather 皆為副詞，因此不能作為答案。

STEP 2 however ＋形容詞／副詞＋主詞＋動詞

根據本句話的句型結構，很容易會將空格到 them 視為副詞子句，因而選擇 (A) Although 作為答案。但是連接詞後方直接連接副詞 poorly，接著又連接主詞和動詞，因此要選擇可以強調副詞的連接詞 (C) However 作為答案。

STEP 3 However 的兩種用法

★測驗中，however 有兩種出題方式：

❶ 當作連接詞使用，引導複合關係副詞子句，表示讓步。
❷ 當作連接副詞使用，在句子中扮演副詞的角色，表示和句點前方的句子屬於轉折的關係。

句子翻譯 不管顧客會對他們多麼不客氣，客服代表仍須以專業精神應對顧客。
字彙 poorly 糟糕地　be required to V 被要求做……　professionalism 專業精神、專業水準
答案 (C) However

PART 6

Questions 131-134 refer to the following instructions.

Why don't you install a Programmable Thermostat?

Save money and energy by installing Homeassistant, our new programmable thermostat, to control heating and air conditioning. This programmable thermostat can save more than 40% of your energy bill by turning on only during the daytime, and automatically shutting off when the desired temperature has been reached. And you can program it **to** — **131** — your home's **temperature** when you are away **and raise** it at a specific time.

The process of programming this thermostat is quite simple and does not consume a lot of time. Begin by pushing the home button of the device and — **132** — long press any blank section of the screen for a few seconds. Select the Choose Option to display the CHOOSE screen and the **selection menu will pop up**. — **133** —. When you're finished, press the OK button **to save your selection**. Your — **134** — will be applied immediately.

131. (A) show
(B) lower
(C) see
(D) review

及物動詞詞彙
→ 選出適當的及物動詞，連接 your home's temperature 作為受詞。

132. (A) simple
(B) simply
(C) simpled
(D) simpler

副詞＋完整句（祈使句）
→ 各類詞性中，副詞可以連接完整句。

133. **(A) Using the drop down arrow, you can select your preferences.**
(B) Before setting your device, check for any ~~missing items~~.
(C) You can ~~return~~ it within 14 days of purchase.
(D) Press the red button on the left to see how much energy it has saved.

句子插入題
→ 確認空格前後的句子。

134. **(A) settings**
(B) savings
(C) ~~screen~~
(D) device

名詞詞彙
→ 選出適合搭配 be applied（適用）使用的名詞。

第 131-134 題 使用說明

您何不裝設程式控制自動調溫器呢？

安裝我們的新型程式控制自動調溫器「家庭助理」，可以控制暖氣與冷氣，以節省您的金錢和能源。這款程式控制自動調溫器可以只在日間開啟，並在達到理想的溫度後自動關閉，讓你省下超過40%的能源費用。而且，您可以在出門時，調低家裡的溫度，並在特定時間才升高溫度。

設定這款自動調溫器相當簡單，而且不會花很多時間。首先，按下裝置上的「home」鍵，然後，只要長按螢幕上的任何空白處幾秒鐘。選擇「Choose」選項以顯示「CHOOSE」螢幕，接著會跳出選單。使用下拉箭頭，您可以選擇偏好設定。完成後，按下OK鍵儲存，您的設定便能立即啟用。

字彙 programmable 程式控制的　thermostat 自動調溫器　save 節省　shut off 關掉　blank 空白的　pop up（尤指突然地）出現　apply 適用

131 動詞詞彙

請由空格後方的受詞來確認適當的及物動詞。

STEP 1 **空格要填入適當的及物動詞，連接後方受詞 temperature（溫度）。**

STEP 2 **空格後方 and 連接的內容為「溫度會在特定的時間上升」。**

由此可以得知空格要填入與調節溫度有關的內容，因此答案要選 (B) lower，意思為「降低」溫度。

132 副詞詞彙

副詞可以連接完整的句子。

STEP 1 **空格前方為 and。**

空格後方連接的句子和前方 Begin 開頭的句子皆為祈使句。

STEP 2 **請掌握句型結構為「祈使句＋ and ＋______＋祈使句」。**

本句話的結構為「完整句 and ______ 完整句」，表示適合填入空格的詞性為副詞，因此答案為 (B) simply（簡單地、僅僅）。

133 句子插入題

題目為句子插入題時請從選項中找出與空格前後內容有所關聯的關鍵字。

STEP 1 題目為句子插入題時，請由空格前後方內容確認答題關鍵字。

本篇文章為操作裝置的說明，空格前方提到按下（select）選擇鍵，空格後方則提到「按下確認鍵儲存所選的內容」，因此空格應填入表示 select 過程的內容，答案要選 (A)。

(A) 使用下拉箭頭，您可以選擇偏好設定。

(B) 在安裝您的裝置前，檢查是否有缺件。→文中並未提到需要確認的項目。

(C) 您可以在購買後 14 天內退回。→這句話適合放在購買規定的後方。

(D) 按下左邊的紅色按鈕，看看它省下了多少能源。

字彙 drop down arrow 下拉箭頭　preference 偏好　missing 丟失的　return 退還

134 名詞詞彙

題目為名詞詞彙題時，請確認相關動詞。

STEP 1 空格位在所有格 your 後方，要填入名詞。

空格為 will be applied 的主詞，請選出適當的名詞填入。

STEP 2 請掌握動詞的性質。

空格前方告知裝置的設定方法，因此後方為「立即啟用你的設定」較為適當。(A) settings「設定」可以連接動詞 apply 的被動語態。

Questions 135-138 refer to the following notice.

> July is high season in Hawaii, so we recommend you make a reservation at your earliest convenience. Hotel **accommodations** here **are** very —**135**—. Reservations will be required with a deposit of $200. This amount will be charged to your credit card upon booking the reservation. Cancellations made more than seven days prior to your scheduled arrival date —**136**— in full.
>
> However, if the reservation is canceled within one week of arrival, it will result in a full charge of the entire —**137**— of your stay booked. —**138**—.

135. (A) restricted ▶限制做某件事
(B) difficult
(C) confirmed
(D) limited ▶數量的限制

136. **(A) will be refunded**
(B) will not be refunded
(C) are refunding
(D) had been refunded

137. (A) room
(B) degree
(C) length
(D) week

138. (A) ~~Also, our new facilities~~ will make your future stays with us even more enjoyable.
(B) This policy applies to early departure as well.
(C) In fact, we will ~~soon open more hotels in July~~.
(D) ~~Thank you for leaving a review~~ of your stay at our hotel.

形容詞詞彙
→ 選出適合説明accommodation（住處）的形容詞。

動詞時態
→ 選出 cancellations 可以連接的語態和時態。

名詞詞彙
→ 選出與 stay（留宿、停留）為同格關係的名詞。

句子插入題
→ 確認空格前後的句子。

第 135-138 題 告示

七月是夏威夷的旅遊旺季，因此，我們建議您盡早預訂。這裡的住宿飯店非常搶手。預訂時需付$200元訂金。這筆金額會在您預訂時，從您的信用卡扣款。在您預定入住日期的七天前取消，可全額退款。

然而，如果在入住日期前一星期內取消，會導致收取您預定住宿期間的全額費用。這項政策也適用於提早退房。

字彙 **recommend** 建議 **reservation** 預訂 **at your earliest convenience** 盡早
require 需要 **deposit** 訂金 **charge** 收費 **cancellation** 取消
prior to 在……之前 **entire** 全部的

135 形容詞詞彙

確認適合搭配形容詞的名詞。

STEP 1 **空格要填入主詞補語。**

空格要填入適當的形容詞，用來說明主詞 hotel accommodations。

STEP 2 **選出適合搭配該主詞的形容詞。**

前方句子提出建議，告知盡可能提早預訂，後方應表明原因較為適當，因此空格要填入 (D) limited（有限的、不多的）。(A) restricted 的意思為「受限制的」，指的是「限制在某個標準內做事」，limited 則是指「數量上有限的」。根據文意，應為飯店客房數量有限，因此答案要選 (D)。

字彙 restricted 受限的　confirmed 確定的

136 動詞時態

請由前後句子的時態來確認動詞時態。

STEP 1 **空格位在主詞後方，要填入適當的主要動詞。**

STEP 2 **空格前方指的是未來的事。**

空格前方假設未來發生的事情（預訂後取消），因此空格要填入未來式。未來式的選項有 (A) will be refunded 和 (B) will not be refunded。而空格後方內容為「但是若於入住前七天以內取消，則要支付全額費用」，前方應為意思相反的內容。因此答案要選 (A) will be refunded，表示「退還費用」。

字彙 refund 退還

137 名詞詞彙

空格被「of ＋名詞」修飾，因此請由 of 後方的名詞確認適合填入空格的名詞。

STEP 1 空格後方為介系詞 of，請務必確認前後方連接的名詞。

(C) length 指「期間」適合搭配 your stay（入住）一起使用。

STEP 2 確認錯誤選項

(D) week 同樣是表示時間的概念，但是填入後會變成「在您入住的一整週」，表示無論預訂幾天的住宿，都得支付一週的費用，並不符合文意。

字彙 degree 程度、等級　length （時間的）期間、（距離的）長度

138 句子插入題

題目為句子插入題時，從選項中找出與空格前後內容有所關聯的關鍵字。

STEP 1 以選項中的 this 或所有格確認前方連接的句子。

空格前方提及取消訂房的注意事項，因此空格內同樣要填入與取消有關的注意事項。

STEP 2 確認選項中的關鍵字。

(A) also 表示前後內容為相似的概念，但是句中提到新的設施（new facilities），因此並不適當；前半段指出「飯店客房數量有限」，(C) 卻提到「more hotels」，因此並不適當；(D) 出現「Thank you for a review」，指的是感謝對方留下入住評論，也不適合填入此空格中。本篇文章告知預訂飯店的相關內容，而空格前方提到取消訂房和費用的條款，因此空格要填入 (B)，指「提前退房也適用相關規定」最為適當。

(A) 此外，我們的新設施會讓你未來入住本飯店期間更加愉快。

(B) 這項政策也適用於提早退房。

(C) 事實上，我們會在七月開更多飯店。

(D) 謝謝您留下對於住宿飯店期間的意見。

Questions 139-142 refer to the following notice.

Notice: Shipping Fragile Items

Thank you for using Florida Logistics. **Our mission —139— **the best and most reliable **service** to all customers. We always handle all our shipments with care and caution, but we do not guarantee special handling for packages even marked "Fragile." Therefore, it is your responsibility to make sure that your contents are protected from any damage that may be caused during the delivery. When you ship your items, we do not recommend using old boxes but new ones. Old and used **ones** do not offer their **—140— rigidity** and adequate protection. In case you use a used box, any labels on it should be removed and any damage such as punctures and tears should be checked. **—141—** may result in damage to the contents. And please remember that it is important to use internal cushioning for items that are fragile. **—142—**. This way, all items **are separated** from each other, so your items will be safe from bumps, vibrations and shocks of any kind.

要求採用此方法將產品分開。

139. (A) provides ▶ 一般事實、習慣、反覆動作
(B) is provided
(C) is providing ▶ 現在一時的狀況
(D) is to provide ▶ be to 不定詞→ 計畫、可能、義務

140. (A) creative
(B) original
(C) ready
(D) various

141. (A) Most
(B) Neither ▶ 兩者皆非（否定）
(C) Others
(D) These ▶ punctures and tears

142. (A) Doing this is ~~not advisable~~.
(B) We can purchase insurance for one single item.
(C) To do so, wrap them individually.
(D) Customers will learn that it is quite unsuitable.

動詞變化

→ 前方提及 our mission 或 goal，表示目的或目標時，請使用 to 不定詞表示未來。

形容詞詞彙

→ 選出適合修飾名詞 rigidity（強度）的形容詞。

代名詞

→ 題目考的是代名詞時，請留意該代名詞要能對應空格前方提及的對象。

句子插入題

→ 確認空格前後的句子。

第 139-142 題 告示

告示：寄送易碎物品

謝謝您選擇佛羅里達物流，我們的使命就是提供最好、最可靠的服務給所有顧客。我們一向小心謹慎地處理我們運送的所有貨物，但我們無法保證，就算標明「易碎品」的包裹也會予以特殊處理。因此，確認您的內容物受到保護，以免受到運送過程可能造成的損害就是您的責任。當您寄送貨品時，我們不建議使用舊箱子，而要用新的箱子。用過的舊箱子已無原來的堅硬，無法給予足夠的保護。假如您使用舊的箱子，請撕掉上面的任何標籤，並檢查任何像是破洞或撕裂的破損。這些都可能會導致內容物受到損害。同時，請記得，易碎品必須要在箱內增加緩衝力。為了達到這個目的，請把物品單獨包裝。如此，所有的物品都彼此分開，您的貨品就能免於任何碰撞、震動和衝擊。

字彙 fragile 易碎的、脆弱的　logistics 物流　reliable 可靠的
shipment 運送、運輸的貨物　guarantee 保證　special handling 特殊處理
responsibility 責任　rigidity 堅硬　adequate 足夠的、適當的　puncture 刺穿
tear 撕裂　bump 碰、撞

139 動詞變化

題目為動詞變化題時，請依照單複數→語態→時態的順序逐一確認。

STEP 1 空格位在主詞後方，要填入適當的主要動詞。

STEP 2 空格後方連接受詞 the . . . service，空格要使用主動語態。

因此，請先淘汰被動語態 (B) is provided。空格前方為特定團體的 mission（任務、目的），適合連接往後將達成的事項。to be 的用法表示「計畫、可能、義務」，因此答案要選 (D) is to provide。

STEP 3 不一定要用現在式表達現在正在發生的事。

(A) provides 為現在式，用於表示一般事實、習慣或反覆動作，特別用來強調無論過去、現在或未來都會重複相同的工作、適用相同的規則，不適合用於表達往後將達成的事情上。(C) is providing 指現在一時的狀況。

140 形容詞詞彙

詞彙題不能單憑選項的中文意思選出答案。

STEP 1 空格要填入適合修飾名詞 rigidity（強度、韌性）的形容詞。

STEP 2 請從空格前後方找出客觀的答題依據，選出符合空格前後文意的答案。

如果只看空格前後的單字，四個選項似乎都能填入空格中，但是千萬不能單憑選項的中文意思選出答案。空格所在句子的主詞為「old and used ones（老舊且用過的箱子）」後方提到無法提供 their（他們的）. . . rigidity（強度）」，因此答案要選 (B) original，表示「原有的／原來的強度」。(D) various（各式各樣的）用來修飾複數命詞、(C) ready 的意思為「準備好的」，兩者搭配名詞 rigidity（強度、韌性）皆不符合文意：(A) creative（有創造力的）也不符合文意。

141 代名詞
代名詞用來代替前方出現過的名詞。

STEP 1 作答 PART 6 中的代名詞考題時，請務必確認空格前方的句子。

空格用來的代替前方的 punctures and tears（破洞和破損），因此答案要選指示代名詞 (D) these。

STEP 2 分析錯誤選項

(B) Neither 表示否定，指「兩者皆非」，不適合作為答案；(C) Others 的意思為「其餘的」，前方要提到 one 或 some，後方才能使用 others 表示其他的人物；(A) Most 的意思為「大多數的」，可以用來指前方對象當中的一部分，不能直接代替前方出現過的名詞。

STEP 3 most 的四大出題重點

❶ the most ＋形容詞／副詞：最高級
❷ the most ＋名詞：many、much 的最高級
❸ 不定代名詞：most ＋ of ＋名詞
❹ 一般形容詞：most ＋名詞「大多數的」

142 句子插入題
題目為句子插入題時，從選項中找出與空格前後內容有所關聯的關鍵字。

STEP 1 解題關鍵為 This way。

空格前方的句子提及注意事項，而空格後方提到「this way（採這樣的方式）可以確保產品的安全」。因此空格要填入明確表達 this way（採這樣的方式）所指的內容，答案要選 (C) 建議要分開包裝。

STEP 2 分析錯誤選項。

(A) 當中使用 this，可以用來代替前方的句子，但是後方提到 not advisable（不希望、不建議），並不符合文意。

(A) 不建議這麼做。
(B) 我們可以為單一物品買保險。
(C) 為了達到這個目的，請把物品單獨包裝。
(D) 顧客會了解這相當不明智。

字彙 advisable 明智的、可取的　wrap 包、裹　individually 單獨地
unsuitable 不合適、不合宜

Questions 143-146 refer to the following e-mail.

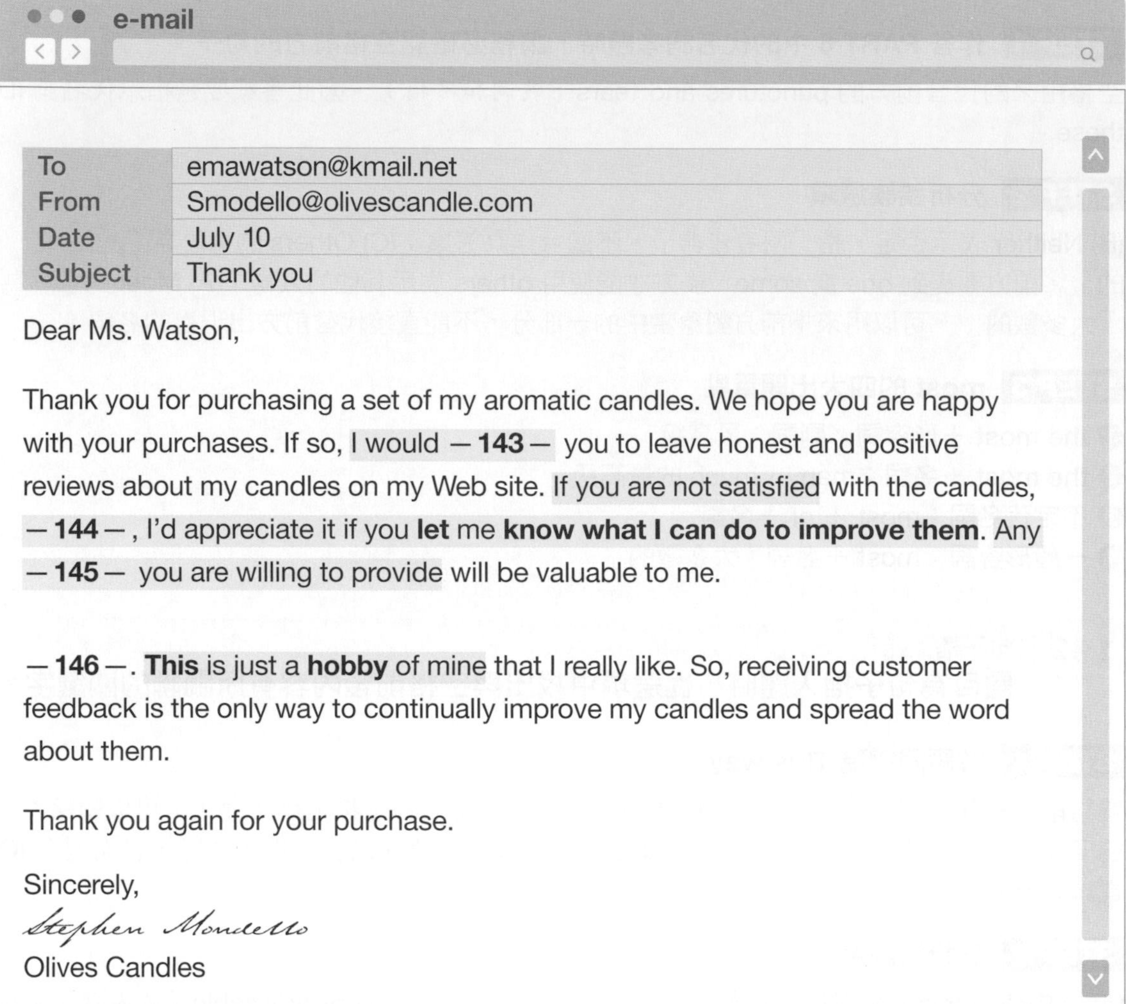

e-mail

To	emawatson@kmail.net
From	Smodello@olivescandle.com
Date	July 10
Subject	Thank you

Dear Ms. Watson,

Thank you for purchasing a set of my aromatic candles. We hope you are happy with your purchases. If so, I would — **143** — you to leave honest and positive reviews about my candles on my Web site. If you are not satisfied with the candles, — **144** —, I'd appreciate it if you **let** me **know what I can do to improve them**. Any — **145** — you are willing to provide will be valuable to me.

— **146** —. **This** is just a **hobby** of mine that I really like. So, receiving customer feedback is the only way to continually improve my candles and spread the word about them.

Thank you again for your purchase.

Sincerely,

Stephen Mondello

Olives Candles

143. (A) like asking
(B) like to ask
(C) have liked to ask
(D) have liked asking

144. (A) in the meantime ▶ 兩個時間點「在期間內」
(B) however ▶ 對比
(C) such as ▶ 介系詞
(D) therefore ▶ 結果

145. (A) proof
(B) ingredients
(C) request
(D) feedback

動詞變化

→ 請熟記「would like to 原形動詞」可以用來表達文章的目的或主旨。

接副詞詞彙題

→ 連接副詞的空格位在句首時，請確認答案能否順利連接空格前後的句子。

名詞詞彙題

→ 選出適當的名詞連接 you are willing to provide。

146. (A) All the candles can ~~be purchased~~ from retail stores in the area.
(B) ~~I regret~~ that there was a mistake in shipping your order.
(C) In order ~~to fulfil customized orders~~, I have a variety of candles in stock.
(D) As you may know from my Web site, I am not a corporate seller.

句子插入題
→ 確認空格前後的句子。

第 143-146 題 電子郵件

收件人	emawatson@kmail.net
寄件人	Smodello@olivescandle.com
日期	七月十日
主旨	謝謝您

親愛的華生女士：

謝謝您購買一組我的香氛蠟燭，我們希望您滿意您所購買的產品。如果滿意，我想請您到我的網站上，就我的蠟燭留下坦率且正面的評價。然而，如果您不滿意蠟燭，若您能告訴我該如何改善，我會很感激。任何您願意提供的回饋意見，對我都很受用。

您可能會從我的網站得知，我不是公司賣家。這只是我真的很喜歡的嗜好。因此，得到顧客的回饋意見，是讓我的蠟燭不斷進步、並宣傳產品的唯一方式。

再次謝謝您的購買。

真誠地
史蒂芬·蒙戴洛
橄欖蠟燭

字彙 aromatic 芳香的 satisfy 滿意 appreciate 感謝、感激
continually 持續地、不停地 spread the word 散布消息

143 動詞變化
would + like to 原形動詞（想要……）

STEP 1 would 後方加上 like，請選出適當的動詞形態。

STEP 2 would 後方加上表示感情狀態的動詞時，不能使用完成式和進行式。

(C) have liked to ask 和 (D) have liked asking 不能作為答案。would like to 後方要連接原形動詞，表示「想要做……」，因此答案要選 (B)。(A) 動詞 like 後方連接動名詞作為受詞時，指的是喜歡動名詞的動作；若填入 like asking，意思會變成「如果是這樣的話，我喜歡提問」，並不適合作為答案。

STEP 3 would have p.p. 指與過去事實相反的假設語氣。

若使用假設語氣，說話者不會依照實際狀況陳述，而是假設相反的情況、或者假定、懷疑、希望或要求無法發生的事情。從屬子句通常會以 if 開頭，主要子句則是使用 would have p.p.，表示與過去事實相反，請特別熟記此用法。

144 連接副詞詞彙
連接副詞用來說明空格前後的關係。

STEP 1 空格前後皆為完整句。

因此，空格要填入適當的連接副詞，連接前後的句子。

STEP 2 確認連接副詞能否順利連接前後的句子。

首先，(C) such as 為介系詞，不能作為答案。空格前方句子提到「如果您對購買的商品不滿意」，後方句子提到「如果您能提出需要改善的地方，我會相當感激您」，這兩句話為對比的關係，因此答案要選 (B) however，表示「然而」。

(A) in the meantime（在期間內）要提到兩個時間點發生的事件，表示一件事發生的期間，又發生另一件事，不適合填入此空格中。(D) therefore 表示子句的結果，因此也不適合作為答案。

145 名詞詞彙
題目為詞彙題時，從空格前後方找出客觀的答題依據，選出符合空格前後文意的答案。

STEP 1 找出能被 you are willing to provide 修飾的名詞。

空格後方為「you are . . . to provide」（您所提供），用來修飾空格，因此整句話為「您所提供的 ______ 對我而言非常寶貴」。而空格前一句話提到「如果您能提出需要改善的地方，我會相當感激您」，由此可以得知適合填入空格的名詞為 (D) feedback，指「回饋、建議」。

(A) proof 為「證據」、(B) ingredients 為「原料」、(C) request 為「要求」，請一併熟記這些單字。

146 句子插入題
題目為句子插入題時，請由空格前後方內容確認答題關鍵字

STEP 1 請熟記下方需要優先確認的解題關鍵字。

❶ 連接詞、連接副詞、介系詞
❷ 指示代名詞、指示形容詞、數量代名詞、人稱代名詞

空格後方連接「This is just a hobby of mine」，空格填入「我不是公司賣家」，連接「這只是我個人的興趣」較為適當，因此答案要選 (D)。

STEP 2 分析錯誤選項

(A) 提到販售商品的地方，但是後方句子以 This is 開頭，因此並不適合填入這句話；(B) 針對運送出錯道歉，這類話語通常會放在文章開頭處；(C) 提到商品的存貨，適合放在廣告文章中。

(A) 所有的蠟燭都可以在這個地區的零售商店買到。
(B) 我很遺憾您的貨品送錯了。
(C) 為了滿足客製化的訂單，我有很多不同的蠟燭現貨。
(D) 您可能會從我的網站得知，我不是公司賣家。

字彙 customized （按顧客要求）訂製的；客製化的

Questions 147-148 refer to the following Web page.

http://www.sudburybroadcasting.co.og

Main	About us	Offers	Events	Contact

Sudbury Broadcasting's Culture

Our organization culture at Sudbury Broadcasting is mission-based. All our employees have a common objective of fertilizing viewers' minds through truthful and fascinating programs.

147 a variety of backgrounds → multiple backgrounds

In order to reflect our audiences who belong to diverse ethnic groups, we actively recruit employees from a **variety** of backgrounds. Sudbury Broadcasting's devotion to its diversity can be also seen in our **Mars Groups**. These groups, made of employees from all different levels of the social groups, have regular **brainstorming sessions** so as to enhance not only productivity but also efficiency.

148 brainstorming sessions → creative solutions

Sudbury Broadcasting provides a wide range of chances for career development and helps keep people motivated and inspired.

陷阱選項 148-B
由 Sudbury Broadcasting 提供，並非由題目關鍵字 Mars Groups 所提供。

147. What is suggested about Sudbury Broadcasting's workers?
(A) They are all highly experienced in a field.
(B) They do not mind working overtime.
(C) They have multiple backgrounds.
(D) They need to regularly attend a training course.

選出符合事實的選項
→ 關鍵字為 Sudbury Broadcasting's workers。

148. What is a purpose of Sudbury Broadcasting's Mars Groups?
(A) To raise funds for the community
(B) To offer ~~a wide range of career opportunities~~
(C) To provide creative solutions
(D) To encourage work-life balance

關鍵字 Mars Groups
→ 從關鍵字前後找出答題線索。

第 147-148 題 網頁

http://www.sudburybroadcasting.co.og

主頁	關於我們	工作機會	活動	聯絡我們

薩伯里廣播的文化

薩伯里廣播的組織文化是以任務為基礎。我們所有的員工都有個共同目標，就是要透過如實而吸引人的節目，豐饒聽眾的心靈。

為了反映我們聽眾的多元族群，我們積極召募來自不同背景的人員。薩伯里廣播對自身多樣性的熱愛還可以從我們的火星群組看出來。這些群組是由來自不同社會群體階層的員工所組成，他們定期集會進行腦力激盪，以求不只增強產能還有效能。

薩伯里廣播提供許多職涯發展的機會，並幫助人們不斷受到激勵與啟發。

字彙 mission-based 以任務為基礎　objective 目的、目標　fertilize 使肥沃、使豐饒　truthful 如實的、真實的　fascinating 吸引人的、迷人的　belong to 屬於　diverse 多樣的、不同的　recruit 招募、吸收　devotion 奉獻、熱愛　diversity 多樣性、差異　regular 定期的、有規律的　brainstorming 腦力激盪、集思廣益　session 會議、集會　so as to V 為了、以便　career development 職涯發展　motivated 受到激勵的　inspired 受到啟發的

147. 關於薩伯里的員工，可由文中得知什麼？

(A) 他們都是某個領域裡的老手。

(B) 他們不介意加班。

(C) 他們來自不同背景。

(D) 他們需要定期參加訓練課程。

STEP 1 題目要求找出相符的事實時，請先整理出各選項的關鍵字，再查看文章內容。

題目關鍵字為 Sudbury Broadcasting's workers，請從文章中找出相關內容，並對照選項的敘述。文中寫道：「In order to reflect our audiences who belong to diverse ethnic groups, we actively recruit employees from a variety of backgrounds.」，提到為了因應不同族群的觀眾，他們僱用各種不同背景的員工。選項將內文的 a variety of backgrounds 改寫成 multiple backgrounds，因此答案要選 (C)。

STEP 2 分析錯誤選項

文中寫道：「These groups, made of employeesfrom all different levels of the social groups, have regular brainstorming sessions」，提到員工會定期開會集思廣益，並非參加訓練課程，因此 (D) 的敘述有誤。

148. 薩伯里廣播火星群組的目的之一是什麼？

(A) 為了幫社區募款

(B) 為了提供多樣化的工作機會

(C) 為了提供有創意的解決方案

(D) 為了鼓勵工作與生活的平衡

STEP 1 **答案通常會出現在關鍵字旁。**

題目關鍵字為 Mars Groups，請從文章中找出相關內容，並對照選項的敘述。文中寫道：「These groups, . . . all different levels of the social groups」與「have regular brainstorming sessions so as to enhance not only productivity but also efficiency」，提到由 Sudbury Broadcasting 的員工組成 Mars Groups，定期開會集思廣益，以提升產能和效率。因此答案要選 (C)，目的為提供有創意的解決方案。

STEP 2 **分析錯誤選項**

文中寫道：「Sudbury Broadcasting provides a wide range of chances for career development」，提到由 Sudbury Broadcasting 提供職能發展的機會，並非由 Mars Groups 所提供，因此 (B) 的敘述有誤。文中並未提到 (A) 和 (D) 的內容。

Questions 149-150 refer to the following text message chain.

●●●○○

Alton Baldwin 10:21 A.M.
Janice, when do you think you can get here? The job applicants have already arrived. We should **start job interviews** in ten minutes.

Janice Bailey 10:22 A.M.
I apologize! The tunnel is still closed. Our taxi had no choice but to take a detour. We should get there in 20 minutes. **Could you** go ahead and **start** without us?

149 start job interviews → speak to a job applicant

Alton Baldwin 10:23 A.M.
All right. We will be meeting Gregg Mclaughlin first.

Janice Bailey 10:24 A.M.
Sure. He is the one I talked about who has some experience at another beverage firm.

Alton Baldwin 10:25 A.M.
Yeah. **I am so surprised** that our firm needs to employ more workers to keep up with orders. **It's growing so fast**.

Janice Bailey 10:25 A.M.
Same here! I'll get there as soon as possible. 150 對前一句話的反應。

149. What does Ms. Bailey want Mr. Baldwin to do?
(A) ~~Publicize~~ an open position
(B) ~~Deal with~~ some orders
(C) Speak to a job applicant
(D) ~~Put off~~ a job interview

Bailey ／要求事項
→ 從 Bailey 的對白中找出要求別人的話語：Could you . . . ?

150. At 10:25 A.M., what does Ms. Bailey mean when she writes, "Same here!"?
(A) She has reviewed the applications.
(B) She has already talked with Mr. Mclaughlin.
(C) She wants the man to arrive as soon as possible.
(D) She is also excited by the firm's rapid growth.

掌握說話者意圖
→ 確認指定句前後的文意。

第 149-150 題 訊息串

艾爾頓・鮑德溫 上午 10 時 21 分
珍妮絲，妳覺得妳什麼時候可以到這裡？應徵的人都已經到了，我們必須在 10 分鐘內開始面試。

珍妮絲・貝利 上午 10 時 22 分
抱歉！隧道仍然封閉，我們搭的計程車不得不繞道而行。我們應該會在 20 分鐘內到那裡，你可以不等我們先開始嗎？

艾爾頓・鮑德溫 上午 10 時 23 分
好，我們會先見葛瑞格・麥克洛芬林。

珍妮絲・貝利 上午 10 時 24 分
沒問題，他是我之前談過、在另一間飲料公司做過的人。

艾爾頓・鮑德溫 上午 10 時 25 分
對，我很驚訝我們公司必須多請人才能應付訂單，公司成長得如此快速。

珍妮絲・貝利 上午 10 時 25 分
我也是！我會盡快趕過去。

字彙 job applicant 應徵者　apologize 道歉　tunnel 隧道
have no choice but to V 不得不、只好　go ahead 進行、開始
experience 經驗　beverage 飲料　firm 公司　keep up with 跟上……、趕上……
Same here! 我也是！／我同意！

149. 貝利女士要鮑德溫先生做什麼？
(A) 公告職缺
(B) 處理一些訂單
(C) 和應徵者談
(D) 延後工作的面試

STEP 1 **文章為線上聊天文時，請務必確認登場人物的工作內容和當前處理工作的狀況。**

本題詢問 Bailey 希望 Baldwin 做什麼事。Bailey 的訊息寫道：「Could you go ahead and start without us?」，請對方在自己不在場的情況下先開始。從這句話中無法得知確切的工作內容，因此請由前方 Baldwin 的訊息確認。Baldwin 的訊息寫道：「The job applicants have already arrived. We should start job interviews in ten minutes.」，提到要和應徵者進行面試。因此答案要選 (C)，要求 Baldwin 和應徵者對談。

STEP 2 **分析錯誤選項**

(B) 的 orders 出現在訊息中：「our firms needs to employ more workers to keep up with orders」，但是並不是 Bailey 要求 Baldwin 的事情，而是僱用員工的原因。

「We should start job interviews in ten minutes」當中提到 job interviews，但是並非延後面試時間，而是直接開始面試，因此 (D) 的敘述並不正確。

150. 上午 **10：25** 時，當貝利女士寫道：「我也是！」，是什麼意思？

(A) 她已審查過應徵者。

(B) 她已經和麥克洛芬林先生談過。

(C) 她要那人盡快到達。

(D) 她對公司的快速成長也很興奮。

STEP 1 **線上聊天文中出現詢問「意圖」的考題時，請確認指定句前後的轉折詞，並選擇較為籠統的敘述作為答案。**

指定句前方寫道：「I am so surprised that our firm needs to employ more workers to keep up with orders. It's growing so fast.」，提到他很驚訝公司成長的如此快速，居然還要僱用更多的員工。接著 Baldwin 便回答：「Same here!」，表示她跟他的想法一樣，因此答案為 (D)。

STEP 2 **分析錯誤選項**

Same here 的意思為「我也是、跟我想的一樣」，用於表示同意對方的看法、或對對方所說的話深有同感，請務必熟記此用法。文中無法得知 (A) 和 (B) 是否正確、而 (C) 為 Bailey 自己想要完成的事。

Questions 151-152 refer to the following flyer.

Immediate Shipping

151 Web site → online
total cost → quote

Do you need your package delivered as soon as possible? We expedite any delivery of items you need to send urgently anywhere in the nation. Just contact us at any time 24 hours a day, and your package will be picked up and processed on the same day. By visiting our **Web site, the total cost** of your delivery request can be calculated. However, keep in mind that the calculated cost is only valid for the day it is estimated. On request, a specific code will be provided, which can be used to **check the status of your shipment** such as its current location and arrival time.

152 status of your shipment
→ track of a package's progress

陷阱選項 151-A
應為 within a day，而非一週以內，因此 within a week 並不正確。

151. What is mentioned in the flyer?
(A) Packages can be delivered ~~within a week~~.
(B) ~~Discounted~~ prices are available for loyal customers.
(C) The quote can be provided online.
(D) A ~~text message~~ is automatically sent upon request.

選出符合事實的選項
→ 答案通常會採換句話說的方式。

152. Why is the specific code issued?
(A) To adjust a shipping schedule
(B) To keep track of a package's progress
(C) To verify shipping insurance
(D) To pay for ~~a delivery service~~

specific code／發送的原因
→ 從文中找出關鍵字 specific code。

第 151-152 題 傳單

立即運送

您需要盡速運送包裹嗎？我們能幫助您加速將貨物送達全國的任何地方。全天無休，請隨時和我們聯絡，您的包裹會在當天收取並處理。造訪我們的網站，可以計算您所有的運送費用。不過，請記得，所計算出的費用只在估算的當天有效。如經索求，將提供一組特定代碼，可用於查對您貨物的狀況，如包裹現在的位置和送達的時間。

字彙 **immediate** 立即的 **package** 包裹 **expedite** 加快 **urgently** 緊急地 **pick up** 取（某物） **process** 處理 **request** 要求 **calculate** 計算 **valid** 有效的 **estimate** 估計、估價 **on request** 經請求、應要求 **status** 情形、狀態 **shipment** 運輸的貨物

151. 傳單中提及何事？

(A) 包裹會在一星期內運送。

(B) 忠實顧客可獲得優惠價格。

(C) 可提供線上報價。

(D) 提出要求後，會自動傳送簡訊。

STEP 1 答案通常會採換句話說的方式。

題目關鍵字為 flyer，請選出和 flyer 的內容相符的選項。首先請分析各選項，確認文中出現答案的位置。本題為題組第一題，因此請從前半段文章中確認答案。當中寫道：「By visiting our Web site, the total cost of your delivery request can be calculated.」，提到可以在網站上計算出配送的總費用。選項將 total cost 和 Web site 改寫成 quote 和 online，因此答案為 (C)。

STEP 2 分析錯誤選項

「your package will be picked up and processed on the same day」當中提到配送的物品當天就會處理，因此 (A) within a week 並不正確。

雖然文中有提到 (D) upon request，但是內文為「On request, a specific code will be provided」，表示會發送特定代碼，並非發送簡訊。

152. 為什麼會發出特定代碼？

(A) 為了調整運送時程

(B) 為了追蹤包裹的運送進度

(C) 為了核對貨物運輸保險

(D) 為了支付運送服務的費用

STEP 1 內文會告知明確的資訊，但是答案會採較為籠統的方式敘述。

題目關鍵字為 why 和 specific code issued，因此請找出發送特定代碼的原因。選項會採較為籠統的方式敘述，因此請先從內文中找出明確的資訊。

文中寫道：「a specific code will be provided, which can be used to check the status of your shipment such as its current location and arrival time」，提到可以用 code 確認配送的狀況，包含現在位置和到貨時間。選項將文中的 the status of your shipment such as its current location and arrival time 改寫成 packages's progress，因此答案為 (B)。

STEP 2 分析錯誤選項

(D) 文中出現 pay 的同義詞 cost：「the total cost of your delivery request can be calculated」，表示可以事先計算出費用，與配送服務無關，因此不能作為答案。

Questions 153-155 refer to the following booklet.

Ruislip-R2Q!
Your lifelong electric device

Thank you for purchasing Ruislip-R2Q, the nation's best rechargeable electric toothbrush. To maintain your device in its best condition, clean your R2Q right after using it by running the part of its head under clear water. —[1]—. Every week, disassemble your R2Q and clean the under parts as instructed in the user handbook. Please be advised that the **brush** should be **replaced** with a **new** one **every other week**. —[2]—.

153 brush → A new part
every other week → regularly

The lithium-ion battery installed in the device makes Ruislip-R2Q last much longer than any other electric products on the current market. —[3]—. You can charge your device any time you wish, but it is best for the battery to recharge your R2Q after it has fully discharged. Please keep in mind that only the charger that comes with your device should be used. Using other chargers from the third party may cause **unexpected malfunctions** not covered by the warranty. —[4]—. Check our Web site for more details : www.ruislipr2q.net/product.info

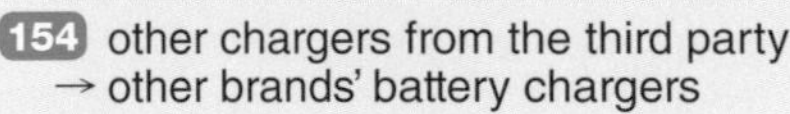

154 other chargers from the third party
→ other brands' battery chargers

155 "This rechargeable battery . . ."

153. What is suggested about the Ruislip-R2Q?
(A) It does ~~not~~ need to be cleaned ~~often~~.
(B) A new part is regularly required.
(C) ~~Some parts~~ should be changed ~~every week~~.
(D) It can be purchased ~~only online~~.

154. According to the booklet, what should users do with their devices to prevent malfunctions?
(A) Bring them to a designated store when it is broken.
(B) Go to a Web site to request a repair service.
(C) Avoid using other brands' battery chargers.
(D) Recharge them after it has fully discharged.

155. In which of the positions marked [1], [2], [3], and [4] does the following sentence best belong?
"This rechargeable battery will last longer than one year, if you perform complete draining every month."
(A) [1]
(B) [2]
(C) [3]
(D) [4]

關鍵字 Ruislip-R2Q
→ 整理出各選項的關鍵字後，再查看文章的內容。

要求事項／後
→ 題目詢問要求事項時，請特別留意後半段文章。

句子插入題
→ 確認句中的指示代名詞、轉折詞。

第 153–155 題 小冊子

Ruislip-R2Q!

您一輩子的電氣設備

感謝您購買 Ruislip-R2Q，全國最好的充電式電動牙刷。為了讓您的機器保持在最佳狀態，使用後要立刻讓 R2Q 刷頭在清水下轉動清洗。每星期把您的 R2Q 拆開，依使用者手冊裡的指示清潔下半部。請留意，刷頭應每隔一星期換新。

機器裡裝的鋰離子電池，讓 Ruislip-R2Q 比目前市面上任何電氣產品壽命都長。如果您每個月把電完全放光，這顆可充電式電池可用超過一年。您可隨時為您的機器充電，但在您的 R2Q 完全沒電後再充電，對電池是最好的。請記得，應該只使用您的機器所附的充電器，使用第三方充電器可能會造成意料之外、不在保固範圍內的故障情事。欲知更多詳細資訊，請上我們的網站：www.ruislipr2q.net/product.info

字彙 **electric** 用電的 **device** 裝置、儀器 **purchase** 購買 **rechargeable** 可充電的 **maintain** 維持 **run** （機器等）運轉 **disassemble** 拆開 **replace** 取代 **every other week** 每隔一週 **lithium-ion** 鋰離子 **charge** 充電 **charger** 充電器 **third party** 第三方 **malfunction** 故障 **cover** 包含、適用於 **warranty** 保固；保證書

153. 關於 Ruislip-R2Q，可由文中得知什麼？

(A) 它不需要常常清潔。

(B) 需要定期換新零件。

(C) 有些零件要每週更換。

(D) 只能上網購買。

STEP 1 請找出選項中與內文不符的單字。

雖然本題關鍵字為 Ruislip-R2Q，但是由於本篇文章從頭到尾都在談論與該產品有關的內容，因此請查看各選項的內容，從中找出錯誤的部分，刪除錯誤敘述後，便能選出正確答案。

「clean your R2Q right after using it」中提到使用過後要立即清洗，因此 (A) 不正確。「Check our Web site for more details」中雖然有提到 (D) 的 online，但是並未提及 purchased 一事，因此不能作為答案。「Please be advised that the brush should be replaced with a new one every other week」中提到建議隔週更換一次刷頭，因此 (C) 的敘述也不正確，答案要選 (B)。

154. 根據廣告小冊，使用者應該怎麼對待機器以避免故障？

(A) 機器故障時，拿到指定店家去。

(B) 上網要求維修服務。

(C) 不要使用其他廠牌的電池充電器。

(D) 在機器完全沒電後再充電。

STEP 1 後半段文章中，會出現要求事項的答案。

本篇文章介紹產品的相關資訊，因此可以推測出後半段會出現要求事項。請由 please 開頭的祈使句／ you should ／ we want you ／ if you want 等句型來確認答案。

文中寫道：「Please keep in mind that only the charger that comes with your device should be used. Using other chargers from the third party may cause unexpected malfunctions」，提到僅能使用本產品附上的充電器，以免發生未預期的故障，因此答案要選 (C)。

STEP 2 分析錯誤選項

雖然「it is best for the battery to recharge your R2Q after it has fully discharged」中有提到 (D) 的 after it has fully discharged，但是與避免故障發生無關，因此不適合作為答案。

155. 下列句子最適合擺在 [1]、[2]、[3]、[4] 哪一處？

「如果您每個月把電完全放光，這顆可充電式電池可用超過一年」

(A) [1]

(B) [2]

(C) [3]

(D) [4]

STEP 1 句子插入題可以根據指示形容詞、指示代名詞或副詞選出答案。

句子插入題要根據上下文意，將題目的指定句插入最適當的空格中，因此請確認題目列出的指定句內容。指定句的關鍵字為 This rechargeable battery 和 last longer，請由關鍵字在文中找出相關的內容。

[3] 前方句子為「The lithium-ion battery . . . last much longer than any other electric products on the current market」，提到產品使用鋰電池的優點。而指定句接著補充說明電池的優點，因此答案要選 (C)。

Questions 156-157 refer to the following advertisement.

Borough
Apparel

All items at our main store in the center of the city are on sale now!

Borough Apparel is replacing everything for next season.

Every summer item is on a clearance sale!

Unique designer accessories

can be purchased at reduced prices.

Every product is eligible for 30 – 60% discount.

Beginning on 15 August until 1 September

Opening hours: 11 A.M. to 8 P.M., Monday through Saturday;

Closed on Sundays.

Our store is on the ground floor of the high-rise building

located at 324 Borough Street.

Check our Web site at: **www.boroughapparel.com**

156 our store . . . on sale
→ I : A business owner

157 in the center of the city
→ in the downtown area

陷阱選項 157-D
main store 指的是總店，由此可以推測出他至少有一家店以上。

156. Who most likely released the advertisement?
(A) A clothing ~~manufacturer~~
(B) A property developer
(C) A business owner
(D) A well-known accountant

Who ／撰寫廣告者
→ 從文章中找出相關內容。

157. What is indicated about Borough Apparel?
(A) It opens ~~seven days~~ a week.
(B) It is located in the downtown area.
(C) It offers a ~~regular~~ sales promotion.
(D) It operates ~~only~~ one store.

關鍵字 Borough Apparel
→ 刪去與內文不相符的選項。

第 156-157 題 廣告

> **博歐服飾**
>
> 我們位在市中心的總店，現在所有品項特價出售！
> 博歐服飾將全面換成下一季的產品。
> 所有夏季衣飾全部清倉大拍賣！
> 與眾不同的設計家配件與服裝全都可以用折扣價格買到。
> 每樣產品都有四到七折的折扣。
> 8 月 15 日起到 9 月 1 日止
> 營業時間：上午 11 時到晚上 8 時，星期一到星期六，星期日休息。
> 我們的店面位於博歐街 324 號大樓的一樓
> 請上網站：www.boroughapparel.com
>
> 字彙 borough 市鎮、大城市中的行政區　apparel 衣服、服裝　on sale 特價出售
> replace 替換　clearance sale 清倉特賣　high-rise building 高層建築物
> located 位於

156. 誰最有可能刊登這則廣告？

(A) 成衣製造商　　(B) 地產開發商
(C) 企業老闆　　(D) 知名的會計師

STEP 1 從文中找出明確的答題線索後，選出最符合的答案。

看到「Borough Apparel」和「All items at our main store in the center of the city are on sale now!」可以得知 Borough Apparel 全部的商品都在特惠中。由此可以確認發表本篇廣告的人應為此間店的老闆，因此答案為 (C)。

STEP 2 分析錯誤選項

文中並未提到 (A) manufacturer，因此不能作為答案。文中也沒有提到 (B) 和 (D) 的內容。

157. 關於博歐服飾，可由文中得知什麼？

(A) 它每週營業七天。　　(B) 它位於市中心。
(C) 它定期舉行特賣促銷。　　(D) 它只經營一家店。

STEP 1 請找出選項中與內文不符的單字。

選項為錯誤敘述時，當中會出現與內文不符的單字，因此請務必仔細找出錯誤的部分。文中寫道：「our main store in the center of the city」，提到總店位於市中心，因此答案為 (B)。

STEP 2 分析錯誤選項

(A) 文中寫道：「Closed on Sundays」，提到週日不營業。
(C) 雖然本篇文章與「sales promotion」有關，但是當中並未提到 regular（定期的）。
(D) 文中提到「main store（總店）」，由此可以推測出不只有一家店鋪。

Questions 158-160 refer to the following letter.

Flora Mckinney
Valerie Supplies Inc.
Churchill Avenue
Watson Town, Regina EQ2 R12

Dear Ms. Mckinney, 收件人：You

160 "... this is ..."

Your final issue of *Luis Weekly* was sent to you last week. However, we have not received your signed renewal contract yet. —[1]—. Over the last four years, *Luis Weekly* has become well-known as a reliable authority in the areas of **fishing equipment, camping news, and the best outdoor activities**. —[2]—. Without doubt, the value of your business can increase by subscribing to **our publication** for £25. —[3]—. Enclosed is a special **offer** for **30 percent off** the yearly subscription rate, which is **only valid for the next 4 weeks**. You would not want to miss a chance to acquire the latest information which should be essential to your business! Don't miss this great offer. —[4]—.

158

159 only valid for the next 4 weeks
→ a limited period of time

陷阱選項 159-D
當中提到提供優惠券，
並非商品禮券。

Sincerely,

Laurence C. Payne 寄件人：I

Subscription Renewal Services

158. What type of business does Ms. Mckinney most likely work for? 收件人：You
(A) A government agency
(B) A publishing company
(C) A leisure goods store
(D) A car rental company

159. According to the letter, what does Mr. Payne offer? 寄件人：I
(A) ~~A free guide~~ for outdoor activities
(B) A discount for a limited period of time
(C) A complimentary copy of a magazine
(D) ~~A gift voucher~~ for future purchases

160. In which of positions marked [1], [2], [3], and [4] does the following sentence best belong?
"We believe that this is not intentional determination, but oversight."
(A) [1] (B) [2]
(C) [3] (D) [4]

收件人 you／職業
→「your business」

寄件人 I／提供
→ 從文中找出「提供」（offer）一詞。

句子插入題
→ 確認句中的指示代名詞和轉折詞，並掌握當中的「this」和「oversight」所指的行為。

第 158-160 題 信件

芙蘿拉・麥金尼
維樂利器材公司
邱吉爾大道
瑞吉納華生鎮 EQ2 R12

親愛的麥金尼女士：

您的最後一期《路易斯週刊》已在上星期寄給您。然而，我們尚未收到您簽名的續期訂單。我們相信，這不是考慮後的決定，而只是疏忽。過去這四年來，《路易斯週刊》已成為釣魚用具、露營新聞和最佳戶外活動方面的可信賴權威。無疑地，您的企業價值會透過以 25 英鎊訂閱我們的刊物而增加。隨信附上訂閱一年打七折的特別優惠價，有效期只有接下來四星期。您不會想要錯過這個機會，這能讓您獲得對您的企業不可或缺的最新訊息！別錯過這麼優惠的價格。

忠誠地
羅倫斯・C・潘恩
續訂服務部

字彙 issue（刊物發行的）期、號　renewal contract 續訂
be well-known as 以……而出名　reliable 可信賴的　authority 權威人士
subscribe 訂閱　publication 出版物、刊物　enclosed 隨函附上的
subscription rate 訂閱費　valid 有效的　essential 必要的、必不可少的

158. 麥金尼女士最可能在哪個行業工作？

(A) 政府機關
(B) 出版公司
(C) 休閒用品店
(D) 租車公司

STEP 1 確認 I／You／第三者以及各自的職業為何。

本篇文章為寄件人 Payne 寄送給收件人 Mckinney 的信件，當中會以代名詞 You 指 Mckinney，請從前半段內文來確認她的職業。當中寫道：「*Luis Weekly* has become well-known as a reliable authority in the areas of fishing equipment, camping news, and the best outdoor activities」和「the value of your business can increase」，提到「Luis Weekly」雜誌以提供釣魚裝備、露營和野外活動的資訊聞名，訂閱雜誌能為 Mckinney 的公司帶來價值。這表示 Mckinney 公司販售的商品與雜誌主題有關，因此答案要選 (C)。

STEP 2 分析錯誤選項

(B) 為寄件人 Payne 任職的公司，並非答案。

159. 根據這封信，潘恩先生提供什麼？

(A) 一位戶外活動的免費嚮導

(B) 限時折扣

(C) 一本免費雜誌

(D) 未來購物的禮品券

STEP 1 人名通常會是重要的關鍵字。

本題關鍵字為 Mr. Payne，請從文章中找出相關內容，再和選項對照。文中寫道：「Enclosed is a special offer for 30 percent off the yearly subscription rate, which is only valid for the next 4 weeks」，提到寄件人 Payne 提供訂閱四週的特別優惠，因此答案要選 (B)。

STEP 2 分析錯誤選項

雖然「*Luis Weekly* has become well-known as a reliable authority in the areas of fishing equipment, camping news, and the best outdoor activities」當中有提到 (A) outdoor activities，但指的是雜誌出名的原因，並非答案。

160. 下列句子最適合擺在 [1]、[2]、[3]、[4] 哪一處？

「我們相信，這不是考慮後的決定，而只是疏忽。」

(A) [1]

(B) [2]

(C) [3]

(D) [4]

STEP 1 題目為句子插入題時，請由空格前後方內容確認答題關鍵字。

句子插入題要根據上下文意，將題目的指定句插入最適當的空格中，因此請務必看懂題目列出的指定句內容。題目關鍵字為 this 和 oversight（疏忽出錯），指出對方不小心做了某個行為，但是並非出自本意，因此請找出此話所指的行為為何。

[1] 前方的句子寫道：「Your final issue of *Luis Weekly* was sent to you last week. However, we have not received your signed renewal contract yet.」，提到自己已將對方訂閱的最後一期雜誌寄出，但是尚未收到對方同意要續訂的合約。因此答案選 (A) 較為適當，可以將指定句視為推測對方尚未提供續訂合約的原因。

Questions 161-164 refer to the following e-mail.

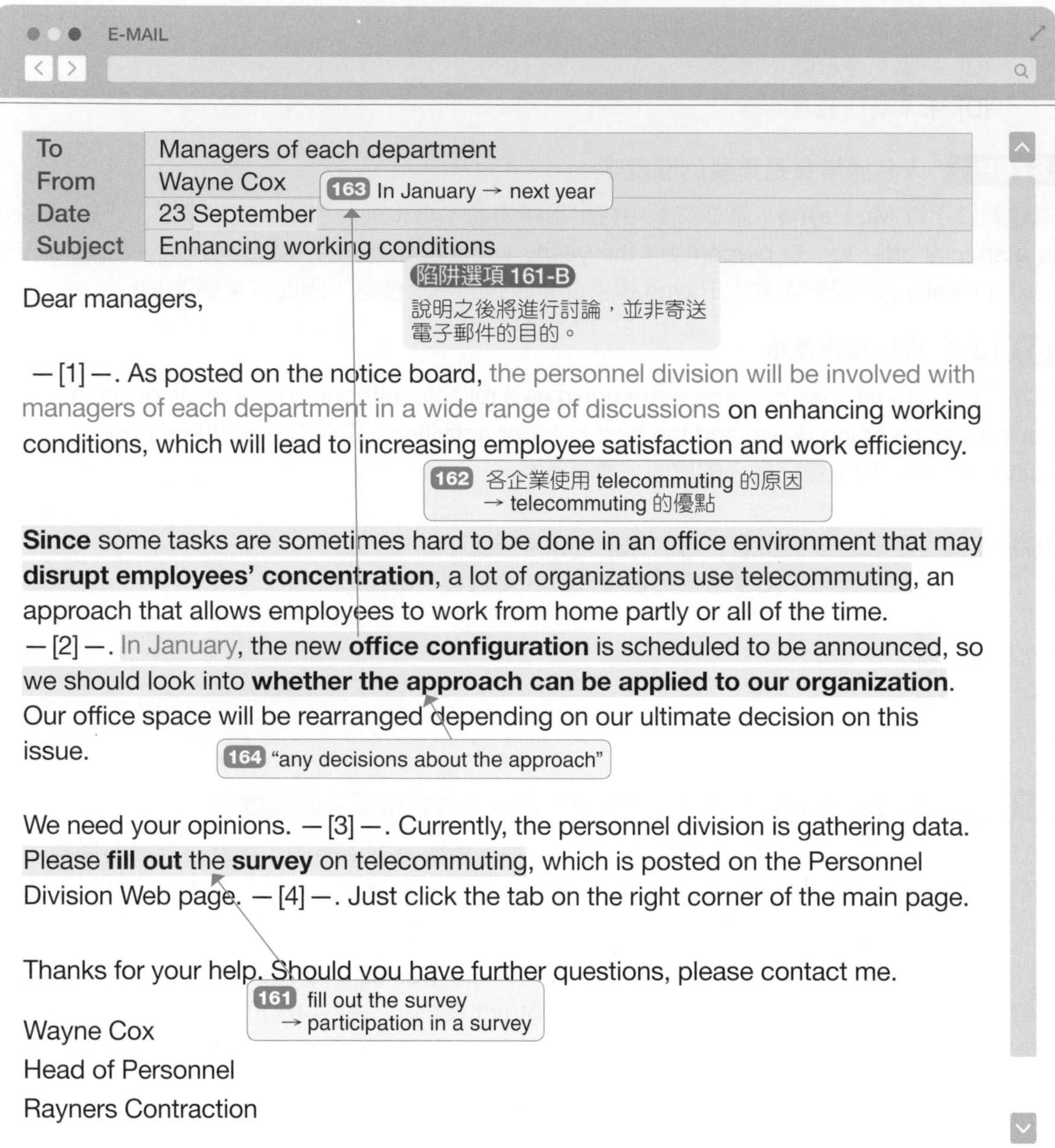

E-MAIL

To	Managers of each department
From	Wayne Cox
Date	23 September
Subject	Enhancing working conditions

Dear managers,

—[1]—. As posted on the notice board, the personnel division will be involved with managers of each department in a wide range of discussions on enhancing working conditions, which will lead to increasing employee satisfaction and work efficiency.

Since some tasks are sometimes hard to be done in an office environment that may **disrupt employees' concentration**, a lot of organizations use telecommuting, an approach that allows employees to work from home partly or all of the time. —[2]—. In January, the new **office configuration** is scheduled to be announced, so we should look into **whether the approach can be applied to our organization**. Our office space will be rearranged depending on our ultimate decision on this issue.

We need your opinions. —[3]—. Currently, the personnel division is gathering data. Please **fill out** the **survey** on telecommuting, which is posted on the Personnel Division Web page. —[4]—. Just click the tab on the right corner of the main page.

Thanks for your help. Should you have further questions, please contact me.

Wayne Cox
Head of Personnel
Rayners Contraction

161. What is the purpose of the e-mail?
(A) To announce ~~new~~ employee policies
(B) To remind staff of an upcoming meeting
(C) To ask for participation in a survey
(D) ~~To increase employee satisfaction~~

162. What is stated as an advantage of telecommuting?
(A) It provides more room for employees.
(B) It can help staff work without distraction.
(C) It lowers overall operating expenses.
(D) It is an environmentally friendly approach.

目的／後半段的要求事項中有 10% 的機率會出現目的

→ 注意後半段文中提出的要求、Please 開頭的句子。

telecommuting 的優點

→ 從文中找出關鍵字 telecommuting。

163. What does the organization plan to do next year?
(A) ~~Redesign~~ a Web page
(B) ~~Recruit~~ a new personnel manager
(C) Carry out its restructuring
(D) Adjust the layout of the office

164. In which of the positions marked [1], [2], [3], and [4] does the following sentence best belong?
"Be advised that any decisions about the approach have not been made yet."
(A) [1] (B) [2] **(C) [3]** (D) [4]

公司往後的計畫／next year
→ 確認提到未來時間點的句子。

插入句子題
→ 確認句中的指示代名詞和轉折詞。掌握指定句中「the approach」所指的東西。

第 161-164 題 電子郵件

收件人	各部門經理
寄件人	韋恩・考克斯
日期	9 月 23 日
主旨	改善工作條件

親愛的經理們：

正如布告欄上所公布的消息，人事部門將和各部門經理就改善工作條件一事進行廣泛討論，這將能夠提升員工的滿足感與工作效率。

在可能會打斷員工專注力的辦公環境下，有些任務可能難以完成，所以許多公司組織採用遠距離工作，一種允許員工部分或全部時間在家工作的方式。新的辦公室配置預定在一月宣布，因此，我們應該研究這種方式是否能應用在我們公司。我們的辦公室空間將依我們在這個議題的最終決定而重新安排。

我們需要你們的意見。請注意，關於這個方式的任何決定都尚未定案。目前，人事部門正在收集資料。請填寫公布在人事部門網站上的遠距離工作調查。只要選擊主頁右邊角落的標籤即可。

謝謝你們的協助。如果還有問題，請與我聯絡。

韋恩・考克斯

人事經理
雷納斯承包

字彙 disrupt 打斷、擾亂　concentration 專注、專心　organization 組織、機構　telecommuting 遠距離工作　approach 方式、方法　configuration 配置　look into 研究、調查　rearrange 重新安排、重新排列

161. 這封電子郵件的目的是什麼？

(A) 宣布新的員工守則

(B) 提醒員工即將召開的會議

(C) 要求參加調查

(D) 提升員工滿意度

STEP 1 **開頭前三句話中，有 90% 的機率會出現目的，其餘 10% 則可能出現在後半段的要求事項中。**

題目詢問目的時，通常要從前半段文章中找出答案。但是本篇文章的前半段並未提及目的，而是針對狀況進行說明，因此請改從後半段文章中尋找答案。後半段文章中寫道：「Please fill out the survey on telecommuting」，由此可以得知本封郵件的目的為要求收件人填寫針對在家工作的問卷調查，因此答案為 (C)。

STEP 2 **分析錯誤選項**

(B) 人事部將對於改善工作環境進行討論，屬於針對狀況的說明，並非目的。

(D) 提升員工的滿意度為進行討論後產生的結果，並非本封郵件的目的。

162. 文中提到遠距離工作的好處是什麼？

(A) 提供員工更多空間。

(B) 有助員工工作，不會分心。

(C) 降低整體的營運費用。

(D) 是種友善環境的方式。

STEP 1 **答案通常會出現在關鍵字旁。**

題目關鍵字為 telecommuting，本題詢問的是在家工作的優點。文中寫道：「Since some tasks are sometimes hard to be done in an office environment that may disrupt employees' concentration, a lot of organizations use telecommuting」，提到使用 telecommuting 的原因為辦公室的環境可能會妨礙員工專心辦公，這表示 telecommuting 的優點為提供員工專心辦公不受打擾的環境，因此答案為 (B)。文中並未提到其他選項的內容。

163. 公司計劃明年要做什麼？

(A) 重新設計網頁

(B) 招募新的人事經理

(C) 進行重組

(D) 調整辦公室的空間布置

STEP 1 關鍵字旁未出現答案時，請確認是否還有其他解題線索。

請從文中找出題目關鍵字 next year。文中寫道：「In January, the new office configuration is scheduled to be announced」，提到一月將公布新辦公室的配置。而撰寫此封郵件的時間為九月，這表示一月指的是明年一月，因此答案要選 (D)。

STEP 2 分析錯誤選項

(A) 雖然文中有提到 Web page，但是並未提到重新設計一事；(B) 僅提到人事部經理，並未提到要僱用新的人。

164. 下列句子最適合擺在 [1]、[2]、[3]、[4] 哪一處？

「請注意，關於這個方式的任何決定都尚未定案。」

(A) [1]

(B) [2]

(C) [3]

(D) [4]

STEP 1 「句子」插入題的解題關鍵為空格前後的轉折詞。

作答句子插入題時，不能僅確認句子插入後文意是否通順，請務必一併確認空格前後方出現的轉折詞。題目列出的指定句中提到「decision about the approach」，因此要將此句話放在提及相同內容的句子後方。[3] 前一段最後提到「our ultimate decision」，再前一句話則提到：「so we should look into whether the approach can be applied to our organization」，表示要調查公司是否適用在家工作的方式，因此答案要選 (C) [3]。

Questions 165-168 refer to the following article.

Halifax Factory to Open

(Brockley, June 21) — Canadian appliance manufacturer, Halifax announced its plan to start operating a **fourth production plant** in Brighten, UK, in October. It will open the facility on Peckham Rye Avenue in Brockley. — [1] —.

168 "The others plants . . ."

"Since **there** are **a lot of experienced and skilled workers** living in the region, the town is the best place to open a new n[...]tor **Isabelle Theron**. She added, "We are e[...]ities in Brighten and are thrilled to expand into this area, getting friendly support from the town." — [2] —.

165 a lot of experienced and skilled workers → The plentiful labor force

166 -based → headquarters

The **Ontario-based** appliance manufacturer also built a plant close to the town of Portland in Australia. — [3] —. Moreover, it has another **plan to contract a factory** in Indonesia **next quarter**. Its management is considering cities such as Medan and Cirebon. — [4] —.

167 contract a factory in Indonesia → expand into Indonesia

165. What benefit of the new location does Ms. Theron mention?
(A) The population growth
(B) The plentiful labor force
(C) The cheap building rental fee
(D) The ~~government~~ support

關鍵字 **new location／Ms. Theron**
→ 從文中找出關鍵字後，再選出與內文相符的選項。

166. Where is Halifax's headquarters?
(A) In ~~Cirebon~~
(B) In Ontario
(C) In ~~Brighten~~
(D) In ~~Brockley~~

關鍵字 **headquarters**
→ 文中使用意思相近的單字 based。

167. According to the article, what does the firm plan to do in the near future?
(A) ~~Close a plant~~ in Brighten
(B) ~~Attract~~ more infrastructure investment
(C) Expand into Indonesia
(D) ~~Acquire~~ another company

未來計畫／後
→ 往後的計畫會出現在後半段。

168. In which of the positions marked [1], [2], [3], and [4] does the following sentence best belong?
"The other plants are in the cities of Haxton, Camden, and Algate."
(A) [1] (B) [2] (C) [3] (D) [4]

句子插入題
→ 確認句中的指示代名詞和轉折詞。

第 165-168 題 文章

哈利法克斯工廠即將開幕

（布羅克利，6 月 21 日）加拿大家電製造商哈利法克斯宣布，位於英國布萊頓的第四家工廠，計劃在十月開始啟用。新工廠將設立在布羅克利派克漢瑞大道。其他的工廠位於哈克斯頓、康登和阿爾蓋特。

「由於許多有經驗且技術純熟的工人都住在這個地區，這個城鎮是開設新工廠的最佳地點，」地區經理伊莎貝兒．塞隆說。她補充道：「我們預料基礎設備會留在布萊頓，很興奮能將業務擴展到這個區域，得到全市的友善支持。」

這家總公司在安大略的家電製造商，也在澳洲靠近波特蘭市的地方蓋了一座工廠。此外，它也計劃下一季與印尼的工廠簽約，管理階層正在考慮棉蘭和井裡汶等城市。

字彙 appliance 家電　manufacturer 製造商　production plant 工廠　facility 設施、機構　manufacturing facility 生產設備　regional director 地區經理　infrastructure facilities 基礎設施　expand 擴張、發展　friendly 友好的、友善的　based 將某地設為總部　contract 訂合約　management 管理部門

165. 塞隆女士提到新地點的好處是什麼？

(A) 人口成長

(B) 充足的勞力

(C) 便宜的大樓租金

(D) 政府的支援

STEP 1 人名通常會是重要的關鍵字。

本題關鍵字為 Ms. Theron，請從文章中找出相關內容，再和選項對照。第二段引用了 Isabelle Theron 所說的話：「Since there are a lot of experienced and skilled workers living in the region, the town is the best place to open a new manufacturing facility」，提到那個區域的優勢為居住很多經驗豐富的技術人員，非常適合作為設立新工廠的地點，因此答案為 (B)。

STEP 2 分析錯誤選項

(D)「getting friendly support from the town」當中有提到 support，但是並非由政府支援，因此不能作為答案。

166. 哈利法克斯的總部位於何處？

(A) 井裡汶

(B) 安大略

(C) 布萊頓

(D) 布羅克利

STEP 1 **答案通常會採換句話說的方式。**

本題要選出與關鍵字 headquarters 有關的內容相符的選項。文中並未出現 headquarters，而是使用意思相近的單字 -based。因此請確認此單字出現的地方，並選出與內文相符的選項。文中寫道：「The Ontario-based appliance manufacturer」，提到家電用品製造商 Halifax 的總公司設在 Ontario，因此答案為 (B)。

STEP 2 **分析錯誤選項**

(C)「its plan to start operating a fourth production plant in Brighten」當中提到 Brighten，但是並非總部，而是計劃設立的第四間工廠，因此並非答案；(A) 計劃於明年簽約的工廠中，有兩間位於印尼的工廠，其中一間位於 Cirebon。

167. 根據本文，這家公司近期計劃做什麼？

(A) 關閉在布萊頓的工廠

(B) 吸引更多基礎建設的投資

(C) 擴展到印尼

(D) 收購另一家公司

STEP 1 **答案通常會採換句話說的方式。**

題目關鍵字 near future 屬於意思較為模糊的單字，文中有極高的機率會採用意思較為明確的單字。文中寫道：「it has another plan to contract a factory in Indonesia next quarter」，提到計劃下一季和印尼的工廠簽約，因此答案要選 (C)。文中並未提及其他選項的內容，因此皆不適合作為答案。

168. 下列句子最適合擺在 [1]、[2]、[3]、[4] 哪一處？

「其他的工廠位於哈克斯頓、康登和阿爾蓋特。」

(A) [1]

(B) [2]

(C) [3]

(D) [4]

STEP 1 **句子插入題可以根據指示形容詞、指示代名詞或副詞選出答案。**

句子插入題要根據上下文意，將題目的指定句插入最適當的空格中，因此請確認題目列出的指定句內容。The others 為不定代名詞，要先提到明確的對象後，才會使用此不定代名詞。由此可以推測出前方會出現明確的地點或地名，因此答案要選 (A) [1]。

STEP 2 **分析錯誤選項**

[4] 前方使用未來式提到未來的計畫，而本題的指定句為現在式，因此並不適合填入該空格中。

Questions 169-171 refer to the following schedule of events.

The Headstone Global Publishing Expo

11-13 October,
Perivale Convention Center, Montreal

Schedule for Thursday, 13 October

The Winds of Change in the Digital Era
1:00 P.M. – 2:00 P.M. Lecture Hall 301

陷阱選項 169-A
debate 並非 interactive activities。

Debate on whether digital media promotes or degrades literacy hosted by Benny Cross.

Beginner Course in Visual Design
2:15 P.M. – 3:15 P.M. Graphic Images Auditorium

169 hands-on experience → interactive activities

Terri Anderson and Killi Ball, experts in visual design, will address useful skills and trainees will gain hands-on experience of what they have learned.

Workshop on E-Publishing
3:30 P.M. – 4:30 P.M. Latimer Center

170 purchase . . . on the Web site → are provided through a Web site

Publishing and advertising e-publications including audio books online. After and before the workshop, attendees will be able to purchase all **accompanying materials on the Web site**.
Presenters: Jancie Bailey, Chief Editor of Canons Books Ltd., and Willard Curtis, Head of Marketing at Canons Books Ltd.

Considering Readers' Views
4:45 P.M. – 6:15 P.M. Hall G1

In order to publicize her new book, "Considering Reader's Views", through a book-signing event, writer Nancy Cole participates in the Headstone Global Publishing Expo to talk about her new topic, answer questions and autograph her books.

171 arrive → come

- Keep in mind that since the number of seats is limited, **arrive** early before the programs you intend to attend start to secure a seat. Reservations are not accepted for any programs. Please be advised that video recordings are prohibited while photos are allowed.
- Purchasing a daily pass for $ 9.50 is required to attend the scheduled programs.
- Refreshments and meals can be purchased at snack bars across Perivale Convention Center. Visit our Web site at www.hgpe_events.com/inf.hotels for information about accommodations.

陷阱選項 171-A
提到可以拍照。

169. Where will publishing expo visitors be able to attend interactive activities?
(A) In Lecture Hall 301
(B) In the Graphic Images Auditorium
(C) In the Latimer Center
(D) In Hall G1

關鍵字 **interactive activities**
→ 文中使用意思相近的單字。

170. What is stated about accompanying supplies for the workshop?

(A) They ~~must be ordered~~ in advance.
(B) They are offered in limited numbers for free.
(C) They are provided through a Web site.
(D) They can be bought ~~at the venue~~.

關鍵字 accompanying supplies

→ 從關鍵字前後找出答題線索。

171. What are publishing expo visitors asked to do?

(A) ~~Avoid~~ taking photos
(B) Come early for programs
(C) Bring their own lunch
(D) ~~Prepare~~ questions before programs

來訪者／被要求事項／後半段

→ 確認後半段中 Keep in mind that 開頭的句子。

第 169-171 題 活動時程

基石全球出版博覽會
10 月 11 – 13 日
蒙特婁派洛威爾會議中心

10 月 13 日星期四日程

數位時代的變革風潮
下午 1 點—2 點 301 演講廳
班尼・克羅斯主持，討論數位媒體究竟提升或降低讀寫能力。

視覺設計初級班
下午 2：15—3：15 圖片影像講堂
視覺設計專家泰瑞・安德森和奇里・鮑爾將講述實用技巧，學員可針對他們的所學，進行實作體驗。

電子出版工作坊
下午 3：30—4：30 拉堤莫中心
出版並廣告促銷如線上有聲書的電子出版品。在工作坊結束之後與開始之前，參加者可以在網站上購買所有隨附的教材。
主持人：坎農書籍有限公司總編輯珍妮絲・貝利，坎農書籍有限公司行銷總監威勒・柯蒂斯

細思讀者觀點
下午 4：45—6：15 G1 廳
為了宣傳新書《細思讀者觀點》，作者南西・柯爾參加了基石全球出版博覽會，透過簽書活動暢談她的新書論點、回答提問並簽書。

- 請記得，由於座位有限，請在欲參加的節目開始之前抵達以確保有座位。任何節目都不接受預訂座位。請注意，不得錄影，但可拍照。

- 參加表定節目需購買 9.50 元的日票。
- 餐點飲料可到派洛威爾會議中心對面的輕食吧購買，住宿資料請上我們的網站：www.hgpe_events.com/inf.hotels 查詢。

字彙 debate 辯論、討論　degrade 降低　hand-on 親自動手的、實務的
accompanying 伴隨的　publicize 宣傳、公布　participate in 參加
autograph 親筆簽名　require 需要、要求　accommodations 住所、住處

169. 出版博覽會的訪客可以到哪裡參加互動活動？

(A) 301 演講廳

(B) 圖片影像講堂

(C) 拉提莫中心

(D) G1 廳

STEP 1 答案通常會採換句話說的方式。

文中通常會將答案改寫成其他意思相近的單字。「interactive activities」指透過相互交流後，進行實作的體驗活動。文中第二個活動——視覺設計初級課程中提到聽完視覺設計的說明後，將進行實作體驗（hands-on experience），等同於 interactive activities 的概念，因此答案要選 (B)。

STEP 2 分析錯誤選項

看到在 (A) 進行的 debate 和 (D) 進行的 answer questions 活動，可能會聯想到 interactive，但是兩者並非以學的東西為基礎進行實作，不屬於 interactive activities 的概念，皆不適合作為答案。

170. 關於工作坊隨附的教材，文中如何描述？

(A) 必須事前訂購。

(B) 免費數量有限。

(C) 可透網站取得。

(D) 可以在會場購買。

STEP 1 答案通常會出現在關鍵字旁。

請從文中找出題目關鍵字 accompanying supplies。文章中間寫道：「attendees will be able to purchase all accompanying materials on the Web site」，提到可以在網站上購買資料，因此答案為 (C)。

STEP 2 分析錯誤選項

(A) 看到文中的 early 可能會聯想到選項中的 in advance，但文中並未提到提前訂購，而是提前到場。

(D) 文中並未提到購買的地方為 at the venue，因此不能作為答案。

171. 出版博覽會的訪客被要求做什麼？

(A) 不要拍照

(B) 在節目開始前提早到

(C) 自備午餐

(D) 在節目之前先想好問題

STEP 1 **後半段文章中，會出現要求事項的答案。**

本題詢問要求來訪者的事項，因此請從後半段文中找出使用 be advised/ please / make sure 祈使句的句型。文中寫道：「Keep in mind that . . . , arrive early」，要求提早到場，因此答案為 (B)。

STEP 2 **分析錯誤選項**

(A) 文中寫道：「while photos are allowed」，提到可以拍照，因此該選項不正確。

(D) 文中僅提到 questions，並未要求要準備。

Questions 172-175 refer to the following online chat session.

●●●○○

Xavier Parker 11:02 A.M.
Hello, all. It is time for us to begin thinking about the department meeting on Thursday. Our sales have been continuously decreasing. I would like us to consider looking at new ways. 173

Tamra Pansy 11:03 A.M.
Right. What do you think we should do?

Xavier Parker 11:04 A.M.
As the demand for **cleaning products** doesn't seem to be strong as it used to be, it could be a good move for us to expand **Wilda Supplies with additional items**. 172

Rhea Maura 11:05 A.M.
There has always been a high demand for small fancy electronics. Let's look into it.

Twila Vonda 11:06 A.M.
I believe that is a good idea. And, probably we should consider toasters.

Tamra Pansy 11:07 A.M.
I can't agree with that more. Electronics such as Blue-tooth speakers and coffee makers can be possible options.

Xavier Parker 11:08 A.M.
Great ideas, everyone. These ideas should be presented at the meeting. **Please research** more **details about manufacturers and estimates** and have those included in the presentation each of you will make. **I'll** need that information later in order to prepare a preliminary budget proposal for the board.

175 details about manufacturers
→ information regarding manufacturers

Twila Vonda 11:09 A.M.
No problem.

174 research more details about . . . estimates
→ collect some information

Xavier Parker 11:10 A.M.
If you have any concerns or questions, please inform me. I'll forward everyone some guidelines by fax.

172. What kind of goods does Wilda Supplies currently sell?
(A) Cleaning supplies (B) Household appliances
(C) Business machines (D) Office appliances

關鍵字 **Wilda Supplies**
→ 從關鍵字前後找出答題線索。

173. At 11:02 A.M., what does Mr. Parker mean when he writes, "I would like us to consider looking at new ways"?
(A) The firm should carry a wider range of products.
(B) The event should address various topics.
(C) The firm has to relocate its main office.
(D) The event should be postponed to another day.

掌握說話者意圖
→ 確認指定句前後的文意。

174. What will Ms. Vonda most likely do next?
(A) Draft a proposal
(B) Fax a document to ~~Ms. Pansy~~
(C) Collect some information
(D) ~~Have~~ a budget ~~approved~~

Ms. Vonda／將要做的事
→ 答案會出現在對方的訊息中，確認使用 Please 開頭，表示勸說或建議的句子。

175. What will Mr. Parker give to the board?
(A) ~~Suggestions for new sales~~ guidelines
(B) More information regarding manufacturers
(C) An invoice of recent orders
(D) A proposal for updating ~~equipment~~

Mr. Parker／未來／the board
→ 確認 Parker 所寫的訊息。

第 172-175 題 線上聊天

查威爾·派克 上午 11 時 02 分
哈囉，各位。我們該開始想想星期四的部門會議了，我們的業績一直下滑，我想要我們大家仔細思考新的方向。

塔瑪拉·潘西 上午 11 時 03 分
對，你覺得我們該怎麼做？

查威爾·派克 上午 11 時 04 分
由於清潔用品的需求似乎不如以往強，對我們來說，以增加其他品項來擴大威達用品的生意可能是個好對策。

蕾亞·莫拉 上午 11 時 05 分
對小巧而別緻電子產品的需求總是很高，讓我們來研究一下。

蒂瓦拉·馮達 上午 11 時 06 分
我覺得這是個好點子。還有，我們或許該考慮烤麵包機。

塔瑪拉·潘西 上午 11 時 07 分
我完全贊同，像是藍牙喇叭和咖啡機這樣的電子產品，也是可能的選項。

查威爾·派克 上午 11 時 08 分
各位的點子都很棒，這些意見應該在會議上提出，請調查更多製造商和估價的資料，然後把這些都放在你們每人要做的簡報裡。我晚一點會需要這些資料，以便準備一份初步預算給董事會。

蒂瓦拉·馮達 上午 11 時 09 分
沒問題。

查威爾·派克 上午 11 時 10 分
如果你們有任何疑慮或問題，請告訴我。我會傳真指導原則給大家。

字彙 **move** 措施、步驟 **expand** 擴大、增加 **additional** 添加的、額外的
look into 研究、調查 **present** 提出、展現 **manufacturer** 製造商
estimate 估價、估算 **preliminary** 初步的 **budget proposal** 預算案
board 董事會 **forward** 發送

172. 威達用品目前販售什麼產品？
(A) 清潔用品
(B) 家用電器
(C) 商用機器
(D) 辦公室用品

STEP 1 答案通常會出現在關鍵字旁。

請從題目關鍵字 Wilda Supplies 附近確認答案。文中寫道：「As the demand for cleaning products doesn't seem to be strong as it used to be. It could be a good move for us to expand Wilda Supplies with additional items.」，提到清潔用品的需求降低，建議 Wilda Supplies 增加販售新的品項。由此可以得知該公司為販售清潔用品的公司，因此答案為 (A)。

173. 上午 11：02 時，派克先生寫道：「我想要我們大家仔細思考新的方向」，意指什麼？
(A) 公司應該出售更多樣的產品。
(B) 活動應該討論各種不同主題。
(C) 公司總部必須搬遷。
(D) 活動應該延後到另一天。

STEP 1 線上聊天文中出現詢問「意圖」的考題時，請確認指定句前後的轉折詞，並選擇較為籠統的敘述作為答案。

指定句前方寫道：「Our sales have been continuously decreasing」，提到銷售量不斷減少，接著寫道：「I would like us to consider looking at new ways」。Parker 在下一段的訊息中又寫道：「expand Wilda Supplies with additional items」，由此可以確認他建議以增加品項來克服當前的問題，因此答案為 (A)。

STEP 2 分析錯誤選項

「It is time for us to begin thinking about the department meeting on Thursday. Our sales have been continuously decreasing」中提到 department meeting，可以改寫成 (B) 的 event，但是討論的主題僅有解決銷售量不佳一項，因此不能作為答案。

174. 馮達女士接下來最可能做什麼？

(A) 草擬提案

(B) 傳真一份文件給潘西女士

(C) 搜集一些資料

(D) 核准預算

STEP 1 **題目詢問未來計畫時，答案通常會出現在另一個人的對白中，以勸說或建議的方式帶出答案。**

本題關鍵字為 Ms. Vonder，詢問她接下來將做的事為何。後半段文章對方的訊息中，會以 ask、require、suggest、need 等動詞提出要求。Parker 的訊息寫道：「Please research more details about manufacturers and estimates」，要求對方仔細調查生產業者和價格。接著 Vonder 回覆 No problem 表示同意，因此答案為 (C)。

STEP 2 分析錯誤選項

(B) 故意將文中的「forward everyone some guidelines by fax」改寫成「fax a document」，但是主詞並不正確。

(D) Parker 的訊息中寫道：「I'll need that information later in order to prepare a preliminary budget proposal for the board.」，當中提到 budget，為 Parker 自己要做的事情，並非要求 Vonda 做的事，因此不能作為答案。

175. 派克先生會給董事會什麼？

(A) 新銷售方針的建議

(B) 更多關於製造商的資料

(C) 近期訂單的出貨單

(D) 更新設備的提案

STEP 1 **文章為線上聊天文時，請務必確認登場人物的工作內容和當前處理工作的狀況。**

本題詢問 Mr. Parker 將在董事會上提供什麼東西，答案會出現在題目關鍵字 Mr. Parker 所寫的訊息中，。Parker 的訊息中寫道：「Please research more details about manufacturers and estimates」和「I'll need that information later in order to prepare a preliminary budget proposal for the board」，麻煩 Vonda 仔細調查生產業者和價格，並表示他需要這些資訊來準備預算表，以便在理事會上提出，因此答案為 (B)。

STEP 2 分析錯誤選項

(A) 雖然 Parker 的訊息中有提到 guidelines，但是與銷售量無關，也不是要在理事會上交出的東西，因此並非答案。文中並未提到 (C) 和 (D) 的內容。

Questions 176-180 refer to the following Web page and e-mail.

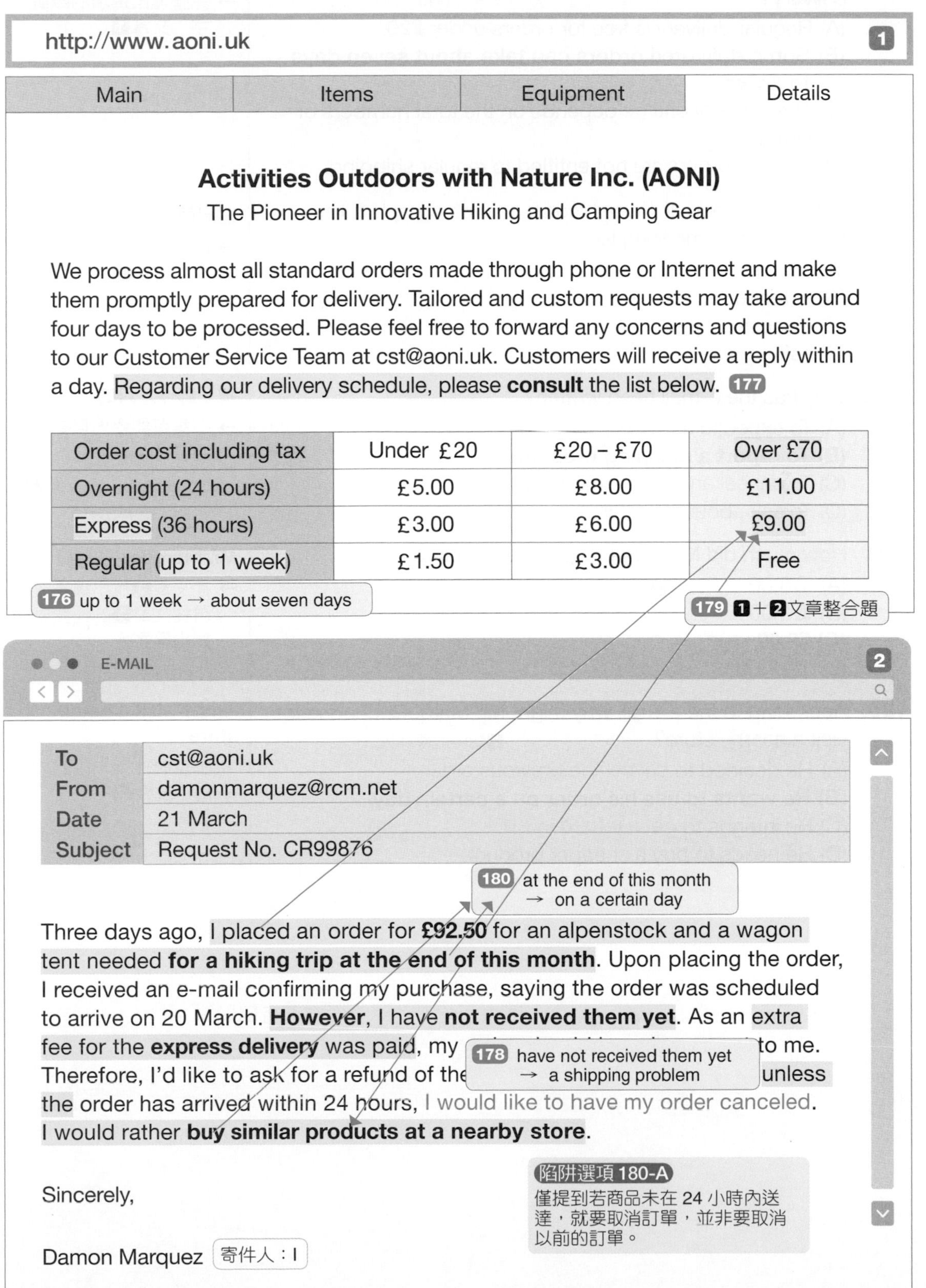

http://www.aoni.uk 1

Main	Items	Equipment	Details

Activities Outdoors with Nature Inc. (AONI)

The Pioneer in Innovative Hiking and Camping Gear

We process almost all standard orders made through phone or Internet and make them promptly prepared for delivery. Tailored and custom requests may take around four days to be processed. Please feel free to forward any concerns and questions to our Customer Service Team at cst@aoni.uk. Customers will receive a reply within a day. Regarding our delivery schedule, please **consult** the list below. 177

Order cost including tax	Under £20	£20 – £70	Over £70
Overnight (24 hours)	£5.00	£8.00	£11.00
Express (36 hours)	£3.00	£6.00	£9.00
Regular (up to 1 week)	£1.50	£3.00	Free

176 up to 1 week → about seven days

179 1+2文章整合題

E-MAIL 2

To	cst@aoni.uk
From	damonmarquez@rcm.net
Date	21 March
Subject	Request No. CR99876

180 at the end of this month → on a certain day

Three days ago, I placed an order for **£92.50** for an alpenstock and a wagon tent needed **for a hiking trip at the end of this month**. Upon placing the order, I received an e-mail confirming my purchase, saying the order was scheduled to arrive on 20 March. **However**, I have **not received them yet**. As an extra fee for the **express delivery** was paid, my ... to me. Therefore, I'd like to ask for a refund of the ... unless the order has arrived within 24 hours, I would like to have my order canceled. I would rather **buy similar products at a nearby store**.

178 have not received them yet → a shipping problem

Sincerely,

Damon Marquez 寄件人：I

陷阱選項 180-A
僅提到若商品未在 24 小時內送達，就要取消訂單，並非要取消以前的訂單。

176. In the Web page, what is suggested about the AONI's delivery?

(A) Regular delivery is ~~free~~ for orders under £20.

(B) Some delivered orders can take about seven days to arrive.

(C) The delivery charge depends on the total numbers of items.

(D) Tailored orders are not entitled to regular shipping.

關鍵字 **AONI's delivery**

→ 先整理出選項的關鍵字：文章❶

177. In the Web page, the word "consult" in paragraph 1, line 5, is closest in meaning to

(A) advise

(B) refer to

(C) discuss

(D) ask

選出同義詞

→ 確認該單字前後的句子：文章❶

178. Why has the e-mail been written?

(A) To ~~expedite~~ a delivery date

(B) To report a shipping problem

(C) To cancel an order ~~immediately~~

(D) To ~~ask about~~ an order status

電子郵件／目的

→ 答案可能會出現在轉折詞後方。

However . . .：文章❷

179. How much did Mr. Marquez pay for shipping?

❷當中的寄件人：I

(A) £5.00

(B) £8.00

(C) £9.00

(D) £11.00

Mr. Marquez ／運費

→ 從文章❷找出線索後，再從文章❶的運費表中找出答案。

180. According to the e-mail, why might Mr. Marquez choose to visit a nearby store?

❷當中的寄件人：I

(A) He ~~decided~~ to cancel the previous order.

(B) He wants to use his order on a certain day.

(C) He intends to get a refund in full.

(D) He needs to buy a cheaper product.

關鍵字 **visit a nearby store**

→ 確認郵件前半段的內容：文章❷

第 176-180 題 網頁與電子郵件

http://www.aoni.uk 1

主頁	品項	設備	詳細資訊

大自然戶外活動公司（AONI）
創新健行與露營用具的先驅

我們處理近乎所有透過電話或網路下單的一般訂單，並迅速撿貨準備運送。客製化與顧客的要求大約需要四天處理。有任何疑慮和問題，請儘管寄信給我們的客戶服務團隊：cst@aoni.uk。顧客會在一天內收到回覆。至於我們的運送時程，請參考下表。

訂單金額含稅	20 英鎊以下	20 到 70 英鎊	70 英鎊以上
隔夜（24 小時）	5 英鎊	8 英鎊	11 英鎊
快遞（36 小時）	3 英鎊	6 英鎊	9 英鎊
一般件（最慢一週）	1.5 英鎊	3 英鎊	免費

2

收件者	cst@aoni.uk
寄件者	damonmarquez@rcm.net
日期	3 月 21 日
主旨	查詢號碼 CR99876

我在三天前訂了月底健行之旅所需的登山杖和旅行車帳蓬，金額是 92.5 英鎊。在下了訂單之後，我收到一封確認購買的電子郵件，說所訂的貨品預定 3 月 20 日送達。然而，我到現在還沒有收到貨品。由於我已支付快遞的額外費用，我的貨品應該已經送來給我了。因此，我要要求退還運費。此外，除非貨品在 24 小時內送達，不然我要取消訂單。我寧願到附近的商店購買類似的商品。

真誠地
戴蒙．馬奎茲

字彙 gear 用具、設備　promptly 快速地、立即地　tailored 客製的
regarding 至於、關於　consult 參考、請教　alpenstock 登山杖
wagon tent 旅行車帳蓬　refund 退費　would rather 寧願

176. 在網頁上，可看出關於 AONI 運費的什麼事？

(A) 普通配送訂單金額 20 英鎊以下免運費。

(B) 有些訂購貨品的送達時間可能要約七天。

(C) 運費依訂購貨品的總數量計算。

(D) 客製化貨品無法以一般件運送。

STEP 1 題目要求找出相符的「事實」時，請先整理出各選項的關鍵字，再查看文章內容。

請找出與題目關鍵字 AONI's delivery 有關的內容後，再對照選項的敘述。由表格可以確認運送相關內容，當中普通配送所需的時間為一週，因此答案為 (B)。

STEP 2 分析錯誤選項

(A) 訂購商品的金額未滿 20 英鎊時，普通配送費用為 1.5 英鎊，並非免運費。
(C) 運費並非取決於訂購商品的數量，而是取決於訂購金額（order cost including tax）。
(D) 文中並未提到客製化商品不適用普通配送。

177. 網頁上第一段、第五行的「consult」一字，意義最接近下列何者？

(A) 勸告

(B) 參考

(C) 討論

(D) 要求

STEP 1 題目考同義詞時，要根據前後文意，選出最適合替換的單字。

請務必要確認該單字在句中所使用的意思，以便找出最適合替換的選項，千萬不能直接選擇與 consult 意思相同的單字。consult 所在的句子提到建議「參考」下方表格，因此答案為 (B) refer to。

178. 為什麼寫這封電子郵件？

(A) 為了加快運送的日期

(B) 為了報告運送問題

(C) 為了立即取消訂單

(D) 為了詢問訂單的狀況

STEP 1 答案會出現在 but、however、unfortunately 等轉折詞後方。

本題詢問撰寫電子郵件的目的。轉折詞前方會針對狀況說明，後方則會告知結論。前半段郵件中提到三天前訂購了商品，接著寫道：「However, I have not received them yet.」，提到尚未收到商品。由此可以得知他的目的為告知對方配送的問題，因此答案為 (B)。

STEP 2 分析錯誤選項

(A) 是對已經超過配送時間提出疑問，因此並非答案。
(C) 郵件中有提到 cancel an order，但是並非 immediately，而是提到 24 小時內未送達。
(D) 郵件中寫道：「I received an e-mail . . . 20 March」，表示 Marquez 已經確認過配送狀態。

179. 馬奎茲先生付了多少運費？

(A) 5 英鎊。

(B) 8 英鎊。

(C) 9 英鎊。

(D) 11 英鎊。

STEP 1 五道題中，至少會有一題必須同時查看兩篇文章的內容，才能選出答案。

第二篇文章為 Marquez 撰寫的電子郵件，當中寫道：「I placed an order for £92.50」，提到訂單金額為 92.50 英鎊。還寫道：「As an extra fee for the express delivery was paid」，表示他選擇的是 express delivery。確認第一篇文章後，可以發現訂購金額超過 70 英鎊時，express 的運費為 9 英鎊，因此答案為 (C)。

180. 根據電子郵件，為什麼馬奎茲先生可能選擇去附近的商店？

(A) 他決定取消之前的訂單。

(B) 他想要在特定日子使用他訂購的物品。

(C) 他想要獲得全額退費。

(D) 他需要買較便宜的產品。

STEP 1 答案通常會出現在關鍵字旁。

從第二篇文章的「I would rather buy similar products at a nearby store」可以找出題目關鍵字 visit a nearby store。當中提到「如果無法在 24 小時以內送達，不如直接在附近店家購買類似的商品」。

另外，郵件開頭寫道：「I placed an order for £92.50 for an alpenstock and a wagon tent needed for a hiking trip at the end of this month.」，提到他訂購了本月底登山旅行要用的商品。由此可以得知他是因為要將訂購的商品用於特定日子，才會選擇到附近店家購買，因此答案為 (B)。

STEP 2 分析錯誤選項

(A) cancel the previous order，但是他尚未確定要取消，因此不能作為答案；(C) 雖然文中有提到 refund，但是他是要求退還 delivery charge，並非 in full，而且此敘述與他去附近店家購買商品無關；文中並未提及 (D) 的內容。

Questions 181-185 refer to the following e-mails.

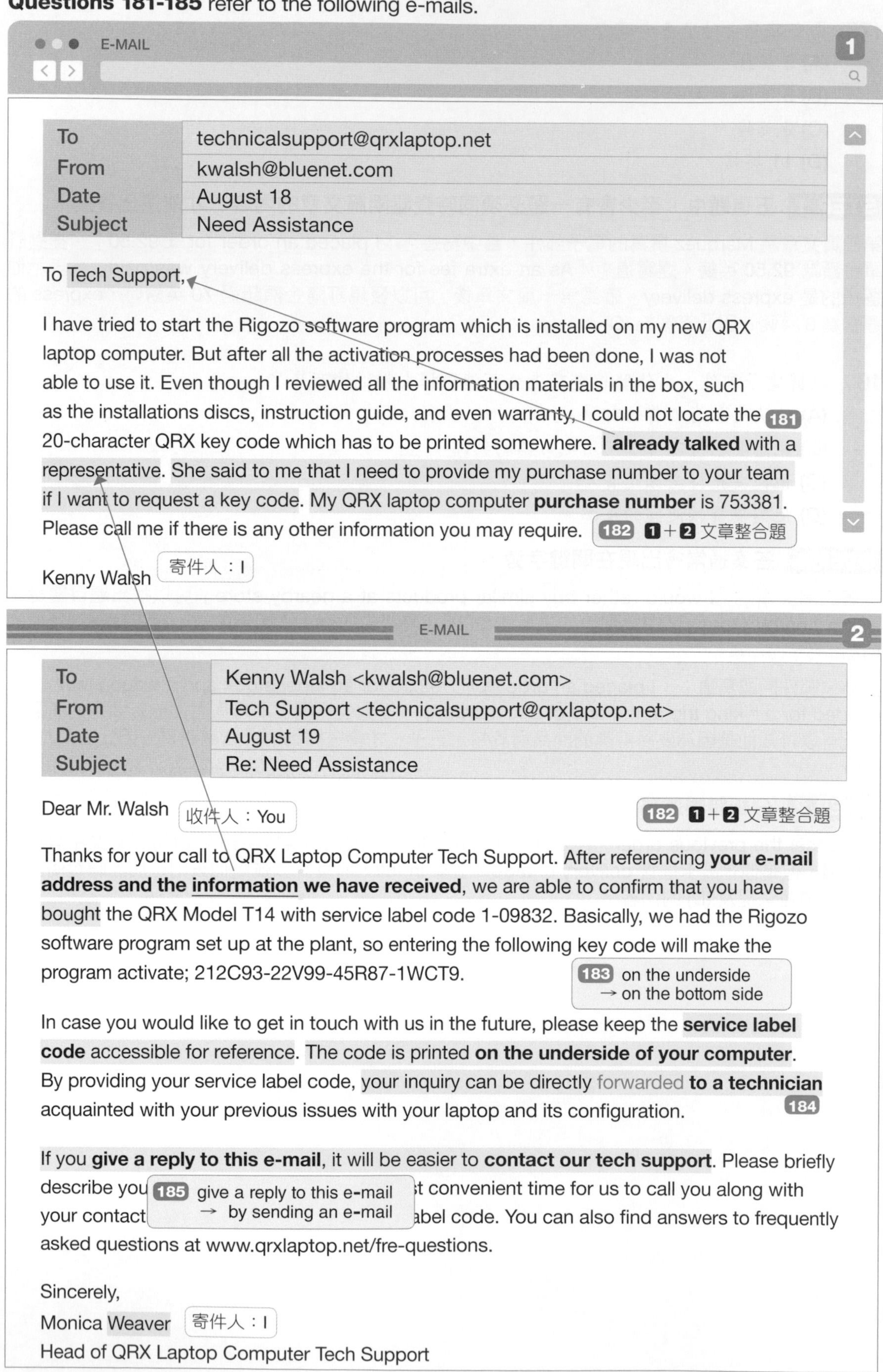

E-MAIL 1

To	technicalsupport@qrxlaptop.net
From	kwalsh@bluenet.com
Date	August 18
Subject	Need Assistance

To Tech Support,

I have tried to start the Rigozo software program which is installed on my new QRX laptop computer. But after all the activation processes had been done, I was not able to use it. Even though I reviewed all the information materials in the box, such as the installations discs, instruction guide, and even warranty, I could not locate the 20-character QRX key code which has to be printed somewhere. I **already talked** with a representative. She said to me that I need to provide my purchase number to your team if I want to request a key code. My QRX laptop computer **purchase number** is 753381. Please call me if there is any other information you may require.

181

182 1+2 文章整合題

Kenny Walsh 寄件人：I

E-MAIL 2

To	Kenny Walsh <kwalsh@bluenet.com>
From	Tech Support <technicalsupport@qrxlaptop.net>
Date	August 19
Subject	Re: Need Assistance

Dear Mr. Walsh 收件人：You

182 1+2 文章整合題

Thanks for your call to QRX Laptop Computer Tech Support. After referencing **your e-mail address and the information we have received**, we are able to confirm that you have bought the QRX Model T14 with service label code 1-09832. Basically, we had the Rigozo software program set up at the plant, so entering the following key code will make the program activate; 212C93-22V99-45R87-1WCT9.

183 on the underside → on the bottom side

In case you would like to get in touch with us in the future, please keep the **service label code** accessible for reference. The code is printed **on the underside of your computer**. By providing your service label code, your inquiry can be directly forwarded **to a technician** acquainted with your previous issues with your laptop and its configuration.

184

If you **give a reply to this e-mail**, it will be easier to **contact our tech support**. Please briefly describe you[r ... mos]t convenient time for us to call you along with your contact [... service l]abel code. You can also find answers to frequently asked questions at www.qrxlaptop.net/fre-questions.

185 give a reply to this e-mail → by sending an e-mail

Sincerely,

Monica Weaver 寄件人：I

Head of QRX Laptop Computer Tech Support

❶當中的寄件人：I

181. What did Mr. Walsh do before writing his August 18 e-mail?

(A) He ~~provided~~ a purchase number.
(B) He ~~changed~~ his computer configurations.
(C) He called to get technical support.
(D) ~~He~~ reviewed answers to previously asked questions.

Mr. Walsh / 過去
→ 確認文章❶中以「I already」開頭的句子。

❷當中的寄件人：I

182. How did Ms. Weaver verify Mr. Walsh's purchase?

(A) By ~~checking~~ a key code previously provided
(B) By using a purchase number and contact information
(C) By inputting a ~~product key number~~
(D) By reaching the ~~software program company~~

Ms. Weaver / verify Mr. Walsh's purchase
→ 從文章❶中確認「information we have received」指的是什麼。

❷當中的收件人：You

183. Where can Mr. Walsh find his service label code?

(A) On the bottom side of his computer
(B) Inside the laptop's ~~warranty~~ statement
(C) Attached to the computer's battery part
(D) On the front cover of the instruction guide

關鍵字 service label code：文章❷
→ 從關鍵字前後方找出答案。

184. In the second e-mail, the word "forwarded" in paragraph 2, line 3, is closest in meaning to

(A) secured
(B) routed
(C) located
(D) advanced

選出同義詞
→ 確認該單字前後的句子。

185. How does Ms. Weaver suggest that Mr. Walsh contact a representative if he has an issue with his item?

(A) ~~By leaving a question~~ on the QRX Web site
(B) By registering for a membership program
(C) By ~~making a phone call~~
(D) By sending an e-mail

Ms. Weaver / contact a representative：文章❷
→ 確認表示勸說或建議的句子。

第 181-185 題 兩封電子郵件

1

收件人	technicalsupport@qrxlaptop.net
寄件人	kwalsh@bluenet.com
日期	8 月 18 日
主旨	需要協助

致技術支援：

我嘗試啟動裝在我的新 QRX 筆記型電腦上的 Rigozo 軟體程式。但是，在試過所有的啟動程序後，我還是無法使用。即使我仔細看過盒子裡的所有資訊，例如安裝光碟、用法指南，甚至是保證書，我也找不到哪裡有印著 20 個字元的 QRX 金鑰密碼。我已經和客服代表談過，她告訴我，如果我想要索取金鑰密碼，我必須提供我的購買序號給你們團隊。我的 QRX 筆記型電腦的購買序號是 753381。如果你們還需要其他資料，請打給我。

肯尼 · 威爾許

2

收件人	肯尼 · 威爾許（kwalsh@bluenet.com）
寄件人	技術支援（technicalsupport@qrxlaptop.net）
日期	8 月 19 日
主旨	回覆：需要協助

親愛的威爾許先生：

感謝您致電 QRX 筆記型電腦技術支援。在參照您的電子郵件信箱地址和我們收到的資訊後，我們得以確定您買了 QRX T14 型，服務標籤代碼 1-09832。基本上，我們在出廠時已安裝 Rigozo 軟體程式，因此，鍵入下列金鑰密碼就能啟動程式：212C93-22V99-45R87-1WCT。

假如您以後想要聯絡我們，請把服務標籤代碼放在手邊以便參考。代碼印在您電腦的底部。藉由提供您的服務標籤代碼，您的問題會直接轉給熟悉您之前電腦與配置問題的技術人員。

如果您回覆這封電子郵件，會更容易聯絡我們的技術支援團隊。請簡單描述您的問題，並說明最方便打給您的時間，還有您的聯絡資料和服務標籤代碼。您也可以在 www.qrxlaptop.net/fre-questions 找到常見問題的答案。

真誠地
莫妮卡 · 威佛
QRX 筆記型電腦技術支援總監

字彙 tech support 技術支援　activation process 啟動程式　installation 安裝
instruction guide 用法說明、操作指南　warranty 保證書
locate . . . 確定……的位置　character 字元　representative 代表　require 要求
reference 參考　set up 安裝（機器）、裝配　plant 工廠　activate 啟動
accessible 容易取得的　for reference 參考　underside 底部　inquiry 問題
forward 轉交、發送　acquainted with 熟悉　configuration 配置　indicate 表明

181. 威爾許先生在 8 月 18 日寫電子郵件之前做了什麼？

(A) 他提出購買序號。

(B) 他更換了電腦的配置。

(C) 他打電話尋求技術支援。

(D) 他仔細察看之前問題的答案。

STEP 1 **請善用題目所提供的線索和文章內有關答案的資訊。**

題目關鍵字為 Mr. Walsh，因此請從第一篇文章中找尋答案。第一篇文章的寄件人為 Walsh，他在郵件中寫道：「I already talked with a representative」，提到他已經和客服聯絡過了。此封郵件的收件人為技術支援部，表示他先前打電話是為了請求技術上的支援，因此答案為 (C)。

STEP 2 **分析錯誤選項**

郵件中有寫出購買序號，提供序號的日期為 18 日，因此 (A) 的敘述不正確；由 Weaver 提及 configuration，且並未提到變更一事，因此 (B) 也不正確。由 Weaver 提出可以瀏覽過往的常見問題，因此 (D) 也不能作為答案。

182. 威佛女士如何查核威爾許先生所買的產品？

(A) 檢查之前提供的金鑰密碼

(B) 利用購買序號和聯絡資料

(C) 鍵入產品金鑰號碼

(D) 聯絡軟體程式公司

STEP 1 **五道題中，至少會有一題必須同時查看兩篇文章的內容，才能選出答案。題目關鍵字和選項內容分別屬於不同文章時，請同時查看兩篇文章。**

題目關鍵字為 Weaver，出現在第二篇文章中，因此請優先確認第二篇文章的內容。當中寫道：「After referencing your e-mail address and the information we have received, we are able to confirm that you have bought . . .」，提到確認 Walsh 的郵件地址和他提供的資料後，確定他購買了商品。

接著請再從第一篇文章中，確認此處的 information 指的是什麼東西。第一篇文章寫道：「I need to provide my purchase number to your team if I want to request a key code. My QRX laptop computer purchase number is 753381.」，表示 Walsh 提供了筆記型電腦的購買序號，因此答案為 (B)。

STEP 2 **分析錯誤選項**

雖然第一篇文章有提到 (A) key code 和 (C) 的 key number，但是文中寫道：「I could not locate the 20-character QRX key code」，並未提到他有提供或輸入號碼，因此不能作為答案；由第一篇文章的 To Tech Support 可以得知 (D) 的 software program company 有誤，因此也不是答案。

183. 威爾許先生可以在哪裡找到他的服務標籤代碼？

(A) 在他電腦的底部

(B) 在電腦的保證書說明文字中

(C) 附在電腦的電池上

(D) 在使用指南的封面上

STEP 1 **答案通常會出現在關鍵字旁。**

題目關鍵字為 service label code，出現在第二篇文章中，表示查看第二篇文章的內容便能找出答案。文中寫道：「please keep the service label code accessible for reference. The code is printed on the underside of your computer」，提到電腦下方印有服務標籤代碼，因此答案為 (A)。

STEP 2 **分析錯誤選項**

「I reviewed all the information materials in the box, such as the installations disc, instruction guide, and even warranty」當中有提到 (B) 的 warranty，但僅表示 Walsh 曾在此處找過條碼，不能作為答案。而文中並未提及其他選項的內容。

184. 在第二封電子郵件中，第二段、第三行的「**forward**」一字，意義最接近下列何者？

(A) 保衛

(B) 發送

(C) 座落於

(D) 前進

STEP 1 **題目考同義詞時，要根據前後文意，選出最適合替換的單字。**

請務必要確認該單字在句中所使用的意思，以便找出意思相同的單字作為答案。「your inquiry can be directly forwarded to a technician」指「將您提出的疑問轉達給工程師」，與選項中 (B) 的意思相同，表示「傳遞」。

185. 如果威爾許先生的產品有問題，威佛女士建議他如何聯絡技術代表？

(A) 在 QRX 網站上留下問題

(B) 註冊登入會員程式

(C) 打電話

(D) 發電子郵件

STEP 1 **聯絡方式、申請方法會出現在後半段文章中。**

題目關鍵字為 contact a representative。回答完 Walsh 的問題後，便會告知他聯絡的方式，因此請確認後半段文章的內容。當中寫道：「If you give a reply to this e-mail, it will be easier to contact our tech support.」，請他回覆此封郵件，便能聯絡技術支援部，因此答案為 (D)。

STEP 2 **分析錯誤選項**

(A)「You can also find answers to frequently asked questions at www.qrxlaptop.net/frequestions」中提到 Web site，但是 leave a question 有誤；(C) 第二篇文章後半段出現 contact，該選項故意改寫成 make a phone call，並非答案。

Questions 186-190 refer to the following leaflet, comment, and e-mail.

1

Learn Business From the Best in Dubai

187 1 + 2文章整合題

The International Dubai Business College (IDBC) can be found in the center of **Dubai's business district**. **This college** provides a wide range of highly informative courses targeted at those who intend to pursue a **master's degree. Students** may explore the city and extend business network[186 master's degree → further education]ke economics, domestic and global sales and marketing, and finance are offered. There are also sessions only for those who intend to pursue a master's degree, involving improving résumés and other relevant materials. Hundreds of students receive help from the college in obtaining acceptance into master's degree courses around the world every year. The college features many highly distinguished lecturers who have expert knowledge in each of their areas, such as Marvin West, General Manager of **Hongkong Financial Consulting**, and E[189 2 + 1文章整合題 Marvin West → General Manager . . . Consulting] (HUB). Please check our Web site at ww... for further details on our excellent course offerings and faculty, or to register.

2

www.idbc.programs.org/comments

Main	Courses	Comments	Contact Info.

Evangeline **Gwen**
November 11

At the moment, I am studying at a business college in Washington. I took one of the business courses at IDBC since I was not able to complete any prerequisite study after acquiring my bachelor's degree.

187 1 + 2文章整合題
Dubai's business district → busy area

During my stay there, even though the public transportation was not convenient, I had no choice but to **commute from the suburb area** due to the incredibly high rent in the area around IDBC. I think there should have been **students housing** or other affordable **accommodation** options. The classes were excellent. **My instructor** was Marvin West. **His classes** were **rather fast paced**, but he covered many subjects in the seven-week course. Yet, I was able to [188 fast paced → rushed through]dying a lot of reading materials provided by IDBC. His commitment to his class was very impressive, and was helpful for me to get ready for joining a master's degree course.

Thank you.

189 2 + 1文章整合題
Ms. Gwen's lecturer → Marvin West

190 3 + 2文章整合題
students housing, accommodation options → dormitory

E-MAIL 3

From	fwells@idbc.org
To	evangelinegwen@skynetmail.com
Date	16 December
Subject	Your comments

Dear Ms. Gwen 收件人：You

190 3 + 2文章整合題
your suggestion → 從文章2確認

Thanks for your comments. Many students have voiced the specific issue you indicated. According to **your suggestion**, we plan to complement it. Those who intend to take courses with IDBC from the beginning of February will receive this new advantage. Please tell anyone willing to take a course with us about this.

Sincerely,

寄件人：I

Frederick Wells

186. For whom is the leaflet intended?
(A) Students who want to improve their résumés for ~~employment~~
(B) Lecturers willing to change their ~~career path~~
(C) People planning to receive further education
(D) Business experts who intend to ~~join an educational institution~~

傳單／For whom
→ 確認文章前半段的內容。

187. What is suggested about students studying at IDBC?
(A) There are internship opportunities for them.
(B) Employment assistance service is available for them.
(C) They go through a busy area to attend their classes.
(D) They can receive financial support.

students studying at IDBC：文章1 + 2
→ Grew：文章2當中的 I

2當中的寄件人：I

188. What does Ms. Gwen mention about her instructor?
(A) ~~He graduated~~ from a business school in Washington.
(B) ~~He provided~~ various reading materials
(C) He presented a lot of examples.
(D) He rushed through his classes.

Ms. Gwen ／ her instructor
→ 確認 Gwen 在文章2中寫的「my instructor」。

2當中的第三者

189. Where does Ms. Gwen's lecturer work when he is not giving lessons?
(A) At the International Dubai Business College
(B) At Hongkong Financial Consulting
(C) At ~~Horace Union Bank~~
(D) At a company in Dubai's business district

Ms. Gwen's lecturer
→ Marvin West：同時查看文章1和2才能解題。

190. How will IDBC be dealing with Ms. Gwen's complaint?
(A) By making a dormitory for students
(B) By providing shuttle bus service
(C) By extending the length of courses
(D) By recruiting additional faculty

Ms. Gwen's complaint：文章2
→ 整合兩篇文章的內容才能解題。

第 186-190 題 傳單、評論與電子郵件

在杜拜最好的學校學商 1

杜拜國際商學院（IDBC）位於杜拜市中心商業區。學院為計劃攻讀碩士學位的人，提供許多資訊豐富的課程。學生可以探索這座城市，並擴展商業人脈。有各種著重內容知識的課程，如經濟學、國內與全球業務及行銷，和財政學。也有只開給打算攻讀碩士學位人士的課程，包含改善履歷表和其他相關資料。每年，來自全世界的數百名學生，在學院的協助下，獲得錄取就讀碩士課程。學院以擁有許多非常卓越的講師為特色，他們在自己的領域上都有專家級的知識，如香港財金諮詢公司的總經理馬文．威斯特，以及何瑞斯聯合銀行總裁布萊恩．懷特。更多關於我們所提供的優秀課程與教師資訊、或欲註冊，請上：www.idbc_programs.org。

---

www.idbc.programs.org/comments 2

主頁	課程	意見	聯絡資料

伊凡潔琳．格溫

11 月 11 日

我目前就讀於華盛頓的一家商學院。我之前在 IDBC 選修一門商業課程，因為我在取得學士學位後，無法完成任何基礎必修課程。

在我修讀期間，即使大眾運輸交通並不方便，但由於 IDBC 週邊的天價租金，我也不得不從市郊通勤。我認為，應該要有學生宿舍或其他可負擔的住宿選擇。課程很棒。我的指導老師是馬文．威斯特，他的上課進度相當快，但七週的課程包含非常多主題。然而，我靠著研讀 IDBC 提供的大量閱讀資料得以跟上進度。他對課程的投入令人非常敬佩，也幫助我準備好就讀碩士課程。

謝謝你們。

3

寄件人	fwells@idbc.org
收件人	evangelinegwen@skynetmail.com
日期	12 月 16 日
主旨	您的意見

親愛的格溫女士：

謝謝您的意見。有許多學生都表達過您所提出的問題。根據您的建議，我們打算將不足處補足。計劃從二月起選讀 IDBC 課程的同學，將會享受到這項好處。請告訴任何願意選讀我們課程的人。

真誠地

佛瑞德里克·威爾斯

字彙 business district 商業區　a wide range of 範圍廣泛的……
informative 提供資訊的、增廣見聞的　targeted 以……為目標（或對象）
intend to V 打算做　pursue 追求、從事　master's degree 碩士學位
extend 擴展　relevant 相關的　obtain 獲得　acceptance 接受
feature 以……為特色　distinguished 傑出的　faculty 全體教師
prerequisite 先決條件、基礎必修課程　bachelor's degree 學士學位
have no choice but to V 不得不做、只好做　affordable 負擔得起
fast paced 進度快速　cover 包含　keep up with 跟上　commitment 投入
voice 表達　complement 補充、使完善

186. 傳單所針對的對象是誰？
(A) 想要改善求職履歷表的學生
(B) 願意改換職業跑道的講師
(C) 打算深造的人
(D) 計劃加入教育機構的商業專家

STEP 1 第一段通常會提到文章針對的讀者。

題目關鍵字為 leaflet，指的是第一篇文章的類型，因此請由前半段來確認這份傳單的讀者。文中寫道：「This college provides . . . pursue a master's degree」，介紹商業大學的課程。由此可以得知，這份傳單是為準備國際杜拜商業大學碩士學位課程的人所撰寫，因此答案為 (C)。

STEP 2 分析錯誤選項

雖然「those who intend to pursue a master's degree involving improving résumés」當中提到 (A) improving résumés，但是目的為取得碩士學位，並非就業，因此不能作為答案；(B) 文中僅提到 lecturers，並未提到 career path，因此並非答案；(D)「lecturers who have expert knowledge in each of their areas, such as Marvin West, General Manager of Hongkong Financial Consulting, and Brian White, President of Horace Union Bank (HUB)」，當中的「lecturers who have expert knowledge」可以改寫成「experts」，但是此處指的是在商業相關領域工作的人，且這些人並非本傳單的讀者，因此並非答案。

187. 關於在 IDBC 就讀的學生，可由文中得知什麼？

(A) 他們有實習的機會。

(B) 他們可以得到協助就業服務。

(C) 他們穿過繁忙的區域去上課。

(D) 他們可以得到財務支援。

STEP 1 題目要求確認與特定人士有關的事實時，請同時查看兩篇文章的內容。

題目關鍵字為 students studying at IDBC，指第二篇文章的 Evangeline Gwen，因此本題是針對此人提問。照理說應該從 Gwen 所寫的評論中確認答案，但是光憑第二篇文章的內容，仍無法選出答案。而本題為題組第二題，因此建議同時查看第一篇文章的內容來確認答案。

第一篇文章寫道：「The International Dubai Business College (IDBC) can be found in the center of Dubai's business district」，提到 IDBC 位在商業區中心。第二篇文章則寫道：「even though the public transportation was not convenient, I had no choice but to commute from the suburb area」，由此可以得知交通不便，但她還是從郊區通勤上課。選項將 Grew 經過的 business district 改寫成 busy area，因此答案要選 (C)。其他選項皆未出現在文章中。

188. 關於格溫女士的講師，她說了什麼？

(A) 他畢業於華盛頓的一家商業院。

(B) 他提供許多不同的閱讀資料。

(C) 他舉了很多例子。

(D) 他的上課進度很快。

STEP 1 確認特定名詞所指的對象。

題目關鍵字為 Ms. Gwen 和 her instructor，這兩個人同時出現在第二篇文章中，因此請從中確認答案。Ms. Gwen 為撰寫第二篇文章的人，當中以代名詞 I 自稱，而 her instructor 則會變成 my instructor，因此請由相關敘述確認答案。

文中寫道：「My instructor was Marvin West. His classes were rather fast paced, but he covered many subjects in the seven-week course.」，提到她的老師為 Marvin West，以及老師上課的速度很快，因此答案要選 (D)。

STEP 2 分析錯誤選項

(A) 文中提及 a business school in Washington 為 Gwen 上課的地方，主詞並非 West，因此不能作為答案；(B)「a lot of reading materials provided by IDBC」中提到 reading materials，但是主詞並不符合，因此並非答案；看內文無法確認 (C) 的內容。

189. 格溫女士的老師不教課時在哪裡工作？

(A) 在杜拜國際商學院

(B) 在香港財金諮詢公司

(C) 在何瑞斯聯合銀行

(D) 在杜拜商業區的一家公司

STEP 1 **題目要求確認與特定人士有關的事實時，請同時查看兩篇文章的內容。**

第二篇文章提到「My instructor was Marvin West」，此人就是題目關鍵字 Ms. Gwen's lecturer，但是此句話後方並未出現任何解題的關鍵字。第一篇文章中也有提到老師的名字，因此請同時查看第一篇和第二篇文章，以便找出答案。

首先，已經在第二篇文章中確認 Gwen 的老師為 Marvin West。第一篇文章寫道：「The college features . . . such as Marvin West, General Manager of Hongkong Financial Consulting」，提到 Marvin West 為 Hongkong Financial Consulting 的總經理。由此段話可以得知他在沒有上課的期間，會在 Hongkong Financial Consulting 上班，因此答案為 (B)。(C) Horace Union Bank 為 Brian White 工作的地方。

190. IDBC 將如何處理格溫女士抱怨的問題？

(A) 設一間學生宿舍

(B) 提供接駁車服務

(C) 延長課程的時間

(D) 招募更多教師

STEP 1 **最後一題的答案通常會出現在第三篇文章中。**

題目關鍵字為 IDBC / dealing with / Gwen's complaint，Gwen 出現在第二篇文章中，因此請從中確認她抱怨的內容為何。第二篇文章寫道：「there should have been students housing or other affordable accommodation options」，提到缺少讓學生居住的地方。

請再由第三篇寄送給 Gwen 的郵件確認 IDBC 如何解決此問題。文中寫道：「According to your suggestion, we plan to complement it.」，提到計劃增加相關設施，表示 IDBC 將增設住宿的地方，因此答案為 (A)。文中並未提及其他選項的內容，因此不適合作為答案。

Questions 191-196 refer to the following advertisement, form, and letter.

1

Looking for Full-time Assistant Chef

191 salad and appetizer items → a limited range of food

The Highgate Bistro is a well established ea... since 1934. We are looking for an assistant cook to arrange **salad and appetizer items** under the direction of the main chef. More than one year of relevant cooking experience is required and a six-month apprenticeship has to have been filled in a high-profile establishment. A high level of ability to create not only new but also traditional sty... 192 1 + 2 文章整合題 ...or the ideal candidate.

To apply, visit www.highgatebistro.net/recruitment.

---

www.highgatebistro.net/recruitment/assistant_chef/apply 2

Name: Amber Ward **E-mail:** a-ward33@skye-mail.net **Phone:** 421-265-3898

Attachment (1): Résumé (√) **Attachment (2):** Reference list (√)

Related Education: Bachelor's degree in Culinary Arts at Goldhawk National University

193 my instructor and mentor → A culinary instructor

Current Employer: Chiswick Restaurant

Position: Assistant Chef (Length of Employment: Seven months)

Previous Employer: Vacation Inn

Position: Apprentice (Length of Employment: Three years)

Previous Employer: Clapham Café

Title: Cook (Length of Employment: Four months)

195 3 + 2 文章整合題 four-month internship → Clapham Café

Cover letter: I would like to fill the position of assistant chef at the Highgate Bistro. I am currently working as an assistant chef for a restaurant cooking traditional style meals. Because the restaurant has neglected to fill th... 192 1 + 2 文章整合題 ...ef, I am taking care of **almost all items** on the menu. I served an **apprenticeship at the well-known Vacation Inn**, working closely with distinguished chef Linda Williams. On top of these, I am capable of creating new innovative recipes as Hazle **Washington (my instructor** and mentor **at Goldhawk National University**) can confirm. Moreover, I won the Great in Creative Award for my East Asian-style seafood recipe, which is served at the moment at the cafeteria in **Goldhawk National University**.

194 Great in Creative Award → Culinary awards

Submit Application

GOLDHAWK NATIONAL UNIVERSITY

3

Department of Culinary Arts

Trevor Vega
Highgate Bistro
2678 Highgate Avenue
Putney, London 32Q1 2N1

Dear Mr. Vega, 收件人：You

This is in reference to Amber Ward's application for employment at Highgate Bistro. As Ms. Washington is away on holiday this semester, she wanted me to assume her role for a while. Ms. Ward, who completed our course in the top three of her class, proved her excellent culinary skills and showed strong initiative to be taught. She was recognized by well-known Chef Sherri **Wade**, who helped Ms. Ward finish her **four-month internship** successfully. I am sure that Ms. Ward will be an invaluable addition to your organization.

195 3 + 2文章整合題
關鍵字 four-month internship

Sincerely,

Horace Warner 寄件人：I

Horace Warner
Head Instructor of Culinary Arts Department

191. What is suggested about the assistant chef position?
(A) It includes working on some ~~weekends~~.
(B) It requires cooking a limited range of food.
(C) It is a six-month ~~contract job~~.
(D) It ~~involves~~ training apprentices.

關鍵字 assistant chef position
→ 從關鍵字前後找出答題線索。

192. What is indicated about Ms. Ward? 2當中的寄件人：I
(A) Some of her recipes have been ~~published in a publication~~.
(B) She led a class on cooking East Asian seafood at a university.
(C) She has already applied at ~~a few establishments~~.
(D) Her qualifications seem to meet the requirements for the job.

Ms. Ward：文章2／文章1
→ 整理出各選項的關鍵字後，再刪除錯誤的選項。

2當中的第三者

193. Who most likely is Ms. Washington?
(A) A culinary instructor
(B) A cafeteria owner
(C) A celebrity chef
(D) A head teacher

Ms. Washington：文章2
→「Washington (my instructor and mentor)」

194. What is true about Goldhawk National University?

(A) A renowned chef is invited every semester as a guest lecturer.

(B) Culinary awards are given to its students.

(C) Cooking seminars are provided for free.

(D) ~~A new chef for~~ its cafeteria will be hired.

Goldhawk National University：文章2

→ 整理出各選項的關鍵字後，再查看文章的內容。

195. Where did Ms. Wade most likely finish her internship?

(A) At ~~Highgate Bistro~~ 3當中的第三者

(B) At Clapham Café

(C) At ~~Vacation Inn~~

(D) At ~~Chiswick Restaurant~~

關鍵字 Ms. Wade / internship

→ 查看文章2和3，並注意關鍵字 four-month。

第 191-195 題 廣告、表單與信件

1

徵全職助理廚師

海格小酒館是信譽卓著的餐廳，從 1934 年起就在戈德斯格林營業至今。我們正在尋找一位助理廚師，在主廚的指導下負責沙拉和開胃菜的準備。需有一年以上相關烹飪經驗，並曾在高知名度的機構完成六個月的學徒期。理想的應徵者需有強大的創造力，不僅能發明創新料理，也能烹煮傳統美食。

意者請上：www.highgatebistro.net/recruitment

2

www.highgatebistro.net/recruitment/assistant_chef/apply

姓名：安珀・華德　　電子郵件：a-ward33@skye-mail.net　　電話：412-265-3898

附件一：履歷表　附件二：推薦人名單

相關學歷：國立高德華大學廚藝系學士

目前僱主：奇斯威克餐廳

職務：助理廚師（在職時間：七個月）

前任僱主：度假飯店

職務：學徒（在職時間：三年）

前任僱主：克萊芬咖啡

職稱：廚師（在職時間：四個月）

求職信：我想要應徵海格小酒館的助理廚師一職。我目前在一家傳統料理餐廳擔任助理廚師。因為這家餐廳疏忽沒聘僱主廚，幾乎菜單上的所有餐點都是我在做。我在著名的度假飯店當學徒，跟隨知名的主廚琳達・威廉斯工作。除了這些經歷之外，我還能發明創新食譜，海佐・華盛頓（我在國立高德華大學的老師兼導師）可以證明。此外，我的東亞風海鮮食譜在創意大賽中贏得傑出大獎，目前國立高德華大學的自助餐廳有供應這道菜。

送出 應徵表格

3

國立高德華大學
廚藝系

崔佛・維嘉
海格小酒館
海格大道 2678 號
倫敦普特尼區，32Q1 2N1

親愛的維嘉先生：

我就安珀・華德應徵海格小酒館工作一事撰寫此信。由於華盛頓女士這個學期休假，她要求我代理她的職務一陣子。華德女士以她班上前三名的成績讀完我們的課程，證明她優秀的烹飪技巧並顯現出強烈的主動學習之心。她受到知名主廚雪莉・韋德認可，韋德主廚幫助華德女士順利完成四個月的實習。我確信，華德女士會成為貴餐廳的寶貴人才。

真誠地
何瑞斯・華納
廚藝系系主任

字彙 established 已確立的　eatery 餐館、小飯館
under the direction of 在……指導（管理）之下　apprenticeship 學徒期
high-profile 高知名度的、受矚目的　establishment 機構、公司
cuisine 菜餚　neglect 忽略　distinguished 傑出的　be capable of 有能力做
at the moment 目前　be away on holiday 去度假　initiative 主動性

191. 關於助理廚師的工作，可由文中得知什麼？
(A) 有些週末要上班。
(B) 有指定要求烹煮的料理。
(C) 是六個月的約聘工作。
(D) 需要訓練學徒。

STEP 1 答案通常會出現在關鍵字旁。

題目關鍵字 assistant chef position 出現在第一篇文章中，請從中確認相關內容。文中寫道：「We are looking for an assistant cook to arrange salad and appetizer items」，提到徵求製作沙拉和開胃菜的助理廚師，表示這個職位需要負責料理指定的菜色，因此答案為 (B)。選項將內文的 salad and appetizer items 改寫成 a limited range of food。

STEP 2 分析錯誤選項

(D) 雖然文中有提到 apprenticeship，但是並未提到助理廚師要指導學徒，因此不能作為答案。

192. 關於華德女士，可由文中得知什麼？

(A) 她的一些食譜曾刊登在刊物上。

(B) 她在大學時教授一門烹煮東亞海鮮的課。

(C) 她已經應徵了幾家公司。

(D) 她的資格似乎符合這個工作的要求條件。

STEP 1 看到針對兩篇文章出題的整合題時，千萬不能只靠單篇文章找尋答案，請務必綜合兩篇文章的資訊，選出最相符的答案。

Ward 所寫的自我介紹中寫道：「Related Education: Bachelor's degree . . . University」和「I am taking care of almost all items . . . chef Linda Williams，表示 Ward 擁有烹飪學士學位，且過去曾於知名 Vacation Inn 的名廚底下擔任學徒。而第一篇文章中寫道：「We are looking for . . . a high-profile establishment」，由此可以得知 Ward 符合 Highgate Bistro 的徵人條件，因此答案為 (D)。

STEP 2 分析錯誤選項

(A) 雖然文中有提及 her recipe，但是無法得知是否有出版。

(B) 文中僅提到 East Asian seafood，並未提到她教過相關課程。

(C) 文中僅提到她曾於其他地方工作過，並未提到她是否還應徵了其他工作。

193. 華盛頓女士最可能是誰？

(A) 廚藝教師

(B) 自助餐廳老闆

(C) 名人主廚

(D) 系主任

STEP 1 題目出現關鍵字時，請在該關鍵字所在文章中找出其他答題資訊。

題目關鍵字為 Ms. Washington，第二篇文章後半段寫道：「Hazle Washington (my instructor and mentor at Goldhawk National University」，提到 Washington 為 Ward 的教授。而第二篇文章前半段寫道：「Related Education: Bachelor's degree in Culinary Arts at Goldhawk National University」，提到 Ward 曾就讀烹飪學系，由此可以推測出 Washington 為烹飪學系的教授，因此答案為 (A)。

194. 關於國立高德華大學，下列何者為真？

(A) 每個學期都邀一位知名主廚當客座講師。

(B) 學生曾獲頒廚藝獎。

(C) 免費提供烹飪研討會。

(D) 自助餐廳將僱用新主廚。

STEP 1 **題目要求找出相符的「事實」時，請先整理出各選項的關鍵字，再查看文章內容。**

選項的關鍵字分別為 (A) chef as a guest lecturer；(B) Culinary awards、students；(C) Cooking seminars、free；(D) new chef、cafeteria、hired，整理完後，再從文中找出相關敘述。

第二篇文章寫道：「I won the Great in Creative Award . . . , which is served at the moment at the cafeteria in Goldhawk National University」，提到他的食譜曾獲獎，並用於 Goldhawk National University 的學生餐廳。由此可以得知 Goldhawk National University 會將烹飪比賽的獎項頒發給在校學生，因此答案為 (B)。

STEP 2 **分析錯誤選項**

文中並未提到 (A) 和 (C) 的內容，因此無法得知是否正確。
(D) 文中僅提到 cafeteria，並未提到要僱用新廚師。

195. 華德女士最可能在哪裡完成實習？

(A) 海格小酒館

(B) 克萊芬咖啡

(C) 度假飯店

(D) 奇斯威克餐廳

STEP 1 **看到針對兩篇文章出題的整合題時，若關鍵字旁未出現答案，請確認該關鍵字旁是否還有其他解題關鍵，並從另一篇文章中找出答案。**

本題關鍵字為 Wade，第三篇文章中寫道：「She was recognized by well-known Chef Sherri Wade, who helped Ms. Ward finish her four-month internship successfully.」，提到 Sherri Wade 協助 Ward 成功完成四個月的實習。第二篇文章提到 Ward 曾在 Clapham Café 工作四個月，由此可以推測出 Ward 是在 Clapham Café 實習，因此答案為 (B)。

STEP 2 **分析錯誤選項**

(A) 為 Ward 應徵的地方；(C) 為 Ward 曾經工作過的地方；(D) 為 Ward 現在工作的地方。

Questions 196-200 refer to the following leaflet and e-mails.

Roger Roofing Materials

1

Over the past few decades, builders and roofers have chosen Roger Roofing Materials for their roofing work including placing and replacing roof panels. Here are some of our best-selling items.

Bertie PRX22: Without any screws, installed with durable clips. Please note that this model should be placed by a skilled professional because aligning the panels tends to be challenging.

Carey PRX31: Best choice for properties whose roofs are steeply sloped. Smooth rainfall drainage is ensured by its slick surface.

Madge PRX01: Sturdy, less time-consuming installation, with a choice of 20 appealing shades.

Marcie PRX12: Quite similar to Madge PRX01, yet with only four shade options (blue, red, green, yellow). In addition, wave patterns are imprinted in it.

Please check out our latest brochure for more pricing information and specifications. Send us an e-mail at customerservice@rogerroofing.net or call us at 220-2235-6654 for any inquiry about our service and products.

Be advise[196 online calculator → online tool] be different depending on roof panel products. Our online calculator is available at www.@rogerroofing.net/overlapdegree to find out the appropriate number of roof panels for your property. Just type the name of the model you would like to purchase with the size of your roof surface.

E-MAIL 2

To	customerservice@rogerroofing.net
From	malloyalisa@lourdesbuildingservice.org
Date	November 19
Subject	Purchase order

T... ern,

197 whether the shade . . . heating up → possibility of retaining heat

I recently submitted an order, #339013, which includes some of your roof panels in dark gray. One of my clients called me to ask a question about **whether the shade** could lead to his gradually-sloped, east-facing rooftop **heating up** in the afternoon, especially during the summer. I informed him that theoretically, bright shades tend to reflect heat a bit better and are definitely not bad choices for warmer climate regions. Is it possible to **give me some advice** as I believe you may have experienced similar issues in the past? He has no intention to switch, and wants to ... ossible.

200 2 + 3 文章整合題

In addition, I heard that you run a **Web site** containing detailed **installation instructions**. I am worried as it is the first time for me to install this type of panel using the screws provided, so I would like to have the information downloaded. Could you give me the link ... instruction page?

198-A

陷阱選項 198-A, B, D
查看內文，並刪去錯誤的選項。

Thank you,
Malloy Alisa 寄件人：I

E-MAIL 3

To	malloyalisa@lourdesbuildingservice.org
From	bernardowood@rogerroofing.net
Date	November 19
Subject	Re: Purchase order

Dear Ms. Alisa, 收件人：You

Thank you for your inquiry about our product and service. In order to reflect sunlight and avoid heat gain, the roof panels are finished with a special coating material. There are several houses in the area that have the same panels in similar shades. But we have not received ... r. Still, we are certainly happy to **provide another model** if the client wants to change his mind. **Please just inform** me no later than tomorrow.

199 provide another model → prepare a different product

As for the Web page you mentioned, **as the manufacturers of the particular models have up-to-date and accurate information** about their products and service, we encourage customers to talk with them directly. So **only** the lists of **contact information** for each manufacturer are **now available** on **our Web site**.

200 2 + 3 文章整合題
the Web page you mentioned → a Web site containing detailed installation instructions

Best Regards,
Bernardo Wood
寄件人：I

196. According to the leaflet, how can consumers decide how many panels to purchase?

(A) By taking advantage of an online tool
(B) By contacting a roofing specialist
(C) By e-mailing a request form
(D) By downloading a special software program

decide／how many panels to purchase
→ 從後半段文章中找出決定方法。

197. What aspect of the roof panels does Ms. Alisa want to learn more about?
❷當中的寄件人：I

(A) Their life compared to other models
(B) Their possibility of retaining heat
(C) Their capability to resist moisture
(D) Their popularity among consumers in a region

Ms. Alisa：文章❷
→「give me some advice」

198. What kind of roof panel did Ms. Alisa most likely purchase for her client?

(A) Bertie PRX22
(B) Carey PRX31
(C) Madge PRX01
(D) Marcie PRX12

文章❶和❷整合題
→ 從文章❶和❷中找出刪去錯誤選項的線索。

❸當中的寄件人：I

199. According to Mr. Wood, why would Ms. Alisa need to contact him again on November 20?

(A) To confirm the status of delivery
(B) To receive a refund
(C) To visit a manufacturer
(D) To prepare a different product

Mr. Wood：文章❸
→ 從時間點「tomorrow」所在的句子找出答題線索。

200. What is indicated about the installation instructions?

(A) They clearly ~~show~~ additional equipment to use.
(B) They used to be on Roger Roofing's Web site.
(C) Ms. Alisa ~~has lost~~ her copy of them.
(D) Roger Roofing ~~will send~~ them to Ms. Alisa by e-mail.

關鍵字 installation instructions：文章❷
→ 再從文章❸確認另一個關鍵字 a Web site。

第 196-200 題 傳單與兩封電子郵件

1

羅傑屋頂建材

過去數十年來，建商和屋頂工人都選擇羅傑屋頂建材進行他們的屋頂工程，包括安裝及更換屋頂板。以下是一些我們最暢銷的產品。

伯蒂 PRX22：不用任何螺絲，採用持久耐用的夾子來安裝。請注意，這款產品應由技術純熟的專家來安裝，因為調校這些頂板成一直線往往是個大挑戰。

凱瑞 PRX31：是屋頂極為陡斜房屋的最佳選擇，光滑的表面可確保雨水排水系統順暢。

麥姬 PRX01：堅固耐久，安裝不耗時，有 20 種吸引人的色調可選。

瑪西 PRX12：和麥姬 PRX01 相當類似，但只有 4 種色調可選（藍、紅、綠、黃）。此外，上面印有波浪花紋。

更多價格資訊及規格，請看我們的最新廣告小冊。對我們的服務和產品有任何問題，請寄電子郵件到 customerservice@rogerroofing.net，或致電 220-2235-6654 給我們。

請注意，重疊率會依屋頂板產品而有不同。可上 www.@rogerroofing.net/overlapdegree，用我們的線上計算器找出您房屋所適用的屋頂板數量。只要鍵入您想購買的型號，以及屋頂面積即可。

2

收件人	customerservice@rogerroofing.net
寄件人	malloyalisa@lourdesbuildingservice.org
日期	11 月 19 日
主旨	訂購單

敬啟者：

我最近送出一份訂單 #339013，裡面包含一些你們的深灰色屋頂板。我的一個客戶打電話給我，問這個顏色是否會造成他那平緩傾斜的面東屋頂在下午變熱，尤其在夏天的時候。我告訴他，理論上，淺色較能反射熱氣，而且在氣候較溫暖的地區，也肯定不是糟糕的選擇。因為我相信你們以前或許也碰過類似的問題，有可能給我一些意見嗎？他不打算改變顏色，可能的話，就維持這個顏色不換。

此外，我聽說你們有個網站，裡面有詳細的安裝指南。我有點擔心，因為這是我第一次用你們提供的螺絲安裝這種屋頂板，因此，我想要下載這項資料。你們可以給我安裝指南網頁的連結嗎？

謝謝你。
瑪洛伊．艾利莎

3

收件人	malloyalisa@lourdesbuildingservice.org
寄件人	bernardowood@rogerroofing.net
日期	11 月 19 日
主旨	回覆：訂購單

親愛的艾利莎女士：

謝謝您詢問關於我們產品與服務的問題。為了反射日光並避免有熱氣，屋頂板最後會上一層特殊的塗料。在那一區有好幾間房子都裝了類似色調的頂板。不過，到目前為止，我們還沒有接到任何關於屋內溫度上升的抱怨。儘管如此，如果客戶想改變主意，我們當然很樂意提供另一款產品。請在明天之前通知我。

至於您提到的網頁，由於該款型號的製造商有他們產品與服務的最新正確資訊，因此，我們鼓勵顧客直接問他們。所以，我們的網站上現在只有每家製造商的聯絡資料。

祝 好

伯納多·伍德

字彙 builder 建築商、建造者　roofing work 屋頂工程　screw 螺絲
durable 耐用的、持久的　align 排成直線　steeply 陡直地
drainage 排水、排水系統　slick 光滑的　appealing 吸引人的　shade 色調、色度
specification 規格　east-facing 朝東的　theoretically 理論上
stick to 固守、不改變某事物

196. 根據傳單，顧客要如何決定該購買多少頂板？

(A) 利用線上工具

(B) 聯絡屋頂工程專家

(C) 用電子郵件寄一份詢問表

(D) 下載一個特別的軟體程式

STEP 1 聯絡方式、申請方法會出現在後半段文章中。

請確認題目關鍵字為 how can consumers decide how many panels。第一篇文章寫道：「Our online calculator is available at www.@rogerroofing.net/overlapdegree to find out the appropriate number of roof panels for your property.」，提到可以上他們的網站確認適當的屋頂板數量，因此答案為 (A)。文中並未提及其他選項的內容。

197. 艾利莎女士想更了解屋頂板的哪方面資訊？

(A) 它們與其他型號相比之下的壽命

(B) 它們保留熱氣的可能性

(C) 它們防潮的能力

(D) 它們受某地區顧客歡迎的程度

STEP 1 題目出現關鍵字時，請在該關鍵字所在文章中找出其他答題資訊。

Alisa 在第二篇文章中寫道：「One of my clients called me to ask a question about whether the shade could lead to his gradually-sloped, east-facing rooftop heating up」，提到顧客詢問屋頂板的顏色是否會影響屋頂的熱度。後方還寫道：「Is it possible to give me some advice」，請對方提供建議。由此可以得知 Alisa 想要知道屋頂板是否會留住熱氣，因此答案為 (B)。

STEP 2 分析錯誤選項

(D) 文中僅提到 region，並未提到在消費者間的人氣。

198. 艾利莎女士最可能幫她的客戶購買哪一種屋頂板？

(A) 伯蒂 PRX22

(B) 凱瑞 PRX31

(C) 麥婭 PRX01

(D) 瑪西 PRX12

STEP 1 看到針對兩篇文章出題的整合題時，請善用題目所提供的線索和文章內所有有關答案的資訊。

Alisa 在第二篇文章中寫道：「includes some of your roof panels in dark gray」，提到購買了深灰色的屋頂板。而 (D) Marcie PRX12 的顏色只有 blue、red、green、yellow，因此並非答案。

文中還寫道：「One of my clients . . . his gradually-sloped」，表示顧客的屋頂朝向東方，斜度偏平緩。而 (B) Carey PRX31 適合較為傾斜的屋頂，因此也不是答案。文章後半段寫道：「panel using the screws provided」，提到需要使用螺絲。而 (A) Bertie PRX22 並不需要使用螺絲，因此也不是答案。綜合上述，答案要選 (C)。

199. 根據伍德先生，艾利莎女士為什麼需要在 11 月 20 日再次和他聯絡？

(A) 為了確認運送狀態

(B) 為了接受退費

(C) 為了拜訪一位製造商

(D) 為了準備好不同的產品

STEP 1 題目出現關鍵字時，請在該關鍵字所在文章中找出其他答題資訊。

請確認題目關鍵字為 Ms. Alisa、contact、November 20，從文中找出與 contact 有關的內容。Wood 在第三篇文章寫道「we are certainly happy to provide another model if the client wants to change his mind. Please just inform me no later than tomorrow」，提到若顧客改變心意，他很樂意提供其他型號的產品，並麻煩對方最晚於明天告知。由此可以得知 Alisa 需要在 11 月 20 日聯絡 Wood 的原因是要請 Wood 準備其他產品，因此答案為 (D)。

200. 關於安裝指南，可由文中得知什麼？

(A) 清楚指出要使用額外的設備。

(B) 以前曾在羅傑屋頂的網站上。

(C) 艾利莎女士遺失了她那一份指南。

(D) 羅傑屋頂會用電子郵件把指南寄給艾利莎女士。

STEP 1 看到針對兩篇文章出題的整合題時，若關鍵字旁未出現答案，請確認是否還有其他解題線索。

請確認題目關鍵字為 installation instructions。Alisa 在第二篇文章後半段寫道：「I heard that you run a Web site containing detailed installation instructions」，提到她聽說 Roger Roofing Materials 的網站上有提供安裝指南。

而第三篇文章中寫道：「As for the Web page you mentioned, . . . So only the lists of contact information for each manufacturer are now available on our Web site.」，提到因為製造商擁有最新最準確的資訊，所以現在網站上只有提供製造商的聯絡資訊。這表示過去 Roger Roofing Materials 的網站上曾提供安裝指南，現在則沒有提供，因此答案為 (B)。

TEST 3
解析

解答 TEST 3

01. (A)	**02.** (D)	**03.** (A)	**04.** (B)	**05.** (A)	**06.** (C)	**07.** (A)	**08.** (B)	**09.** (A)	**10.** (C)
11. (B)	**12.** (A)	**13.** (C)	**14.** (A)	**15.** (A)	**16.** (B)	**17.** (B)	**18.** (A)	**19.** (A)	**20.** (C)
21. (B)	**22.** (A)	**23.** (B)	**24.** (C)	**25.** (A)	**26.** (B)	**27.** (B)	**28.** (B)	**29.** (A)	**30.** (C)
31. (C)	**32.** (D)	**33.** (A)	**34.** (D)	**35.** (B)	**36.** (C)	**37.** (A)	**38.** (B)	**39.** (A)	**40.** (B)
41. (A)	**42.** (C)	**43.** (A)	**44.** (C)	**45.** (D)	**46.** (B)	**47.** (A)	**48.** (C)	**49.** (C)	**50.** (D)
51. (B)	**52.** (C)	**53.** (C)	**54.** (C)	**55.** (A)	**56.** (C)	**57.** (D)	**58.** (B)	**59.** (A)	**60.** (C)
61. (B)	**62.** (D)	**63.** (A)	**64.** (C)	**65.** (B)	**66.** (A)	**67.** (C)	**68.** (B)	**69.** (A)	**70.** (C)
71. (D)	**72.** (A)	**73.** (D)	**74.** (B)	**75.** (A)	**76.** (D)	**77.** (B)	**78.** (A)	**79.** (D)	**80.** (D)
81. (C)	**82.** (A)	**83.** (D)	**84.** (A)	**85.** (D)	**86.** (B)	**87.** (A)	**88.** (C)	**89.** (C)	**90.** (A)
91. (C)	**92.** (D)	**93.** (C)	**94.** (A)	**95.** (B)	**96.** (B)	**97.** (D)	**98.** (D)	**99.** (C)	**100.** (C)
101. (B)	**102.** (D)	**103.** (C)	**104.** (B)	**105.** (C)	**106.** (B)	**107.** (A)	**108.** (B)	**109.** (C)	**110.** (B)
111. (A)	**112.** (A)	**113.** (C)	**114.** (C)	**115.** (C)	**116.** (D)	**117.** (D)	**118.** (D)	**119.** (B)	**120.** (D)
121. (B)	**122.** (A)	**123.** (A)	**124.** (A)	**125.** (D)	**126.** (B)	**127.** (D)	**128.** (D)	**129.** (A)	**130.** (D)
131. (D)	**132.** (C)	**133.** (C)	**134.** (D)	**135.** (B)	**136.** (D)	**137.** (D)	**138.** (B)	**139.** (C)	**140.** (D)
141. (B)	**142.** (B)	**143.** (C)	**144.** (C)	**145.** (D)	**146.** (D)	**147.** (A)	**148.** (D)	**149.** (B)	**150.** (D)
151. (C)	**152.** (D)	**153.** (B)	**154.** (A)	**155.** (C)	**156.** (B)	**157.** (A)	**158.** (B)	**159.** (C)	**160.** (C)
161. (C)	**162.** (D)	**163.** (A)	**164.** (C)	**165.** (C)	**166.** (D)	**167.** (B)	**168.** (D)	**169.** (B)	**170.** (C)
171. (B)	**172.** (B)	**173.** (C)	**174.** (B)	**175.** (C)	**176.** (A)	**177.** (C)	**178.** (C)	**179.** (D)	**180.** (A)
181. (C)	**182.** (D)	**183.** (A)	**184.** (C)	**185.** (A)	**186.** (D)	**187.** (C)	**188.** (B)	**189.** (D)	**190.** (B)
191. (B)	**192.** (C)	**193.** (C)	**194.** (B)	**195.** (C)	**196.** (D)	**197.** (C)	**198.** (C)	**199.** (D)	**200.** (B)

PART 1

1

(A) A woman is examining some items.
(B) A woman is trying on a jacket.
(C) A man is purchasing some merchandise.
(D) A man is labeling some clothes.

(A) 女子正在查看物品。
(B) 女子正在試穿夾克。
(C) 男子正在購買商品。
(D) 男子正在替衣服貼標籤。

字彙 examine 檢查、檢視　try on 試穿　merchandise 商品　label 貼標籤

01 照片背景為餐廳、購物中心、市場、商店等日常生活場景。

照片以超市為背景時，答案通常會是「查看」（examine、study、inspect、look at）或手推車（cart）。

STEP 1 照片分析

❶ 雙人照片
❷ 女子正在看商品
❸ 女子圍著圍巾
❹ 男子拿著商品

STEP 2 聽到照片中未呈現的單字時，請立即刪去該選項。

(A) A woman is examining some items. ▶ 答案

(B) A woman is ~~trying on~~ a jacket.
▶女子身上已穿著夾克。

(C) A man is ~~purchasing~~ some merchandise.
▶男子並未做出購買商品的動作。

(D) A man is ~~labeling~~ some ~~clothes~~.
▶男子並未做出貼標籤的動作。

STEP 3 刪去法 POINT

❶ 若聽到照片中未出現的名詞或動詞，皆為錯誤的描述。
❷ 男女雙人照片→請確認男女主詞是否連接適當的動作或狀態。
❸ 多人照片→請確認主詞的單複數是否搭配適當的動詞。

2

(A) A man is drinking from a bottle.
(B) A man is stocking shelves with some beverages.
(C) There are some seating areas in the room.
(D) There are vending machines side by side in the lounge.

(A) 男子正用瓶子喝飲料。
(B) 男子正在補貨上架飲料。
(C) 房間裡有一部分是座位區。
(D) 販賣機並排設立在休息區裡。

字彙 stock 補貨上架　beverage 飲料　seating area 座位區　vending machine 販賣機　side by side 並排

02 當畫面重點以背景為主時，請仔細聆聽事物的狀態。

▶ 照片中有人，不代表答案一定是針對人物的描述。
▶ 雖然有時針對照片中最顯眼的行為描述的選項即為正確答案，但是有時答案反而是針對意想不到的部分進行描述的選項。

STEP 1 照片分析

❶ 單人照片
❷ 男子正在使用自動販賣機
❸ 照片中有很多台自動販賣機

STEP 2 聽到照片中未呈現的單字時，請立即刪去該選項。

(A) A man is ~~drinking from a bottle~~.
▶ 男子並未做出喝的動作。

(B) A man is ~~stocking shelves~~ with some beverages.
▶ 男子並未做出把飲料上架的動作。

(C) There are ~~some seating areas~~ in the room.
▶ 照片中沒有出現座位。

(D) There are vending machines side by side in the lounge. ▶ 答案

STEP 3 人＋物照片的刪去 POINT

❶ 確認主詞是人還是物，並聽清楚動詞為何。
❷ 聽到主詞為人時，請確認該主詞的動作和狀態。
❸ 聽到主詞為物時，請確認該事物的位置和狀態。

3

(A) A man is using some laboratory equipment.
(B) A man is taking off his glove with the other hand.
(C) They're clearing off a table.
(D) They're writing something down on a notepad.

(A) 男子正在使用一些實驗室設備。
(B) 男子正用手脫另一隻手的手套。
(C) 他們正在清理桌面。
(D) 他們正在筆記本上記事情。

字彙 laboratory equipment 實驗室設備　take off 脫去（衣物等）　clear off 清理（平面）

03 請確認雙人照片中人物的共同動作和各自的動作。

▶ 一般來說，雙人照片的答案會是兩人的共同動作，但有時也會以描述其中一人的動作作為答案。

STEP 1 照片分析

❶ 雙人照片
❷ 男子正在使用實驗器具。
❸ 男子戴著手套。
❹ 女子拿著筆記本正在記錄著什麼。
❺ 男女兩人皆戴著眼鏡、身穿實驗室服。

STEP 2 聽到照片中未呈現的單字時，請立即刪去該選項。

(A) A man is using some laboratory equipment. ▶ 答案

(B) A man is ~~taking off~~ his glove with the other hand.
▶ 男子正戴著手套。

(C) They're ~~clearing off a table~~.
▶ 照片中並未出現清理桌子的人。

(D) ~~They're~~ writing something down on a notepad.
▶ 只有女子一人在寫東西。

STEP 3 雙人照片的 POINT

❶ 照片為雙人照片時，請依序觀察人物的「共同之處→個別細節」。
❷ 觀看照片的方向請由左方看至右方。
❸ 若選項以雙方拿著或給對方的物品作為主詞時，通常會使用進行被動式的用法。
❹ 主詞為物品時，請由周遭事物的狀態判斷答案。

照片類型	出題頻率前五高的正確答案
雙人照片的情況	❶ 描述兩人的共同動作或狀況
	❷ 描述單人或兩人的動作細節
	❸ 描述人物的外貌、外型等
	❹ 描述兩人身旁物品的動向或狀態
	❺ 描述周遭（地點）的狀況或物品狀況

4

(A) The drawers of the chest have been left open.
(B) There are cabinets above a computer monitor.
(C) Curtains have been closed in front of a window.
(D) All of the bookshelves are filled with documents.

(A) 衣櫃的抽屜沒關。
(B) 電腦螢幕上方有些小櫥櫃。
(C) 窗簾是闔上的。
(D) 書架上全都擺滿了文件。

字彙 chest 衣櫃　be filled with 被……塞滿了

04 請由句末的「介系詞＋名詞」確認物品的位置。

▶ 無人物品照通常會針對名詞的位置和背景畫面進行描述。
▶ 介系詞片語「介系詞＋名詞」可以用來表示地點。而在 PART 1 中，介系詞片語會放在句末，因此即便聽到正確的名詞，也請務必聽到最後，確認是否為正確描述。

STEP 1 照片分析

❶ 室內物品照
❷ 窗簾為拉開的狀態。
❸ 架上擺了幾樣東西。

STEP 2 聽到照片中未呈現的單字時，請立即刪去該選項。

(A) The drawers of the chest have been left ~~open~~. ▶ 櫃子抽屜並未處於開啟的狀態。
(B) There are cabinets above a computer monitor. ▶ 答案
(C) Curtains have been ~~closed~~ in front of a window. ▶ 窗簾為拉開的狀態。
(D) ~~All~~ of the bookshelves are filled with documents. ▶ 書架上並沒有全擺滿文件。

STEP 3 表示位置的介系詞一覽

▶ **in front of**：
位在某物前方、或往某物前方移動
There is a truck in front of the building.
建築物前有一台卡車。

▶ **on**：位於……上方
There are some books on the shelves.
書櫃上有一些書。

▶ **beside**：位於……旁邊
（＝ next to、close to、by）
A man is walking beside the bicycles.
男子正在腳踏車旁行走。

▶ **over**：在（某個空間）的上方、越過
There is a bridge over the river.
河的上方有一座橋。

He is carrying a bag over his shoulder.
他的肩上揹了一個包包。

▶ **above**：位在比某物更高的位置
There is a picture above the fireplace.
壁爐上方有一幅畫。

▶ **under**：位於……下方
There are cabinets under the counter.
吧檯下方有櫥櫃。

▶ **through**：從一方通過另一方、貫穿
Light is shining through the window.
燈光照射穿過窗戶。

▶ **at**：和某物極為接近的狀況
A man is standing at the copier.
男子正站在影印機旁。

▶ **against**：垂直方向緊靠著
There are two beds against the wall.
有兩張床緊挨著牆壁。

A ladder is leaning against the building.
一架梯子倚靠著建築物。

▶ **along**：人或物沿著 shore（岸邊）、street（街道）、railway（鐵路）等
A man is walking along the shore.
男子正沿著岸邊行走。

5

(A) Boards are propped against the wall.
(B) All the doors have been closed.
(C) A ladder is being placed on the floor.
(D) A floor is being polished with a brush.

(A) 板子靠牆撐著。
(B) 門全都關上了。
(C) 一個梯子正被擺放在地上。
(D) 一片地板正在被刷亮。

字彙 **be propped against** 靠……支撐著　**polish** 磨光；擦亮

05 熟記無人照片的兩大陷阱重點。

▶ 物品照刪去法重點

1. 若聽到人物名詞，該選項則不能作為答案。
2. 大部分的「be being p.p.」用法不能做為答案。

STEP 1 照片分析

❶ 室內物品照
❷ 照片中出現梯子。
❸ 門板倚靠著牆壁。
❹ 地上擺著一些東西。

STEP 2 聽到照片中未呈現的單字時，請立即刪去該選項。

(A) Boards are propped against the wall. ▶ 答案

(B) All the doors have been ~~closed~~.
▶ 門並未處於關閉的狀態。

(C) A ladder ~~is being placed~~ on the floor.
▶ 照片中沒有出現擺放梯子的人。

(D) A floor ~~is being polished~~ with a brush.
▶ 照片中沒有出現刷地板的人。

STEP 3 物品照刪去法 POINT

❶ 請確認主要事物的位置和狀態、以及周遭事物和背景畫面。

1. 確認主要事物的位置和狀態。
2. 確認周遭事物。
3. 確認地點和背景畫面。
4. 若題目為無人照片，選項卻出現人物名詞時，屬於錯誤描述，請立即刪去該選項。
5. 請特別留意，錯誤選項中可能會提及照片中未出現的事物。

❷ be being p.p. 不能作為答案。

- 「事物主詞＋ be being p.p.」表示「某人針對某物做某個動作」，因此此用法不適用於無人照片，屬於錯誤的敘述。
- 〔例外〕display（陳列）表示一種持續的狀態，因此即使照片中沒有人，仍可以使用進行被動式。

6

(A) Billboards are being posted along a building.
(B) Some stairs have been divided by a handrail.
(C) Some people are descending some stairs.
(D) Some people are crossing a street.

(A) 有人正在沿著建築物張貼廣告牌。
(B) 一部分的樓梯被扶手給隔開了。
(C) 有些人正在下樓梯。
(D) 有些人正在穿越馬路。

字彙 billboard 告示牌；廣告牌　post 張貼　handrail 扶手　descend 走下　cross 穿越

06 照片中同時出現人物和事物

▶ 照片為〈人物＋事物〉時，若選項以事物作為主詞，後方通常會使用進行被動式 be being p.p.。
▶「事物主詞＋ be being p.p.」＝「人物正在對事物做某個動作」

STEP 1 照片分析

❶ 照片為〈人＋物〉
❷ 人們正在下樓梯。
❸ 建築物掛著廣告牌。

STEP 2 聽到照片中未呈現的單字時，請立即刪去該選項。

(A) Billboards ~~are being posted~~ along a building.
　▶ 照片中沒有出現張貼廣告牌的人。

(B) Some stairs have been ~~divided~~ by a handrail.
　▶ 樓梯中間沒有扶手。

(C) Some people are descending some stairs. ▶ 答案

(D) Some people are ~~crossing a street~~.
　▶ 照片中沒有出現過馬路的人。

STEP 3 照片中同時出現人物和事物的 POINT

❶ 判斷人物和背景的比例各占多少。
❷ 確認照片中的地點，以及周遭事物的位置與狀態。
❸ 請務必熟記與照片中的事物特徵有關的單字。
❹ 請特別留意，錯誤選項中可能會出現與人物動作不相干的動詞。
❺ 請特別留意，錯誤選項中可能會提到照片中沒有的事物。

07. When is *Eddie*, the newest movie, coming out?
(A) There is a schedule on the Web site.
▶ 以地點回答 When 問句
(B) Its ~~setting~~ was in Berlin. ▶ 相關單字 x
(C) He's ~~coming~~ today. ▶ 相同單字 x

07. 那部最新的電影《艾迪》什麼時候出啊？
(A) 官網上有上映時間。
(B) 場景在柏林。
(C) 他今天會來。

08. Why has the flight been delayed for over an hour?
(A) It ~~takes about three hours~~ to arrive in Rio de Janeiro. ▶ 適用 How long 問句
(B) Should we take a train instead? ▶ 反問對方方法
(C) A taxi to the ~~airport~~. ▶ 相關單字 x

08. 為什麼班機延誤超過一個小時？
(A) 抵達里約熱內盧需要三個小時。
(B) 我們應該要改搭火車嗎？
(C) 一台往機場的計程車。

09. What do you usually do on the weekend mornings?
(A) I go to the Yardly Boulevard for brunch.
▶ 具體回答出做什麼事情
(B) I ~~usually~~ work the evening shift. ▶ 相同單字 x
(C) ~~No~~, today isn't a national holiday.
▶ 不能用 Yes 或 No 回答

09. 你週末早上通常都做什麼？
(A) 我去庭院大道吃早午餐。
(B) 我通常上晚班。
(C) 不，今天不是國定假日。

10. Sophia Ping will be the main singer for this jazz festival, won't she?
(A) In the ~~concert hall~~. ▶ 相關單字 x
(B) The sound effects were very ~~fantastic~~.
▶ 適用 How 問句
(C) Yes, I'm really looking forward to it.
▶ 用 Yes 加上附和回答附加問句

10. 蘇菲亞．平是這次爵士節的主唱，不是嗎？
(A) 在演奏廳裡。
(B) 音效很棒。
(C) 對啊，我真的很期待。

11. The initiative of Palcon Industries should be discussed.
(A) ~~To reduce~~ the air pollution. ▶ 適用 Why 問句
(B) I'm free tomorrow afternoon. ▶ 表示同意
(C) It ~~was~~ going well. ▶ 時態有誤

11. 應該來好好談一談友同企業的起步。
(A) 以便減少空汙。
(B) 我明天下午有空。
(C) 過得很順利。

12. What's the weather like in Sao Paulo at this time of year?
(A) It's like early spring in Korea. ▶ 說明天氣
(B) I visited there ~~to go sightseeing~~. ▶ 適用 Why 問句
(C) It's ~~based on~~ the daily routine. ▶ 適用 How 問句

12. 每年的這個時候聖保羅的天氣如何？
(A) 就像是韓國早春的時候。
(B) 我到那裡去觀光。
(C) 這取決於每日的例行工作。

13. I can't handle this new drilling machine.
(A) It is helpful ~~to dig a hole~~. ▶ 相關單字 x
(B) I think it's ~~in the warehouse~~.
▶ 適用 Where 問句 | 相關單字 x
(C) When are you available for me to stop by?
▶ 提出往後的行動

13. 我不會操作這台新的鑽孔機。
(A) 它拿來挖洞很好用。
(B) 我想它應該放在倉庫裡。
(C) 你哪時方便讓我過去看一下？

14. Where are the packaging tools?

(A) I don't work on this team.
▶表達「我不知道」

(B) ~~A large box.~~
▶適用 What 問句｜相關單字 x

(C) It costs ~~$1,000~~.
▶適用問句 How much is it?

14. 包裝用品放哪去了？

(A) 我不是這個團隊的人。

(B) 一個大箱子。

(C) 這要一千元。

---

15. Would it be better to alter the length of this uniform?

(A) I think it fits well. ▶間接回答

(B) Fill out a ~~form~~. ▶發音相似 x

(C) It comes in ~~red and black~~. ▶相關單字 x

15. 把這件制服的長度改一下會不會比較好？

(A) 我覺得它很合身。

(B) 填寫表單。

(C) 它有紅色和黑色。

---

16. Why didn't Molly leave for New York yesterday?

(A) ~~For sightseeing~~. ▶相關單字 x

(B) She had a scheduling conflict. ▶回答出具體原因

(C) It's an ~~exciting place~~.
▶相關單字 x｜適用 How 問句

16. 為什麼茉莉昨天沒有去紐約？

(A) 去觀光。

(B) 她行程衝到了。

(C) 這地方蠻刺激的。

---

17. I got the results of the survey conducted by the focus group.

(A) They have ~~focused~~ on that. ▶發音相似 x

(B) That was quick. ▶附和直述句的內容

(C) It is applied to a ~~group~~ rate. ▶相同單字 x

17. 我收到焦點訪談的研究成果了。

(A) 他們一直很注意那件事。

(B) 很快耶。

(C) 這適用團體費率。

---

18. Isn't your store closed for this holiday?

(A) No, we are open all year round.
▶以 No 回答加上補充說明

(B) ~~In the storage folder~~. ▶適用 Where 問句

(C) The grand ~~opening~~ was September 1.
▶相關單字 x｜適用 When 問句

18. 你們店這次節日不放假嗎？

(A) 對，我們全年無休。

(B) 在檔案夾裡。

(C) 九月一日盛大開幕。

---

19. I'll have my car fixed by the mechanic today.

(A) I'll give you a ride to work then. ▶告知下一步動作

(B) The ~~machine~~ is easy to assemble. ▶相關單字 x

(C) He can't ~~fax~~ it. ▶發音相似 x

19. 我今天會去找技師修車子。

(A) 我到時載你去上班。

(B) 這機器蠻好組裝的。

(C) 這個他沒辦法傳真。

---

20. Marc, you're going to attend the conference next month, right?

(A) A flight ~~attendant~~. ▶發音相似 x

(B) ~~Refer to~~ the product list. ▶適用 What 問句

(C) No, my request was denied.
▶以 No 回答加上補充說明

20. 馬克，你準備參加下個月的會議，對嗎？

(A) 一名空服員。

(B) 請參考產品目錄。

(C) 沒有，我的請求被拒絕了。

21. **Why didn't you meet** the contractor this afternoon?

(A) ~~Right next to~~ the post office. ▶適用 Where 問句
(B) We found a better contractor. ▶回答原因
(C) ~~That's a good plan~~. ▶適用表示勸說或建議的問句

21. 你今天下午為什麼沒有和承包商開會？
(A) 就在郵局旁邊。
(B) 我們找到更好的承包商。
(C) 這是個好計畫。

22. I **don't know how to operate** this electronic lecture desk.

(A) Jenny used it last class. ▶表達「我不知道」
(B) ~~That would be great~~. ▶適用表示勸說或建議的問句
(C) To increase the efficiency of the ~~lecture~~.
▶相同單字 x｜適用 Why 問句

22. 我不知道怎麼操作這張數位講桌。
(A) 珍妮上一堂課有用。
(B) 那樣會很棒。
(C) 讓講課更有效率。

23. **I am surprised at the traffic** in this part of the city.

(A) That ~~was~~ a good idea. ▶主詞有誤｜適用 How 問句
(B) It will be worse during rush hour.
▶提出往後的狀況
(C) ~~He~~ was disappointed with that road. ▶主詞有誤

23. 城裡這區的交通讓我很驚訝。
(A) 這是個好主意。
(B) 尖峰時刻會更糟。
(C) 他對那條路很失望。

24. **What benefits do I receive** if I get a membership to your supermarket?

(A) ~~Within~~ five business days. ▶適用 When 問句
(B) A wide range of ~~fresh produce~~. ▶相關單字 x
(C) Here are some guidelines. ▶間接回答

24. 成為你們超市的會員，我會得到什麼好處？
(A) 五個工作天內。
(B) 各式各樣的新鮮農產。
(C) 這裡有一些說明。

25. **Wasn't he awarded** the prize last month?

(A) You mean our business partner?
▶以反問方式確認事實
(B) ~~A discounted price~~. ▶發音相似 x
(C) It ~~will~~ be held ~~in the Plaza Hotel~~.
▶時態有誤｜適用 Where 問句

25. 他上個月不是得獎了嗎？
(A) 你是說我們的商業夥伴嗎？
(B) 優惠後的價格。
(C) 將在廣場飯店舉行。

26. Do you think **we should ask another vendor** for office furniture?

(A) Some ~~chairs and desks~~. ▶相關單字 x
(B) I haven't heard any complaints. ▶間接回答
(C) It ~~rose by 15%~~. ▶適用 How much 問句

26. 你覺得我們應該要問問看其他辦公家具的廠商嗎？
(A) 一些桌椅。
(B) 我沒有接獲任何抱怨。
(C) 漲了 15%。

27. **How many copies** of the reports for the shareholders' meeting **should I prepare**?

(A) ~~Colorful images~~, please.
▶相關單字 x｜適用 What 問句
(B) I thought Rachel was making those. ▶間接回答
(C) ~~For~~ a higher ~~stock~~ price.
▶適用 Why 問句｜相關單字 x

27. 股東會上我需要準備多少份報告？
(A) 請用彩色圖片。
(B) 我以為那些瑞秋會準備。
(C) 為了哄抬股價。

TEST 3 PART 2 中譯 & 解析

28. Make sure to leave your belongings at the front desk.

(A) The ~~2 P.M~~ tour. ▶ 適用 When 問句
(B) Don't worry, I will. ▶ 使用「I will」回答
(C) It ~~belongs~~ to you. ▶ 發音相似 x

28. 記得要將隨身物品寄放在服務台。
(A) 下午兩點的行程。
(B) 別擔心，我會的。
(C) 這是你的東西。

---

29. Do you know who was nominated public relations manager of Colinsworth?

(A) We're still looking to fill the position.
▶ 表示「尚未決定」
(B) This facility is open for the ~~public~~. ▶ 相同單字 x
(C) No, ~~she~~ is in charge of it. ▶ 主詞有誤

29. 你知道是誰被提名為柯林斯沃斯的新公關經理嗎？
(A) 我們還在找人填補這個職缺。
(B) 這個設施對外開放。
(C) 不，這是她負責的。

---

30. Please send the marketing files to our client by 2 P.M.

(A) In a ~~filing cabinet~~. ▶ 適用 Where 問句 | 相關單字 x
(B) The ~~market~~ is closer. ▶ 相關單字 x
(C) I'll mark that on my schedule. ▶ 告知往後的行動

30. 請在下午兩點前把銷售資料寄給我們的客戶。
(A) 在檔案櫃裡。
(B) 那個市場比較近。
(C) 我會記在我的行程表上。

---

31. I don't want to eat at the French restaurant.

(A) Oh, I'm going to get ~~take-out~~.
▶ 相關單字 x | 適用 Which 問句
(B) ~~A lunch~~ with some colleagues.
▶ 適用 What 問句 | 相關單字 x
(C) But, I heard a new chef is there now.
▶ But ＋補充說明

31. 我不想在法國餐廳吃飯。
(A) 喔，我會外帶。
(B) 和一些同事共進午餐。
(C) 不過，我聽說那裡現在有新廚師。

07 【When 問句】最新回答方式——告知來源或位置表示「I don't know」。

題目分析 **When is *Eddie*, the newest movie, coming out?**

本題問句為「電影何時上映？」，詢問未來要發生的事情。

選項分析

(A) There is a schedule on the Web site. ▶ 答案

題目為以 When 開頭的問句，詢問未來的時間點「電影何時上映？」，可以用「我不知道」作為答案。該選項回答「網站上有時刻表」，告知對方可以確認資訊之處，故為正確答案。在新制測驗中，When 問句會回答地點作為答案，請特別留意。

(B) Its setting was in Berlin. ❹ 相關單字陷阱

setting 與題目句中的 movie 有所關聯，屬於陷阱選項。

(C) He's coming today. ❹ 相同單字陷阱

重複使用題目句中的 coming，屬於陷阱選項。值得留意的是，題目句中要提到特定人士，答句才能出現 He 或 She。而題目句中的 Eddie 指的是新上映電影的片名。

08 面對不利的狀況，藉反問方式提出替代方案。

題目分析 **Why has the flight been delayed for over an hour?**

本題為以 Why 開頭的問句，詢問「飛機為何延遲」。由解題關鍵「Why / flight / delayed」可以確認問題的核心。

選項分析

(A) It takes about three hours to arrive in Rio de Janeiro. ❷ 適用其他問句

回答「約三小時才會到」，應搭配以 How long 開頭，詢問所需時間的問句較為適當。

(B) Should we take a train instead? ▶ 答案

本題以 Why 問句詢問飛機延遲的原因，該選項提出其他方法反問對方，故為正確答案。值得留意的是，以反問方式回答時，通常會詢問與往後行動相關的問題、告知對方其他方法、或者提出疑問釐清現況。

(C) A taxi to the airport. ❹ 相關單字陷阱

airport 與題目句中的 flight 有所關聯，屬於陷阱選項。

09 問句為〈What ＋助動詞〉開頭時，答題關鍵為後方的主要動詞。

題目分析 **What do you usually do on the weekend mornings?**

What 問句的答題關鍵為名詞或動詞，若以〈What ＋助動詞〉開頭時，請務必聽清楚後方連接的動詞。由關鍵字「What / you / do」可以確認問題的核心。

選項分析

(A) I go to the Yardly Boulevard for brunch. ▶ 答案

題目詢問「週末上午通常會做些什麼？」，該選項回答「去 Yardly Boulevard 吃早午餐」，明確回答出會做什麼事情。

(B) I usually work the evening shift. ❹ 相同單字陷阱

重複使用題目句中的 usually，屬於陷阱選項。該選項應搭配以 When 開頭，詢問何時工作的問句較為適當。

(C) No, today isn't a national holiday. ❶ 不能以 Yes 或 No 回答

What 問句不能使用 Yes 或 No 來回答。請務必由〈What ＋助動詞＋主詞＋動詞〉當中的動詞，找出相關聯的回答。

10 【否定疑問句或附加問句】肯定回答 Yes，否定則回答 No。

題目分析 **Sophia Ping will be the main singer for this jazz festival, won't she?**

本題為附加問句，解題關鍵為「Sophia Ping / will be / main singer」，詢問該女子是否為主要歌手。

選項分析

(A) In the concert hall. ❹ 相關單字陷阱

concert hall 與題目句中的 jazz festival 有所關聯，屬於陷阱選項。該選項應搭配以 Where 開頭的問句較為適當。

(B) The sound effects were very fantastic. ❷ 適用其他問句

形容詞 fantastic 表達感受，應搭配以 How was 開頭，詢問對方想法或感受的問句較為適當。另外，sound 與題目句中的 singer 有所關聯，屬於答題陷阱，請特別留意。

(C) Yes, I'm really looking forward to it. ▶ 答案

回答附加問句時可以使用 Yes 加上依據、同意、附和，或者告知往後行動。本題詢問「Sophia Ping 是主要歌手對吧？」該選項回答「對，我真的非常期待」，附和對方所說的話，故為正確答案。

11 直述句中以 should 表示建議或義務。

題目分析 **The initiative of Palcon Industries should be discussed.**

本題的解題關鍵為「The initiative / should / (be) discussed」。直述句的答案通常會明確表示同意的話語，或是告知對方同意的原因、想法、補充說明，請務必留意這類內容。

選項分析

(A) To reduce the air pollution. ❷ 適用其他問句

回答中使用 to 不定詞，表示目的或理由，應搭配 Why 問句較為適當。

(B) I'm free tomorrow afternoon. ▶ 答案

本題以直述句告知「應該討論一下」，該選項回答「我明天下午有空」，表示同意對方所說的話。

(C) It was going well. ❺ 時態有誤

答句和題目句的時態必須一致才行。本題題目句的時態為未來式，但該選項卻使用過去式回答，因此不能作為答案。

12 答題關鍵為 What 後方連接的名詞。

題目分析 **What's the weather like in Sao Paulo at this time of year?**

本題的解題關鍵為「What's / weather」。有別於其他 Wh- 問句，what 問句無法單靠疑問詞 what 判斷出答案，請務必聽清楚後方的名詞或動詞。

選項分析

(A) It's like early spring in Korea. ▶ 答案

「和韓國初春的天氣差不多」，明確告知對方天氣狀況，故為正確答案。

(B) I visited there to go sightseeing. ❷ 適用其他問句

to go sightseeing 表示「原因或目的」，應搭配以 Why did you visit 開頭的問句較為適當。

(C) It's based on the daily routine. ❷ 適用其他問句

回答「取決於每日的例行工作」，應搭配以 How 開頭，詢問手段或方法的問句較為適當。

13 藉反問告知對方解決問題的下一步動作。

題目分析 **I can't handle this new drilling machine.**

本題的解題關鍵為「I can't handle」，由直述句告知問題所在。值得留意的是，回答可能會以「由我來……」、「你應該要……」、「往後的狀況」告知對方下一步的動作。

選項分析

(A) It is helpful to dig a hole. ❹ 相關單字陷阱

該回答與題目句中的 drilling machine 有所關聯，屬於陷阱選項。

(B) I think it's in the warehouse. ❷ 適用其他問句

warehouse 與題目句中的 machine 有所關聯，屬於答題陷阱。該選項應搭配 Where 問句較為適當。

(C) When are you available for me to stop by? ▶ 答案

題目以直述句表示問題為「我不會操作鑽孔機器」，而該選項回答「何時方便過去看一下」，告知對方解決問題的下一步動作，故為正確答案。

14 若選項表示「我不知道」，通常就是正確答案。

題目分析 **Where are the packaging tools?**

本題為 Where 開頭的問句，詢問包裝用具放在哪裡。解題關鍵為「Where / are / tools」。

選項分析

(A) I don't work on this team. ▶ 答案

除了「I don't know」之外，「不是我負責的」也算是表明「我不知道」的回答方式，為正確答案的機率極高。本題詢問「包裝用具放在哪裡」，該選項回答「我不是這個團隊的人」，等同於回答「我不知道」，故為正確答案。

(B) A large box. ❹ 相關單字陷阱

box 與題目句中的 packaging 有所關聯，屬於答題陷阱。該選項回答名詞，應搭配 What 問句較為適當，請特別熟記。

(C) It costs $1,000. ❷ 適用其他問句

該選項應搭配詢問價格的問句「How much is it?」較為適當。

15 回答 Be 動詞或助動詞問句時，省略 Yes 和 No，間接表明狀況。

題目分析 **Would it be better to alter the length of this uniform?**

本題為以助動詞開頭的問句，解題關鍵為「Would it / be better / to alter」。回答中可以省略 Yes 和 No，告知對方下一步的動作、或間接説明狀況。

選項分析

(A) I think it fits well. ▶ 答案

本題詢問「制服長度是不是要修改一下比較好」，該選項「我認為很合身」，代替 No 的概念，間接説明狀況，故為正確答案。

(B) Fill out a form. ❹ 相似發音陷阱

form 和題目句中 uniform 的發音相似，屬於答題陷阱，請特別留意。

(C) It comes in red and black. ❹ 相關單字陷阱

顏色 red and black 和題目句中的 uniform 有所關聯，屬於陷阱選項。

16 以狀況不太適合當作理由回答 Why didn't . . .?

題目分析 **Why didn't Molly leave for New York yesterday?**

本題的解題關鍵為「Why didn't . . . leave」，以否定句詢問對方理由，因此答案會回答不能做的理由。

選項分析

(A) For sightseeing. ❹ 相關單字陷阱

sightseeing 與題目句中的 New York 有所關聯，屬於答題陷阱。雖然該選項回答了原因，但是不適合用來回答問句「為何她沒有前往……？」。

(B) She had a scheduling conflict. ▶ 答案

本題詢問「為何 Molly 沒有前往紐約？」，該選項回答「與她原定行程有衝突（scheduling conflict）」，以狀況不太適合當作理由，故為正確答案。

表示狀況不太適合的常見用法		
• busy 忙碌	• work late 工作得晚	• have a meeting 要開會
• traffic jam 塞車	• bad weather 壞天氣	• out of ink 沒墨水了

(C) It's an exciting place. ❷ 適用其他問句

當中出現形容詞 exciting，應搭配 How 問句較為適當。另外，exciting place 與題目句中的 New York 有所關聯，屬於答題陷阱，請特別留意。

17 回答直述句時，可以表示同意或者附和。

題目分析 **I got the results of the survey conducted by the focus group.**

本題的解題關鍵為「I / got / the results」，最常用來回答直述句的方式為表示同意或附和對方。

選項分析

(A) They have focused on that. ❹ 相似發音陷阱

focused 與題目句中 focus 的發音相似，屬於答題陷阱。另外，值得留意的是，題目中並未出現與 They 相對應的特定人物或事物。

(B) That was quick. ▶ 答案

本題直述句表示「收到了問卷調查的結果」，該選項回答「速度真快」，表示附和，故為正確答案。

(C) It is applied to a group rate. ❹ 相同單字陷阱

重複使用題目句中的 group，屬於答題陷阱。該選項應搭配以 How 或 What 開頭的問句較為適當。

18 請務必小心發音相似的單字和有所關聯的單字。

題目分析 **Isn't your store closed for this holiday?**

本題為否定疑問句，欲向對方確認事實。肯定事實回答 Yes，否定則回答 No，並在後方加上其他想說的話。

選項分析

(A) No, we are open all year round. ▶ 答案

本題詢問「節日沒有休息嗎？」，該選項先回答 No 表示否定，接著再補充說明「全年無休」，故為正確答案。

(B) In the storage folder. ❷ 適用其他問句

該選項回答地點，因此應搭配 Where 問句較為適當。

(C) The grand opening was September 1. ❹ 相關單字陷阱

opening 與題目句中的 closed 有所關聯，屬於答題陷阱。該選項應搭配 When 問句較為適當。

19 針對問題提出替代方案。

題目分析 **I'll have my car fixed by the mechanic today.**

本題的解題關鍵為「I'll / have / car / fixed」，當中使用使役動詞 have 表示要把車子拿去修理。回答可以使用「Let's . . .」、「You should . . .」、「I will . . .」等句型表達下一步的動作。

選項分析

(A) I'll give you a ride to work then. ▶ 答案

本題以直述句表示「今天要把我的車子拿去修理」，該選項回答「我到時載你去上班」，告知對方下一步動作，故為正確答案。

(B) The machine is easy to assemble. ❹ 相關單字陷阱

machine 與題目句中的 mechanic 有所關聯，屬於答題陷阱。

(C) He can't fax it. ❹ 相似發音陷阱

fax 與題目句中 fixed 的發音相似，屬於答題陷阱。

20 新制測驗中，附加問句常以 right 結尾。

題目分析 **Marc, you're going to attend the conference next month, right?**

本題為附加問句，以 right 結尾，向對方確認某事是否屬實。

選項分析

(A) A flight attendant. ❹ 相似發音陷阱

attendant 與題目句中 attend 的發音相似，屬於答題陷阱。且該選項回答名詞，應搭配 What 問句較為適當，請特別留意。

(B) Refer to the product list. ❷ 適用其他問句

該選項應搭配以 What 或 How do I know 開頭的問句較為適當。

(C) No, my request was denied. ▶ 答案

本題詢問對方下個月是否會參加會議，該選項以 No 表示否定，故為正確答案。

21 說明不做特定行動的原因。

題目分析 **Why didn't you meet the contractor this afternoon?**

本題的解題關鍵為「Why / didn't / meet」。Why 問句不能用 Yes 或 No 來回答，答案通常是原因或解釋。

選項分析

(A) Right next to the post office. ❷ 適用其他問句

回答地點，適合搭配以 Where 開頭的問句較為適當。

(B) We found a better contractor. ▶ 答案

本題詢問「為何你不和承包商見面？」，該選項回答「我們找到更好的人選」，告知對方原因，故為正確答案。

(C) That's a good plan. ❷ 適用其他問句

該選項回答「這是個好計畫」，表達肯定的答覆，應搭配表示勸說或建議的問句較為適當。

22 間接表示「我不知道」。

題目分析 **I don't know how to operate this electronic lecture desk.**

本題的解題關鍵為「don't know / how / operate」，以直述句表達「我不知道該如何操作」。若要否定直述句的內容，通常會回答「我也不知道」、「我也反對」，請特別留意這類回答方式。

選項分析

(A) Jenny used it last class. ▶ 答案

該選項回答「上堂課 Jenny 有用過」，婉轉建議對方向用過的人請教，等同於表示「我不知道」，故為正確答案。

(B) That would be great. ❷ 適用其他問句

該選項回答「那很不錯」，表達肯定對方的話，應搭配表示勸說或建議的問句較為適當。

(C) To increase the efficiency of the lecture. ❹ 相同單字陷阱

重複使用題目句中的 lecture，屬於陷阱選項。該選項應搭配 Why 問句較為適當。

23 同意對方想法並補充說明。

題目分析 **I am surprised at the traffic in this part of the city.**

本題為直述句，解題關鍵為「I / surprised / traffic」。回答可以告知對方未來的狀況。

選項分析

(A) That was a good idea. ❺ 時態有誤

題目句的時態為現在式，但該選項卻使用過去式回答，兩者時態不一致，因此不能作為答案。該選項應搭配問句「How was it?」較為適當。

(B) It will be worse during rush hour. ▶ 答案

本題以直述句表示「沒想到交通狀況竟是如此」，而該選項回答「上下班時間更可怕」，補充說明，故為正確答案。

(C) He was disappointed with that road. ❸ 主詞有誤

題目句中並未出現 He 或 She 可以對應的人物，因此不能作為答案。

24 請特別留意間接說明狀況或迴避型的答覆。

題目分析 **What benefits do I receive if I get a membership to your supermarket?**

本題的解題關鍵為「What benefits / I / receive」，詢問有什麼好處。

選項分析

(A) Within five business days. ❷ 適用其他問句

該選項回答「在五個工作日內」，表示為期多久，應搭配 When 問句較為適當。

(B) A wide range of fresh produce. ❹ 相關單字陷阱

fresh produce 屬於販賣的商品，與題目句中的 supermarket 有所關聯，但與好處無關，因此不能作為答案。

(C) Here are some guidelines. ▶ 答案

本題詢問「我可以獲得什麼好處」，該選項採間接回答的方式，告知對方「請參考這裡的說明」，故為正確答案。

25 反問對方確認是否屬實。

題目分析 **Wasn't he awarded the prize last month?**

本題的解題關鍵為 Wasn't he awarded，問句以 Be 動詞開頭，確認某事是否屬實。

選項分析

(A) You mean our business partner? ▶ 答案

該選項回答「你指的是我們的商業夥伴嗎？」，以反問方式向對方確認題目句中的 he 指的是否為商業夥伴，故為正確答案。

反問的回答方式主要分為以下四種：

❶ 以 Wh- 問句詢問相關細節
❷ 以反問方式確認某事與否屬實
❸ 提出疑問以釐清狀況
❹ 詢問方法

(B) A discounted price. ❹ 相似發音陷阱

price 與題目句中 prize 的發音相似，屬於答題陷阱。

(C) It will be held in the Plaza Hotel. ❺ 時態有誤

答句和題目句的時態必須要一致才行。本題題目句的時態為過去式，但答句卻用未來式回答，因此不能作為答案。該選項應搭配 Where 問句較為適當。

26 Do you know / think ＋直述句……？

題目分析 **Do you think we should ask another vendor for office furniture?**

請仔細聆聽「Do you think / know」後方的內容，以便找出答案。本題的解題關鍵為「we should ask another vendor」。

選項分析

(A) Some chairs and desks. ❹ 相關單字陷阱

該回答與題目句中的 furniture 有所關聯，屬於答題陷阱。若回答為名詞，應搭配 What 問句較為適當，請特別留意。該選項應搭配問句「What should I order?」。

(B) I haven't heard any complaints. ▶ 答案

本題詢問「是否該詢問其他供應商」，該選項回答「我並沒有聽到它有任何負評」，間接表示他認為沒必要再找其他供應商。

(C) It rose by 15%. ❷ 適用其他問句

該選項回答「上升了 15%」，應搭配以 How much 開頭的問句較為適當。

27 請特別留意最新的回答方式 I thought。

題目分析 **How many copies of the reports for the shareholders' meeting should I prepare?**

本題為以 How many 開頭的問句，詢問「應該要準備多少份」。解題關鍵為「How many copies / should I prepare」。

選項分析

(A) Colorful images, please. ❹ 相關單字陷阱

colorful images 與題目句中的 copies 有所關聯，屬於答題陷阱。該選項應搭配 What 問句較為適當。

(B) I thought Rachel was making those. ▶ 答案

本題以 How many 問句詢問「應該要準備多少份」，該選項使用 I thought，採間接回答的方式表示「我以為是由 Rachel 負責準備」。I thought 句型的意思為「我以為……結果不是」，屬於假設的概念，是新制測驗中常見的用法。

(C) For a higher stock price. ❷ 適用其他問句

stock 與題目句中的 shareholders 有所關聯，屬於答題陷阱。另外，該選項回答原因，應搭配 Why 問句較為適當。

28 回答對方的建議或要求。

題目分析 **Make sure to leave your belongings at the front desk.**

本題以直述句提出要求，解題關鍵為「leave your belongings」。題目為直述句時，答案經常會以 I will 句型回答「我會這麼做」、「我會確認看看」，請特別留意這類回答方式。

選項分析

(A) The 2 P.M. tour. ❷ 適用其他問句

該選項回答時間，應搭配 When 問句較為適當。

(B) Don't worry, I will. ▶ 答案

本題要求對方「將隨身物品寄放在櫃台」，該選項回答「I will」，表示「我會這麼做」，故為正確答案。

(C) It belongs to you. ❹ 相似發音陷阱

belongs 與題目句中的 belongings 的發音相似，屬於答題陷阱。請特別留意這類發音或意思相近的陷阱。

29 題目為「Do you know ＋疑問詞……？」時，答題關鍵為疑問詞。

題目分析 **Do you know who was nominated public relations manager of Colinsworth?**

本題為間接問句，請務必聽清楚中間的疑問詞和後方內容，以便找出答案。解題關鍵為「who is nominated / manager」。

選項分析

(A) We're still looking to fill the position. ▶ 答案

本題屬於 Who 問句，詢問「任命誰為負責人」，該選項回答「我們還在找人」，表示尚未決定，故為正確答案。題目為 Who 問句時，常見的回答方式有「我沒聽說這件事」、「我還沒決定好」或「我不知道」，請務必熟記。

(B) This facility is open for the public. ❹ 相同單字陷阱

重複使用題目句中的 public，屬於答題陷阱。該選項應搭配問句「Who is the facility open for?」較為適當。

(C) No, she is in charge of if. ❸ 主詞有誤

本題開頭為 Do you know，乍看之下可以回答 No 表示否定。但是題目句中並未提及與 she 相對應的人物，因此不能作為答案。

30 間接表示未來某一天會做。

題目分析 **Please send the marketing files to our client by 2 P.M.**

本題以直述句要求對方做事，解題關鍵為「Please / send / files」。

選項分析

(A) In a filing cabinet. ❷ 適用其他問句

該選項回答地點，應搭配 Where 問句較為適當。另外，a filing cabinet 與題目句中的 files 有所關聯，屬於答題陷阱。

(B) The market is closer. ❹ 相關單字陷阱

market 與題目句中的 client 有所關聯，屬於答題陷阱。

(C) I'll mark that on my schedule. ▶ 答案

本題請對方「在兩點前寄送檔案」，該選項回答「我會記在我的行程表上」，間接表示同意對方的要求，故為正確答案。

31 以 but 反駁對方的想法。

題目分析 **I don't want to eat at the French restaurant.**

本題使用否定的直述句，表示「我不想吃」。在新制測驗中，經常會以 but 回答，請特別熟記。另外，題目為助動詞開頭的問句時，回答也常在 Yes 或 No 後方加上 but，用來補充說明事實。but 的意思為「不過、但是」，帶有轉折之意。

選項分析

(A) Oh, I'm going to get take-out. ❹ 相關單字陷阱

take-out 與題目句中的 restaurant 有所關聯，屬於答題陷阱。該選項應搭配以 Which 開頭，要求選擇其一的問句較為適當。

(B) A lunch with some colleagues. ❷ 適用其他問句

a lunch 與題目句中的 eat 有所關聯，屬於答題陷阱。另外，該選項回答名詞，應搭配 What 問句較為適當。

(C) But, I heard a new chef is there now. ▶ 答案

本題以直述句表示「我不想去法國餐廳吃飯」，該選項使用 but 加上補充說明「聽說那裡新來了一位廚師」，故為正確答案。

PART 3

Questions 32-34 refer to the following conversation.

M Hello, Melissa. This is Marcus from Delvin Telecommunications. I was told that you called me yesterday. I'm sorry I was out of the office for a conference. 32-C

W 32 Hello, Marcus. I was calling because a suite of offices that you're apt to like is on the market. It's located on Stockton Avenue and can accommodate up to 50 people. I think it could be perfect for you. 32-A

M 33 Umm, actually the number of our employees is 40, so that would be bigger than we need.

W I know, but during our last conversation you mentioned your company might expand. I think it would be better for you to get a more spacious office.

M You're right. When can I see the property? I'm available for this afternoon.

W 34 How about 4 P.M.? For your reference, I'll send a copy of the floor plan and the address of the property. 34-C

32. What is the main topic of the conversation?
(A) Reviewing market ~~trends~~
(B) Taking a job training
(C) ~~Going to a conference~~
(D) Renting office space

主旨／前
→ 注意聆聽第一句對白。

33. What is the man concerned about?
(A) The office size (B) The deadline
(C) The market conditions (D) ~~The location~~

男子／擔憂的事
→ 注意聆聽 but、actually、however 開頭的句子。

34. What will the woman do next?
(A) Consult a ~~book~~ (B) Refer to the Web site
(C) Send a ~~report~~ **(D) Email some information**

女子／未來／後
→ 注意聆聽女子提及 I'll . . . 的對白。

第 32-34 題 對話

男：哈囉，梅麗莎。我是戴爾文電信的馬庫斯。我接獲通知您昨天有來電。很抱歉我昨天去開會，人不在辦公室。

女：哈囉，馬庫斯。我打電話是因為市面上有可能適合您的辦公室。位於史塔克頓大道上，可以容納50人。我認為完全符合您的需求。

男：嗯，我們公司實際上只有40名員工，所以比我們需要的大了點。

女：我知道，不過上次你有提到公司可能擴編，我想辦公室空間大點對您比較好。

男：您是對的，什麼時候方便去看看？我今天下午有空。

女：下午四點怎麼樣？我會寄平面圖和地址給您參考。

32. 對話主旨是什麼？
(A) 檢討市場趨勢 (B) 接受職訓
(C) 去開會 (D) 租辦公室

33. 男子在意的事情是什麼？
(A) 辦公室大小 (B) 截止日期
(C) 市場局勢 (D) 地點

34. 女子接下來將會做什麼？
(A) 查書
(B) 參考官網
(C) 寄份報告
(D) 用電子郵件寄送一些資訊

32 若題目詢問主旨或目的，答案會出現在開頭前兩句話。

STEP 1 題目詢問對話主旨時，千萬不要從頭到尾默默聽完整篇對話後，才開始選答案。務必要先看完選項內容，如此一來只要聆聽前半段對話，便能找出答案。

對話中説道：「I was calling because a suite of offices that you're apt to like is on the market.」，女子打電話想告知對方想要辦公室空出來了，因此答案為 (D) Renting office space。

STEP 2 陷阱選項和錯誤選項

(A) Reviewing market trends ▶ 雖然對話中有提到「market」，但是並未提及市場趨勢。
(B) Taking a job training
(C) Going to a conference ▶ 為男子沒接電話的原因。
(D) Renting office space ▶ 答案

33 直接由本人口中說出問題和擔憂的地方。

STEP 1 由另一名說話者提出問題，再由題目中說話者的回答帶出問題所在。

本題詢問男子擔憂的事為何，因此請仔細聆聽男子的對白。女子先説道：「It's located . . . can accommodate up to 50 people」，提到這個辦公室最多可以容納 50 人。而後男子回答：「actually the number of our employees is 40, so that would be bigger than we need.」，提到員工數量為 40 人，因此他擔心辦公室有點過大。這段話表示男子擔憂的事為 (A) The office size。

STEP 2 陷阱選項和錯誤選項

(A) The office size ▶ 答案
(B) The deadline
(C) The market conditions ▶ 出現在女子的對白中，並非答案。
(D) The location

34 後半段對話中，未來資訊的答案會出現在 I'll . . . 後方。

STEP 1 題目詢問下一步動作（未來資訊）時，答案通常會出現在當事人所說的話當中。

女子提到她的下一步動作：「I'll send a copy of the floor plan and the address of the property.」，提到她會將建築物平面圖和地址寄給男子，因此答案為 (D) Email some information。選項將對話中的單字 floor plan 和 address 改寫成較為廣義的單字 information。

STEP 2 陷阱選項和錯誤選項

(A) Consult a book ▶ 聽到「copy」可能會聯想到「book」。
(B) Refer to the Web site
(C) Send a report ▶ 女子寄給男子的是 floor plan 和 address，因此該選項不正確。
(D) Email some information ▶ 答案

字彙 out of the office 不在辦公室內　conference 會議　suite 有傢俱的房型
be apt to V 可能適合做、傾向做　on the market 市面上　accommodate 容納
up to 最多達……　the number of ……的數量　expand 擴張　spacious 空間大的
property 房產、地產　reference 參考　floor plan 平面圖

Questions 35-37 refer to the following conversation.

W	Hi, Thomas. I've just received a call from our client, Colide Waters. They want us to change the packaging design for their new mineral waters. So can you work on the revisions right away? I know it's not a lot of time, but they'd like to see something by tomorrow.	35-D
35		
M	I was just leaving for the annual packaging fair in Liverpool. Well, I can ask Morin to update me later. Can you tell me what exactly they want to change?	
36		
W	Sure, here's the request. They want simpler packaging.	
M	Okay, I'll just email it to my team. 37	
W	Perfect. Thank you for helping me.	

35. Where do the speakers work?
(A) At a law firm
(B) At a design firm
(C) At an advertising agency
(D) At a water ~~manufacturer~~

職業／前
→ 注意聆聽提及 we 的對白。

36. Why does the man say, "I can ask Morin to update me later"?
(A) He wants to ~~update~~ the policy.
(B) He needs to process the work ~~later~~.
(C) He plans not to attend an event.
(D) He disagrees with a ~~request~~.

男子／掌握說話者意圖
→ 刪去與指定句字面上意思相同的選項。

37. What will the man do next?
(A) Inform his coworkers
(B) ~~Contact~~ his client
(C) Send a ~~sample~~
(D) ~~Print~~ a design

男子／未來／後
→ 注意聆聽男子提到 I'll . . . 的對白。

第 35-37 題 對話

女：嗨，湯瑪斯。我剛剛接到碰撞活力水客戶的來電。他們想要我們更換新礦泉水的包裝設計，所以你可以馬上修正嗎？我知道時間不多，不過他們明天就想看到東西。

男：我才剛動身前往利物浦的年度包裝展覽。嗯，我等會可以請莫林告訴我最新狀況。妳可以確切告訴我他們想換什麼嗎？

女：當然，他們的請求就是想要更簡單的包裝。

男：好，我現在就把它轉寄給我的團隊。

女：太好了，感謝你的協助。

35. 談話者在哪裡工作？
(A) 法律事務所
(B) 設計工作室
(C) 廣告代理商
(D) 礦泉水製造商

36. 為什麼男子說：「我等會可以請莫林告訴我最新狀況」？
(A) 他想要更新政策。
(B) 他需要晚點再處理工作。
(C) 他不打算出席活動。
(D) 他不同意某項要求。

37. 男子接下來會怎麼做？
(A) 通知同事 (B) 聯繫客戶
(C) 送出樣本 (D) 印出設計

35 前半段對話中會談到職業或地點。

STEP 1 答案會出現在前兩句話中，以 our/your/this/here 加上表示地點或職業的名詞。

本題詢問說話者們任職的地點。女子說道：「They want us to change the packaging design for their new mineral waters.」，提到客戶要求他們更改包裝設計，因此說話者們任職於 (B) At a design firm。

STEP 2 陷阱選項和錯誤選項

聽到 client 可能會聯想到法律事務所、廣告公司、礦泉水生產業者。因此必須由「change the packaging design」來確認說話者任職的公司。

(A) At a law firm
(B) At a design firm ▶ 答案
(C) At an advertising agency
(D) At a water manufacturer
▶ 提到客戶要求更改包裝設計，因此該選項不正確。

36 請先刪除與引號內字面意思相同的選項。

STEP 1 題目詢問說話者意圖時，答案不會是引號內指定句字面上的意思。

指定句前方，男子說道：「I was just leaving for the annual packaging fair in Liverpool.」，提到他正準備前往 Liverpool，接著又說道：「我等等再麻煩 Morin 告訴我最新狀況。」由此段話可以推測男子不會去參加活動，因此答案為 (C)。

STEP 2 陷阱選項和錯誤選項

(A) He wants to update the policy. ▶ 重複使用對話中的「update」。
(B) He needs to process the work later. ▶ 重複使用對話中的「later」。
(C) He plans not to attend an event. ▶ 答案
(D) He disagrees with a request. ▶「request」和對話中「ask」的意思相同。

37 後半段對話中，未來資訊的答案會出現在 I'll . . . 後方。

STEP 1 **題目詢問下一步動作（未來資訊）時，答案通常會出現在當事人所說的話中。**

男子提到他的下一步動作：「I'll just email it to my team.」，提到他會將客戶 Colide Waters 的要求寄給他們部門的員工，因此答案為 (A) Inform his workers。

STEP 2 **陷阱選項和錯誤選項**

(A) Inform his coworkers ▶ 答案
(B) Contact his client ▶ 先前已經接到客戶的聯絡，因此該選項不正確。
(C) Send a sample ▶ 男子要寄「request」給員工，並非「sample」。
(D) Print a design
▶ 雖然對話中有提到「design」，但客戶想要更改設計，因此該敘述有誤。

字彙 packaging 包裝　revision 修正版　fair 展覽會　update 更新；為……提供最新資訊
request 請求；需求

Questions 38-40 refer to the following conversation with three speakers.

M	Julie and Kate, I was looking forward to seeing you both. How was your trip to Hong Kong?	38-C
W1 38	Hi, Shane. It was good. Can you believe it? We made ten contracts during the expo.	38-A
M	Wow, that's great. Kate, you joined our company last month. Wasn't it your first trip for an international expo?	
W2 39	Yes, and I made several mistakes during the demonstrations because it was not that easy for me to present in front of many people. Thankfully, Julie helped me a lot. Anyway, I think it was a good opportunity to learn about our business.	39-B
M 40	Actually, I'm working on some guides for new employees on how to present our products effectively. You can take one on your next trip.	40-A 40-D
W1	That sounds great, Shane.	

38. Why did the women travel to Hong Kong?
(A) To negotiate a merger　**(B) To get new business**
(C) To take some time off　(D) To deliver some merchandise

女子／Hong Kong／出差原因／前
→ 注意聆聽女子的對白：過去式。

39. What does Kate say about the trip?
(A) She had some problems during her presentation.
(B) She just helped her coworker do them.
(C) She has lots of overseas experience.
(D) She had a good time with her family.

關鍵字 Kate ／ trip
→ 注意聆聽關鍵字前後的內容。

40. What is the man working on?
(A) A sales report　**(B) Presentation materials**
(C) A product sample　(D) A project proposal

男子／working on ／後
→ 注意聆聽後半段男子的對白。

第 38-40 題 對話

男　：茱莉和凱特，我很期待見到妳們倆。妳們的香港行如何啊？

女1 ：嗨，夏恩。很好啊。你相信嗎？我們在展覽上一共簽了十份合約。

男　：哇，這樣很棒。凱特，妳上個月才來公司。這不是妳第一次參加國際展覽嗎？

女2 ：對啊，展示的時候我出了不少差錯。因為要在很多人面前做簡報，對我來說沒那麼簡單。還好，茱莉幫了我大忙。總之，我覺得這是個了解公司的好機會。

男　：是啊，我正在弄一些給新進員工的指南，教他們怎麼有效地簡報我們的產品。下次出差妳們可以帶一份。

女1 ：聽起來不錯喔，夏恩。

38. 為什麼兩位女子會去香港？
(A) 去談併購
(B) 要開發新客戶
(C) 把一些假休掉
(D) 去送貨

39. 凱特針對這趟行程說了什麼？
(A) 她簡報時有些問題。
(B) 她剛幫同事做些事。
(C) 她海外經驗豐富。
(D) 她在家和家人過得很愉快。

40. 男子正在忙什麼？
(A) 銷售報告　(B) 簡報資料
(C) 樣品　(D) 計畫提案

38 題目以 Why 詢問時，對話會重複使用題目句的內容並於後方提及原因。

STEP 1 聆聽對話時，請仔細聆聽 why 後方的關鍵字，其後方將會出現答案。

本題 why 後方的關鍵字為 travel to Hong Kong，詢問女子前往香港的原因，因此答案會出現在女子的對白中。男子詢問女子出差到香港的狀況，第一名女子回答：「We made ten contracts during the expo.」，提到在展覽期間簽了十個約。由此段話可以得知女子前往香港為的是進行新的事業，因此答案為 (B) To get new business。

STEP 2 陷阱選項和錯誤選項

(A) To negotiate a merger ▶ 聽到「contract」可能會誤選該選項。
(B) To get new business ▶ 答案
(C) To take some time off ▶ 聽到「trip」可能會誤選該選項。
(D) To deliver some merchandise

39 三人對話題組的第二題通常會指定某個人，並針對此人提問。 ▶Kate、trip

STEP 1 若題目中出現特定人物的名字，聆聽對話時，請特別留意此人為哪一名說話者。

男子說道：「Kate, you joined our company last month. Wasn't it your first trip for an international expo?」，向 Kate 詢問她第一次出差的狀況。接著 Kate 回答：「Yes, and I made several mistakes during the demonstrations」，提到她在發表的時候失誤了幾次，表示發表時出了點小問題，因此答案為 (A)。

STEP 2 陷阱選項和錯誤選項

(A) She had some problems during her presentation. ▶ 答案
(B) She just helped her coworker do them. ▶ 為 Julie 做的事，並非 Kate。
(C) She has lots of overseas experience.
▶ 聽到「Hong Kong」可能會聯想到「overseas」。
(D) She had a good time with her family.

40 題目中提及男子，因此答案會出現在男子的對白中。

STEP 1 若題目針對男子提問，答案會在男子的對白中。

本題詢問男子目前負責的工作，因此答案會出現在男子的對白中。男子説道：「I'm working on some guides for new employees on how to present our products effectively.」，提到他正在製作一些説明，幫助新進員工可以更有效率地發表自家產品。説明指的是發表資料，因此答案為 (B) Presentation materials。

STEP 2 陷阱選項和錯誤選項

(A) A sales report ▶ 聽到「guides」可能會聯想到「report」。
(B) Presentation materials ▶ 答案
(C) A product sample ▶ 雖然對話中有提到「products」，但是並未提到「sample」。
(D) A project proposal ▶ 聽到「guides」可能會聯想到「proposal」。

字彙 look forward to Ving 很期待做某件事　make a contract 簽約　expo 展覽會
make a mistake 犯錯　demonstration 展示　work on 從事於　guide 指南
effectively 有效地

Questions 41-43 refer to the following conversation.

W Kevin, have you finished the proposal for Alloy's Apparel? **41-B**
M Well, I got a call from the manager yesterday, and he told me they
41 wanted to increase the budget for social media.
W Hmm . . . they must believe that's more efficient. What about the
42 monthly budget? Do they want to increase it?
M No, they want to reduce it by 20% for other ads instead. So today **42-B**
43 I have to review all the reports from our agencies and reallocate **42-D** **43-C**
funds.

41. What is the conversation mainly about?
(A) A budget for advertising
(B) A proposal for ~~new business~~
(C) An upcoming sale
(D) Accounting procedures

主旨／前
→ 注意聆聽第一句話。

42. What does the man mean when he says, "They want to reduce it by 20% for other ads instead"?
(A) A total amount of budget has been ~~changed~~.
(B) A new ~~advertising~~ method should be added.
(C) A plan should be revised.
(D) A report has some ~~errors~~.

男子／掌握說話者意圖
→ 注意指定句前後文意。

43. What does the man say he will do next?
(A) Review some documents
(B) Replace a file
(C) ~~Contact~~ another agency
(D) Reserve a meeting room

男子／未來／後
→ 注意聆聽男子提到 I have to 的對白。

第 41-43 題 對話

女：凱文，你做好合金服飾的企畫了嗎？

男：嗯，我昨天接到經理的電話，他告訴我他們想要增加社群行銷的預算。

女：嗯……他們想必認為這樣比較有效。那每個月的預算如何？他們有增加嗎？

男：沒有，他們想要減兩成，改買其他廣告。所以我今天得看一次所有代理商的報告並重新分配資金。

41. 會話的主旨為何？
(A) 廣告預算 (B) 新業務的企畫
(C) 即將到來的促銷 (D) 會計程序

42. 男子說：「他們想要減兩成，改買其他廣告」，意思為何？
(A) 總預算額已經被改了。
(B) 需要加入新的廣告方法。
(C) 計畫需要變更。
(D) 報告裡有些錯誤。

43. 男子說他下一步要做什麼？
(A) 檢閱一些文件
(B) 換掉一個檔案
(C) 聯絡另一家代理商
(D) 預約一間會議室

41 若題目詢問主旨或目的，答案會出現在開頭前兩句話。

STEP 1 題目詢問對話主旨時，千萬不要從頭到尾默默聽完整篇對話後，才開始選答案。務必要先看完選項內容，如此一來只要聆聽前半段對話，便能找出答案。

男子說道：「I got a call from the manager yesterday and he told me they wanted to increase the budget for social media.」，表示他接到經理的電話，提到 Alloy's Apparel 公司想要提高預算，因此對話主旨為 (A) A budget for advertising。

STEP 2 陷阱選項和錯誤選項

(A) A budget for advertising ▶ 答案
(B) A proposal for ~~new business~~
▶ 雖然對話中有提到「proposal」，但是並未提到「new business」。
(C) An upcoming sale
(D) Accounting procedures

42 請先刪除與引號內字面意思相同的選項。

STEP 1 聽完指定句引號前後方句子後，再選出較為廣義的敘述作為答案。若選項使用與引號內相同的單字、或是字面意思相同的敘述，來表達說話者意圖時，通常不會是正確答案。

指定句前方說道：「Do they want to increase it?」，女子詢問提高月季預算的部分處理得如何。男子回答：「No」之後，才接著出現題目的指定句，這表示指定句和前方句子表達的概念相反。而後又說道：「So today I have to review all the reports from our agencies and reallocate funds」，提到為解決這個問題，他得將代理商的報告通通看過一遍。這表示 Alloy's Apparel 公司想要的跟男子預期的有出入，為此他將重新擬定新計畫，因此答案為 (C)。

STEP 2 陷阱選項和錯誤選項

(A) A total amount of budget has been changed.
▶ 重複使用對話中的「budget」，而且當中並未提及要更改總額。

(B) A new advertising method should be added. ▶ 使用同義字「add」。

(C) A plan should be revised. ▶ 答案

(D) A report has some errors. ▶ 雖然對話中有提到「report」，但並未提到「errors」。

43 後半段對話中，未來資訊的答案會出現在 I'll . . . 後方。

STEP 1 題目詢問下一步動作（未來資訊）時，答案通常會出現在當事人所說的話當中。

男子提到他的下一步動作：「I have to review all the reports from our agencies and reallocate funds.」，提到他得將代理商的報告通通看過一遍，因此答案為 (A) Review some documents。

STEP 2 陷阱選項和錯誤選項

(A) Review some documents ▶ 答案

(B) Replace a file

(C) Contact another agency ▶ 雖然對話中有提到「agency」，但是並未提到要聯絡。

(D) Reserve a meeting room

字彙 proposal 提案、企畫　budget 預算　efficient 有效的　monthly 每月的
review 複審；檢視　agency 代理商　reallocate 重新分配

Questions 44-46 refer to the following conversation.

W Hi, Peter. I heard from today's department meeting that there will be
44 maintenance on our computer system during the last weekend of June. 44-A 44-B
M Really? So, what do we need to do for the maintenance?
W This time the operating system will be updated. So all the employees
45 won't be able to work from Friday night to Sunday afternoon on that
46 weekend. Can you send an e-mail to remind the rest of our team?
M Sure. I'll take care of that.

44. What will take place at the end of June?
(A) ~~A department meeting~~
(B) A repair of a ~~heating~~ system
(C) Computer maintenance
(D) Implementation of a ~~revised company policy~~

關鍵字 the end of June
→ 注意聆聽關鍵字前後的內容。

45. What should the employees be aware of?
(A) They have to bring warmer clothing.
(B) They should ~~turn off~~ their computers when they leave.
(C) They need to ~~return~~ the laptop computers to the company.
(D) They will not be able to work on a weekend.

關鍵字 employees／要求事項
→ 注意聆聽祈使句、或提及 should 的對白。

46. What is the man asked to do?
(A) ~~Return~~ his computer
(B) Write an e-mail
(C) Ask for an ~~estimate~~
(D) Submit a vacation request

男子／被要求的事／後
→ 注意聆聽女子要求或建議對方的對白。

第 44-46 題 對話

女：嗨，彼得。我在今天的部門會議聽說，我們的電腦系統在六月最後一個週末要進行維護。

男：真的嗎？所以為了維護，我們需要做什麼嗎？

女：作業系統這一次將會升級。所以全體員工那個週末從星期五晚上開始到星期天下午都不能工作。你可以寄封電子郵件提醒我們團隊的其他人嗎？

男：當然，包在我身上。

44. 六月底將會發生什麼事？
(A) 部門會議
(B) 暖氣系統維修
(C) 電腦維護
(D) 公司修改的一項政策上路

45. 員工需要注意什麼？
(A) 他們需要帶保暖衣物。
(B) 他們離開時應該關電腦。
(C) 他們需要繳回公司的筆電。
(D) 他們週末將沒辦法工作。

46. 男子被要求做什麼事？
(A) 繳回他的電腦
(B) 寫封電子郵件
(C) 要到一份估價單
(D) 提交休假需求

44 題目中出現關鍵字時，答案會在該關鍵字前後的句子。▶ the end of June

STEP 1 若題目中出現特定的關鍵字，聆聽對話時，勢必會於該關鍵字前後聽到答案。一般來說會先聽到關鍵字，再聽到答案的內容，但在新制測驗中，有時反而會先聽到答案的內容，之後才聽到關鍵字。

本題的關鍵字為 the end of June，對話中說道：「there will be maintenance on our computer system during the last weekend of June.」，提到六月最後一週將進行電腦系統維護，因此答案為 (C) Computer maintenance。

STEP 2 陷阱選項和錯誤選項

(A) A department meeting ▶ 今日已舉行過部門會議。

(B) A repair of a heating system ▶ 重複使用「computer system」當中的「system」。

(C) Computer maintenance ▶ 答案

(D) Implementation of a revised company policy
▶ 將進行電腦系統維護，並沒有要實施修改後的公司規定。

45 請一邊預測答案出現的位置，一邊觀看選項。▶ employees

STEP 1 對話會依序出現答案線索，因此務必要按照題目順序，將注意力放在該題目列出的選項上，並仔細聆聽對話中是否提及選項中的單字或相關單字。

本題的關鍵字為 employees，詢問員工需要知道什麼事情。對話中說道：「So all the employees won't be able to work from Friday night to Sunday afternoon on that weekend.」，提到由於電腦系統更新，員工在週五晚上到週日下午將無法工作，因此答案為 (D)。

STEP 2 陷阱選項和錯誤選項

(A) They have to bring warmer clothing.

(B) They should turn off their computers when they leave.
▶ 雖然對話中有提到「computers」，但並未提到與「turn off」有關的內容。

(C) They need to return the laptop computers to the company.
▶ 聽到「computers」可能會聯想到「laptop computers」。

(D) They will not be able to work on a weekend. ▶ 答案

46 題目使用被動語態時，答案會出現在另一方以 You 開頭的對白中。

STEP 1 題目詢問建議、要求、或未來計畫時，答案會出現在後半段對話中。請注意聆聽表示間接建議的句子「由我來……」、以及直接勸說或建議對方的句子「請你……」。

最後一段對話，女子說道：「Can you send an e-mail to remind the rest of our team?」，請男子寄郵件通知其他員工電腦系統更新一事，因此男子被要求的事為 (B) Write an e-mail。

STEP 2 陷阱選項和錯誤選項

(A) Return his computer ▶ 僅談論到電腦系統更新一事，並未談到歸還電腦。
(B) Write an e-mail ▶ 答案
(C) Ask for an estimate ▶ 女子並未向男子要求報價單。
(D) Submit a vacation request

字彙 maintenance 維護　operating system 作業系統　update 升級　remind 提醒
rest 其餘的

Questions 47-49 refer to the following conversation.

W	Hi, Daniel. We're doing fairly well since we opened two months ago, don't you think?	
M 47 48	Yeah. I've already found several good reviews online. They are satisfied with our seafood and very reasonable prices. Nobody can beat our prices.	
W	Right. And the view from the seats is fantastic as well. But, I think we should think about the next step at this point. What do you think will make our business more profitable in the next season?	48-B
M	Do you have any ideas?	
W 49	Well, why don't we add a new menu? You know, seaweed is well known as being good for your health.	49-B
M	That sounds good. I'll call and consult with our vendors in the fish market right away.	47-D

47. Where do the speakers most likely work?
(A) At a restaurant　(B) At a hotel
(C) At a medical clinic　(D) At a ~~fish market~~

職業／前
→ 注意聆聽前半段對話提及 we 或 our 的對白。

48. According to the man, what do customers like about the business?
(A) The quality of the service
(B) The ~~convenient~~ location
(C) The reasonable prices
(D) The business hours

關鍵字 customers ／ like
→ 注意聆聽提及第三人稱代名詞 they 的對白。

49. What does the woman mean when she says, "Seaweed is well known as being good for your health"?
(A) She hopes to ~~change her business~~.
(B) She has some concerns about the man's ~~health~~.
(C) She wants to use a certain ingredient.
(D) She is about to explain nutritious food.

女子／掌握說話者意圖
→ 刪去與指定句字面上意思相同的選項。

第 47-49 題 對話

女：嗨，丹尼爾。你不覺得開業兩個月以來，我們做得相當不錯嗎？

男：是啊。我找到了好幾個不錯的網路評價。他們很滿意我們的海鮮和實惠的價格，我們的價位無人能敵。

女：對，座位的景觀也是好極了。但我想我們應該就此思考下一步。你覺得什麼會讓我們下一季的利潤更好？

男：妳有什麼想法嗎？

女：嗯，不如加個新菜色吧？你也知道，海藻對健康有益，出了名的。

男：聽起來不錯，我馬上就打電話請教我們在漁市場的供應商。

47. 談話者最可能是在哪裡工作？
(A) 餐廳 (B) 飯店
(C) 診所 (D) 漁市場

48. 根據男人的說法，客戶喜歡這個商家裡的什麼東西？
(A) 服務品質 (B) 位置便利
(C) 價格實惠 (D) 營業時間

49. 女子說：「海藻對健康有益，出了名的」，是什麼意思？
(A) 她希望轉行。
(B) 她有點在意男子的健康。
(C) 她想要使用某個特定的食材。
(D) 她即將解釋營養的食物。

47 前半段對話中會談到職業或地點。

STEP 1 答案會出現在前半段對話中，以 our/your/this/here 加上表示地點或職業的名詞。

對話中說道：「They are satisfied with our seafood and very reasonable prices.」，這表示說話者們在販售海鮮的地方工作，因此答案為 (A) At a restaurant。

STEP 2 陷阱選項和錯誤選項

(A) At a restaurant ▶ 答案
(B) At a hotel
(C) At a medical clinic
(D) At a fish market ▶ 雖然後半段對話中有提到，但指的是男子打電話給魚販業者。

48 題目中出現人名或公司名稱時，對話中會使用第三人稱代名詞表示。

STEP 1 對話中，重複提及前方出現的專有名詞或一般名詞時，會使用第三人稱代名詞（he / she / they / it）來代替。

本題詢問讓顧客滿意的點，請由男子的對白確認答案。男子說道：「I've already found several good reviews online. They are satisfied with our seafood and very reasonable prices.」，後句中的 they 指的就是留下評論的顧客。男子提到顧客對於他們販售的料理和合理的價格非常滿意，因此答案為 (C) The reasonable prices。

STEP 2 陷阱選項和錯誤選項

(A) The quality of the service
(B) The convenient location ▶ 聽到「point」可能會聯想到「location」。
(C) The reasonable prices ▶ 答案
(D) The business hours

49 請先刪除與引號內字面意思相同的選項。

STEP 1 聽完指定句前後方句子後，再選出較為廣義的敘述作為答案。若選項使用與引號內相同的單字、或是字面意思相同的敘述，來表達說話者意圖時，通常不會是正確答案。

指定句前方說道：「Why don't we add a new menu?」，建議加入新的菜單，而後推薦使用海藻作為材料。指定句表示她想使用海藻加入新菜單中，因此答案為 (C)。

STEP 2 陷阱選項和錯誤選項

(A) She hopes to change her business.

▶ 由「**Why don't we add a new menu?**」可以得知她是想加入新的菜單，因此該選項不正確。

(B) She has some concerns about the man's ~~health~~. ▶ 重複使用指定句中的「**health**」。

(C) She wants to use a certain ingredient. ▶ 答案

(D) She is about to explain nutritious food.

▶「**Seaweed**」、「**good for your health**」字面上的意思等同於「**nutritious food**」。

字彙 **fairly** 相當地 **review** 評價 **reasonable** 合理的 **profitable** 獲利的 **seaweed** 海藻 **consult with** 向……請教 **vendor** 供應商 **fish market** 漁市場

Questions 50-52 refer to the following conversation with three speakers.

M 50	Thank you for coming here, Sarah and Merriam. As you all know, our book sales have been decreasing over the past year. I'd like to discuss the issue and try to come up with solutions. Sarah, do you have an idea for how to increase our sales?	50-C
W1 51	Well, how about publishing e-book versions? With the popularity of affordable tablets, there has been a demand for e-books.	
W2	That's true. We're still publishing only printed versions of books. Other local publishing competitors have launched e-books through their Web sites.	51-A
W1	It will cost a lot to create electronic versions of all the printed books, but we'll be able to continue reproducing them at no extra charge.	
M 52	I like the idea. I'll make some arrangements and ask for a consultation.	52-A 52-B

50. According to the man, what is the problem?
(A) A machine is not working properly.
(B) A meeting is canceled.
(C) A book has an ~~error~~.
(D) Sales are disappointing.

男子／問題
→ 注意聆聽第一段男子的對白。

51. According to Sarah, what will most likely change at the business?
(A) A ~~printing machine~~
(B) A version of book
(C) A launching date
(D) A safety procedure

Sarah ／變更事項
→ 注意聆聽 Sarah 所說的話。

52. What will the man do next?
(A) Arrange for ~~a meeting~~
(B) Ask for ~~investment~~
(C) Schedule a consultation
(D) Report to the management

男子／未來／後
→ 注意聆聽男子提及 I'll . . . 的對白。

第 50-52 題 三人對話

男 ：感謝妳們來這裡，莎拉、梅立恩。妳們都知道，我們的書去年一整年的銷量下滑了。我想要討論這件事，找出解決辦法。莎拉，妳有什麼主意可以增加銷售嗎？

女1：嗯，不如試著出版電子書版本？平價平板愈來愈普及，電子書的需求已經出現。

女2：這是真的。我們現在還是只有出版印刷書籍。當地競爭的同業都已經透過各自的官網開賣電子書了。

女1：所有印刷書都出電子版會花不少錢，不過後續重製我們就沒有額外開銷。

男 ：我喜歡這個想法，我會再安排一下，並找人諮詢。

50. 根據男子的說法，發生了什麼問題？
(A) 有機械運作失常。
(B) 有場會議取消。
(C) 書中有錯誤。
(D) 銷量令人失望。

51. 根據莎拉的說法，什麼東西最有可能改變這門事業？
(A) 一台印刷機
(B) 書的版本
(C) 開賣日期
(D) 安全程序

52. 男子接下來將要做什麼？
(A) 安排一場會議
(B) 尋求投資
(C) 安排諮詢
(D) 回報管理高層

50 直接由本人口中說出問題和擔憂的地方。

STEP 1 若題目詢問問題為何，答案通常會出現在第一和第二段對白中。

本題詢問男子提到什麼問題，因此請仔細聆聽男子的對白。男子說道：「our book sales have been decreasing over the last year.」，提到書籍的銷售量下跌，因此答案為 (D)。

STEP 2 陷阱選項和錯誤選項

(A) A machine is not working properly.
(B) A meeting is canceled.
(C) A book has an error. ▶ 雖然對話中有提到「book」，但並未提到「error」。
(D) Sales are disappointing. ▶ 答案

51 三人對話題組的第二題通常會針對某個人提問。

STEP 1 題目可以詢問某名說話者碰到的問題、擔憂的事或建議為何。通常會用 the woman/man 或人名來指定某個說話者，並針對此人提出問題。

男子提出問題，同時提到 Sarah，詢問她的想法。這表示接著回話的人為 Sarah。她說道：「how about publishing e-book versions?」，提議出版電子書版本，等同變更出版形式，因此答案為 (B) A version of book。

STEP 2 陷阱選項和錯誤選項

(A) A printing machine ▶ 聽到「publish」可能會聯想到「print」。
(B) A version of book ▶ 答案
(C) A launching date
(D) A safety procedure

52 後半段對話中，未來資訊的答案會出現在 I'll . . . 後方。

STEP 1 題目詢問下一步動作（未來資訊）時，答案通常會出現在當事人所說的話當中。

男子提到他的下一步動作：「I'll make some arrangement and ask for a consultation.」，提到他將此構想統整過後，會去諮詢看看，因此答案為 (C) Schedule a consultation。

STEP 2 陷阱選項和錯誤選項

(A) Arrange for ~~a meeting~~ ▶ 會議應該改成諮詢。
(B) Ask for ~~investment~~ ▶ 對話中並未提到要投資。
(C) Schedule a consultation ▶ 答案
(D) Report to the management

字彙 come up with 找到　affordable 平價的　demand 需求　local 當地的
competitor 競爭對手　launch 開始　reproduce 重製
at no extra charge 沒有額外開銷　make an arrangement 安排　consultation 諮詢

Questions 53-55 refer to the following conversation.

W 53	Hello, this is Ashlee Rice calling. Last week, I applied for the online marketer position. I was wondering when my application will be reviewed.	53-B
M 54	Hello, Ms. Rice. I'm sorry we're scheduled to accept applications until today. Then we'll proceed to the next step. But if you don't mind, can you tell me about yourself now?	
W	Well, I'm majoring in business management and I have one semester left before graduation.	
M	Hmm . . . but as you probably know, you need some prior work experience.	
W 55	Sure. I had several jobs while I was studying. I've already completed two internship programs. The first one was in Canada, and the other one was at your company last year.	
M	Oh, that's interesting. What kind of work did you do in Canada?	

53. According to the woman, what happened last week?
(A) She ~~posted~~ a job opening.
(B) She applied to be a ~~volunteer~~.
(C) She provided some documents for a job.
(D) She developed a new Web site.

女子／關鍵字 last week／前
→ 注意聆聽過去式句子。

54. Who most likely is the man?
(A) ~~A job applicant~~
(B) A business consultant
(C) A personnel manager
(D) A real estate agent

男子／職業／前
→ 注意聆聽男子的對白。

55. What does the man imply when he says, "That's interesting"?
(A) He wants to hear more about the woman's experience.
(B) He agrees to take an interview.
(C) He enjoyed the discussion about ~~a job trend~~.
(D) He accepts the woman's suggestion.

男子／掌握說話者意圖
→ 注意指定句前後的文意。

第 53-55 題 對話

女：哈囉，我是艾希莉·萊斯。我上個星期應徵了網路行銷的職位。我想知道應徵申請什麼時候會審查。

男：哈囉，希斯女士。我很抱歉，應徵收件預計到今天才會結束。然後我們才會進行下一個階段。如果您不介意的話，現在可以自我介紹嗎？

女：嗯，我主修企業管理，再一學期就畢業了。

男：嗯……但您應該知道，您必須要有工作經驗吧。

女：當然，我讀書的時候就做過幾份工作了。我完成了兩次實習計畫。第一次是在加拿大，另外一次則是去年在貴公司。

男：喔，很有趣。您在加拿大是做什麼的？

53. 根據女子說法，上週發生了什麼事？
(A) 她發布了徵才需求。
(B) 她應徵做志工。
(C) 她為了求職提供了一些文件。
(D) 她開發了新網站。

54. 這個男人最有可能的身分是？
(A) 求職者 (B) 企業顧問
(C) 人事經理 (D) 房仲

55. 男子說：「很有趣」的意思為何？
(A) 關於女子的經驗他想瞭解更多。
(B) 他同意要接受訪談。
(C) 他樂於討論就業趨勢。
(D) 他接受女子的建議。

53 題目中出現關鍵字時，答案會在該關鍵字前後的句子。 ▶ last week

STEP 1 **若題目中出現特定的關鍵字，聆聽對話時，勢必會於該關鍵字前後聽到答案。一般來說會先聽到關鍵字，再聽到答案的內容，但在新制測驗中，有時反而會先聽到答案的內容，之後才聽到關鍵字。**

本題的關鍵字為 last week。對話中說道：「Last week, I applied for the online marketer position.」，提到她應徵了網路行銷一職。這表示她繳交了履歷表應徵工作，因此答案為 (C)。

STEP 2 **陷阱選項和錯誤選項**

(A) She posted a job opening. ▶ 聽到「apply for」可能會聯想到「job opening」。
(B) She applied to be a volunteer. ▶ 應徵「online marketer position」，並非志工服務。
(C) She provided some documents for a job. ▶ 答案
(D) She developed a new Web site.

54 前半段對話中會談到職業或地點。

STEP 1 **答案會出現在前半段對話中，以 our/your/this/here 加上表示地點或職業的名詞。**

本題詢問男子的職業，因此請注意聆聽男子的對白。男子說道：「I'm sorry we're scheduled to accept applications until today.」，男子提到他負責與應徵工作相關的工作，這表示他任職於人事部門，因此答案為 (C) A personnel manager。

STEP 2 **陷阱選項和錯誤選項**

(A) A job applicant ▶ 指對話中的女子，並非男子的職業。
(B) A business consultant
(C) A personnel manager ▶ 答案
(D) A real estate agent

55 題目詢問引號內的說話者意圖時，請確認指定句前方的連接詞。

STEP 1 題目詢問說話者意圖時，指定句通常是對前一人說的話的答覆或反應，因此若選項包含前一人對白中的「特定單字」或相關敘述，就是正確答案。另外，若指定句前方有連接詞時，請務必分清楚答案應表達正面還是負面的意涵。

指定句前方說道：「I've already completed two internship programs. . . . the other one was at your company last year.」，女子簡單說明自己的實習經歷。而指定句後方說道：「What kind of work did yo do in Canada?」，由此話可以看出男子對女子此項經歷有興趣，因此答案為 (A)。

STEP 2 陷阱選項和錯誤選項

(A) He wants to hear more about the woman's experience. ▶ 答案
(B) He agrees to take an interview.
(C) He enjoyed the discussion about a job trend.
▶ 男子並未對就業趨勢感興趣，而是想了解女子的實習經歷，因此該選項不正確。
(D) He accepts the woman's suggestion.

字彙 be scheduled to V 預定要做　proceed 繼續　if you don't mind 如果您不介意的話
major in 主修　prior 先前的　work experience 工作經驗

Questions 56-58 refer to the following conversation with three speakers.

W1	Good morning. May I help you?	
M 56	Hi, my name is Darrell O'Brien, and I'm a reporter from *Hamilton Monthly Review*. I'm supposed to interview Dr. Nunez at 10:00.	56-A
W1 57	OK, but she is in a meeting at the moment. Can I see your identification? I just need to check all the visitors' appointments.	
M	Sure, here it is.	
W1	Her meeting will be finished soon. Oh, here she is now. Dr. Nunez, this is Darrell O'Brien, your 10:00 appointment.	58-A
W2 58	Hi, Mr. O'Brien. Thanks for coming. I'm so sorry, but I need a few more minutes to wrap up the meeting. Jane, could you take him to my office?	58-C

56. What is the purpose of the man's visit?
(A) To ~~review~~ an estimate
(B) To inspect safety standards
(C) To conduct an interview
(D) To ~~pick up an ID card~~

目的／男子來訪／前
→ 注意聆聽第一段對話。

57. What does the man agree to do?
(A) ~~Sign up for~~ an event
(B) Provide ~~contact information~~
(C) Perform a regular checkup
(D) Show his identification

男子／同意
→ 注意聆聽女子要求男子的事。

58. What will Dr. Nunez most likely do next?
(A) She will ~~cancel an appointment~~.
(B) She will get back to a meeting.
(C) ~~She will take the man to her office~~.
(D) She will lead an inspection.

關鍵字 Dr. Nunez ／未來／後
→ 注意聆聽第三人稱代名詞和未來式句子。

第 56-58 題　三人對話

女1：早安，有什麼能協助您的嗎？

男　：嗨，我叫作戴瑞．歐布萊恩，我是《哈米爾頓每月評論》的記者。我應該在10點訪問努涅茲博士。

女1：好的，不過她現在正在開會。我可以看一下您的識別證嗎？我只是需要確認所有的訪客安排。

男　：當然，請看。

女1：她的會議很快就會結束。喔，她正好來了。努涅茲博士，這是戴瑞．歐布萊恩，跟您約在10點見面。

女2：嗨，歐布萊恩先生。感謝您前來。非常抱歉，但我還需要一點時間結束會議。珍，可以請妳帶他到我的辦公室嗎？

56. 男子訪問的主要目的為何？
(A) 檢視估價單　(B) 檢查安全標準
(C) 進行訪問　(D) 領取識別證

57. 男子同意做什麼？
(A) 報名參加活動　(B) 提供聯絡資訊
(C) 定期檢查　(D) 出示識別證件

58. 努涅茲博士接下來最有可能做什麼？
(A) 她將取消一場會面安排。
(B) 她將回去開會。
(C) 她會把男子帶到辦公室。
(D) 她會主導檢查。

56 三人對話題組的第一題，通常會詢問三人的職業或對話主旨。

STEP 1 題目詢問主旨或目的時，答案通常會出現在對話開頭部分。

本題詢問男子來訪的目的，因此請注意聆聽男子的對白。男子說道：「I'm supposed to interview Dr. Nunez at 10:00.」，提到他要專訪 Nunez 博士，因此答案為 (C) To conduct an interview。

STEP 2 陷阱選項和錯誤選項

(A) To review an estimate ▶「review」和「interview」的發音相似。
(B) To inspect safety standards
(C) To conduct an interview ▶ 答案
(D) To pick up an ID card ▶ 雖然對話中女子要求男子出示「ID card (identification)」，但男子來訪的目的並非領取 ID card。

57 題目詢問某人同意的事項時，請確認此人同意前方說話者什麼事情。

STEP 1 答案會在男子表示同意的前一句對白。

女子 1 說道：「Can I see your identification?」，要求男子出示身分證。而後男子回答：「Sure, here it is.」，表示男子同意女子的要求，因此男子同意的事項為 (D) Show his identification。

STEP 2 陷阱選項和錯誤選項

(A) Sign up for an event
▶ 雖然對話中有提到「event（指 interview）」，但是並未提到「sign up for」。
(B) Provide contact information ▶ 並未要求男子提供聯絡方式。
(C) Perform a regular checkup
(D) Show his identification ▶ 答案

58 三人對話的最後一題，通常會詢問未來計畫或建議。

STEP 1 若題目詢問往後將發生的事情，答案為 I'll . . . 或 Let's . . . 後方連接的第一個動詞。

本題詢問 Nunez 的下一步動作，因此答案會出現在 Nunez 的對白中。女子說道：「but I need a few more minutes to wrap up the meeting.」，提到距離會議結束還有一小段時間，因此答案為 (B)。

STEP 2 陷阱選項和錯誤選項

(A) She will cancel an appointment. ▶ 她僅提到會議尚未結束，並未表示要取消約定。
(B) She will get back to a meeting. ▶ 答案
(C) She will take the man to her office. ▶ 為另一名女子 Jane 要做的事，並非 Nunez。
(D) She will lead an inspection.

字彙 be supposed to V 應當　at this moment 目前　identification 身分識別
appointment 約會　wrap up 完成；結束

Questions 59-61 refer to the following conversation and calendar.

W	Hi, Samuel. You know, we recently installed new spinning and weaving	59-B
59	machines at our factory. For safety reasons, we need to have a safety	59-C
	training workshop. I'm wondering when the workshop could be held.	
M	Let's check this week's calendar. Well, how about this day? There will be	
60	a staff meeting, so all of our floor employees will already be gathered.	
W	In addition, because it will be in the morning, we'd better provide them with breakfast.	
M	That sounds good. Also, I'd like to recommend the Mom's Sandwich	
61	next to our factory. It offers a variety of sandwiches and beverages	61-C
	which taste more delicious than at nearby stores.	
W	All right. Then, I'll ask Kendra to email the workshop notice to all employees and call the store to place an order.	

	Monday	Tuesday	Wednesday	Thursday
9-10			Staff meeting	
10-11	Team building			
11-12		Directors' meeting		Survey day
13-14				

59. According to the woman, what did the business do?
(A) It replaced some equipment.
(B) It hired new employees.
(C) It changed safety policies.
(D) It had a meeting with a client.

女子／關鍵字 **business**／前
→ 注意聆聽第一段對話：過去式。

60. Look at the graphic. On which day will the workshop be held?
(A) Monday
(B) Tuesday
(C) Wednesday
(D) Thursday

圖表資訊／ **workshop**
→ 由圖表確認選項以外的資訊。

61. What is suggested about Mom's Sandwich?
(A) It offers reasonable prices.
(B) It is located nearby.
(C) It has only one menu item.
(D) It owns its own farm.

關鍵字／ **Mom's Sandwich** ／後
→ 注意聆聽第三人稱代名詞

第 59-61 題 對話與日曆

女：嗨，山謬。你知道的，我們工廠安裝了新的紡紗織布機。出於安全考量，我們需要舉行安全訓練的工作坊，我想知道什麼時候方便舉行。

男：來看一下這週的行事曆。嗯，這天怎麼樣？這時候會有一場員工會議，我們全體員工本來就會集合。

女：除此之外，因為要辦在早上，我們最好能提供早餐。

男：聽起來不錯。這樣我想推薦我們工廠旁邊的媽媽三明治。三明治和飲料的選擇很多，味道比鄰近店家好很多。

女：好唷。然後我會請卡德拉向全體員工寄出工作坊公告，還有打電話向店家訂餐。

	星期一	星期二	星期三	星期四
9-10 點			員工會議	
10-11 點	團隊共識建立			
11-12 點		經理會議		市調日
13-14 點				

59. 根據女子說法，這間公司做了什麼？
(A) 更換部分設備。
(B) 聘僱新員工。
(C) 更改安全政策。
(D) 和一位客戶開會。

60. 參考圖表，工作坊將在哪天舉行？
(A) 星期一
(B) 星期二
(C) 星期三
(D) 星期四

61. 對話中關於媽媽三明治，提到了什麼？
(A) 它的價格實惠。
(B) 位於附近。
(C) 只有唯一一種菜色。
(D) 有自家農場。

59 題目針對過去提問時，答案會出現在前半段對話中。

STEP 1 對話會依序出現答題線索，因此聆聽對話時，請按照題目順序，將注意力放在選項上。

前半段對話中，會出現與過去有關的內容。因此請注意聆聽第一段女子的對白，從過去式句子中找出答案。女子說道：「we recently installed new spinning and weaving machines at our factory.」，提到安裝了紡織機器，因此答案為 (A)。

STEP 2 陷阱選項和錯誤選項

(A) It replaced some equipment. ▶ 答案
(B) It hired new employees. ▶ 重複使用對話中的「new」。
(C) It changed safety policies. ▶ 雖然對話中有提到「safety」，但並未提到「policies」。
(D) It had a meeting with a client.
▶ 雖然對話中的「workshop」可以改寫成「meeting」，但是當中並未提到「clients」，因此不能作為答案。

60 對話中不會提到選項列出的圖表資訊。

STEP 1 圖表題的選項不會直接出現在對話當中。

本題詢問舉辦工作坊的時間。男子說道：「how about this day? There will be a staff meeting, so all of our floor employees will already be gathered」，而後女子說道：「it will be in the morning.」。綜合這兩句話，表示男子建議的那天上午有員工會議，因此答案為 (C) Wednesday。

61 題目中出現關鍵字時，答案會在該關鍵字前後的句子。
▶ Mom's Sandwich

STEP 1 若題目中出現特定的關鍵字，聆聽對話時，勢必會於該關鍵字前後聽到答案。一般來說會先聽到關鍵字，再聽到答案的內容，但在新制測驗中，有時反而會先聽到答案的內容，之後才聽到關鍵字。

本題的關鍵字為 Mom's Sandwich。對話中說道：「I'd like to recommend the Mom's Sandwich next to our factory.」，提到該店家位於說話者工作地點工廠旁邊，因此答案為(B)。選項將對話中的 next to 改寫成 nearby。

STEP 2 陷阱選項和錯誤選項

(A) It offers reasonable prices.
(B) It is located nearby. ▶ 答案
(C) It has only one menu item.
▶ 對話中提到店家提供「**a variety of sandwiches and beverages**」，因此該敘述不正確。
(D) It owns its own farm. ▶ 對話中並未提到。

字彙 **install** 安裝　**spinning and weaving machine** 紡紗織布機　**wonder** 想知道
a variety of 各式各樣的　**notice** 通知　**place an order** 下訂單

Questions 62-64 refer to the following conversation and screenshot.

M Hey, Melissa. I've been trying to send a file, but my computer can't access the Internet for some reason. 63-B 63-D
W Really? That's strange. Mine is working properly. Well, would you like me (63) to send it instead?
M I'd really appreciate that. Here, it's on this memory card. It was made on (62) November 3.
W All right. Let me see. I found it. To whom do you want to send it?
M All of our marketing employees including Mr. Song, the team director.
W Okay. By the way, I'm going to the Romario Italian Restaurant which is (64) located on Northern Boulevard for lunch. Would you like to join me?
M I'd love to.

Documents Folder		
Title	**Date**	**Size**
Palcon's strategy	2015-11-07	32KB
Employee schedule	2015-11-02	92KB
Payroll records	2015-11-04	120KB
Sales projections	2015-11-03	2.2GB

62. Look at the graphic. What file is the man suggesting?
(A) Palcon's strategy
(B) Employee schedule
(C) Payroll records
(D) Sales projections

圖表資訊／男子／資料夾名稱
→ 由圖表確認選項以外的資訊。

63. How will the woman help the man?
(A) By forwarding an e-mail
(B) By ~~printing~~ a document
(C) By calling a colleague
(D) By ~~fixing~~ a computer

女子／協助方式
→ 注意聆聽女子勸說或建議對方的話。

64. What will the man do next?
(A) Go to the ~~office~~
(B) Have a ~~meeting~~
(C) Have lunch
(D) Park his car

男子／未來／後
→ 注意聆聽後半段對話中的未來式句子。

第 62-64 題 對話與螢幕截圖

男：嘿，梅麗莎。我一直試著傳送檔案，不過我的電腦因為某些原因連不上網。
女：真的嗎？奇怪了。我的電腦很正常。嗯，還是你要我代替你上傳？
男：感謝妳願意這麼做。這裡，檔案在這張記憶卡上，11月3號做的。
女：好喔，讓我看看。找到了，你想要寄給誰？
男：我們全體行銷人員，包括團隊主管宋先生。
女：好。順道一提，我正要去北大道的羅馬里奧義大利餐廳吃午餐。你想要一起去嗎？
男：好啊。

檔案夾		
名稱	日期	大小
友同公司策略	2015 年 11 月 7 日	32KB
員工行程	2015 年 11 月 2 日	92KB
薪資紀錄	2015 年 11 月 4 日	120KB
銷售預測	2015 年 11 月 3 日	2.2GB

62. 參考圖表，文中提到的應該是哪個檔案？
(A) 友同公司策略
(B) 員工行程
(C) 薪資紀錄
(D) 銷售預測

63. 女子將如何協助男子？
(A) 轉發電子郵件
(B) 列印文件
(C) 打電話給同仁
(D) 修理電腦

64. 男子接下來將會做什麼？
(A) 到辦公室
(B) 開會
(C) 吃午餐
(D) 停車

62 對話中不會提到圖表題的 (A)–(D) 選項內容。

STEP 1 圖表題的選項不會直接出現在對話當中。

請特別留意，對話中提及與圖表相符的內容才是正確答案。本題詢問男子提到的資料夾名稱為何。男子說道：「I've been trying to send a file」，提到資料夾。

下段對話中，男子又說道：「It was made on November 3rd.」，提到完成時間為 11 月 3 日。確認表格後，可以發現符合該日期的資料夾名稱為 (D) Sales projections。

63 確認題目中是否提及 man / woman / speakers。

STEP 1 題目針對女子提問時，答案會出現在女子的對白中。

本題詢問女子如何協助男子，因此女子的對白中應會出現建議對方的句子。由此可以推測出男子會於前方提出問題，而女子則於後方提出建議，以解決該問題。第一段對話中，男子說道：「I've been trying to send a file, but . . .」，提到他本來打算寄送檔案，卻沒能成功，提出問題點。而後女子回答：「Would you like me to send it instead?」，詢問是否要改由自己寄出，這表示女子要幫男子寄送資料，因此答案為 (A)。

STEP 2 陷阱選項和錯誤選項

(A) By forwarding an e-mail ▶ 答案
(B) By printing a document
▶ 雖然聽到「file」可能會聯想到「document」，但是對話中並未提到列印一事。
(C) By calling a colleague
(D) By fixing a computer ▶ 雖然對話中有提到電腦的問題，但是並未提到「fix」一事。

64 後半段對話中，未來資訊的答案會出現在 I'll . . . 後方。

STEP 1 題目詢問下一步動作（未來資訊）時，答案通常會出現在當事人以 I'll . . . 開頭的對白中。但是若為難度較高的考題，則會採同意對方建議或要求的方式來表達，因此請務必聽清楚對方建議或要求的內容為何。

一般來說，要由最後一句男子的對白，確認男子的下一步動作。男子說道：「I'd love to.」，表示同意前方女子的建議。而女子最後一句話說道：「I'm going to the Romario Italian Restaurant which is located on Northern Boulevard for lunch. Would you like to join me?」，提到她要去吃午餐，詢問男子是否要一同前往。由男子的回答「I'd love to.」，表示他同意這個建議，因此答案為 (C) Have lunch。

STEP 2 陷阱選項和錯誤選項

(A) Go to the office ▶ 男子要一同前往餐廳，因此該敘述有誤。
(B) Have a meeting ▶ 男子要去餐廳吃午餐，因此該敘述有誤。
(C) Have lunch ▶ 答案
(D) Park his car

字彙 access 連結　properly 正常地　appreciate 感謝　director 主管

Questions 65-67 refer to the following conversation and spreadsheet.

M 65	Linda, how's the new inventory management software working out? It has been almost a month since the committee approved your request to buy it.	
W 66	It's nice. The software facilitates managing books which are checked out in our library. Each time books are removed, it can also calculate the due date and inform users of it by text message.	66-D
M	So, with this new software, we can update the status of books for both our librarians and users, right?	
W 67	Exactly. And I can search for a status just by entering keywords in a spreadsheet. For example, look what happens when I type "due." See? **Two items** are due to be returned today.	

Title	Date checked out	Date due
The Unicorn, Book 7	October 1	October 5
The Temperature of Love	October 2	October 5
Her Name is Matilda	October 3	October 8

65. What did the business recently do?
(A) Hire more employees
(B) Purchase some software
(C) ~~Check~~ the inventory
(D) ~~Inspect~~ the system

過去／前
→ 注意聆聽過去式句子。

66. According to the woman, how can users find the due date?
(A) By reading a text message
(B) By calling a business
(C) By visiting a business
(D) By checking ~~their e-mails~~

女子／關鍵字 due date
→ 注意聆聽女子提及關鍵字 due date 的對白。

67. Look at the graphic. When is the conversation taking place?
(A) October 1
(B) October 2
(C) October 5
(D) October 8

圖表資訊／後
→ 由圖表確認選項以外的資訊。

第 65-67 題 對話與試算表

男：琳達，新的庫存管理軟體運作得怎麼樣？自從委員會批准妳的採購需求以來，已經過了將近一個月了。

女：很好，這套軟體方便管理圖書館借閱的書本。書被拿走時，它就會計算到期日並透過簡訊通知使用者。

男：所以有了新軟體，我們就可以同時向圖書館員和使用者更新書籍狀況，對嗎？

女：正是如此，而且我只要在試算表中輸入關鍵字就可以搜尋情況。舉例來說，我輸入「到期日」看看會怎樣。有看到嗎？有兩本書今天會歸還。

名稱	借出日	到期日
《獨角獸》第七集	10 月 1 日	10 月 5 日
《相愛的溫度》	10 月 2 日	10 月 5 日
《她名為瑪蒂達》	10 月 3 日	10 月 8 日

65. 這間公司最近做了什麼？
(A) 增聘員工
(B) 採購某些軟體
(C) 確認庫存
(D) 檢查系統

66. 根據女子說法，使用者要如何得知到期日？
(A) 看簡訊
(B) 打電話詢問公司
(C) 訪問公司
(D) 收電子郵件

67. 參考圖表，何時進行了這場會話？
(A) 10 月 1 日 (B) 10 月 2 日
(C) 10 月 5 日 (D) 10 月 8 日

65 題目針對過去提問時，答案會出現在前半段對話中。

STEP 1 題目針對過去提問時，請注意聆聽前半段對話。

本題詢問這間企業最近做了什麼事。對話中說道：「how's the new inventory management software working out? It has been almost a month since the committee approved your request to buy it.」，提到約莫一個月以前，購買了新的庫存管理軟體，因此答案為 (B) Purchase some software。

STEP 2 陷阱選項和錯誤選項

(A) Hire more employees

(B) Purchase some software ▶ 答案

(C) Check the inventory

▶ 雖然對話中有提到「inventory」，但問題為是否啟用，並非詢問確認與否。

(D) Inspect the system

▶「system」可以表示庫存管理軟體，但是對話中並未提到「inspect」。

66 題目中出現關鍵字時，答案會在該關鍵字前後的句子。 ▶ due date

STEP 1 若題目中出現特定的關鍵字，聆聽對話時，勢必會於該關鍵字前後聽到答案。一般來說會先聽到關鍵字，再聽到答案的內容，但在新制測驗中，有時反而會先聽到答案的內容，之後才聽到關鍵字。

本題的關鍵字為 due date。對話中說道：「it can also calculate the due date and inform users of it by text message」，提到新軟體的特色為計算到期日，並以簡訊通知使用者。這表示使用者可以藉由 (A) By reading a text message 確認還書日期。

STEP 2 陷阱選項和錯誤選項

(A) By reading a text message ▶ 答案
(B) By calling a business
(C) By visiting a business
(D) By checking their e-mails ▶ 對話中提到確認簡訊，並非確認電子郵件。

67 對話中不會提到圖表題的 (A)–(D) 選項內容。

STEP 1 圖表題的選項不會直接出現在對話當中。

本題詢問對話發生的時間點。對話中說道：「look what happens when I type "due." See? Two items are due to be returned today」，女子提到輸入「到期」兩字，就會顯示今天要歸還的書有兩本。確認表格後，可以發現 October 5 有兩本要歸還的書，因此答案為 (C)。

字彙 inventory management 庫存管理 work out 運作 committee 委員會 approve 准許 facilitate 有助於 check out 借出 remove 取走 calculate 計算 inform A of B 向 A 通知 B status 情況；狀態 type 輸入 due 到期

Questions 68-70 refer to the following conversation and price list.

M Thank you for calling Lyndhurst Institute. How may I help you?

W Hello, I'm Dr. Samantha Fanulli from Durittle Veterinary Clinic. I want
68 to register for next week's veterinary research conference, but I haven't been able to access your Web site since this morning.

M I'm sorry for the inconvenience, Dr. Fanulli. Due to unexpected demand, our Web site is down. So I can take your registration over the phone. Will you be attending the conference for both days? 68-C

W No. I'm just interested in the **first day**.

M All right. Well, if you are **a member** of Lyndhurst Institute, you can
69 save on the registration fee. If you want to become a member, I can process your application right now. Just give me your name and 70-D 70-B
70 contact information.

W Sounds perfect. **I'll do that**.

Day 1 only	Members $85 Non-members $100
Day 2 only	Members $110 Non-members $125
Both days	Members $160 Non-members $170

68. What problem does the woman mention?

(A) A contract has expired.
(B) A Web site is not working.
(C) ~~A demand for registration is higher.~~
(D) Research ~~has some errors.~~

女子／問題／前
→ 注意聆聽第一段女子的對白和 but 出現的地方。

69. Look at the graphic. How much will the woman most likely pay?

(A) $85
(B) $100
(C) $110
(D) $125

圖表資訊
→ 由圖表確認選項以外的資訊。

70. What does the man ask the woman to provide?

(A) The number of attendees
(B) Her membership ~~number~~
(C) Identification information
(D) A ~~deposit~~

男子／要求／後
→ 注意聆聽男子勸說、建議、或要求對方的話。

第 68-70 題 對話與價格表

男：感謝您致電林德赫斯特機構，請問您需要什麼協助嗎？

女：哈囉，我是杜立德獸醫診所的醫生薩曼莎．芳努利。我想要登記參加下個星期的獸醫學研究會議，但我今天早上開始一直連不上你們的官網。

男：芳努利醫師，很抱歉造成不便。因為有緊急需求，我們的網站下架了。所以我可以透過電話接受您的登記，您將參加兩天的會議嗎？

女：不，我只對第一天的感興趣。

男：沒問題。嗯，如果您是林德赫斯特機構的會員，可以省下登記費用。如果您想成為會員，我現在可以馬上處理您的申請，只要給我您的姓名和聯絡資訊。

女：聽起來很棒，我要。

第一天	會員 85 元美金
	非會員 100 元美金
第二天	會員 110 元美金
	非會員 125 元美金
兩天	會員 160 元美金
	非會員 170 元美金

68. 女子提到什麼問題？
(A) 一項合約到期了。
(B) 官網無法運作。
(C) 登記的需求比較高。
(D) 研究有些錯誤。

69. 根據圖表，女子可能要付多少錢？
(A) 美金 85 元
(B) 美金 100 元
(C) 美金 110 元
(D) 美金 125 元

70. 男子要求女子提供什麼？
(A) 來訪人數
(B) 她的會員號碼
(C) 身分認證資訊
(D) 訂金

68 直接由本人口中說出問題和擔憂的地方。

STEP 1 若題目詢問問題為何，答案通常會出現在第一和第二段對白中。

本題詢問女子提出什麼問題，因此請注意聆聽女子的對白。女子說道：「I want to register for next week's veterinary research conference, but I haven't been able to access your Web site since this morning.」，提到她想報名參加研討會，卻連不上網站。這表示女子碰到的問題為 (B) A Web site is not working。

STEP 2 陷阱選項和錯誤選項

(A) A contract has expired.

(B) A Web site is not working. ▶ 答案

(C) A demand for registration is higher.

▶ 雖然有提到「demand」，但為男子提及的問題，因此該選項不適當。

(D) Research has some errors.

▶ 雖然對話中有提到「research」，但是女子的問題為無法順利進入網站，因此該敘述有誤。

69 若題目針對表格、傳單等圖表資訊提問時，答題關鍵在於確認與對話內容是否相符。

STEP 1 題目出現表格、傳單等圖表資訊時，詢問的是圖表中與對話內容相符的部分。

本題詢問女子要付多少錢。女子說道：「I'm just interested in the first day.」，而後男子說道：「if you are a member of Lyndhurst Institute, you can save on the registration fee.」。這兩段話表示女子只想報名第一天，而男子建議她加入會員。另外，對話最後，女子又說道：「Sounds perfect.」，表示她答應加入會員。確認表格後，可以發現會員報名第一天的費用為 (A) $85，故為正確答案。

70 題目詢問要求或建議時，解題關鍵在後半段對話中，以 You 說明。

STEP 1 向對方要求或建議某事時，會使用句子「請你……」。

本題詢問男子要求女子提供什麼東西，因此請注意聆聽男子的對白。男子說道：「Just give me your name and contact information.」，要求對方提供姓名和聯絡方式。這表示男子請女子提供的是 (C) Identification information。選項將對話中的 name and contact information 改寫成較為廣義的說法 Identification information。

STEP 2 陷阱選項和錯誤選項

(A) The number of attendees

(B) Her membership number ▶ 聽到「member」可能會誤選該選項。

(C) Identification information ▶ 答案

(D) A deposit ▶ 聽到「registration fee」可能會誤選該選項。

字彙 institute 機構　veterinary 獸醫學　veterinary clinic 獸醫診所　access 使用；進入　inconvenience 不便　due to 因為；由於　unexpected 意料之外的　save 節省　process 進行；處理　contact information 聯絡資訊

PART 4

Questions 71-73 refer to the following talk.

As you know, one of the biggest events in Carlisle, the Fifth Soccer
71 Match, will be held at Carlisle Stadium at the beginning of next
month. As a part of preparation for the event, there will be road
resurfacing work and marching band practice until the end of this
month. Therefore, Main Street where the construction will take place,
72 will be blocked from nine to noon every morning for two weeks. To
reduce any inconvenience for citizens, the Transport Authority will
provide shuttle buses which stop at the subway stations between
City Hall and Carlisle Stadium. The buses will come every 10 minutes,
73 with the last one departing at 11:40, and will take 20 minutes to get
to the stadium. For more information about the bus schedule and
other events, visit www.carlisle.go.kr.

71-A,B,C

73-C

71. What kind of event will take place next month?
(A) A ~~conference~~
(B) A ~~concert~~
(C) A ~~festival~~
(D) A sports match

活動／ **next month** ／前
→ 注意聆聽第一句話。

72. Why won't Main Street be available during a particular time?
(A) The road will be resurfaced.
(B) ~~The sewage system will be fixed~~.
(C) The road will be blocked ~~by snow~~.
(D) The site will be inspected.

關鍵字 Main Street ／無法使用的原因
→ 確認關鍵字前後的內容。

73. When will the last bus of the day arrive at Carlisle Stadium?
(A) 11:00
(B) 11:20
(C) 11:40
(D) 12:00

關鍵字 last bus ／未來／後
→ 注意聆聽後半段數字部分。

第 71-73 題 談話

如您所知，卡萊爾的當地一大活動第五屆足球賽，下個月初將在卡萊爾體育館舉行。為了籌備這項活動，到這個月底為止，這裡將進行道路重新鋪設的工程，並有儀仗隊的排練。因此，主要大街將進行施工，並在這兩週的每天早上九點到正午實施封街。為了減少市民的不便，交通當局將在市政大廳和卡萊爾體育館之間的地鐵站提供接駁公車。公車間隔10分鐘，末班車為11點40分發車，抵達體育館會花費20分鐘的時間。如需查詢公車時刻表和其他活動資訊，請上www.carlisle.go.kr。

71. 下個月將舉行哪一類型的活動？

(A) 會議　(B) 演奏會
(C) 節慶　(D) 運動比賽

72. 為什麼主要大街在特定時間內將不能使用？

(A) 道路要重鋪。
(B) 汙水系統整修。
(C) 道路將被積雪阻塞。
(D) 該場址要接受檢查。

73. 當天的末班車會在何時抵達卡萊爾體育館？

(A) 11:00　(B) 11:20
(C) 11:40　(D) 12:00

71 題目中出現關鍵字時，答案會在該關鍵字前後的句子。 ▶ next month

STEP 1 若題目中出現特定的關鍵字，聆聽獨白時，勢必會於該關鍵字前後聽到答案。一般來說會先聽到關鍵字，再聽到答案的內容，但在新制測驗中，有時反而會先聽到答案的內容，之後才聽到關鍵字。

獨白中說道：「the Fifth Soccer Match, will be held at Carlisle Stadium at the beginning of next month」，出現關鍵字 next month，提到下個月將於 Carlisle Stadium 舉辦足球比賽。選項 (D) 將獨白中的 Soccer Match 改寫成 A sports match。

STEP 2 陷阱選項和錯誤選項

(A) A conference　(B) A concert
(C) A festival　(D) A sports match ▶ 答案

72 題目以 Why 詢問時，獨白會重複使用題目句的內容並於後方提及原因。

STEP 1 聆聽獨白時，請仔細聆聽 Why 後方的關鍵字，其後方將會出現答案。

Why 後方的關鍵字為「won't . . . be available」，表示本題詢問的是無法使用的原因。獨白中說道：「there will be a road resurfacing work」與「Main Street . . . will be blocked」，提到 Main Street 被封閉是因為要重新鋪設路面，因此答案為 (A)。

STEP 2 陷阱選項和錯誤選項

(A) The road will be resurfaced. ▶ 答案
(B) The sewage system will be fixed. ▶ 聽到「blocked」可能會誤選該選項。
(C) The road will be blocked by snow. ▶ 並非因為天候導致道路封閉。
(D) The site will be inspected.

73 四個選項都是日期、星期或地點時，屬於難度較高的考題。 ▶ last bus

STEP 1 題目的四個選項都列出時間或地點時，代表獨白中會提到兩個以上的時間或地點，因此算是難度較高的考題。

獨白中說道：「The buses will come every 10 minutes, with the last one departing at 11:40, and will take 20 minutes to get to the stadium」，提到最後一班巴士的發車時間為 11 點 40 分，抵達目的地要花費 20 分鐘的時間，因此答案為 (D)。

STEP 2 陷阱選項和錯誤選項

(A) 11:00　　(B) 11:20
(C) 11:40 ▶ 為最後一班巴士的發車時間。　　(D) 12:00 ▶ 答案

字彙 match 比賽　stadium 體育館　resurfacing 重新鋪路　marching 遊行　block 封阻
transport authority 交通當局　depart 出發；啟程

Questions 74-76 refer to the following telephone message.

Rachel, it's Mario. I heard that your company **won** an international
74 **award for your** new variety of sparkling **red wine**, Rosso
Spumante, in Rome **last month**. Congratulations! As you know, our
store has a plan to expand the drink product lines which we carry. 74-C,D 75-B
So my supervisor, **Mr. Powell**, is interested in your wines, especially
75 the sparkling wine varieties, and **he** would like to have a meeting 75-D 76-A,B
with you soon. He will be at the **International Wine Fair in France** 75-C
76 **until next Tuesday. From the following day, he will be at his**
desk for the rest of the week. So please let me know when you
will be available. I'm looking forward to seeing you soon.

74. What did Rachel's company do last month?
(A) It gathered customer reviews.
(B) It received an award.
(C) It expanded ~~its office~~.
(D) It announced a merger.

關鍵字 last month／前
→ 注意聆聽關鍵字前後的句子。

75. What does Mr. Powell want to do?
(A) Have a meeting with a business
(B) Expand to an ~~international market~~
(C) ~~Visit a fair in France~~
(D) Give a woman some advice

關鍵字 Mr. Powell
→ 注意聆聽關鍵字前後的句子。

76. Why does the speaker say, "He'll be at his desk for the rest of the week"?
(A) To ~~recommend~~ a suitable meeting time
(B) To suggest ~~changing~~ a meeting time
(C) To complain about some tasks
(D) To indicate that he will work

掌握說話者意圖
→ 確認指定句前後的文意。

第 74-76 題 電話留言

瑞秋，我是瑪利歐。我聽說妳們公司新的氣泡紅酒系列品項「閃爍玫瑰」上個月在羅馬贏得國際獎項。恭喜！妳知道的，我們店計劃擴大現有的飲料產品線。所以關於妳的紅酒，我的主管波威爾先生很感興趣，特別是氣泡品項，也想要儘快跟妳會面。他到下週二前都會在法國的國際酒展。接著下個星期的其他時間他都會待在辦公室，所以請讓我知道妳何時方便，我期待很快就可以跟妳見面。

74. 瑞秋的公司上個月做了什麼？
(A) 收集顧客意見。 (B) 獲獎。
(C) 擴建辦公室。 (D) 宣布合併。

75. 波威爾先生想要做什麼？
(A) 和一間公司開會
(B) 開拓國際市場
(C) 到法國參展
(D) 給一名女性一些建議

76. 為什麼說話者會說：「下個星期的其他時間他都會待在辦公室」？
(A) 建議適合的開會時間
(B) 建議更改開會時間
(C) 抱怨部分職務
(D) 暗示他有上班

74 題目針對過去提問時，答案會出現在前半段對話中。 ▶ last month

STEP 1 **第一題的關鍵字與過去有關時，請務必由前半段獨白中，找出過去式的句子。**

本題的關鍵字為 last month。獨白中說道：「your company won an international award for your new variety of sparkling red wine, Rosso Spumante, in Rome last month」，提到公司上個月以新的紅酒產品贏得了國際獎項，因此答案為 (B)。

STEP 2 **陷阱選項和錯誤選項**

(A) It gathered customer reviews.
(B) It received an award. ▶ 答案
(C) It expanded its office.
▶ 獨白中僅提到 Mario 的店擴張 drink product lines，因此該敘述不正確。
(D) It announced a merger. ▶ 聽到「expand」可能會聯想到「merger」。

75 題目中出現人名或公司名稱時，獨白中會使用第三人稱代名詞表示。 ▶ Mr. Powell

STEP 1 **獨白中，重複提及前方出現的專有名詞或一般名詞時，會使用第三人稱代名詞（he / she / they / it）來代替。**

本題的關鍵字為 Mr. Powell。獨白中說道：「my supervisor, Mr. Powell, is interested in your wines, especially the sparkling wine varieties, and he would like to have a meeting with you soon」，說話者 Mario 提到自己的主管想和 Rachel 開個會，因此答案為 (A)。

STEP 2 陷阱選項和錯誤選項

(A) Have a meeting with a business ▶ 答案

(B) Expand to an international market

▶ Powell 提到擴張 drink product lines，因此該選項不正確。

(C) Visit a fair in France ▶ 並非他想要做的事，而是計劃好要做的事。

(D) Give a woman some advice

76 題目中出現指定句詢問說話者意圖時，答案會是說明較為籠統的選項。

STEP 1 指定句主要作為承先啟後的角色，表達說話者的意圖，因此要先確認前後文的意思，才能理解指定句真正的意思和說話者的意圖。

指定句前方説道：「He will be at the International Wine Fair in France until next Tuesday」，提到主管 Powell 出差至下週二。而指定句正前方連接：「From the following day」從隔天開始，這表示他強調從隔天週三開始工作，因此答案為 (D)。

STEP 2 陷阱選項和錯誤選項

(A) To recommend a suitable meeting time

▶ 雖然獨白中有提到「meeting」，但並未建議適合的時間。

(B) To suggest changing a meeting time

▶ 雖然獨白中有提到「meeting」，但是並未提到變更時間。

(C) To complain about some tasks

(D) To indicate that he will work ▶ 答案

字彙 international 國際的　carry 現有出售　supervisor 主管　following day 隔天
rest 其餘的人或事　look forward to V-ing 期待做某事

Questions 77-79 refer to the following speech.

	First of all, let me thank you all for coming here today. Today is the second day of the new employee orientation session, and **I'll be**	
77	**giving** you some useful **information about** working in the **Accounting** Department. Then, after the lunch break, I'll introduce each mentor, all of whom are senior employees. During the meeting, they will give you a tour of the company's facilities, including the employee lounges and fitness center. Before I forget, I want to tell you something. We've	78-B
78	**recently changed** the payroll policy. The original paydays were on the	
79	15th and 30th, but **the 30th is always a busy day at our company**. So we decided to **move the** dates to the 1st and 15th. Also, at the end of the day, I'll give you survey forms so that we can collect your feedback about our orientation. Please fill them out and submit them in the box on the desk outside of this room. Now, let's get started.	79-B 78-C

77. What kind of department do the listeners work for?
(A) Advertising **(B) Accounting**
(C) Sales (D) Research

78. What does the speaker say has recently changed?
(A) A payday
(B) A meeting ~~location~~
(C) A survey
(D) A hiring process

79. What does the speaker imply when she says, "The 30th is always a busy day at our company"?
(A) To encourage employees
(B) To delay the date
(C) To ask for ~~overtime~~
(D) To explain an excuse

聽者／職業／前
→ 注意聆聽獨白開頭前兩句話。

關鍵字 recently changed
→ 注意聆聽關鍵字前後的句子。

掌握說話者意圖
→ 請務必確認前後的文意。

第 77-79 題 演講

首先，感謝各位今天來到這裡。今天是新人引導課程的第二天，我會給你們一些在會計部門工作的實用資訊。等等午休過後，我會介紹每一位導師，他們都是資深員工。會面時，他們會帶著你們在公司內進行導覽，包括員工休息區和健身中心。怕我忘記，我想先跟你們告知一些事項。我們最近修改了薪資政策，原來的發薪日是15號和30號，不過在30號公司裡總是很忙，所以我們決定把發薪日移到1號和15號。今天結束時，我們也會發放問卷，蒐集你們對於引導課程的回饋意見。請填寫完畢後，繳交至這間房間外那張桌子上的箱子裡。現在，就讓我們開始吧。

77. 聽講的人在哪個部門工作？
(A) 廣告 (B) 會計
(C) 業務 (D) 研究

78. 講者說最近改變了什麼？
(A) 發薪日 (B) 開會地點
(C) 問卷調查 (D) 聘僱流程

79. 當講者說：「30號公司裡總是很忙」，她在暗示什麼？
(A) 激勵員工 (B) 延期
(C) 要求加班 (D) 解釋理由

77 前兩句話會以代名詞（I / You / We）或地方副詞（here / this ＋地點名詞）告知職業或地點。▶ 聽者的職業

STEP 1 前兩句話會聽到 our / your / this / here 加上表示地點或職業的名詞。

本題詢問聽者工作的地點。獨白中說道：「I'll be giving you some useful information about working in the Accounting Department.」，說話者提到會提供對方在會計部門工作的相關資訊，因此聽者工作的地點為 (B) Accounting。

STEP 2 陷阱選項和錯誤選項

(A) Advertising
(B) Accounting ▶ 答案
(C) Sales
(D) Research

78 題目中出現關鍵字時，答案會在該關鍵字前後的句子。▶ recently

STEP 1 **若題目中出現特定的關鍵字，聆聽獨白時，勢必會於該關鍵字前後聽到答案。一般來說會先聽到關鍵字，再聽到答案的內容，但在新制測驗中，有時反而會先聽到答案的內容，之後才聽到關鍵字。**

本題的關鍵字為 recently。獨白中說道：「We've recently changed the payroll policy. . . . So we decided to move the date to the 1st and 15th」，提到發薪日改成 1 號和 15 號，因此答案為 (A) A payday。

STEP 2 **陷阱選項和錯誤選項**

(A) A payday ▶ 答案
(B) A meeting ~~location~~ ▶ 雖然獨白中有提到「meeting」，但是並未提到「location」。
(C) A survey ▶ 雖然獨白中有提到，但是說話者要求聽者填寫的東西，並非變動事項。
(D) A hiring process

79 題目中出現指定句詢問說話者意圖時，答案會是說明較為籠統的選項。

STEP 1 **指定句主要作為承先啟後的角色，表達說話者的意圖，因此要先確認前後文的意思，才能理解指定句真正的意思和說話者的意圖。**

指定句前方說道：「We've recently changed the payroll policy. The original paydays were on the 15th and 30th」，提到要更改發薪的日期，原本的日期為 15 號和 30 號。而指定句後方說道：「So we decided to move the date to the 1st and 15th」，由此可知指定句表達的是從 30 號更改成 1 號的理由，因此答案為 (D)。

STEP 2 **陷阱選項和錯誤選項**

(A) To encourage employees
(B) To delay the date ▶「date」與指定句中「day」的發音相似。
(C) To ask for overtime
(D) To explain an excuse ▶ 答案

字彙 session 課程　accounting department 會計部門　mentor 導師　senior 資深的
give a tour of 給予導覽　facility 設施　employee lounge 員工休息區　payroll 薪資
payday 發薪日　survey form 問卷表　so that 如此一來　fill out 填滿

Questions 80-82 refer to the following talk.

	Good morning, everyone. First of all, thank you for coming in so early today. As you know, today is our second **restaurant's** grand	
80	**opening**. So I want all of you to be on the ball and pay attention to everything from A to Z. James, the centerpiece you have placed on	81-B
	each table is enchanting, and I really appreciate it. All of you just got the uniforms Maria ordered. I think they look fine. Before you start	81-D
81	working, please change into **them**. Also, Cathy Paluza, head chef	80-C
	from our main restaurant, has developed a new menu for the winter	
82	season. She has made some samples and would like to collect your	81-A 82-B
	feedback. Please taste them and fill out the survey forms which have been laid on the counter.	

80. What is the speaker mainly talking about?

(A) A job interview (B) A flower shop
(C) A ~~new~~ chef **(D) A business opening**

主旨／前
→ 注意聆聽前兩句話的內容。

81. What does the speaker tell the listeners to do?

(A) Order some ~~samples~~
(B) Decorate the business
(C) Put on their uniforms
(D) ~~Review~~ their uniforms

要求聽者的事
→ 注意聆聽提及 please 的句子。

82. Why did Cathy Paluza make some samples?

(A) To get some opinions from staff
(B) To collect ~~some money~~
(C) To offer them for free
(D) To try them on

Cathy Paluza ／原因／後
→ 注意聆聽試做菜色的原因。

第 80-82 題 談話

大家早安。首先，感謝你們今天這麼早到。你們知道的，今天是我們第二家餐廳盛大開幕的日子。所以我希望你們全都保持機靈、徹頭徹尾留意每一件事。詹姆士，你在每張桌子中間放的擺飾很迷人，我真的很欣賞。你們大家剛剛收到的制服是瑪莉亞訂的，我覺得看起來很棒。開工前，請記得換上它。另外，來自餐廳本店的主廚凱西．帕路札已為冬季開發了新菜單。她做了其中幾道，想要蒐集你們的意見。請吃吃看，然後填寫放在櫃檯的問卷表。

80. 講者主要在談論什麼？
(A) 工作面試 (B) 花店
(C) 新廚師 (D) 新事業開張

81. 講者要聽者做什麼？
(A) 訂樣品 (B) 裝飾公司
(C) 穿上制服 (D) 檢查制服

82. 為什麼凱西．帕路札試做了一些菜色？
(A) 要從員工那獲取一些意見
(B) 要湊點資金
(C) 要免費提供
(D) 要試穿看看

80 若題目詢問主旨或目的，答案會出現在開頭前兩句話。

STEP 1 題目詢問主旨或目的時，答案有 90% 的機率會出現在對話開頭部分。

開頭簡單打完招呼後，接著說道：「today is our second restaurant's grand opening」，提到今天為第二家餐廳的開幕日，因此答案為 (D) A business opening。

STEP 2 陷阱選項和錯誤選項

(A) A job interview
(B) A flower shop
(C) A new chef ▶ 雖然後半段獨白中有提到「chef」，但並未提到「new」。
(D) A business opening ▶ 答案

81 題目詢問要求或建議時，答案會位在後半段獨白中，並以 please 告知。

STEP 1 獨白中經常使用 If you 或 please 來表達建議的內容，請務必熟記。

獨白中說道：「All of you just got the uniforms Maria ordered. I think they look fine. Before you start working, please change into them.」，要求大家穿上 Maria 訂購的制服，因此答案為 (C) Put on their uniforms。

STEP 2 陷阱選項和錯誤選項

(A) Order some samples
▶ 雖然獨白中有提到「order」，但是訂購的是「uniform」，而非「samples」。
(B) Decorate the business ▶ 為已經發生過的事。
(C) Put on their uniforms ▶ 答案
(D) Review their uniforms ▶ 雖然獨白中提到制服，但並未提到「review」。

82 題目以 Why 詢問時，獨白會重複使用題目句的內容並於後方提及原因。

STEP 1 聆聽獨白時，請仔細聆聽 Why 後方的關鍵字，其後方將會出現答案。

Why 後方的關鍵字為「make some samples」，表示本題詢問的是 Cathy Paluza 試做菜色的原因。獨白中說道：「She has made some samples and would like to collect your feedback」，提到她做了幾道菜，想要聽聽員工們的意見，因此答案為 (A) To get some opinions from staff。

STEP 2 陷阱選項和錯誤選項

(A) To get some opinions from staff ▶ 答案
(B) To collect some money
▶ 雖然獨白中有提到「collect」，但後方連接的是「your feedbacks」。
(C) To offer them for free
(D) To try them on ▶ 出現在要求穿上制服的片段，與試做菜色無關。

字彙 first of all 首先　grand opening 盛大開幕　be on the ball 機靈　from A to Z 徹頭徹尾　centerpiece 餐桌中央擺飾　place 放置　enchanting 迷人的　appreciate 欣賞　counter 櫃檯

Questions 83-85 refer to the following talk.

	Good morning, everyone. My coworker Collins and I've been asked to	
83	talk to you about the handbooks for our all-in-one systems **for smaller**	83-C
	businesses. I was told that we've **recently received** phone calls from	
84	users who say that the set-up instructions are rather **confusing** and	
	don't match the sketches. What I'd like to do today is to make some	84-C
	suggestions on how we can make our handbooks more user-friendly. For	84-B
85	your convenience, I've prepared some handouts with the **details** for you	85-A
	to refer to. **Collins**, the handouts are in your folder. After the presentation,	
	I'd like you to share your ideas.	

83. By whom is the handbook used?

(A) Journalists (B) Teachers
(C) Engineers **(D) Business owners**

84. What did the speaker recently receive?

(A) Complaints (B) ~~Handbooks~~
(C) ~~Sketches~~ (D) Samples

85. Why does the speaker say, "The handouts are in your folder"?

(A) To arrange something properly
(B) To correct some errors
(C) To make his coworker surprised
(D) To ask for some assistance

handbook／對象／前
→ 注意聆聽介系詞 for。

關鍵字 recently receive
→ 注意聆聽關鍵字前後的句子。

掌握說話者意圖
→ 注意聆聽指定句前後的文意。

第 83-85 題 談話

大家早安。我的同事柯林斯和我被要求和你們談談，關於我們提供給小型企業的那套整合式全功能系統手冊。我被告知最近我們收到了用戶來電表示，組裝的說明和圖例不符讓人不解。我今天想要給予一些建議，該如何讓我們的使用手冊更人性化。為了你們方便，我準備了一些詳細的講義給你們參考。柯林斯，講義在你的文件夾裡。簡報之後，我想要大家分享自己的看法。

83. 手冊是要給誰用的？
(A) 記者 (B) 老師
(C) 工程師 (D) 企業主

84. 講者最近收到什麼？
(A) 投訴 (B) 說明書
(C) 圖例 (D) 樣品

85. 講者為什麼說：「講義在你的文件夾裡」？
(A) 為了把某事安排妥當
(B) 為了修正一些錯誤
(C) 為了使同仁感到驚訝
(D) 為了尋求一些協助

83 題目詢問對象時，答案會出現在開頭前兩句話。

STEP 1 聆聽前半段獨白時，請注意提及表示職業的名詞和 you 的句子。

本題詢問誰是使用 handbook（手冊）的對象。獨白中說道：「I've been asked to talk to you about the handbooks for our all-in-one systems for smaller businesses」，提到手冊針對小型企業使用的系統進行解說，因此使用該手冊的對象為 (D) Business owners。

STEP 2 陷阱選項和錯誤選項

(A) Journalists
(B) Teachers
(C) Engineers ▶ 聽到「system」可能會聯想到「engineers」。
(D) Business owners ▶ 答案

84 題目中出現關鍵字時，答案會在該關鍵字前後的句子。
▶ recently receive

STEP 1 若題目中出現特定的關鍵字，聆聽獨白時，勢必會於該關鍵字前後聽到答案。一般來說會先聽到關鍵字，再聽到答案的內容，但在新制測驗中，有時反而會先聽到答案的內容，之後才聽到關鍵字。

本題的關鍵字為 recently receive。獨白中說道：「we've recently receive phone calls from users who say that the set-up instructions are rather confusing and don't match the sketches」，提到收到使用者的來電，表示看不懂安裝過程，還有圖片和實際內容不一致的狀況，這表示為使用者碰到的問題，因此答案為意思相近的說法 (A) Complaints。

STEP 2 陷阱選項和錯誤選項

(A) Complaints ▶ 答案
(B) Handbooks ▶ 為企業老闆使用的東西，並非說話者。
(C) Sketches ▶ 電話中提到的內容，並非答案。
(D) Samples

85 題目中出現指定句詢問說話者意圖時，答案會是說明較為籠統的選項。

STEP 1 指定句主要作為承先啟後的角色，表達說話者的意圖，因此要先確認前後文的意思，才能理解指定句真正的意思和說話者的意圖。

指定句前方說道：「I've prepared some handouts with the details for you to refer to」，說話者提到會準備好更為詳細的說明供聽者參考。而指定句正前方以「Collins」開頭，表示說話者要求 Collins 幫忙取出放在他資料夾內的資料，因此答案為 (D) To ask for some assistance。

STEP 2 陷阱選項和錯誤選項

(A) To arrange something properly
(B) To correct some errors ▶ 聽到「handout」可能會聯想到「errors」。
(C) To make his coworker surprised
(D) To ask for some assistance ▶ 答案

字彙 handbook 手冊　all-in-one system 整合式全功能系統　set-up 組裝；安裝
instruction 指示　confusing 讓人困惑的　match 相符　make a suggestion 提出建議
user-friendly 易於使用的　convenience 便利　refer to 參考　handout 講義

Questions 86-88 refer to an excerpt from a meeting.

86	The first agenda for today's meeting is an update on sales for our new line of **video game consoles**. Since introducing them only two weeks ago, I've been surprised that the sales have been dramatically increasing. As you know, we have applied a promotion offering an extra flash memory card for a limited time.	
87	To be honest, I didn't have much confidence that this **promotion** would be **helpful**, **but** look at these numbers. So, as indicated, we'll definitely be continuing this promotion until the end of the year. The other item on the agenda is that our 10th annual company picnic will be postponed. According to the weather forecast, there will be rain next Friday when the outdoor picnic was to be held in Kensington Park.	87-B 87-C 87-D
88	What do you think of the **5th of May** for the picnic?	

86. What industry do the listeners most likely work in?
(A) Accounting **(B) Electronics**
(C) Engineering (D) Logistics

聽者／職業／前
→ 注意聆聽開頭前兩句話。

87. What does the speaker imply when she says, "But look at these numbers"?
(A) Sales are higher than expected.
(B) A ~~different~~ promotion is necessary.
(C) Some ~~figures~~ must be corrected.
(D) A location for the event will not be ~~spacious~~.

掌握說話者意圖
→ 注意聆聽指定句前後的文意。

88. What does the speaker ask the listeners about?
(A) What to bring
(B) Who to invite for the event
(C) When the event should be held
(D) How to get to the ~~convention~~

詢問事項／後
→ 注意聆聽問句。

第 86-89 題 會議摘錄

今天開會的第一個議題，要來看看我們電玩遊戲機新上市的銷售情況。自從兩週前開賣，銷售量急遽成長讓我很驚訝。你們都知道，我們用閃卡當作贈品做限時促銷。說真的，我並不是很有自信這次促銷會有幫助，不過看到這些數字，我們到年底確實都應該繼續這項促銷。另一項會議議程，是我們公司第十屆的年度野餐延期了。根據氣象預報，下週五，也就是在肯辛頓公園辦戶外野餐當天會下雨。改在5月5號野餐的話，你們有什麼看法嗎？

86. 聽者最有可能在什麼產業工作？
(A) 會計 (B) 電子
(C) 工程 (D) 後勤

87. 當談話者說到「不過看到這些數字」，指的是什麼？
(A) 銷售高得超乎預期。
(B) 需要其他促銷方案。
(C) 有些數據需要修改。
(D) 活動場地的空間不夠大。

88. 說話者問聽者什麼？
(A) 要帶什麼
(B) 要邀請誰來參加活動
(C) 哪時候辦活動
(D) 如何到會場

86 前兩句話會以代名詞（I / You / We）或地方副詞（here / this ＋地點名詞）告知職業或地點。▶ 聽者的職業

STEP 1 前兩句話會聽到 our / your / this / here 加上表示地點或職業的名詞。

本題詢問聽者工作的地點。獨白中說道：「The first agenda for today's meeting is an update on sales for our new line of video game consoles.」，表示聽者任職於與遊戲機有關的公司，因此答案為 (B) Electronics。選項將獨白中的 video game consoles 改寫成較為廣義的說法 Electronics。

STEP 2 陷阱選項和錯誤選項

(A) Accounting　　(B) Electronics ▶ 答案
(C) Engineering　　(D) Logistics

87 題目詢問引號內的說話者意圖時，請確認指定句前後方的連接詞。

STEP 1 本題詢問指定句在對話中代表的意思，因此請確認前後對白的內容，並找出最符合的答案。另外，若指定句前方有連接詞時，請務必分清楚答案應表達正面還是負面的意涵。

指定句前方說道：「To be honest, I didn't have much confidence that this promotion would be helpful」，說話者表達自己真實的想法，提到他本來對於宣傳活動的效果沒什麼自信，而後方指定句以 but 開頭，為表示轉折語氣的連接詞，代表宣傳有實質效果，賣得比預期的好，因此答案為 (A)。

STEP 2 陷阱選項和錯誤選項

(A) Sales are higher than expected. ▶ 答案
(B) A different promotion is necessary. ▶ 為指定句後方句子的含意。
(C) Some figures must be corrected. ▶「figures」和指定句中「numbers」的意思相同。
(D) A location for the event will not be spacious.
▶ 活動地點在 Kensington Park，但並未提到其空間大小。

88 獨白中會依序出現答案線索。

STEP 1 題目句使用 ask about 提出疑問或問題，因此請注意聆聽獨白中的問句。

本題詢問說話者提出什麼疑問。獨白最後說道：「What do you think of the 5th of May for the picnic?」，詢問野餐日改成 5 月 5 日如何，表示他向聽者詢問對活動舉辦時間的想法，因此答案為 (C)。

STEP 2 陷阱選項和錯誤選項

(A) What to bring ▶ 聽到「picnic」可能會聯想到該選項，但獨白中並未提到。
(B) Who to invite for the event
(C) When the event should be held ▶ 答案
(D) How to get to the convention

字彙 agenda 議程　update 更新
video game console 電玩遊戲機
extra 加贈的　to be honest 老實說
confidence 自信
company picnic 公司野餐
postpone 延期　outdoor 戶外的
What do you think of 你的看法為何

Questions 89-91 refer to the following broadcast and map.

Now for the Rapid City sports news. **Yesterday** evening, **the**
89 **championship basketball game** between the Cups and the Bears
was fierce and thrilling. As you already know, the Bears won the game, which was the first time since their team's founding. To celebrate the win and show appreciation to their fans, the Bears will have a big festival in Ontario Arena this Friday. A spokesperson for the Bears said there will be dance performances with team players and a variety of shows for their fans, such as a K-POP Cover Dance. To get a ticket, please **visit**
90 the Bears' **Web site** at www.bearsteam.com and sign up. Also, there is
construction for one of the parking areas at the arena so remember that
91 you **can't access Main Street**. Next is today's weather forecast. Over to
you, Sharon.

90-B

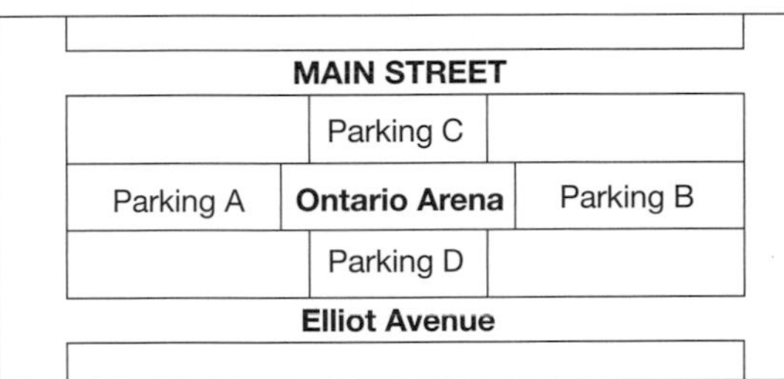

89. According to the speaker, what happened yesterday?
(A) A concert
(B) A festival
(C) A competition
(D) Construction

90. What will the interested listeners most likely do next?
(A) Visit a Web site
(B) Get a signature
(C) Call a program
(D) Use public transportation

91. Look at the graphic. Which parking area will be closed?
(A) Parking area A
(B) Parking area B
(C) Parking area C
(D) Parking area D

關鍵字 yesterday／前
→ 注意聆聽關鍵字前後的句子。

聽者／未來
→ 注意聆聽 please 開頭的句子。

圖表資訊／ parking area ／ closed
→ 注意聆聽距離和比賽場地。

第 89-91 題 廣播與地圖

現在是拉皮德城運動新聞時間。昨天下午，獎盃隊與熊隊的籃球冠軍賽戰況激烈又驚險。眾所皆知，比賽由熊隊勝出，這可是他們成軍以來的頭一遭。為了慶祝勝利並向粉絲表達感謝，熊隊這個星期五將在安大略體育館大肆慶祝。熊隊發言人表示，現場將有舞蹈表演，球員將一起登場，還有為觀眾所準備的各種表演秀，像是韓樂模仿舞蹈。如果想得到入場券，請上熊隊官網www.bearsteam.com並且註冊。另外，因為體育館的其中一個停車區正在施工，所以請記得，主要大街不能通行。緊接著是今天的氣象預報，把時間交給雪倫。

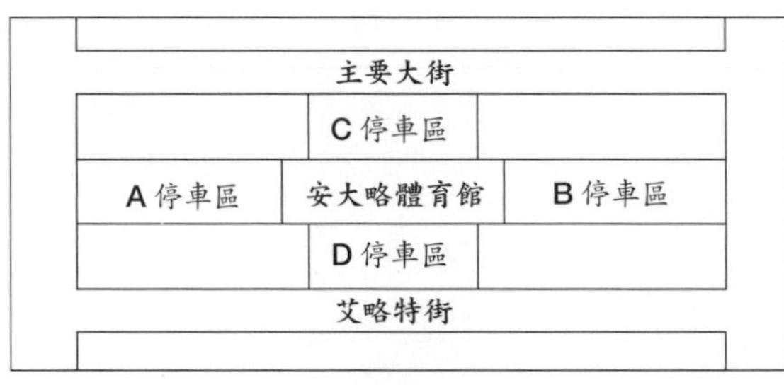

89. 根據說話者的說法，昨天發生了什麼事？
(A) 一場音樂會 (B) 一場慶典
(C) 一場比賽 (D) 施工

90. 感興趣的聽眾接下來最有可能做什麼？
(A) 上網站查看
(B) 得到簽名
(C) 打電話給節目
(D) 利用大眾運輸工具

91. 參考圖表，哪個停車區將會封閉？
(A) A 停車區 (B) B 停車區
(C) C 停車區 (D) D 停車區

89 題目中出現關鍵字時，答案會在該關鍵字前後的句子。 ▶yesterday

STEP 1 **若題目中出現特定的關鍵字，聆聽獨白時，勢必會於該關鍵字前後聽到答案。一般來說會先聽到關鍵字，再聽到答案的內容，但在新制測驗中，有時反而會先聽到答案的內容，之後才聽到關鍵字。**

本題的關鍵字為 yesterday。獨白中說道：「Yesterday evening, the championship basketball game between the Cups and the Bears」，提到昨晚進行了一場籃球冠軍賽，因此答案為 (C) A competition。選項將獨白中的 championship basketball game 改寫成 competition。

STEP 2 **陷阱選項和錯誤選項**

(A) A concert
(B) A festival
(C) A competition ▶答案
(D) Construction

90 題目針對未來提問時，答案會出現在後半段獨白中。

STEP 1 **請注意聆聽祈使句和 you will 開頭的句子。**

本題詢問聽者下一步的行動，因此請從後半段獨白中，找出告知聽者的話。獨白中說道：「To get a ticket, please visit the Bears' Web site at www.bearsteam.com and sign up.」，提到有興趣購票的人，請進入網站，因此答案為 (A) Visit a Web site。

STEP 2 陷阱選項和錯誤選項

(A) Visit a Web site ▶ 答案
(B) Get a signature ▶ 聽到「team players」可能會聯想到「signature」。
(C) Call a program
(D) Use public transportation

91 圖表題選項 (A)–(D) 的內容不會直接出現在獨白當中。

STEP 1 獨白中不會提及選項列出的停車區域，因此請確認其他部分來找出答案，也就是要聆聽距離或表示地點的介系詞。

獨白中說道：「there is construction for one of the parking areas at the arena so remember that you can't access Main Street」，提到比賽場地周邊有一個停車區域正在施工，因此不能靠近 Main Street，表示答案為靠近 Main Street 的區域 (C) Parking Area C。

字彙 now for 現在是　fierce 激烈的　thrilling 驚險的　founding 成立　appreciation 感謝　spokesperson 發言人　access 通行　Over to you. 交給你了

Questions 92-94 refer to the following talk and schedule.

Good morning, everyone. First, I'd appreciate your hard work. This is
92 the busiest season of the year and many seminars are being hosted in our hotel, so I ask all of you to concentrate on operating these smoothly. Before today's shift begins, I'd like to remind you of a change in today's seminar schedule. The Interpersonal and Analytical Skills seminar is going to be held according to schedule. However, the **Sapphire Hall** which
93 was reserved for one of today's sessions hasn't been prepared yet. Also, the number of attendees is lower than the organizer expected, so we've decided to change the room to Ruby Hall. Because it is a last-minute change, please escort attendees for the seminar to the right place. And
94 as a part of celebrations for Halloween **this week**, we will distribute some candy to the customers who want it.

92-A
94-B

Seminars	Place
Interpersonal and Analytical Skills	Diamond Hall
Planning and Writing a Blog	Emerald Hall
Information and IT Literacy	Sapphire Hall
Effective Negotiation	Prestigious Room

TEST 3 PART 4 中譯&解析

92. Where do the listeners work?
(A) At a conference center (B) At a restaurant
(C) At a newspaper **(D) At a hotel**

93. Look at the graphic. Which session has been changed?
(A) Interpersonal and Analytical Skills
(B) Planning and Writing a Blog
(C) Information and IT Literacy
(D) Effective Negotiation

94. What will the employees do this week?
(A) Give out some sweets
(B) Distribute ~~some vouchers~~
(C) Apply a discount
(D) Conduct a survey

聽者／職業／前
→ 注意聆聽開頭前兩句話。

圖表資訊／ session ／ changed
→ 注意聆聽獨白中提及的地點。

關鍵字 this week ／未來／後
→ 注意聆聽關鍵字前後的句子。

第 92-94 題 談話與行程表

大家早安。首先我想感謝各位這麼努力工作。這一季是今年最忙的一季，接下來還有很多研討會要在我們飯店舉行，所以我想請你們大家專心投入，讓它們都能順暢進行。今天的值班開始前，我想提醒你們今天的研討會行程有變動。人際與分析技術的研討會將照計畫走。但是為了今天一項課程所保留的藍寶石廳還沒有準備好。而且，與會人數比主辦單位預期來得少，所以我們決定改到紅寶石廳舉行。因為這項變動很緊急，請務必引導與會者到正確的場地。還有，為了慶祝這週的萬聖節，我們會發一些糖果給想要糖果的客人。

研討會	地點
人際與分析技巧	鑽石廳
部落格規畫和寫作	翡翠廳
資訊與資訊科技識讀	藍寶石廳
有效溝通	尊榮房

92. 聽者在哪裡工作？
(A) 會議中心
(B) 餐廳
(C) 報社
(D) 飯店

93. 請參考圖表，哪項課程有異動？
(A) 人際與分析技巧
(B) 部落格規畫和寫作
(C) 資訊與資訊科技識讀
(D) 有效溝通

94. 員工這週將會做什麼？
(A) 送出一些糖果
(B) 發送禮券
(C) 祭出折扣
(D) 進行問卷調查

92 前兩句話會以代名詞（I / You / We）或地方副詞（here / this ＋地點名詞）告知職業或地點。▶ 聽者的職業

STEP 1 前兩句話會聽到 our / your / this / here 加上表示地點或職業的名詞。

本題詢問聽者工作的地點。獨白中說道：「This is the busiest season of the year and many seminars are being hosted in our hotel」，提到聽者工作的飯店內舉辦很多場研討會，因此聽者工作的地點為 (D) At a hotel。

STEP 2 陷阱選項和錯誤選項

(A) At a conference center ▶ 聽到「seminars」可能會聯想到「conference center」。
(B) At a restaurant
(C) At a newspaper
(D) At a hotel ▶ 答案

93 圖表題選項 (A)–(D) 的內容不會直接出現在獨白當中。

STEP 1 獨白中不會提及選項列出的研討會名稱，因此請確認其他部分來找出答案，也就是要聆聽表示地點的單字。

獨白中說道：「However, the Sapphire Hall which was reserved for one of today's sessions hasn't been prepared yet. Also, the number of attendees is lower than the organizer expected, so we've decided to change the room to Ruby Hall.」，提到研討會原本要在 Sapphire Hall 舉行，但是因為場地尚未準備完畢，因此決定改到另一個場地，這表示更動地點的研討會為 (C) Information and IT Literacy。

94 題目中出現關鍵字時，答案會在該關鍵字前後的句子。 ▶ this week

STEP 1 若題目中出現特定的關鍵字，聆聽獨白時，勢必會於該關鍵字前後聽到答案。一般來說會先聽到關鍵字，再聽到答案的內容，但在新制測驗中，有時反而會先聽到答案的內容，之後才聽到關鍵字。

本題的關鍵字為 this week。獨白中說道：「as a part of celebrations of the Halloween this week, we will distribute some candy to the customers who want it」，提到為慶祝本週的萬聖節，將準備糖果發送給客人。選項將單字 candy 改寫成通稱 sweets，因此答案為 (A) Give out some sweets。

STEP 2 陷阱選項和錯誤選項

(A) Give out some sweets ▶ 答案
(B) Distribute some vouchers ▶ 發送的東西為「candy」，並非「vouchers」。
(C) Apply a discount
(D) Conduct a survey

字彙 concentrate on 專心致志於　operate 運作；進行　shift 值班　interpersonal 人際間的　analytical skill 分析技巧　according to 根據　schedule 時程　attendee 與會者　organizer 主辦者　last-minute 最後一刻的　celebration 慶祝　distribute 發放

Questions 95-97 refer to the following announcement and brochure.

Attention, Fityou Shoes store shoppers. It's time to get your shoes 95-D
at the lowest prices of the year. We'll have a huge selection of shoes
95 **in preparation for the** new season! So we are going to have a big 
clearance sale in our four locations. Here, at this store, you'll get 25 97-A
96 percent off on **sneakers**, including running shoes. But you'll see other
different discounted items for each store location in our leaflet. Also, if
you get a membership card, you'll receive another 10 percent off. Visit our
97 Web site **to become a member** of our Fityou Shoes Shopper Program and
sign up to start saving and find more information on our shop.

Fityou Shoes 25% Discount until This Weekend!	
Sale Item	**Store Location**
Sandals	Peterborough
Sneakers	Kingston
Ankle boots	Rochester
High tops	Kitchener

95. Why is Fityou Shoes having a sale?
(A) To ~~celebrate~~ a new season
(B) To make room for stock
(C) To attract more tourists
(D) To ~~close~~ the store

Fityou Shoes／原因／前
→ 注意聆聽前兩句話。

96. Look at the graphic. At which store location is the announcement being made?
(A) Peterborough
(B) Kingston
(C) Rochester
(D) Kitchener

圖表資訊／店面位置
→ 注意聆聽特價的品項。

97. Why should listeners visit a Web site?
(A) To shop for more items
(B) To check for job openings
(C) To participate in a survey
(D) To become a member

聽者／進入 Web site 的原因
→ 注意聆聽祈使句前後的內容。

第 95-97 題 宣告與小冊子

「就適你」鞋店的顧客注意囉！用今年的最低價格買新鞋就趁現在。下一季我們準備推出大量精選鞋款！因此，在我們的四間店鋪將有清倉大拍賣。在本間店裡，購買運動鞋，包括慢跑鞋在內將享有75折的折扣。您也可以參考傳單上其他店鋪的折扣品。如果您持有會員卡還可以再享10%折扣。請上官網加入就適你鞋店的會員計畫，註冊後即刻開始省錢，並能獲得更多店鋪銷售資訊。

就適你鞋店 75 折折扣 僅到本周末為止！	
銷售商品	店鋪位置
涼鞋	彼得伯勒
運動鞋	金斯頓
短筒靴	羅徹斯特
高筒運動鞋	基秦拿

95. 為什麼就適你鞋店有拍賣活動？
(A) 為了慶祝換季 (B) 為了騰出庫存空間
(C) 為了吸引更多遊客 (D) 為了把店收掉

96. 參考圖表，發布這則公告的店鋪在哪裡？
(A) 彼得伯勒 (B) 金斯頓
(C) 羅徹斯特 (D) 基秦拿

97. 為什麼聽眾應該上官網看看？
(A) 以便購買更多產品 (B) 以便查詢職缺
(C) 以便參加市調 (D) 以便成為會員

95 題目以 Why 詢問時，獨白會重複使用題目句的內容並於後方提及原因。

STEP 1 聆聽獨白時，請仔細聆聽 Why 後方的關鍵字，其後方將會出現答案。

Why 後方的關鍵字為「have a sale」，表示本題詢問的是舉行特賣的原因。獨白中說道：「We'll have a huge selection of shoes in preparation for the new season! So we are going to have a big clearance sale」，提到為迎接新的一季，將提供多款鞋類的清倉折扣。這表示要賣掉存貨，騰出放置新商品的空間，才會舉行特賣，因此答案為 (B) To make room for stock。

STEP 2 陷阱選項和錯誤選項

(A) To celebrate a new season ▶ 準備迎接新的一季，並非慶祝。
(B) To make room for stock ▶ 答案
(C) To attract more tourists
(D) To close the store ▶ 雖然獨白中有提到「store」，但並未提到要歇業。

96 圖表題選項 (A)–(D) 的內容不會直接出現在獨白當中。

STEP 1 **獨白中不會提及選項列出的店面位置，因此請確認其他部分來找出答案，也就是要聆聽特價的品項。**

獨白中説道：「Here, at this store, you'll get 25 percent off on sneakers」，說話者提到運動鞋類的折扣為七五折，因此該廣播通知的地點在 (B) Kingston。

97 題目針對 Web site 提問時，後半段獨白中，通常會出現表示原因或方法的句子。

STEP 1 **請注意表示原因的用法：「to ＋原形動詞」。**

Why 後方的關鍵字為「visit a Web site」，表示本題詢問的是聽者進入網站的原因。獨白中説道：「Visit our Web site to become a member of our Fityou Shoes Shopper Program and sign up」，請聽者進入 Fityou Shoes 網站加入會員，因此答案為 (D) To become a member。

STEP 2 **陷阱選項和錯誤選項**

(A) To shop for more items ▶ 聽到「clearance sale」可能會誤選該選項。
(B) To check for job openings
(C) To participate in a survey
(D) To become a member ▶ 答案

字彙 in preparation for 為……做準備　clearance sale 清倉拍賣　location 地點　leaflet 傳單　sign up 註冊

Questions 98-100 refer to the following announcement and graph.

98 Let's begin today's meeting. As you know, **we** have tried to develop a new line of **cereal**. A month ago, we conducted a survey of focus groups to understand their needs. We received a lot of suggestions for developing a new item and have organized the results to show the four most-mentioned topics. So let's take a look at those results now. As
99 you can see, **one feature was most important to the focus group members**. We'd like to focus on that. Most of the people surveyed showed concern about calories, so management has decided to develop a new product with low calories and high protein. So, we will start working on that immediately. Let's **come up with** ideas for the
100 new product. After our discussion, please submit your ideas to Sara in Research and Development. 100-B

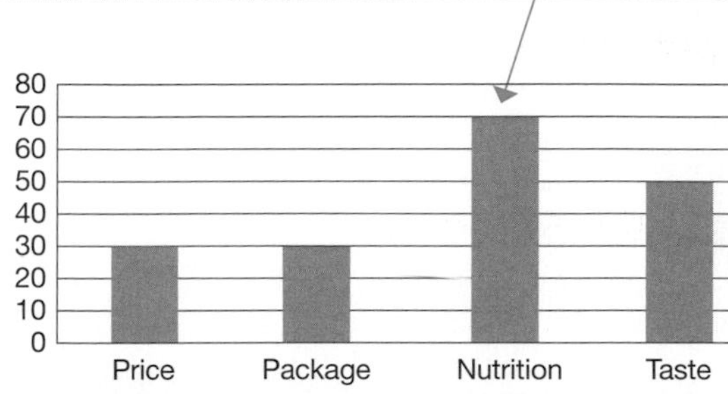

98. What product does the company sell?
(A) Glasses (B) Shoes
(C) A drink **(D) A cereal**

販售商品／前
→ 注意聆聽前半段獨白。

99. Look at the graphic. Which feature will the company begin to work on?
(A) Price (B) Package
(C) Nutrition (D) Taste

圖表資訊／ will work on
→ 注意排序和最高級的用法。

100. What will the listeners do next?
(A) Sign up for a workshop (B) Submit ~~their preferences~~
(C) Work on brainstorming (D) Return to the office

聽者／未來／後
→ 注意聆聽提及未來的句子。

第 98-100 題 宣告與圖表

讓我們開始今天的會議吧。你們知道的，我們試著開發新的穀物產品線。我們在一個月前做了焦點團體調查來了解需求。針對新產品的開發，我們接獲很多建議，也把四個最常提到的主題整理出來。現在請各位看一下這個結果。你們可以看到，對焦點團體的成員來說，有一項特色是最重要的，我們打算專攻這一塊。受測者大多都很關心熱量，因此，管理階層決定要開發低熱量、高蛋白的產品。所以，我們將馬上開始行動，一起為新產品集思廣益一下。討論完後，請把你們的點子轉達給研發部門的莎拉。

98. 這間公司販賣什麼產品？
(A) 眼鏡 (B) 鞋子
(C) 飲料 (D) 穀物

99. 參考圖表，公司將會開始著手哪項產品特色？
(A) 價格 (B) 包裝
(C) 營養 (D) 口味

100. 聽者接下來會做什麼？
(A) 登記參加工作坊 (B) 提供個人偏好
(C) 開始腦力激盪 (D) 返回辦公室

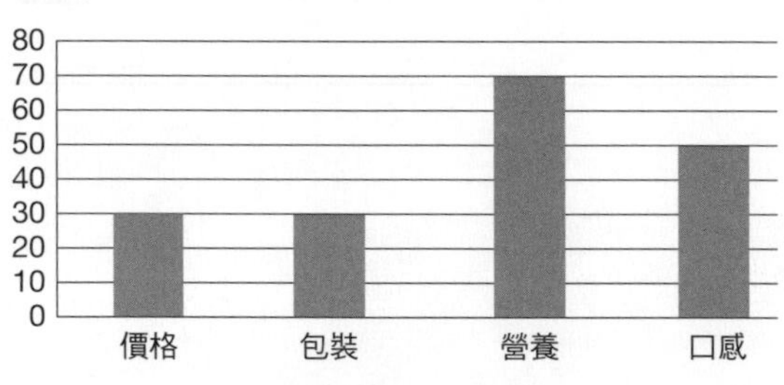

98 前兩句話會以代名詞（I / You / We）或地方副詞（here / this ＋地點名詞）告知販售的商品或聽者的職業。▶ 販售商品

STEP 1 前兩句話會聽到 we / you / this 加上名詞。

本題詢問該公司販售什麼商品。獨白中說道：「we have tried to develop a new line of cereal」，由此可知說話者和聽者皆任職於開發穀物麥片的公司，因此該公司販售的商品為 (D) A cereal。

STEP 2 陷阱選項和錯誤選項

(A) Glasses
(B) Shoes
(C) A drink
(D) A cereal ▶ 答案

99 圖表題選項 (A)–(D) 的內容不會直接出現在獨白當中。

STEP 1 圖表的作用為「比較」，因此請從排序、最高級、數量等用法確認答案。

獨白中說道：「one feature was most important to the focus group members. We'd like to focus on that」，提到要把重點放在大家最為重視的項目上。確認圖表後，可以發現數值最高的項目為 (C) Nutrition。

100 獨白最後提到 Let’s、next、from now 等字詞時，表示未來的計畫。

STEP 1 後半段獨白中，會使用 I will 或 Let's 表示下一步動作。

獨白中說道：「Let’s come up with ideas for the new product」，提到讓我們一起來思考有關新商品的點子，表示要一同討論。選項將獨白中的 come up with ideas 和 discussion 改寫成 brainstorming，因此答案為 (C) Work on brainstorming。

STEP 2 陷阱選項和錯誤選項

(A) Sign up for a workshop

(B) Submit their preferences

▶ 要求提出新商品的點子，並未提到偏好的商品，因此該選項不正確。

(C) Work on brainstorming ▶ 答案

(D) Return to the office

字彙 conduct a survey 做調查 focus group 焦點團體 take a look at 看一下
focus on 專注於；專攻 concern 關切 protein 蛋白質 come up with 想出

101 (At the company's tenth year celebration), Shane's Italian Cuisine / will provide /
介系詞片語 主詞 1 動詞 1
--------- / which / consists of / various Italian menus / offered (at the restaurant).
受詞 1 關係代名詞主格 動詞 2 受詞 2 分詞 介系詞片語

動名詞當作不可數名詞使用時，通常被視為單數。
provide + ________ + (which consists of various Italian menus)

STEP 1 空格要填入動詞 provide 的受詞。

空格要填入名詞，而 (A) cater 和 (C) caters 皆屬於動詞形態，因此不能作為答案。(D) catered 可以作為動詞的過去式或過去分詞，當作分詞使用時，句中要有被它修飾的名詞，因此 (D) catered 並非答案。選項中只有動名詞 catering 可以當作名詞使用，因此答案為 (B) catering。

STEP 2 動名詞形態的名詞屬於不可數名詞。

若名詞和動名詞的意思不同時，通常名詞是**可數名詞（C）**，動名詞則為**不可數名詞（UC）**。

funds / funding	[C] 資金／ [UC]（提供）資金
process / processing	[C] 過程／ [UC] 處理中
house / housing	[C] 住家／ [UC] 住宅；提供住宿
advertisement / advertising	[C] 廣告／ [UC] 廣告；廣告業
seat / seating	[C] 座位／ [UC] 座位；就座
market / marketing	[C] 市場／ [UC] 市場行銷
plan / planning	[C] 計畫／ [UC] 計劃中

※ spending（開銷）和 recycling（回收）也曾出現在考題中。

句子翻譯 在公司的十週年慶祝活動上，「夏恩義式佳餚」將會承辦宴席，其中包含了許多在餐廳供應的義大利餐點。

字彙 celebration 慶祝
consist of 包含
catering 承辦宴席；提供餐點

答案 (B) catering

102 After / the president of the company / had passed away, / his son/,
連接詞 主詞 1 動詞 1 主詞 2
(the --------- living relative of the president) / inherited / his properties.
同格 動詞 2 受詞 2

形容詞前方可以放置形容詞。
the + ________ + living relative (of the president)

STEP 1 空格要填入適合修飾 living relative 的單字。

空格要修飾形容詞 living。主要子句已經有動詞 inherited，而 (C) select 也是動詞，因此不適合作為答案。

STEP 2 副詞不能修飾分類形容詞。

形容詞分成表示名詞的性質或狀態的**一般形容詞**、和表示名詞種類的**分類形容詞**。副詞可以修飾性質或狀態，卻不能修飾種類，因此不能使用副詞修飾分類形容詞，請特別留意這一點。

空格後方為 living relative，意思為「尚健在的親屬」，此處的 living 屬於分類形容詞，表示親屬的生或死，因此空格不能填入副詞，而是要填入形容詞，來修飾名詞 relative。

(D) sole 的意思為「唯一的」，填入後表示「能繼承他財產的對象只有兒子一人」，故為正確答案。(A) sheer 的意思為「純粹的」，強調名詞的大小、程度或數量時，才會使用該形容詞；(B) stark 帶有負面的意思，主要被用於描寫風景或狀態（處境）時，不能修飾親戚，因此並非答案。

STEP 3 形容詞的順序規則：將形容詞放在名詞前方的順序

形容詞的順序								+	名詞
數量	想法	大小	性質／外觀	新／舊	顏色	材料	所屬／目的／種類		
序數→奇數	主觀形容詞	事實（客觀形容詞）							

句子翻譯 在公司總裁過世後，他唯一的親屬兒子繼承了他的遺產。

字彙 pass away 過世　relative 親屬；親戚　inherit 繼承　stark 荒涼的；嚴峻的

答案 (D) sole

103 The number of customers / (who visited the store) / has increased /
主詞　形容詞子句（主格）　動詞
tremendously / --------- the unprecedented sale / it has offered / (for a limited time).
副詞　名詞（受格）　形容詞子句（省略 that）　介系詞片語

for 狀態持續一段時間 vs. during 動作發生於一段特定的時間
__________ + the unprecedented sale

STEP 1 動詞的數量＝連接詞／關係代名詞＋ 1

本句話有三個動詞，而連接詞和關係代名詞有 who 以及 sale 和 it has offered 之間省略的關係代名詞 that，因此不需要再填入其他連接詞。在完整句中加入名詞時，要使用介系詞來連接名詞。選項中，(B) though 和 (D) while 皆為副詞子句連接詞，因此不能作為答案。

STEP 2 選出可以表達時間或一段時間的介系詞，用來修飾 unprecedented sale。

(A) since 當作介系詞使用時，要連接表示過去特定時間的名詞，因此不適合作為答案；(C) during 要連接一段特定的時間，指「那段期間」發生的事情，故為正確答案。

句子翻譯 在商店提供史無前例的限時特賣期間，來店顧客數急遽地增加。

字彙 tremendously 極大地；非常　unprecedented 空前的

答案 (C) during

104 The change / (in the firm's board committee) / --------- / better working conditions /
主詞 1　介系詞片語　動詞 1　受詞 1
(for the employees) / as / the members of the board / have decided to shorten /
介系詞片語　連接詞　主詞 2　動詞 2
working hours / and / raise wages.
受詞 2　對等連接詞 and 表並列關係 (decided to) ＋動詞＋受詞

一個句子當中必定要有一個主要動詞。
The change + __________ + better working conditions

STEP 1 請先蓋住「介系詞＋名詞」片語後，再分析句型的結構。

連接詞為 as，而「主要動詞的數量＝連接詞數量＋ 1」，因此空格要填入主要動詞。選項中，(A) promising 並非主要動詞該有的形態，因此不能作為答案。

STEP 2 **請由從屬子句的時態，來確認主要子句的時態。**

從屬子句的時態為現在完成式，以 as 說明事情發生的原因或理由。(D) would have promised 為 would have p.p.，屬於假設語氣，表示與過去相反的事實，不能作為答案。

若以主要子句表示未來的結果，可以填入未來式，但是動詞 promise 作為不及物動詞使用時，後方不能連接受詞；作為及物動詞使用時，用法為「promise ＋人物＋事物」，改寫成被動語態的話，主詞不能使用事物 change，因此 (C) will be promised 不能作為答案。綜合上述，答案要選 (B) promises 來表示現在的結果。

句子翻譯 隨著董事會成員決定縮短工時與加薪，董事會的這項改革將承諾員工能有更好的工作環境。

字彙 board committee 董事會　wage 薪水

答案 (B) promises

105 --------- / the firm / to avoid bankruptcy, / the workers / did / their best / (in united efforts) / but / they / could not evade / the crisis.

名詞 (the firm)　to 不定詞片語 (to avoid bankruptcy)　主詞 1 (the workers)　動詞 1 (did)　受詞 1 (their best)　介系詞片語 (in united efforts)　連接詞 (but)　主詞 2 (they)　動詞 2 (could not evade)　受詞 2 (the crisis)

由後方連接的名詞選出適當的介系詞。

_________ + the firm

STEP 1 **「____＋名詞，完整句」當中，要將____＋名詞組合成副詞片語。**

(D) Forward 當作副詞使用時，後方不能連接名詞，因此不能作為答案。其餘三個選項皆為介系詞，請找出填入空格後符合句意的選項。

STEP 2 **選出介系詞之前，請先確認後方適合連接的名詞種類。**

(A) Onto 的意思為「到……之上、往……方向」，後方要連接表示地點的名詞，通常會搭配表示移動的動詞一起使用。然而，空格後方連接 to 不定詞的動詞為 avoid，並非表示移動，因此不適合作為答案。(B) Until 會搭配表示時間點的名詞，因此也不能作為答案。

STEP 3 **弄清楚 to 不定詞和名詞之間的關係。**

空格後方為 firm，to 不定詞的動作為避免破產，而 firm 為該動作的執行者。因此答案要選 (C) For，用來表示 to 不定詞意義上的主詞。

句子翻譯 為了使公司避免破產，職員聯合盡了最大的努力，但他們仍無法逃離危機。

字彙 bankruptcy 破產　in united efforts 協力做……　evade 迴避；避免

答案 (C) For

106 As / the marketing department / has been augmented/, Raymond Spencer / has been transferred / (to the new section) / --------- his former division.

連接詞 (As)　主詞 1 (the marketing department)　動詞 1 (has been augmented)　主詞 2 (Raymond Spencer)　動詞 2 (has been transferred)　介系詞片語 (to the new section)　受詞 (his former division)

根據慣用語選出適當的介系詞。

transferred + to the new section + _________ his former division

STEP 1 完整句＋ to 名詞＋____＋名詞

空格位在完整句後方，要填入介系詞，來連接後方的名詞。動詞為 has been transferred，而空格前後方分別出現形容詞 new 和 former，代表由之前的地點換到新的地點，因此答案要選 (B) from，用來連接起點 his former division。「transfer from A to B」表示「從 A 搬遷、調動至 B」，請務必熟記此用法。

STEP 2 分析錯誤選項

(A) in 指存在或包含在某個地點或特定空間內，不適合用於表示 Raymond Spencer 調至新的部門；(C) across 表示離開原來所在的地點，因此不適合作為答案；(D) of 表示同格關係、當中的一部分或組成要素，且 of 後方連接的名詞範圍通常會比前方連接的名詞範圍更廣，但是 section 和 division 同樣都屬於「部門」，因此不能作為答案。

句子翻譯 隨著行銷部門擴編，雷蒙史賓塞已從原部門被調至新部門。

字彙 augment 擴大；增加　former 先前的

答案 (B) from

---

107 (After years of hard work and successful results in important contracts),
介系詞片語

Kristi / now / has / --------- / (over her colleagues and superiors).
主詞　副詞　動詞　受詞　介系詞片語

找出適當的「名詞＋介系詞」組合（pair）。
has + ________ + over her colleagues and superiors

STEP 1 **空格要填入及物動詞 has 的受詞，並搭配後方介系詞 over 一起使用。**

雖然 (B) consequence 和 (C) significance 都可以放在動詞 have 後方，但是兩者後方不能連接介系詞 over，而是要搭配 for 一起使用，表示「帶來……影響（意義）」，因此不能作為答案。(D) reaction 通常會放在動詞 experience、bring、cause 後方，連接介系詞 to、in、against 後，再加上表示狀況或事件的名詞，因此也不能作為答案。

(A) authority 的意思為「權力」，可以放在動詞 have 後方，連接介系詞 on、of、over 後，再加上受影響的人物名詞作為受詞，故為正確答案。

STEP 2 名詞搭配介系詞的組合

1. 介系詞＋名詞＋介系詞		
• in combination with 和……結合 • in comparison with 和……比較 • by means of 透過……的方式 • in conjunction with 和……一道 • in compliance with 和……相符 • in observance of 遵照……	• with the exception of 除……之外 • in charge of 負責…… • in accordance with 依據…… • at the rate of 以……的速度 • in addition to 在……之餘 • in response to 作為……的回應	• in view of 從……的觀點 • on behalf of 身為……的代表 • as a result of 作為……的結果 • in excess of 超過……

2. 名詞＋介系詞		
• advance in ……的進步 • effect/impact on 對……造成影響 • commitment to 承諾去 • proximity to 接近…… • question about/concerning 詢問／關切……	• demand/request/call for 要求／請求／籲求 • emphasis on 強調…… • concern with 和……有關 • alternative to 作為……的替代	• exposure to 與……有接觸 • concern about/for/over 對……的關注 • dedication to 致力於 • regret for 為……感到遺憾 • access to ……的管道
3. 介系詞＋名詞		
• under construction 正在施工中 • for free 免費 • in advance 提前 • on schedule 照表	• beyond repair 無法修復 • without a doubt 毫無疑問 • upon request 根據要求	• in third 在第三位 • in writing 以書面方式 • in duplicate 一式兩份 • in place 到位

句子翻譯 在多年努力簽得重要合約後，克莉絲蒂現在擁有比同事與上級更大的權力。

字彙 contract 合約　colleague 同事　superior 上級

答案 (A) authority

108 The lounge / may be --------- / (by anyone with a small entrance fee) / but /
主詞 1　動詞 1　介系詞片語　連接詞
the lack of information / (about the place) / holds / people back /
主詞 2　介系詞片語　動詞 2　受詞 2
(from using the service).
介系詞片語

將空格與句中的單字相互連結，並找出答案。
The lounge + may be ________ + by anyone with a small entrance fee

STEP 1 千萬不能只依賴單字意思來解題。

本句話為被動語態，而空格後方並未出現受詞，因此空格要填入及物動詞的過去分詞，才符合本句話的句意和文法結構。

STEP 2 解題時，請先將被動語態改成主動語態。

改寫成主動語態後為「Anyone with a small entrance fee may ______ the lounge」。

(A) informed 的受詞要連接人物，因此不能作為答案。(C) prevented 的用法為「prevent A from B」，意思為「阻止、預防 A 做 B」，受詞可以連接人物或事物，但是主詞「支付入場費用的人」並不適合搭配受詞「休息室」一起使用，因此不能作為答案。

(D) advanced 當作不及物動詞使用時，無法轉換成被動語態；當作及物動詞使用時，若表示「預付」的意思，受詞要連接表示金錢的名詞；若表示「提出」的意思，受詞則要連接表示想法、理論、計畫的名詞，無論是哪一種，皆不適合填入本句空格中，因此也不是答案。

STEP 3 釐清空格和後方介系詞片語的關係，以便選出答案。

選項中，只有 (B) accessed 適合搭配介系詞片語 with a small entrance fee（支付入場費用），意思為「進入」。

句子翻譯 任何人只要支付小額入場費皆能進入休息室，但由於大家對於該場所所知甚少，所以很少人使用該服務。

字彙 hold back 阻止；抑住　inform 通知　access 接近；通道

答案 (B) accessed

109 We / are / one of the leading companies / (in furniture manufacturing)
(We：主詞1；are：動詞1；one of the leading companies：主格補語1；(in furniture manufacturing)：介系詞片語)

--------- / it / took / us / ten years / to get where we are now.
(---------：連接詞；it：虛主詞；took：動詞2；us：受詞1；ten years：受詞2；to get where we are now：真主詞)

以 even though 表示與期待相反。

. . . leading companies + ________ it took us ten years to get where we are now

STEP 1 空格要填入副詞子句連接詞，連接前後兩個完整句。

從屬子句要以 (C) even though 連接，表示與主要子句的事實相反，故為正確答案。

STEP 2 分析錯誤選項

(A) since 為表示時間的副詞子句連接詞，用於表示過去特定時間發生的事情，影響至今、或是用來表示原因，與 because 為同義詞；(B) before 表示主要子句的時間早於從屬子句的時間，因此不能作為答案；(D) instead 不能連接句子，因此也不是答案。

STEP 3 even though / although vs. but——分辨與轉折語氣 but 的差異。

- 驚訝或與期待相反的內容＋ even though / although ＋事實、期待
- 適時、期待＋ but ＋補充與事實不符的內容、推測或預想的內容

雖然 although 和 but 的意思相似，但前者通常會於減輕主要子句內容的影響力或效果時使用。

→ You can use my adapter although I'm not sure it is compatible with yours.
　你可以使用我的轉接器，不過我不確定是否與你的相容。

句子翻譯 我們是家具製造業的領頭公司之一，不過這花了我們十年才達到現在的規模。

字彙 leading 主要的

答案 (C) even though

110 (Before funding the project), / the corporation / sent / experts / to have /
介系詞片語 主詞 動詞 受詞 to 不定詞片語 1
the proposed product / ------ / to estimate its potential value and verify compliance /
受詞 受詞補語 to 不定詞片語 2
(with the national standards).
介系詞片語

確認使役動詞 have 的受詞和受詞補語間的關係。
have + the proposed product + __________

STEP 1 空格要填入受詞補語，補充說明名詞 the proposed product。

空格作為使役動詞 have 的受詞補語，因此要填入原形動詞或過去分詞，補充說明 the proposed product。選項皆為過去分詞（形容詞），與名詞 the proposed product 互為被動關係，請從中選出最適當的單字。

STEP 2 找出適合連接受詞 proposed product 的動詞。

當句型結構為 S+V+O+OC，受詞補語為主動語態時，表示受詞和受詞補語的動作為主動關係。但是受詞補語為過去分詞時，則要看動詞和受詞間的關係，確認受詞 the proposed product 適合搭配的動詞（選項的過去分詞）。

(A) invested 的意思為「投資」，受詞要連接投資的對象，像是股票、資產、或物品；(C) conducted 的意思為「引導、指揮、實施」，後方要連接表示特定活動或表演的名詞，不適合連接 product；句首為介系詞片語 Before funding the project，表示在投入資金以前，填入 (D) developed 後，表示「開發產品」並不適當，因此答案要選 (B) assessed。

句子翻譯 在投資該計畫之前，企業派送了專家衡量提案商品，以評估該產品的潛在價值、並確保符合國家規定。
字彙 estimate 評估 verify 驗證 compliance with 和……相符 assess 估價
答案 (B) assessed

111 The regulars of Isaac Design / who spend more than $20,000 a year
主詞 形容詞子句（主格）
/ will be --------- of / any upcoming fashion shows / (with invitations).
動詞 受詞 介系詞片語

必考題型「通報／告知＋人物受詞」。
The regulars + will be + __________ of any upcoming fashion shows . . .

STEP 1 選項皆為過去分詞時，屬於被動語態考題。

選項皆為過去分詞時，表示本題的句子為被動語態。請選出適當的單字，搭配後方介系詞 of 一起使用。

STEP 2 解題時，請先將被動語態改成主動語態。

改寫成主動語態後為「People will _______ the regular of Isaac Design . . . of any upcoming fashion show . . .」，受詞為人物 the regulars（常客），因此要選出適合搭配該名詞的動詞 p.p.。

(B) regulated 及物動詞，意思為「規定、調整」，受詞會使用表示活動或過程的名詞；(C) announced 通常會連接 that 子句，而 announce 後方連接人物名詞作為受詞時，意思為「通報……的到達」，並不適合搭配後方的介系詞片語，因此不能作為答案；(D) determined 要連接表示決定或結論的名詞，因此也不是答案。

notify 屬於「通報／告知」類動詞，後方可以加上「人物＋ of ＋事物」或「人物＋ that 子句」。本句話為被動語態，人物名詞要移至主詞的位置，事物名詞則放在 of 的後方，因此答案要選 (A) notified。

句子翻譯 在「艾薩克設計」每年消費超過 20,000 美元的常客，將獲邀參加任何即將舉行的時裝秀。
字彙 regular 老顧客 upcoming 即將到來的
答案 (A) notified

112 Most of the customers / (of our mattress store) / decide / to buy the product
主詞 介系詞片語 動詞 受詞
/ that they --------- comfortable / (after lying on it for a short time).
形容詞子句（受格） 介系詞片語

由連接詞數量判斷動詞的數量。
that they ________ comfortable

STEP 1 本題要選出適當的動詞填入空格中。

句中的 that 為關係代名詞／連接詞，主要動詞為 decide。為符合「主要動詞的數量＝連接詞數量＋ 1」，空格要填入動詞。

STEP 2 關係代名詞 that 後方連接主詞，因此該關係代名詞為受格。

空格後方連接形容詞 comfortable，說明的是 that 子句前方先行詞 product 的狀態，因此答案要選 (A) find。

(C) relax 作為不及物動詞時，意思為「放鬆」，後方不能連接受詞，也不會使用形容詞修飾，而是使用副詞作修飾，因此不能作為答案；(B) stay 作為完全不及物動詞使用時，後方不會連接形容詞，而是要用副詞作修飾；作為不完全不及物動詞使用時，意思為「保持……狀態」，指的是持續維持某種狀態。但是後方的介系詞片語為「暫時躺了一會兒後」，表示主詞感受到的舒適感為暫時性的狀態，因此不適合作為答案；(D) spend 的用法有「spend sth on sth」和「spend 時間／金錢＋ Ving」，因此也不是答案。

句子翻譯 在我們床墊店的多數顧客，都會購買在稍微試躺過後覺得舒服的床墊。
字彙 lie 躺臥
答案 (A) find

113 Paul Academy, / a non-profit online organization, / is dedicated / to making /
主詞 同格 動詞 介系詞片語
their program / --------- / (to children) / (who live in inadequate conditions)
making 的受詞 介系詞片語 形容詞子句（主格）
(by allowing them to receive quality online learning experiences.)
動名詞片語

看似要填入副詞，但是副詞並非答案。
making + their program + ________

STEP 1 動詞 make 可以作為完全及物動詞或不完全及物動詞。

若為完全及物動詞，受詞後方的空格要填入副詞，但是 (D) educationally 不能修飾動作，而是用來修飾狀態，因此不能修飾動詞片語或整個句子。綜合前述，本題的 make 不完全及物動詞。

STEP 2 作為不完全及物動詞使用時，受詞補語可以使用名詞或形容詞。

受詞補語可以填入名詞，表示和受詞為同格關係；或填入形容詞，用來修飾受詞，因此答案要選形容詞 (C) educational。(A) educates 和 (B) educate 皆為動詞形，不能作為答案。

句子翻譯 非營利線上組織「保羅學院」致力於幫助貧困孩童學習，並確保他們能夠獲得優質的線上學習體驗。
字彙 non-profit 非營利的　dedicate 貢獻於　inadequate 不適當的
答案 (C) educational

114 Jacob's sales records / have been (steadily) --------- / since / he / entered
主詞 1　動詞 1　連接詞 主詞 2　動詞 2
/ the company; / this phenomenon / answers / the question
受詞 2　主詞 3　動詞 3　受詞 3
(of why companies think highly of experienced workers).
介系詞＋名詞子句修飾 the question

現在完成進行式表示從過去一直持續到現在。
Jacob's sales records have been steadily ________ + since 完整句

STEP 1 關鍵在於確認空格適合填入的詞性。

空格前方出現 have been，(A) improve 和 (B) improves 皆為主要動詞，因此不能作為答案。若填入 (D) improvement，本句話會變成「S+V+SC」句型，而主詞 sales records 和主詞補語要為同格的關係，因此 (D) 也不能作為答案。

STEP 2 副詞 steadily 和連接詞 since

空格後方為連接詞 since，用於表示過去特定時間點發生的事影響至現在，而分號前方的主要動詞為 have been，表示時態為現在完成式。答案要選 (C) improving，表示一種持續的狀態「銷售業績持續變好」。

句子翻譯 雅各的銷售紀錄從進公司以來就穩定地持續成長；這個現象解釋了為什麼企業偏好有經驗的職員。
字彙 sales record 銷售紀錄　steadily 穩定地　phenomenon 現象　think highly of 對……評價高
答案 (C) improving

115 (In large companies like ---------), / it / is / nearly impossible /
虛主詞 1
介系詞片語　名詞　動詞 1　主詞補語 1
虛主詞 2 → 動詞 2　真主詞 2　to pass by 的受詞
to get to know every single employee, / so / (it) / is / normal / to pass by / strangers.
真主詞 1　連接詞　主詞補語 2

找出省略的名詞，就能選出正確的所有格代名詞。
In large companies like ________

STEP 1 介系詞 like 後方要連接名詞。

空格為介系詞 like 的受詞，要填入名詞，而 (B) our 為人稱代名詞的所有格，扮演形容詞的角色，因此不能作為答案；(D) we 為主格代名詞，要放在主詞的位置，因此也不能作為答案；介系詞 like 針對前方名詞舉例，(A) us 為人稱代名詞的受格，表示人物，因此不是答案。答案要選 (C) ours (= our large company)，在大型企業中，以自家公司為例。

STEP 2 **比較所有格代名詞和其他人稱代名詞的差異**

所有格代名詞可以放在句中主詞、受詞或補語的位置，因此請務必找出它在句中代指哪一個名詞，才能分辨出與其他人稱代名詞的差異。

★滿分重點——所有格代名詞後方不能連接名詞。

All the hiring procedures are handled by _____ affiliated agency. (we/our/ours/ourselves)
千萬不要一看到介系詞，就認為後方要連接名詞，馬上選擇可以作為名詞使用的所有格代名詞或反身代名詞。請務必稍微多想一下，空格後方連接的是名詞片語（affiliated agency），因此答案要選所有格 our，修飾該名詞片語。

句子翻譯 在像我們這樣的大公司裡，要認識每一位員工是不可能的，所以身邊經過陌生人是很正常的。
字彙 nearly 幾乎　get to know 掌握；認識
答案 (C) ours

116 The president of the charity organization, / Eduseed, / visits / the school /
主詞 1　同格　動詞 1　受詞 1
(he has built in Burma) / --------- / to restock the supplies / (that have run out).
形容詞子句（受格、省略 that）　to 不定詞片語　形容詞子句（主格）

考題中現在式搭配的頻率副詞。
. . . visits the school he has built in Burma + _________

STEP 1 **空格前方連接完整句，因此空格要填入副詞。**

STEP 2 **本句話中的主要動詞為 visits，屬於現在式。**

to 不定詞表示動詞的目的，加上主要子句的時態為現在式，答案要選副詞 (D) regularly，來表示動詞屬於日常中有規律、經常性的動作。(A) shortly 意思和 soon 相同，通常會搭配未來式一起使用；(B) deeply 的意思為「（往下方、裡面）深處」，該副詞只能用來修飾形容詞和副詞；(C) finely 的意思為「微小、精緻地」，通常會用來修飾動詞 cut（切）或 craft（製作），因此不能作為答案。

句子翻譯 慈善機構「教育種子」的總裁會定期參訪他在緬甸蓋的學校，以補齊用完的物資。
字彙 restock 進貨　run out 用盡
答案 (D) regularly

117 Quality, reputation and service / are usually given / high priority / (by many business
主詞 1　動詞 1　受詞 1　介系詞片語
owners) / --------- / these / are / easy / (for the customers) / to inspect.
主詞 2　動詞 2　主詞補語　意義上主詞　to 不定詞

常考連接詞 because / since vs. so that
完整句 + _________ + 完整句

STEP 1 **空格前後各連接一個完整的句子，因此要填入副詞子句連接詞。**

選項皆為副詞子句連接詞，因此請根據意思和句型結構，找出最適合填入的選項。(C) as if 為假設語氣用法，若後方連接現在式，則會變成推測，並非假設語氣。主要子句表示一般常見的事實，若從屬子句表示不確定的內容，兩者無法呼應，因此不能作為答案。

STEP 2 釐清主要子句和從屬子句的關係。

空格後方連接的子句為主要子句（結果）的原因，因此答案要選 (D) since。主要子句表示原因、從屬子句表示結果時，才能填入 (B) so that，因此該選項並非答案；(A) when 為表示時間的副詞子句連接詞，不符合句意。

STEP 3

※ **because / since vs. so that**

主要子句的動詞	連接詞	從屬子句的動詞
（結果）時間晚於從屬子句	because、since	（原因）時間早於主要子句（過去）
（原因）時間早於從屬子句（過去）	so that	（結果）時間晚於主要子句
（過程）時間早於從屬子句（過去）	in order that	（目的）時間晚於主要子句

※ **since vs. as vs. because**

❶ 與 because 相比，使用 since 和 as 時，說話的重點在於結果，而非理由。尤其當理由為已知的事實時，會使用 since。
❷ 與 because 相比，since 屬於更為正式的用法。
❸ since 子句通常會放在主要子句的前方。若放在主要子句後方使用時，since 前方要加上逗點。（若 since 子句擺在前方，則要在主要子句前方加上逗點。）

句子翻譯 品質、名譽與服務通常是許多企業主優先重視的事，因為這三者顧客可以很容易得知。
字彙 priority 優先事項　inspect 檢查；調查
答案 (D) since

118 Ms. Greenhill, / --------- vehicle / had been destroyed / (in a bad accident),
主詞 1　主詞 2　動詞 2　介系詞片語
had to take / public transportation / until / she / could afford / a new car.
動詞 1　受詞 1　連接詞　主詞 3　動詞 3　受詞 3

whose 是唯一可以連接完整句的關係代名詞。
_________ vehicle + had been destroyed

STEP 1 本句話中需要加入連接詞或關係代名詞。

本句話中有三個動詞（had been destroyed、had to take、could afford），因此需要兩個連接詞或關係代名詞。而當中只有看到一個連接詞 until，表示空格需要再填入一個連接詞或關係代名詞。

STEP 2 關係代名詞 whose 為例外，後方要連接完整句。

空格後方連接 vehicle had been destroyed，動詞為不及物動詞，並使用被動語態，屬於結構完整的句子，因此答案要選 (D) whose。套入原來的句子中為 whose vehicle = Ms. Greenhill's vehicle。關係代名詞 (A) who 和 (B) whom 後方要連接不完整的句子、(C) whoever 為複合關係代名詞，因此皆不能作為答案。

句子翻譯 葛林希爾女士的汽車在一場嚴重意外中損毀，在她能夠再買一輛新車之前，她都必須搭乘大眾交通工具。
字彙 destroy 破壞；摧毀　public transportation 公共交通運輸　afford 負擔得起
答案 (D) whose

119 We / ensure / that / our newly released automated sprinklers and mowers /
主詞 1 動詞 1 連接詞 主詞 2
are / much faster than those --------- / (by hand).
動詞 2 受詞補語 介系詞片語

「those who ＋動詞」vs.「those ＋分詞」vs.「only those ＋介系詞片語」
those + __________ + by hand

STEP 1 先確認句子的結構

代名詞 those 後方可以使用形容詞修飾（後位修飾）。複數名詞 those 指的是 sprinklers and mowers，而選項皆為過去分詞形，因此請先思考動詞和受詞的關係。也就是説，答案的動詞要能連接該名詞作為受詞。(A) accepted 通常會連接表示提議（offer）、邀請（invitation）、辭職（resignation）、道歉（apology）、建議（advice）的名詞作為受詞，因此不適合作為答案。

STEP 2 找出比較的對象

句中比較的對象為 newly released automated sprinklers and mowers 和 those 後方的內容，要選出意思和 newly 相反，且適合加上 by hand（手動）的形容詞，因此答案為 (B) operated，意思為「運轉」。

(C) publicized 的意思為「公布、宣傳」，受詞通常會連接表示公告內容或資訊的名詞；(D) intensified 作為及物動詞使用時，受詞會連接增強的對象，而 (C) 和 (D) 後方皆不適合連接句中的介系詞片語，因此不能作為答案。

STEP 3 those 六大出題模式

❶ those who ＋不完整句（複數動詞）	關係代名詞 who 代替人物
❷ those ＋（who ＋ be 動詞）＋分詞	V-ing / V-ed 分詞省略關係代名詞
❸ Those ＋介系詞＋名詞＋動詞＋受詞	以介系詞片語「with ＋名詞」修飾 those
❹ 介系詞＋ those who . . . ＋動詞＋受詞	for、except、with
❺ 副詞＋ those（介系詞片語／ who . . .）＋動詞＋受詞	大多會以 only 修飾
❻ those ＋複數名詞→指示形容詞	後方連接複數名詞變成指示形容詞 例 those applicants who

句子翻譯 我們保證，我們新發售的自動灑水器與割草機比用手工操作的機型還要快速。
字彙 ensure 確保 by hand 用手工
答案 (B) operated

120 Once / you / get to / Highway No. 65 / (which leads --------- to the city center),
連接詞 主詞 1 動詞 1 受詞 1 形容詞子句(主格)
/ it / will take / less than half an hour / (from the airport to our office).
主詞 2 動詞 2 受詞 2 介系詞片語

副詞可以修飾名詞以外的其他詞性。
Highway No. 65 + which leads + ------- + to the city center

STEP 1 空格位在動詞和介系詞片語之間，要填入副詞，修飾前方動詞。

選項中只有 (D) straight 為副詞。

TEST 3 PART 5 中譯&解析

STEP 2 動詞和介系詞片語之間不能填入形容詞。

形容詞可以放在名詞前方修飾名詞，而 (A) straightened 與 (B) straightening 皆為分詞形，不適合作為答案。逗點前方有兩個連接詞（once 和 which），因此句中要有三個動詞才行。句中的動詞有 get、leads、will take，不需要額外的動詞，而 (C) straighten 為動詞，因此也不能作為答案。

句子翻譯 一旦您開上 65 號高速公路，它能直達市中心，從機場到敝辦公室將花不到半小時的時間。
字彙 get to the highway 到達高速公路　straighten 弄直　straight 筆直的
答案 (D) straight

121 It / will take / months / to negotiate the --------- / (to the urban development issue in downtown Chicago) / since / most building owners / voted (against it).
（虛主詞 It；動詞 1 will take；受詞 1 months；真主詞 1 to negotiate the ---------；介系詞片語 (to the urban development issue in downtown Chicago)；連接詞 since；主詞 2 most building owners；動詞 2 voted；介系詞片語 (against it)）

確認適合搭配句中及物動詞使用的名詞。
negotiate + the __________ to the urban development issue

STEP 1 空格要填入動詞 negotiate 的受詞。

動詞 negotiate 通常會連接「合約書、交易、條約」等名詞當作受詞，因此空格適合填入主要在協商的事物，答案為 (B) resolution。

STEP 2 分析錯誤選項

(A) occasion 當作可數名詞使用時，意思為「時刻、時機」；當作不可數名詞使用時，則表示事情發生的「起因、問題」，套入後表示協商都市開發問題的原因，並不適當；(C) impression 後方不會連接介系詞 to，而是連接 of，表示對人事物的印象；(D) situation 指「情況、局面」，而問題在於房屋所有人表示反對，因此該選項也不適合作為答案。

句子翻譯 由於大部分的建築擁有者都持反對票，芝加哥市區的都市發展議題將要花上數個月來協商決議。
字彙 negotiate 協商　urban 城市的　vote against 投票反對　resolution 決心；決議
答案 (B) resolution

122 The texts and images / (in the brochure) / have been provided / --------- / (of the Tourism Administration Department).
（主詞 The texts and images；介系詞片語 (in the brochure)；動詞 have been provided；介系詞片語 (of the Tourism Administration Department)）

確認由兩個單字以上組成的介系詞片語。
have been provided + __________ of someone

STEP 1 被動語態為完整句時，通常會省略「by ＋主詞（執行動作者）」。

空格前方為完整句，使用及物動詞 provide 的被動語態，空格位在完整句和 of 之間。形容詞無法單獨使用，因此 (B) courteous 不能作為答案。

STEP 2 by courtesy of 當中的 by 可以省略。

by courtesy of 的意思為「經……同意、承蒙……好主意」，可以省略 by，因此答案要選名詞 (A) courtesy。(C) courteously 為副詞，不適合作為答案；(D) courteousness 的意思為「有禮貌、謙恭」。

句子翻譯 小冊子裡的文字與圖片是由觀光行政局所核准提供。

字彙 courtesy 禮貌　courteous 有禮的

答案 (A) courtesy

123 (Only after realizing the importance of satisfying the local customers,) / Jessie, / the owner
分詞構句 主詞 同格
of Jess Café / --------- (on serving various Asian foods) / has developed / a localized menu.
介系詞片語 動詞 受詞

分辨動詞和動狀詞的差異。
主詞 + __________ + 動詞 + 受詞

STEP 1 一個句子中至少要有一個動詞。

題目句由主詞 Jessie 和動詞 has developed 所構成，而 (C) is focused 和 (D) focus 皆為動詞，因此不適合填入空格中。

STEP 2 空格連接介系詞 on，且修飾前方名詞，因此請選擇動狀詞填入空格中。

分詞 (A) focused 加上後方介系詞 on，可以用來修飾前方名詞 the owner of Jess Café，故為正確答案。

STEP 3 to 不定詞通常用來修飾「計畫、努力、目的、意圖、時間」等名詞。

★常考「名詞＋ to 不定詞」：

ability to V 做……的能力	attempt to V 嘗試做……
effort to V 努力做……	right to V 有權利做……
opportunity/chance to V 有機會做……	way to V 有辦法做……
decision to V 決定做……	willingness to V 願意做……
time to V 做……的好時機	plan to V 打算做……
authority to V 有權力做……	proposal to V 提議做……

句子翻譯 在意識到滿足當地顧客的重要性後，專注於供應亞州料理的傑西咖啡店店主傑西，開發了一份在地化菜單。

字彙 local 在地的　localize 在地化

答案 (A) focused

124 (--------- given above), / any claims / (for refund) / will be rejected, / as /
分詞構句 主詞 1 介系詞片語 動詞 1 連接詞
the customer / is accountable for / all damages / (to the product after purchase).
主詞 2 動詞 2 受詞 2 介系詞片語

連接詞後方省略主詞＋ be 動詞變成「連接詞＋分詞構句」。
__________ given, 完整句

STEP 1 確認適合填入空格的詞性。

選項只有介系詞和連接詞兩種詞性，空格後方沒有名詞，直接連接分詞 given。而 (D) For 為介系詞，後方要連接名詞，因此不能作為答案。

STEP 2 空格要填入副詞子句連接詞，連接省略「主詞＋ be 動詞」的分詞構句。

(B) While 為副詞子句連接詞，表示時間時，意思為「當……的時候」；表示讓步時，意思則為「然而」。(C) After 的意思為「……之後」，為表示時間的副詞子句連接詞，不適合填入空格中。(A) As 為副詞子句連接詞，意思為「依照、如同」，as given above 表示「如同上方所述」，為常見的用法，請務必熟記。

句子翻譯 如上所述，顧客應當負責產品購買後的損壞，因此所有退款申請將予以駁回。
字彙 claim 主張　be accountable for 為……負責
答案 (A) As

---

125 (Due to their modest stipend), / anyone / usually / working /
介系詞片語　主詞　副詞　分詞
(under twenty hours a week) / is / --------- / (from the income tax).
介系詞片語　動詞　介系詞片語

be 動詞＋形容詞 vs. 過去分詞
主詞 + be 動詞 + __________ + 介系詞片語 (from the income tax)

STEP 1 空格位在 be 動詞後方，要填入主詞補語，補充說明主詞的狀態。

空格要填入適當的形容詞，和後方介系詞 from 一同補充說明主詞 anyone 的狀態。 (D) exempt 為形容詞，加上介系詞 from 的意思為「免除」，故為正確答案。(A) subject 當作形容詞使用時，用法為「be subject to ＋名詞」，意思為「容易受到……的影響、遵守（法規）、繳交（罰金）」，不適合作為答案。

STEP 2 及物動詞連接事物名詞，再改成被動語態

主詞為動作的執行者時，屬於主動語態；主詞為動作的承受者時，屬於被動語態（be + p.p.）。(B) operated 為 operate 的過去分詞（p.p.），operate 作為及物動詞使用時，意思為「營運」；(C) built 為 build 的過去式或過去分詞，build 作為及物動詞使用時，意思為「建設」。改成被動語態時，主詞不會使用人，因此不能作為答案。

句子翻譯 由於薪資微薄，每週工作時數低於 20 小時的人免徵所得稅。
字彙 modest stipend 微薄薪資　income tax 所得稅
答案 (D) exempt

---

126 The Green Belt Action, / in which / construction of buildings and destruction of nature
主詞 1　關係副詞　主詞 2
/ are strictly prohibited, / is / part of an effort / to preserve more --------- / for wildlife
動詞 2　動詞 1　主詞補語　to 不定詞片語　意義上主詞
/ to dwell and reproduce in.
to 不定詞片語

確認適合連接名詞的動詞和修飾該名詞的片語。
preserve + more __________ + (for wildlife) + to 不定詞

STEP 1 「及物動詞＋形容詞＋名詞」

空格為 to 不定詞 preserve 的受詞，要填入名詞，表示可以被保存的對象。

STEP 2 以 to 不定詞修飾名詞

空格要填入適當的名詞，搭配後方用來修飾該名詞的 to 不定詞，因此答案要選 (B) space，表示「可以居住和繁殖的空間」。(A) benefit 指「利益、好處、津貼」；(C) project 指「計畫、課題、目標」；(D) journey 的意思為「旅行、旅程」，三者皆不適合作為答案。

句子翻譯 「綠帶行動」嚴格禁止建築建物與破壞自然，是為了讓野生動物有更多生存空間居住與繁殖。
字彙 prohibit 禁止 preserve 保留 dwell 居住；棲息 reproduce 繁殖
答案 (B) space

127 Ms. Lewis / is / --------- / that / Timothy, / (under her supervision), / will smoothly carry out / orders / assigned (to him).

主詞 1 動詞 1 連接詞 主詞 2 介系詞片語 動詞 2 受詞 2 分詞 介系詞片語

be 動詞＋形容詞＋ that 子句
主詞 + be 動詞 + ______ + that 子句

STEP 1 空格位在 be 動詞後方，要填入主詞補語，補充說明主詞的狀態，後方再連接 that 子句。

答案要選 (D) confident，意思為「有自信的、確信的」，填入後表示「Lewis 確信業務交由 Timothy 負責，將會進行得很順利」。

STEP 2 動詞連接 that 子句的用法

將及物動詞 (A) designated 改成被動語態後，後方不會連接 that 子句，其用法為「be designated sth」和「be designated as/for sth」，因此不能作為答案；(B) remembered 使用主動語態時，後方才能連接 that 子句，因此也不能作為答案；(C) important 為形容詞，後方加上 that 子句時，用法為「it is important that」。

STEP 3 常考「be 動詞＋形容詞＋ that 子句」

• be aware that 意識到……	• be clear/obvious that ……是顯然的
• be sure/confident/convinced that 確信／自信／相信……	• be appropriate that ……是適當的
• be optimistic/positive that 對……抱持樂觀	• be essential that ……至關重要
• be natural that ……是很自然的	• be important that ……是重要的
• be possible/true that ……有可能／是真的	• be inevitable that ……是不可避免的
	• be likely/unlikely that ……是很可能的／不可能的

句子翻譯 路易斯女士有信心，在她的督導下，提摩西能夠順利地執行分配到的指令。
字彙 supervision 監督 order 命令 assign 安排
答案 (D) confident

128 The shareholders / hurriedly disposed of / their shares / --------- /
主詞 1 動詞 1 受詞 1
they / would sink / (in price) / once / the corruption / (in their firm) / received / coverage.
主詞 2 動詞 2 介系詞片語 連接詞 主詞 3 介系詞片語 動詞 3 受詞 3

主要動詞的數量＝連接詞數量＋ 1
主詞＋動詞＋ ________ ＋主詞＋動詞

STEP 1 句中出現三個主要動詞時，需要兩個連接詞。

本句話中有三個主要動詞 disposed of、would sink、received，連接詞卻只有 once 一個。而 (A) as for 為介系詞、(B) meanwhile 和 (C) for example 為連接副詞，都不能作為答案。因此答案要選 (D) because。

STEP 2 連接副詞並非連接詞，而是副詞。

❶ 轉換話題：(in the) meantime 在此同時、meanwhile 同時、by the way 順道一提
❷ 舉例說明：for example / for instance 舉例來說、in particular / specifically 特別是
❸ 不然：otherwise 否則；不同樣地；在其他方面
1. The bank will renew the contract unless notified otherwise.
除非有另行通知，否則銀行將更新合約。
2. They won although expected otherwise.
雖然與預期不同，他們還是獲勝了。
3. This is only the traditional area in the otherwise modern city.
這只是這個相對現代的城市中較為傳統的區域。
❹ 補充：besides / furthermore / moreover / above all / in addition / as well 此外
❺ 順序：then / thereafter 然後
❻ 選擇／放棄：instead / alternatively 取而代之的是
❼ 同樣、相似地：likewise 同樣地
❽ 結果：accordingly / consequently / hence / therefore / thus / as a result / finally 結果
❾ 讓步：nonetheless / nevertheless / however 然而

句子翻譯 股東們迅速拋售他們的股份，因為一旦公司的貪污消息被報導出來，股價將會大幅下跌。
字彙 dispose of 捨棄 share 股份 once 一旦 coverage 報導 receive coverage 獲得報導
答案 (D) because

129 The critics / highly praised / the seemingly profound film,
主詞 1 動詞 1 受詞 1
/ admiring its unique filming techniques and original methods of plot unfolding,
分詞構句
/ while / the audience reviews / suggest / ---------.
連接詞 主詞 2 動詞 2

suggest / indicate / instruct + otherwise
主詞＋及物動詞＋副詞

STEP 1 及物動詞 suggest 後方連接副詞的情況

suggest 為及物動詞，後方要連接受詞，但是選項皆為副詞。(B) in contrast 的意思為「與……相比」，後方要連接介系詞 to 或 with；(D) on the contrary 的意思為「相反地、對立地」，為連接副詞，不適合作為答案；(C) instead 為副詞，意思為「作為替代、反而」，因此也不能作為答案。

STEP 2 請務必熟記 otherwise 的用法

(A) otherwise 當作副詞使用時，意思為「用別的方法、除此以外」，用法為「. . . say/think/decide/suggest/indicate + otherwise」，表示「並非那麼說／想／決定／使人想起／暗示」，因此答案要選 (A)。

★更多 otherwise 的出題重點：

1. unless otherwise noted / unless instructed otherwise 除非另外告知／除非另外指示
2. 例外：「冠詞＋ otherwise ＋形容詞＋名詞」

例 an otherwise happy life 一個原本幸福美滿的人生

句子翻譯 評論家對這部看似深奧的電影讚譽有加，欣賞其獨特的拍攝手法與原創的劇情走向，然而觀眾的評論卻與之不同。

字彙 unfolding 展開

答案 (A) otherwise

---

130 Mr. Rogers / --------- / the proposals, / but / he / has / no other choice
主詞 1　受詞 1　連接詞　主詞 2　動詞 2　受詞 2
but to decline them / (due to the financial burden) / (they will bring him).
介系詞片語　形容詞子句（受格）（省略 that）

找出決定答案的關鍵依據。
主詞＋ ＿＿＿＿ ＋受詞（the proposals）

STEP 1 後方以連接詞 but 連接，因此空格要填入及物動詞，連接受詞（the proposals）。

在多益測驗中，(A) appeals 常會當作不及物動詞使用，後方要連接介系詞 to；(B) focuses 也會當作不及物動詞使用，後方要連接介系詞 on；(C) relates 當作不及物動詞使用時，後方要搭配介系詞 to 一起使用；當作及物動詞使用時，用法為 relate A to B。

STEP 2 答題關鍵為表示轉折的 but。

but 後方出本題的解題重點 decline，這表示前方句子中，必須使用帶有「同意、批准」之意的動詞。(D) endorses 的意思為「公開支持、認可」，故為正確答案。

★常考「不及物動詞＋介系詞」

• concentrate on 專注於……	• go through 經過……	• deal with 處理……
• care for 關心……	• benefit from 從……得到好處	• refrain from 克制……
• succeed in 在……取得成功	• enroll in 報名參加……	• focus on 專注於……
• check in 辦理登記	• differ in 在……有所不同	• rely on 依賴……
• interfere with 干擾到	• wait for 為……等待	• look into/through 調查／識破
• talk about 談到	• contend with 對……感到滿意	• apologize to 向……道歉
• consist of 包括……	• compete with 與……競爭	• listen to 聽……
• object to 反對……	• lay off 資遣	• look for 尋找……

句子翻譯 羅傑斯先生贊同這項提案，然而卻不得不駁回，因為這項提案將帶給他們沉重的財務負擔。

字彙 have no other choice but to V 別無選擇只能做……　appeal 求助；訴諸；上訴

答案 (D) endorses

PART 6

Questions 131-134 refer to the following e-mail.

E-MAIL

From	williamr_thomas@abcsprts.com
To	jamesburns@kaum.net
Date	June 23
Subject	Scale barbecue grills

Dear Mr. Burns,

主題：回覆對方的訊息——針對對方的要求提出解決方式

We have received your message and checked your record. It states that you ordered **three barbecue grills** (model no. SCT-250) through our TV home shopping channel on June 17 and they were scheduled to arrive June 22. We are sorry to hear that you have not yet received — **131** —. Usually it takes no more than three or four days to deliver items.

— **132** —. According to **this information**, your grills should arrive on June 23. If you do not receive your order by then, please — **133** — us.

動詞

We apologize for the inconvenience this has caused you. Obviously, it does not happen very often. I want to emphasize that **this situation** is very — **134** — .

主詞　補語

Thank you.

William R. Thomas

ABC Sports International

131. (A) ones ▶ 不定代名詞
(B) it ▶ 單數
(C) some ▶ 一部分
(D) them ▶ Three barbeque grills

代名詞
→ 確認空格代替前方什麼東西。

132. (A) ~~Visit our store~~ to purchase an additional item.
(B) ~~Thank you~~ for your feedback.
(C) We were able to track your order.
(D) Unfortunately, the items you ordered are ~~not available at the moment~~.

句子插入題
→ 確認空格前後的句子。

133. (A) contacting
(B) contacted
(C) contact
(D) contacts

動詞詞彙
→ 一個句子中至少要有一個動詞。

134. (A) interesting
(B) similar
(C) impossible
(D) unusual ▶ It does not happen very often.

形容詞詞彙
→ 從前一句話中找出 This situation 所指的事情。

第 131-134 題 電子郵件

寄件人	williamr_thomas@abcsprts.com
收件人	jamesburns@kaum.net
日期	6 月 23 日
主旨	規模烤肉架

敬愛的伯恩斯先生，

我們收到您的訊息並查詢了您的紀錄，其中載明，您於 6 月 17 日經由我們的家用電視購物頻道，訂購了三組烤肉架（型號 SCT-250），商品預計在 6 月 22 日抵達。我們很遺憾聽到您說還沒有收到它們。通常物流時間不會超過三到四天。

我們能夠追蹤您的訂單。根據追蹤資訊，您的烤肉架應該會在 6 月 23 日送達。如果到時候您仍沒收到貨，請和我們聯絡。

造成您的不便我們非常抱歉，這種事顯然不常發生，我想再度強調這種情形是相當罕見的情況。

感謝您。

威廉斯 R. 湯瑪士
ABC 運動國際

字彙 state 載明　be scheduled to V 被安排好要做某事　usually 通常
take 花費（時間、金錢）　apologize for 為……道歉　cause 造成
obviously 顯然　emphasize 強調

131 代名詞
代名詞用來代替前方出現過的名詞。

STEP 1 請先確認空格代替前方什麼名詞。

根據文意，代名詞代替的是 three barbecue grills，而 (B) 只能代替單數名詞，因此不能作為答案；(C) some 表示一小部分，填入後並不符合文意；(A) ones 為不定代名詞，並非代替前方出現過的名詞，而是表示與前方名詞同類的其他名詞，不適合填入空格中。綜合上述，答案要選 (D) them。

132 句子插入題
題目為句子插入題時，請從選項中找出與空格前後內容有所關聯的關鍵字。

STEP 1 看到句子插入題時，請注意空格前後是否出現指示形容詞或代名詞。

空格後方出現 this information，為「指示代名詞＋名詞」，因此請選出提及相關內容的句子。this information 後方告知對方訂購商品到貨的時間，由此可以得知 this information 與訂購商品有關。因此答案要選 (C)「我們追蹤了您的訂單」，填入後最符合前後文意。(A) 為針對加購的說明；(B) 為針對顧客意見表的回覆；(D) 為針對訂購商品的回覆。

(A) 請來店面選購其他商品。

(B) 感謝您的意見回饋。

(C) 我們能夠追蹤您的訂單。

(D) 很遺憾，您訂購的商品缺貨。

字彙 track 追蹤　at the moment 目前

133 動詞詞彙
一個句子中至少要有一個動詞。

STEP 1 空格要填入主要動詞。

if 子句後方只出現 do not receive，表示此句話中還需要一個動詞。

STEP 2 句子為祈使句，省略主詞。

空格要填入動詞，但是前方並未連接主詞，表示這句話為祈使句。空格要填入原形動詞，因此答案為 (C) contact。

134 形容詞詞彙
根據整篇文章的文意，找出最適合填入的答案。

STEP 1 本題要選出適當的形容詞作為補語。

四個選項皆符合文法規則，因此請確認 this situation 所指的事情為何。前半段文中提到訂購商品尚未到貨，並寫道：「it does not happen very often」，提到這種情況並不常見。由此可以得知 this situation 指的是 unusual（不常有、稀奇的）事情，因此答案要選 (D)。值得留意的是，(C) impossible（不可能的）指的是不會發生的狀況或無法處理的狀況。

Questions 135-138 refer to the following customer review.

I bought some fabrics at Trago's Textile Inc. last week. When I first called to ask some of the options they offered, the representative was very knowledgeable and helpful. So, I **ordered** some printed cotton and linen in bulk over the phone. **Unfortunately, I** probably — **135** — here for fabric **anymore**. The workers at the warehouse apparently didn't care about the — **136** — of the fabric they loaded onto my truck. Some of it was **damaged and stained**. — **137** —. They did let me replace some of the fabric there, but I had to return to their store with the damaged ones. Next time **I** will find a place that will let **me** — **138** — **my own fabric**. And I strongly recommend that you avoid doing business with Trago's Textile.

訂購商品的問題

Mary T. Barra

135. (A) did not shop
(B) will not be shopping
(C) may not have shopped
(D) could not have shopped

136. (A) category
(B) width
(C) price
(D) quality

137. (A) There was a long line of waiting for a refund.
(B) I couldn't carry them by myself.
(C) They recommended a repair shop.
(D) About half of what I got looked used.

138. (A) design
(B) choose
(C) provide
(D) cut

動詞時態

→ 選出適當的時態，使得 Unfortunately 前後句子為對比的關係。

名詞詞彙

→ 選出最適當的名詞作為 didn't care about 的受詞。

句子插入題

→ 善用連接副詞或代名詞。

動詞詞彙

→ 選出最適當的動詞連接受詞 my own fabric。

第 135-138 題 顧客評論

我上個星期在燕子織品公司買了一些布。我第一次打電話過去問他們有提供哪些選擇的時候，對方代表知識豐富而且樂於助人。我便透過電話訂購了一些印花棉布和大批的亞麻。很遺憾的是，我可能再也不會在這裡買布了。倉庫人員很顯然不在乎他們放到我卡車上的布料品質。有一些已經汙損了，我拿到的布有一半看起來已經被使用過。他們讓我在那裡換了其中一些，但我還是得把壞掉的帶回店裡。下一次我會找個可以讓我自己選布料的地方。我強烈建議你們避免和燕子織品做生意。

瑪麗 T. 芭拉

字彙 textile 織品　option 選擇　representative 代表　knowledgeable 知識淵博的
helpful 樂於助人的　printed 印花的　in bulk 大量的
over the phone 經由電話　apparently 顯然地　care about 對……在乎
load 裝貨　damaged 被毀損的　stained 被弄髒的　replace 替換
do business with 和……做生意

135 動詞詞彙

題目為動詞詞彙題時，請留意連接詞和其他的動詞。

STEP 1 作答 PART 6 的時態題時，請先確認前後句子的時態後，再選出正確答案。

前一句話寫道：「So, I ordered . . .」，提到先前訂購了商品。而 Unfortunately 為表示轉折的詞，後方要提出不滿的意見，因此答案要選 (B) will not be shopping，以未來式表達「再也不想在此購買」。(D) could not have shopped 屬於假設語氣，表示與過去相反的事實；(C) may not have shopped 表示對過去的推測。

136 名詞詞彙

詞彙題不能單憑選項的中文意思選出答案。

STEP 1 請從空格前後方找出客觀的答題依據，選出符合空格前後文意的答案。

如果只看空格前後的單字，四個選項似乎都能填入空格中，但是千萬不能單憑選項的中文意思選出答案。本題要選出最適當的名詞作為 care about（介意、在乎）的受詞。空格下一句話提到一部分布料有破損，還有污漬在上面，提出布料品質的問題，因此答案要選 (D) quality，表示「不太在乎布料的品質」。(A) category 指「種類」；(B) width 指「寬度」；(C) 指「價格」。

137 句子插入題
請由空格前後方內容確認答題關鍵字。

STEP 1 題目為句子插入題時，請先整理出各選項的關鍵字，再從空格附近找尋關鍵字。

空格前方提出訂購商品的問題，以 some of it 表示一部分商品的情況。下一句話要表達該商品的其他問題較為適當，因此答案要選 (D)。

(A) 排隊要退款的隊伍很長。→適合放在提及直接到店內購買的內容後方。
(B) 我沒辦法自行搬運。→空格前方提到訂購商品的品質，因此不適合在後方提及搬運。
(C) 他們推薦了一間修理店。→空格後方提到換貨一事，因此不適合在前方提及修理店。
(D) 我拿到的布有一半看起來已經被使用過。

138 動詞詞彙
請務必完全理解整篇文章的內容。

STEP 1 本題要選出適當的及物動詞，連接受詞 my own fabric。

乍看之下，四個選項似乎都能填入空格中，因此請務必掌握整篇文章的目的、狀況和時間點，才能選出正確答案。前方提出對於訂購商品的不滿，包含倉庫員工提供有瑕疵的商品、以及要求她將商品載回去換貨。因此答案適合選 (B)「挑選」，表示下一次（next time）她要到可以自行挑選布料的商店。

Questions 139-142 refer to the following letter.

> Dear Henry's Fun
>
> This letter is **to** serve as proof of your registration **—139—** confirm your participation in the 10th International **Toy Fair**, from July 10 to July 16. Since you participated in last year's fair, **Henry's Fun** will be offered **—140— booths** at a reduced rate. Please be aware that we have made small changes in regard to preparing your space. This year, all participants must have their booths ready by 9 P.M. on July 9. **—141—**. Tables and chairs needed will be provided by the organizer. On the day, you will need to visit our office next to the main entrance before you begin setting up your booths.
>
> 攤位準備工作的細節
>
> We appreciate your choosing to **participate** in our **—142—**.
>
> Gregory Anderson, Coordinator

139. (A) rather than ▶ 而不是……
(B) therefore ▶ 連接副詞
(C) and also ▶ 而且也是
(D) in case ▶ 連接詞

140. (A) rent
(B) rents
(C) renting ▶ 受到修飾的名詞為分詞形態時，表示意義上的主詞，帶有主動和進行的概念。
(D) rental

141. (A) The ~~final schedule~~ will be posted on our Web site.
(B) All trash and packing materials should also be removed by that time.
(C) The ~~Rex Toy~~ will be ~~located~~ next to our office.
(D) The number of ~~participants~~ has increased over the last ten years.

142. (A) contest
(B) event
(C) research
(D) course

連接詞詞彙

→ 看到連接詞詞彙題時，請確認句中動詞、以及連接詞引導的子句。

形容詞 vs. 分詞

→ 請以形容詞為先。

句子插入題

→ 請由空格前後方內容確認答題關鍵字。

名詞詞彙

→ 請確認該名詞指前一句話中的什麼東西。

第 139-142 題 信件

敬愛的「玩心亨利」：

這封信係證明您已完成登記，並且確認您在 7 月 10 日到 7 月 16 日期間將參加第十屆國際玩具展。因為「玩心亨利」去年曾參展過，您的租用攤位將享有折扣。請注意，關於您的空間準備有點小變動。今年所有的參展者必須在 7 月 9 日晚上 9 點前整理好攤位。所有的垃圾和包裝材料在這個時間以前都必須清空。所需的桌椅由主辦單位提供。當天開始擺設您的攤位前，您需要到我們主要入口旁的辦公室一趟。

我們感謝您選擇參加我們的活動。

格雷戈里·安德森 統籌

字彙 serve as 當作……用　registration 登記　confirm 確認　participation in 參加……
fair 商展　organizer 主辦方　set up 擺設

139 連接詞詞彙
對等連接詞後方可以省略重複的部分。

STEP 1 選出前方沒有動詞，後方可以直接連接原形動詞的轉折詞。

空格後方連接原形動詞 confirm，因此要填入對等連接詞。(D) in case 為副詞子句連接詞，引導「主詞＋動詞」組合而成的子句，不適合作為答案。(B) therefore 為連接副詞，不能直接連接原形動詞，請特別留意這一點。

選項中只有 (A) rather than（而不是……）和 (C) and also（而且也是）為對等連接詞。根據句型結構，空格連接 to serve 和 confirm，依序列出來信的目的，因此答案要選 (C) and also，表示「此封信證明您已經成功報名，同時也確認貴公司會參加」。

140 形容詞詞彙
「形容詞 vs. 分詞」時，請優先選擇形容詞。

STEP 1 當空格要填入形容詞，選項卻同時出現形容詞和分詞時，請以形容詞為先。

空格要填入形容詞，修飾後方名詞 booths，因此答案為 (D) rental（出租的）。rent 作為名詞使用時，指「租金」；作為動詞使用時，指「出租」，因此 (A) 和 (B) 皆不是答案。

STEP 2 明確選出適合修飾名詞的詞性

❶ 形容詞	＋名詞	→描述名詞的狀態、大小、種類、顏色等一般形容詞。
❷ 過去分詞	＋名詞	→名詞表示分詞意義上的受詞，帶有被動或完成的概念。
❸ 現在分詞	＋名詞	→名詞表示分詞意義上的主詞，帶有主動和進行的概念。
❹ 名詞	＋名詞	→組成複合名詞，指出名詞的類型或種類，前方不能加上冠詞、也不能使用複數形態。

141 句子插入題
請由空格前後方內容確認答題關鍵字。

STEP 1 題目為句子插入題時，請先整理出各選項的關鍵字，再從空格附近找尋關鍵字。

前一句話提到「在 7 月 9 日晚上 9 點以前完成攤位的準備工作」，後方接著補充說明攤位準備工作的相關細節較為適當。因此答案要選 (B)，表示「在這個時間以前（by the time），垃圾和包裝材料也都要（also）清理乾淨」。(D) 提到參展者數量增加、(C) 指出 Rex Toy 公司的位置，皆不適合填入空格中；雖然最終日程表（final schedule）可以與前方提到的時間點做連結，但是前方還提到今年起開始實施，與日程表沒有任何關聯，因此 (A) 也不太適合填入空格中。

(A) 最後的時程表會在我們官網上公布。
(B) 所有的垃圾和包裝材料在這個時間以前都必須清空。
(C) 雷克斯玩具位於我們辦公室旁邊。
(D) 參與者人數在過去十年間增加了。

142 名詞詞彙
從文中找出明確的答題線索後，選出最符合的答案。

STEP 1 確認空格前後的答題線索後，選出同義詞、或是意思最為相近的單字作為答案。

空格位在「感謝您參加我們的 ______」，以此句話作為信件的結尾。第一句話提到此封信為參加 International Toy Fair 的確認信，而與 Fair（博覽會）意思最為相近的單字為 (B) event（活動），故為正確答案。

(A) contest 指兩人以上進行的競爭或競賽、(C) research 的意思為「研究」，皆不適合作為答案。(D) course 指「過程、進程」，不適合代替 fair。

Questions 143-146 refer to the following article.

Jackson City
Educational Committee Approved Funds

通知已核准將經費用於計畫上。

Special community programs with advanced technology —**143**— to the local residents of Jackson City. On Wednesday, the Jackson City Council announced that its "Local Hi-Tech Program" **proposal was approved** by the board of the City Education Committee. —**144**—.

Each community library in the city will be allotted $1,000,000 for the purchase of tablet computers. Library users will be allowed to take home the tablets —**145**— **of the time** for library programs, but they will be available only —**146**— its opening hours. 不可數名詞 可數名詞

143. (A) came
(B) were coming
(C) are coming
(D) come

動詞時態
→ 確認其他動詞的時態和整篇文章的時態。

144. (A) Residents are looking forward to the ~~final decision~~.
(B) The tablets ~~will be donated~~ by local businesses.
(C) The vote took place on Tuesday, August 10.
(D) Nevertheless, the programs will be the same as previous ones.

句子插入題
→ 請由空格前後方內容確認答題關鍵字。

145. (A) none ▶ 否定
(B) many ▶ 複數名詞
(C) all
(D) some

代名詞
→ 選出適當的代名詞表示 of 後方的一部分。

146. (A) at ▶ +時間點
(B) to ▶ +路線、方向
(C) for ▶ +數詞
(D) during ▶ +一段時間

介系詞詞彙
→ 由後方連接的名詞選出適當的介系詞。

第 143-146 題 文章

傑克森市
教育委員會核准經費

結合進階科技的特別社區課程即將來到傑克森市市民面前。傑克森市議會星期三宣布，市政教育委員會已通過市府的「在地高科技課程」計畫，該投票已於 8 月 10 日星期二進行。

市內每間社區圖書館將分配到 1 百萬美元以供採購平板電腦。圖書館的使用民眾獲准基於課程需求，得以在部分時間把平板帶回家，但只有圖書館開放時間內平板才可供借用。

字彙 advanced 進階的　announce 宣布　approve 通過　board 董事會
committee 委員會　allot 分配　available 可供使用的

143 動詞時態
題目為動詞時態題時，請確認其他動詞的時態。

STEP 1 請先確認整篇文章的時態為過去還是未來。

空格所在的句子沒有動詞，因此空格要填入主要動詞。主詞為 programs，空格下句話提到計畫的企畫書已獲核准（was approved），表示往後將施行此計畫。因此答案要選 (C) are coming，以 come 的現在進行式表達未來即將發生的事。

144 句子插入題
請由空格前後方內容確認答題關鍵字。

STEP 1 題目為句子插入題時，請先整理出各選項的關鍵字，再從空格附近找尋關鍵字。

空格前一句話提到計畫已獲教育委員會核准，後方適合連接「投票已於 8 月 10 日星期二舉行」，因此答案為 (C)。

(A) 提到期待 final decision，但是文中已提出結論，因此並不適合；(B) 與計畫獲准的內容無關，應放在第二段針對計畫的說明較為適當；(D) 文中並未提到與 previous ones 相對應的對象，因此不能作為答案。

(A) 市民很期待最終決議出來。
(B) 平板將由當地商家贊助。
(C) 該投票已於 8 月 10 日星期二進行。
(D) 然而，課程會和之前都一樣。

145 代名詞
由 of 後方的名詞確認答案為 one of、most of、all of。

STEP 1 空格要填入不定代名詞，表示 of 後方名詞的一部分。

請依照 of 後方的名詞選出適當的不定代名詞。of 後方的名詞為 the time，為不可數名詞。(B) many 用於表示複數名詞，因此請先刪去此選項。其他的選項皆符合文法規則，但是根據文意，表示「允許在圖書館計畫中的一部分時間，將平板電腦帶回家中」較為適當，因此答案要選 (D) some。

(A) none 表示否定，指「沒有任何的」；(C) all 指所有的時間，看似可以作為答案，但是後方有提到「only . . . its opening hour」，表示僅限特定的時段，因此不能使用 all。

146 介系詞詞彙
由後方連接的名詞選出適當的介系詞。

STEP 1 題目考介系詞時，請先確認空格後方的名詞。

空格後方連接名詞 its opening hour，表示特定一段時間，選項中只有 (D) during 可以連接該名詞。(C) for 也可以連接一段時間，但是用於表達狀態持續一段時間，一般會搭配數詞使用，請特別留意；(A) at 要連接時間點；(B) to 要連接動線或方向，不適合搭配可數名詞使用，請特別留意。

PART 7

Questions 147-148 refer to the following information.

Odessa Culinary Institute Guidelines for filling out a purchase order request

* List product codes if available, and describe the item or items in detail.
* Tick the box marked "No substitutes" if a specific brand is needed, and provide a clear reason in the vicinal space.
* Indicate the name of the supplier including the contact information or Web address.
* Order requests with no signature **will not be processed**, so submit the signed form to the purchasing department.
* Thoroughly look through your expense report.

147 will not be processed → must be provided

Once the order has been filled, the **expense of the purchase** will be allocated to your divisional budget.

148-D the expense of the purchase → funding

陷阱選項 147-B, C, D
並沒有規定要滿足所有的要求事項。

147. According to the information, what detail must be provided in every request?
(A) A signature
(B) A supplier's contact information
(C) A product code
(D) A reason for requesting a particular brand

must be provided／request
→ 從文中找出與關鍵字有關的內容：not be processed

148. What is suggested about the Odessa Culinary Institute's purchasing department?
(A) It ~~has information~~ on local suppliers.
(B) It ~~requires budget reports~~ from every division.
(C) It ~~searches for less expensive~~ items for divisions.
(D) It provides funding to each division's budget.

關鍵字 purchasing department
→ 整理出題目和各選項的關鍵字後，再查看文章的內容。

第 147-148 題 資訊

奧德賽餐飲學院申請採購單的填寫說明

* 盡可能明列產品編號並描述物品或詳述細節。
* 如果需要指定特定品牌，勾選註記「不可替換」的欄位，並在附近空白處提供明確理由。
* 列出供應商的名稱，且包括聯絡資訊和官網網址。
* 訂單如果沒有簽名將不受理，因此請將簽署過後的表單交到採購部門。

* 徹底瀏覽你的經費報告。

訂單一旦填寫，採購費用將分配到你的部門預算裡。

字彙 culinary 餐飲的　fill out 填寫　purchase order 採購單　request 需求
list 列出　product code 產品編號　in detail 仔細地　tick 打勾勾
substitute 替代品　vicinal 鄰近的　thoroughly 徹底地　look through 瀏覽
expense report 支出費用報告　allocate 分配　divisional 部門的

147. 根據文中資訊，在每一次提出請求時，哪項細節是必要的？

(A) 簽名
(B) 供應商的聯絡資訊
(C) 產品編號
(D) 需要特定品牌的原因

STEP 1 答案通常會出現在關鍵字旁。

題目關鍵字為 must be provided in every request，請從內文中找出相關內容，並和選項對照。文中寫道：「Order requests with no signature will not be processed」，提到如果訂購要求上沒有簽名，就沒辦法受理。由此可以得知一定要提供簽名，因此答案為 (A)。

STEP 2 分析錯誤選項

(B) 文中寫道：「Indicate the name of the supplier including the contact information or Web address.」，建議標出供應商的名稱，包含聯絡方式或網址，屬於選填事項，並非必填項目，因此不能作為答案。

(C) 文中寫道：「List product codes if available」，建議提供產品編號，因此也不是一定要提供的項目。

(D) 文中寫道：「if a specific brand is needed」，提到若需要特定品牌的商品，要填寫明確的原因，因此也不是必填項目。

148. 關於奧德賽餐飲學院，文中提到什麼？

(A) 它有當地供應商的資訊。
(B) 它的每個部門都需要提出經費報告。
(C) 它為部門尋找比較不貴的產品。
(D) 它為每一個部門的預算提供經費。

STEP 1 題目要求找出相符的事實時，請先整理出各選項的關鍵字，再查看文章內容。

請從內文中找出與題目關鍵字 purchasing department 相關的內容。文中寫道：「so submit the signed form to the purchasing department」，提到將訂購要求交給採購部門。由此可以得知由採購部門負責處理這類需求。文中還寫道：「the expense of the purchase will be allocated to your divisional budget」，提到會將採購費用撥至部門的預算中。由此可以得知採購部門負責撥出預算提供各部門資金，因此答案為 (D)。

Questions 149-150 refers to the following notice.

Modern Beauty Apparel

149 Item Return → a policy ※ Item Return Requests

- **Within five days of purchase**, customers may return clothes for store credit only. All returns must be accompanied by original receipts.

150 within five days of purchase → a certain period

- Clothes must be in an unused and unworn condition with the attached tags when they are returned.

- Sales of clothes at reduced prices are final. Customer requests for returns or refunds will not be accepted.

陷阱選項 150-A, B
(A) 提到退貨時要提供收據
(B) 只能換成店內抵用金

149. What is the main reason the notice has been posted?
(A) To announce a sales event
(B) To inform customers of a policy
(C) To publicize a recent relocation
(D) To promote a new product

目的／前
→ 選項會採較為籠統的說法表示主旨和目的。

150. What is mentioned about products to be returned?
(A) ~~No~~ receipt is required for some clothes.
(B) ~~Cash~~ refunds may be given to some customers.
(C) The store ~~resells~~ them at discounted prices.
(D) They cannot be returned after a certain period.

關鍵字 products to be returned
→ 刪去與內文不相符的選項。

第 149-150 題 告示

現代美人服裝

※ 退貨需求

– 顧客可在購買五天內將衣服退貨，只能換成店內抵用金。所有退貨均須持原收據辦理。

– 退貨時，衣物須沒有被使用或穿過，且所附標籤完整。

– 特價衣物售出後，顧客要求退貨或退款將不受理。

字彙 return request 退貨需求　within 在……期間內　store credit 店內抵用金
original 當初的；原來的　accompany 伴隨　attach 附帶

149. 張貼告示的主要原因為何？

(A) 宣布拍賣活動　(B) 向顧客告知一項政策
(C) 公告近期搬遷　(D) 推銷新產品

STEP 1 開頭前兩句話有 90% 的機率會出現文章的目的。

本題詢問本篇公告的目的。文中寫道：「Item Return Requests」，提到退貨的要求，接著在下方列出退貨的相關政策規定。由此可以得知本篇公告的目的為告知顧客規定，因此答案為(B)。

STEP 2 答案通常會採換句話說的方式。

選項將文中的 item return requests 改寫成 an policy。

150. 關於被退貨的產品，文中提到什麼？

(A) 部分衣物不需要有收據。　(B) 部分可能可以拿到現金退款。
(C) 店家會用特價重新販賣。　(D) 特定時間過後將不能退貨。

STEP 1 題目要求找出相符的「事實」時，請先整理出各選項的關鍵字，再查看文章內容。

請先整理出各選項的關鍵字，分別為 (A) No receipt；(B) Cash refunds；(C) resells；(D) cannot、a certain period。文中寫道：「Within five days of purchase, customers may return clothes for store credit only.」，提到在購買五日之內，可以退貨，並換成店內抵用金。(D) 指過了特定時間就不能退貨，故為正確答案。選項將文中的 within five days of purchase 改寫成 a certain period。

STEP 2 請找出選項中與內文不符的單字。

(A) 文中寫道：「All returns must be accompanied by original receipts.」，提到退貨時，一定要攜帶收據，因此該敘述有誤。

(B) 文中寫道：「for store credit only」，表示只能退換成店內抵用金，因此該敘述有誤。

(C) 文中並未提到 resells，無法得知是否為轉售。

Questions 151-152 refers to the following article.

BERMONDSEY TOWN, August 11- The council of Bermondsey Town is currently looking through proposals from commercial property developers for establishing a business district on a 31,000-square-meter parcel of land **to the north of town**.

The **business district** is to be located in proximity to **Highway R21**, on the land where some Bermondsey Town companies **once operated**, such as Anerley **Automobile Manufacturer**, Charing Furniture, Inc., and Penge Appliance. 152-C The facilities will use integrated cutting-edge energy-efficient systems. The town also has a plan to build residential apartment complexes in the vicinity of the site within three years.

151 Automobile Manufacturer
→ Vehicles used to be produced

"We are excited about this chance to draw new businesses to our town," said town council member Virgil Valdez. "The business district will be in an excellent location 152-B close to various dining establishments and accommodations, as well as a major transportation system. Once the initial stage of the design is done, space will be divided based on occupants' needs," he added. 152-A Since the region's train station, situated just fifteen kilometers away in Northolt, was expanded, most of the development plans in Bermondsey Town have been expedited.

陷阱選項 152- A, B, C
請刪去內文提到的選項。

151. What is indicated about the northern area of Bermondsey Town?
(A) There ~~was once~~ a train station there.
(B) It ~~has been~~ a residential district.
(C) Vehicles used to be produced there.
(D) An appliance business ~~will start~~ its operations there.

選出相符的事實。
→ 關鍵字為 northern area of Bermondsey Town。

152. What aspect of the business district is NOT stated?
(A) The ~~closest major transportation~~ system
(B) Its ~~vicinity~~ to some ~~dining businesses~~
(C) Its ~~energy-saving building~~ technology
(D) The total number of complexes to be constructed

aspect / Not
→ 看到 NOT question 時，請善用刪去法。

第 151-152 題 文章

伯蒙德鎮 8 月 11 日 ——伯蒙德鎮議會目前正在審閱商用不動產開發商的提案，他們打算在鎮上北部 3 萬 1 千平方公尺的土地上建設商業區。

商業區將設在 R21 公路附近，當地過去曾有一些伯蒙德鎮上的公司營運。像是阿納利汽車製造商、查靈家具股份有限公司和彭奇家電。整體建設將採用高端的整合節能系統。市鎮並有計畫在三年內於鄰近位置建造公寓住宅社區。

「我們很高興鎮上有機會吸引到新公司。」鎮議員維吉爾．瓦爾迪茲表示。「商業區的地點非常棒，不少餐飲、住宿業者以及距離主要運輸系統都很近。」

「一旦初期設計完成，空間會根據廠商需求分配。」他補充說。因為只有 15 公里遠、位於諾霍特的地方火車站擴建了，加快了伯蒙德鎮大部分的發展計畫。

字彙 council 議會　look through 瀏覽；查閱　commercial property 商用不動產
business district 商業區　square-meter 平方公尺　parcel 一塊；一片
in proximity to 靠近　facility 場所　integrate 整合　cutting-edge 高端的
energy-efficient 節能　residential 居住的；住宅的　complex 建築群
vicinity 鄰近地區　draw 吸引　dining establishment 餐飲業
accommodation 住宿業　occupant 占有者；承租者　situate 位於

151. 關於伯蒙德鎮北部，文中提到什麼？

(A) 那裡過去曾有火車站。

(B) 一直以來是住宅區。

(C) 以前在那裡製造交通工具。

(D) 一間家電行將在那裡開業。

STEP 1 關鍵字旁未出現答案時，請確認是否還有其他解題線索。

請先確認題目關鍵字為 the northern area。文中寫道：「The council . . . to the north of town」，提到最近正在審閱在城鎮北部地區設置商業區的提案書。接著寫道：「The business district is to be located in proximity to Highway R21, on the land where some Bermondsey Town companies once operated, such as Anerley Automobile Manufacturer」，表示有關在城鎮北部地區設置商業區，預計會設在 Highway R21 附近，還提到 Highway R21 以前曾設有 Anerley Automobile Manufacturer（汽車製造業者）。由此段話可以得知城鎮北部以前曾為生產汽車的地方，因此答案為 (C)。

STEP 2 分析錯誤選項

(A) 文中寫道：「the region's train station, situated just fifteen kilometers away in Northolt」，僅提到火車站設在距離 15 公里遠的地方，無法得知過去是否有火車站。

(B) 文中寫道：「The town also has a plan to build residential apartment complexes in the vicinity of the site」，僅提到 a residential district，表示預計在附近蓋住宅公寓，無法確認該區域是否為住宅區。

(D) 文中僅提到該區域曾有 Penge Appliance 公司，無法得知是否將有家電業者在此營運。

152. 關於商業區，沒有提及哪一方面的事情？

(A) 最接近的主要運輸系統

(B) 鄰近餐飲業者

(C) 節能建築科技

(D) 總共要興建的建築群數量

STEP 1 **看到 NOT Question 時，請善用刪去法。**

本題詢問文中未提及的選項，因此將內文對照選項內容，刪去相符的敘述後，便能找出答案。

(A)「the region's train station, situated just fifteen kilometers away.」中提到火車站設在距離 15 公里遠的地方。

(B)「The business district will . . . , close to various dining establishments」中提到商業區離餐廳很近。

(C)「The facilities will use integrated cutting-edge energy-efficient systems.」中提到設施將使用最新科技節能系統。

(D) 文中僅提到 complexes，並未提到預計要蓋多少棟建築，因此答案為 (D)。

Questions 153-154 refer to the following text message chain.

●●●○○

Clare Tamika 11:02 A.M.
One of the tenants from the apartment complex at 2642 Sudbury Hill called to inform me that she would like to **move out** at the beginning of June, **but her lease is supposed to end at the end of July**.

153 move out at the beginning of June → early termination of a lease

Lorene Miranda 11:03 A.M.
In that case, according to the lease agreement, tenants wanting to move out before the lease ends have to pay a penalty for the early leave. However, if they can find new tenants right away, occasionally some landlords may waive the penalty. **Why don't you contact the landlord** and ask whether they intend to grant an exemption?

Clare Tamika 11:04 A.M.
Since there are some people currently looking for rental properties in the town on our list, it could be worth trying that.

154

Lorene Miranda 11:05 A.M.
Absolutely, you shouldn't have difficulty finding new tenants as the Sudbury Hill apartment is a very popular one. Keep me informed of the progress.

Clare Tamika 11:07 A.M.
Okay. I will keep in touch.

陷阱選項 153-D
文中僅提到 move，並未提到要搬去其他鄰近的公寓。

153. What is the tenant most likely trying to do?
(A) Request a maintenance service
(B) Make the early termination of a lease
(C) Put a property on the market
(D) Move to ~~a different apartment nearby~~

154. At 11:04 A.M., what does Ms. Tamika most likely mean when she writes, "It could be worth trying that"?
(A) She intends to contact the landlord.
(B) She is aware that a penalty should be charged.
(C) She wants to let the tenant know her responsibility.
(D) She will persuade the landlord to renovate the property.

關鍵字 tenant
→ 請從關鍵字前後找出答題線索。

掌握說話者意圖
→ 掌握指定句前後的文意，並確認指定句中的「that」指的是什麼事。

第 153-154 題 訊息串

克萊爾·塔密加 上午 11:02
薩德伯里丘 2642 號的公寓社區一個住戶打電話通知我說，她想要在六月初搬走，但她的租約應該是七月底才會結束。

羅琳·米蘭達 上午 11:03
這種情況下，根據租約，住戶想要在租約到期前提早搬走需要付違約金。不過，如果他們可以馬上找到新住戶，部分屋主有時候就會不收罰金。妳何不聯絡一下屋主，問問看他們想不想通個人情？

克萊爾·塔密加 上午 11:04
因為在我們名單上，有些人目前正在鎮上找房子租，這蠻值得試試看的。

羅琳·米蘭達 上午 11:05
一點也沒錯，薩德伯里丘公寓社區非常受歡迎，妳找住戶應該不會有困難。有什麼進度隨時通知我。

克萊爾·塔密加 上午 11:07
好的，我會保持聯絡。

字彙 tenant 住戶　complex 建築群　lease agreement 租約　penalty 罰金；違約金
occasionally 有時候　waive 免除　intend to V 打算做……
grant an exemption 給予豁免　property 房地產　worth 值得
keep A informed of B 讓 A 知道 B 的進度　keep in touch 保持聯絡

153. 住戶現在最有可能做什麼？
(A) 要求維修服務
(B) 提早終止租約
(C) 在房市上賣房產
(D) 搬到鄰近的另一間公寓

STEP 1 答案通常會出現在關鍵字旁。

請先確認關鍵字 tenant。文中寫道：「One of the tenants . . . she would like to move out at the beginning of June, but her lease is supposed to end at the end of July」，提到有個房客打算於六月初搬家，但是她的租約到七月底才到期。由此可以得知房客想要提早結束合約，因此答案為 (B)。

STEP 2 分析錯誤選項

(D) 文中僅提到 move，並未提到 a different apartment nearby，無法得知她是否要搬去其他鄰近的公寓。

154. 上午 11:04 時，當塔密加說道「這蠻值得試試看的」，最有可能的意思是？

(A) 她打算聯絡屋主。

(B) 她知道可能要支付罰金。

(C) 她想要讓房客知道她的責任。

(D) 她將說服屋主整修那間房子。

STEP 1 線上聊天文中出現詢問「意圖」的考題時，請確認指定句前後的轉折詞，並選擇較為籠統的敘述作為答案。

前方 Miranda 的訊息寫道：「Why don't you contact the landlord and ask whether they intend to grant an exemption?」。對於此項提議，Tamika 回答：「Since . . . , it could be worth trying that」，由此回覆可以得知指定句中的 that 指的是 Miranda 建議 contact the landlord 一事，而她同意和房東聯絡這項提議。由此可以得知 Tamika 打算和房東聯絡，因此答案為 (A)。

Questions 155-157 refer to the following e-mail.

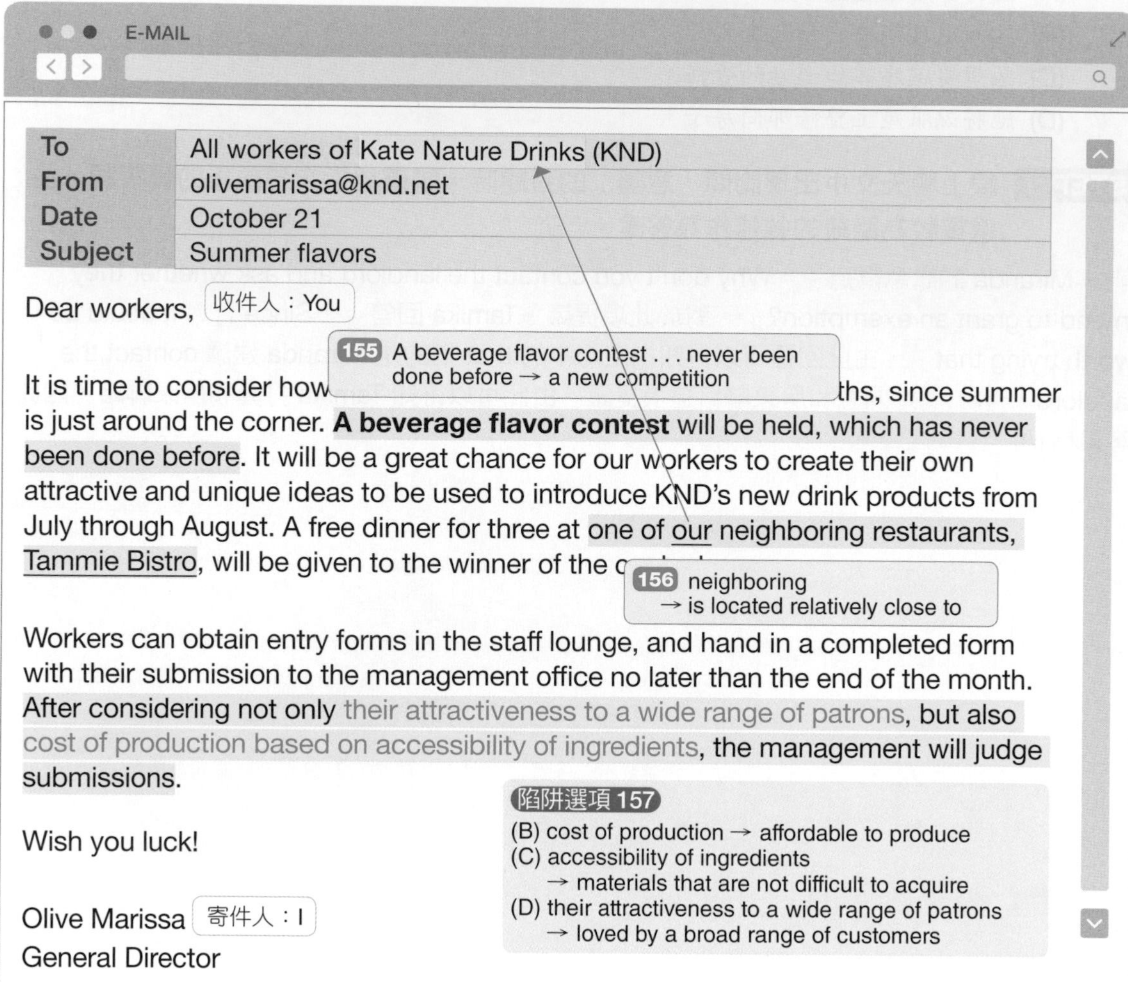

E-MAIL

To	All workers of Kate Nature Drinks (KND)
From	olivemarissa@knd.net
Date	October 21
Subject	Summer flavors

Dear workers, 收件人：You

155 A beverage flavor contest . . . never been done before → a new competition

It is time to consider how ... ths, since summer is just around the corner. **A beverage flavor contest** will be held, which has never been done before. It will be a great chance for our workers to create their own attractive and unique ideas to be used to introduce KND's new drink products from July through August. A free dinner for three at one of our neighboring restaurants, Tammie Bistro, will be given to the winner of the c...

156 neighboring → is located relatively close to

Workers can obtain entry forms in the staff lounge, and hand in a completed form with their submission to the management office no later than the end of the month. After considering not only their attractiveness to a wide range of patrons, but also cost of production based on accessibility of ingredients, the management will judge submissions.

陷阱選項 157
(B) cost of production → affordable to produce
(C) accessibility of ingredients
→ materials that are not difficult to acquire
(D) their attractiveness to a wide range of patrons
→ loved by a broad range of customers

Wish you luck!

Olive Marissa 寄件人：I
General Director

155. What is the main purpose of the e-mail?
(A) To report a recent increase in drink sales
(B) To announce a new production policy
(C) To introduce a new competition
(D) To ~~encourage employees to sample~~ new beverage products

156. What is suggested about Tammie Bistro?
(A) It is only open during summer months.
(B) It is located relatively close to the drink company.
(C) It ~~has recently introduced~~ a new menu item.
(D) It uses ~~seasonal ingredients~~ for its menu.

157. What is NOT stated as a feature of great beverage products?
(A) They should have appealing packaging.
(B) They should be affordable to produce.
(C) They should use materials that are not difficult to acquire.
(D) They should be loved by a broad range of customers.

目的／前
→ 確認前半段文章的內容。

關鍵字 Tammie Bistro
→ 找出文中的關鍵字後，再選出與內文相符的選項。

NOT ／ beverage products 特色
→ 看到 NOT Question 時，請整理出選項的關鍵字，再與內文對照，刪去文中提及的選項。

第 155-157 題 電子郵件

收件人	凱特天然飲全體員工
寄件人	olivemarissa@knd.net
日期	10 月 21 日
主旨	夏季口味

敬愛的員工，

夏季就要到來，該來想想怎麼在這幾個月增加銷量了。我們即將舉行前所未有的飲料風味大賽，這將是個好機會，讓我們員工發想自己的點子、創造吸引人而且獨一無二的飲料，作為凱特天然飲七月到八月推出的新產品。優勝者將獲得鄰近一家餐廳塔米耶餐酒館的三人晚餐免費招待。

員工可以在員工休息區取得參賽表格，填寫好了以後，最晚請在月底前把申請書交到經理辦公室。

申請者將由高層進行評審，不只將考量對於廣大熟客的吸引力，也會根據食材取得難易度來考量成本。

祝好運！

奧麗芙·瑪莉莎
總經理

字彙 just around the corner 即將來臨　beverage 飲料　flavor 口味
obtain 取得　entry form 參賽表　staff lounge 員工休息區　hand in 繳交
submission 申請　management office 經理辦公室
attractiveness 吸引力　a wide range of 範圍廣大的　patron 熟客；老主顧
accessibility 取得難易程度　ingredient 食材

155. 這封電子郵件的主旨為何？
(A) 報告最近飲料銷量增加
(B) 公告新的產品政策
(C) 介紹新的比賽
(D) 鼓勵員工試喝新飲料

STEP 1 開頭前兩句話有 90% 的機率會出現文章的目的。

請由前半段文章的內容確認目的。文中寫道：「A beverage flavor contest will be held, which has never been done before.」，提到將首次舉辦飲料風味大賽。由此可以得知本文的目的為告知大家有新的比賽，因此答案為 (C)。

STEP 2 答案通常會採換句話說的方式。

選項將文中的「A beverage flavor contest will be held, which has never been done before.」改寫成 a new competition。

156. 關於塔米耶餐酒館，文中提到什麼？
(A) 只有在夏天幾個月開張。
(B) 和飲料公司的位置較近。
(C) 最近推出新菜色。
(D) 用季節食材入菜。

STEP 1 **答案通常會出現在關鍵字旁。**

請從文中找出題目關鍵字 Tammie Bistro。文中寫道：「at one of our neighboring restaurants, Tammie Bistro」，提到 Tammie Bistro 為公司附近的餐廳。

STEP 2 **our 指寄件人加上收件人。**

本篇文章為公司高層 Olive Marissa 寄給 Kate Nature Drinks 全體員工的郵件，由此可以得知 our 指的是 Kate Nature Drinks 公司。因此答案要選 (B)，表示餐廳鄰近飲料公司。

157. 關於好飲料的特點，文中沒有提到哪一點？
(A) 包裝必須吸引人。
(B) 製作需要能夠負擔得起。
(C) 要使用不難取得的材料製作。
(D) 要被廣大顧客所愛。

STEP 1 **看到 NOT Question 時，請善用刪去法。**

看到 NOT Question 時，請先確認題目和選項的關鍵字，刪除與內文相符的選項後，便能找出答案。

請先確認題目關鍵字為 a feature of great beverage products。文中寫道：「After considering not only their attractiveness . . . , the management will judge submissions」，提到 (B) affordable to produce、(C) materials that are not difficult to acquire、(D) be loved by a broad range of customers。文中並未提及 (A)，故為正確答案。

STEP 2 **答案通常會採換句話說的方式。**

(B) **cost of production** → affordable to produce
(C) **accessibility of ingredients** → materials that are not difficult to acquire
(D) **attractiveness to a wide range of patrons** → be loved by a broad range of customers

Questions 158-160 refer to the following flyer.

Could you use a holiday?

Come to Birds' Hill!

Several-time Winner of Travel Advice's
"[...] Holiday Spot"

159 several-time
→ more than one time

What Birds' Hill offers!

The beautiful nature! Experience the great views with plenty of wildlife throughout Sloane For[...] 158 You can enjoy **hiking and biking along approximately 20km of trails** around the area. Our experienced guides can help you explore **the beauty of the area's nature** or you can wander on your own.

陷阱選項 160-A, D
僅提到報名後可以參加，並未提到是否要額外收費。

We also have indoor and outdoor **sport facilities** [...]us sports such as football, baseball, tennis, and basketball. Come to our game room and enjoy chess and card games. By registering, you can rent a boat on the lake or experience a horse back ride when the weather is nice.

You can spend the evening reading and unwinding at our modern, relaxing library if you would like to have some quiet time. From the latest best sellers to classic literature, every visitor will be happy with our wide selection. A variety of movies are available, which you can check out and watch at your own place.

160 guided tours → get a guide

With the exception of guided tours, our daily package includes all services and activities provided at Birds' Hill. Please feel free to contact us for further price information.

158. What most likely is Birds' Hill?
(A) A sports facility
(B) A public park
(C) A wildlife preserve
(D) A holiday resort

關鍵字 **Birds' Hill**

159. What is suggested about Birds' Hill?
(A) It offers sport ~~lessons~~ for free.
(B) It is run by a ~~nonprofit organization~~.
(C) It has received awards more than one time.
(D) It has ~~recently opened~~ a movie theater.

選出相符的事實
→ 關鍵字為 Birds' Hill。

160. Why do the visitors probably pay an additional fee?
(A) To ride a horse
(B) To rent a bicycle
(C) To get a guide
(D) To use a boat

additional fee ／ why
→ 請從文中找出與關鍵字 additional 有關的內容。

第 158-160 題 傳單

您假日想要怎麼過？
來鳥之丘吧！
旅遊建議的「必訪假日景點」屢屢奪標

鳥之丘有什麼呢！

美麗的大自然！觀賞美景還有豐富野生動植物遍布的斯隆森林。您可以沿著約 20 公里長的步道享受健行或單車行，我們經驗豐富的嚮導能帶你探索在地自然之美，您也可以自行漫遊。

我們也有室內和戶外的運動設施，您可以從事各種運動，像是足球、棒球、網球和籃球。到我們的遊戲室下棋或玩各式的卡牌遊戲。如果是好天氣，您可以在湖邊登記租船或者體驗騎馬。

如果您想要片刻安靜，可以花一個下午在我們現代、輕鬆的閱覽室裡閱讀放鬆。從最新最暢銷的書籍到古典文學都有，我們的廣泛選書，讓每位來客都很享受。有多種電影可供欣賞，您也可以借回自己的地方看。

除了導覽觀光外，我們的每日包裝行程包括所有鳥之丘提供的服務和活動。欲知更多價格資訊，歡迎隨時聯絡我們。

字彙 several-time 多次的；屢次的 spot 景點 approximately 大約 trail 步道
wander 漫遊 unwind 放鬆 relaxing 輕鬆的 classic literature 古典文學
check out 借出 exception 例外
feel free to V 自在地去做……；隨時歡迎去做……

158. 鳥之丘最有可能是什麼？

(A) 運動設施
(B) 公園
(C) 野生動植物保護區
(D) 度假村

STEP 1 從文中找出明確的答題線索後，選出最符合的答案。

前半段文中寫道：「You can enjoy hiking and biking along approximately 20km of trails around the area. Our experienced guides can help you explore the beauty of the area's nature or you can wander on your own.」，提到可以沿著「二十公里長的步道」健行或騎腳踏車，還有導遊帶你一同探索「自然之美」。

另外還寫道：「We also have indoor and outdoor sport facilities . . . 」，提到室內和戶外都設有「運動設施」。綜合上述線索，可以推測出 Birds' Hill 應為公園，因此答案為 (B)。

159. 關於鳥之丘，文中提到什麼？

(A) 免費提供運動課程。

(B) 由非營利組織經營。

(C) 多次獲獎。

(D) 最近新開了電影院。

STEP 1 題目要求找出相符的「事實」時，請先整理出各選項的關鍵字，再查看文章內容。

請先整理出各選項的關鍵字，分別為 (A) sport lessons；(B) nonprofit organization；(C) awards；(D) opened a movie theater，再從文中找出相關敘述。標題寫道：「Several-time Winner」，表示得過很多次獎，因此答案要選 (C)。

STEP 2 分析錯誤選項

雖然文中有提到 sport facilities，但是並沒有提到不用收費，因此 (A) 的敘述有誤；(B) 文中未提及任何相關內容；(D) 文中僅提到可以看電影，無法得知電影院是否為最近開幕。

160. 遊客為什麼有可能要額外付費？

(A) 去騎馬

(B) 去租腳踏車

(C) 去找嚮導

(D) 去使用船

STEP 1 答案通常會出現在關鍵字旁。

請先確認題目關鍵字為 an additional fee。文中寫道：「With the exception of guided tours, our daily package includes all services and activities provided at Birds' Hill.」，提到一日行程除了導遊導覽之外，包含其他所有的服務和活動的費用。由此段話可以推測出申請嚮導導覽需要額外付費，因此答案為 (C)。

STEP 2 分析錯誤選項

文中僅提到報名後可以參加 (A) ride a horse 和 (D) use a boat，無法確定是否要額外付費。

Questions 161-163 refer to the following e-mail.

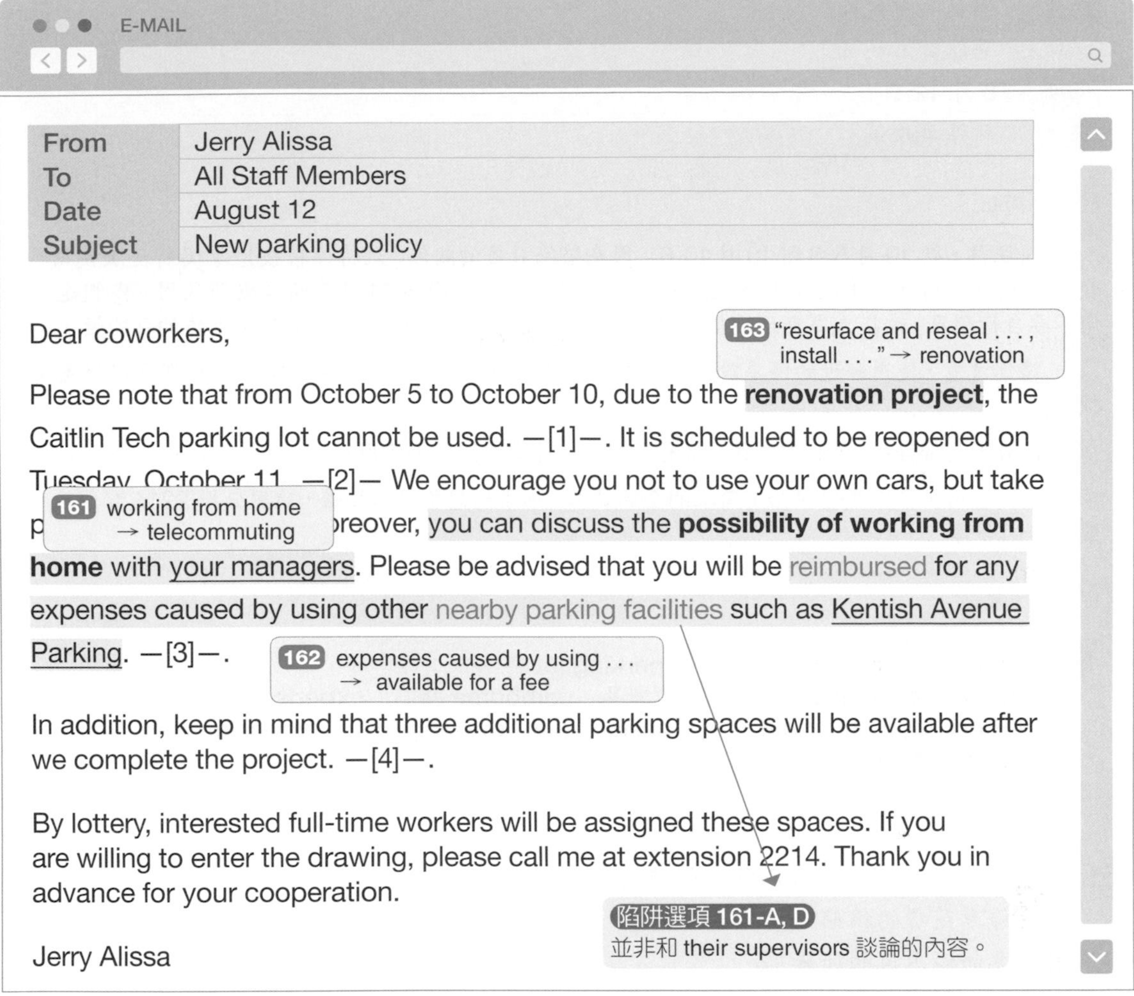

E-MAIL

From	Jerry Alissa
To	All Staff Members
Date	August 12
Subject	New parking policy

Dear coworkers,

Please note that from October 5 to October 10, due to the **renovation project**, the Caitlin Tech parking lot cannot be used. —[1]—. It is scheduled to be reopened on Tuesday, October 11. —[2]— We encourage you not to use your own cars, but take p[...]. Moreover, you can discuss the **possibility of working from home** with your managers. Please be advised that you will be reimbursed for any expenses caused by using other nearby parking facilities such as Kentish Avenue Parking. —[3]—.

161 working from home → telecommuting
162 expenses caused by using . . . → available for a fee

In addition, keep in mind that three additional parking spaces will be available after we complete the project. —[4]—.

By lottery, interested full-time workers will be assigned these spaces. If you are willing to enter the drawing, please call me at extension 2214. Thank you in advance for your cooperation.

Jerry Alissa

161. According to the e-mail, what can workers talk about with their supervisors?
(A) The reimbursement for parking expenses
(B) Participating in a lottery drawing for a parking space
(C) The likelihood of telecommuting
(D) Finding nearby parking facilities

關鍵字 their supervisors
→ 從文中找出關鍵字後，再選出與內文相符的選項。

162. What is indicated about Kentish Avenue Parking?
(A) It is owned by Caitlin Tech.
(B) It will be reopened on October 11.
(C) It has lately been renovated.
(D) It is available for a fee.

關鍵字 Kentish Avenue Parking
→ 從文中找出關鍵字後，再選出與內文相符的選項。

163. In which of the positions marked [1], [2], [3], and [4] does the following sentence best belong?
"We plan to resurface and reseal the parking lot, and install a new fence."
(A) [1] (B) [2] (C) [3] (D) [4]

句子插入題
→ 從上下文確認答題線索。

第 161-163 題 電子郵件

寄件人	傑利．阿麗莎
收件人	全體員工
日期	8 月 12 日
主旨	新停車政策

敬愛的同仁，

請注意，從 10 月 5 日到 10 月 10 日，因為整修計畫的關係，凱特林科技停車場將無法使用。我們計劃重整路面和重劃停車格，並安裝防護欄。預計在 10 月 11 日星期二重新啟用。我們建議您不要自行開車，改搭大眾交通運輸工具。此外，您也可以和您的主管討論在家工作的可能性。

請您注意，使用鄰近的停車設施，像是肯提許大道停車場，所產生的任何開銷都可以報支請款。

此外，也請留意，等到完工後，將有另外三個停車空間可供使用。

空間會用抽籤方式安排給有需求的全職員工。如果您想要參加抽籤，請用分機 2214 聯繫我。感謝您的合作。

傑利．阿麗莎

字彙 note 注意　renovation 整修　parking lot 停車位；停車格
public transportation 大眾運輸工具　reimburse 補貼　expense 支出
lottery 抽籤　full-time 全職　assign 安排　drawing 抽籤　extension 擴展；擴建
cooperation 合作

161. 根據電子郵件，員工可以和主管談論什麼事？
(A) 停車花費的報銷
(B) 參加停車位的抽籤
(C) 在家工作的可能性
(D) 找附近的停車設施

STEP 1 答案通常會出現在關鍵字旁。

請先確認題目關鍵字為 their supervisors。文中寫道：「you can discuss the possibility of working from home with your managers」，your managers 指的就是 their supervisors，當中提到員工可以和主管討論可否在家工作，因此答案為 (C)。

STEP 2 答案通常會採換句話說的方式。

答案選項將文中的 working from home 改寫成 telecommuting。雖然文中有提到 (A) The reimbursement for parking expenses 和 (D) nearby parking facilities，但是並不是要和主管談論的內容。

162. 關於肯提許大道停車場，文中提到什麼？

(A) 為凱特林科技所有。

(B) 將在 **10** 月 **11** 日重新啟用。

(C) 近期剛剛整修好。

(D) 可供付費使用。

STEP 1 答案通常會出現在關鍵字旁。

請先確認題目關鍵字為 Kentish Avenue Parking。文中寫道：「any expenses caused by using other nearby parking facilities such as Kentish Avenue Parking」，提到停在鄰近的收費停車場，例如 Kentish Avenue Parking。由此可以得知 Kentish Avenue Parking 要付費才能停車，因此答案為 (D)。

163. 下列句子最適合擺在 [1]、[2]、[3]、[4] 哪一處？

「我們計劃重整路面和重劃停車格，並安裝防護欄。」？

(A) [1]

(B) [2]

(C) [3]

(D) [4]

STEP 1 題目為句子插入題時，請由空格前後方內容確認答題關鍵字。

要插入空格的指定句為「We plan to resurface and reseal the parking lot, and install a new fence.」，為停車場翻修工程計畫的相關細節。[1] 前方寫道：「due to the renovation project, the Caitlin Tech parking lot cannot be used」，提到 Caitlin Tech 停車場正在進行翻修工程，無法使用。指定句適合放在提及翻修工程 [1] 的後方，因此答案要選 (A)。

Questions 164-167 refer to the following article.

The Communication Fair Plans Announced by Pauline

SOUTHFIELD (23. July)- Pauline, one of the leading conglomerates in the communication industry, announced yesterday that they are not going to introduce its newest mobile phone lines at this quarter's two-day-long Southfield Communication Fair in October. —[1]—.

The fair has been generally considered one of the most **integral** events 165 this quarter for the communication industry, in which the country's leading companies hold well-prepared presentations to boast about their latest collections. The fair has brought in much media attention and been popul 167 「hence」的依據 rsonnel. These days, however, interest of the general public has not been as strong as it used to be. —[2]—.

The CEO of Pauline, Rhonda Webb, clearly said at the press conference in the main office that the determination to skip this quarter's presentation at the fair does not reflect that Pauline will give up participating in the event. —[3]—. "We will have no public presentation, but there will be busines

164 through social media, Web site → Use the Internet

retail deale Webb added. "**In order to publicize our latest mobile phones and services**, we will intentionally expose the public to them not only through **social media** but also through our **main Web site** during the fair."

Ms. Webb replied, when asked about the new marketing strategy, that Pauline aims to increase interest in its new items and services through giving information to present users before launching them to the public. Moreover, by forgoing showing off its new items and services at the fair, Pauline will be able to **avoid being rated by consumers in comparison to its competitors**. "People will enjoy the

166 avoid being rated → reluctant to be evaluated

cts on its own 4]—.

164. According to the article, what will Pauline do during the Communication Fair?

(A) ~~Hold~~ a press conference
(B) ~~Film~~ a presentation to post on its Web site
(C) Use the Internet to promote new products
(D) ~~Collaborate~~ with other companies in presentations

165. In the article, the word "integral" in paragraph 2, line 2, is closest in meaning to

(A) complete
(B) incorporated
(C) significant
(D) installed

關鍵字 Pauline ／ during the Communication Fair

→ 從關鍵字前後找出答題線索。

選出同義詞

→ 確認該單字前後的句子。

166. What is the main reason Pauline intends to use the new strategy?
(A) It is looking for a site for the ~~next quarter's fair~~.
(B) Its ~~marketing budget~~ has been cut.
(C) Its new products and services are ~~not ready yet~~.
(D) It is reluctant to be evaluated against other companies.

關鍵字 use the new strategy
→ 整理出題目和選項的關鍵字後，再查看文章的內容。

167. In which of the positions marked [1], [2], [3], and [4] does the following sentence best belong?
"Professionals in the industry, hence, did not seem surprised at Pauline's announcement."
(A) [1] **(B) [2]**
(C) [3] (D) [4]

句子插入題
→ 確認句中的指示代名詞和轉折詞：hence。

第 164-167 題 文章

寶琳企業宣布通訊大展計畫

南菲爾德（7 月 23 日）——通訊業主要集團寶琳企業昨天宣布，將不會在 10 月為期兩天的南菲爾德通訊當季大展上介紹他們最新的手機產品。

這個大展被普遍認為是通訊業者非常重要的當季活動。大展上國內各大領導企業將播映精心準備的簡報以推銷最新的商品系列。大展向來吸引大量媒體關注且大受業界人士的喜愛。然而近日來一般民眾的興趣已不可同日而語。似乎也是因為如此，寶琳企業的聲明並沒有讓業界專業人士感到意外。

寶琳執行長朗達・韋伯在總部記者會上明確表示，決定跳過這季的簡報並不代表寶琳企業放棄參展。「我們沒有公開簡報，但在展上我們還是會和零售商和配送夥伴召開相關的商務會議。」韋伯補充。「為了宣傳最新款手機和最新服務，我們不只將特意透過社群媒體，也會在大展期間透過我們官網讓大家知道。」

韋伯女士被問到新的市場策略時答道，寶琳在公開亮相前率先把資訊呈現給使用者，目標是要讓新品和新服務受到更多關注。而且，寶琳放棄在大展上炫耀新品和新服務，也能夠避免被消費者用來和競爭業者比較。「人們將能親身體驗寶琳的新產品。」韋伯強調。

字彙 conglomerate 集團 quarter 一季 integral 不可或缺的
boast 吹捧；以……為傲 personnel 人員 general public 一般大眾
press conference 記者會 main office 總部 skip 跳過 retail dealer 零售商
distribution 配送 publicize 公布；宣傳 intentionally 特意地
expose 使……接觸到 launch 新品發表 forgo 放棄
show off 吸引大家注意；炫耀 rate 評比 in comparison to 和……做比較

164. 根據文章，寶琳在通訊大展將會做什麼？

(A) 召開記者會

(B) 側錄簡報把影片放在官網

(C) 用網路推銷新產品

(D) 和其他公司合作做簡報

STEP 1 答案通常會出現在關鍵字旁。

請從文中找出題目關鍵字 Pauline do during the Communication Fair。

The CEO of Pauline 所說的話為：「In order to publicize our latest mobile phones and services, we will intentionally expose the public to them not only through social media but also through our main Web site during the fair.」，提到為了宣傳最新的手機和服務，將在展覽期間利用社群媒體和網站來展示自家產品。由此段話可以得知在展覽期間，Pauline 公司將利用網路宣傳新產品，因此答案為 (C)。

STEP 2 分析錯誤選項

已經開過記者會，因此 (A) 的敘述有誤；文中提到不會進行簡報，因此 (B) 和 (D) 也不正確。

165. 文中第二段、第二行的單字「integral」，意思最接近下列何者？

(A) 完全的

(B) 合併的

(C) 重要的

(D) 安裝好的

STEP 1 題目考同義詞時，要根據前後文意，選出最適合替換的單字。

請務必要確認該單字在句中所使用的意思，以便找出最適合替換的選項，千萬不能直接選擇與 integral 意思相同的單字。根據文意，句子的意思為展覽被視為最「重要的」活動之一。integral 最適合換成選項中的 significant，因此答案要選 (C)。

166. 寶琳使用新策略的主因為何？

(A) 正在找下一季大展的位置。

(B) 行銷預算被砍了。

(C) 新產品和服務還沒準備好。

(D) 不願被拿來和其他公司評比。

STEP 1 答案通常會採換句話說的方式。

請從文中找出題目關鍵字 new strategy。文中寫道：「Ms. Webb replied, when asked about the new marketing strategy」，提到 Webb 回答了新的市場策略。

後方又寫道：「by forgoing showing off our new items and services at the fair, Pauline will be able to avoid being rated by consumers in comparison to its competitors」，提到 Pauline 公司不會在展覽上展示新的產品和服務，如此一來可以避免消費者拿自家產品與其他競爭公司作比較。

由此段話可以得知，Pauline 公司使用新市場策略是因為不願和其他公司作比較，因此答案為 (D)。選項將文中的 avoid being rated 改寫成 reluctant to be evaluated。

167. 下列句子最適合擺在 [1]、[2]、[3]、[4] 哪一處？
「似乎也是因為如此，賓琳企業的聲明並沒有讓業界專業人士感到意外。」？

(A) [1]　(B) [2]　(C) [3]　(D) [4]

STEP 1 「句子」插入題的解題關鍵為空格前後的轉折詞。

請務必一併確認空格前後方出現的轉折詞，以便插入適當的空格中。商業文章習慣會一次說明完一種資訊，因此請確認每一段的主題，並將句子插入最適當的段落。

指定句中出現 hence，請找出與此相對應的原因。[2] 前方寫道：「however, interest of the general public has not been as strong as it used to be」，提到已經不像過去一樣能引起大眾的興趣。由此可以得知指定句適合填入 [2]，表示導致產生 hence 後方所連接的內容，因此答案要選 (B)。

Questions 168-171 refer to the following information.

Amersham Communication, Ltd.
Weekly Discussion

In the business world, havin[168 efficient way to accomplish that goal → work more efficiently]s can be a good approach to getting jobs pro... to use staff members' time in the most productive way. In order to help to find the **most efficient way to accomplish that goal**, here are a few questions to consider.

"What is the main reason for having a meeting?"
There must be a clear purpose of a meeting that could **lead employees to reach an agreement on a common issue**, to improve their business abilities, and to find out [169 reach an agreement on a common issue → make a decision] ...plishments. But holding a meeting only to address ...ded.

"When is the most appropriate time to meet?" 170
It is natural to put off a meeting when **important data and figures** are not ready **or** an **essential person** is not able to attend. However, the meeting should not be called off if doing so is not unavoidably necessary.

"Are there any other alternatives for how to reach the goal?"
E-mail can be an excellent **way to be debriefed on information or report** updates. If only a few team members are re[171 be debriefed → be reported]would be better to hold an informal small gathering at a location every member can easily access.

"What will occur if the meeting does not take place?"
Prior to calling off or rescheduling the meeting, it is important to think about what would happen. What could be missed? Would the cancellation provoke any issues among other participants or managers? You have to check whether there is enough information for members to have the task completed or find a better solution if they suggest that the meeting is not necessary.

168. What is the information about?

(A) What the best way to make a speech is
(B) How customer satisfaction can be increased
(C) Why more employees need to be hired
(D) How employees can work more efficiently

開頭前兩句話會談到目的。
→ 確認前半段文章。

169. What is mentioned as an ideal reason to schedule a meeting?

(A) To ~~deliver~~ general ~~information~~
(B) To help employees make a decision
(C) To hold a ~~training session~~ for new hires
(D) To promote positive ~~relationships~~ among ~~employees~~

關鍵字 reason to schedule a meeting
→ 從文中找出關鍵字後，再選出與內文相符的選項。

170. The word "essential", in paragraph 3, line 2, is closest in meaning to

(A) fundamental (B) intrinsic
(C) critical (D) simple

選出同義詞
→ 確認該單字前後的句子。

171. According to the information, how should information be reported?

(A) By contacting employees ~~by telephone~~
(B) By e-mailing employees messages
(C) By ~~sending letters~~ to staff members
(D) By ~~publishing~~ a weekly ~~newsletter~~

How should ／ be reported
→ 找出提及方法 way 的句子。

第 168-171 題 資訊

阿默舍姆通訊股份有限公司
每週討論

在商業界，和同事或客戶開會是能讓工作確切完成的好方法。然而，重要的是要能最大效用地使用員工的時間。為了找到最有效率的方法來達成目標，得考慮以下幾個問題。

「開會的主要原因是什麼？」

必須要有明確的會議目的，其可引導員工針對共同議題達成協議、改善他們的業務能力、或是找出達到成就的更好方法。但如果只是為了說明不迫切的新狀況，應該要避免舉行會議。

「何時最適合開會？」

如果重要的數據和圖表還沒準備好、或是重要人物無法出席，推遲會議是自然而然的事。然而，除非有無法避免的情事，否則不應該取消開會。

「有替代方案來達成目標嗎？」

電子郵件是匯報資訊或報告進度非常好的方法。如果需要參加會議的團隊成員很少，那麼在每個人都很容易到達的地點舉行非正式的小型會議比較好。

「如果沒有開會，將會發生什麼事？」

取消或重新安排會議之前，應當思考會發生什麼事。會錯過什麼？取消會不會造成與會人士或主管的麻煩？如果大家建議沒有必要開會，必須確保資訊是否充分讓每位成員完成任務、或是找到更好的解決方法。

字彙 approach 方法　productive 有效用的　efficient 有效率的　accomplish 完成　reach an agreement 達成協議　address 說明　urgent 迫切的　put off 推遲　figure 圖表　call off 取消　debrief 聽取匯報　provoke 導致

168. 這則資訊談的是什麼？

(A) 發表演說最好的方法

(B) 如何讓客戶感到更滿意

(C) 為什麼需要聘僱更多員工

(D) 如何讓員工工作更有效率

STEP 1 開頭前兩句話有 90% 的機率會出現文章的目的。

本題詢問文章的主旨和目的。本篇文章類型為 information，前半段寫道：「In order to help to find the most efficient way to accomplish that goal, here are a few questions to consider.」，提到藉由以下幾個問題，幫助大家找出達成目標最有效率的方法。由此可以得知本篇文章談論的是員工該如何增進工作效率，因此答案為 (D)。

STEP 2 答案通常會採換句話說的方式。

答案選項將文中的 the most efficient way to accomplish the goal 改寫成 work more efficiently。

169. 文中提到了哪個非常適合安排開會的理由？

(A) 宣布整體資訊

(B) 協助員工做決定

(C) 為新進員工舉辦訓練課程

(D) 正向提昇員工的人際關係

STEP 1 答案通常會出現在關鍵字旁。

請先確認題目關鍵字為 an ideal reason to schedule a meeting。整理出各選項的關鍵字分別為 (A) deliver、information；(B) help、make a decision；(C) training session；(D) relationship、employees 之後，再從提及題目關鍵字的地方找出相關內容。

文中寫道：「There must be a clear purpose of a meeting that could lead employees to reach an agreement on a common issue」，提到開會的目的為協助員工在合作議題上達成共識。由此段話可以得知安排會議的理由應為協助員工做決定，因此答案為 (B)。

STEP 2 答案通常會採換句話說的方式。

答案選項將文中的 reach an agreement on a common issue 改寫成 make a decision。

170. 文中第三段、第二行的「essential」，意思最接近下列何者？

(A) 根本的

(B) 內在的

(C) 關鍵性的

(D) 簡單的

STEP 1 同義詞考題考的並非只是找出意思相同的單字。

同義詞考題中的選項通常都是該單字的同義詞，因此請確認該單字在句中所使用的意思，以便找出最適合替換的選項，千萬不能直接選出意思相同的單字。

單字所在句子為：「It is natural to put off a meeting when important data and figures are not ready or an essential person is not able to attend.」，提到如果尚未準備好重要資料或數據，或者當中有「重要的」人無法參加會議時，自然會將會議延期。因此答案要選 (C) critical，意思為「重要、重大的」。

171. 根據文中資訊，資訊應該怎麼報告？

(A) 用電話聯絡員工

(B) 寄電子郵件訊息給員工

(C) 寄信給員工

(D) 發行每週業務通訊

STEP 1 答案通常會出現在關鍵字旁。

請先確認題目關鍵字為 how 和 be reported。文中寫道：「Email can be an excellent way to be debriefed on information or report updates」，提到欲提供資料或更新報告書時，傳送電子郵件是一種極佳的方式。由此可以得知文中建議透過電子郵件傳遞資料，因此答案為 (B)。

STEP 2 分析錯誤選項

文中並未提及 (A)、(C)、(D) 的內容。

Questions 172-175 refer to the following online chat discussion.

●●●○○

Jillian Araceli 1:12 P.M.
Good afternoon, everyone. Is there any news on the Fulham Community Park proposal we submitted last week?

Tammy Woods 1:13 P.M.
I contacted Ms. Fulham yesterday. She told me that the final decision was to be made by Tuesday, but I haven't heard from her yet.

Jillian Araceli 1:14 P.M.

172 soil, flower, plants → Landscaping

That's sooner than expected. Although the **soil** has been prepared, unless the **flowers** and **plants** are ordered by today, they won't arrive in time for the deadline she asked.

Maggie Wilson 1:15 P.M.
We've already put in the order. We placed it this afternoon.

Jillian Araceli 1:15 P.M.
That's not really good. If we are not awarded the contract, we are required to pay for them even though they are not necessary any more. **Do we have enough time** to cancel the order before they are shipped to us?

173

Maggie Wilson 1:16 P.M.
I believe they may choose us again as they contracted us last year. Let me see.

Jillian Araceli 1:17 P.M.
Tammy, could you call Ms. Fulham and check how it is going?

Maggie Wilson 1:17 P.M.
No need to worry. **We can call off the order** by this evening with no cancellation fee.

175 call off the order → withdraw an order

Tammy Woods 1:18 P.M.
I think we should, Jillian. I just talked with **Mr. Kim** on the phone. He told me they closed the deal, but **Ms. Fulham chose to work with Richmond Family**.

174 Ms. Fulham chose to work with Richmond Family → another company won the contract

Jillian Araceli 1:19 P.M.
That's a shame. But let's not be disappointed. There should be better jobs waiting for us.

172. What type of industry do the people most likely work in?
(A) News media
(B) Landscaping
(C) Business consulting
(D) Career development

people／職業
→ 確認訊息中提及職業的句子。

173. At 1:16 P.M., what does Ms. Wilson mean she will do when she says, "Let me see"?
(A) Pay for ~~shipment~~
(B) Draft an ~~estimate~~
(C) Check a schedule
(D) Call off a delivery

掌握說話者意圖
→ 確認指定句前後的文意。

174. Why did Mr. Kim contact Ms. woods?
(A) ~~To order~~ more supplies
(B) To notify her that another company won the contract
(C) To inform her that ~~Ms. Fulham is not available~~
(D) To let her know about ~~an extra fee~~

關鍵字 Mr. Kim
→ 從出文中找出關鍵字後，再選出與內文相符的選項。

175. What will Ms. Wilson most likely do next?
(A) ~~Revise~~ a proposal
(B) ~~Contact~~ Ms. Fulham to thank her
(C) Withdraw an order
(D) ~~Call~~ a managerial meeting

Ms. Wilson／未來／後
→ 從後半段文中找出 Wilson 之後要做的事。

第 172-175 題 線上聊天

吉利安・阿瑞切利 下午 1:12
大家午安，我們上星期提交的富勒姆社區公園一案，有任何消息嗎？

湯米・伍茲 下午 1:13
我昨天聯絡了富勒姆女士，她跟我說星期二會做出最後決定，但她還沒給我答覆。

吉利安・阿瑞切利 下午 1:12
這比預期來得快。泥土雖然準備好了，但除非今天訂好花和植物，否則會趕不上她要的期限。

瑪姬・威爾森 下午 1:15
我們已經下好訂單了，今天下午下單的。

吉利安・阿瑞切利 下午 1:15
這真的不太妥，如果合約沒有批給我們，這些就沒用了，可是我們還是得為它們付錢。在它們寄來以前，時間夠我們取消訂單嗎？

瑪姬・威爾森 下午 1:16
我相信他們會再次選擇我們，畢竟他們去年也讓我們承包，讓我看看。

吉利安・阿瑞切利 下午 1:17
湯米，可以請你打給富勒姆女士確認狀況如何嗎？

瑪姬・威爾森 下午 1:17
不需要擔心，我們可以在今晚取消訂單也不用付註銷費。

湯米・伍茲 下午 1:18
我想我們得這麼辦，吉利安。我剛剛和金先生通電話，他告訴我結案了，可是富勒姆女士選擇和李奇蒙家族合作。

吉利安・阿瑞切利 下午 1:19
真遺憾，不過不要沮喪，還有更好的案子等著我們。

字彙 community 社區 soil 土壤 in time 準時 put in the order 提出訂單
award the contract 批出合約 ship 運送 cancellation fee 註銷費
close the deal 完成交易；結案 That's a shame. 真遺憾；真慚愧

172. 這些人最有可在哪個產業工作？

(A) 新聞媒體 (B) 景觀美化
(C) 企業諮詢 (D) 職涯發展

STEP 1 **從文中找出明確的答題線索後，選出最符合的答案。**

本題詢問文中人物的職業。文中寫道：「Although the soil has been prepared, unless the flowers and plants are ordered by today.」，提及明確的線索 soils、flowers、plants。由此可以推測出他們從事的工作與園藝造景有關，因此答案要選 (B)。

173. 下午 1:16 時，威爾森女士說「讓我看看」，意指她要做什麼？

(A) 付運費　(B) 擬估價
(C) 確認行程　(D) 取消送貨

STEP 1 **線上聊天文中出現詢問「意圖」的考題時，請確認指定句前後的轉折詞，並選擇較為籠統的敘述作為答案。**

Araceli 在訊息中寫道：「Do we have enough time to cancel the order before they are shipped to us?」，之後 Wilson 對此問題回答：「Let me see.」，由此可以得知 Wilson 將確認是否有足夠的時間取消訂單，因此答案為 (C)。

174. 金先生為什麼聯絡伍茲女士？

(A) 訂更多產品　(B) 通知她另一家公司贏走合約
(C) 告知她富勒姆女士沒空　(D) 讓她知道有額外費用

STEP 1 **答案通常會出現在關鍵字旁。**

Woods 在訊息中寫道：「I just talked with Mr. Kim on the phone. He told me they closed the deal, but Ms. Fulham chose to work with Richmond Family.」，提到她剛和 Kim 通過電話，得知他們公司成功獲得那筆生意，Fulham 決定和 Richmond Family 共事。由此段話可以得知 Kim 打電話給 Woods 是為了告訴她與別家公司成功簽約一事，因此答案為 (B)。

STEP 2 **分析錯誤選項**

(C) Ms. Fulham is not available 是指 Fulham 女士沒有空，並非答案。

175. 威爾森女士接下來最有可能做什麼？

(A) 修改提案　(B) 聯絡富勒姆女士感謝她
(C) 取消一份訂單　(D) 召開主管會議

STEP 1 **內文會告知明確的資訊，但是答案會採較為籠統的方式敘述。**

本題詢問 Wilson 之後要做什麼事。Wilson 在訊息中寫道：「We can call off the order by this evening with no cancellation fee.」，提到今晚以前都可以免費取消訂單。

而後 Woods 在訊息中寫道：「I just talked with Mr. Kim on the phone. He told me they closed the deal, but Ms. Fulham chose to work with Richmond Family.」，提到沒能成功取得和 Fulham 的合約。由此段話可以推測出 Wilson 將負責取消訂單，因此答案為 (C)。

STEP 2 **分析錯誤選項**

文中提到已經提交企畫書，因此 (A) 的敘述不正確；文中並未提到 (B) 和 (D) 的內容，因此也不適合作為答案。

Questions 176-180 refer to the following e-mails.

E-MAIL 1

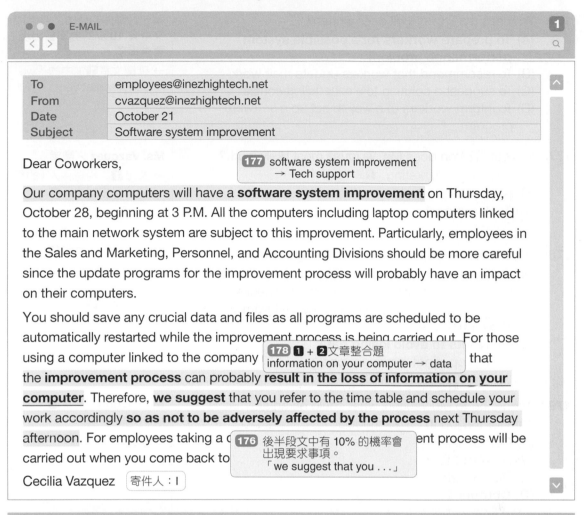

To	employees@inezhightech.net
From	cvazquez@inezhightech.net
Date	October 21
Subject	Software system improvement

Dear Coworkers,

177 software system improvement → Tech support

Our company computers will have a **software system improvement** on Thursday, October 28, beginning at 3 P.M. All the computers including laptop computers linked to the main network system are subject to this improvement. Particularly, employees in the Sales and Marketing, Personnel, and Accounting Divisions should be more careful since the update programs for the improvement process will probably have an impact on their computers.

You should save any crucial data and files as all programs are scheduled to be automatically restarted while the improvement process is being carried out. For those using a computer linked to the company [178 1 + 2 文章整合題 information on your computer → data] that the **improvement process** can probably **result in the loss of information on your computer**. Therefore, **we suggest** that you refer to the time table and schedule your work accordingly **so as not to be adversely affected by the process** next Thursday afternoon. For employees taking a [176 後半段文中有 10% 的機率會出現要求事項。「we suggest that you . . .」] ent process will be carried out when you come back to

Cecilia Vazquez 寄件人：I

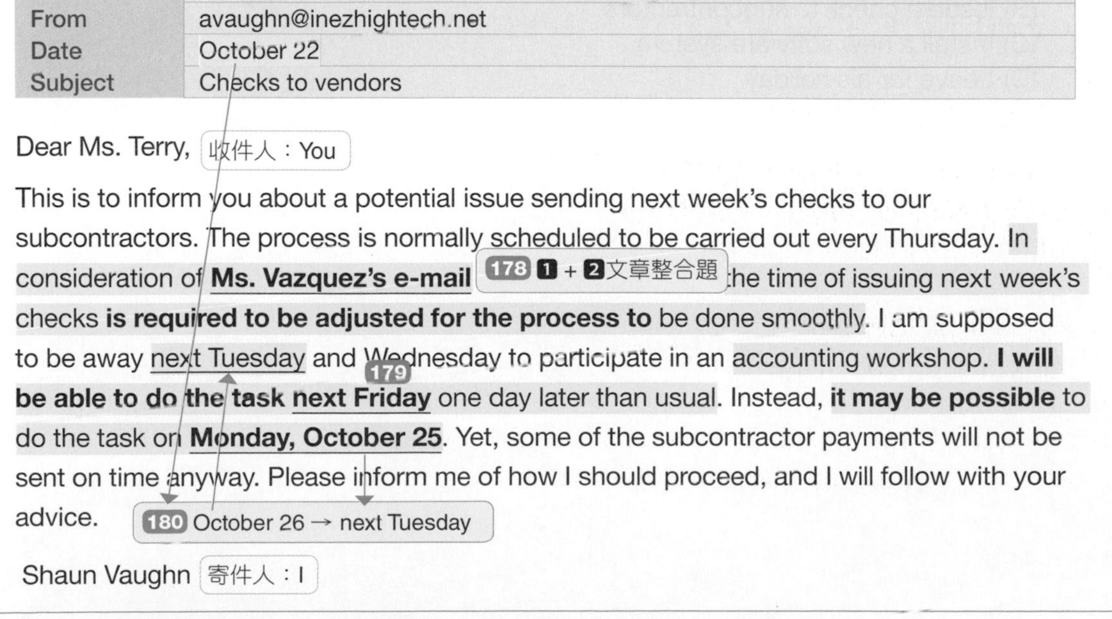
E-MAIL 2

To	jterry@inezhightech.net
From	avaughn@inezhightech.net
Date	October 22
Subject	Checks to vendors

Dear Ms. Terry, 收件人：You

This is to inform you about a potential issue sending next week's checks to our subcontractors. The process is normally scheduled to be carried out every Thursday. In consideration of **Ms. Vazquez's e-mail** [178 1 + 2 文章整合題] the time of issuing next week's checks **is required to be adjusted for the process to** be done smoothly. I am supposed to be away next Tuesday and Wednesday to participate in an accounting workshop. **I will be able to do the task next Friday** one day later than usual. Instead, **it may be possible** to do the task on **Monday, October 25**. Yet, some of the subcontractor payments will not be sent on time anyway. Please inform me of how I should proceed, and I will follow with your advice.

179

180 October 26 → next Tuesday

Shaun Vaughn 寄件人：I

TEST 3 PART 7 中譯&解析

176. Why has the first e-mail been written?

(A) To prepare workers for a possible system performance problem

(B) To recommend that workers update their work

(C) To suggest a solution to a ~~scheduling conflict~~

(D) To inform workers of ~~a way to set up~~ a software program

第一封郵件的目的／後半段文中有 **10%** 的機率會出現要求事項。

→ 確認文章❶當中的「we suggest that you . . .」。

177. In what division does Ms. Vazquez most likely work?

(A) Sales and Marketing ❶當中的寄件人：I

(B) Accounting

(C) Tech support

(D) Personnel

Ms. Vazquez ／職業

→ 文章❶：從寄件人 I 的相關資訊中找出答案。

❷當中的寄件人：I

178. What most likely is the reason Mr. Vaughn intends to reschedule a job?

(A) He wants to adjust the time of issuing checks.

(B) He received a prompt payment request from subcontractors.

(C) He wants to avoid losing data.

(D) His laptop is not working properly.

Mr. Vaughn：文章❷

→ In consideration of Ms. Vazquez's e-mail：同時查看文章❶解題。

❷當中的寄件人：I

179. According to Mr. Vaughn, what could be an alternative date for the job to be rescheduled?

(A) October 21

(B) October 22

(C) October 28

(D) October 29

Mr. Vaughn：文章❷、alternative date

→ 答題關鍵為 later than usual。

❷當中的寄件人：I

180. What is Mr. Vaughn planning to do on October 26?

(A) Attend a training session

(B) Issue a check to subcontractors

(C) Install a new software system

(D) Leave for his holiday

Mr. Vaughn：文章❷

→ 確認 October 26 是星期幾。

第 176-180 題 兩封電子郵件

1

收件人	employees@inezhightech.net
寄件人	cvazquez@inezhightech.net
日期	10 月 21 日
主旨	軟體系統改善

敬愛的同仁，

我們公司的電腦將在 10 月 28 日星期四，從下午三點開始進行軟體系統改善。所有連接到主要網路系統的電腦，包括筆電都是改善對象。特別是業務暨行銷部、人事部和會計部門的員工要更加留意，因為改善過程中的軟體升級可能影響他們的電腦。

你應該要把重要資料和檔案存檔，因為所有程式在改善過程中將按程序自動重啟。至於電腦連結到公司內網系統的同仁，請注意改善過程可能會造成你們電腦上的資訊消失。所以我們建議你們參考時程表去安排工作，以免在下星期四下午受到影響。當天休假的同仁，改善過程會在你們回來工作時再執行。

塞西莉亞・瓦茲奎茲

2

收件人	jterry@inezhightech.net
寄件人	avaughn@inezhightech.net
日期	10 月 22 日
主旨	給賣家的支票

敬愛的泰瑞女士，

此信是要通知您，下個禮拜發給外包廠商的支票會遇到潛在問題。這個流程通常安排在每個星期四進行。我昨天收到瓦茲奎茲女士的電子郵件，為了讓流程順利進行，下週發支票的時間需要調整。

我下週二和三要去參加會計研討會，應該不會在辦公室。我預計比平常晚一天、在下週五做這件事。比起這樣，也許我可以在 10 月 25 日週一先做，但這樣對部分外包廠商可能無法準時付款。請知會我應該怎麼進行，我會按照您的建議去做。

尚・沃恩

字彙 be subject to 受……影響／支配　have an impact on 對……造成影響
crucial 重要的　result in 導致　adversely 不利的　potential 潛在的　issue 問題
subcontractor 外包廠商　carry out 實行　in consideration of 考量……
adjust 調整　payment 付款　proceed 繼續進行

176. 為什麼會寫第一封電子郵件？

(A) 讓員工準備因應系統運作的問題

(B) 建議員工更新工作狀況

(C) 提出撞行程的解決辦法

(D) 通知員工安裝軟體的方法

STEP 1 開頭前三句話中，有 90% 的機率會出現目的，其餘 10% 則可能出現在後半段的要求事項中。

當前半段文章以較長的篇幅說明狀況時，請改從後半段文中找尋要求或請求的事項。第一封郵件前半段說明軟體系統將進行修正。而後半段寫道：「we suggest that you refer to the time and schedule your work accordingly so as not to be adversely affected by the process next Thursday afternoon」，建議調整這段時間的工作日程表，以免受到影響。由此可以得知撰寫此封郵件的目的是希望員工不會在系統修正時發生問題，因此答案為 (A)。

STEP 2 分析錯誤選項

(C) 文中僅提到 schedule，並未提出如何解決 scheduling conflict。

(D) 文中僅提到 software，並未告知安裝方法。

177. 瓦茲奎茲女士最可能在哪個部門工作？

(A) 業務與行銷　　(B) 會計

(C) 技術支援　　(D) 人事

STEP 1 從文中找出明確的答題線索後，選出最符合的答案。

題目關鍵字 Vazquez 為撰寫第一封郵件的人。前半段寫道：「Our company computers will have a software system improvement」，告知員工們公司電腦軟體系統將進行改善工作。由此可以推測出，此人應任職於與電腦軟體系統有關的技術支援部，因此答案為 (C)。

STEP 2 分析錯誤選項

文中提到 (A)、(B)、(D) 部門需要特別留意電腦系統改善時帶來的影響，並非答案。

178. 最可能是什麼原因讓沃恩先生得重新安排工作？

(A) 他想要調整給支票的時間。

(B) 他接到外包廠商即刻付款的要求。

(C) 他想避免遺失資料。

(D) 他的筆電無法正常運作。

STEP 1 針對兩篇文章出題的整合題——五道題中，至少會有一題必須同時查看兩篇文章的內容，才能選出答案。

請先確認題目的解題關鍵為 reason Mr. Vaughn . . . to reschedule。第二篇文章中，Vaughn 寫道：「In consideration of Ms. Vazquez's e-mail . . . , the time of issuing next week's checks is required to be adjusted」，提到考量到 Vazquez 所寫的郵件，應該要調整開支票的時間。

STEP 2 **關鍵字旁未出現答案時，請確認是否還有其他解題線索。**

第一篇文中寫道：「Our company computers will have a software system improvement on Thursday」，提到星期四將進行軟體系統修正工作。下一段還寫道：「the improvement process can probably result in the loss of information on your computer」，告知系統改善過程中，可能會導致資料遺失。由此內容可以得知調整時間為的是避免數據資料消失，因此答案要選 (C)。

179. 根據沃恩先生的說法，重新安排工作的日子可能是？

(A) 10 月 21 日
(B) 10 月 22 日
(C) 10 月 28 日
(D) 10 月 29 日

STEP 1 **題目詢問價格、費用或日期時，請從文中找出所有相關資訊，依序整理後，選出最適當的答案。**

請先確認題目關鍵字為 alternative date for the jobs。第二篇文章中，Vaughn 寫道：「I will be able to do the task next Friday one day later than usual.」，提到預計比平常晚一天，於週五可以完成工作。而本封郵件於 10 月 22 日寄出，當中還寫道：「it may be possible to do the task on Monday, October 25」，由此可以得知 10 月 25 日為星期一，那麼下週五便是 10 月 29 日，因此答案為 (D)。

180. 沃恩先生 10 月 26 打算做什麼？

(A) 參加訓練課程
(B) 給外包廠商開支票
(C) 安裝一套新軟體系統
(D) 去休假

STEP 1 **關鍵字旁未出現答案時，請確認是否還有其他解題線索。**

請先確認關鍵字 10 月 26 日為星期幾。Vaughn 於 10 月 22 日撰寫郵件並寄出，當中寫道：「it may be possible to do the task on Monday, October 25」，由此可以得知 10 月 25 日為星期一，那麼 10 月 26 日便是星期二。郵件中間還寫道：「I am supposed to be away next Tuesday and Wednesday to participate in an accounting workshop.」，提到下週二和三他將參加會計研討會。由此可以得知 Vaughn 將於 10 月 26 日參加研討會，因此答案要選 (A)。

STEP 2 **答案通常會採換句話說的方式。**

答案選項將文中的 an accounting workshop 改寫成 a training session。

STEP 3 **分析錯誤選項**

(B) 文中提到將於下週五 10 月 29 日或週一 10 月 25 日開出支票給合作公司，因此該選項並非答案。

Questions 181-185 refer to the following e-mails.

E-MAIL 1

185-C

To	All our present customers
From	marketing@inezpublication.con
Date	Friday, 21 October
Subject	Final Chance! These Copies W

陷阱選項 185-B, C, D
(B) Once again it's time . . . , Our Yearly Sale → a clearance sale each year
(C) To: All our present customers → keeps track of every customer's purchase record
(D) Photo Shoot Text Book → carries publications about photography

Dear Valued Customer,

185-B

Here is surprising news for you! Once again it's time to hold our clearance sale on various collections of Inez Publication's books. All the copie print, so do not miss this great opportunity to acquire exce your life more pleasant. Our Yearly Sale Pamphlet will soon be mailed to you, **but by visiting our Web site**, you **can check** out the **list of collections** on sale **sooner**. Placing an order through our Web site is recommended in order to purchase the copies you would like before they are out of stock. All purchases will be delivered for free until next week, and if **more than four books** are ordered, we will **gift-wrap** your books with no charge. Take advantage of this special chance!

181 by visiting our Web site → use the online pamphlet

184 ❶ + ❷文章整合題 Mr. Schultz 的訂單：三本

Lauren Stone

Inez Publication S

182 ❶ + ❷文章整合題 you have purchased publications → he has ordered some items

Notice: This e-mail is being sent to you **since you have purchased publications from Inez Publication**. If our information about sales is not necessary for you anymore, just respond to this e-mail with the subject "No Subscription."

E-MAIL 2

Dear Mr. **Schultz**,

182 ❶ + ❷文章整合題 關鍵字 Mr. Schultz

We appreciate your purchase. The below products will be delivered within 4-7 business days through the TRO Mail Service. Please be advised that **no refund** for **any item** will be issued.

183 no refund → non-refundable

Placed Order: 24 Oct 1:15 P.M.

Item No.	Quantity	Book title 185-D	Price per unit	Total
32118	1	Photo Shoot Text Book: With Various Skills	$11.50	$11.50
44312	1	Contemporary Photograph Collection	$9.00	$9.00
98031	1	The Photography Software for Amateurs	$15.50	$15.50
		Gift Packing		$6.00
		Delivery Fee		-
		Total		$42.00

184 ❶ + ❷文章整合題 Mr. Schultz 的訂單：三本

181. What is the reason customers would use the online pamphlet rather than the print pamphlet?
(A) To be exempt from shipping fee
(B) To look through a wider range of books
(C) To search for books earlier
(D) To acquire a revised price list

online pamphlet：文章❶
→ 從關鍵字前後找出答題線索。

182. What is suggested about Mr. Schultz?
(A) He is running his own business.
(B) He has collected a wide selection of photographs.
(C) He needed some books for his photography course.
(D) He has ordered some items from Inez Publication before.

Mr. Schultz：文章❷
→ 請留意提及代名詞 he 的句子。

183. What is most likely true about the items ordered?
(A) All of them are non-refundable.
(B) ~~One of them~~ will not be delivered in October.
(C) Some of them are rare books.
(D) Most of them will be available in an electronic version.

the items ordered：參考文章❷的表格
→「no refund for any item」

184. What should Mr. Schultz have done to get an additional benefit from the special offer?
(A) Use the online order system
(B) Obtain a student discount coupon
(C) Order more publications
(D) Submit his order before October

Mr. Schultz：文章❷、an additional benefit：文章❶
→ 請整合兩篇文章的答題線索。

185. What is NOT suggested about Inez Publication?
(A) It can deliver books abroad.
(B) It holds a clearance sale each year.
(C) It keeps track of every customer's purchase record.
(D) It carries publications about photography.

NOT Question
→ 刪去文中提及的選項，選出正確答案。

第 181-185 題 兩封電子郵件

1

收件人	我們現有的全部客戶
寄件人	marketing@inezpublication.com.ca
日期	10 月 21 日 星期五
主旨	最後機會！這些書將絕版！

敬愛的貴客：

為您報上驚喜的大消息！又到了伊內茲出版社書籍大出清的時候了。所有拍賣書籍都將絕版，所以不要錯過這個大好機會，買到超棒的書、讓您的生活更充實。我們很快就會把年度拍賣的銷售手冊寄給您，不過上我們官網查看年度選書更快速，建議您在售罄前到官網下單搶購。凡在下週前購買皆免運費。如果訂購超過四本，我們將為您免費包裝。好好利用這個特別的機會大賺特賺！

羅倫·史東

伊內茲出版社業務經理

提醒：本封信件寄給您係因您曾向伊內茲出版社購書。如果您已不再需要我們的銷售資訊，請以「取消訂閱」為主旨回覆此郵件。

2

敬愛的舒茲先生：

感謝您的購買。下列產品將在四到七個工作天經由 TRO 郵寄服務送達。請注意所有商品均不得退款。

訂購時間：10 月 24 日 下午 1:15

商品號碼	數量	書本名稱	單位價格	總價
32118	1	攝影教典：各種技巧	$11.50	$11.50
44312	1	當代攝影選輯	$9.00	$9.00
98031	1	業餘人士的攝影軟體	$15.50	$15.50
禮品包裝				$6.00
運費				-
總金額				$42.00

字彙 copy 書冊　once again 又再　out of print 絕版　acquire 購得
pleasant 愉快的　yearly 年度　place an order 下訂單
in order to V 為了做……　purchase 購買　out of stock 沒有庫存
for free 免費　gift-wrap 禮品包裝　with no charge 不用付費
take advantage of 利用……　appreciate 感謝　business days 工作天
issue 發放　price per unit 單位價格

181. 出於什麼原因，顧客會使用線上手冊而非紙本？

(A) 為了免運費

(B) 為了看更多類型的書

(C) 為了提早找書

(D) 為了取得修改價格後的清單

STEP 1 答案通常會出現在關鍵字旁。

請先確認題目關鍵字為 reason 和 use the online pamphlet，並從文中找出相關內容。第一篇文章寫道：「Our Yearly Sale Pamphlet will soon be mailed to you, but by visiting our Web site, you can check out the list of collections on sale sooner.」，提到不久後就會寄出年度銷售手冊，但是如果直接造訪網站，將能更快確認商品清單。由此內容可以得知選擇使用線上手冊，而非紙本手冊的原因是想更快找到書籍，因此答案為 (C)。

STEP 2 分析錯誤選項

文中提到有各類書籍，但是目的並非提供閱覽，因此 (B) To look through a wider range of books 並不正確。

182. 關於舒茲先生，文中提到什麼？

(A) 他自己開店。

(B) 他蒐集很多精挑細選的照片。

(C) 他為了攝影課需要一些書。

(D) 他之前曾在伊內茲出版社買書。

STEP 1 看到針對兩篇文章出題的整合題時，從文中找出明確的答題線索後，選出最符合的答案。

由第二篇文章可以確認 Schultz 購買了優惠書籍。第一篇文章針對書籍庫存清倉優惠說明，當中寫道：「This e-mail is being sent to you since you have purchased publications from Inez Publication.」，提到先前有購買過書籍的人才會收到此封郵件。由此可以得知 Schultz 以前曾在 Inez Publication 買過書，因此答案為 (D)。

STEP 2 分析錯誤選項

雖然 Schultz 購買的書籍都與照片有關，但是無法從文中確認 (B) 和 (C) 是否正確，因此不能作為答案。

183. 關於訂購商品，何者最可能為真？

(A) 所有商品不得退款。 (B) 其中一本在十月不會寄出。

(C) 部分是稀有書籍。 (D) 其中大多都有電子版本。

STEP 1 題目要求找出相符的「事實」時，請先整理出各選項的關鍵字，再查看文章內容。

第二篇文中寫道：「Please be advised that no refund for any item will be issued.」，提到所有的商品都不提供退貨。由此可以得知訂購商品都不能退貨，因此答案為 (A)。

STEP 2 分析錯誤選項

(B) 第一封郵件的寄送時間為 10 月 21 日，當中寫道：「All purchases will be delivered for free until next week.」，由此句話可以得知十月份會配送所有的訂單。第二篇文中寫道：「Placed Order: 24 Oct 1:15 P.M.」，表示 Schultz 於 10 月 24 日訂購。上方寫道：「The below products will be delivered within 4-7 business days」，提到預計於工作日 4 至 7 日內送達，由此可以得知十月分內會到貨。

184. 舒茲先生應該怎麼做，才能從這筆特別訂單得到更多好處？

(A) 使用網路訂購系統 (B) 取得學生折價券

(C) 訂購更多書 (D) 在十月前訂購

STEP 1 針對兩篇文章出題的整合題——其中一篇文章列出優惠或會員資格條件時，另一篇文章會提及特定人物的條件，請務必整合相關資訊以便找出答案。

請先確認關鍵字為 an additional benefit。第一篇文中寫道：「if more than four books are ordered, we will gift-wrap your books with no charge」，提到如果購買四本以上的書籍，將提供免費包裝服務。查看第二篇文中便能確認 Schultz 只訂購了三本書。這表示如果他想要獲得額外的優惠，就必須再多訂一本書，因此答案要選 (C)。

STEP 2 分析錯誤選項

透過網站只能更快確認有販賣哪些書，因此 (A) 不正確。文中並未提及 (B) 和 (D) 的內容。

185. 關於伊內茲出版社，文中沒有提到什麼？

(A) 可以把書寄到國外。

(B) 每年都會大出清。

(C) 持續追蹤每位客戶的購買紀錄。

(D) 有攝影的書籍。

STEP 1 看到 NOT Question 時，請善用刪去法。

(B) 第一篇文中寫道：「Once again it's time to hold our clearance sale」，提到 Inez Publication 又將展開庫存清倉優惠。加上後方寫道：「Our Yearly Sale Pamphlet . . .」，由此可以確認為年度庫存清倉優惠；(C) 第一篇文章為寄給曾經消費的顧客的郵件，這表示他們有保留顧客的消費紀錄；(D) 由 Schultz 的購買明細可以確認他買的是與照片有關的書籍，因此答案為 (A)。

Questions 186-190 refer to the following notice, advertisement, and e-mail.

1

TO All LCG Fitness Trainers
FROM Stacey Carroll
DATE September 18
SUBJECT Promotional offer

188 1 + 2文章整合題

Dear Fitness trainers,

As mentioned earlier, we are planning to **offer students the 30 percent** summer discount on an annual basis if they register during the first two weeks of November since a lot of Loughton College students are expected to be in the city during the winter season. In addition, LCG Fitness is thinking about offering two different types of special rates to new members and those who want to continue their membership during the upcoming winter (From Nov 1 to Dec 1).

Before the final decision on the two possible offers is made, we are soliciting our staff's opinions. One would be a family discount option. If a current LCG member's family member (age over 17) registers for membership, they will be eligible for a 20 percent reduced rate.

The other option would be to let Diamond-level members' friends or acquaintances use LCG's facilities for free from 9 A.M. to 2 P.M. on Tuesdays and Wednesdays. They would be allowed to use the whole gym, including the swimming pool. But, the badminton courts would be res[...] in order to avoid worsening **the already long wait**.

187 the already long wait
→ in high demand in the center

Please consider these possible options and **reply** by October 10 with the one which [...] our members as well as us.

186 Please consider these possible options
→ ask employees for suggestions

Thanks for your assistance in advance.

Stacey Carroll
Head of Marketing
LCG Fitness Center

陷阱選項 189-A, C
從文中找出選項的關鍵字後，刪去錯誤的敘述。
(A) family member (age over 17)
(C) Diamond- and Crystal-level members

188 1 + 2文章整合題：更動事項
1 the first two weeks of November → 2 between November 1 and December 10

2

Winter Special Offers

Welcome Loughton College students!

Register between November 1 and December 10 to take advantage of a 30% discount on your winter membership at **any level** and receive a complimentary **plastic water bottle.**

Work out with a friend or an acquaintance every Tuesday and Wednesday:

189 Register → when they sign up
any level → Crystal-level members

Starting on November 1, all Diamond- and Crystal-level members are allowed to invite a friend or an acquaintance with no additional charge on Tuesdays and Wednesdays. In order to use LCG's facilities, they have to sign in and present their valid ID at the reception desk.

LCG Fitness Center

E-MAIL 3

TO	Kerry Bush <kerrybush@lcgfitnesscenter.net>
FROM	Joann Bradley <joannbradley@lcgfitnesscenter.net>
DATE	December 11
SUBJECT	Re: The number of the new members

Kerry,

I appreciate you forwarding the report as usual. I was excited about the number of both Diamond- and Crystal-level members, which all rose by 13 percent after we had begun the winter promotion.

Most of them are from Loughton College and have registered for Diamond- memberships. This means that we should consider planning to launch another promotional offer for students when the spring semester starts. It is said that the **gym** in **the college** is scheduled to **be refurbished** during the following year. So, many students are going to search for [190 be refurbished → be remodeled] ince other fitness facilities which can be deemed our competitors are several kilometers away from the college, if we provide shuttles for students to get to and from our center, they will be more likely to come to LCG Fitness Center.

I will keep you informed. Thank you.

Joann Bradley,
Sales Director
LCG Fitness Center

186. What is the main reason the notice has been written?
(A) To report a schedule change
(B) To recognize employees for their hard work
(C) To publicize a new discounted rate
(D) To ask employees for suggestions

目的／後半段文中有 **10% 的機率會出現要求事項。**

→ 注意文章❶後半段以 Please 開頭的要求。

187. What is indicated about the badminton courts?
(A) They are scheduled to be refurbished soon.
(B) They are located near the main building.
(C) They are in high demand in the center.
(D) They used to be a swimming pool.

badminton courts：文章❶

→ 整理出題目和選項的關鍵字後，再查看文章內容。

188. What aspect of the promotional offer for the students has changed since September?
(A) The discount percentage for students has been reduced.
(B) The registration period for the promotional offer was lengthened.
(C) Students do not need to pay their membership fee monthly.
(D) Students can try the fitness facilities twice a month for free.

promotional offer ／ students ／ since September

→ 請找出文章❶和❷的相關資訊後，再進行比較。

189. What is suggested about LCG Fitness Center?
(A) Fee discounts are available to every family member.
(B) It stays open late on Tuesdays and Wednesdays.
(C) ~~Students~~ are permitted to invite their friends and acquaintances.
(D) Crystal-level members can obtain plastic bottles when they sign up.

LCG Fitness Center
→ 確認文章2的內容。

190. According to the e-mail, what will most likely happen at Loughton College?
(A) The community will be allowed to use its gym for ~~a nominal fee~~.
(B) The fitness facility for students will be remodeled.
(C) ~~Additional fitness trainers~~ will be recruited.
(D) The new semester will start ~~in the winter~~.

Loughton College／未來：文章3
→「is scheduled to . . .」

第 186-190 題 通知、廣告與電子郵件

1

收件人	LCG 塑身教練
寄件人	史黛西・卡羅爾
日期	9 月 18 日
主旨	促銷優惠

敬愛的各位健身房教練：

誠如稍早提過的，因為預計會有很多勞頓學院的學生在冬天進城，若他們在 11 月上半登記的話，我們計劃提供他們 30% 的年度夏日折扣。

此外，LCG 健身房正在考慮要提供給新會員、以及有意在接下來的冬天（從 11 月 1 日到 12 月 1 日）續辦會員者兩種不同的特別優惠。

我們想在決定兩個最終優惠版前先徵求員工意見。其一可能是家庭折扣方案，如果有現存的 LCG 會員，他的家庭成員（超過 17 歲）加入會員的話，就適用減免 20% 的費率。

另一個則是讓鑽石級會員的朋友或認識的人，在星期二和三的早上 9 點到下午 2 點免費使用 LCG 的設施。他們被准許使用健身房，包括游泳池在內。不過，羽球場還是僅限我們既有會員使用，避免讓現在排隊等候的情況更糟。

請考慮這些可能選項，你覺得哪一個同時對會員及我們都有好處，請在 10 月 10 日前回覆。提前感謝你的協助。

史黛西・凱羅爾
行銷長
LCG 健身中心

2

冬季特惠

歡迎勞頓學院的學生！

於 11 月 1 日到 12 月 10 日間報名登記，任何等級都將享有冬季會員 30% 折扣，還能獲贈一個塑膠水瓶。

和友人或認識的人，每個星期二、三一起健身：
從 11 月 1 日起的星期二和三，所有鑽石級和水晶級會員都獲准邀請一位朋友或認識的人，無須另外付費。欲使用 LCG 設施，他們需要在櫃檯登記並出示有效身分證件。

LCG 健身中心

3

收件人	凱莉．布希 <kerrybush@lcgfitnesscenter.net>
寄件人	瓊安．布萊得利 <joannbradley@lcgfitnesscenter.net>
日期	12 月 11 日
主旨	回覆：新會員的人數

凱莉：

感謝妳提交的報告。我很興奮，鑽石級和水晶級會員的人數，自我們開始冬季優惠已經整整成長了 13%。

其中大多都是勞頓學院的學生，且註冊成為鑽石級會員。這代表我們應該開始為春季學期開始，計劃下一個學生促銷方案。據說，學院的健身房將在明年安排整修，所以很多學生會開始找健身的替代場所。因為可被視為競爭對手的其他健身設施，都距離學院有好幾公里遠，如果我們提供學生往返我們中心的接駁車，將會讓他們更想來 LCG 健身中心。

我將隨時跟妳報告進度，感謝妳。

瓊安·布萊得利
業務長
LCG 健身中心

字彙 on an annual basis 以年為基礎的；年度　continue 繼續　solicit 徵求
family member 家庭成員　register for 登記註冊　membership 會員
be eligible for 有獲得……的資格　acquaintance 認識的人　facility 設施
restrict 限制　beneficial 有利的；有好處的　complimentary 贈送的
work out 健身　additional charge 額外付費　sign in 註冊　promotion 促銷
launch 開始　refurbish 整修　search for 尋找　deem 認為

186. 寫這篇通知的主因為何？

(A) 回報行程異動

(B) 肯定員工辛勤工作

(C) 宣布新的折扣費率

(D) 詢問員工的建議

STEP 1 開頭前三句話中，有 90% 的機率會出現理由或目的，其餘 10% 則可能出現在後半段文章中。

商業文章的目的通常會出現在前半段文章中，但是當前半段文章以較長的篇幅說明狀況或是首次寄送郵件的狀況時，則會在後半段提及文章重點，因此請改從後半段文章中找尋要求或請求的事項。

第一篇文章後半段寫道：「Please consider these possible options and reply by October 10 with the one . . .」，請大家思考一下可行的選項，並於 10 月 10 日以前回覆。而本篇文章是由 LCG Fitness Center 的行銷部主管寫給健身中心教練的公告，由此可以得知他撰寫本文的目的為詢問員工們的建議，因此答案為 (D)。

STEP 2 分析錯誤選項

文中並未提及 (A) 和 (B) 的內容，因此不能作為答案；雖然文中有提到 reduced rate，但是本篇公告的目的並非告知 a new discounted rate（最新優惠價格），因此 (C) 也不正確。

187. 關於羽球場，文中提到什麼？

(A) 很快就會安排整修。 (B) 位於主建築附近。
(C) 在中心裡被使用的需求多。 (D) 過去曾是游泳池。

STEP 1 答案通常會出現在關鍵字旁。

請先確認題目關鍵字為 badminton courts。第一篇文中寫道：「the badminton courts would be restricted to our current member in order to avoid worsening the already long wait」，提到由於羽球場本來就得花很多時間排隊，為了避免這種情況更加惡化，僅限現在的會員使用。由此內容可以得知在健身中心內，很多人都想使用羽球場，因此答案為 (C)。

STEP 2 答案通常會採換句話說的方式。

答案選項將文中的 the already long wait 改寫成 in high demand。(D) 文中並未提到羽球場以前曾是游泳池，因此不能作為答案。

188. 哪項學生折扣的內容從九月開始變動？

(A) 給學生的折扣比例減少了。
(B) 促銷登記的期間延長了。
(C) 學生不需要每個月付會員費。
(D) 學生每個月可以免費試用健身設施兩次。

STEP 1 看到針對兩篇文章出題的整合題時，從文中找出明確的答題線索後，選出最符合的答案。

請先確認題目的解題關鍵為 promotional offer for the students has changed since September，並從文中找出在九月之後，提供給學生的促銷活動產生了什麼改變。

第一篇文章為九月撰寫的公告，當中寫道：「we are planning to offer students the 30 percent summer discount on an annual basis if they register during the first two weeks of November」，提到若學生於十一月前兩週申請入會，將提供七折的夏季優惠。

但是第二篇廣告卻寫道：「Welcome Loughton College! Register between November 1 and December 10 to take advantage of a 30% discount」，提到優惠期間為 11 月 11 日到 12 月 10 日為止。綜合兩篇文章的內容可以確認九月之後，提供給學生的促銷活動期間有所變動，因此答案為 (B)。

STEP 2 **分析錯誤選項**

(A) 提供給學生的 discount percentage 為 30%，並未改變；(D) 週二和週三免費招待 Diamond 等級的會員於帶朋友或熟人前來健身中心使用。

189. 關於 LCG 健身中心，文中提到什麼

(A) 每名家庭成員都享有折扣費用。

(B) 在星期二、三通常開到很晚。

(C) 學生獲准邀請朋友或認識的人。

(D) 水晶級會員登記時可以獲得塑膠水瓶。

STEP 1 **「題目要求找出相符的「事實」時，請先整理出各選項的關鍵字，再查看文章內容。**

本題針對 LCG Fitness Center 提問。請先整理出各選項的關鍵字，分別為 (A) Fee discounts、every family member；(B) stay open late；(C) invite、friends and acquaintances；(D) plastic bottles、sign up，再從文中找出相關敘述。

第二篇文章為針對 Loughton College 學生的廣告，當中寫道：「Register . . . your winter membership at any level and receive a complimentary plastic water bottle」，提到不管是哪個等級的會員，只要申請入會就能得到免費的塑膠水瓶。這表示 Crystal 等級的會員申請時，同樣可以得到水瓶，因此答案為 (D)。

STEP 2 **分析錯誤選項**

(A) 第一篇文中寫道：「If a current LCG member's family member (age over 17) register for membership, they will be eligible for a 20 percent reduced rate.」，提到若家人為現任 LCG 會員，且申請者年滿 17 歲時，可以獲得入會費用八折的優惠。而 (A) 表示適用所有的家人，並不正確。

(B) 文中並未提及相關內容，因此不能作為答案。

(C) 第二篇文中寫道：「all Diamond- and Crystal-level members are allowed to invite a friend or an acquaintance」，提到免費招待 Diamond 和 Crystal 等級會員的朋友和熟人，因此該選項也不正確。

190. 根據電子郵件，勞頓學院裡最可能發生什麼事？

(A) 社區獲准以低廉費用使用健身房。

(B) 學生運動設施將要整修。

(C) 會聘僱其他健身教練。

(D) 新學期冬天開始。

STEP 1 **關鍵字旁未出現答案時，請確認是否還有其他解題線索。**

請先確認題目關鍵字為 Loughton College。第三篇文中寫道：「Most of them are from Loughton College」，提到 Loughton College。後方又寫道：「It is said that the gym in the college is scheduled to be refurbished during the following year」，提到明年大學內的體育館將進行整修。此處的 the college 指的就是前方提過的 Loughton College，因此答案為 (B)。

STEP 2 **答案通常會採換句話說的方式。**

答案選項將文中的 the gym 和 be refurbished 改寫成 the fitness facility 和 be remodeled。文中並未提到 (A) 和 (C) 的內容。「when the spring semester starts」指的是計劃於春季學期開始時，推出其他的學生促銷活動。而 (D) 提到新學期於冬季開始，並不正確。

Questions 191-195 refer to the following leaflet, course description, and phone message.

1

A new class at Renaissance Art Glass (RAG)
Creating Unique Colorful Stained Glass
Instructor: Barbara Brown
Price: £115

The class will be held for five successive **Wednesday nights**, f[193 1 + 2 文章整合題]0 P.M., beginning on September 9. It requires no previous experience, **but registration** is limited **only to our current members of the** community's arts associations.

[194 1 + 3 文章整合題：registration]

Familiarize yourself with the basic level of making stained glass artworks and take one of those you have made with you. Designing, glass-cutting, color selection, framing, and more will be included in the subjects of each class. You can design your own style or simply select from among a variety of sample patterns.

[191 the five-week period, for each of their projects → Not, be brought all at once]

Those who registered for the class can buy mate[rials] be advised that they are available **as required** over the **five-week period** to make sure that attendees purchase the appropriate tools and supplies **for each of their projects** and also have the cost of the materials spread out. Similar tools and supplies are available elsewhere, **but** attendees should **realize** that quality is not the same. Using the best supplies makes the end outcome different. [192]

Unique Colorful

Stained Glass

2

195 2 + 3文章整合題
其他關鍵字：brushes

Subjects	Week	Tools and Supplies
Workroom Safety; Orientation and learning and practicing "glass-cutting" techniques and skills	1	glass cutter, cutting oil, protective goggles and industrial gloves, pliers, and ruler with metal edge
Designing patterns and glass or selecting from samples	2	glass, several pieces of thick paper, a pair of scissors, and color pens
Shaping your own style through grinding and cutting glass	3	industrial gloves, protective goggles
Applying enamel to glass panel according to the patterns you have created or chosen	4	enamel paint, enamel brushes, utility knife
Coating and framing	5	coating compound, frame

193 1 + 2文章整合題

Please note that for students who **need** more time and **an instructor's tips**, the workroom at RAG is open **on Friday** from 11 A.M. to 5 P.M. In case you need time with an instructor after these hours, you are required to contact us in advance or be ready to work on your own in the workroom.

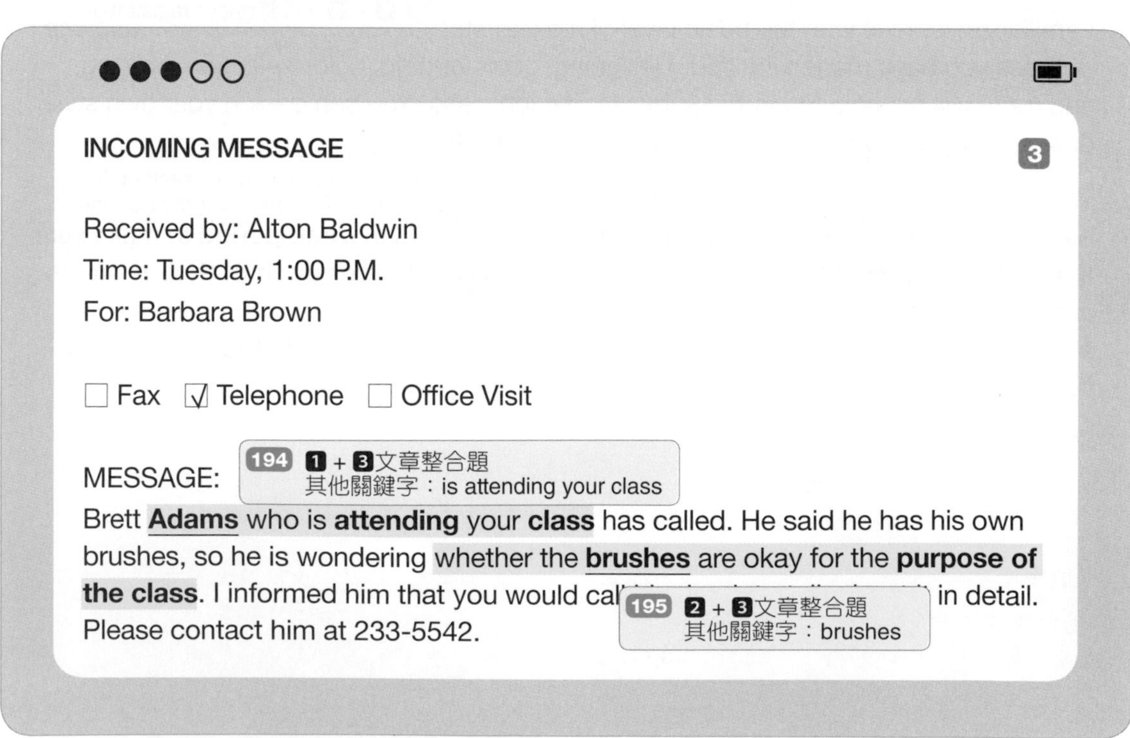

INCOMING MESSAGE

3

Received by: Alton Baldwin

Time: Tuesday, 1:00 P.M.

For: Barbara Brown

☐ Fax ☑ Telephone ☐ Office Visit

194 1 + 3文章整合題
其他關鍵字：is attending your class

MESSAGE:

Brett **Adams** who is **attending** your **class** has called. He said he has his own brushes, so he is wondering whether the **brushes** are okay for the **purpose of the class**. I informed him that you would cal[...] in detail. Please contact him at 233-5542.

195 2 + 3文章整合題
其他關鍵字：brushes

191. What is indicated about the tools and supplies needed for RAG's new class?

(A) They are getting ~~cheaper~~ these days.

(B) They are not required to be brought all at once.

(C) They are not available in other supply stores.

(D) They will ~~be distributed by~~ the class instructor.

關鍵字 **tools and supplies ／ RAG's new class**

→ 確認文章1的內容。

192. In the leaflet, the word "realize" in paragraph 3, line 5, is closest in meaning to

(A) sell (B) cash

(C) know (D) achieve

選出同義詞

→ 從文章1中確認該單字前後的句子。

193. What does the course description imply?

(A) ~~Attendees~~ can leave their ~~opinion~~ after their class.

(B) RAG ~~recently renovated~~ its workroom.

(C) Attendees can get help even outside class hours.

(D) A class has been ~~rescheduled~~ to another day.

the course description

→ 文章1和2

194. What is indicated about Mr. Adams?

(A) He ~~has purchased~~ all the tools and supplies.

(B) He is a member of a local association.

(C) He ~~had to miss~~ the orientation.

(D) He ~~has supplied materials~~ to RAG.

關鍵字 Mr. Adams：文章3

→ 善用關鍵字前後的線索找出答案。

「is attending your class」

→ 文章1「registration」

195. To which class session does the phone message most likely refer?

(A) Week 2 (B) Week 3

(C) Week 4 (D) Week 5

電話留言：文章3

「brushes」

→ 文章2

第 191-195 題 傳單、課程描述與來電訊息

1

文藝復興藝術玻璃（RAG）的新課程
創造獨一無二的花窗玻璃
指導老師：芭芭拉‧布朗
價格：115 英鎊

課程將從 9 月 9 日開始，時間為晚間 7 點至 10 點，連續五個星期三。無經驗可，但限社區藝術協會現有會員才能登記參加。

讓您熟悉花窗玻璃的製作基礎，並帶走一樣自己的作品。每堂課的主題包括設計、玻璃切割、選色、裝框等。您可以用自己的風格、或者從各式樣款中擇一來設計。

報名課程者可用約莫 155 英鎊的價格從 RAG 購買材料。請留意，五週課程期間如有需要都能購買，以確保參加者能買到符合計畫的工具和耗材，並且能夠分攤材料成本。類似的工具和耗材別的地方也買得到，不過上課的人應該會了解到品質不一樣，使用最好的耗材會讓成果大不相同。

獨一無二的彩色花窗玻璃 2

主題	週次	工具和耗材
工作室安全；入門、學習和練習玻璃切割的技術和技巧	第一週	玻璃切割刀、切削油、護目鏡和工業手套、鉗子、金屬鑲邊尺
設計圖案和玻璃或選定樣式	第二週	玻璃、多張厚紙、一把剪刀、色筆
透過研磨與切割形塑自我風格的玻璃	第三週	工業手套、護目鏡
用搪瓷在玻璃面繪製你所發想或選定的圖樣	第四週	瓷漆、瓷漆刷、多用途刀
鍍膜與裝框	第五週	鍍膜塗料、邊框

請注意，如果學生需要較多時間或指導老師的建議，RAG 的工作室在星期五早上 11 點到下午 5 點開放使用。假使你在這之後仍需要時間找指導老師，必須事先和我們聯絡，否則就得準備好自己在工作室作業。

來電留言 3

接收者：奧爾頓・鮑德溫
時間：星期二下午 1 點
致：芭芭拉・布朗

☐傳真　☑電話　☐辦公室訪問

留言：

妳班上的布列特・亞當斯來電，表示他有自己的刷子，所以想知道他的刷子是否合乎課程需求。我通知他妳會回電詳細說明。請致電 233-5542 聯絡他。

字彙 stained glass 花窗玻璃　successive 連續的　registration 登記
association 協會；公會　familiarize 使熟悉……　artwork 藝術品
glass-cutting 玻璃切割　selection 精選　spread out 分攤　attendee 參加者
outcome 成果　orientation 入門　grind 研磨　workroom 工作室　in detail 詳細地

191. 關於 RAG 新課程所需的工具和耗材，文中提到什麼？

(A) 最近愈來愈便宜。　(B) 不需要一次買齊。
(C) 在其他商店買不到。　(D) 將由指導老師發配。

STEP 1 答案通常會出現在關鍵字旁。

請先確認關鍵字 tools and supplies。第一篇文中寫道：「they are available as required over the five-week period to make sure that attendees purchase the appropriate tools and supplies for each of their projects」，提到報名課程者需要購買五週課程的道具和用品，並依照當週課堂所需攜帶必要的用具，這表示不需要一次買齊所有的用品，因此答案為 (B)。

STEP 2 分析錯誤選項

(A) 文中並未提及近期的價格；(C)「Similar tools and supplies are available elsewhere」當中提到可以在其他地方買到；(D) 文中並未提及相關內容。

192. 傳單中第三段、第五行的「realize」意思最接近下列何者？

(A) 販賣 (B) 換成現金
(C) 知道 (D) 獲得

STEP 1 題目考同義詞時，要根據前後文意，選出最適合替換的單字。

千萬不能只是單純選出意思相同的選項，而是要找出適合替換至句中空格的單字。realize 在句中表示參加課程者必須「知道」品質並不相同，因此答案為 (C) know。

193. 課程描述指出下列什麼？

(A) 課程學員課後可以留下意見。
(B) RAG 最近整修了工作室。
(C) 課程學員可以在課程以外的時間得到協助。
(D) 有一堂課被調課。

STEP 1 針對兩篇文章出題的整合題——由題目關鍵字找出的內容不夠明確時，請再查看另一篇文章找出答案。

請先確認題目關鍵字 course description。第二篇文章為課程說明，當中寫道：「Please note that for students who need more time and an instructor's tips, the workroom at RAG is open on Friday from 11 A.M. to 5 P.M.」，告知如學生需要更多的時間和老師的協助，請記得 RAG 工作室的開放時間為週五上午 11 點至下午 5 點。

而第一篇文中寫道：「The class will be held for five successive Wednesday nights, from 7 P.M. to 10 P.M.」，提到上課時間為週三傍晚 7 點至 10 點。由此內容可以得知課程參加者可以在課程以外的時間獲得協助，因此答案為 (C)。

194. 關於亞當斯先生，文中提到什麼？

(A) 他已經買好所有工具和耗材。
(B) 他是當地協會的一員。
(C) 他不得不錯過入門課程。
(D) 他供應材料給 RAG。

STEP 1 針對兩篇文章出題的整合題——請善用題目所提供的線索和文章內有關答案的資訊。

請先確認題目關鍵字 Adam。第三篇文中寫道：「Brett Adams who is attending your class has called.」，表示 Adams 有參加課程。而第一篇文中寫道：「registration is limited only to our current members of the community's arts associations」，提到僅限社區藝術協會會員報名課程。綜合兩者內容可以得知 Adams 為社區協會的會員，因此答案為 (B)。

195. 來電留言談到的最有可能是哪一門課程？

(A) 第二週

(B) 第三週

(C) 第四週

(D) 第五週

STEP 1 針對兩篇文章出題的整合題——關鍵字旁未出現答案時，請確認是否還有其他解題線索，再從另一篇文章找出答案。

請確認題目關鍵字為 phone message 和 class session。第三篇文章為 phone message，當中寫道：「he is wondering whether the brushes are okay for the purpose of the class」，提到他想知道課堂上是否可以使用自己的刷子。請再由第二篇的表格確認課堂上要準備的物品，當中第四週課程要用到刷子，因此答案為 (C)。

Questions 196-200 refer to the following e-mails and quote.

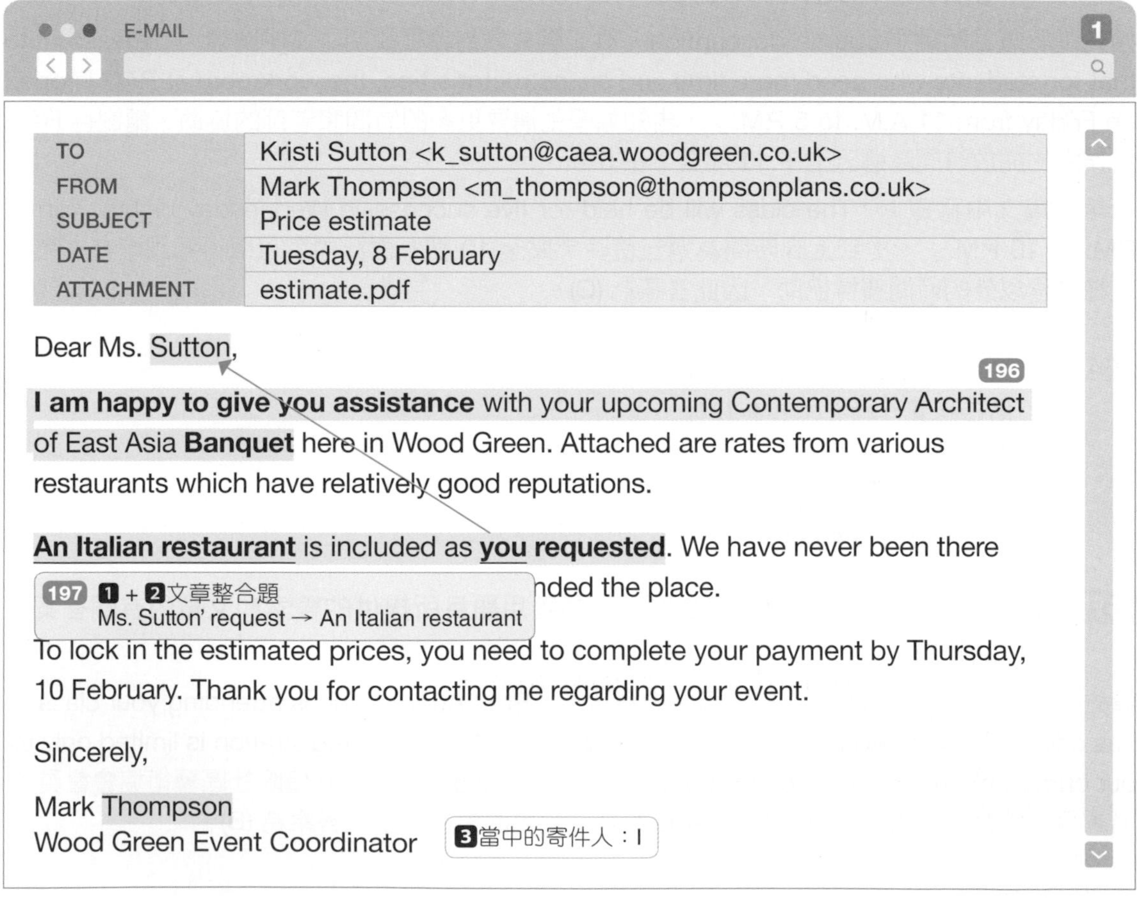

E-MAIL 1

TO	Kristi Sutton <k_sutton@caea.woodgreen.co.uk>
FROM	Mark Thompson <m_thompson@thompsonplans.co.uk>
SUBJECT	Price estimate
DATE	Tuesday, 8 February
ATTACHMENT	estimate.pdf

Dear Ms. Sutton,

196 **I am happy to give you assistance** with your upcoming Contemporary Architect of East Asia **Banquet** here in Wood Green. Attached are rates from various restaurants which have relatively good reputations.

An Italian restaurant is included as **you requested**. We have never been there [...]nded the place.

197 1 + 2文章整合題
Ms. Sutton' request → An Italian restaurant

To lock in the estimated prices, you need to complete your payment by Thursday, 10 February. Thank you for contacting me regarding your event.

Sincerely,

Mark Thompson
Wood Green Event Coordinator

3當中的寄件人：I

2

Rate Estimate for Dining Options

197 1 + 2文章整合題
其他關鍵字：An Italian restaurant

Banquet type: *Six courses*
Date of Event: *15 May*

Prepared for: *Contemporary Architect of East Asia Banquet*
Number of Diners: *30*

* *All listed prices below include the meal, beverages, tax, and tips.*

Restaurant	Total cost	Price per diner	Type of Cuisine	Special features
Elm Cuisine	£660	£22	Chinese	198 customizable → be personalized
Abbey House	£810	£27	Middle Eastern	Its catering menu is fully-**customizable**
Benessere Paranzo	£930	£31	Italian	Up to 35 seats available in its private banquet hall
Seafood Castle	£1,110	£37	Japanese	Provides live classic music
All Saints Table	£1,230	£41	Steak and Salad	Public **transportation** within walking distance

199 2 + 3文章整合題
3 conveniently accessible to the area's transportation
→ 2 Public transportation within walking distance

E-MAIL 3

TO	Mark Thompson <m_thompson@thompsonplans.co.uk>
FROM	Kristi Sutton <k_sutton@caea.woodgreen.co.uk>
RE	Payment
DATE	Thursday, 10 February

Dear Mr. Thompson,

We deeply appreciate your excellent help in arranging the banquet. Today, I have paid the full amount through your Web site. The fully-customizable menu is appealing, **but** we are more conscious about a location which should be **conveniently accessible to the area's transportation**.

199 2 + 3文章整合題

Since the location has been decided, **we now** need **your recommendation for a printer** for the invitation. Also, the decorations have to be discussed, but we will be able to talk about them at the next meeting on 20 February. At the meeting, it will be really helpful if you give us advice on finalizing the design of the event and selecting an appropriate photographer.

Sincerely,
Kristi Sutton

200 need your recommendation for a printer → submit a print order

196. What is suggested about Mr. Thompson? ❶當中的寄件人：I

(A) He is ~~running~~ his own ~~travel agency~~.
(B) He is a ~~restaurant manager~~.
(C) He ~~used to have~~ an Italian ~~restaurant~~.
(D) He is involved in arranging a banquet.

Mr. Thompson
→ 注意文章❶當中的寄件人I。

197. What restaurant did Mr. Thompson ❶當中的寄件人：I based on Ms. Sutton's request?

(A) Abbey House ❶當中的收件人：You
(B) Elm Cuisine
(C) Benessere Paranzo
(D) Seafood Castle

Mr. Thompson：文章❶
→ Ms. Sutton's request
→ An Italian restaurant：請一併確認文章❷的內容。

198. What is indicated about Abbey House?

(A) Its price is the most affordable available.
(B) It can provide musical entertainment for free.
(C) Its menu items can be personalized.
(D) It has a separate dining area for a special event.

Abbey House
→ 答案在文章❷的表格中。

199. How much most likely has Ms. Sutton paid?

(A) £660 (B) £930
(C) £1,110 **(D) £1,230**

Ms. Sutton：文章❸
transportation：文章❷

200. According to the second e-mail, what will Ms. Sutton most likely do next?

(A) Buy some office equipment
(B) Submit a print order
(C) Search for the photographers
(D) Create the design

Ms. Sutton／未來
→ 文章❸：確認寄件人I最先要做的事。

第 196-200 題 兩封電子郵件與估價單

1

收件人	克莉斯蒂・蘇頓 <k_sutton@caea.woodgreen.co.uk>
寄件人	馬克・湯普森 <m_thompson@thompsonplans.co.uk>
主旨	估價
日期	2 月 8 日，星期二
附件	估價.pdf

敬愛的蘇頓女士：

我很高興在綠林這裡即將登場的亞洲當代建築餐會上給您協助。附件是幾家不同餐廳的費用，相對來說評價都還不錯。

基於您的要求，其中也包括一間義大利餐廳。雖然我們之前沒去過那裡，不過我有一名同事推薦。

為了把估價定下來，您需要在 2 月 10 日週四前完成付款。感謝您為了活動聯繫我。

誠摯的，
馬克・湯普森
綠林活動策畫

餐飲項目估價

2

餐會類型：六菜
活動日期：5 月 15 日

準備給：亞洲當代建築餐會
用餐人數：30

以下表列的價格都包括餐點、飲料、稅和小費。

餐廳	總消費	個人消費	菜色類型	特色
榆餐	英鎊 660	英鎊 22	中式	可坐戶外庭院座位區
寺之家	英鎊 810	英鎊 27	中東式	餐飲可完全客製化
健康餐館	英鎊 930	英鎊 31	義大利式	私人宴會廳座位高達 35 席
海鮮城	英鎊 1110	英鎊 37	日式	提供現場古典樂演奏
全聖席	英鎊 1230	英鎊 41	牛排和沙拉	用走的就能抵達大眾運輸工具

3

收件人	馬克・湯普森 <m_thompson@thompsonplans.co.uk>
寄件人	克莉斯蒂・蘇頓 <k_sutton@caea.woodgreen.co.uk>
主旨	付款
日期	2月10日，星期四
附件	估價.pdf

敬愛的湯普森先生：

我們深深感謝您為餐會安排給予大力相助。我今天剛透過您的網站把所有款項付清。完全客製化的菜色很誘人，不過，我們更在意地點前往搭乘當地大眾運輸方不方便。因為地點已經決定好了，我們現在需要您建議印邀請函的廠商。布置也還需要討論，但我們可以在2月20日下一次會議上談談。會議上如果您能針對活動設計和適合的攝影師給出最終決定的建議，將對我們受用無窮。

誠摯的，
克莉斯蒂・蘇頓

字彙 upcoming 即將到來的　rate 費率；費用　relatively 相對的
reputation 名聲；聲望　estimate 估價　complete 完成　payment 付款
regarding 關於　diner 用餐者　list 列表　per 每一　patio 庭院
catering 提供餐飲　customizable 可客製化的　up to 最高達
within 在……期間內　appreciate 感謝　appealing 吸引人的
conscious 注意的；有意識的　accessible 可接近的；易達到的　finalize 最後確定

196. 關於湯普森先生，文中提到什麼？
(A) 他現在經營自己的旅行社。
(B) 他是一名餐廳經理。
(C) 他曾開過義大利餐廳。
(D) 他參與餐會的安排。

STEP 1 題目要求找出相符的「事實」時，請先整理出各選項的關鍵字，再查看文章內容。

請先確認題目關鍵字 Thompson，並整理出各選項的關鍵字分別為 (A) running、travel agency；(B) restaurant manager；(C) used to have、restaurant；(D) arranging a banquet。

第一篇文章為 Thompson 所寫的電子郵件，當中寫道：「I am happy to give you assistance with your upcoming Contemporary Architect of East Asia Banquet」，提到很開心能協助對方宴會活動相關事宜。接著又寫道：「Attached are rates from various restaurants which have relatively good reputations.」，提到附件為餐廳的價格表。由這兩句話可以得知此人在準備宴會，因此答案為 (D)。

STEP 2 分析錯誤選項

文中並未提及 (A) 的內容；文中僅提到附件中包含義式餐廳的價格，並未提到他擁有一間餐廳，因此 (C) 的敘述不正確。

197. 哪一家餐廳是湯普森先生根據蘇頓女士的要求列上的？

(A) 寺之家　(B) 榆餐

(C) 健康餐館　(D) 海鮮城

STEP 1 針對兩篇文章出題的整合題——關鍵字旁未出現答案時，請確認是否還有其他解題線索，再從另一篇文章找出答案。

請先確認題目關鍵字 Ms. Sutton's request。第一篇文章為 Thompson 寄給 Sutton 的電子郵件，當中寫道：「An Italian restaurant is included as you requested」，由此話可以得知 Sutton 要求的餐廳為 An Italian restaurant。確認第二篇的表格後，可以發現 Italian restaurant 為 Benessere Paranzo，因此答案要選 (C)。

198. 關於寺之家，文中指出什麼？

(A) 價格為市面上最實惠。

(B) 免費提供音樂相關的娛樂。

(C) 菜色可以個人化。

(D) 為了特別活動有一個獨立用餐區

STEP 1 答案通常會採換句話說的方式。

請先確認題目關鍵字 Abbey House，從第二篇的表格中可以找到 Abbey House。當中提到 Abbey House 的特色為「Its catering menu is fully-customizable」，表示餐廳提供客製化菜單，因此答案為 (C)。選項將文中的 customizable 改寫成 be personalized。

STEP 2 分析錯誤選項

(A) most affordable available 為 Elm Cuisine 的特色。

(B) musical entertainment 為 Seafood Castle 的特色。

(D) separate dining area 為 Benessere Paranzo 的特色。

199. 蘇頓女士最有可能要付多少錢？

(A) 英鎊 660 元

(B) 英鎊 930 元

(C) 英鎊 1,110 元

(D) 英鎊 1,230 元

STEP 1 針對兩篇文章出題的整合題——關鍵字旁未出現答案時，請確認是否還有其他解題線索，再從另一篇文章找出答案

請先確認題目關鍵字 Sutton。第三篇文章為 Sutton 所寫的郵件，當中寫道：「I have paid the full amount . . .」，提到已經線上支付全額。後方接著寫道：「The fully-customizable menu was appealing, but we are more conscious about a location which should be conveniently accessible to the area's transportation.」，提到雖然客製化餐單很吸引人，但是更偏好交通方便的地方。

請再確認第二篇的表格，找出特色為交通便利的餐廳。All Saints Table 的特色為交通便利，而此餐廳的價格為 1230 歐元，由此可以確認 Sutton 付了 1230 歐元，因此答案為 (D)。

200. 根據第二封電子郵件，蘇頓女士接下來最有可能做什麼事？

(A) 採買辦公室用品
(B) 提出印刷訂單
(C) 找攝影師
(D) 做出設計

STEP 1 從文中找出明確的答題線索後，選出最符合的答案。

本題詢問根據第二封電子郵件，Sutton 之後將會做什麼事。Sutton 在郵件中寫道：「Since the location has been decided, we now need your recommendation for a printer for the invitation.」，提到已經決定好地點，希望對方推薦印刷邀請函的業者，由此內容可以推測出 Sutton 之後將下訂印刷，因此答案為 (B)。

STEP 2 分析錯誤選項

2 月 20 日會議中才會針對 (C) 討論，時間比下訂印刷晚，因此不能作為答案。